DAMSELS AND DEMONS
THE ADVENTURES OF EDMUND AND ELEANOR
VOLUME THREE
by Ashley Mayers

First Printing: 2019
ISBN 978-1-943918-20-1
International Print Edition

Grass Roof Publishing
P.O. Box 14908
San Francisco, California, 94114
www.GloriousVictories.com

Also by Ashley Mayers:
THE SITA CHRONICLES:
    Red Sapphire
    Violet Sapphire
    White Sapphire
    Golden Sapphire
    Cerulean Sapphire
    Green Sapphire
    Black Sapphire
THE GLORIOUS VICTORIES OF ELEANOR MACLEOD:
    The Cursed Baron
    Angels in Disguise
    Damsels and Demons
    Eastward Beyond the Sky
    Before Midnight Ends
THE RIDDLE

Notes from the Publisher:

The Glorious Victories of Eleanor MacLeod is a new five-book epic that adds another layer to the rich fantasy world created by Ashley Mayers and first published in 2015-16 in her seven-book modern multicultural epic, *The Sita Chronicles*.

Damsels and Demons, the third book of Eleanor MacLeod's story, continues the modern story from *The Sita Chronicles*, in juxtaposition to Eleanor's prequel epic unfolding in the 1920s. As an homage to the genres that Ashley Mayers found most fascinating as a young reader herself, each book in Eleanor's epic plays with elements of a classic genre. *Damsels and Demons* incorporates elements of a modern fairy tale with a unique Ashley Mayers twist.

Throughout this series, it is the author's intention to give enough background for an uninitiated reader to develop a relationship with the world of *The Sita Chronicles*, while introducing them to several new heroines whose stories haven't yet been told. Both series fit together as puzzle pieces, creating unique insights into characters who are lovingly developed over the combined set of twelve books. All five books of Eleanor's story are intended to be read in order.

This series, like *The Sita Chronicles*, is a completely original, multicultural saga with roots in Hindu mythology. It exists in a world not dissimilar to ours, where Avatars (deities on Earth), Rakshasas (shapeshifting demons originating on Venus), and Yakshas (shapeshifting nature spirits) are real. While knowledge of Hinduism is not required to enjoy this series, a short glossary is provided in the back of the book to offer readers more context on Hindu cultural references.

TABLE OF CONTENTS

PROLOGUE

Ellie sat alone in the headmaster's office, eyeing the gold-plated awards hanging on the wall behind the imposing administrative desk and perusing the various titles of pedagogical theory placed prominently on the mahogany bookshelves all around, attempting to keep herself calm as she reran her speech in her head over and over again.

She had actively avoided discussing her alien origins publicly since the First Contact announcement almost a year earlier, and mostly she'd gotten away with it. After all, there were several other Rakshasas of Venus who were far more outgoing and interesting than she was, including her own father. To her great relief, the public and the press were more than happy to keep their attention focused on the most newsworthy (and gossip-worthy) headlines, from which she had so far mercifully escaped.

But now, as the good big sister that she was (and had always secretly wanted to be throughout her lonely childhood), she'd agreed to speak to her adopted human brother's class of curious ten-year-olds about her experiences as a teenager during World

War II. She'd regretted her decision the moment she'd agreed, but if her father, who was intensely shy by nature, could flit about the world as the leader that he had finally become with only a few hints here and there of his struggle, mostly given away by his tendency towards human blushing, then surely she could address a group of ten-year-olds... *surely*.

She was startled as a light knock distracted her, and then she tensed as someone swung open the door. She'd been hiding away in the headmaster's office to avoid the inevitable hubbub that followed her everywhere she went, despite the fact that after eighty years the setting still made her somewhat nervous, as if she were waiting to be punished for some infraction she didn't think she'd committed. Her unusually fiery hair that she'd always embraced wholeheartedly as a connection to her mother made her instantly recognizable, and despite the press's general focus on the other Rakshasas, an alien was an alien—even she understood why everyone was so intrigued. If she weren't the intensely ordinary alien herself, she too would have found the idea highly curious.

A tall, handsome Indic man clad in a well-fitted suit entered the room and closed the door behind him.

"Are you the famous Ellie MacLeod?" he asked with a lilting Anglo-Indian accent.

"Aye," she agreed reluctantly as she stood up. "I don't sign autographs or pose for alien selfies, if that's what you're after. I am here strictly on business, and I will be needed any second in the auditorium."

He grinned. With a subtle wiggle, his disguise dissolved, revealing only a fleeting moment of violet metallic plasma, and then her father was standing before her, inspecting his fair hands proudly.

"I really had you that time, didn't I, Ellie-bean?"

"Dad!" she exclaimed as she rushed to engulf him into a hug. "I didn't think you'd be here! Aren't you supposed to be in Mexico rebuilding the rural hospitals with Supriya?"

He squeezed her lovingly, and she relished the familiarity of his frigid temperature. "My talented wife has it entirely under control. She is even leading classes for the villagers on basic emergency medicine. When the word got out, people started coming from miles and miles away to attend. You should have seen it, Ellie-bean! She delivered twins in a tent with only some towels and a bucket of water!"

"She is remarkable, isn't she?" Ellie winked.

Seeing her father so intensely in love with a partner who was just as extraordinary and overly modest as he was, was almost enough to pull Ellie out of the general malaise she'd been secretly battling for months… Almost.

"She is," Edmund agreed proudly as he hugged her again. "She didn't need my help with the rest of the project, and I couldn't resist coming to support you in your first speech."

"It's just to Charlie's classmates," she shrugged as a wave of nerves returned.

"A speech is a speech. I avoided public speaking for sixty years myself, and I didn't have a gawking audience looking for the tiniest hint of alien behavior to contend with. I'm so proud of you for not letting it deter you, Ellie-bean."

Ellie pulled him into another hug and pushed back tears. She hadn't realized until that moment how much she'd been missing him. He sensed her change in mood, and pulled away.

"What's wrong, Ellie-bean?" he asked with concern as he wiped her first tear away, like he had done when she was a little girl.

She swallowed hard, annoyed at herself for crying in front of her father after the ninety years she'd spent growing up.

"I don't know… I guess it's just nerves," she said as he pulled her into another hug.

"Ellie-bean, they're just a group of school children. You'll be wonderful! Just pretend they're your kindergarteners. You were a wonderful teacher before our alien coming out party, and I'm sure you will be one again today," Edmund reassured her.

"A hundred clever ten-year-olds and twenty kindergarteners are hardly the same thing, Dad."

"Well, even if you don't give the most impressive speech, it won't matter." He changed his tactic. "Kuveni volunteered to run security when she found out what you'd agreed to do. She's already disabled everyone's phones, so there won't be a single illicit recording of your speech; although, I can make one just for you if you want one. Supriya's been coaching me in how to use these blasted smartphones."

He pulled a phone out of his pocket and dropped it straight onto the ground as he attempted to unlock it.

Ellie smiled at his predictable demonstration of technical incompetence. Given how close he was to his bi-centennial, he'd done an admirable job of keeping up with the times—so much so that when they were reporters together in the 1960s, he had taught her everything she needed to know about the complicated recording equipment they were using, but now, she couldn't blame him for falling behind. Things were just changing too fast.

"Blimey, I hate these tiny screens!" he exclaimed. "Whatever happened to buttons and knobs and good old-fashioned type-writers? I need some tactile feedback from my technology!"

"I know exactly what you mean." Ellie reached down and collected his phone for him.

"Thanks, Ellie-bean." He took it back, and then he guided her to sit beside him on the leather couch across from the headmaster's desk. "I feel like I'm about to get an earful from the headmaster."

"I was thinking exactly the same thing," Ellie agreed as she finally relaxed. "It reminds me of the time they called me into the office to tell me that I'd received the highest marks on the national exams. The headmaster was delayed in a meeting while I sat in the hallway waiting, and I was convinced for an hour that they'd discovered… never mind…" She trailed off as Edmund's attention was piqued.

"That they'd discovered what, Ellie-bean?" His tone was not the least bit concerned, only intrigued. "I didn't realize you'd ever done anything worthy of being called into the headmaster's office! What did you get away with?"

Ellie stared before her, debating what to say.

"Ellie-bean, it's been seventy-two years since you graduated. I'm rather proud that you got away with something. I myself got away with many silly pranks when I was a young lieutenant in the army in the 1890s. Did I ever tell you about the time the chaps were going on and on about the poor dental care of the natives? No matter how many times I told them the dark color of the locals' teeth was intentional, they simply wouldn't believe me until I proved it. I slipped a pinch of henna into their tooth powder, and those chaps didn't know what hit them! It took weeks for the color to come out, but they never said one more word about it."

Ellie smiled. "I don't think you ever told me that, actually."

"I didn't want to set a poor example. It was a rather cruel prank, when I think back on it. A few of them were genuinely worried the color would never come out, no matter how much I reassured them that it would… but tell me, Ellie. What were you afraid the headmaster had discovered? It certainly couldn't have been that bad."

Ellie took a deep breath. "I was afraid someone had discovered that… that I was an alien." She cringed as she said it, as she had never once confessed to her father that she had known about her Rakshasa plasma since long before he revealed his origins to her.

Edmund worked unsuccessfully to hide his surprise, but Ellie knew him too well. "But… but, Ellie-bean…" She watched as he catalogued various thoughts and memories in his head.

"I fell out of one of the lindens when I was a lass, Dad. On my eighth birthday. I broke my arm—a very nasty break, actually–

—and my Rakshasa plasma came to the rescue. I didn't tell you because I was afraid you wouldn't let me play in the woods alone again."

"But… but, Ellie… if you'd told me…" He wasn't able to hide his grimace. "You were right. I wouldn't have let you play in the woods alone again… I would have been tormented by the idea of you getting hurt… But… but, if I'd known you'd inherited my self-healing talents…" A look of great sadness worked its way onto his face. "We might have had many more honest years together. You might have had an honest childhood."

"Woulda–Shoulda–Coulda. Who knows what would have actually happened, Dad. We had a lovely time together all those years, and now we've had many decades to appreciate being honest with each other. The contrast is necessary for the appreciation, or so you've said."

Edmund took Ellie's hand into his. "I love you, Ellie-bean."

Ellie leaned over and hugged him. "I love you, Dad. I'm sorry I didn't tell you."

"I'm sorry I was such an overbearing father that you didn't feel like you could tell me the truth, Ellie-bean."

"Overbearing isn't the right word… more like a champion worry-wart," Ellie tried to bring back some humor.

Edmund was too distracted to follow her lead. "But, Ellie… when I told you my secret after the fire, you still never said anything about your own plasma. Why didn't you tell me you knew? I thought for two decades after that that I might lose you in a human lifetime."

She thought carefully about her answer. "I suppose I didn't want to get your hopes up. I knew that you were much more alien than I was. It took hours for my arm to heal, but you were a freshly healed young man just minutes after that fire. I thought that if my plasma wasn't strong enough to heal me like yours healed you, I didn't want you to be surprised by losing me. I thought it would

6

make the whole thing worse, like the surprise you felt when you lost Mum."

As words escaped him, Edmund pulled her into another hug, and the ball in her throat returned. She always cried when he cried, but this time her emotion wasn't just rooted in the shared tragedy that had defined their relationship her whole life. This time, her emotions were driven by something far more ordinary. It had been so long since they'd spent any mundane time together without crowds or family or magical shenanigans to distract them that suddenly she felt an overwhelming pang of longing for the mostly uneventful life they'd been living before destiny had decided that it was time for the Age of Truth.

"I'm sorry, Ellie-bean," he whispered. He pulled away from her and wiped a violet tear back into his skin. "I shouldn't have let my melancholy distract you before your speech."

"It's not you, Dad…" Ellie wiped a violet tear from her eye.

"Then tell me, Ellie-bean. Tell me what's making you sad." Edmund took her hand gently into his, and she nestled into his arms, leaning her head against his cold chest, as she had done so many times throughout her life when she was sad.

Ellie smiled wistfully at the nostalgic familiarity of the feeling. "It's just… I don't know. It's a lot of things, I suppose. I miss you, Dad. I miss this. I miss us alone together in a library chatting about everything that comes to mind. It hasn't happened since those MI-5 snipers shot you. It was like our whole world just dissolved that day, and it never came back."

"I'm sorry, Ellie. I've been rather self-absorbed with all the changes in my life this past year. I should have paid closer attention to how you were feeling."

Ellie's heart broke at the grimace of guilt that blanketed her father's expression.

"Dad, please don't feel guilty. I'm really glad to see you so happy. I've *never* seen you this happy, not in my entire life. You should be reveling in it every minute. You, more than anyone ever, have earned some unburdened happiness."

"Still, Ellie. I can be happy and thoughtful of your needs at the same time," Edmund argued.

"I'm ninety, Dad. I shouldn't need you to coddle me." Ellie didn't like that somewhere deep down, she really did miss being coddled. She pushed the feeling aside and forced herself to return to cheer. "I've had lots of wonderful things to keep me busy. I love my life with Angus and Duncan at the MacLeod ancestral home in Elphinstone. My photography gallery on Princes Street is doing so well that I'm thinking of opening another one in London, and all the while Kuveni has done a bang-up job of keeping me connected to all of you… and it's not like our life before was perfect. I don't miss spending a single moment with Grace… who's here, by the way. Did you see her when you came in? Charlie said that she came because she wanted to hear my speech! Can you believe the nerve?!"

Edmund worked hard to not give away the degree of his extreme distaste for dealing with his ex-wife. "No, I didn't realize she was here… I snuck into the office without checking out the audience. Kuveni told me you were waiting in here, away from the crowds." He straightened his posture and prepared himself for a mature, fatherly statement. "Despite her cold temperament, I do believe that Grace loves you, Ellie. She asks about you every time we meet to hand over Charlie."

"She had a funny way of showing it all those years," Ellie humphed.

"Grace was never good with feelings. I'm sorry I let her tyranny ruin our beautiful time together. Marrying her was one of the biggest mistakes of my life."

"Dad, we all make mistakes. I didn't bring her up to hassle you. I brought her up because I was reminding myself that the times I'm longing for so desperately weren't really that great. I know logically that the world has changed for the better. I don't have any excuse for feeling nostalgic for how things were before… It's just… I suppose I've never really liked change very much."

"You are the daughter of the Preserver of the Universe. It is natural for you to dislike change, you know," Edmund pointed out. "I suppose you can blame me for that. It's rather ironic, actually. You have me to blame for most of the changes in your life, don't you? I haven't been particularly good at preserving things."

"I blame *destiny*." Ellie and her father rolled their eyes in unison as she said it, and then she smiled. "I love you, Dad. Please, don't let me get you down. I always feel a bit off when there's a lot of change, and I suppose I've been thinking a lot about the past as I've been putting my speech together. Plus, there was that manuscript from Supriya about you and Mum getting married. It changed a lot about how I thought of her… about both of you. Not for the worse, but still, it changed things."

"Ah, the manuscript…" Edmund blushed. "I hope it wasn't disappointing? Or, perhaps too detailed? I almost asked Supriya to censor it, but your mother really did want you to know everything."

"It was perfect, Dad. I read it so many times the pages began to fray. I've been meaning to thank Supriya for sending it. I just can't believe that you had so many wild adventures that you never told me about. I mean, hostages on the Orient Express! Pirates! Spies! You and Mum were both so interesting! And I can't believe that she knew Mélusine and Kuveni so intimately, and you never figured it out!"

"Neither can I," Edmund admitted. "It's rather shameful when I think back on it, although your mother seemed to recognize a certain distaste for the truth in me that was certainly accurate. I was quite active in avoiding certain realities that I didn't want to know about. I was mostly just desperate for some confirmation that Vibhi was my father; everything else was secondary. I suppose my childhood in the orphanage made me desperate for a family more than anything else—more than even learning what species I was."

"They were all very good at refusing to answer your questions. It's not like you didn't ask."

"Yes, yes, you're right. I didn't remember how tenacious I was in my questioning until I read Supriya's manuscript. I had your mother to thank for that. As the manuscript made abundantly clear, I was not naturally inquisitive... at least about myself. I could have spent months researching a historical question, but somehow I didn't have the same drive for digging into my own history. I think Vibhishana was right—I simply wasn't ready to know. Speaking of which..."

Edmund wiggled awkwardly and pulled a thick manuscript from a hidden pocket in the back of his well-fitted suit jacket.

"Geez, Dad, did you carry that all the way from Mexico like that?!" Ellie exclaimed.

"I did. It was nestled between my back and my wings. Neha taught me the technique a few months ago, and I've found it extremely useful ever since." Edmund smiled as he presented it to her. "Supriya sends it with love. It covers the rest of my honeymoon with your mother in India. There were so many adventures, they took up an entire manuscript."

Ellie stared at it with equal parts excitement and anxiety.

"Oh, and Supriya had to consult some surprising sources to get some extra details. She and I were both very surprised at how many of our loving relatives made their way into the story this time. I'll give you a clue—Rahul had quite an interesting perspective from when he was just a boy and Eleanor and I happened to join the Patels for a banquet at the maharaja's palace in Baroda."

"Really?!" Ellie exclaimed. "I can't even roll my eyes at destiny's role in that one!"

"Neither can I. I was utterly shocked when Supriya gave me the manuscript to read. There was so much that happened that I wasn't privy to, that reading the manuscript made it feel like it was someone else's story entirely."

"I've been wondering about that… I've been wondering how strange it is for you to read them… and for Supriya to write them about you and another woman. She's been quite a good sport about all of it."

"Supriya is a wonderful sport about many things," Edmund agreed. "But she isn't just doing this out of familial duty. She loves you and Eleanor just as much as I do." Ellie threw him a skeptical look. "That statement is literally true, Ellie. You see, because we are both Rakshasas…" Edmund trailed off with a deeper red blush as he thought better of his revelation.

"Because you are both Rakshasas?" Ellie coaxed. "Come on, Dad. I've been reading saucy accounts of your honeymoon escapades with Mum. Just tell it to me straight."

He smiled as she parroted one of her mother's favorite phrases, and sucked up his discomfort. "Rakshasas have unique ways of bonding with each other. When we exchange our plasma, our consciousness becomes one. We feel what the other feels, including our love for others. It is unlike anything else I've ever experienced, and it is a beautiful gift for us to be able to share our emotions in that way. If ever you find yourself with a worthy Rakshasa companion, you will learn how it feels for yourself."

"Huh… the idea of being with another Rakshasa never even crossed my mind… I suppose there are plenty hopping about now, although not so many in human form…"

"Only a *worthy* one," Edmund reiterated with a burst of fatherly worry. "You share all of your emotions with your partner when you do it. Exchanging your plasma with an unworthy partner is unpleasant and can be outright dangerous, or so Mélusine warned."

"Don't worry, Dad. I had one murderous, abusive wanker in my life, and one was enough."

Edmund squeezed her hand. "You will know when you are with someone worthy, Ellie-bean. Trust yourself. I had never felt anything like how I felt when I met your mother. She made me feel like I was flying many decades before I could do it literally, but it took me over a hundred years to reach that point."

Ellie pulled him into another hug. "Thanks, Dad."

As he pulled away, the door opened, and a grey-haired man in a navy blue suit bearing the school's crest stepped inside. He glanced across the room to the chair where Ellie had been sitting, and then startled as he spotted them sitting on the couch.

"Colonel?" he asked with nervous excitement. "We didn't realize you would be here! If you'd told us you were coming, we would have prepared!"

"No extra preparation was necessary in the slightest, Dr. Higgins," Edmund reassured him as he stood up and shook his hand amicably. "I will be in disguise today. Ellie does not need her father to steal the limelight when she has so many more interesting things to say than I do."

He closed his eyes, and with a subtle wiggle, he returned to the handsome Indic form he had used when he arrived.

"Good lord," Dr. Higgins murmured.

"I reckon that if this form was good enough to convince my own daughter, it should work sufficiently for our needs today," Edmund said as he observed his transformation with satisfaction.

"It really is very good, Dad. It looks completely natural. Much better than that blond surfing bloke you tried back in August."

Edmund smiled. "Yes, that form was a bit outrageous. I've found that they must feel natural to look natural. This one is based on how I imagined Abdul Barr must have looked as a young man. Using it reminds me of what a kind, thoughtful teacher he was. But, that's enough of that. I suspect there is an impatient audience awaiting your words of wisdom, Ellie."

Dr. Higgins nodded his agreement. "Charlie and Anders are in the front row, and Grace is standing in the back. I should warn you, though, that the audience is a little bigger than just Charlie's class…" He threw them both an apologetic glance as he broke the

12

news. "Rumors got out around the school that you were coming, you see, and Charlie thought you wouldn't mind…"

Ellie sighed her concession loudly. "In for a penny, in for a pound, I suppose."

"There are a few empty seats for teachers beside Charlie in the front row, Colonel, if you'd like to take one of those," Dr. Higgins quickly moved the conversation along.

"You'll be wonderful, Ellie," Edmund whispered as he squeezed her hand. He took the manuscript and returned it to his hidden pocket. "I'll keep it safe for you until we're all celebrating together after your speech. Sabrina and Amy are preparing a family feast at the Rutherford house for later."

Ellie took a deep, calming breath, and with her supportive father by her side, she followed Dr. Higgins through the stone hallways of the prestigious school, readying herself to take one tiny step towards coming out of her shell. She hoped that her mother would approve, and she wished intensely as she often had as a girl that her mother could be there with her.

I'm here, Ellie-bean, and you will be wonderful. Trust yourself.

Ellie shivered at the odd sensation of hearing her mother's voice echo in her head. She straightened her posture and took another deep breath.

"I'm ready," she declared.

Ellie took her position at the podium and watched as Edmund took his seat next to Charlie, who looked momentarily annoyed by the stranger's intrusion until Edmund whispered something into his ear, and his eyes lit up. Edmund offered his hand, and Charlie subtly took it, looking over his shoulder to glance around the room at the hundreds of peers gathered behind him. With a shared little whispered joke in Hindi between father and son, Charlie ignored the pre-adolescent embarrassment that was resonating in his head and settled in to enjoy every moment of his unexpected reunion with his exceptionally busy father.

Ellie shook her head with bemusement as a wave of whispers spread through the crowd. Her father was still not particularly adept at disguising his identity, no matter how skillful his shapeshifting abilities had become. She watched as Charlie's best friend, Anders, noticed their exchange and began wiggling excitedly, working his hardest to keep his special knowledge to himself.

Edmund also noticed Anders's attention and leaned over to whisper a hello, at which point the crowd went wild with excitement, and Edmund realized his error. He threw Ellie an apologetic glance and then looked around the room at the consequences of his poorly executed farce. Ellie's nerves exploded as many hundreds of children became unruly, and as Dr. Higgins fell into a panic at the degenerating situation, Edmund took a deep, calming breath, rolled his shoulders, and dissolved his disguise, to a chorus of thrilled squeals from the audience.

He squeezed Charlie's hand and stood up to address the crowd. "I can see that you are all too clever for my unskilled farce. As most of you have undoubtedly realized, I am Colonel Edmund Marriner. I have joined you today to listen to the fascinating historical insights that Ellie has thoughtfully prepared for you. Now, I will be seated silently with my son, Charlie, in the front row, and you had best all buckle down and prepare yourselves for the most interesting lecture you'll ever hear in your lives."

As he moved to sit back down, a crumpled piece of paper flew across the room and hit him in the chest. Charlie cringed as Edmund reached down to pick it up. He unfolded the paper, read its contents, glanced back at Ellie and then down at Charlie, who was shaking his head with shame, and then he nimbly hopped up to stand beside Ellie at the podium.

Charlie watched, mortified, as Ellie read the note and threw her father a surprised look of disapproval, and then a subtle look of pity towards Charlie. His months of keeping the many mean comments of his classmates from his unknowing alien family had just come to an end.

"It would seem that someone in the audience is proudly ignorant," Edmund declared. He held up the note and read it for all to hear. "'Go home, filthy demons.' Not really the most poetic of insults, is it?"

He smiled supportively at Charlie, and then glanced towards Dr. Higgins, whose face was red with anger as he scanned the audience for any evidence of the culprit.

"For most of my life, I would have found an attack like this to be quite debilitating. It isn't pleasant for anyone, even us, to be the subject of ridicule," Edmund addressed the audience calmly. "But, I have learned in my two hundred years that when the voice of reason remains silent, it creates a void for others to fill. So, I shall address the fearful ramblings that have made it difficult for your minds to accept the truth that is right before you, and help rid you of your struggle so that you can fully appreciate what Ellie has to say."

Ellie offered him a supportive nod, and he continued on determinedly.

"Firstly, we are home, my young friends. Rakshasas have been on Earth for billions of years, since before humans evolved from single-celled organisms. We made Earth the planet that you know today. If you do not know what I'm talking about, you should join the three billion people who have watched Neha's scientific lecture about it on the internet. Additionally, as you are all certainly aware, Ellie and I are both part human, and we were born here, as were countless generations of our ancestors—Rakshasas and humans alike. Thirdly, we are impeccably clean, far cleaner than humans are, since microbes will not come near us. And fourthly, Rakshasas are not demons."

"You are too! It was all over the tele!" A teenaged boy with a crackling voice and a red face covered in painfully peeling acne yelled from the back of the crowd. "You had spikes and fangs and everything!"

"That is quite enough!" Dr. Higgins boomed. "The next student who interrupts will be expelled!"

Charlie looked down, as if he was hoping for the floor to swallow him whole.

"That level of discipline should be reserved for more of an offense than speaking one's honest mind, Dr. Higgins," Edmund said calmly. "I suspect that our loud peer in the back is not the only one with these ideas. Is he?"

Edmund glanced around the crowd assessingly, stopping for an extra moment as he noticed his ex-wife standing by the door. She looked pained as he made eye contact, undoubtedly reminded of the same ignorant accusation she had thrown at him on the fateful day she had learned his secret and they had finally annulled their excruciating marriage.

"They are not demons," Grace declared as she kept her eyes locked on Edmund. It was the first time she had uttered the words aloud, and Ellie assessed her curiously, spotting the rosary in her right hand. "They are agents of God."

Edmund smiled genuinely as he glanced down at Charlie, who looked as surprised as Ellie was at the development.

"But you admitted it! You even turned into a demon in the video online!" a pale girl from the middle of the audience called. The girls around her whispered disapprovingly.

Ellie braced herself, as she knew that there was only one reaction to expect from her father at a baiting like that. She threw Charlie a commiserative look, and together they watched with resignation as Edmund brought forth his demonic form, covering his human body with a layer of bright multi-colored patches across his skin and black spikes to match his black eyes and fangs, while maintaining his impeccably-fitted suit. The entire audience exploded into gasps, cheers, and jeers.

Edmund looked apologetically towards his ex-wife, realizing his error in pushing her most intense button just moments after she'd made a concession that he had never expected to witness. He channeled his embarrassment into his lecture.

"This form is indeed grotesque," he declared as he held out his ghoulish hands before him. "It is understandable why humans and Rakshasas alike believed for many centuries that it was demonic in nature. But it is the Age of Truth now. We know that the origin of this form has a far more mundane explanation. My people created this form to prevent *you*, my friends, and your ancestors from attempting to eat us. Early humans were just as savage as the most frightening beasts on Earth, and after tens of thousands of years attempting to live in harmony side by side with cannibalistic humans, my people still fall back on this form when we are threatened. These spikes…" He held out his green and yellow hands before him, inspecting the black spikes jutting from his wrists and pausing for an extra-long moment to observe his black, claw-like fingernails, "for all intents and purposes are just the same as porcupine quills. They are a predatory deterrent, and they exist to protect *us* from *you*."

"It was also for their own good," Ellie chimed in. She was startled as she realized she'd just accidentally made a declaration before their large audience. She cleared her throat and spoke more authoritatively, imitating her father's tone. "The bright colors are a deterrent to warn humans that we are poisonous. If you try to consume us, you will die. It really is a fair warning, if you think about it. I can't imagine anyone getting close enough that the spikes are necessary."

Edmund smiled, nonchalantly revealing his fangs. "I wouldn't come close to a creature that looks this grotesque if I weren't one myself. Would you, Ellie?"

"I personally think it's a good deterrent," she agreed as she glanced to the audience. "Do you agree?" The students nodded and finally relaxed at their conversational tone.

He closed his eyes and subverted his demon, returning to his handsome, youthful human form.

"I was rather horrified when I woke up one morning, and I looked like that. Can you imagine? Looking perfectly human for a good two hundred years, and then waking up one morning with spikes, claws, and fangs?"

He paused to let the students envision the idea for themselves.

"But I am certainly not the only one on Earth who woke up one day and was frightened by what I saw. There comes a time in everyone's life when he or she must overcome some type of unpleasant physical condition. When how we look on the outside does not at all match how we feel on the inside. In my case, my condition was bloody terrifying!"

Some of the students laughed at his enthusiasm, while others looked pensive, including his acne-ridden detractor in the back, as they considered his assertion.

"But, my wise daughter Ellie here has kindly reminded me over the years that there is no point in stewing over unfortunate things we cannot change about ourselves, even when those things are as ghastly as mine are."

He paused as he considered how much he was willing to share. He looked around the audience who was now listening intently, landing his gaze once again on Grace.

"I thought when my monstrous form first surfaced, and for quite some time afterwards, that it was a karmic punishment for the wickedness of my father, whose many evil deeds you are all certainly aware of at this point. What I didn't realize until later was that having such a grotesque form was a blessing, not a curse. It was a perfect tool to help me demonstrate to all of you—to the entire human race—that creatures as frightening as we are could save the world. It was only my beastly form that enabled me to convince you that an Avatar of Light does not always have to look like a beautiful, glowing angel."

As Grace's eyes teared up, Edmund finally moved his attention to the rest of his audience.

"We must all make meaning from our circumstances, even the unpleasant ones. It is now one of my sacred duties to guide humans and Rakshasas alike to fully understand that, and I shall now conclude my impromptu lecture by thanking the ruffian in the crowd for his insult." He stared down a young blond boy, only a year or two older than Charlie, until the boy looked away. "I trust that no one here will be repeating it or anything similar to my son ever again." The students shivered as a subtle burst of power emanated off of him. "And now, my young friends, you are lucky enough to have the exceptionally rare opportunity to hear Ellie's stories about being just about your age at the dawn of World War II. Those of you who are wise will not let the unimportant detail of our foreign race distract you from learning the many useful things that Ellie has to teach you."

He smiled and offered her a salute, and then returned to his seat next to Charlie. He offered his hand to his son once again, and Charlie squeezed it.

"You were great, Dad," Charlie whispered.

"I would have stepped in sooner if I'd known they'd been giving you trouble, Charlie," Edmund whispered back. "You can tell me *anything* from now on. You know that, right?"

"I know, but sometimes a man has to fight his own battles."

Edmund smiled at Charlie's grown-up response.

"You are certainly right about that," Edmund agreed.

"Sometimes it's still good to have my dad's help, though," Charlie added as he sighed with contentment and relaxed as the pulsating cold of Edmund's hand made him feel like he was home. Edmund reveled in a moment of closeness that he knew would become even more fleeting as Charlie's childhood dissolved, and he fought back a bout of melancholy at the idea.

Ellie smiled as they settled in, and Charlie offered her a thumbs-up. She took a deep breath and readied herself for her prepared speech.

"My name is Eleanor Ariadne MacLeod Marriner. I am a Rakshasa of Venus, and yet, you and I are far more similar than we are different. When I was your age, I cared about the same things that you do—school, friends; hopes, dreams; sneaking onto the train to London to go to the shows when I was supposedly studying with my friends…" She glanced at her father and smiled as she revealed a secret she had kept from him for seventy-five years, and he smiled supportively back. "And then one night on the radio, as I sat in my father's library slaving away on an essay about ego-maniacs in Shakespeare's histories, the announcement came: Hitler had invaded Poland. That was when I knew the world would never be the same again. Little did I know how intensely it would change, but that was just the beginning of the story…"

Ellie settled into her speech and smiled with secret satisfaction as the students listened intently and nodded emphatically at each of her well-crafted points, but in the back of her mind, just as if it were Christmas Eve, she felt burning anticipation for what was to come. There was a new story waiting for her in Supriya's manuscript. She hoped sincerely that the tragedy of her mother's ending would not work its way into the story just yet, after all, they were still just halfway through their honeymoon.

Don't worry, Ellie-bean. A wild Indian adventure awaits, her mother's voice murmured.

I'm ready.

PART ONE
NAMASTE, INDIA

CHAPTER 1 – THE PRODIGAL RETURN

April 3, 1923

The Arabian Sea, just off the coast of Bombay

"Dearest, can you believe we're finally in India?!" Edmund swooned as the steamer chugged its way towards a hazy land mass in the distance.

They sat cuddled together on a velvet divan just inside the balcony of their suite, watching the approach. The late-afternoon heat and humidity were so intense that even the strong breeze produced by the steamer's high speed no longer provided the relief that Eleanor had come to depend on throughout the last few days of travel on the Arabian Sea.

"I can certainly believe we're in the tropics," Eleanor replied unenthusiastically as she wiped a flood of sweat off of her forehead, dabbing the area under her wide-brimmed sun hat with a handkerchief that had already gathered a grotesque mix of brown sweat and black and red smudged makeup from its days of constant use.

She'd spent so much time anticipating the pleasures of this part of the journey that she hadn't given one thought to the potential discomforts of the tropics. But, ever since they'd commandeered their passenger liner back from the pirates and returned it to its charted course away from the dangerous coastline of Somalia, the temperature had increased several degrees every hour, and her Scottish temperament was not keeping up.

She looked up at her happy husband, who didn't seem bothered by the change in the slightest.

"Is it too hot for you, dearest?" Edmund asked concernedly as another drip of sweat ran down Eleanor's face before she could wipe it away.

"I am a wild Scottish thistle, darling. We grow best in cold, windy rain." She tried to keep her tone positive, despite her rare bout of self-consciousness about her unattractive state.

"Yes… yes, of course, dearest. I had a Scottish colleague in the British Indian Army at one point, a highlander, in fact. Captain Ferguson was a very strange bloke. He did not have the temperament for India's heat either. At every possible opportunity, he hopped away from the regiment to lounge about beside whatever watering hole happened to be close by."

"Well, I suppose that means you'll know where to find me if I disappear on you," Eleanor quipped.

Edmund did not find it humorous, as he was already preoccupied with silent self-castigation at his personal responsibility for her plight.

"I'm sorry, dearest. It didn't occur to me that the heat would overwhelm you… I didn't plan very well at all, in fact. April and May are always the hottest months of the year in India. They call it summer here, because it is the dry season before the monsoon comes to cool things down."

He pulled her into his arms, and she relished his cool body, although as the temperature had risen over the last few days, she had noticed that his frigidity had subsided as well. She wondered from time to time if perhaps one source of his love of India was

24

that the humid heat of the air kept him naturally warmer than the cool climate of England did.

Eleanor sighed with contentment. "I'm enjoying your cool arms immensely, Edmund. They are the perfect respite from the incessant heat."

"Captain Ferguson never had the privilege of cooling himself in my arms." He tightened his grip as he let her pull him back into his cheer. "As long as I keep myself properly hydrated, I have never had a problem with the heat. I will, perhaps, bathe in cold water from now on, so that I can serve as your personal cooling valet."

"I will take any excuse to spend time in your arms, darling." Eleanor reached up to kiss him gently on the lips, and he pulled her into a more passionate embrace. As she fought off a momentary bout of lightheadedness (as she often did when he embraced her with the full power of his divine love), she noticed something that she had never noticed before. "Are you not the least bit hot, darling? Not at all? I don't see a drop of sweat anywhere on you."

Edmund shifted uncomfortably at her question. "I feel the heat, and sometimes it irritates my skin, but I don't sweat, dearest. Not at all, and I never have. Haven't you noticed? We've been in the heat of passion many times already…"

Eleanor paused to catalogue her memories. He was certainly right. She'd never witnessed him sweat at all, but she'd only known him since it had been cold! They'd met in October! She'd always assumed that it simply wasn't hot enough, or perhaps she hadn't even really thought about it at all. The idea was so utterly foreign that it hadn't even crossed her mind.

"No, darling, I never noticed… but please, Edmund. Don't be self-conscious about it. It's a rather pleasant trait, don't you think? Men smell so grotesque when they're walking around in thick fabrics on hot days. I find it incredibly attractive that you will never smell like a burly, sweaty bloke."

Edmund pulled her into his arms for another passionate embrace.

"Shall we test the boundaries of your pleasant trait in the heat of passion?" Eleanor suggested naughtily as she copped an enticing feel.

Edmund's entire body perked up at the idea, but as she led him hastily into the bedroom for one final honeymoon go-around before their ship pulled into port, a timid knock at the door interrupted their pleasant plan.

"Just a minute!" Eleanor called.

Edmund took several deep, calming breaths to force his excitement to disperse.

"I'm sorry, darling, I suppose we'll have to continue our fun later tonight."

Eleanor led him to the door and waited for his nod of approval. As she swung it open, their two newest friends whom they'd met by chance during their fateful ride on the Orient Express, (the only couple on Earth who knew Edmund's secrets, and their veritable allies in fighting off a troop of pirates and spies alongside the mysterious help that Edmund's powerful guardians had provided) stood before them.

"G'day mates!" Oz declared jovially. "It looks like we're about to reach your port of call!"

"We wanted to say goodbye before parting ways," Yvie added as she pulled Eleanor into enthusiastic French cheek kisses.

"You are welcome to visit us anytime in Perth, with an excuse or without one." Oz reiterated the generous offer he'd already made several times. "Here's my calling card. Now, don't be strangers, mates."

"You know..." Eleanor's face lit up as an idea occurred to her. "The ship is staying in Bombay for two days. You could disembark with us and let Edmund show you around the city. He is the most expert guide you will ever meet, I suspect."

"What a wonderful idea!" Edmund exclaimed. "Do come! You won't even need to bring your luggage! You can stay here on the ship! We will be staying with a very dear friend of mine whom I've known for years and years. I'm sure that he will be glad to meet you."

"I have always wanted to see India," Yvie admitted.

"Let's do it!" Oz agreed. "Thank you kindly for the invitation."

"Oh, this will be so wonderful!" Edmund exclaimed.

Eleanor loved his childlike enthusiasm, and as the ship sounded its resonating call into port, Edmund pulled Eleanor into a romantic dip, and Oz and Yvie laughed and clapped at the sight.

"I'm glad to see you're back to a proper honeymoon, mates!" Oz said as Edmund steadied Eleanor and took her hand tightly into his.

"Colonel!" Mr. Valov exclaimed as he rushed towards them from the elevator. "It's time to disembark!"

Edmund looked to Eleanor with surprise. "The ship is here for two days, Mr. Valov. Is there some urgency of which I am not aware?"

Mr. Valov looked at Oz and Yvie, and then relaxed as he reconsidered the circumstances. "I suppose there isn't. To be honest, I'm rather surprised to see that you're... er... clothed and ready to go. I assumed I'd need to rally you."

Edmund laughed as a subtle blush worked its way onto his face. "A fair assumption, Mr. Valov. But Oz and Yvie have beaten you to your task, and they will be joining us in Bombay for a little excursion. Can you see to our luggage in the meantime? We will be staying with Mr. Ravi Bidkar at his home on Malabar Hill. He is sending a car to collect us at the port, but with Oz and Yvie joining us, you might need to hail a separate taxi."

"I will see to it, Colonel," Mr. Valov agreed. Eleanor caught a hint of annoyance in his expression, whether at the cumbersome request or at his exclusion from their party, she wasn't entirely certain. "Do you happen to have Mr. Bidkar's address?"

"Hrm…" Edmund's posture deflated. "I can't say that I do. He has always sent a car for me… but he is rather well-known in Bombay. Perhaps you can ask around? Or you could leave the luggage here and join us in the car for the journey, and then return for our luggage later tonight? I'm sure he'd be happy to send a man or two to assist you. His staff is rather large, and they are always exceedingly helpful."

"I will figure something out, Colonel. Please do not worry about me." Mr. Valov shifted with subtle discomfort, and then lowered his voice. "You had best keep a bit mum about your friendship with the Bidkars, if you don't want to cause trouble for yourself with the army, Colonel. Times have changed."

Mr. Valov threw Eleanor a subtle look of warning, and her interest was piqued.

"Why is that, Mr. Valov?" she asked innocently. She knew he was in dangerous territory, straddling his true identity as a Secret Service spy while pretending to be Edmund's exceptionally skilled butler, and yet she couldn't help but nudge him into clarifying what he meant with his rather specific warning.

"It is of no matter," Edmund replied quickly on his behalf. "Mr. Valov, you will have to fill me in on your familiarity with my friend's reputation at a later date. We don't want to keep his car waiting."

The fact that Edmund appeared to know what Mr. Valov was talking about enflamed Eleanor's curiosity even more, and suddenly a wave of impatience about learning every detail of their upcoming Indian adventure bombarded her. Until that moment, she had maintained no idea of who they were going to meet or where they were going to go in India, other than the obvious sojourn to Hyderabad to visit the old city where Edmund had spent the happiest years of his childhood apprenticing for the kind old Muslim painter. Edmund had done such an unusually good job of keeping the details secret from her, that she hadn't wanted to push him, but now. *Now*, she had to know!

"Edmund, darling, are we going to be staying with a revolutionary?" she teased.

"Come on," Edmund suggested as he took her hand. "We don't want to be late."

"Good lord," she murmured. She hadn't meant her statement literally. She threw Mr. Valov a nervous look, and he shrugged his concession and followed Oz and Yvie as they all made their way to the elevator.

"I will meet you with your luggage at the Bidkars' later today," Mr. Valov said as he closed the grate for them.

Eleanor's nerves picked up as the elevator worked its way to the deck, while Edmund was practically bursting with excitement.

"Oh, I can't wait for you all to see how colorful and different it is!" he exclaimed giddily. "The world feels more alive in India!"

"Thank you for inviting us to tag along, mate," Oz said as he squeezed Yvie's hand.

They all waited quietly as the elevator reached its destination, and Eleanor felt slightly lightheaded as Edmund held her hand tightly in his. It was a similar feeling to how she felt when he kissed her with his full unburdened passion, and she contemplated the odd truth that he loved the place in a similar way to how he loved his wife. She had never met a man, or a woman, for that matter, whose love was so intensely tangible, and she loved him even more for it.

When they reached the deck, Edmund practically skipped with glee towards the gangplank, and Eleanor took a deep breath of hot, humid air, and readied herself for the ride.

Edmund completely ignored the cheerful staff offering them grateful and friendly goodbyes, as he was entirely focused (with a wide happy smile on his face) on the wild scene before them.

"Come on, dearest! We're here!"

He pulled her along into a sea of humanity adorned in sparkling, beaded silks of every imaginable color. Children darted about amongst the crowd, yelling a harsh song to offer their porter services 'for a very good price!,' while cows lounged lazily right in the middle of the hubbub, carefully undisturbed by all who scurried around the busy port.

Eleanor held on tighter to Edmund as various vendors swooped in to aggressively offer their services.

"Do you need a ride, Mister? Madame? The best price in town!" a man with only a few teeth hissed in English as he stood before them, holding up a very rickety rickshaw covered in fading painted designs and frayed fabric flourishes.

"Lady, lady! Chestnuts! Chestnuts!" a boy yelled as he pushed a bag of chestnuts into her face.

"Tours! Tours of India! I will take you anywhere! Everywhere! See the magic of India!" an old Muslim man in a fez held out a card with text in a language Eleanor didn't recognize.

"No, thank you," she refused.

His eyes lit up at her acknowledgement, and he quickly began jabbering in a foreign tongue while offering her a ripped, yellowing pamphlet from his pocket.

"Edmund, darling?"

She looked up at Edmund, who stood with his eyes closed, breathing in the rich bouquet of scents—spices, incense, manure, chestnuts, diesel, smoke, fresh jasmine—she couldn't bear to interrupt his communion with the chaos around them.

She threw an apologetic glance towards Oz and Yvie, who stood beside them, hand in hand, taking in the chaos with wonder for themselves.

A large family holding hands as they moved through the crowd worked their way around them, but stopped to stare as they noticed Eleanor's fiery red hair and unusually pale skin. As they stood ogling, the group behind them joined in, and then another group, and within only a few seconds, Eleanor was the center of attention for a very large and growing audience. She blushed with embarrassment and then shifted uncomfortably, as she noticed their attention move from her hair down to her bare legs that were showing underneath her fashionable lavender and ivory lace sundress. They began to point and whisper as their attention moved on to Yvie's similarly short skirt.

"Edmund, darling," Eleanor called desperately, pulling him back to attention with a jerk of his arm. "Darling, I think we are garnering too much attention. Where should we go?"

Edmund startled as her reminder wrested him from his reverie. "I'm so sorry, dearest! I don't know what came over me!" He looked around the attentive audience, and then looked down at her. "Blimey, I should have thought of this sooner."

"Thought of what?" Eleanor asked nervously.

"Indian women never show their bare legs. I'm sorry, dearest. I should have advised you to wear trousers. It's just... before the war, British women didn't wear short skirts, so it never crossed my mind to warn you... Come, we must go to the road where the car is waiting."

With a look of determination, Edmund guided her through the crowd. She grabbed Yvie's hand and pulled them along, as the hordes of people parted in subtle deference to Edmund's powerful presence.

When they finally reached a wide avenue filled with scores of rickshaws, sleek cars (as well as some very fascinating homemade approximations of cars), and colorfully decorated carriages, all surrounded by scurrying pedestrians, an army of men pulling rickshaws spotted their position and veered across traffic to greet them.

"We are not in need of a ride," Edmund declared. He switched his announcement into several Indian languages in a row, but after a few moments of surprise at his fluency in their local tongues, the rickshaws decided to hedge their bets and continue their approach anyway.

"Welcome to India, darling," Edmund said sheepishly.

"I suppose the adventure has officially begun," Eleanor murmured.

For the first time in her life, Eleanor wasn't entirely certain that she was interested in more adventure.

CHAPTER 2 – OLD FRIENDS MEET NEW

As Edmund prepared himself to address the army of disobedient rickshaw drivers more authoritatively, the door of one of the closest sleek, black cars swung open, and a strikingly beautiful young Indian woman with bright brown eyes and long, silky black hair held back from her face in a complicated pile of braids and plates, stood up gracefully.

She was dressed in a green and red sari made up of copious layers of fine silk draped with perfect pleats that flowed beautifully with the weight of the heavy gold and jewels embedded in its borders. Her elaborate gold jewelry, encrusted with red and green gems, and including a thoroughly exotic piece that connected one of her dangling earrings with a ring in her nose, jangled as she took a moment to make sure that her outfit was in place before she threw one commanding look at the army of rickshaws and yelled something at them in Marathi. They immediately dispersed. Eleanor observed with silent fascination that the woman's arms were tattooed with intricate designs all the way from her fingertips up to her forearms. The sight was as foreign as anything she could have imagined.

"Edmund?!" the woman exclaimed with perfect British English. "You've hardly changed at all!"

"Good lord. Shruti?" Edmund called.

Simultaneous excitement and nerves exploded inside of Eleanor at his familiarity with the exceptionally beautiful young woman, but Shruti did not allow Eleanor's nerves to get the best of her for long.

"Uncle Edmund, we never thought we'd see the day when you'd become a married man! Shakti has finally smiled upon you!"

As she reached their position, she put her hands together and offered them a polite *namaste* bow, and Edmund returned her gesture.

"You must be the famous Eleanor MacLeod! The woman who saved our beloved Edmund from a lifetime of loneliness and longing!"

Edmund blushed, and Eleanor smiled self-consciously.

"You are even more beautiful than I imagined. Shakti was very generous, wasn't she?" Shruti winked at Edmund, but avoided any sort of physical greeting with either of them.

Eleanor noticed the trend immediately, and she wondered if they had already stumbled upon yet another of Edmund's Yakshini guardians whom she hadn't met yet.

"It is a pleasure to meet you," Eleanor replied politely. "I have never met a woman from Edmund's past before."

Shruti and Edmund both burst into laughter.

"It sounds strange, doesn't it, Uncle Edmund? A woman!" Shruti giggled.

"The last time I saw Shruti, she was still just a girl," Edmund explained. "I can't believe I've been away long enough that she has become a woman."

"My father wanted to join me to welcome you, but he was held back with business, as usual. He will greet you later at home.

34

But, I believe, perhaps, we will have the pleasure of more than just your company tonight?" Shruti glanced at Oz and Yvie who had been watching the entire exchange in polite silence.

"Oh, yes. Of course! Please forgive me!" Edmund exclaimed as his face turned red with a deep blush of embarrassment. "Oz and Yvie Helmsworth, this is Miss Shruti Bidkar. Eleanor and I met Oz and Yvie on the Orient Express, and we've been great friends for the last several thousand miles. I hope you don't mind that I've invited them along? They will head off to their home in Australia when the steamer leaves port day after tomorrow."

"A friend of Edmund's is a friend of ours," Shruti reassured them. "It will be our privilege to host you while you are in Bombay."

"Thank you kindly for the offer, but we were planning to return to our room on the ship later tonight," Oz demurred.

"Nonsense. Our home is hours from the ship in traffic," Shruti countered.

"Is it really? It takes hours to get to your home from here?" Edmund interrupted to ask. Shruti sighed with resignation as she nodded her agreement. "But it's so close!"

Shruti shrugged. "The city has been growing too fast for its own good. Every day there are new settlements of migrants coming in from the countryside. They come looking for work, but there isn't a good place for them to live, so they set up encampments wherever the authorities will let them, which is mostly in the low-lying areas where no one should live. It's very sad to watch. Father has tried various methods to help them establish themselves in a more sustainable way—he even worked with some Parsi friends to make a foundation to help them—but so far, there are just too many people for our little island. You should see it during monsoon now. It's a nightmare for people displaced by the flooding every time, and even the British authorities don't know what to do about it. They've gone far too long without your sage advice, Uncle Edmund. We all have." Shruti shed her serious tone, and Edmund blushed slightly at the compliment.

"Bombay is an island?" Eleanor asked curiously. She hadn't noticed as she'd watched their arrival into port.

"It used to be several islands. Seven, if I'm not mistaken. Almost no one lived here. It is remarkable how busy it is now, isn't it, Shruti?" Edmund glanced around at the rickshaws blocking every lane of traffic in the wide street as the drivers watched them curiously. "It is much busier than it was when I left for the war."

"I suppose we don't notice the change so much when we are here every day, but you are right, Uncle Edmund. We used to be one of the only cars on the road, and now look at it!" Shruti gestured for the remaining rickshaws to disperse and then returned her attention to Oz and Yvie. "Stay with us. You will never know more luxury. Even Uncle Edmund said that our house was the most beautiful residence he'd ever had the pleasure of sleeping in, and I don't think he was simply flattering us. Were you, Edmund?"

"I never flatter without cause," Edmund winked.

Oz and Yvie slipped into whispers to discuss the invitation, and then they both smiled.

"Don't mind if we do!" Oz agreed on their behalf.

"As long as we really aren't a burden," Yvie added.

"Not at all," Shruti reassured them seriously. "It will be wonderful for us to get to know you."

Oz reached out his hand for a polite handshake, and Shruti watched the gesture and smiled without offering him her hand.

"You have never been to India before, have you, Mr. Helmsworth?" she asked.

"Fair dinkum," Oz admitted as he looked to Edmund for some evidence of his faux pas.

"We do not shake hands," Shruti explained. "A young, virtuous woman such as myself, especially does not shake the hand of a man she is not related to. It is our way."

36

She put her hands together into another *namaste* and offered him a bow. "This is how we greet each other."

Oz mirrored her gesture, and she smiled with approval.

"Why, Yvie, I reckon we aren't in France anymore," Oz said jokingly.

Yvie smiled. "*Oui, oui,* Ozzy, you are *absolutement* correct."

"You are French, Mrs. Helmsworth?" Shruti asked excitedly.

"*Oui,*" Yvie replied. "And you may call me Yvie."

"Oh, how exciting! Uncle Edmund, you have answered my prayers again! Yvie, I would like very much to talk about French dance with you. I run a ballet school these days, and I have only been able to study the theory in books. I'm quite sure my pronunciation of the positions is wretched."

"You run the school now?" Edmund asked curiously. "What about your mother? I hope her health isn't failing?"

Shruti sighed with resignation. "My father didn't have the heart to tell you, Edmund. Mother died five years ago."

Edmund looked like the news had plowed right over him. "I'm sorry," he whispered.

Shruti sighed and swallowed hard. "She died quickly, after only three days of fever. It was a long time ago now. But, we mustn't speak of sad things on such a happy occasion. Father is most excited to see you. Come. Let's take a little tour of the city in the car on the way home."

Shruti guided them to the car and then took a moment to assess their options. There was only one bench in the back seat, certainly not big enough for five people.

"If you don't mind, we'd like to sit up front with the chauffeur to get a better view of all the sights," Oz suggested.

"*Oui,* I love sitting up front!" Yvie seconded.

Eleanor winked her thanks to Yvie, as she and Oz climbed into the cramped seats beside the middle-aged, impeccably dressed Indian chauffeur donning an enormous red turban, leaving the back seat open for them.

Shruti urged Edmund inside, then Eleanor, and then she pulled the layers of her silk sari into the car and closed the door. As Shruti ducked awkwardly to avoid the wide brim of Eleanor's sun hat, Eleanor took it off and threw it into the boot.

"That hat is absurdly large, isn't it?" Eleanor whispered.

"Think nothing of it," Shruti reassured her. "Foreigners must be very careful to protect themselves from our tropical sun."

"Nice to see you again, Harjeet!" Edmund addressed the driver. He switched their conversation into Punjabi, while Harjeet maneuvered the car into the slow crawl of the main lanes of traffic.

After a few minutes, Edmund and Harjeet burst into hearty laughter, and their jovial conversation came to an end. Edmund took Eleanor's hand into his, and she relished the pulsating cold of his grip.

As another river of sweat dripped down Eleanor's face, Shruti noticed her problem and offered her a silk handkerchief. "You have arrived at the hottest time of year, I'm afraid. The weather was quite pleasant a few months back. I hope you aren't too parched. It will be at least an hour, probably two, before we reach home."

"I am perfectly fine," Eleanor reassured her as she dabbed the sweat from her face. Shruti gestured for her to keep the handkerchief. "Thank you so much for your hospitality."

"It is I who must thank you for allowing me the opportunity to meet my new auntie in person," Shruti countered amicably. "I wasn't joking before. I never thought I'd see the day that Edmund Marriner would fall in love. It just goes to show that Shakti's will is unpredictable."

"Shakti?" Eleanor asked curiously.

"The goddess," Shruti explained. "She is the underlying energy that animates the universe."

"You worship a goddess?" Eleanor asked with surprise. The idea of a modern society worshipping a female deity had never even crossed her mind.

"I am her," Shruti replied nonchalantly.

"You are a goddess?" Eleanor asked. She glanced at Edmund to observe his reaction, but he only gazed out the front window at the haphazard traffic with a look of peaceful contentment in his expression.

"You are her, too," Shruti explained. "You see, she manifests on Earth in many different ways. She is creation and change, love and time, and every other aspect of human life that we hold dear. I am an agent of Shakti with a specialty in creative energy. I channel her whenever I choreograph a new dance. My mother was an agent of Shakti with a specialty in transformation, just like Parvati, the benevolent female aspect of Shiva, although my mother wasn't always benevolent. Boy did she have a fiery temper! My father used to call her Durga when she was angry." Shruti laughed at the idea. "Durga is one of the most powerful manifestations of Shakti, you see. She is a warrior who slays demons and such in our scripture. I always thought that calling my mother Durga should be a compliment, but it only ever made her angrier when he called her that." Eleanor noticed Edmund smiling nostalgically. "I am quite sure that if you were able to transform our dearest Edmund from an ascetic into a householder, you too are an agent of great and powerful change, Eleanor—change that touches all of the people you encounter in ways you don't even realize. Do you have a fiery temper as well?"

Eleanor smiled. "I must admit that I do."

"I knew it!" Shruti exclaimed triumphantly. "I can always tell. Not everyone is an agent of Shakti, you know. Only very special people. But I knew that anyone good enough to be Edmund's wife had to be bursting with Shakti's energy."

Eleanor thought about the idea fancifully. It seemed almost like a game—identifying which form of goddess best described those around her. With so many choices, she wondered if everyone could find an aspect they related to. "It is nice for you to find such a sense of personal meaning in your religion. My mother has always been very religious, but I have never been a strong proponent myself. I've found that in practice, most religious people are intensely hypocritical."

Shruti grinned. "Shakti sent you a perfect match, didn't she, Edmund?"

Edmund squeezed Eleanor's hand. "She did."

"Hinduism is not as simple as Christianity," Shruti continued her explanation casually. "There are many different forms of the deities, and many different sects who see them quite differently. Many Hindus prefer to connect with the male manifestations of the deities, like Rama or Krishna, two of Lord Vishnu's human avatars. I feel connected to Shakti, personally, and her manifestations as the female Creators—Brahmani and Saraswati––but my mother always felt more strongly connected to Lord Shiva the Transformer, even after she married my father, who believes that Lord Vishnu, the Preserver of the Universe, is the primary form of God. My father has always been a dedicated preservationist himself, just like Edmund. My mother always thought that was why they got on so well."

"So your mother and your father were opposites?" Eleanor asked curiously.

"A transformer and a preserver make a very powerful match. Together my mother and my father made a perfectly balanced pair—a manifestation of the deity Harihara—and I think, Eleanor, that you and Edmund do too."

Eleanor baited her gentle husband. "What do you think of that, darling? Are we a perfectly balanced pair, together forming a Hindu deity?"

"I could never keep any of it straight, myself." Edmund politely avoided a direct answer to the question. "Hinduism is just as foreign as every other religion to me. I prefer to keep my mind focused on ideas that are rooted in reality."

Eleanor looked to Shruti to observe her reaction to Edmund's seemingly insulting response. Shruti smiled. "It is reassuring to me that you haven't changed one bit, Edmund. I expected nothing less." She leaned in confidingly to Eleanor. "My family has always been unusually liberal when it comes to religion, and unlike those incessant Christian missionaries, Hindus tend to care very little about what other people believe. It only matters when those people try to limit our rights to worship as we wish. But, that is enough of politics for now. We are headed towards the Haji Ali mosque now. You will be able to see it from the beach where we will stop the car, but you won't be able to go inside half naked like that."

Eleanor looked down at her bare legs and worked to temper a tone of annoyance. "Edmund failed to mention that my dress would be taboo here."

"It doesn't surprise me. He wasn't particularly focused on women's fashions as an ascetic, were you, Edmund? My mother always joked that he was more chaste than any priest in the world."

"I appreciated the craftsmanship of women's fashions as much as the next man," Edmund replied with a hint of defensiveness. "But I cannot argue with your mother's pessimism on the chastity of priests. Or their morality, for that matter, and she certainly knew far more than anyone else about that."

"My mother was a devadasi," Shruti explained when it was clear that Eleanor didn't understand what he was talking about.

"Devadasi?" Eleanor asked.

"There really is no foreign equivalent to the term. Historically, they were of a somewhat high position in society, but nowadays they are thought of more often as prostitutes." Eleanor couldn't hide her surprise, and Shruti took her predictable reaction in stride. "My mother was a highly skilled dancer whose performances connected worshippers with God and kept an ancient tradition alive. She was, however, also required to bring the priests closer to God through other physical means that she detested and that were not voluntary."

"Poor woman," Eleanor murmured.

"My mother was the child of a devadasi herself," Shruti explained. "If my father had had any living relatives, surely he would never have gotten away with marrying her, but there was no one to protest, and so when he fell in love with her after one conversation during a business trip to Madras, he brought her back to Bombay and gave her the means to celebrate God through dance without submitting herself to the earthly desires of lascivious men. He helped her create a school where she could teach girls Bharatnatyam—Indian classical dance—to celebrate our ancient traditions without the sacrifices that she had been forced to make. She even changed the costume for the dances, wearing bridal attire so that there would be no question as to the modesty of the movements. In her heyday, she had several hundred students, including many Brahmin girls. It proved to everyone in Indian society that the dance could be separate from the sex. If only the *firangs* had paid closer attention."

"*Firangs?*" Eleanor asked.

"Foreigners. I shouldn't have said it like that to you, though. It doesn't have a particularly positive connotation. The idea of virtuous *firangs* who respect our culture is quite foreign to many of us. Edmund has served as our shining example for decades."

"The Scots have a similar word for the British. We call them sassanacks. I'm not sure where it comes from, but I think it means exactly the same thing. My mother complained for weeks when she learned I was marrying a sassanack."

"I'm not sure what my mother would have said if I'd told her I wanted to marry a *firang*. The idea is so grotesque, I haven't even considered it." Eleanor looked to Edmund for his reaction, but he did not appear to be offended. Shruti noticed her attention, and a hint of embarrassment at her insult entered her expression. She rushed to explain. "You see, the British banned Bharatnatyam back in 1910, and it was a great blow to us. That was why we had to change our school into a ballet school. The British missionaries had no problem with the same dance moves when they were performed in tutus with French words. My family has not held them in high esteem ever since, except for Uncle Edmund, of course. He is an honorary member of the family."

"The British banned Indian dance?" Eleanor sighed with disappointment. "They banned Scottish highland dance as well when they were trying to conquer our spirit."

Shruti squeezed Eleanor's hand affectionately. "I didn't know the Britishers had ever done anything so foolish to people who looked so similar to them. We are sisters in arms, Eleanor, aren't we?"

Edmund shifted uncomfortably. "Best not repeat that phrase so loudly, Shruti. Since the war, the government has gotten stricter about snuffing out subversion. We just had a very violent reminder of the lengths they are willing to go to find it, and their definitions of subversion are very lax. You must not use such incendiary language."

"In my own car?" Shruti asked skeptically. "Edmund, we are among friends!"

"I suppose you're right," he conceded. "I suppose I'm being a bit paranoid. But we have had several unpleasant experiences recently in which we learned that the walls have ears. I do not want anything happening to you and your father, Shruti."

"When we do not have the freedom to speak our minds in our own car, we will not have any reason to live, Edmund," Shruti shot back with a hint of teenaged idealism.

Edmund straightened his posture, and he suddenly looked more fatherly than Eleanor had ever seen him. "Tides come and go, Shruti. I have been around longer than you can imagine, and I have seen many regimes rise and fall."

"Really, which ones?" Shruti asked with genuine curiosity. Eleanor felt Edmund's pulse pick up.

"Why, we were just in Turkey, as one example. With just a few years of that wretched war, the Ottoman Empire fell after a thousand years. For a pittance, we stayed in a palace that was the sultan's just a few years back, and all of his lovely old clothing was still there covered in dust, as if he was going to return for it."

Eleanor was thoroughly impressed by his quick thinking, although she wondered how much of that story he actually believed after the lies that she and Mr. Valov had told him about the true proprietors of the former palace.

"The French regimes have changed practically every decade," Yvie chimed in from the front seat. "Every time they change, we feel great hope or despair. In the end, many of us are still around, waiting for an age of true peace. I'd hoped it was finally here after that wretched war, but I think our recent experiences have proven that there is more fighting to come."

Edmund grimaced at the idea, and then he gathered his wits. "My point, Shruti, is that there is great value in keeping yourself alive and free, so that when the tides turn again, you will be around to take advantage of it. When India is finally independent, she will need people like you to revive all that has been lost."

Shruti sighed contentedly. "Edmund, you have always known how to talk us down from the precipice." She leaned in confidingly to Eleanor. "Only Uncle Edmund could calm my mother when the fire of Durga was burning within her."

"I only convinced her of perfectly sound logic."

"You should have seen the rage my mother was in when the announcement came that despite all of Uncle Edmund's efforts, the British had banned Bharatnatyam. I thought she might burst into flames right there in the living room. After everything she'd been through, and the years she'd taken to rebuild her life after leaving the temple, I was worried it might be the final blow. Edmund sat talking with her for an hour, and by the end she was perfectly content. By the next day, she'd changed the school's sign to say 'Ballet,' and by the next week, the British were lauding us for our *modernity*." Shruti rolled her eyes.

"Your mother must have been incredibly resilient." Eleanor felt a pang of sadness that she hadn't had the chance to meet the woman. She had a sneaking suspicion that they would have been great friends. Then she felt a wave of melancholy at the idea of Shruti losing her mother. She pushed it away.

"My mother was exceedingly resilient," Shruti agreed. "And brilliant and kind and beautiful, too. She wanted me to understand where she'd come from, so that I could appreciate the life I didn't have to live."

"It was very wise of her to be honest with you," Edmund replied. "I wish that I knew more about my mother."

"Did your mother die when you were young, Edmund?" Shruti asked curiously. "You've never mentioned anything about your parents in our years together, have you?"

Eleanor squeezed Edmund's hand supportively as he debated his response. "I never knew my parents," he finally confessed. "I spent my early childhood in an orphanage, in fact. There is a man I've met many times whom I believe to be my father, but he wouldn't admit that it was true, even when he attended our wedding a few weeks back. I suppose that confirms my suspicion that I'm a bastard."

Shruti reached over and placed her hand on top of Edmund's and Eleanor's as they were intertwined tightly in Eleanor's lap. Eleanor felt carefully for any hint of Yakshini warmth (just in case), but Shruti's hand felt entirely human.

"My mother knew it the day we met you, Edmund. She was very perceptive about these things. No one, British or Indian, with a perfectly impeccable past would have dared to do what you did knowing what you knew. Your burden freed you to accept us as we truly were. It was a remarkable thing, actually, very rare indeed."

"What did you do, darling?" Eleanor asked excitedly.

"That is a story best told with my father's help," Shruti laughed. "He and Uncle Edmund are extremely entertaining when they tell it together."

"I can't wait!" Eleanor exclaimed.

"I will remind them at dinner to tell it. The most important result of the story was that Uncle Edmund came into our lives. We had many fun times after that. He stayed with us whenever he stopped through Bombay on leave, and he even taught me to play cricket against my mother's wishes."

"Why didn't she want you to play? Because you were a girl?" Eleanor asked. The idea seemed strange, given the many trials her mother had overcome.

Shruti sighed with ambivalence. "She was afraid that it would distract me from my more important studies. I relished disobeying her, and Uncle Edmund was a terribly good accomplice. He even got my father and the servants to join us. I don't think she ever found out about those midnight cricket games in the garden. If she did, she never said one word about them."

"She knew," Edmund revealed. "The first time we attempted it, she watched us play from one of the upstairs windows. She told me the next morning that she hadn't realized how much you cared when she'd disallowed it, but that she was glad she'd said no, because you were enjoying it so much more as a secret between daughter and father. She was a wonderful woman."

"Yes, she was," Shruti sighed.

They sat in silence for many minutes, looking out the window at the beautiful chaos all around, until they reached a particularly busy intersection, and their car came to a complete stop as a chorus of shouting brought their attention to a man in the center of the traffic circle whose cart of coconuts had just been hit by a sput-sputting dusty black car. The man's arm was bleeding, but he jumped unwisely around the stalled cars and carriages, chasing after his coconuts.

While several other vendors and rickshaw drivers shouted on the man's behalf, the back window of the culprit's car rolled down, and a red-faced, balding British man shouted with a thick cockney accent: "Out of the way! There's a reason for rules, you know! No carts on the roads, you bloody coolies!"

46

As his insult echoed, more vendors and rickshaw drivers worked their way against traffic (in any direction they could fit) towards the scene.

Edmund squeezed Eleanor's hand and then hopped out of the car. "Stay here. I'll be right back."

"Edmund, darling, it's not your fight!" Eleanor protested.

"Since when did Edmund Marriner respond to an argument like that?" Shruti laughed. "Stay here and don't worry. This will be resolved straightaway."

She gave some orders to the driver in Hindi, and then stepped out of the car to join Edmund in the completely stopped traffic.

Eleanor popped her head out of the window to watch and listen.

"I sure hope he has better luck than he did on the Orient Express," Oz said as he looked past the driver's position, ready to jump to Edmund's aid.

The vendors and rickshaw drivers parted with deference as Shruti approached the injured man, while Edmund made his way straight to the culprit's car window.

"I am Colonel Edmund Marriner of the British Army, and I would like you to explain to me, sir, how you think you are helping this situation?"

"They aren't supposed to have carts on the roads!" the man argued.

"How long have you been in India, sir?" Edmund asked. "One day or two?"

"I'm sorry?"

"I'm asking what short period of time you have been in India, because if you had been here for any extended period of time, you would have realized by now that this is not Britain. These men have pushed their carts on the roads since long before the British arrived, and telling them they can no longer do so in order to make room for your hired car is not going to change their behavior. Running them over and shouting insults at them, however, will reiterate what they already know: that they don't like the British Raj one bit."

"But... but... that's... that's treason against the Crown and the Empire!" the man stuttered.

"Yes, and the result of American treason against the Crown was the United States of America." Edmund paused for his point to sink in. "Now, as the good British citizen that you are, I suggest that you desist from making a public ass of yourself in the center of Bombay, and tell your driver to be more careful not to run over a man who is going about his daily business simply because you don't like the fact that he's there."

While the man huffed and puffed, Edmund leaned in and barked some orders in Hindi at the driver, who nodded his head in emphatic agreement.

Eleanor was intensely aroused by her gentle husband's surprisingly forceful tone. She had seen glimpses of his leadership before, but now he was in his element, and she suddenly realized that for the first time, she was witnessing him in the full glory of the man he'd been before the war had ruined him. She wondered if married women would have as much trouble getting positions as nurses in India as they did in Britain... An idea crossed her mind for the first time... She pushed it away. They'd only been in the country for an hour; it was too soon to begin fantasizing about moving across the world.

Edmund approached Shruti, who was rallying several rickshaw drivers to collect the coconuts back onto the man's cart, and they exchanged a few quick words. To the shock of the curious bystanders, Edmund joined the men in their efforts to collect the coconuts.

"Your hubby sure isn't shy about getting his hands dirty," Oz laughed as he watched Edmund reach carefully underneath a pair of impatient carriage horses to gather up three rogue coconuts. "If you ever come to Perth, we'll have to take you out to the ranches for some cattle-wrestling!"

48

"I'm sure he would love it," Eleanor said as she relaxed at the seemingly mundane turn of events.

When the last of the coconuts were gathered up, Edmund pushed the cart alongside the injured man straight through the stopped traffic to their car. He quickly loaded every single coconut into the boot of the car, and Shruti paid the injured man, offering him some strict, final orders as she pointed at his bleeding arm.

As soon as Edmund and Shruti were back in the car, traffic began moving.

"Thank you for indulging us," Edmund said as he finished wiping his hands with a handkerchief and then gathered Eleanor's hand back into his. "I have always felt the need to intervene in situations like that; otherwise, they will just happen again and again. Hopefully that brute will heed my advice."

"You were very convincing, darling." Eleanor worked hard not to pull him into a kiss. He squeezed her hand lovingly.

"What do you plan to do with the coconuts? Will you cook with them?" Yvie asked.

"He would have had a hard time selling the bruised coconuts," Shruti explained. "And losing an entire supply like that would have been very bad for him, so I bought them at face value as a charity. I suggested he spend some of the money on a doctor, but he will do what he wants. We will take the coconuts to the beach now and give them to the people who live in the tents there."

"People live in tents on the beach?" Eleanor asked. "Permanently?"

"They move when the coppers come by, and then they return. It has been that way since the beginning. They will appreciate the coconuts."

"That is very thoughtful of you," Eleanor said genuinely.

"It is a small gesture compared to what we normally do. My father and I sponsor free public meals every week in the areas with the greatest poverty. Those are more useful than a boot full of coconuts, but nothing we do is ever really enough."

"You sound wonderfully charitable to me," Yvie chimed in.

"We cannot appreciate the luxurious life we have, if we do not look out for those who aren't so lucky," Shruti replied.

"If only more people felt that way," Eleanor sighed.

"Yes, it is a tragic similarity between Britain and India that so few of the privileged look out for those less fortunate, or so Uncle Edmund tells us. My father and I have never been to Britain ourselves. We've never had the need or the desire, except for your wedding, of course. We were about to buy our tickets when Edmund called my father up and asked about a honeymoon visit instead. You should have seen how happy he was; I thought he might burst! And I was rather grateful to avoid escorting him to Britain, to be honest. He doesn't tend to travel well."

They sat quietly looking out the car windows until they reached a rocky shoreline, and the car stopped beside a tall barrier of boulders.

"If you'd like to take a look at the Haji Ali mosque from afar, you can stand on those rocks there," Shruti advised. "The mosque is one of the oldest structures in Bombay, I think. It is on a tidal island—you can only get there when tide is low. Some medieval Islamic saint made it, but I don't remember his name or his story. If you're curious, you can ask Babri, who is my head seamstress. She is the only Muslim in our household, and she might know more about it than I do, although, it's anyone's guess what she might say."

Edmund hopped nimbly out of the car and helped Eleanor up, while the driver got out and climbed up the rocks, calling something out towards the beach beyond.

"We'd best take a quick look before they come for the coconuts, dearest, and then you and Yvie should get back in the car before they see your short dresses."

Edmund hastily helped Eleanor up the rocks.

They stood together, while Oz and Yvie joined them, gazing out over the hazy water and squinting to see the white domed

50

structure. Eleanor could barely keep her eyes open as the sun beat down on her, and as she spotted a horde of curious respondents to the chauffeur's call approaching from a large tent encampment many hundreds of meters down the beach, she decided she'd seen enough.

"Edmund, darling. I think I'd like to get back in the car." A wave of nausea overwhelmed her. Suddenly, she felt like her throat was closing and she couldn't escape the heat.

"Yes, of course, dearest." Edmund must have sensed her trouble, and he escorted her back into the shade of the car, which was now intensely hot itself without the breeze of the car's movement to keep it cool. "Are you alright?"

"I think I'm overheating." Eleanor hated to admit her debilitating deficiency in the regular climate of the place Edmund loved so much.

Edmund pulled her into his cool arms. "Is that better, dearest?" He held his cool hands on her forehead and her chest. She nestled in and took a deep breath.

"I'm sorry, darling." Tears of frustration worked their way into the corners of her eyes. "I don't want to be a distraction to you, but it's just so bloody hot! I'm wilting."

Edmund kissed her on the forehead.

"It is entirely my fault, Eleanor. It didn't even occur to me that it would be the height of summer when we arrived. Most British people can't bear the Indian heat."

He held up his hand to show it to her. "You see there? Even I can't bear it. My skin is already irritated."

Eleanor observed the subtle evidence of flaking, and then guided his hand back onto her chest.

"I love you, Edmund. I will figure out how to not let the heat overwhelm me, but I think I need a bit of practice first."

Oz rushed Yvie into the car and closed the door, and then rushed around the boot alongside the chauffeur to begin gathering up the coconuts.

"*Il fait trop chaud!*" Yvie exclaimed. "It is wickedly hot! It's not even this hot in Australia! Oh, Ellie, are you alright? Your color looks off."

"I'm overheated," Eleanor said as she nestled deeper into Edmund's arms. "But luckily I have a personal cooling valet at my disposal."

"Rest," Yvie advised. "We will get you some water and salts when we arrive at Shruti's house, and then you'll be fine."

Eleanor nodded her agreement and let herself give into her fatigue. As she closed her eyes, the sound of the grateful recipients of the coconuts mixed with gentle waves crashing on shore and a polite conversation between Edmund and Yvie, until the excursion was complete, and the car was back on its way.

"I'm sorry, Eleanor. I should have brought you some water," Shruti whispered. "We will be home soon."

Eleanor mumbled a half-awake apology, and then returned to peaceful slumber punctuated by the subtle pulsating of Edmund's power.

The most mundane trial of their honeymoon adventure had just begun.

Eleanor stirred and struggled to open her eyes as the scent of fresh rain infused her senses. The car had finally stopped, and she took a moment to remember where she was as Edmund gently squeezed her hand.

"Dearest, we're here."

Eleanor sat up from her position with her head nestled against Edmund's cool chest. They were the only ones left in the car.

"Is it raining?" Eleanor asked groggily.

"Yes, it has been gently sprinkling for about half an hour. Are you alright, dearest? Are you still too hot?"

Eleanor's throat was dry and her head was pounding, but the temperature was no longer so oppressive. In fact, it was outright comfortable.

"No, darling. This weather is much more bearable. I think I just need some water with rehydration salts and rest."

"We will get you some straightaway. Shall I help you out of the car?"

"Yes, darling. Thank you." Eleanor loved him so much for asking, especially when she knew that his chivalrous instincts to coddle her must have been going mad with desperation to whisk her straight to bed.

"Welcome!" A jolly voice boomed as Edmund escorted Eleanor towards a structure that could hardly be called a house. It looked more like a palace than any ordinary house she'd ever seen, but somehow the grandeur felt entirely natural. Huge white marble columns held up beautifully mosaicked domed ceilings above open-aired hallways that surrounded a verdant garden filled with exotic tropical flowers. The garden was open to the sky, and yet fully integrated into the home, allowing the gentle pitter patter of the rain to echo through the marble hallways that led like mazes into many different wings beyond. The enormous leaves looked as if they were straight out of a fairy tale, and their color was even more vibrant with the muted light and fresh coating of rain.

Edmund squeezed Eleanor's hand excitedly as their host approached from one of the many hallways. She did her best to stand up straight and hide her discomfort, but as the man approached, she couldn't stifle a small gasp at his appearance.

He wore an elaborate beaded Indian sherwani suit in gold and ivory with a matching turban, but his face and his hands were so grotesquely scarred from old burns that she could hardly make out any feature that had been born to him. His left eye did not open at all, and his flesh looked as if it had melted and then healed over it, while his nose was hardly present, and his turban, unlike those of the many Sikhs she'd met, covered a completely bald, scarred head. She could, however, make out a jovial smile on his crooked mouth. If she was going to be perfectly honest with herself, he looked quite a bit like her childhood vision of ogres from the stories her father had told her at bedtime. She pushed the mean idea away and smiled, forcing herself to look at him in the eye.

"Welcome to India!" he exclaimed with perfect British English as he reached their position and pulled Edmund into a friendly hug. Edmund hugged him tightly back. When they were finished, he stepped back and took a look at Eleanor, offering her a polite *namaste*. "And you must be the lovely Eleanor. I am so happy to meet you. Edmund has told me so much about you that the telephone operators are taking bets on whether you are a Devi or an Apsari!"

Eleanor was at a rare loss for words.

"Ah, I can see that your overly polite husband has not done either of us any favors by keeping to himself the obvious detail that I am rather difficult to look at," Mr. Bidkar declared. "Please, think nothing of it. I am dressed like a maharaja so that you have something better to look at than my face." He burst into laughter, and Eleanor smiled awkwardly. "You needn't feel one hint of pity, my dear. This condition you see before you has been most useful for helping me build my empire. My trading partners are so keen to get away from me that they cave far too early in our negotiations, every time... Ah, and I see that our dearest Edmund has gathered up some more virtuous *firangs* to present as an exhibit of evidence that he is not the only one?" He looked to Oz and Yvie, and burst into laughter at his uncouth joke. "Welcome to India, my friends. Our home is your home. You may call me Ravi."

He reached forward and shook Oz's hand. Oz smiled and shook it back, pausing to look down at his hand with a moment of puzzlement.

"The burns are four decades old now, my dear chap," Ravi explained. "It was a tragic train accident. I was the only one in my family to survive. Dreadfully bad timing it was, too. I was on my way to meet my fiancée in Poona. She wasn't so interested in the arrangement after the fact, I'm afraid. But, all's well that ends well. Isn't that how the phrase goes, Edmund? Lord Vishnu works in mysterious ways."

"I'm sorry to hear that, Ravi, but I was actually confused by your greeting," Oz admitted. "Shruti told us that Indians do not shake hands."

"Did she?!" Ravi burst into another round of jolly laughter. "Yes, yes, she was not lying, my dear chap. We have a more traditional greeting that we prefer, but I have observed that the British find our greetings to be too foreign. It butters them up a bit when I shake their hands. Good for diplomacy and trade relations, if you know what I mean. But, if I'm not mistaken, you're not British, are you?"

"I'm Australian."

"Australian! Why, then you must be the descendent of a convict!" Ravi waited just long enough for Oz to squirm, and then he burst into another round of laughter. "I hope I have offended you enough that you will feel free to offend me at your leisure. It will be more fun this way, I promise."

"Good on ya, mate," Oz replied, rather taken aback.

Shruti rushed towards them from another hallway with four young servants behind her dressed in colorful traditional clothing, two men and two women, each carrying large carafes of water.

"Father, we mustn't keep them waiting in the foyer like this. Eleanor is struggling with the heat."

Shruti gestured to one of the maids, who crouched down and presented a carafe to Eleanor with her eyes averted. Eleanor took it, finding the formality of the situation even more awkward than the British equivalent, but she quickly took a small sip. She almost choked on the sour taste.

"Oh, I'm sorry. I should have warned you, Eleanor. There are rehydration salts in the water."

Eleanor forced herself to take several more sips.

"Thank you, I'm already feeling better."

The other servants used the same gesture to present their carafes to Edmund, Oz, and Yvie, and Eleanor watched curiously to see if Edmund would consume the offering with his regular superhuman thirst. He took a few polite swallows, holding back his instincts, until Oz began chugging his down as if it were a contest night at the pub, and Edmund used his lead as an excuse to do the same.

"Looks like I finally bested you, Colonel. You are welcome to challenge me for the title any time." Oz covered his mouth as a belch worked its way up, and Yvie shook her head with minor embarrassment at his manners.

"You can bet I will," Edmund smiled gratefully. A burst of love for their thoughtful allies rolled over Eleanor, and she took a few more sips of the liquid.

Yvie turned to Eleanor and inspected her color. "You're looking better, Ellie. Drink the rest of the water slowly but steadily. You don't want to overwhelm your body."

Eleanor felt Edmund relax as her prognosis improved.

"Now, first things first," Shruti declared. "We have a very special evening planned, but Eleanor and Yvie cannot attend dressed as they are. Babri is waiting in my chambers to help us get them dressed properly for the occasion. Father, perhaps you can entertain Edmund and Oz in the meantime? Don't forget that dinner will be early tonight."

"Yes, yes, Shruti dear. Always running the household like a British Army base," he laughed. "Edmund, you will feel right at home!"

"I always feel at home here," Edmund agreed amicably.

Ravi pulled him into another affectionate hug. "Come, I have two bottles of fine aged cognac that I won off of a French trader in Pondicherry three years ago. He couldn't even bear to look at my poker face!" He laughed heartily. "I've been saving them for your prodigal return."

"Will you be alright, dearest?" Edmund asked Eleanor one last time.

"I will be perfectly fine, darling. Go enjoy your reunion. Although, perhaps you can save a few sips of the cognac for Yvie and me to taste later."

Edmund nodded his agreement, and then pulled her into a parting kiss. The servants gave off subtle murmurs of shock, but Shruti and Ravi both clapped with excitement.

"What a beautiful gift it is to see you united with your other half, Edmund," Ravi said happily. "I never thought I'd see the day!"

"Neither did I," Edmund winked.

Shruti took Eleanor's hand. "Come, we have work to do." She stopped as she looked down and noticed Eleanor's feet. "Oh, and take off your shoes. You must *always* take off your shoes in an Indian household. The servants will store them for you."

Eleanor slipped off her heels and looked over to Edmund who had already removed his shoes without a word from Ravi.

"Edmund never needs to be reminded," Shruti whispered as she noticed Eleanor's attention. "He is a very unusual *firang*. Now, come!"

She grabbed Eleanor's and Yvie's hands and guided them through several marble corridors marked by more hidden gardens of tropical flowers and softly babbling fountains, past altars to exotic multi-armed deities piled high with jasmine garlands, and finally into a vast marble room built up against the hillside. On one side, the breeze blew in through an open-aired garden where more exotic plants collected the gentle rain, and on the other, a mosaicked terrace opened out onto a sweeping view of a small bay and the city of Bombay stretching out onto another peninsula beyond.

"It's beautiful," Eleanor murmured. She could hardly believe the space had been created without Yakshini magic.

"Father hired the most brilliant architect in India for the design," Shruti explained. "Even in the summer, the open garden allows the breeze to pass through and the heat to escape. I suppose you won't get to experience that feeling today. It is very strange weather now. It feels almost unnatural."

Eleanor made another mental note to thank Kuveni for her help later.

"Now, come, Eleanor. Sit on my chaise and drink your water. You must recover so we can all go to Elephanta tomorrow. Father has been planning the excursion for weeks."

"Are there elephants there?" Yvie asked curiously as she took a seat in a neighboring chair.

"No. It is a rather silly foreign name, actually. We call it Gharapuri. It means 'city of caves,' which is more apt. The Portuguese called it Elephanta because of a statue of an elephant by the village, but it is really a series of temples carved into the hillside. My mother believed that they were built by Lord Shiva himself, and so when there was an idea thrown around to build houses on the island, my father stepped in on her behalf and paid off those with influence to leave it alone. Now there are just a few villages that have been there forever, and a set of British Army barracks that were built a long time ago, although luckily they don't care much about the temples. They just want to keep their canons manned to protect the harbor."

"An island? How far away is it?" Eleanor asked. She wasn't particularly keen on the idea of getting back on a boat.

"It is only 10km away. It is practically in the Bombay harbor. We will take our yacht, and we will have the caves all to ourselves to explore. The locals like my father very much because he has been a great preservationist on their behalf... and because he brings them food and supplies every time we visit. It helps them ignore his scars."

"Both of your parents seem utterly remarkable," Eleanor said as she took several pensive sips. "I don't know if I've ever witnessed such resilience."

"I often wonder if I could be as resilient as they are," Shruti admitted. "I've never faced a trial as difficult as theirs. I hope I never have to..." She gave into a moment of melancholy, and then she smiled, clapped her hands, and called: "Babri, we're ready for you!"

A middle-aged woman with streaks of white in her long, frizzy black hair, clad in a red and orange silk outfit made up of a flowing floor-length skirt and a matching blouse with especially flamboyant, puffy sleeves paired with a bright orange and white spotted scarf tucked into it so artfully that it almost looked like a sari, rushed in from a carved wooden door on the far end of the room, followed by three teenaged girls wearing colorful saris.

Babri stopped to observe Eleanor's porcelain white skin and fiery red hair with puzzlement. "Is it real?" she asked with a thick accent and husky voice as she reached forward to feel one of Eleanor's wavy tendrils. "You are like a doll!"

"Tsk!" Shruti hissed as she slapped Babri's hand. "How rude, Babri!"

"My hair is real," Eleanor said self-consciously. "The color is unusually red, even compared to others where I am from in Scotland. It runs in my family."

Babri rubbed her hands together excitedly. "What colors shall we use, memsahib? So many choices for such an unusual *firang*! We mustn't use red… no, no, no. Red won't work at all. Perhaps green? Yes, green will go well. Or perhaps purple!"

"Babri, why don't you go collect the fabrics that we already have on hand, and we will let Eleanor and Yvie choose their own," Shruti suggested.

Without an acknowledgment, Babri rushed past Yvie, back through the door from which she'd come.

Shruti laughed. "I hope you'll forgive her. Babri is a bit… er… simple, but she is a genius when it comes to making clothes. She will have both of you dressed like maharanis in time for dinner, and by morning she will have an entire wardrobe for you."

"She will sew something for us? In just a few hours?" Eleanor asked with surprise.

"If she gets a good start, it won't even take an hour," Shruti winked.

"I hope we can watch," Yvie giggled.

"Babri will be very pleased to have an appreciative audience," Shruti agreed.

Babri rushed back in through the door with her arms full of colorful, elaborately embroidered silks and immediately began spreading them across the chaise around Eleanor.

When she was finished, she whisked Eleanor up and tugged at her dress. "Take it off! You must take off that shirt! What happened to your trousers? Never mind. We must see the waist! The bust! But there is nothing to see, skinny doll! Nothing to see at all! *Geldi, geldi chello!* We must make due, but we have no time, no time to waste…"

"She won't need to measure you. She will be able to make a lehenga like hers that will fit perfectly just by looking at you in your undergarments. You too, Yvie."

"Perhaps the sleeves could be more like yours?" Eleanor dared to ask.

Shruti laughed and then gave Babri instructions in Hindi. "Babri likes to experiment. I've told her to make something tasteful, but a lehenga will still be better for you, so you don't have to learn how to drape a sari like mine. It takes years of practice to do it perfectly." Shruti looked past Babri to another one of the servants. "Bring two of my best silk robes for them, Gita."

The girl bowed and rushed away.

"Those dresses really do look odd. Are they really the western fashion now? What woman wants to show off her knees? They are so unflattering!" Shruti exclaimed. "At least mine are."

"Well, the silk stockings are meant to cover them," Eleanor explained.

"Ha! Yes, of course. Just as they cover the legs of our little ballerinas. It is hardly modest to see the shape of a lady's body clearly through the fabric… but, I suppose to each their own.

Christians have been upset by our Hindu fashions for centuries because they reveal the stomach. We see nothing wrong with it at all."

Gita returned with two of the most elaborately embroidered robes Eleanor had ever seen, one in a beautiful cerulean, and the other in a bright emerald green.

Shruti helped Eleanor up, and another servant girl rushed to collect her half-finished carafe of water.

"Please bring us some chai and sweets, Sheena," Shruti requested with an air of natural authority that Eleanor found strangely captivating. The girl bowed and left the carafe on a side table beside the chaise.

Shruti smiled encouragingly while Gita held out the green robe. Eleanor self-consciously slipped off her dress, and another servant girl took it straight out of her hand. Yvie followed her lead, and quickly they were wrapping themselves in the soft silk of the robes.

"Have the shirts laundered immediately, Navi," Shruti ordered. The girl bowed and scurried away.

"Open the robes!" Babri screeched. "No time to waste!!!"

Eleanor and Yvie were so startled by her tone that they obeyed without protest. Babri circled them making various humphing noises and muttering to herself in Hindi.

"We will make it work in time for dinner, Inshallah…"

"Babri, you are Muslim?" Eleanor asked as she observed her revealing lehenga. "Are you… er … allowed to dress like that?"

Babri burst into husky laughter without answering the question. "Skinny doll asks too many questions!"

"She does not go out on the street dressed like that," Shruti explained on Babri's behalf. "She covers her hair with a scarf and wears a longer choli—a top—that covers her stomach. In here, though, she gets to wear whatever she wants. I let her experiment with her own fashions using the fabrics that I don't end up liking for myself."

"Memsahib is very generous," Babri said as she squeezed Eleanor's waist, and Eleanor squealed. "Skin and bones, this doll is…"

"Tsk!" Shruti hissed.

Babri ignored her. "Choose your fabric, skinny doll, *geldi, geldi!*" she declared instead.

Eleanor and Yvie fingered the delicate beading and intricate embroidery of the silks.

"Are you sure it's no trouble?" Yvie asked. "These silks are lovely. Too lovely for a whim."

"Nonsense!" Shruti exclaimed. "In India we have so much beautiful fabric that I hardly notice it anymore. These aren't even very good, really. They're the leftovers that I couldn't decide what to do with. You will be doing me a favor by helping me get rid of them."

Eleanor picked up a midnight blue silk that shimmered with hues of purple in the muted light. "This one would be lovely, wouldn't it?"

As Yvie leaned over to take a look, Babri ripped it from her hands and rushed to the corner of the room, sitting herself down cross-legged, and yelling her orders at the servant girls in Hindi. The girls scrambled to collect Babri's sewing supplies from the closet.

"She is a woman on a mission," Shruti laughed.

As Yvie held up a deep turquoise silk that turned almost yellow with the angle of the light, Shruti clapped her approval, grabbed the fabric, and skipped over to place it in the queue on the floor next to Babri.

"Now, what shall we do while Babri works?" Shruti looked around the room assessing their options. "Yes! Yes, yes, yes!" She clapped her hands excitedly. "How about some mehendi! I'm an expert at mehendi. My students always have me do their bridal designs. Oh Eleanor, we will make you look just like an Indian bride! Edmund won't know what hit him! We were sad for him, missing the opportunity for a Hindu wedding since they are really so much fun, but now he can see you looking just like the Indian bride he's dreamed about his whole life!"

"Did he tell you that himself?" Eleanor asked with piqued interest and a hint of nerves. "Did he tell you that he always dreamed of marrying an Indian bride?"

Shruti suddenly looked concerned. "I'm sorry, Eleanor. I was speaking out of turn."

"Well, did he?" Eleanor pushed. "Was it a literal dream or a just a fancy? Please, Shruti. You must tell me."

"He only mentioned it once or twice," Shruti hedged. "I'm sure he was just humoring us as he always does. You are the best bride for him in the entire world, Eleanor. I honestly can't believe how perfectly suited you are to each other."

Eleanor thought back to his pleasant dreams of flying with the wings he had not yet learned how to use in the waking world. It was clear that those dreams were some sort of instinctual prompt, preparing him for the day when he would be ready. She did not want to think about any other instinctual prompts that might be floating about in his unconscious, half-human head. Kuveni had sworn that there wasn't some Rakshasa princess bride awaiting him... she'd *sworn* it...

"*Coucou*, Eleanor?" Yvie whispered. "Are you alright?"

"Yes. Perfectly fine," she lied as she took a deep breath and put on a fake smile.

"I'm sorry, Eleanor," Shruti reiterated.

"I'm not offended, Shruti," Eleanor reassured her. "Now, tell me more about this mehendi, you called it?"

Shruti smiled. "It is like this." She held out her tattooed hands, showing Eleanor the intricate designs that went all the way up her arms. "It is from a dye made of the roots of the henna plant. It will keep the design on your skin for a few weeks, and then it will disappear."

"So it's not permanent?" Eleanor asked.

"It is as ephemeral as everything else in this world," Shruti replied philosophically. Then she giggled. "That's not true. It's much more ephemeral than most things. It allows us to play with different designs each time. Oo! If you'd like, I can incorporate Edmund's initials into the design! That's what we do for weddings. Then the groom can find his initials when he is inspecting you in the bridal chamber." Shruti giggled again at the thought.

"Aye, alright," Eleanor agreed.

Shruti clapped her hands excitedly. "Oh Eleanor, you will look so exotic like this. I can't even imagine how striking the mehendi will be on your fair skin. You will be the talk of the town."

"That is certainly true," Eleanor laughed. "The British women won't have any idea what to say!"

"We will shock them together!" Shruti exclaimed. "Yvie, I will do yours too, if you'd like. We will have a henna party!"

"*Mais oui*. It sounds like fun!" Yvie agreed.

"Gita, please fetch my supplies."

One of the servant girls disappeared into the closet and quickly returned with a basket filled with cones that looked vaguely like something a baker would use to decorate a cake. Shruti positioned Eleanor's arm loosely on the table by the chaise, but then she stopped as she noticed the grime that had stuck to Eleanor's skin during her hours of sweating in the incessant heat.

"Navi, please wash Eleanor's arms and feet in preparation," Shruti said to the servant girl who had just returned from taking their dresses to the laundry. The girl disappeared through another door and quickly returned with a washbasin and a sponge. Eleanor felt slightly awkward as she held out her arms and watched the girl obediently wash her with delightfully cool water, but the sensation felt so good that she gave in and relaxed as the girl finished up her duties. "Now change the water and do Yvie please."

Navi obeyed without a word.

Shruti positioned Eleanor's arm again. "Now, you will need to stay in position for a while. Perhaps ten or twenty minutes for the palms, and then the same for the other side, and then we will do your feet."

"Can you really do all that in so little time?" Eleanor asked curiously as she eyed the intricacy of Shruti's own mehendi.

"Oh yes. It will be easy for me. My students joke that I'm the fastest mehendi artist in India, and I'm used to doing it on myself. It will be much easier with both hands."

Eleanor settled in and watched while Shruti set up her supplies, glancing past her to Babri who was already determinedly cutting the silk.

As soon as Shruti began, Eleanor was puzzled. The substance was thick and wet and an ugly color of dark brown on her skin, letting off a subtle tingling sensation not dissimilar to eucalyptus, but with a completely unfamiliar herbal scent.

Shruti noticed her attention. "The paste will need to dry, and then we will rub lime and sugar on it to get the color to settle. Normally, a bride would keep it on all night, but we have too much to do, and the paste is annoying to have on for too long, because it begins to flake all over the place, and it's dastardly difficult to clean up. By the time Babri is finished with her work, we will use coconut oil to help us wipe the crusted paste off, and the dye will begin to set. It will get darker for a day or two after that, but you will be free to use your hands during dinner."

Eleanor nodded her agreement, and Shruti set about creating her intricate artwork on Eleanor's skin at a speed not dissimilar to Babri's frenetic stitching.

"Well, now, a silent henna party is no fun at all," Shruti declared without looking up from her work for a second. "I will tell you the story of how we met Uncle Edmund, so that when he and my father tell it later at dinner, you will know what is true and what isn't."

"I'm intrigued!" Eleanor exclaimed.

"Me too!" Yvie seconded. She nodded her silent thanks as Sheena presented her with a steaming cup of aromatic spiced milky tea and a plate of biscuits.

Shruti smiled. "Well, it all started when my mother and I were walking home from the dance school one evening. I was just about to turn seven years old. We were running dreadfully late, and my father was hosting an important dignitary, and so we didn't bother to change out of our dance costumes, which meant that we were both dressed as Tamil brides. Normally Harjeet would have driven us, but he was busy collecting the Sultan of Malacca at the port, and the school really wasn't so far from home, and so we planned to take a regular rickshaw. Well, it turned out that there was a festival that evening on the other side of town, and so there were no rickshaws to be found, and we were stuck making the trek on our own in the monsoon, which had come very inconveniently a week earlier than expected. We were soaked through and through as soon as we started our walk in earnest."

"How do these colorful silks do in the rain?" Eleanor asked curiously.

"Not well," Shruti confided. "They become very sticky and difficult to walk in, not to mention the lack of modesty... That is actually an important detail, because as we were walking through the streets, we made our way into one of the foreign parts of town, where normally we would never have gone, especially not alone, and we were approached by two drunken British officers. They followed us, yelling harassments, and as we attempted to escape through an alleyway (which we didn't know well because we had never once walked there before), my mother took a wrong turn, and we found ourselves cornered. My mother, like the lioness that she was, stood in front of me and prepared to fight them off, but I screamed my lungs out, and Edmund eventually answered my call and came to our rescue.

"With a few swift movements, he had both of the drunken officers wrangled on the ground. I had never seen two men disabled so quickly, and it hardly took Edmund any effort at all! He was like Lord Vishnu defeating the demon Bali! He lectured them about honor for a bit—I'm sure you can imagine that—and they argued that they'd done nothing wrong because my mother was just a madame, pimping out young girls—me—for money!"

"No!" Eleanor exclaimed. "The scoundrels!"

"The British were never able to tell the difference between a devadasi and a prostitute. It was no different on that occasion. One drunken soldier demanded that my mother admit that she was a devadasi, and she did. She tried to explain the distinction to Edmund in the broken English she was still learning from my father, but he switched into fluent Tamil, which utterly shocked her, and she proceeded to explain the long, complicated history of the devadasi and her subsequent position as the virtuous wife of a highly successful trader. He told her that it wasn't his place to judge, which displeased her mightily, since it indicated that he didn't really accept her argument, and so she invited him to come home with us to see for himself. He took it as a proposition and refused her invitation, focusing instead on gathering up the drunken soldiers and escorting them away from us for disciplinary action."

"He must have blushed when he thought your mother was propositioning him," Eleanor laughed.

"Oh yes. It was so rosy on his fair skin; we'd never seen anything like it. She found it endearing."

"So do I," Eleanor agreed. Shruti repositioned Eleanor's hands to begin her mehendi on the other side.

"But then how did you become friends, if Edmund didn't believe your story?" Yvie asked.

"Well, when we showed up dreadfully late to greet the Sultan of Malacca, soaked to the bone and covered in layers of soot and dirt, my mother quickly explained to my father what had come to pass, and he was livid, of course, at those scoundrels. He sent us upstairs to bathe and rest (and to get our haggard presence out of

68

the way of his business dealings), and at about two o'clock in the morning when his trade deal had been signed, he woke us up and asked us to tell him every detail. By noon the following day, he'd used his influence to uncover who the exceptionally tall, Tamil-fluent British soldier was who'd rescued us, and he set out to prove to Edmund that my mother was, in fact, not a prostitute or a pimp."

"What a strange mission to embark upon," Eleanor said as she glanced over at Babri who was hastily sewing up the sleeves of a blouse. She couldn't believe the woman had made it so quickly, but her efforts appeared to be entirely human.

"It was not the first time he'd done it, actually. My father was very motivated to prove to the world that a devadasi could be a virtuous wife and mother. I think it was their efforts together that allowed the school to build its impeccable reputation."

"How remarkable," Eleanor murmured.

Shruti refocused on Eleanor's mehendi for a few minutes as she finished up a particularly intricate geometric design on the palms, and then she crouched on the floor and continued her story as she began her work on Eleanor's feet.

"So, at lunchtime, my parents dressed up in their finest, most expensive, most modest traditional clothing, hopped in our motorcar (which was especially fancy back in those days, since only the richest, most influential people had them), and they went down to the building where Edmund was taking a break from some sort of army policy meetings. My father is rather well-known in Bombay, even among the British, since he's very easy to recognize, and so the guards let him into the building and set about helping him find Edmund, who was taking tea with some colleagues. Using his perfect English (he has always been very good at languages, just like Edmund), my father introduced himself and reintroduced my mother in front of the entire pack of army officers, and right there in front of everyone, he invited Edmund to our home for dinner as thanks for his role in rescuing us from the dregs of the British

Colonial Army. Edmund didn't refuse, despite the ridicule of some of his colleagues, and that evening we hosted him for the first time of many."

"What a lovely ending," Yvie sighed.

"My mother believed that the monsoon came early that year because God wanted us to meet Uncle Edmund. He did so much for us over the years—so many things that he didn't have to do. He even brought Lord Kitchener himself to our home the following year, trying to convince him to use the army's influence to keep Bharatnatyam from being banned. We put on the show of our lives to convince him, but in the end, he told Edmund that it wasn't the army's place to get involved in social policy. We couldn't disagree with him on that, although Edmund was very disappointed that his plan hadn't worked." She looked up from her mehendi to glance at the wet garden. "Perhaps God wanted you to see Elephanta tomorrow, Eleanor. Now it won't be too hot."

"I think perhaps you're right," Eleanor agreed.

"What about this story do you think Edmund will omit when he tells it?" Yvie asked curiously.

"He will not be so heroic," Shruti replied as she returned to her efforts. "And he will not admit that he thought my mother was propositioning him."

"I think you're right, but I suppose we shall see," Eleanor smiled.

"Done! I think that was a record!" Shruti exclaimed. "Babri, are you finished with one?"

"You win, memsahib. I still need to hem the skirt," Babri called without looking up.

"We like to race," Shruti explained. "It makes all of our work more of a game. Yvie, shall we see if I can beat Babri twice?"

"You can't!" Babri exclaimed. "I will win!"

Shruti laughed. "We shall see."

"*C'est magnifique,*" Yvie murmured as she leaned in to observe the highly intricate details of the henna that was cracking on Eleanor's skin.

"Sheena, please dab Eleanor's henna with lime and sugar," Shruti ordered. As soon as Sheena arrived with the tray of supplies, Shruti began her work on Yvie. "Now try not to move for as long as you can, Eleanor. In fact, it might be better for you to lie back and rest. Babri probably won't be done for another hour, and we'll have to wait for Yvie's henna to dry before we do anything else."

"Rest, Eleanor," Yvie reiterated. "You are still recovering from a heat stroke."

"Do you think it was that bad?" Eleanor asked as she eyed her half-empty carafe of water.

Gita noticed her plight and rushed to help her drink some. She felt rather childish requiring the help of a servant to hold up the carafe, but she was certainly not going to use her own hands, and she did not want to miss out on any other experiences because her unaccustomed Scottish temperament couldn't bear the heat.

"Now, Yvie, tell me all about France," Shruti changed the subject. "Are the palaces there as grand as the ones here?"

"I think they are similar," Yvie said as she glanced around the grandiose space.

"Which is the grandest palace in France? Here I think it might be the Maharaja's palace in Mysore. That is not too far from here by train. Perhaps Eleanor and Edmund will even be able to visit it. My father offered to give them an introduction."

Eleanor wondered if Edmund's secret itinerary was simply a tour of the greatest luxuries of India, afforded to him by his uniquely amicable nature. She pushed back a flash of what her sisters would think if they could see the odd reality of her strange new life.

Eleanor refocused on the conversation as Yvie turned over her hands for Shruti's second stage of design. "The grandest palace in France used to be Versailles, but it has crumbled a bit since the *ancien régime*."

"How did you say that?" Shruti asked.

"*Ahn-cyahn reh-jeem*," Yvie said slowly. "French is very hard to pronounce for foreigners."

"So is Marathi; it's one of the local languages. My father is Marathi, so I speak Marathi, Hindi, English, and Tamil from my mother. Tamil is even more difficult than Marathi, but Hindi is rather easy, I think. It has some similarities to English in its grammar."

"Your accent in English is much better than mine. I have no excuse. My grandfather was English," Yvie replied.

"I learned from my father. He speaks so many languages, I can't even keep track. That's one reason he's so successful as a trader. Now, tell me, Yvie, is the 't' pronounced at the end of *ballet*? It isn't, is it?"

"*Non*," Yvie replied. "We rarely pronounce the final consonants. There are several consistent rules you can use when you are reading French words out loud…"

Eleanor finished drinking down her entire carafe, and she nodded her appreciation to Gita, who dutifully took it and rushed it away through one of the doors. She laid back, letting her arms dangle off the sides of the chaise without touching anything, closed her eyes, and listened to Shruti and Yvie dive into an impromptu lesson on French pronunciation.

To the gentle patter of rain in the tropical garden, Eleanor whispered her thanks to Kuveni for the reprieve from the heat, and slept.

CHAPTER 4 – A REVOLUTIONARY EVENING

Eleanor awoke to the gasps and giggles of Shruti and her maids.

"*C'est magnifique!*" Yvie exclaimed as she twirled around in front of the mirror, observing herself approvingly in her new lehenga.

"Excellent work, Babri," Shruti declared. Eleanor noticed as she opened her eyes fully that Shruti had also changed into an even more elaborate green silk sari with gold-threaded paisley designs encrusted with sparkling jewels that were matched perfectly by a delicate complementary design on the sleeves of her blouse.

"Memsahib is pleased!" Babri exclaimed. "Yes, memsahib is very pleased. Babri did well."

"How extraordinary," Eleanor murmured.

"Ah! The sleeping beauty has awakened!" Yvie exclaimed. "I was beginning to worry! You've been asleep for two and a half hours!"

Eleanor sat up and examined her hands. The crusty henna had all been removed, and the designs were now directly on her skin in a dark color of orange. Yvie's looked very similar.

"You were sleeping so soundly, Sheena was able to wash your henna right off," Shruti explained.

"I suppose I was tired," Eleanor said as she observed the elaborate designs on her hands. They looked thoroughly exotic, and it only occurred to her at that moment that she hoped Edmund would like them—she was committed now. "I haven't had much sleep these past few weeks, with so many better things to do in bed."

Shruti squealed with excitement. "Shakti really has smiled upon you both! Now, come! Dinner is almost ready, and we shouldn't be late. We have a very special performance planned for afterwards, and some of my students will be arriving early to get into their costumes."

"Are you going to do a ballet performance?" Eleanor asked.

"No. We are going to do Bharatnatyam," Shruti said excitedly. "We used the ballet school as a front to continue teaching Bharatnatyam. Tonight's performance won't be entirely traditional so that each girl can play a distinct part—in that way it will be more like a ballet—but the choreography and the story will be the best ever in India! Tonight, in honor of Lord Vishnu (and because it's my father's favorite), we will perform an entire Hindu epic."

"Oh, which one, my lady?!" Gita interrupted. "Can we watch?!"

"You may," Shruti agreed. "We will perform Valmiki's *Ramayana.*"

"How wonderful!" Sheena exclaimed. "Will Hanuman fly?"

"I won't spoil the surprise." Shruti smiled coyly, obviously excited by the enthusiasm of her maids. "Don't worry, Eleanor. I will translate everything for you so you will know what's going on. It is a very colorful piece. There are flying monkeys and shapeshifting demons, and Lord Vishnu's seventh avatar will slay

74

Ravana, the ten-headed Rakshasa king. The costume for that took months to make."

"I'm sorry, what did you just say?" Eleanor's heart began racing. "The *Rakshasa* King Ravana?"

"Oh, a Rakshasa is a demon," Shruti explained nonchalantly. Eleanor worked hard to hide her reaction. "And Ravana was the Rakshasa king of Lanka, which is called Ceylon these days, although my father still uses the ancient name. Lord Vishnu came to Earth as Lord Rama to end Ravana's scourge, but Ravana managed to kidnap Lord Rama's wife! Can you believe the nerve?! But I won't give too much of the plot away yet, it will ruin the surprise. This may be the only performance the girls will ever do for anyone other than their parents."

"How nice that we get to experience it," Yvie said as she twirled around again, clapping happily at the flow of her new skirt, completely unaware of the panic attack that was brewing inside of Eleanor.

Her mind raced. She knew the name Ravana. Kuveni had let it slip more than once. *Ten-headed demon king…* The words echoed in her mind. Was she really going to sit beside her unsuspecting husband to watch a performance of schoolgirls acting out the slaying of his evil father? Or worse, a propaganda piece that laid out the idea that all Rakshasas were evil demons to the world? But the ending must have been wrong… Ravana hadn't been slayed in ancient times… He was around in 1818 to produce a bastard child while masquerading as King George IV of England… a bastard child who would be watching the epic unfold before his eyes with no clue that it had any connection to him whatsoever…

"Are you alright, Ellie?" Yvie asked. "Are you still feeling ill?"

"I'm perfectly alright," Eleanor lied again. She worked to focus on the mundanity of the situation. "Are you sure it's safe to perform a banned artform here? You will hardly be able to deny what you're doing if you have elaborate costumes," Eleanor asked as she thought back to their violent encounters with the British spy organizations on the steamer to Bombay.

"We will be performing among friends in our own home. If it is not safe, India has been lost entirely. Now come, let's get you dressed, Eleanor! I can't wait to see how beautiful you look in the lehenga, and then there will be the jewelry, too! I have matching sets for every color and thousands and thousands of bangles! Although, you won't need a necklace, I think. The one you have is so stunning."

Eleanor looked down at the sparkling green sapphire pendant that served as her talisman to summon Mélusine.

"The ring is stunning too, almost like a Ceylon sapphire," Shruti said as she reached forward to gently inspect it. "Did Edmund choose it?"

"It was his mother's." Eleanor regretted the words as soon as they came out of her mouth.

"His mother's?" Shruti asked astutely. They both remembered the conversation in the car when Edmund had admitted his questionable origins.

"She died when he was born. The ring was passed down through a family friend who surprised us at our wedding." Eleanor was rather pleased that the explanation was not a lie in the slightest.

"How nice that you can both have a connection to her now," Shruti said politely. Eleanor was grateful that she dropped the subject. "Now, come. Let's get you dressed!"

Shruti clapped her hands, and Eleanor let Gita and Sheena undress her and help her into the new skirt and blouse. Eleanor smiled bemusedly as she noticed the thick layer of padding Babri had added to her blouse to perk up her otherwise boyishly flat bust.

"Don't forget the dupatta, skinny doll! We must hide your bones!" Babri rushed towards her and presented a wide, black sheer silk scarf with beaded silver stars embroidered into the border that perfectly matched the border of her new blouse. Without asking for permission, Babri roughly tucked it into the waist of her skirt, and then twirled Eleanor around, draping it over her front and pinning it to the top of her skirt so that Eleanor's thin stomach was covered by gracefully folded layers of silk.

"Oh, Ellie, you look *très jolie*!" Yvie exclaimed. "How fun this is!"

"It really is beautiful," Eleanor agreed as she twirled around, watching the shimmering midnight blue silk pouf in the mirror. She glanced over at Babri's pleased expression. "I can't believe you made it so quickly."

"I did! I did! Memsahib saw me do it!" Babri protested, misunderstanding Eleanor's praise.

"Oh yes, of course, I believe you!" Eleanor corrected herself. "Babri, you are a true genius."

Babri smiled widely. "Allah has smiled on both of us today."

Shruti took Eleanor's and Yvie's hands and led them into one of the wooden doors that the servants had been traversing. Inside, a wall of jewelry from floor to ceiling glistened with a special spotlight pointed right at it.

"Biordinar!" Eleanor exclaimed.

"*C'est magnifique*!" Yvie seconded. "Like Ali Baba's treasure!"

Shruti giggled. "None of it's real. This is all costume jewelry. My real jewelry is kept under lock and key. Please, take whatever you want."

Shruti quickly set about compiling a special selection of black, silver and blue bangles to match Eleanor's lehenga.

"It does feel royal, doesn't it?" Eleanor said as Shruti offered her some heavy diamond earrings.

Shruti quickly began smoothing out Eleanor's messy hair and pulling it into a simple half-up style, letting her red wavy tendrils fall naturally all around her neck while parting the middle for a special jewel that attached to her hair and dangled down the front of her forehead.

"This is called a *maangtikka*," Shruti explained. "It is one of my favorite accessories, and I've never seen any of the *firang* women wear anything like it."

"Neither have I," Eleanor agreed.

As Babri compiled a set of jewelry for Yvie, Eleanor took a deep breath, appreciating the novelty of the experience. Never in her life had she been so dressed up, not even on her wedding day. Now, playing around with girlfriends trying on fancy clothes and sparkling jewelry felt like a luxury that her teenaged self, with the burden of her family's future weighing heavily on her shoulders, wouldn't have ever dreamed could be hers. Suddenly, the idea overwhelmed her.

"Thank you, Shruti. Yvie, Babri… It's all lovely," Eleanor said as she fought back tears.

"It is nothing," Shruti said matter-of-factly. "It is absolutely nothing compared to the gift you have given us by marrying our dearest Edmund and coming with him back to India. Now, we have no time to waste. Your husband awaits you!"

Shruti clapped excitedly as she led them out of the room, and the maids followed closely, giggling in anticipation of the big reveal.

Twilight was falling, and the rain had turned into a comfortable humid warmth with a cool breeze.

"Wait here," Shruti whispered as they approached a brightly lit dining room. "I will announce you."

"Shruti, my dear!" Ravi exclaimed. "We were on time per our commandant's orders, but where were the ladies?!"

"The wait will be worth it, I promise!" Shruti said excitedly. "Might I present to you, two blushing Indian brides?"

Eleanor and Yvie giggled in anticipation and stepped together into the banquet hall.

"Good lord," Edmund murmured.

"Strewth!" Oz exclaimed. "Yvie, you look like an Indian princess!"

Eleanor felt the heat of a rare blush rush into her cheeks. "Do you like it, darling?"

"I have never dreamed of a vision half as lovely as you are right now, Eleanor. I don't have words to describe it," Edmund whispered.

Eleanor smiled with genuine relief. "Good. Because Shruti said the henna will be on my arms for a couple weeks."

Edmund took her hand and inspected the intricate lines. "You did this, Shruti? The artistry is exceptional."

"I learned from the best! Edmund taught me how to draw when I was little," she explained. "He was the most patient tutor in the world."

"I am grateful to reap the rewards of both of your hard work," Eleanor said as Edmund took the palm of her hand to his mouth and kissed it. A shiver ran down her spine.

As he finished, he paused as he noticed something on her forearm. A wide smile spread across his face. "I found my initials. Does that mean that Eleanor is officially my bride?"

"They are hidden on her legs too," Shruti said slyly. "You will have to look for them there later tonight."

"Indeed, I will," Edmund said with another rosy blush.

"Come, sit. We are running late now." Shruti guided them to the table. "Edmund, we've had the chef prepare navrattan korma, paneer makhani masala, and subzi dum biryani for you, all without turmeric, like always. Hopefully you will find them satisfying enough without meat."

"I'm sure they will be as delicious as ever," he said as he pulled out Eleanor's chair for her. He paused distractedly as she sat down.

"What is it, darling?" she asked self-consciously.

"I am having one of those moments... it feels wonderful and frightening at the same time. It feels as if it cannot possibly be real that you are here with me right now, sitting beside me as my wife."

"It is real, darling," Eleanor reassured him. "Perhaps getting some delicious curries into you will help convince you."

He sat down beside her, and she smiled as he poured her a glass of cognac from a dusty bottle that was already positioned in front of her place-setting.

"My wife requested a taste of one of Mr. Bidkar's finest wins at poker," Edmund said happily as he poured another glass for Yvie and then collected two that had already been poured for himself and Oz.

"Don't Shruti and Ravi want some?" Eleanor asked.

"We don't drink alcohol," Shruti replied.

"So you won these cognacs just for Edmund?" Eleanor asked as she sniffed the rich caramel scent wafting off of the crystal glass. "In case he ever came to visit again?"

"God sent me a drunken Frenchman who was bad at poker so that we would have something to serve when Edmund brought his enchanting wife to meet us," Ravi corrected her. "I knew God must have a plan, and I was surely correct! Lord Vishnu works in mysterious ways!"

The rest of the group sat down at the table, and Yvie's loud jewelry clanked against the porcelain plate.

"Indian princesses must have to practice to wear all this jewelry!" Yvie laughed.

A large staff rushed through a set of double doors, carrying a series of silver platters. Eleanor heard Edmund's stomach growl loudly as they unveiled the steaming curries.

"This smells scrumptious!" Edmund exclaimed.

He waited politely for everyone to be served, but as soon as the footman behind him placed a stack of steaming, buttered, freshly-baked flatbreads on the bread-plate beside him, he lost his battle with his manners and quickly set about devouring his entire serving with just his right hand using the graceful manners of his childhood, before anyone else had taken a single bite. Shruti and Ravi watched the spectacle without a hint of surprise, only satisfaction. Ravi gestured to the footman closest to Edmund, who silently served him another portion.

"So, Edmund, you and Father must tell us all how you met," Shruti prompted slyly as she took her first bite, using a similar eating style to the one Edmund was using to combine the rice and the curry in her right hand.

Eleanor watched Ravi curiously as he did the same, and it suddenly occurred to her that they had not noticed exactly how unusual Edmund's Hyderabadi table manners were for an English soldier. She looked at her place-setting again and gratefully noticed the presence of a spoon—the only item of cutlery on the table. As she picked it up, Oz and Yvie followed her lead, and they set about awkwardly trying to guess what an appropriate use of the spoon would look like.

Edmund, in the meantime, cleaned his fingers politely with a lime in a fingerbowl, and then wiped them on his napkin and cleared his throat as the servants swooped in to replace his fingerbowl with another. "How did we meet, Ravi? Will we agree this time?"

"Certainly not," Ravi declared jovially.

"Well, at least we agree on something," Edmund smiled. "Many years back, in 1909, I think it was? I was in Bombay for a conference of mind-numbing meetings about army policy when I happened to walk by two damsels in distress on my way back to the rowdy barracks where I was obliged to stay during my visit. I stepped in and disciplined the two drunken officers responsible, and then Ravi and Reya hopped by the conference the next day to thank me for my troubles. The rest is history, I suppose."

Shruti threw Eleanor and Yvie a satisfied glance at her accurate prediction of Edmund's omissions.

"No, no, no!" Ravi interrupted. "You have it all wrong!"

Shruti winked, reminding them of her other prediction—that they would be more entertaining telling the story together.

"Pray, Sri Bidkar, do offer your testimony to the court," Edmund saluted jokingly.

Ravi took a deep breath, readying himself to tell his version of the story with his deepest, most melodramatic voice. "The monsoon came early. So early that the Sultan of Malacca changed his route, taking the passage between India and Lanka instead of going around. Varuna led him straight here! He arrived in Bombay three days sooner than he was supposed to, and during Eid, of all times! Now, if that doesn't prove that Allah and Lord Vishnu are one and the same, I don't know what does!"

"I don't believe that evidence would hold up in a court of law," Edmund pointed out.

"I believe in a higher court," Ravi countered. "God sent those distractions so that Reya and Shruti would encounter the ruffians, and Edmund would swoop in unexpectedly just like Jatayu the vulture flew in to help Lord Rama. He saved the day!"

"Am I a vulture in tonight's metaphor? Did I have wings, or did I fly without them?" Edmund asked amicably. Eleanor wondered if Kuveni or Mélusine were listening to how close the conversation was getting to the truth. "I believe last time I was a lion, and the time before that I was a turtle."

"No, no, no. You were Kurma, Second Avatar of Vishnu, who simply *happened* to be a turtle," Ravi argued matter-of-factly. "Last time you were Narasimha, Fourth Avatar of Vishnu. He is half man, half lion. It is entirely different than being a full lion, believe me."

Shruti giggled at her father's seriousness on the matter. "Have you encountered many half-man-half-lions for comparison?" she asked with a straight face.

"I haven't had the need. Everyone knows what Narasimha is like. Lord Vishnu's avatar swooped in to defeat the evil Rakshasa Hiranyakashipu. He used the brains of a man and the brawn of a lion. It was a divinely brilliant plan."

"The brains of a man and the brawn of a lion… that sounds about right to me, mate," Oz said as he held up his cognac glass for an amicable toast.

"Edmund didn't like the metaphor when he was slaying a demon," Shruti interjected.

"One must be careful about who they consider a demon." Edmund gave away slightly more emotion in his statement than Eleanor knew he wanted to show. "Those who are different are not necessarily evil."

"Exactly!" Ravi exclaimed. "So this time you are Jatayu! A vulture who swoops in to save Lord Rama himself! I mean, who would have thought that a *vulture* of all creatures would turn out to save the day?"

"Jatayu doesn't have the happiest ending, though, Father," Shruti pointed out.

"Well, that part wasn't in the metaphor," he countered. "Edmund was a downright hero, I tell you. There are many stories to compare it to, and one of these days, I will find one that Edmund likes."

"I await the day." Edmund paused to whisper a thank you as the footman served him his third serving. "What matters is that Shruti and Reya were perfectly alright in the end, those two drunken ruffians were sent back to Britain for punishment, and I met these friends whom I have missed dearly these last nine years."

Ravi reached across the table to take Edmund's left hand into his. "That is what matters most, isn't it, my dear chap?"

"It appears we agree on two things tonight. I believe that is a record," Edmund smiled.

They sat in peaceful silence eating for several minutes until the commotion of an arriving car indicated that the next stage of the evening was about to commence. Shruti stood up. "That will be Sona, she's always early. Enjoy your dinner, everyone. I will come and get you when the performance is ready to begin."

"Ravi, tell us more about what you were doing in Pondicherry when you won this excellent cognac," Yvie asked politely.

"Now, *that* was a story, let me tell you…"

Eleanor smiled as Ravi dove right into a series of increasingly tall tales, and Edmund devoured more curry than she'd ever seen him eat (even more than on their wedding day), with the silent help of his attentive footman.

She and Yvie shared the bottle of cognac, pouring their own tastes without much regard for the volume consumed, until Eleanor felt rather tipsy, and the booming laughter of the group at one of Ravi's many climactic points made her realize that she had stopped paying attention.

"We're ready for you!" Shruti announced.

Eleanor leaned on Edmund as she stood up.

"Are you alright, dearest?" he asked concernedly.

"I think I might have just reached my limit of cognac," Eleanor admitted.

Edmund wrapped his arm around her waist and supported her as they walked side by side into a grand sitting room with a full stage set up before an imposing fireplace.

Several rows of beamingly proud parents dressed in their finest saris and suits looked up at them as they made their way to the front row.

She heard several women gasp with excitement as they spotted her and Yvie's outfits, and she took a deep breath, ordered herself not to show one hint of the tipsiness she was feeling, and sat up straight next to Edmund. Shruti took a seat between her and Yvie, readying herself to translate.

As soon as they were all seated, the lights in the room dimmed, and a spotlight turned on. Eleanor looked around to the back of the room to spot two servants in charge of the enormous electrical device. She wondered how much Shruti had spent on such an unusual item.

"We welcome you to this performance of *The Ramayana of Valmiki*, the greatest epic of all time, told through the holiest ancient traditions of the Indian people, in honor of Reya Bidkar, whose tutelage and tenacity has kept Bharatanatyam alive against all odds. May it last until Satya Yuga, the ultimate Age of Truth," a woman in a sparkling purple sari announced in English from her position on the edge of the stage.

Eleanor squeezed Shruti's hand while Edmund looked over and offered her a supportive smile, and as the narrator switched into a foreign tongue, Shruti sniffled and then began translating the narration:

"Once upon a time, in the ancient land of India, in the Great Kingdom of Ayodhya, there was a kind and fair king. This king was beloved by all, but was sad because he had no children…"

Eleanor looked over to Edmund, whose attention was already wandering to the craftsmanship of the elaborate stage decorations, while several adorable little girls rushed out onto the stage in creatively embellished costumes, enacting a scene of great drama with graceful yet purposeful movements.

It looked quite a bit like ballet to her, although there was something more exotic about it, and not just because of the rich fabrics and foreign cuts of the costumes or the unfamiliar tonality of the music that was being performed by a trio of elderly women crouched in the corner on a padded platform playing a veena, a shehnai, and a set of drums. The drums and the veena were both structured around beautifully crafted gourds upon which Edmund landed his focus. He began subtly tapping his fingers in her palm to the beat of the drums. The effect was odd, and Eleanor wasn't sure that she liked it as the tapping reverberated through her, leaving her slightly queasy. She pulled her hand away, and Edmund looked down, noticing for the first time his subconscious movements as he continued his tapping on his knee. He blushed slightly and offered her a silent apology, but he did not stop his commune with the rhythm of the music, and Eleanor wondered whether the tick was beyond his control. As he sighed contentedly and continued on with his tapping, she let her attention return to Shruti's translation.

She became increasingly impressed by the performers' stamina as the epic continued on and on, with one chapter flowing straight into the next, almost like the *Arabian Nights*, weaving in side plots that seemed decidedly peripheral until poof—the greater meaning became clear. She began paying closer attention to the game of the storytelling, until she was distracted by the twists in the dancers' movements. Time after time, just as she thought she could anticipate their next move, they did something utterly surprising, and she found their choreography so mesmerizing that she began to tune out Shruti's translation until the name *Ravana* boomed so clearly from the narrator that she couldn't ignore it.

"And Sita took pity on the poor man and invited him to cross the threshold, but ah ha! As soon as he was inside, Ravana revealed his true demonic nature and captured her! His ploy had worked! Sita would be his!"

Five girls stood in a row, each with an extra papier maché head attached to their necks, fluttering their arms about, creating the exotic image of the so-called ten-headed demon Eleanor had been anticipating ever since Shruti's revelation of the subject-matter hours earlier. She looked to Edmund, who was highly entertained by the optical illusion they were attempting to create, and he squeezed her hand happily, as the little girls did their best to imitate the frightening monster of their imaginations.

"And so, Ravana spirited Sita away to Lanka, but Lord Rama would not have it. He would not let the evil demon king kidnap his wife. War was coming!"

As the little girl tasked with impersonating Hanuman hopped onto the stage in her best impression of a monkey, the entire house shook, and Shruti looked around, startled. A loud crash echoed through the marble hallways from one of the open-aired gardens, and as Shruti and Ravi stood up to investigate, Eleanor, Edmund, Oz, and Yvie rushed to follow.

"Please continue," Shruti said calmly to the performers as she led the posse hastily out of the room. "What could that have been?" she hissed as soon as they were out of earshot. "I've never heard anything so loud in this house. It was like an earthquake!"

Edmund sniffed the air, and his eyes turned black.

"Say your mantras, darling," Eleanor whispered before Shruti or Ravi could notice.

He closed his eyes and whispered his personal reminder to cling to his humanity, and when he reopened them, they were back to their human hazel.

"There is fresh blood here," Edmund said as he sniffed some more, landing his gaze on a large-leafed tropical flower towards the back of the closest garden. Next to it, the basin of a trickling fountain was filled with bright red blood.

"Good lord," Eleanor muttered. "Not again."

The ladies hiked up their skirts to keep them clean as the entire group followed Edmund into the garden, paying no heed to their bare feet as they squished their way through the muddy dirt. Edmund whispered his mantras more heatedly. Dripping from the leaves of several neighboring plants was more fresh blood than any reasonable benevolent excuse could explain, but there was no trace of a victim, or a culprit.

"Are you alright, old chap?" Ravi asked as Edmund leaned up against the wall of the garden, refusing to face them while he worked his hardest to get himself back under control.

"Perfectly fine," he lied. "The scent of blood has made me ill ever since the war."

"I can understand that," Ravi said supportively. "Do what you must, old chap. I'm sure we can take it from here if you'd like to excuse yourself."

"I just need a minute." Edmund kept his eyes closed as he spoke.

"This is all very strange," Oz said as he crouched down to inspect the base of the fountain. "It doesn't look broken. No one's body was thrown against it."

"But where is the rest of the evidence?" Yvie said as she examined the bloody plants without touching them. "Not one leaf has been crushed."

They kneeled down together to inspect the soil.

"There are footprints here," Oz said as he pointed. "Men's footprints. It looks like they were wearing fancy shoes."

"*Oui*, look at the heels," Yvie pointed. "But there is no blood in the soil. How did it land only in the fountain?"

They both glanced along the ground to the closest marble hallway.

Eleanor tiptoed carefully to the edge of the garden, squinting for any evidence of mud on the marble floors, but there was none. It was absolutely clean. "There aren't any footprints here." She moved on to examining the marble pillars. "I don't see any evidence of soil or blood at all."

"Perhaps they took their shoes off before they went to seek help?" Yvie suggested.

"But help after what? This is a lot of blood," Oz said as he leaned in to re-examine the bloody water.

"Perhaps it was some sort of accident," Shruti suggested hopefully. "Where is Hari? Maybe the gardener cut himself. I suppose he could have stopped the bleeding before he left the garden, and then he carried his boots with him to not dirty the floor. Father, perhaps you can go check on him in the men's quarters?"

"I will go right now," Ravi agreed.

"I'll go with you, mate. I was a medic in the war," Oz suggested.

"That is very kind, thank you. It's this way." Ravi guided him out of the garden.

"Shall I join you?" Edmund asked unenthusiastically.

"I think we've got it covered, mate. There's no need for the lion's brawn just yet." Oz threw a knowing glance towards Eleanor. She nodded her appreciation of his help.

As soon as Oz and Ravi disappeared into the dark hallway, Eleanor made her way to Edmund's side.

"Are you alright, darling?" She held his cheek in her hand, blocking Shruti's view as she checked on his eyes. With one more round of aggressive mantras, the black dissolved, and his human hazel was once again intact.

"Very good, darling," Eleanor whispered. "It looks like you're making progress."

Edmund finally turned around to face Shruti. "I'd best get away from all this blood."

Eleanor held his hand tightly as they tiptoed out of the garden, leaving a trail of muddy footprints behind them. Shruti followed, guiding them around the corner, to the edge of another grand sitting room with a large harp right in the middle of an elaborate persian carpet. She flagged down one male servant who was watching the performance through the open doorway and whispered some orders to him in Marathi. He nodded and disappeared down the hallway.

"The girls and their parents will get suspicious if we don't return. I'm sure Father will take care of it in no time," Shruti whispered. "But first we must make ourselves presentable."

Eleanor recognized the same false calm in Shruti's voice that she herself was so seasoned at producing.

"Darling, do you feel up to it?" Eleanor asked as a chorus of little girls roaring echoed in from the performance room.

"Yes. Yes, I mustn't be entirely useless," he agreed.

"You are never useless, Uncle Edmund," Shruti reassured him. "And you are doing me a great favor. If all the men were missing, they'd know something was amiss."

The male servant returned with three more servants, each carrying washbasins and towels. They crouched down at their feet and began washing off the mud from the garden. When they were finished, the servants used the towels to wipe up the trails of muddy footprints, but as the mud smeared, Eleanor contemplated exactly how strange it was that there was absolutely no evidence of the victim or the culprit anywhere in the halls surrounding the garden.

"Come, we mustn't be away too long," Shruti whispered. She guided them back into the makeshift theater and smiled reassuringly to the parents as they sat down. Eleanor took Edmund's hand, hoping desperately that there would be some mundane explanation for the odd occurrence.

The narrator continued the story unfazed, and Shruti reluctantly returned to translating.

"Just as it seemed that all hope was lost, a visitor arrived, a *Rakshasa* visitor, the brother of the demon Ravana himself, Vibhishana, but he was not a villain, no, he was an unexpected ally, a virtuous demon, and a bearer of important secrets…"

Eleanor's attention was piqued as a little girl dressed in a beautiful violet costume, quite different from the other Rakshasa costumes, danced onto the stage.

"Huh…" It was the first time that she had ever encountered Vibhi's official role in the story. It sounded rather believable, in fact…

She looked over to Edmund to see if he was paying attention, but his focus was still entirely on the odd mystery in the garden as he glanced over to where Ravi and Oz had headed.

They sat for the rest of the long performance paying only partial attention, which felt especially interminable to both of them as they waited for Ravi and Oz to return. When it was over, and the dancers were bowing to their cheering parents, they offered their polite congratulations, and made their escape, while Shruti managed the dispersion of the crowd.

"Do you think everything is alright?" Yvie asked nervously. "What could have possibly caused the noise?"

"I don't have any clue. I really am a dreadful detective," Edmund whispered dismally. "I was hoping this part of our honeymoon would not be littered with dark mysteries."

"It is not your fault, Edmund," Eleanor said sternly. "Do not take personal responsibility for whatever this is. I'm sure it has a perfectly rational explanation that has nothing to do with you."

"I hope you're right," he whispered. "I don't want to bring danger to everyone I love. It didn't used to be that way, and it had better not start now…"

"I'm sure that it won't, darling. You help those you love out of difficult situations that they otherwise would not survive at all."

"It's true," Yvie seconded. "We would all have been shot on the Orient Express by those revolutionaries if you hadn't saved us."

Edmund looked pained at the memory, and then he relaxed slightly as he accepted the truth of her argument.

They all perked up as Oz and Ravi approached from around the corner of a dark hallway.

"Well, was he alright, Ozzy? Was it the gardener?" Yvie asked.

"He was sleeping like a baby and had been for hours, I'm afraid," Oz reported. "It's good for him, I suppose, but it means the blood wasn't his. We searched the entire house. Every single room, every garden, every hallway. There is nothing. I'm not sure what we do now." He looked to Ravi.

"We do nothing," Ravi whispered. "No police. No army. No excuse for any stranger to enter this house. I will bring in my own investigators and give them free rein while we are away at Elephanta tomorrow. If there is something to find, they will find it." He smiled and shook off his obvious concern as Shruti approached. "Shruti, the performance was wonderful. Your mother would have been so proud. Did the girls and their parents enjoy it?"

"Yes, they were all very pleased with themselves… But, Father, was Hari alright?" She didn't let him distract her for one second.

"He was perfectly fine. I will call in the Singhs tomorrow to investigate. We did our own search and found no evidence of anything amiss. If there is something to find, they will find it. In the meantime, you must all rest up. We will leave in the morning when the tide is optimal, and we will be out all day. Come, old chap, I will show you to your bridal chambers myself."

"Ravi..." Edmund interrupted as a troubling thought occurred to him. "Have you heard from my butler, Mr. Valov, today? Did he come by with our luggage?"

"We received a call this afternoon that he was held back on the ship. He said he'd be by tomorrow. I gave him directions and offered to send a car, but he said he would make his own way. Strange accent, that chap has. Russian?"

"Czech," Edmund replied. Eleanor could see concern working its way into Edmund's expression.

"Don't worry, Edmund. Babri will be working all night. We will have a perfect wardrobe for all of you by morning," Shruti reassured him, misunderstanding the source of his concern (or skillfully deflecting it to something more mundane).

"Oh, she doesn't have to do that!" Eleanor exclaimed.

"Oh, she loves it," Shruti laughed. "It is the only thing that keeps her mind properly occupied. She often works at night, and the more work, the more of a game it is for her to get it finished. Your best payment will be to shower her with praise in the morning. Then she will sleep all day in my bed while we are out, and she will be perfectly fine by evening. It is much better than anything she knew before we took her in. We found her living on the streets."

"How horrible!" Eleanor exclaimed.

"It is not an uncommon story. Her parents couldn't marry her off, and after a while they gave up on her completely. I was lucky to have stumbled upon her. She has been as much of a blessing for us as we have been for her."

"You are underestimating the impact you've had on her," Edmund replied.

"I wonder who I learned that from," Shruti winked.

"Come, my friends. Do not let these trivialities distract you from your honeymoon." Ravi gestured for them to follow him.

"I will show you to your rooms, Oz and Yvie. We have put you far away from Edmund and Eleanor, so that they can make as much noise as they'd like," Shruti whispered.

"Sounds like a right bonza idea," Oz agreed.

Eleanor took Edmund's hand as they followed Ravi through several hallways lit only by flickering torch-light until they reached a set of wooden doors open to a series of marble chambers very similar in luxury and layout to Shruti's, with a similarly magical view of the twinkling city glittering from across the dark water of the bay.

"How lovely," Edmund whispered. "I didn't realize you had such grand bedrooms here."

"This room is reserved for married couples. I am so glad that you will finally enjoy its charms, Edmund." Ravi took Edmund's hand into both of his and shook it affectionately. "I will send someone to wake you up when it is time for you to get ready. We will take breakfast on the yacht so we won't lose any time. I can't wait to show you the caves! They were your idea, you know, old chap. Reya was in a tizzy over the plans to develop the island, and you are the one who suggested I pay our way into their protection. It worked like a charm."

"I'm glad to hear it." Edmund smiled, finally letting himself relax.

Ravi offered them a final bow and left them alone.

After one moment of contemplation, Edmund whisked Eleanor up into his arms, and she squealed with surprise.

"I cannot ignore another opportunity to carry my bride over the threshold," he declared as he carried her into the bridal chamber. "Eleanor MacLeod, I still cannot believe the great fortune that you are my wife!"

"I love you, Edmund." Eleanor enticed him into a kiss.

The elaborate canopied bed was covered in richly scented jasmine and marigolds, and a steaming turkish bath was waiting for them in a large bathroom just beyond.

"Shall I search your mehendi for my initials?" Edmund asked as he put her down and took her hand into his.

"Is that what you have always dreamed about doing?" Eleanor asked, as Shruti's intel about his dream of an Indian bride worked its way back into her head.

Edmund stopped to think about her question. "I suppose I have found the idea alluring. I never thought I'd get to do it myself, and certainly not with a Scottish bride. You are so open, Eleanor. You are so much more interesting than I thought anyone could be."

"Thank you, darling," Eleanor said as she gave up on her minor mission.

"Do you think we should be worried about the blood in the garden?" he asked as the thought distracted him.

"I think we've done everything we can do about it for now." Eleanor guided him into the bathroom. "Let's not let it ruin our first night in India together."

Edmund put his large hands around her bare waist between the blouse and the skirt of her flowing lehenga, and she felt him perk up with excitement.

"Undress me, Edmund," she whispered as she reached up onto her tiptoes to lick his lips. "It's time to inspect your bride."

And together, as the lights of Bombay twinkled in the unusually mild humid air, and the Bidkars tended to the many complicated details of the world around them, Edmund and Eleanor set about exploring the many exotic pleasures of their Indian bridal evening.

Eleanor awoke from her position nestled in her gentle husband's cold, naked arms, and it took her a moment to remember where she was. A strange herbal scent wafted off of her arms, and she looked down to spot the dye of the henna settling in much darker than it had been the night before. The Bidkars... The henna... India.

A loud banging on the door startled her, but Edmund didn't stir.

"Darling," she whispered as she ran her fingers gently along his nipples until they hardened, and he sighed contentedly. "Darling, it's time to wake up."

Edmund gasped in his awakening Rakshasa breath.

"Good morning, dearest. I was having the most pleasant dream..." He trailed off as he noticed the henna on her arms, and he took her hand to his mouth and kissed it. "You and I were dancing at our wedding, but it wasn't our real wedding. It was an

Indian wedding… and then the crowds disappeared, and I ravaged you right there on the wet lawn."

Eleanor reached up to entice him into a naughty french kiss. "I wish I were there to enjoy it with you."

A louder, more aggressive knock on the door wrested them from their romantic moment.

"Wake up, skinny doll!" Babri shouted. "Your new clothes are ready. Memsahib is waiting!"

"We'd better listen to her. Babri might just push her way in here," Eleanor whispered. "Just a minute!" she called.

She hopped out of bed and threw Edmund a silk robe while she gathered hers up from the floor. As soon as she'd tied the loose belt, she pulled open the door, and Babri—covering her hair with a loose blue scarf and wearing a more modest lehenga than she had the night before, with a long-sleeved, knee-length choli that didn't show a hint of her stomach or her arms—pushed her way inside without a word of request or apology.

Babri carried a stack of neatly folded garments, all made of rich violet silk, covered in thousands of black sparkling beads. "This salwar kameez is for you, skinny doll."

She held up a pair of baggy silk trousers and a long, flowing dress-like shirt with a matching black and violet dupatta scarf. She forced them into Eleanor's hand so that she could present Edmund with his.

"And this suit is for the giant."

She presented a kurta made of the exact same violet material along with a pair of flowing, baggy silk trousers that tapered at the bottom. It had the same sparkling black beadwork, and Eleanor giggled as Edmund held the suit up for his own inspection.

"Why thank you, Babri. I am sure to be the talk of the town on our excursion today." Eleanor could see that he was working hard to keep a straight face.

Babri's face lit up at the compliment.

"Thank you, Babri. They're lovely," Eleanor said politely. "Did you work all night on these?"

"No, I made two more," she said proudly. "French doll and yellow-haired man got theirs already. Now dress! Memsahib is waiting! Sahib is impatient about the tide! Shall I dress you?"

She reached forward and ripped at the belt of Eleanor's robe, and Eleanor slapped her hand gently to stop her. "Thank you for the offer, Babri, but your help is not necessary. My husband will dress me." Babri's eyes lit up with excitement at the idea. "You can tell Ravi and Shruti that we will be there in a few minutes."

Babri skipped to the door. "Memsahib says to wear the jewelry from last night again today. You must look proper to meet Lord Shiva."

"Lord Shiva? I didn't realize you had such a famous dignitary on our itinerary, darling," Eleanor teased.

"He never responded to my inquiries," Edmund winked. "I suppose he must have replied directly to Ravi. I'm glad I will be properly attired for our meeting."

Babri did not understand the sarcasm of their exchange, and smiled once again at the compliment.

"Thank you, Babri. The clothes are wonderful," Eleanor reiterated.

Babri skipped away happily. Eleanor closed the door, and then held out the suit before her again.

"It really is remarkable how quickly she made these… If only her stylistic decisions were a bit… more stylish."

"I don't know what you mean," Edmund said as he tied up the drawstring of the silk pants and pulled on the heavy kurta with a comfort that indicated that he had done something similar many times before. "I think they are the height of fashion."

Eleanor giggled as he twirled around. She was surprised by his lack of self-consciousness on the matter, and she suddenly loved him even more for it. She was quite sure that he was the only

British man on Earth who would put on such a flamboyant foreign outfit and seriously consider wearing it outside.

"Look at the artistry of the beading, dearest. Can you imagine how long it must have taken someone to sew in each and every one of these?"

Eleanor reached forward to inspect the beaded paisley designs on his sleeve. "I love that you see so many layers of beauty in everything, darling. You really are so unusual in that way." She reached up and stole a kiss. "It looks strangely natural on you, actually."

Edmund looked down at his outfit. "I suppose it reminds me of my childhood in Hyderabad. It was stylish for men there to wear much more interesting fabrics than men in Britain have ever worn in my lifetime. Although, Abdul Barr and I never wore anything so grand. These heavily beaded silks were reserved for the Nizam and his court. Do you think Babri made me a turban with a matching violet feather?"

"I can only hope," Eleanor giggled.

She let her silk robe fall to the ground and stood for a moment as Edmund ran his cold fingers along her naked breasts until a wave of goosebumps erupted. He leaned in for a tantalizing kiss, arousing her so much that she suddenly felt a pang of pain in her loins, but as Babri's voice echoed in the hallway beyond, he dutifully helped her pull on the flowing fabric of her matching suit. As soon as the drawstring of her trousers was tightened, she wrapped her legs around his, and he happily took her cue and dipped her into a long, romantic kiss.

"You look lovely, dearest." He finally let her go, and she steadied herself from a moment of lightheadedness.

"It seems rather practical, actually," Eleanor said as she twirled around in front of the mirror. "These trousers allow freedom of movement, while still giving the stylistic effect of the flowing fabric from the dress. Do you think this fashion will ever make it to Europe?"

"We can only hope. Perhaps you will be the one to introduce it." He readjusted her scarf so that it was draped over her shoulders across the front of her top. "This is how the Indian women wear it."

"So you were paying attention," Eleanor teased him.

Edmund blushed. "It is hard for me not to appreciate beauty in all its forms."

Eleanor kissed him again, and then popped into the bathroom for a few minutes of private preparations while her gentle husband waited patiently.

When she was finished, he pulled her into a final kiss, and then escorted her through the open-aired marble hallways, past several verdant gardens where a number of serious Sikh men had already started their detailed investigation at the behest of Ravi Bidkar, and finally to the front entryway where they had arrived the day before. Two sleek black cars were lined up in a row awaiting their use. Harjeet sat awaiting his orders in the driver's seat of the first car, while a younger Sikh man in a matching uniform looked rather bored as he sat waiting in the second car.

She glanced down the drive, past the forested hill dotted with topiary and altars, to an elaborate golden gate she hadn't noticed upon their arrival. The house really was a palace, by every reasonable definition. She thought fleetingly about how Ravi's horrific condition had given him the means for such luxury… or about how he had not let his condition stop him from achieving it. She wasn't sure which one was more true. She hoped that whatever odd occurrence had happened during the dance recital would not inconvenience the Bidkars, and she hoped even more avidly that it did not have anything to do with Edmund.

"I'm glad to see we weren't the only ones who got the royal treatment!" Oz exclaimed, breaking her out of her unpleasant thoughts.

Eleanor giggled. Oz and Yvie's outfits matched theirs verbatim in style (highlighting to Eleanor how handsome

Edmund's tall, muscular body was in comparison to Oz's stockier, shorter one), except that Oz and Yvie's had been concocted in a dark blue silk covered in silver and blue beads.

"Princely brothers, I'd say we are," Edmund laughed. "Perhaps princely brothers married to two lovely sisters?"

Shruti laughed as she approached the group and rushed to greet them, wearing her own matching suit in emerald green, covered in thousands of sparkling green and gold beads.

"Oh, you all look splendid!" she exclaimed. "Very exotic. I've never seen *firangs* donning our clothing like this. What a treat! I hope you consider wearing them all the time. They really do look better than those drab brown suits that are so popular in Europe. Oh, and the mehendi! Eleanor, it is so dark on your skin! It hardly looks real!"

She clapped her hands, and Gita and Sheena rushed to her side, carrying four pairs of intensely beaded, pointy-toed shoes that looked like they were right off the stage of a *Scheherazade* ballet.

"You can't go out on a hike barefoot!" Shruti exclaimed as Sheena and Gita presented the offerings with respectful bows. "Edmund, yours are the right size, I believe, although I'm sorry for the absurdity. It was quite a feat to get so many pairs of shoes made in the middle of the night, but I had the cobbler use your slippers that we had made for you last time as a model. They were so big that he thought they were for one of the demon dance costumes, so he added some extra flourishes." She poked at two large golden poufs that had been added to the pointed toes, creating the effect of a medieval court jester's shoes. "Why he thought Rakshasas would have especially big feet is a bit of a mystery, but what's done is done..."

Eleanor hid her anxiety at the reference, and instead focused on wiggling on the sparkling shoes. She laughed as Edmund managed to squeeze his on.

"If only I'd had these for our wedding, dearest. They would have made my dress uniform so much more exciting!"

Everyone laughed as Edmund did a little jig, and Eleanor felt a burst of love for his confident good sportsmanship.

"Come, come!" Ravi boomed as he clapped his hands, rushing towards them from a hallway beyond, clad in a similarly elaborate outfit to the one he'd been wearing the day before in gold and white. "Open the gates. We are leaving now, while the tides are still on our side!"

Ravi slipped on his own sparkling shoes, and then escorted Edmund and Eleanor to the back seat of the first car, while Shruti followed his lead and escorted Oz and Yvie to the back seat of the second car.

"You look marvelous, old chap. Both of you are a vision!" Ravi said happily as he threw himself down in the front seat and Harjeet sped off. "You are going to have so much fun today, and the weather has obliged us beautifully. It is really quite temperate for this time of year."

Eleanor took in a satisfied breath of the cool humidity and the scent of the wet earth wafting up from the garden. She reminded herself once again to thank Kuveni for it later.

"Now, it will be a few minutes before we get to the harbor, but never you worry. I have all the gossip on every neighbor we'll be passing to keep you entertained on our drive. Why, that house just there belongs to the Maharaja of Gondal. He and his wife use it as a second home when they are visiting Bombay from Gujarat. He has quite a mind for business, although he's a bit too much of an opportunist for my taste, and his wife was never particularly kind to Reya…"

Eleanor sat back and held Edmund's cold hand tightly in hers, letting Ravi's words wash over her as she felt the subtle lull of Edmund's pulsating power. They rode for far longer than Ravi's 'few minutes' estimate, and by the time they actually reached the dock where an enormous modern white yacht awaited them with a staff of at least twenty people watching their approach curiously, gasping and whispering as they spotted the exotic vision of

Edmund and Eleanor in their Indian clothing, Ravi's jovial commentary morphed into a panicked hurry.

"Quick, my friends, please be careful boarding the yacht, but we must go as soon as the other car arrives. The tide is almost too low." He urged them towards the boat and began yelling orders at the staff.

Edmund and Eleanor stood watching from the deck of the ship as several different servants insisted that they take some chai.

Ravi became more and more agitated as they waited for the second car. When it finally pulled up, Shruti hopped out and opened the doors for Oz and Yvie.

"Sorry, Father," she called. "There was a minor accident that had to be sorted, but we're here now."

She escorted Oz and Yvie right onto the boat, and without a second wasted, it pulled away from the dock.

"I was worried sick," Ravi whispered as he pulled Shruti into a hug.

"We were perfectly fine, Papa. You mustn't worry yourself over such minor things. It isn't good for your heart."

"Come. Let's take our breakfast on the deck. It will take less than an hour to get to Elephanta now," Ravi said as he took Shruti's hand and squeezed it.

Edmund held Eleanor steady on the stairs as the yacht swayed from side to side in the choppy water, and she was grateful when they reached the top deck and she spied a lovely table that was set underneath an enormous white canvas umbrella for shade. The staff rushed to pull out their chairs, and as Eleanor sat down, she gratefully noticed a sweating carafe of iced water in front of every person's place-setting.

"We must not repeat the mistakes of yesterday," Shruti whispered into Eleanor's ear. "Please, drink all that you can stomach. There is plenty more in the kitchen, and they are on orders to refill your glass as often as you empty it."

Several more servants reached forward to lift up a series of silver covers, revealing a platter of spongy white disks that looked vaguely similar to crumpets, an aromatic steaming red sauce with chunks of onion and potato, and a burbling batch of creamy yellow curry that made Edmund's stomach growl.

"We also have marmite and toast, if you'd prefer," Shruti offered. "I know curry for breakfast is quite foreign to *firangs* (other than Edmund, of course), so I had the staff collect some staples from the British import store."

"Those pancakes look mighty scrummy to me," Oz replied.

"They are called idlis, and they are made out of a rice and lentil batter, so I think they are healthier than British pancakes, or so Uncle Edmund tells us," Shruti explained. "We normally dip them in sambar, which is the red sauce there, but Uncle Edmund likes to dip them in Punjabi curry, so we had the chef make that yellow creamy curry there just for him. Idlis are normally more of a southern dish, but we can't help but indulge Uncle Edmund's whims. We also have coconut chutney which is quite mild, and cucumber raita, there, which is a yogurt dish, in case you find the sauces too spicy. I recommend drinking masala chai while you eat. The milk will help with digestion."

"Normally you shouldn't drink anything while you eat," Ravi interjected as he sat down beside her and offered idlis to each person. "But you'd better listen to Shruti. She knows more about accommodating foreign temperaments than I do. She has an entire class of British ballet dancers now. Thirty students, I think."

"Thirty-four, actually. I'm going to split them into two groups next season. They are not part of the Bharatnatyam underground, of course."

Shruti finished taking two idlis and placed the rest on Edmund's empty plate, as he had already (of course) finished his first serving. She gestured for the servants to replace the serving dish with a fresh one, and she winked at Eleanor as Edmund noticed his indiscretion and self-consciously slowed down his pace.

"Thirty-four students," Ravi sighed. "It really is an accomplishment, Shruti dear... Although, as I always say, one of your own is worth hundreds of other people's."

Shruti rolled her eyes.

"One of your own what?" Edmund asked.

"Children. He means children," Shruti said with annoyance. "Father decided quite a while back that he'd like some grandchildren, but I have not yet obliged him."

"You are rather young," Eleanor pointed out.

"Thank you, Eleanor. I agree. Besides, children are not a solution to boredom. They should be the product of a responsible, loving marriage, and for that, one must have a responsible, loving husband."

"What was wrong with the Maharaja of Mysore's brother? He was so polite!" Ravi leaned in confidingly to Edmund. "He was very taken with her."

"He was forty!" Shruti exclaimed.

Ravi buckled down for an argument that he had obviously made many times before. "Wisdom should not be underestimated, Shruti dear. Look at Edmund here. He is the best husband in the world, because he had enough time to become a man before he got married, just like I did."

"Do you not think that girls should have time to become women before they get married?" Eleanor asked.

"Shruti is a woman!" Ravi argued. "Shruti has been so responsible with running our household and the school these last five years that she has the experience of a woman twice her age!"

"Well, when I find the right husband, I will consider your request, Father," Shruti said diplomatically. "Until then, you will have to occupy yourself with your business matters as always."

Ravi sighed melodramatically and popped another idli into his mouth. "I will keep praying then, Shruti dear. Lord Vishnu works in mysterious ways."

They all sat for a few moments of silent eating before Shruti changed the subject.

"Yvie was most helpful yesterday in explaining to me the nuances of the French language that I had been finding entirely confounding. I didn't think there was a language that was harder to pronounce than Tamil, but French might be it."

"Oh yes, *ze French*..." Ravi did his best impression of an exaggerated French accent. "*Zat reminds me of a time in Pondicherry when I made a deal wiz a very angry frog...*"

"Father," Shruti hissed.

"What?" he protested. "*Ze story will be worz it*, I swear."

Eleanor glanced at Yvie, who was too entertained by his uncouth impression to be offended, and then she relaxed and settled into the friendly mundanity of the meal, watching slyly to keep a silent count on behalf of Edward Rutherford's game to note exactly how many idlis Edmund ended up consuming (twenty-four, for the record, to the great entertainment of the servers).

In what felt like no time at all, the yacht was pulling up into a muddy mangrove forest to a small dock. Before them was a thickly wooded island made up of layers of rolling hills. A large group of villagers dressed in colorful but simple garb were jumping up and down, shouting their enthusiastic welcome, while a strikingly large number of monkeys were similarly welcoming, dancing around with wild screeches on the roof of the small hut attached to the dock. The sight was as exotic as any Eleanor could have imagined, and the fact that no one else seemed to find the presence of the monkeys remotely notable added to the effect.

"Father is very popular here," Shruti laughed. "Come. We should try to reach the caves before the height of midday. We do not need you to overheat again, Eleanor, even when Shakti has blessed us with this lovely breeze."

Eleanor found the idea that they were all going to hike in their elaborate outfits rather absurd, but as Shruti and Ravi did not seem to find anything strange about the idea at all, she kept her thoughts to herself, and instead focused on the nice sensation of the cool grip of Edmund's hand in hers.

"Take this." Shruti offered her a silk parasol, and she took her hand out of Edmund's to hold it. "Use it, Eleanor, or you will be burned by the time we get to the caves." She handed another one to Yvie, and then prepared her own.

Shruti shouted thanks to the villagers, who cheered happily back, and quickly, with eight servants following them carrying what appeared to be enough supplies for an entire regiment of the army, they were off on their journey.

As they walked, the rustling of creatures in the bush just beyond sent a shiver down Eleanor's spine, but as she glanced to Shruti and Ravi, who didn't seem bothered by the sounds in the slightest, she worked hard to ignore her instincts.

"Are there snakes here?" Yvie asked with a hint of nerves. Eleanor was glad that she wasn't the only one who was worried about the wildlife.

"There are cobras from time to time," Shruti replied nonchalantly.

"*Mon dieu*," Yvie muttered.

"Don't worry, they are just as unenthusiastic about looking at my face as humans are," Ravi laughed. "They always scurry out of the way when we come through."

"This place is quite wild for being so close to Bombay. I'm surprised I've never made it here before," Edmund commented as the path narrowed.

Ravi began using his carved ivory walking cane to gently escort several creepily large red and black striped spiders out of their way. Each time, he guided the spiders onto his cane and then urged them onto neighboring branches, keeping each and every one alive.

"The British have been helpful in preserving it, actually. They like that the island's position is strategic for protecting the harbor, and so they have kept it reserved for a small army garrison, who have mostly stayed out of the caves, except for a few vandals and miscreants…" He trailed off as he relegated a look of anger at the thought. "I assumed that you had something to do with protecting it, Edmund. You didn't?"

"You give me too much credit, Ravi, like always. I'm not personally responsible for every reasonable judgment made by the British Army, you know."

Ravi laughed. "I suppose there must be a few more like you, old chap. They're just few and far between."

"Father," Shruti hissed with embarrassment.

He brushed her off and continued with what he was going to say. "We have done what we could to keep too much foreign interest away from the caves. The last thing we need is some egotistical archaeologist digging them up for his own personal glory. The caves are holy to us, you see. We'd rather those who do not appreciate their meaning stay away completely."

"I suppose then, I am not particularly qualified to enter," Edmund replied.

"You will appreciate their meaning, old chap, even if you don't believe the scripture," Ravi countered. "They contain some of the most impressive ancient works of art in India. There was a reason Reya believed they'd been created by Lord Shiva himself. I have no doubt you will respect their artistry more than any other *firang* in the world."

"I am grateful for the privilege."

Eleanor focused on keeping her parasol in place without tripping in the uncomfortable shoes for what felt like an interminable walk up an increasingly steep hillside, until they reached an old stone wall that was almost entirely obscured by thick vines and blooming tropical flowers. The path led to a spot where the wall had already crumbled into ruins.

Eleanor held her breath as the bushes rustled with the movement of many creatures moving towards them with increasing speed and urgency, but she laughed with relief as a family of monkeys finally popped up out of the foliage and climbed up onto the ruins.

"Good lord," Edmund muttered.

"Hello, my friends!" Ravi addressed the monkeys.

He reached into his pockets and handed them each a guava, but as the littlest monkey devoured his in one loud slurp, the largest monkey of the pack took the offering and threw it straight at Edmund's head with a decidedly unwelcoming hiss.

Ravi and Shruti were both dumbfounded by the development, while Oz burst into laughter. "Looks like he doesn't like you, mate."

"The feeling is mutual," Edmund said testily as he wiped the sticky substance off of his face.

Another group of monkeys hopped up onto the wall from the underbrush, lining up behind their comrades. The largest of the pack hissed at Edmund, and two smaller ones began squawking heatedly.

"Is this normal behavior for them? Do they guard the caves?" Eleanor asked.

"There are always a lot of monkeys here." Shruti reached into her pockets and threw another handful of guavas to the monkeys. The largest monkey caught two at once, and a savage fight erupted as three smaller males attempted to steal them. "But I've never seen them so riled up. Usually they are very calm and welcoming."

"Monkeys and I do not tend to get along." Edmund threw a look of extra warning towards Eleanor, implying that there was more to the story. "If I'd known there would be a colony of them here, I might have refused the excursion completely."

"Oh, come now, old chap, it can't be that bad!" Ravi argued. "Let's get moving. We are almost there, and we must get the ladies out of the sun."

He guided them through the opening in the wall, but as Edmund stepped through, all of the monkeys screamed with wild protestations. With more rustling in the underbrush indicating their growing numbers, Edmund pushed forward, working his hardest to ignore them.

They hiked hastily through several more crumbling walls until they reached an open grassy courtyard up against a steep hillside. Imposing stone pillars and grand staircases flanked the entrances to a series of dark caves that were carved right into the earth, while the peaceful trickling of water flowing somewhere beyond intermixed disconcertingly with the squawking of unhappy monkeys and the screeching of kites circling in the air above them.

"How extraordinary," Eleanor murmured. "They really built the temples right into rock, didn't they?"

"It looks like they've seen better days," Oz said as he nodded towards a particularly dilapidated pillar that was barely recognizable from the pile of rubble around it.

"The Portuguese soldiers used them as target practice," Shruti explained. "And they didn't even spare the religious carvings inside. There are some scenes that are completely unrecognizable now."

"*Quelle horrible!*" Yvie exclaimed. "Those brutes!"

Shruti sighed. "It is another reason we have tried to keep foreigners away. How anyone could possibly see this site and decide to destroy it is beyond me, no matter what their religious beliefs are."

"I agree," Edmund said pensively. "Thank you for bringing us here."

"Come, my friends!" Ravi declared. "You haven't even seen the best parts yet. There are such wonderful carvings inside. Entire stories of the most powerful of gods cut right into the walls."

He clapped his hands and called something to the servants, two of whom dug through their packs and rushed to light a set of torches. They presented both to Ravi, and he handed one to Edmund.

"The Ardhanarishvara is just in there towards the back on the left. It is a form of the Transformer made up of two perfect halves of Lord Shiva and his wife, Parvati. It was Reya's favorite. She always referred to it as God's self-portrait." Ravi gave into a nostalgic sigh. "And then we will go see the Nataraja—dancing Shiva, whose cosmic energy stomps down the dwarf of ignorance…"

"How poetic!" Eleanor exclaimed.

"I think so too. It has always been my favorite," Shruti confided.

"And then we will see several scenes from the marriage of Lord Shiva and Parvati," Ravi continued. "Those will be perfect for your honeymoon! Oh, and we can't miss the lingam; it is the most holy of all of the carvings, and I've brought a puja to offer on your behalf, so your marriage will be as blessed as mine was."

"Really, Ravi, that isn't necessary," Edmund protested.

"Indulge me, old chap." He snapped his fingers at one of the servants who immediately put down his pack and began digging through it, removing first a heavy garland of jasmine and marigolds, then a coconut, a stick of incense with a small metal burner, three metal bowls of white, yellow, and red powder, and a metal pot that looked vaguely like a teapot, but with a longer spout. "No, don't put them on the ground!" Ravi exclaimed. He snapped his finger at another servant who rushed to gather them up.

Suddenly, a chorus of angry screeching echoed from all directions, and a shiver ran down Eleanor's spine.

"Father, have you ever seen the monkeys so agitated? It is like they are Sugriva's army, positioning themselves for battle," Shruti asked nervously as hundreds of monkeys surrounded them, jumping up and down on the grassy outcrops overhanging the temple entrances.

"I warned you that monkeys and I don't get along, Ravi. They've always had it out for me. We must leave before the situation gets any worse." Edmund closed his eyes and whispered his mantras, which only made Eleanor more worried.

"Nonsense. We have come here for years and years, and we've never once had a problem. I'm sure they'll calm down as soon as we're in the caves."

Edmund took Eleanor's hand and held the torch in the other, but as they followed Ravi towards the entrance of the closest temple, several monkeys swooped down from the rocks above.

What happened next went by so quickly that Eleanor could hardly keep the order of it straight.

One monkey grabbed Edmund's torch, while another ripped at his arm until a piece of his sleeve tore right off, flinging a shower of black beads across the ground.

As the monkey wrapped its legs and tail around Edmund's arm, he chucked it off with all of his might, slamming the monkey against the rocks with a thud and a crunch. The creature's crushed body landed on the ground, and the entire primate army shrieked ferociously.

A third monkey swooped down, bearing its fangs, but as it took a beastly bite right out of Edmund's forearm, he swatted it off and cradled his gaping wound with his other hand so that Ravi and Shruti would not see his violet Rakshasa plasma as it oozed to the surface.

As Shruti and Ravi argued in Marathi, six of the eight servants dropped their supplies and ran at their fastest speed away from the scene.

"Come back! They're not Sugriva's army!" Shruti called.

Ravi followed up her entreaty with outraged shouting in Marathi that made Eleanor cringe. She hadn't heard a similar tone since she'd told her mother she was moving out of the house to study nursing...

As soon as it was clear that the servants were not going to return, she turned her attention on the remaining two, who began dutifully digging through the packs for more torches.

Oz and Yvie both rushed over to examine Edmund's ugly wound. Edmund flinched as they approached, and then he remembered the unusual reality that he did not need to hide his secrets from them, and he let them watch as his Rakshasa plasma did its work.

"I hope you don't have to worry about rabies, mate. That's a doozey," Oz whispered.

"I will be perfectly fine. I just need a moment to collect myself," Edmund whispered.

Eleanor caught a glimpse of Edmund's black eyes.

"Darling, calm yourself," she whispered as she rubbed his back soothingly. "Everything is going to be alright. You just have to remain calm and cling to your humanity, and we will all work together to get out of this mess."

Yvie threw her a look of shared concern as she glanced over at Ravi and Shruti, who were still engaged in an increasingly heated argument. But Eleanor's panic about the Bidkars noticing Edmund's inhuman traits was suddenly overwhelmed by the grotesque gagging and squawking of the monkey who had imparted the wound.

Several monkeys swarmed around to watch as the culprit crouched into a fetal position, let out one final, blood-curdling scream, and then stiffened into a corpse. A drop of Edmund's violet metallic plasma dripped from its mouth, scurried across the ground and up Edmund's shoes, and disappeared into his skin just between his ankle and his trousers.

"Good lord," Eleanor murmured.

"*Mon dieu*," Yvie whispered.

"Bloody hell," Edmund hissed. "Do you think they saw that?"

As the monkeys' shrieks became even more fierce, a large group led by several muscular males began swinging down the carved pillars at the entrance to the caves, honing in on their position.

"The monkeys sure did," Oz whispered.

Shruti, with a freshly lit torch in her left hand, rushed towards them, offering no evidence that she or her father had seen any of the incriminating scene. "You must come, Eleanor. We must let the men deal with this."

"Go!" Edmund whispered. "Eleanor, dearest, go with Shruti to safety!"

"Wait, what? No!" Eleanor protested. "Not this again!"

"This is not a place for women!" Shruti grabbed Eleanor's hand and yanked her towards the closest cave.

"Yvie, go with them!" Oz exclaimed. "If they did this to Edmund, they can do it to you! We don't have any weapons!"

As Yvie protested angrily in French, Eleanor grabbed her hand, and with the exceptional strength afforded by her lifetime of Bharatnatyam practice, Shruti fought off the monkeys with her torch and dragged her two wards against their wills into the closest temple.

"Let's see how you like fire, you little buggers!" Oz exclaimed.

Eleanor caught one last glimpse of the valiant men's battle as Oz began an absurd pantomime of a fencing match, wielding the torch against a swarm of screaming monkeys.

"Shruti, we have to help them!" Eleanor's fiery Celtic temper was burrowing its way to the surface. "Yvie and I are modern women! We both know how to fight!"

"What will hiding in this cave even do for us?" Yvie added angrily. "We will be trapped in here while the monkeys eat them alive! They will come for us next!"

"Do not worry, my children," an elderly woman interrupted them. Her voice echoed in perfect English from the darkness beyond. Eleanor, Yvie, and Shruti threw each other looks of total confusion. "Lord Kalki will defeat my army in good time. They have been gunning for a good fight for centuries, and Rakshasas have always been their favorite targets. Many will not be able to believe that Lord Kalki and their Rakshasa foe are one and the same, but the ones who cannot see the truth will be the first to parish. All will be as it should."

"Rakshasa foe…" Eleanor murmured. Her mind began racing. Whoever the voice in the darkness was, she knew Edmund's secret.

"*Qu'est-ce que c'est?*" Yvie whispered as she squinted to see into the darkness.

"Who are you?" Shruti called. "Reveal yourself!"

"Never fear, my children. I am a friend. Your men will be thoroughly distracted with violent frivolities while we discuss more important things."

"This isn't funny!" Shruti swung the torch around, looking for the source of the voice. "My father will have your head for this. These caves are sacred! They are not to be used for blasphemous games."

"Do not worry, my child. This is not a game."

"Tell us who you are," Shruti demanded. "Come out of the darkness and face us!"

She walked deeper into the cave, holding up the flickering torch before her. But, before any of them could make out the figure of the mysterious woman, the earth began shaking, and an ominous rumble exploded into deafening crashes as the pillars at the front of the temple collapsed, bringing huge hunks of the rock ceiling down with them.

They struggled to maintain their balance, but one by one, as the shaking continued with greater and greater intensity, the women fell to the ground.

When the quake finally subsided, they were engulfed in darkness, and the entrance to the cave was completely encompassed in a puff of dust and debris. Massive boulders blocked every inch of their escape route, and Eleanor cringed as she heard Edmund's desperate cries calling her name from just beyond, followed by Ravi calling for Shruti, and Oz calling for Yvie.

"What just happened?" Eleanor murmured.

As the dust began to settle, one eerily glowing yellow light lit up deep in the cave beyond. Eleanor managed to stand up and help Yvie off the ground, but as they approached Shruti's position, several flickering fire torches illuminated themselves along the walls of the temple.

At the far end of the cave, on a throne carved directly into the rock, sat a regal primate woman. She was the size of a human but her physicality was distinctly that of a monkey, and she wore only a tall golden crown, accessorized by heavy golden necklaces over her large bare breasts.

"Welcome, my daughters. I am Uma, Avatar of Shakti. It is time for us to plant the first seeds of the Age of Truth."

CHAPTER 6 – UMA

"*Mon dieu,*" Yvie whispered.

"Blimey," Eleanor muttered. She had a sneaking suspicion that the entire episode had Edmund's mysterious divine destiny written all over it. She looked back towards the completely sealed entrance to the cave and sighed with resignation. She knew enough about Edmund's mad world to realize that there was no point in trying to escape.

"You can't be the Avatar of Shakti!" Shruti exclaimed. "You aren't even human! You are... you are a *Vanara*! A... a... a real one, not just like those ordinary monkeys outside..." Shruti trailed off to consider the implications.

Uma smiled. "Very good. I am a Vanara. There are not so many of us left."

"The Avatar of Shakti can't possibly be a Vanara, can she?" Shruti murmured more to herself than to the mysterious queen before them.

"Like the daughter of a devadasi cannot be a leader in her society?" Uma asked. "Or the daughter of a polygamist cannot be the worthy wife of a god?" She addressed her statement to Eleanor. "Or a woman born of an aristocratic line cannot dirty her hands as a nurse?" She looked to Yvie. "We are told that too many things cannot possibly be true. Don't you think?"

Uma gathered a golden trident from its resting position against the rock behind her, and Eleanor gasped as a large tiger stirred from its curled-up position beside Uma's throne.

"*Mon dieu*," Yvie hissed as she took a step back. Eleanor followed her lead. "How can this possibly be real?"

The tiger sat up and stretched languidly, and then lay itself back down right at Uma's feet. Shruti took one more minute to observe the odd surroundings, and then she dropped to the ground in full prostration.

"Please forgive me, Your Holiness," she whispered. "My ignorance is inexcusable. But how… how have you come to this place? My father and I have been here hundreds of times and we've never seen you."

"I come and go as I please, my child. It is quite easy to avoid the humans who have come in recent years, thanks to your father's efforts. You must thank him on my behalf for his protection of my temple."

"It is his honor, Your Holiness," Shruti whispered.

"I know. He is just as worthy as you are of touching divinity, my child. Now, please stand. We have more important things to discuss." When Shruti refused to comply, Uma's voice became more authoritative. "That is an order, my child."

Eleanor shivered. It was far more acute, but the power that emanated off of Uma was not dissimilar to the power that emanated off of Edmund, except that there was an edge to it, a subtle element of morbidity that Edmund's lacked. It felt strangely familiar, and her mind raced trying to place it.

118

"I can see that you sense my power, Eleanor," Uma said curiously as Shruti gathered herself up off the ground and straightened out her dusty outfit to stand beside Eleanor and Yvie with her eyes averted. "As I have waited for you throughout the centuries, I have often wondered how you would be. You are more perceptive than I expected… and your coloring is very strange indeed."

"I am from Scotland, on the other side of the world," Eleanor replied self-consciously as Uma stared at her red hair for slightly too long for comfort.

"Yes, yes, of course you are. The prophecies were very clear on that account. I should not be so surprised that you look so strange, but let us not be distracted by unimportant details. It is your unusual perceptiveness that interests me most. Tell me, my child, have you ever encountered anyone whose power feels like mine does?"

Eleanor closed her eyes and focused on the waves of morbid power emanating off of Uma, until suddenly the answer became clear. "Huh…" she murmured. "It just keeps getting more and more complicated, doesn't it?"

"Yes?" Uma coaxed.

She hesitated as she glanced at Shruti.

"Please speak honestly, my child. We are planting the seeds of the Age of Truth. There shall be no secrets in my temple today."

"You feel very similar to Vibhishana," Eleanor whispered.

"*Lord* Vibhishana?" Shruti's eyes widened. "Eleanor, you *know* Lord Vibhishana? You've met him?"

Eleanor glanced to Uma again. "Aye, we've met."

Uma smiled. "You indeed have the power to sense the true avatars, Eleanor. It is a very powerful gift, and one that no human has ever had before. This changes everything."

"Great…" Eleanor was getting rather tired of ominous declarations.

"That is exactly what it is." Uma ignored Eleanor's sarcastic tone. "The ability to sense the avatars is a great boon, one that has brought those who are not worthy of it to ruination."

"The avatars?" Shruti asked.

"Lord Vibhishana is my counterpart." Uma pointed to a carving on the other side of the chamber, illuminated by gentle flickering firelight. "Together, he and I comprise all aspects of the Transformer, he as the Immortal Avatar of Shiva, and I as the transformative incarnation of Shakti. I am the Avatar of Parvati, Kali, or Durga, depending on how much of a battle needs to be fought. These days, though, I spend most of my time here in merciful silence. The wrath of Durga has not been evoked in centuries."

"Lord Vibhishana is Lord Shiva..." Shruti murmured. "I thought Lord Shiva could not have an avatar because he is formless..."

"Lord Shiva works in mysterious ways," Uma replied. "And Lord Vibhishana is not trapped in one single form. He is one of very few corporeal beings who can change his form at will."

"Because he is a Rakshasa?" Shruti asked. "But I thought he stopped being a demon when Lord Rama anointed him!"

"We cannot change what we are, my child." Uma looked down at her primate body. "It is a fundamental truth of life on Earth for Rakshasas, humans, and Vanaras alike."

"No wonder he is a Chiranjivi..." Shruti said as she worked through the idea out loud. "But the epics never said he was that important... the *Avatar* of Shiva... that means he was as powerful as Lord Rama himself in *The Ramayana*... but then why would he not have just smited his brother for all of his wrongdoings? Why wouldn't he have stopped Ravana with a snap of his finger?"

Uma laughed heartily. "The world is not so simple, my child, even for the gods. Eleanor knows that truth better than any other human, I suspect."

"Eleanor?" Shruti whispered. "Why Eleanor?"

120

"So you know Vibhishana then, Uma?" Eleanor skillfully deflected the conversation away from herself.

"Oh yes," Uma replied with a hint of sadness. "But it is not our fate to be joined in this life. We have both been ascetics throughout the entire six hundred years of my time on Earth."

"How sad," Eleanor murmured.

"One must not fight destiny. It is a hopeless battle that only leads to more misery," Uma reminded her. "Besides, one can achieve a certain type of spiritual awakening through foregoing earthly temptations. We have both used this time to reflect quietly on our divinity, as we were always meant to."

"How do you know what is meant to be?" Eleanor asked. The question had been needling her for months. "How do you know what destiny's decree even is? How do you know when you're fighting it?"

"I have my sources." As Uma noticed Eleanor's disappointment in her evasive answer, she closed her eyes for a moment of contemplation, and then she softened her demeanor. "We must look into ourselves, Eleanor, and interpret the facts around us as we see fit. That is all any of us can do, even someone as powerful as I am."

"And what exactly were the facts that led you to believe that it is not your fate to be joined with Vibhishana?"

As she asked the question, Eleanor was bombarded by an explosion of nerves at the various references she'd encountered (including Shruti's unwitting revelation the night before), indicating that Edmund was destined for an Indian bride who was most certainly not her.

Uma sensed Eleanor's underlying meaning, and smiled reassuringly. "If it were our destiny to be together, Vibhishana and I would not have been born of two species that find each other utterly grotesque. *I* would not have been born a Vanara. But in the next life... Oh, in the next life, we will revel in the pleasures of being one. The fire of my fiercest aspects will animate him to ascend to his true sacred throne. For now, though, we must both embrace our patience. But, you, Eleanor, will revel in the pleasures of a beautifully soulful marriage with the worthiest of men before you connect me with my next incarnation. I'm not entirely sure how. The prophecies were not very clear on that point."

"I've been warned not to let the prophecies drive my behavior." Eleanor let the dire warnings Mélusine had repeated time and again work their way back into her mind.

"You have been given very sage advice. Although, the others do not have the skill that I have at managing the knowledge of the prophecies. They do not have the discipline of an ascetic, nor the foresight of the Oracle nestled within them." Uma's eyes glowed a momentary bright green. "It is time."

"Time for what?" Eleanor's heart raced as she threw Yvie a nervous look, while Shruti only whispered more vehement prayers.

"I am the Vanara Oracle, my daughters, and I have been waiting for this moment for three hundred years. The prophecies foretold that a virtuous *Tridevi* was destined to arrive at my doorstep, and that together they would release me from the burden of my sacred throne."

"*C'est trop fantastique,*" Yvie murmured.

"We aren't avatars, are we?" Shruti asked with a hint of hope in her voice.

"You are not. But that does not mean that you do not channel the energy of Shakti in your human deeds every day. You, Shruti Bidkar, already know that you are a creator. And you, Yvette, have embraced the energy of the Preserver as a skilled healer, and Eleanor… Eleanor, you are an exceptional transformer. I have always thought that your purpose was to come here to facilitate my transformation, but I can see now that I misinterpreted the prophecies. There is much more happening than I ever imagined. Destiny is in motion."

"I've heard that one before," Eleanor muttered.

"Yes… yes, I'm sure you have. Lady Mélusine is a very wise interpreter of the prophecies. You should continue to heed her advice."

"Is she an avatar of Shakti?" As soon as the words came out of her mouth, Eleanor realized what she had known since the first time she and Mélusine had met. Mélusine emanated the same power as Edmund and Vibhishana, the same power as Uma, only it was different, somehow warmer and softer.

Uma smiled. "Does her power feel the same as mine?"

Eleanor closed her eyes and thought back to the subtle pulsating power she'd noticed the very first time Mélusine had revealed her true Rakshini nature back in Basingstoke.

"Not exactly. I have never met anyone else who felt exactly like her. There is something especially motherly about it."

"Your senses are very acute. They are more finely tuned than others who have shared this gift. You must use this skill to your advantage, Eleanor. You are right that Lady Mélusine is a powerful avatar, but she does not know her own destiny yet. She is just as blind as Edmund is for now, and I will not add to your burden by giving you another sacred secret that you will be forced to keep."

"Edmund?" Shruti murmured.

"Thank you," Eleanor whispered. "My burden is often too heavy to bear."

Uma's expression turned to sympathy, and she took another moment to collect her thoughts. "You indeed carry a heavy burden, my child. I didn't realize that you would be the human wife of Lord Kalki… that you would be so powerful, so pivotal. Your fate is far more important than releasing me from my throne, Eleanor. You are the woman whose unconditional love will ignite Lord Kalki's love for the human race. You are the key to *everything*."

That was the first time Eleanor realized that Lord Kalki was the official name of Edmund's divine destiny. She was glad it had a name, something that made it distinctly separate from the man she loved in the present. As for her important fate as the key to *everything,* Eleanor could only sigh. She didn't know what good such knowledge could possibly do for her, or for the world.

"Lord Kalki?" Shruti whispered. "Does that mean... no, it can't... it can't possibly mean... *Edmund Marriner* is Lord Kalki?"

"He is," Uma confirmed.

"But he isn't even a Hindu! Edmund doesn't believe in any god!" Shruti exclaimed.

"Who is Lord Kalki?" Yvie whispered. "I thought Edmund was an angel."

"That is a Christian way of putting it," Eleanor whispered. "It is not totally inaccurate either."

"Lord Kalki is the Tenth and Final Avatar of Vishnu. He is the ultimate incarnation of the Preserver of the Universe!" Shruti exclaimed. "He will awaken those who are capable of virtue and strike down those who darken the world with their greed!"

"Lord Kalki will lead creatures of all faiths into the Age of Truth, and he will not do it alone," Uma said calmly. "But he has not ascended yet. It is much too early. Almost a century too early."

"A century," Eleanor murmured. She was somewhat glad to hear it, even though it underscored her own mortality. She would certainly be dead by the time he'd get around to his ultimate divine ascension.

"Give or take," Uma clarified. "It is difficult to be exact when the calendars keep changing."

"But Lord Kalki was supposed to be born in Shambhala!" Shruti exclaimed.

"Lord Kalki was supposed to be born in a center of great spiritual power, deep in the land of the conquerors," Uma corrected her. "Do you know who the conquerors were when the Kalki Purana was written?"

"It was a Khan," Shruti whispered. "They came from the North, near Mongolia, did they not, Your Holiness?"

"Very good," Uma praised. "But the sages did not understand the timing, did they, my child? Lord Kalki didn't come back then, when the Khans were India's Raj. Lord Kalki has come now."

"Britain," Shruti whispered. "My god, Edmund is from Britain, the land of the conquerors!"

"You must always remember, my child, that the scriptures are subject to the flaws of human interpretation. It is why you must hold on most deeply to the greater truths that the stories represent."

"Yes, Your Holiness… but… but… I don't understand. What have I done to deserve the counsel and friendship of Lord Kalki?"

"Look within yourself, my child. Think carefully about what Edmund Marriner needs from you. You will know the answer."

"He hasn't needed anything from us! Not from anyone in my family. He has only ever helped us!" Shruti exclaimed. "We have done nothing to deserve his kindness!"

"You have given him true friendship," Eleanor said as she took Shruti's hand. "It is a rare and beautiful gift that he does not take lightly."

A loud crash resonated from the collapsed entrance to the cave, and a puff of dust encompassed them. Eleanor coughed and blinked with her eyes watering until the dust settled.

"Lord Kalki is getting desperate." Uma glanced past them. "He is using his full Rakshasa strength and speed to break his way through the rock. He has given up on hiding his talents from his old friend. I will have to let him in soon, or he will begin to suspect that our circumstances are not entirely natural."

"Rakshasa strength…" Shruti whispered. "I don't understand."

"You asked for an opportunity to earn your position in Lord Kalki's court," Uma replied. "Now I have given it to you."

"I don't understand," Shruti reiterated.

"Edmund is a Rakshasa," Eleanor whispered. "He is half, to be precise, through his father. His father is…" She looked to Uma, who nodded her support, "his father is Ravana."

"The ten-headed demon king from last night's recital?" Yvie asked with surprise. "*Certainement non.*"

"It is true," Uma confirmed.

"*Pauvre* Edmund!" Yvie exclaimed. "Does that make him an angel and a demon at the same time? It makes sense, actually…"

"Lord Kalki is Ravana's son…" Shruti whispered. "None of the puranas said anything about that… They didn't say anything *at all* about that…"

"It surprised many of us," Uma admitted. "But it is what it is. When Edmund learns of the truth himself, it will be more painful than anything you can imagine, but that time is not here yet." Uma looked to all three of them. "It is not time for Edmund to know the truths that have been revealed to you today. He is not ready. I have chosen you because you are worthy of keeping his secrets."

The cave shook again as Edmund threw himself against the rock, blasting a small hole of daylight into a crevice between two boulders.

"Eleanor?!" he called desperately. "Eleanor, dearest? Please answer me!"

"Edmund, darling, we're all fine!" she called.

"Yvie?!" Oz called.

"*Oui,* Ozzy. *Ça va!*" she added.

"Shruti?!" Ravi sobbed.

"Papa, I'm perfectly safe!" she called.

"Lord Kalki will break through on his third try," Uma informed them. "Now, quick, Eleanor, you must release me from my throne."

She rushed forward and slammed her trident into Eleanor's hand.

"What? No!" Eleanor exclaimed as she refused to take it. "You want me to kill you?"

126

"It is your destiny," Uma declared as the cave shook with her power.

"It most certainly is not!" Eleanor countered. "I will never do anything wicked just because someone thinks it's my destiny, not even you."

She struggled as Uma tried to force the trident into her grip. She accepted the weapon for one moment until Uma was satisfied, and then she cheekily dropped it onto the ground in front of her. Shruti gasped and whispered quiet, fearful prayers at Eleanor's blasphemy, but she held her ground.

"I'm not going to kill you. If you want to die, you will have to do it yourself."

Uma reached down calmly and collected the weapon, and Eleanor flinched as she pointed it straight at her chest.

"I'm quite sure that it is not your destiny to murder Lord Kalki's human wife in cold blood," Eleanor said with her head held high, hoping dearly that Vanaras could not taste fear like Rakshasas could. "I don't see how murdering me could possibly free you from your sacred throne."

Uma held her position, as Eleanor felt more and more desperate, and Yvie eyed the dark passages for any escape route they might have missed after the cave in.

"Please, my lady. I beg you. Spare her," Shruti whispered as she dropped to her knees.

For one fleeting moment, the trident exploded into a bright green glow, and Eleanor almost collapsed as a burst of heat rushed through her. Yvie rushed to catch her, and as she regained her senses, Uma was smiling contentedly.

"Eleanor, you are the strongest human I have ever had the pleasure of meeting. It is no wonder you are Lord Kalki's muse. Trust your instincts, my child. They are impeccable. I will see you in the next life."

Without a moment wasted, Uma thrust the trident right through her own abdomen, and all three women screamed as Uma collapsed onto the ground.

"Good lord," Eleanor whispered. She and Yvie both kneeled down to inspect the trident that remained lodged straight through Uma's limp body, without a hint of blood anywhere. It glowed an eerie, unnatural green, and as Eleanor tugged at it to remove it from Uma's flesh, the green dissolved. Seconds later, the entire trident disappeared, as if it had never been there. Eleanor blinked several times to get her bearings, and then she ran her fingers along Uma's bare flesh.

"She's still warm," she whispered as she picked up Uma's wrist to take her pulse. The gesture seemed absurd given the circumstances, but somehow it made her feel better, as if human medicine had some rational place in the madness. "She has no pulse."

"She appears to be dead." Yvie held her hand over Uma's mouth, feeling for breath. "Is there a way to know for sure with this… eh… species?"

"You know as much as I do about this species," Eleanor replied. "It's just as mad to me as it is to you… speaking of madness…"

Uma's sleeping tiger stirred and stood up for a final languid stretch, eyeing each of them in due turn. All three women backed away from Uma's body slowly, making their way towards the blocked entrance.

"Nice kitty," Yvie squeaked.

"Edmund, darling, I think it's time to get us out of here!" Eleanor called.

With a growl of despair, the tiger pounced onto Uma's body, and they both disappeared into a flash of green light. Even with all of the magical shenanigans she had witnessed, the sight was still the most bewildering Eleanor had ever seen.

"*C'est trop incroyable,*" Yvie whispered.

Shruti only prayed a series of frenzied mantras.

"Stand back, Edmund's going in for another round!" Oz called through the hole from the other side.

"*Viens*. We must give Edmund the space he needs to rescue us," Yvie whispered as she pulled Shruti out of her frenzy, and they scurried away from the entrance.

Eleanor held her breath, hoping that Edmund's desire to rescue her would not push him so far that he would mortally wound himself.

With a deafening crash, Edmund burst through the rock, landing in the middle of the temple with deep wounds cut into his bare hands, his arms, and his chest.

Eleanor rushed to his side as he collapsed unconscious onto the ground and his violet metallic plasma worked its way to the surface of his wounds.

"My god," Shruti whispered as she stared at the unbelievable spectacle.

"Edmund, darling?" Eleanor whispered as she gathered his head into her lap and stroked his hair. "Edmund, darling, we're all safe and sound. Focus on healing yourself."

Oz gathered Yvie into his arms, and she sighed as he pushed her up against the cave wall, embarking upon a frenzied, juicy reunion kiss.

Ravi rushed straight to Shruti and burst into tears as he gathered her into his arms. "Shruti... He... He... We... We... You... You... I thought I'd lost you!"

"You didn't lose me, Papa. I'm right here," she whispered as she hugged him back.

"God... God answered my prayers!" he cried. "Lord Vishnu himself gave Edmund the strength to save you! You wouldn't believe it, Shruti. Edmund ran faster than the eye could see! You should have seen how many Vanaras he defeated at once!"

Shruti glanced down at Edmund's unconscious body, pausing for a long moment to watch his Rakshasa plasma heal his human flesh. Finally, she lowered her voice. "Father, Edmund *is* Lord Vishnu. He is Lord Kalki!"

"Lord Kalki…" He paused to consider the idea. "But he can't be! Lord Kalki is nothing like Edmund! He is supposed to be from Shambhala! And where is his white horse and his divine weapon?!"

"Father, he is the commander of the king's cavalry. Surely he has ridden a white horse at some point! And he's a soldier! He used to always carry a sword in uniform, remember!"

"But he'd take it off when he'd come inside! He said he didn't want to bring a vehicle of violence into our home! Lord Kalki should always carry his divine weapon to protect the weak and virtuous!"

"Father, we mustn't be so literal in our expectations," she whispered as she threw an embarrassed look towards Eleanor. "Besides, he hasn't ascended yet. He doesn't even know who he is! Shakti herself revealed the truth to me just now, while we were trapped in her temple. She said that we must focus on transcendent truths, not literal facts!"

Ravi moved to argue, and then he stopped. He glanced over to watch the alien sight of Edmund's violet plasma filling in his gaping wounds, and then he catalogued his memories in his head. He gasped, and then gulped with fear.

"My god, Shruti. What have we done? We've been treating Lord Kalki like a regular *firang* soldier! I've insulted him so many times, I can't even count them!"

"That is exactly what he wants," Eleanor interjected. "It is what he needs. You must not treat him any differently now that you know the truth."

"You knew?" Ravi asked with disbelief. "You knew you were marrying Lord Kalki? What about Padma?"

Eleanor's heart almost exploded. "Padma?" she asked with her greatest impression of calm.

"Padma! Lord Kalki's consort!" he exclaimed.

"Father, please. The puranas are not entirely literal. It turned out that Lord Kalki was from the conquering land of Britain, not Mongolia, and there were many other details that were wrong. Big, important details! Surely the sages got that one wrong too."

"Padma…" Eleanor murmured.

"Father, Eleanor has met Lord Vibhishana," Shruti whispered. "Shakti said she has a very special fate!"

"Lord Vibhishana lives?" Ravi struggled to process the intel. "Yes, yes, of course he lives… I have wondered from time to time what he's been doing as a Chiranjivi all these centuries… You know Lord Vibhishana?" He returned his attention to Eleanor. "You've met him, in the flesh?"

"He is really very normal for how famous he is." Eleanor almost laughed at the understatement.

"How does a *firang* know such things?" Ravi murmured to himself.

"Apparently, I have a very special fate," Eleanor shrugged. "I know a great many things, including many things that Edmund does not know about himself yet." She glanced at Shruti, noting that she had strategically omitted the detail of Edmund's Rakshasa lineage. "Ravi, you cannot tell Edmund that he is Lord Kalki. It is not time yet. Great misery will stalk you if you reveal to him things he is not ready to know."

As Edmund's Rakshasa plasma finished up its healing work and dissolved into his perfectly smooth skin, he took in his awakening Rakshasa breath and sat up.

"Eleanor?" he asked groggily.

"I'm perfectly alright, darling." She smiled and squeezed his hand.

He pulled her straight into his arms for a passionate kiss, and she shivered at his delightful frigidity. It was a sensation she had already come to miss.

"I'm right here, darling." She kissed him again.

"I thought I'd lost you," he whispered into her ear. "I don't ever want to feel like that again. It was like my soul had been crushed along with you."

"You didn't lose me," she whispered back.

She refused to think about the ugly reality of her own mortality. The day would come when he would lose her for good.

"I'm right here," she said instead as she caressed his face.

She noticed suddenly that there was a vibrancy to him that seemed different than before. In fact, he looked slightly younger than she had ever seen him. Not the teenaged version of himself that he so often feared would surface with a mortal wound, but a new vibrancy nonetheless. The crow's feet at the corners of his eyes seemed smoother, his arms more muscular, and his grey hair that had been peppered with black was surely now black hair peppered with grey.

She kissed him again and let him revel in the beauty of their reunion until she felt a bout of lightheadedness and pulled away.

He looked up self-consciously to Shruti and Ravi. "I suppose there is no rational excuse I can give you for what you've seen. I am not entirely human, but I'm really very ordinary."

Ravi and Shruti were at an utter loss for words.

"I hope that I have proven enough to you over the years that you will not think me some sort of demon," Edmund added uneasily. "It would be a great shame for us to lose our friendship after so many years."

"No... no, of course you're not a demon, my lord. Of course not!" Ravi said as he dropped to his knees.

Shruti threw Eleanor a knowing look and held her tongue. Eleanor appreciated her judgment on the matter mightily.

Edmund looked even more pained at Ravi's showing of piety. "You should call me Edmund like you always have. I am not a god. I am really a very ordinary man with a few unusual talents. It is very important to you and to me that you do not let this incident interfere with the colorful stories you've built up in your head about your benevolent god. They have nothing to do with me, and I will not allow myself to be responsible for disappointing you."

Ravi moved to protest, but Shruti interrupted him. "Father, we've all been through a great ordeal today. Let Uncle Edmund rest."

"Yes... yes, I suppose you're right," Ravi agreed. He watched with silent awe as Edmund hopped up nimbly and then pulled Eleanor into his arms.

"I suppose we should return to the yacht," Eleanor said as she gathered her wits.

"Let's hurry. I don't want you to get sunburned, Eleanor," Shruti said as she guided her father out of the cave.

Eleanor gasped as her eyes adjusted to the bright light of midday outside, and she observed the remnants of the men's bloody battle. The ground was littered with crushed, dead monkeys, while Edmund's elaborate Indian shirt was spread across the courtyard in tatters.

"There were a few violent moments, although I am rather glad that they were monkeys and not men," Edmund whispered.

"Me too," Eleanor agreed.

She looked up towards the rocks above the cave entrances where the remaining monkeys bowed in deference.

"It looks like they didn't all incur your wrath?" she asked.

"Yes, some of them had the sense to give up when I killed their comrades. If only humans had the same sense."

Without another word, they walked back down the path through the bush. An eerie silence permeated the woods, and Eleanor could feel Edmund's anxiety at the prospect of losing the special relationship he had with the Bidkars.

When they reached the dock, Edmund blushed but said nothing as the villagers gasped at his scandalously topless appearance, but they dropped into total silence as Ravi shouted a few words at them on Edmund's behalf. Eleanor hoped that he hadn't just announced that their messiah had arrived... She relaxed slightly as he and Shruti disappeared onto the bridge of the yacht to begin the preparations for their return journey.

"How're you feeling, mate?" Oz asked as Edmund sat down on an elaborate divan just inside the yacht's extravagant living room. "Those wounds looked like your worst yet."

"Oh, I've had worse," Edmund chuckled. "Believe me."

"It all seems bloody painful to me," Oz replied.

"Yes, being stabbed through the stomach with two swords at once is really quite unpleasant," Edmund admitted.

"Fair dinkum," Oz murmured. "I reckon it is."

"Although, bullet wounds to the thigh, I think, are possibly more painful to rectify, because they're harder to get out than the swords. Today's injuries were really quite easy to heal without any weapon to remove afterwards."

"You must be quite the expert, mate." Oz worked to hide his bewilderment at Edmund's honest admission. "So you think you're fully recovered?"

Edmund straightened his posture and took in a deep breath. "I'm feeling perfectly fine. Better than fine, in fact. To be honest, I feel a bit strange."

"Really, darling. How?" Eleanor asked as she sat down beside him and took his hand into hers.

Edmund scrunched his nose as he thought about it. "I suppose I feel a bit younger than I did earlier. A bit more energetic than I have felt since before the war. It's strange, though…"

"What's strange, darling?"

"I was worried that I didn't have the same strength that I used to. That if only I were a bit younger I could break through the rock…" Edmund inspected his hands. "Do I look younger?"

"A bit," Eleanor admitted. As a subtle panic worked its way onto his face, she rushed to clarify. "Perhaps five or ten years younger. You still look much older than a young cadet. I'm sure that only the people who know you best will notice at all."

"But how could that have happened..." Edmund ran his memories through his mind again. "I never just get slightly younger. It's always been all or nothing..."

"It is a nice development, isn't it, darling?" Eleanor asked as she stole a gentle kiss. "Now we look even more similar in age." She leaned in and whispered into his ear. "Later tonight we will have to test your fresh vigor in bed."

Edmund blushed and took a deep, calming breath to keep his excitement at the idea under control.

"Well, more power to ya, mate. You saved us again, and I'm pretty sure no one will believe this story, not even as a tall tale." Oz slapped Edmund amicably on the back and then took a seat on the divan across from them and gestured for Yvie to sit in his lap.

She took a seat on his knee and squealed as he squeezed her waist naughtily. "A right damsel in distress you were this time, Yvie. You'll have to admit that the white knights swooped in to save the modern sheilas just this once!"

Yvie moved to protest, and then she thought the better of it. "Just this once, Ozzy."

They sat in restful silence, listening with vague interest as Ravi yelled at the disobedient servants who had left them before the battle, and Shruti ordered the rest of the staff to prepare an impromptu serving of chai, until the footsteps of both of their hosts converged. They paused in the hallway to whisper heatedly, and then Shruti rushed in before her father and offered her unspoken apology for whatever he was about to do.

"My lord... Edmund, may I please have a word?" Ravi asked as he held his turban in his hands, revealing his scarred, bald head. "Privately?"

Oz and Yvie stood up. "There is chai on the deck," Shruti whispered as she gestured for them to follow her.

Eleanor felt Edmund's heart racing, but as Ravi looked at her desperately, she stood up, unsure of whether she should leave her gentle husband alone with him for whatever unwise move he was about to make.

She decided to hedge her bets, and as Ravi took a seat on the floor at Edmund's feet, she nodded to Shruti to leave them alone, and then she waited, standing in the stairwell where only Edmund could see her, ready to intervene at his behest.

"Ravi, I am not a lord," Edmund whispered. "Please stop calling me that."

"Yes... yes, I will try, my lord..." Edmund cringed at his immediate failure. "I mean Edmund... old chap?" Ravi looked skeptically for his approval, and he smiled encouragingly. "I know that it will displease you for me to ask this. Every fiber of my being tells me to leave it alone. Shruti told me to leave it alone. But I cannot live with myself if I do not ask..."

Edmund reached down and guided Ravi out of his position of prostration and onto the divan across from him.

"You may ask me anything your heart desires, my friend, but you must forgive me when my answers disappoint you," Edmund said gently.

"Yes... yes... I will forgive you, Edmund. I promise I will forgive you..." Edmund nodded for Ravi to continue. "You see, the thing is... what I saw in the temple... the power that you had... I mean, you are perfectly healed after those horrible injuries..." Ravi reached forward and touched Edmund's bare chest, and he startled at the frigidity.

"I am always very cold after I've healed," Edmund explained.

"Yes... yes, of course..." Ravi looked as if he was struggling to work the detail into the tapestry of his story. "You see, the thing is... I had always thought that the accident was a punishment, you see... for my premarital indiscretions, and that Lord Vishnu preserved my life in the way that he did to teach me the error of my ways, and I have learned them, Edmund. Oh, how I have learned how wrong I was for the things I did before the accident. And Lord Vishnu knew that I had paid my karmic dues; he *must*

136

have known. He acknowledged it when he sent me Reya. She saw me, Edmund. Without pity or fear, she was the first person who had ever really seen me for me since the accident… And then Lord Vishnu blessed us with Shruti, even though Reya thought she was too old to have children, and Shruti wasn't just a child! She was the most perfect gift God could have ever given to Earth! To me! Lord Vishnu made my life happier than I ever thought was possible, and I did everything I could to honor him. Everything, Edmund, you must believe me… and so, I am so ashamed to ask, but I cannot help myself because I am so weak and selfish…"

"Just spit it out, old chap," Edmund said as he glanced over to Eleanor.

"Can you heal me?" Ravi whispered. "Can you heal the burns?"

A look of utter devastation crossed Edmund's face.

"I cannot heal you, Ravi. I told you I'm not a god," Edmund said with his best impression of calm authority.

"Yes… yes. You did tell me that… But… but, Edmund, would you… would you perhaps try to heal me anyway? Perhaps you don't know that you can do it yet. Have you always been able to move faster than the eye can see? Have you always been able to beat through a boulder with your bare hands?"

Edmund considered his suggestion thoughtfully. "It is true that I have not always been able to do the things that I can do now."

Eleanor's heart began racing. An intense fear that Ravi was tempting some sort of massive punishment from destiny rushed through her.

"But, Ravi, I don't even know how I would go about trying. How does someone heal someone else? My body heals itself. I do not do anything consciously," Edmund said pragmatically.

"The legends say that Lord Vishnu can heal with the touch of his hands," Ravi suggested nervously. "Perhaps you could try that?"

Eleanor could see the pity in Edmund's eyes at the earnest desperation of Ravi's request. "If I try it and it doesn't work, will you agree that I am just an ordinary man with a few special talents and treat me just as you always have?"

"I will, my lord," Ravi whispered.

Ravi shivered but said nothing as Edmund placed his frigid hands on his, closed his eyes, and whispered. "Heal. Heal, my friend. Let the burns melt away..." As his entreaty made no impact, he switched his commands into a series of increasingly foreign tongues, landing on the very strange hissing one that she had heard him use only a few times before when his brain was most addled.

He moved his hands to various locations—on Ravi's chest, his forehead, and the top of his head—repeating his mantras more emphatically until finally, with a deep sigh of concession, he gave up.

"I'm sorry, my friend," Edmund whispered. "I have proven to both of us what I already knew was true."

Eleanor's heart broke as she noticed a violet tear in the corner of his eye that he quickly absorbed back into his skin before Ravi could notice. When Ravi finally looked up at him, tears were streaming down his scarred face. He sniffled, and then collected his turban from the floor and returned it to his head.

"I will never forget that you tried, old chap," he whispered. "Never."

They sat in silence until Edmund took a deep breath and straightened his posture. "Ravi, you are aware that I am not an expert in religious matters, but might I offer you some advice anyway?"

"Anything," Ravi whispered. "Please, Edmund. Tell me anything!"

Edmund thought carefully about his words. "I have been around for quite a while. Longer than you might guess."

"How long?" Ravi looked up at him reverentially.

"A little bit over a century," Edmund revealed. "Quite a long time on a human scale, although I have recently learned that there are others who have been around far longer."

"A century…" Ravi whispered.

Edmund swallowed his nerves and pushed forward. "My point is that as I have lived my life, I have seen many horrific things happen to good people, and many wicked scoundrels living in the lap of luxury without one hint of the error of their ways crossing their selfish minds. Perhaps, you should not be looking so literally for God's will in your circumstances."

They both sat in a long, contemplative silence until Edmund decided on his next words.

"You, more than anyone else I have ever met, have made the most of your horrific circumstances. You have used them to your advantage, and you have built an empire that you have used to perpetuate all sorts of peaceful causes. It was your strength I thought of when the boys around me were succumbing to horrific chemical burns in the trenches."

"*My* strength…" Ravi whispered.

"Your resilience gave me hope that some of them would triumph like you did, and I needed that knowledge, Ravi. I needed it to keep me from going mad."

"Then there was meaning to it. More meaning than I ever realized… a more profound meaning…" Ravi gave into another round of tears.

"Perhaps you should be looking for the meaning of your triumph within yourself, my friend… and you should certainly give yourself the credit that you deserve. You did not just sit around praying to be healed, did you?"

"It didn't work," Ravi admitted. "I tried for months after the accident until I decided that it was God's will that I would not be a full man ever again."

Edmund paused to consider Ravi's honest admission. "Well, I will be forever grateful that you found the strength within yourself to rebuild your life. You have given me great inspiration, and you would never have met Reya if you hadn't taken your own initiative. Shruti wouldn't be here now. Think of the beauty that your own personal initiative has brought to the world."

"I could not have done it without Lord Vishnu's help," Ravi said as he wiped the last tears from his eyes. "It was true then, and it is just as true now. Lord Vishnu works in mysterious ways."

"I suppose we will just have to agree to disagree, like we always do," Edmund sighed. "I do wish I could heal you, though, Ravi. I really do. But I was not lying when I told you that I am really very ordinary."

"The monkeys didn't think so," Ravi sniffled.

After a moment of silence, Ravi cracked a crooked smile, and Edmund joined him gratefully.

"I reckon they didn't," Edmund agreed as he helped Ravi up.

Edmund pulled Ravi into a brotherly hug, and Ravi held on, despite a violent shiver that rushed down his spine.

"I am grateful to have you as a friend, Ravi," Edmund said as he let go.

Ravi moved to respond, but he couldn't speak through a final round of tears. Instead, he wiped them away self-consciously, while he slapped Edmund on the back, nodding his profuse agreement.

Eleanor tiptoed up the staircase and out the door to the deck, while Edmund escorted Ravi up the stairs behind her. As they approached, Shruti watched them with hopeful anticipation, followed by a moment of disappointment, which morphed into relief.

"Well, it looks like everything's all sorted then?" Oz asked cheerfully.

"It is," Ravi agreed as he sat down next to Shruti, and she squeezed his hand.

"Now tell us, heroes of the hour, how did you defeat Sugriva's army?" Shruti asked. "How many monkeys did you fight off at once?"

"It was at least twenty," Edmund replied as he drank down an entire cup of tea in one gulp and the servants rushed in to pour him another.

"Twenty?! I'd reckon it was closer to fifty!" Oz declared.

"It was certainly seventy," Ravi added.

"Maybe even a hundred?" Eleanor baited them playfully.

"Why, I reckon it was!" Oz laughed.

"Edmund led us into battle like Lord Kalki on his white horse wielding the sword of righteousness!" Ravi exclaimed.

Shruti and Eleanor both threw him disapproving looks.

"So, in this metaphor, I am just a man on a horse with a sword?" Edmund asked.

"A very special man," Ravi replied as he glanced at Eleanor.

"I think you've found a metaphor I can agree with, old chap," Edmund said as he slapped Ravi's back.

"I knew the day would come!" Ravi exclaimed.

"Here, here," Edmund said cheerfully as he held out his tea cup in a toast and drank down his second serving.

"And what were you sheilas up to while the men were busy in battle? Were you trying to scratch your way out of the cave? Bloody bad trot that there was an earthquake right then and there, wasn't it?"

"We were confronting a tiger," Yvie replied truthfully. "And having a little chat with the monkey queen whose army you were battling outside."

"That's just what I thought you were up to!" Oz laughed.

Eleanor took Edmund's hand into hers. It was already pulsating with warmth from the tea.

"Are you alright, darling?" she whispered into his ear.

"I don't know whether I wished more that I could or that I couldn't heal him," he whispered back.

"It is a burden that I cannot even imagine," she whispered.

"I suppose I will sleep easier tonight knowing that the burden isn't mine. It can't be, can it? One should not feel guilty about a talent that isn't his."

"No, darling. You shouldn't feel one hint of guilt. You saved us, all of us. That is all that should be in your mind. You were our knight in shining armor, and this time, there is absolutely no denying it."

"I love you so much, Eleanor," Edmund whispered as he kissed her. "I can't imagine my life without you now. The idea is utterly unbearable."

"Don't imagine it, darling. Just appreciate that we are here together now, in the present, on our honeymoon, in your beloved India." She snuck a final kiss, and then together, with their hands held tightly in one another's, they rejoined the amicable conversation.

For the moment, destiny's creed was satiated, but Eleanor had an intensely uneasy feeling that its appetite would return hungrier than ever.

As it turned out, she wasn't wrong.

CHAPTER 7 – VIGOR

By the time they arrived back at the house, another mid-afternoon rainstorm was in full swing. Ravi had spent the entirety of their return trip in the motorcar muttering to himself, only stopping every so often to ask Edmund seemingly random questions. "And silver is better than gold when it comes to English silverware, am I right, old chap?" "And if there were ten servants, they could each carry a pack, and that would look more symmetrical than if there were only eight servants and two had to carry two packs, don't you think, Edmund?" "And red wine is better than champagne to accompany a meal, isn't it, old chap?"

Edmund just held Eleanor's hand tightly in his, gazing out the window and answering Ravi's questions with polite yeses or nos.

When they finally arrived, Ravi hopped out of the car with renewed vigor. "I've got some business to take care of, old chap. Please do whatever you want in the house. Think of it as yours entirely."

Before Edmund could thank him or protest, Ravi was clapping his hands, and several manservants were rushing to his side, taking orders as he charged down one of the many marble hallways and disappeared.

Eleanor squealed as Edmund pulled her into a deep romantic dip. She gave into his especially passionate embrace, and when he finally returned her to a standing position, she leaned woozily against him.

"Shall we go test the extent of your youthful vigor now?" she suggested naughtily.

A wide grin spread across Edmund's face, and he laughed giddily. "Yes, dearest, let's!"

But, as he grabbed her hand and led her hastily towards their room, the second car with Shruti, Oz, and Yvie pulled up the drive, and he stopped for a moment to watch them. Eleanor could tell that he was debating whether it would be too rude to skip off for a honeymoon tryst without even greeting them, and she was hoping he'd find it within his Victorian manners to indulge his whim after their exceptionally trying day.

Eleanor startled as she felt a sudden shiver run down his spine.

"Is something wrong, darling?" Eleanor asked as she looked up at him.

As Oz, Yvie and Shruti got out of the car, Oz practically knocked Yvie over as they stopped to stare at the sight.

"Strewth," Oz murmured.

Eleanor barely stifled another squeal. There, instead of her mature English soldier, stood his youthful doppelganger. Every wrinkle was gone, every gray hair was now a solid jet black, and every ounce of spare fat had dissolved into his tall, muscular body that looked a bit lanky without any of his middle-aged weight to balance out his excessive height. He looked barely twenty, if not slightly younger. Despite the fact that he was exceptionally handsome as a young man, the extreme inconvenience of the development set Eleanor's mind racing for any reasonable solution.

"I feel a bit odd," Edmund said as he held out his hands to inspect them. "Colder than normal. Do I look different?"

As a group of servants approached to greet Shruti, an acute panic exploded inside of Eleanor.

"Come, darling. Let's go to our room. I'm sure we can work everything out there." Eleanor guided Edmund into the far hallway towards their bridal chamber.

"So, Yvie, do the French take afternoon tea like the British do?" Shruti asked with feigned enthusiasm as she distracted the servants' attention from Edmund's position.

"It is not such a ritual as it is for the British, but the Aussies love it," Yvie replied loudly as she followed Shruti's lead.

"I reckon I could use some sweets," Oz added.

Eleanor was intensely relieved that she had such worthy allies.

"Please, follow me to the music room. We will take our tea there," Shruti suggested. She hissed some assertive orders to the servants who rushed ahead of them, leaving Edmund and Eleanor alone.

"Come on, darling," Eleanor reiterated as she grabbed his hand.

She guided him swiftly away from the foyer, making a beeline for their bridal chamber. As soon as they were inside, she slammed the door behind them.

"How are you feeling, darling?" she asked as she ran her finger along his rosy cheek. She couldn't ignore how strikingly handsome he was as a young man—far more handsome than the old, grainy black and white photographs from his most recent youth in the 1890s had implied. "Are you still feeling odd?"

He placed his large hands around her waist, and a strange, almost primal glimmer of acute desire entered his expression. "To be honest, dearest, all I can think about is ravishing you. The feeling is completely overwhelming all of my other senses."

Eleanor felt a strange fluttering inside of her, a certain type of anxious excitement that she hadn't felt in years... decades even...

since she was a young woman, readying herself to make love for the first time.

He crushed her into a tongue-filled kiss and guided her across the room, pushing her up against the wall for a rougher go-around.

Eleanor was so turned on by his unusual vigor that she couldn't bring herself to inform him of the plight he was still unaware of, and while she felt a pang of guilt for taking advantage of his unburdened return to youth, she felt such a burning desire in her loins that she pushed all other thoughts away, focusing only on the unexpected pleasure afforded by their predicament.

Edmund reached around her to unbutton the top of her salwar kameez, but after a few failed attempts, he lost his patience and ripped the back of her top wide open. She giggled as he threw it across the room.

As he kneeled down to suckle her freshly naked breasts, she pulled the drawstring of his trousers and released him entirely from the burden of clothing. He was even more attractive now that she could appreciate him in his full naked glory, and she moaned with no regard for anyone else in the house as he pulled her drawstring, moving his attention and his skilled tongue down from her breasts to her most sensitive areas.

"Good lord, Edmund, you are so good at this, darling. You are playing... me... like... an instrument..." She could barely speak through her sighs of pleasure, and her encouragement only increased his vigor until she was shaking from an intense orgasm. He didn't give her a moment to calm down. Instead, he guided her to the bed, threw her on top of the silk sheets, and entered her.

Until that moment, Eleanor had never experienced the full pleasures of youthful vigor combined with mature skill in a lover, and the feeling drove her positively mad. As he held himself up with his muscular arms, returning his attention to her breasts while he rode her with the perfect amount of force, they sighed and moaned in unison until another orgasm exploded in her loins, and he smiled with his triumph, and kept going.

For his third round, he slowed down his pace and held himself tantalizingly above her with a sly grin until she felt like she might die from desire, and then he thrust straight into a position so pleasurable that she hadn't even known such a feeling was possible. Each time he repeated the game with more and more vigor until he pushed her over the edge for the longest, most intense orgasm she'd ever felt in her life.

Finally, as she shook and moaned and sighed with pleasure, he joined her over the edge with his own loud moans.

"Oh Eleanor," he whispered as he collapsed beside her and gathered her into the nook of his arm. "Have you ever felt anything so satisfying?"

"Never, darling," she agreed as she ran her fingers through the black hair on his cold, smooth chest.

"Eleanor, dearest, do you prefer me a bit younger?" Edmund asked as he glanced at his hands again. He paused to observe them, and Eleanor quickly gathered them into hers. She wasn't ready to deal with reality yet, and she was quite sure that he wasn't either.

She thought quickly and then began her careful effort to ease him into the truth. "Edmund, darling, I love you every way you are. Young or old, human or Martian. You should be the age that you want to be."

"It's not like I have a choice on the matter." He commandeered one of his hands back and ran his finger along her naked breast until a delightful round of goosebumps erupted.

Eleanor struggled for a moment to decide what to say. His current state had not been brought on by a mortal wound, and so her scientific conclusion was that he had once again accidentally stumbled into some unintentional form of shapeshifting. Suddenly, an idea occurred to her... Maybe, just maybe, she could coax him into solving his predicament completely...

"I think, perhaps, darling, you have more control than you realize. You became younger today before you broke through the rock, didn't you? You said you were wishing you were a bit younger, and then poof—you were. Were you thinking about your youthful vigor before we came in here to celebrate it?"

"I suppose I was," Edmund admitted. "I was wondering how much more vigorous I could be, since you already drive me wild with desire."

"You were certainly more vigorous, darling," Eleanor said as she leaned in for a gentle kiss. "But I do love how distinguished you are in your natural older form. Looking as if you're in your forties or fifties is easier in life, isn't it? People treat you as if you're already established. You don't need to earn respect from your elders in the same way, not to mention your military career. You've invested quite a lot in it, and it would be a shame if you had to give it up, all for some extra vigor in bed, don't you think? You're really quite vigorous at every age."

"Are you saying you prefer me how I was?" Edmund asked with a burst of nerves.

Eleanor squirmed. Was she really going to attempt to get them out of this mess without him even realizing that he looked like a teenager? He thought they were talking about a difference of a few years in his age, not the drastic change that he had accidentally enacted in his horny haste.

"I love you at every age, Edmund. I was just saying that I think you have more control over your physical age than you realize. Perhaps it doesn't take a mortal wound for you to change. It would be quite convenient if you could change how you look and feel at your whim, don't you think?"

"I suppose," he said unenthusiastically. "I have no idea how I would go about doing it. What if I accidentally made myself into a teenager again?"

"We would figure it out." Eleanor hoped that she wasn't lying as she reassured him. She pushed her anxiety away as she leaned over to kiss him again. "Perhaps we should take a little nap and let our bodies calm down from that delightful honeymoon dessert, and then we can think more clearly about it."

"I am rather fatigued," Edmund admitted.

"You've been very busy today, darling," Eleanor reminded him. "It's not every day you break through a boulder with your bare hands."

"It didn't used to be every day, but now I'm not so certain." Edmund couldn't hide his frustration at the idea.

"I'm sure things will calm down soon enough, darling, and then we'll both be longing for the days of our exciting honeymoon adventure."

"I suppose." Edmund yawned as she nestled into his arms.

Just a wee cat nap before we face the firing squad, Eleanor convinced herself.

And in the arms of her unknowingly youthful husband, Eleanor slept.

"Psst…"

Eleanor stirred. The room was dark. A pleasant humid breeze blew in from the open terrace. Eleanor took a moment to assess her surroundings. She was completely disoriented.

The creak of the door wrested her from her position in Edmund's arms, but she realized to her embarrassment that they were both still naked, and she scrambled to cover them both with the silk sheets.

"Eleanor!" Shruti whispered. "I'm so sorry to disturb you. I'm not looking, I swear. I brought you both robes and some clothing you can wear to dinner. Is Edmund awake yet?"

Eleanor looked over at her peacefully sleeping husband, but the room was so dark she couldn't make out anything but his profile. He took in a satisfied breath, turned over, and returned to his dreams.

Eleanor sat up, assessed her options, and then scampered naked over to Shruti and wrapped herself in one of the robes. Shruti grabbed her hand and pulled her into the hallway.

"Tell me what I should do, Eleanor," Shruti whispered as soon as the door was closed. "How are we going to explain Edmund's miraculous return to youth?"

"I have no bloody clue," Eleanor admitted. "This is the first time it's ever happened on a whim like that. He's only ever gotten younger after he's been mortally wounded, but it would seem some part of him is experimenting with abilities he doesn't consciously know he has."

"It sounded like you were both enjoying your experiments," Shruti whispered.

Eleanor blushed. "Yes, I suppose we were. If ever you find that elusive combination of expert skill and youthful vigor, I suggest you take advantage of it."

Shruti giggled. "Perhaps Shakti will smile upon me someday."

"I'm sure she will," Eleanor agreed.

Shruti became more serious at Eleanor's comment. "It means a lot to me, Eleanor, that someone as special as you are—someone whom Uma was waiting to meet for hundreds of years—thinks it's possible for me to fall in love. I've grown up assuming that no reasonable man would marry me, given my family's history, and I've been dreadfully afraid of gold-diggers—men who care more about my father's money than anything else. But seeing you together, knowing that Edmund, Lord Kalki, *Ravana's son*, found a woman who loves him entirely for who he is, gives me great hope for the future."

"I'm not really that special," Eleanor demurred. "At least not compared to others. I suppose my standards have changed a lot in the last few months as I've watched Edmund stumble upon all sorts of strange things about himself."

"How odd his life must be," Shruti murmured.

"I still have trouble imagining it," Eleanor agreed.

"He is so lucky to have you, Eleanor." Shruti took her hand and squeezed it. "He was always so alone, and it broke our hearts to see him that way. He always seemed like he was waiting for his other half, but I had no idea how alone he truly was until now. You are such a gift to him, and to us."

"I hope that's true. I often feel like a horrible wife," Eleanor admitted.

"What? No! You're a wonderful wife!" Shruti exclaimed. "You're so accepting of everything about him! You're an even better wife than my mother was! She was always bothered by so many of my father's habits!"

"We just haven't been married long enough for nitpicking," Eleanor shrugged. "But I lie to him all the time. He doesn't even know that he looks like a teenager right now. I didn't have the heart to tell him, because I knew he would fall into a dangerously anxious state. I'm so good at it now, I've stopped noticing when the lying begins. It's shameful, really."

"Uma told you it isn't time for him to know everything," Shruti reminded her.

"Somehow that doesn't make me feel any better when I'm making up another story to keep my husband trapped in ignorance… Speaking of which, I'd better get moving on the newest one. I suppose I can't hide this from him. Maybe I'll guide him into the bathroom where he can see himself in the mirror, but *blimey*, he's going to be upset. He'll have to leave his job, of course, and I'll have to make up excuses for why he isn't visiting my family… maybe we can join Oz and Yvie in Perth after all…"

"How awful! What pain his secrets cause both of you!"

"Well, by the grace of many gods, I knew exactly what I was getting into. Several of Edmund's guardians warned me of his divine fate before we tied the knot."

"Many gods…" Shruti murmured. "Such as?"

"Probably more than I realized at the time," Eleanor answered vaguely. "Lord Vibhishana gave me some advice, as did several others I probably shouldn't mention by name."

"I'm sorry, I didn't mean to pry," Shruti said as she worked to curtail her curiosity. "Eleanor, you'd better come up with a plan.

We don't have much time. Dinner will be ready in about fifteen minutes, and my father has invited the Maharaja of Gwalior and his wife to join us. Harjeet went to collect them at their holiday home down the road already, so they'll be back any minute now. My father is trying to arrange passage for you two to get to Agra on the maharaja's private train. It will be much more pleasant than a public train."

"Blimey, there will be an audience of strangers..." Eleanor muttered.

"I tried to convince Father not to invite them, but he didn't see the state Edmund was in! He was completely focused on using his influence to arrange all sorts of amazing honeymoon experiences for you."

Eleanor smiled at the idea. "Your father is a very good friend."

"He is," Shruti agreed. "Although, his actions are not entirely out of friendship anymore. They are rooted in piety. He would do anything for Lord Kalki, Eleanor. You must help Edmund tread carefully. My father will do *anything* that he says now without question. Speaking of which..."

Shruti tiptoed across the hallway and gathered up a stack of clean, colorful silk Indian clothing from its position on an ivory chaise, topped by an elaborate golden turban with pearls and diamonds sewn all around the base.

"I told my father not to do this," Shruti said with subtle annoyance. "He has offered his most princely turban for Edmund to wear to dinner tonight. He wants Edmund to be wearing a crown of sorts." She rolled her eyes. "My father has a very specific idea of how the gods should be, Eleanor. It's why I omitted the Rakshasa part of the story completely. But Edmund should not wear this turban, especially not with the Maharaja of Gwalior visiting. It will be very odd to guests that you and Edmund are wearing Indian clothing at all, but if he is dressed like a bona fide maharaja, it could seem as if you are mocking them."

"I see..."

"You can just leave it in your room. I will have Babri collect it while you're at dinner and return it to my father's closet."

"That takes care of the turban, I suppose, but not the teenager who is sharing my bed…"

"What are you going to do?"

Eleanor sighed with stress. "I haven't decided yet."

"Well, the maharaja doesn't know what to expect. He didn't see Edmund before. The bigger problem will be the servants…"

"Blimey, I'd forgotten about them…"

As the bed creaked inside the room, Eleanor gathered up Shruti's offering of clothing.

"I don't know what to do yet. Can you come back in a few minutes?"

Shruti nodded her agreement.

"Dearest?" Edmund called.

"Thank you, Shruti," Eleanor whispered.

"I will help you however I can," Shruti reiterated.

Eleanor slipped back into the room and closed the door behind her. "Darling, close your eyes, I'm going to turn on the lights."

She flipped on the electric light switch and waited for a moment for Edmund's eyes to adjust. Sitting up in the bed was the husband she had married, fully returned to the latter part of middle-age with his grey hair speckled with black, the crow's feet at the corners of his eyes, and a more balanced body weight.

"Shruti brought us clothing to wear to dinner, darling," Eleanor explained. "Apparently, it will be ready soon, and Ravi has invited the Maharaja of Gwalior and his wife to join us."

Edmund scrunched his nose. "The Maharaja of Gwalior, you say? That name sounds familiar…" Edmund looked down at his body. "I'm back to my old self again, aren't I?"

"You are, darling." Eleanor couldn't have been happier with the development, and she sat down next to him and enticed him into a kiss. "Does it feel different?"

"It feels older," Edmund replied with ambivalence. "My body does not feel as spry or energetic, but I suppose I feel more natural this way. I've spent years getting used to it."

"Well, I love you at all ages, darling."

He kissed her again, and then he spied the elaborate turban topping off the stack of clothing.

"Oh, Ravi sent this along to go with your new outfit from Babri. Shruti said you shouldn't wear it, though. Ravi is just being overly accommodating."

Edmund picked it up and put it on his head, and Eleanor giggled. The turban wasn't big enough to fit on Edmund's head, so he balanced it precariously and then let it fall off gently back into his hands.

"Perhaps in Hyderabad I will procure one of my own," he winked as he placed it on the bedside table.

Commotion from the other side of the house echoed.

"We'd better get moving," Eleanor said as she laid out the new offerings on the bed. An emerald green lehenga with gold and silver beaded flowers all over it was paired with a matching emerald green sherwani for Edmund.

Edmund gathered her hand into his and kissed her palm. "Your henna is looking lovely."

He was right. The dye was now a very dark color of brown, and the intricate designs were popping very distinctly from her fair skin.

"I'll have to thank Shruti again for her artistry at dinner," she said as she wiggled awkwardly into the lehenga. She shivered as Edmund buttoned up the back of her blouse and then kissed her neck with his cold lips.

"Perhaps I should drink some chai before I meet the maharaja," Edmund said self-consciously as he pulled on the new trousers.

"I find the feeling of your cold skin to be utterly delightful, darling."

154

Eleanor reached around him and squeezed his bum before he had a chance to put on his elaborate shirt. They almost lost themselves in another round of honeymoon pleasure, but Shruti's gentle knock at the door broke them out of their stupor before all of their clothes were strewn across the floor.

"The maharaja and the maharani are here," Shruti called through the door.

"Just a minute!" Eleanor called back. She giggled as she pulled her skirt back up and Edmund rushed to pull on his shirt. As soon as they were decent, Eleanor rushed to open the door.

Shruti moved to say something, and then held her tongue as she looked Edmund up and down.

"Right then, okay…" Shruti said as she recalculated her next move. "You both look lovely. Eleanor, perhaps I can help you with your hair. It needs a bit of… er… taming. Oh, and Edmund, your butler just arrived. He is very worried about you. Perhaps you can go ease his mind?"

"Yes, yes, of course!" Edmund was positively giddy at the news that Mr. Valov was safe and sound.

"He's in the front entryway with your trunks. The porters will bring them around to your room, and there is a spare room by the kitchen that he can use as his own until you leave tomorrow."

"Tomorrow?" Edmund asked disappointedly. "I thought we were going to stay a few more days."

"You are welcome to stay as long as you want, but the Maharaja of Gwalior is heading home tomorrow morning, and the steamer is leaving port at noon with the Helmsworths. We thought that perhaps you might enjoy the unique luxury of riding on the maharaja's private train. Gwalior is only a few hundred miles south of the Taj Mahal, so you won't be going out of your way at all. Plus, a private train is safer than a public one, which matters quite a bit to my father."

"Yes, yes, I can imagine," Edmund agreed.

"You are, of course, also welcome to stop through our home in Bombay on your way out of India, or anytime you'd like. Uncle Edmund, you and Eleanor are a true part of our family now, if that isn't too much of a presumption. You should think of our home as your home."

Edmund pulled her into a cold hug.

"It is a great privilege, Shruti." He let her go, and she dutifully held in a shiver.

"Now, Eleanor, come. Let us fix your hair before you meet the maharani. She's incredibly fashionable." Shruti grabbed Eleanor's hand and gestured towards the bathroom.

"I'll go greet Mr. Valov," Edmund said excitedly.

He kissed Eleanor goodbye, and then skipped out of the room. If she didn't know that Edmund had so much more vigorous youthful energy pent up inside of him, she'd think that he was still at the height of his physicality, especially compared to any other man who appeared to be in the latter half of middle age. She sighed lovingly.

"Tell him I said hello!" Eleanor called.

"Will do, dearest!" As soon as Edmund slammed closed the door to their chambers, Shruti guided Eleanor into the bathroom.

"I find it very reassuring that Lord Kalki feels so much love for his butler," Shruti said as she immediately set about attempting to tame Eleanor's wild hair. She sat Eleanor down at the edge of the bathtub. "It means he is not the least bit aristocratic in that snobby way that keeps the masses subjugated just because of their lineage."

"Edmund cares very deeply about many people, including those who are less fortunate than he is. I have never met anyone who exudes love in the way that he does. It makes me fall in love with him again each time I observe it."

"And yet he isn't weak." Shruti worked Eleanor's hair into a reasonable half-up do and began pulling pins out of a hidden pocket in her sari to solidify it. "So many people think that loving men are weak. With the power of Lord Kalki and Ravana, I'm sure Edmund could kill anyone with the flick of his wrist, and yet he chooses not to."

"You're right. Being forced to kill during the war was the worst thing that could have happened to him. Those deaths haunt him… all of the men he's killed haunt him."

"Yes… yes, I suppose he must have killed scores of men already," Shruti murmured. "It is very hard to imagine. He seems so gentle and kind."

"It is hard for me too, even now." She tried to push the image of Edmund's bloody victory on the Orient Express from her mind, but it stuck like mud. "I've seen it."

"You've seen him kill?" Shruti asked as she stopped what she was doing to address Eleanor.

"In defense of the innocent, of course," Eleanor clarified quickly. "Just like he killed those monkeys. The carnage was similar, except that he killed worthless human bolshies who were going to kill everyone on our train in Bulgaria. They killed a priest right in front of us before he was willing to indulge his darker strengths."

"Poor Edmund!" Shruti exclaimed.

"I was so angry at them for putting him in that position, I might have killed them myself if I'd had a gun," Eleanor admitted. "My killing would have been vengeful, though. Edmund didn't stoop to vengeance. He only focused on justice, just as you would expect."

"I'm grateful he had the strength to save you. Did he save Oz and Yvie too? They didn't seem particularly surprised by today's revelations." Shruti's tone became casual as she returned to finishing off Eleanor's hair by pinning the elaborate mangtikka jewel so it could dangle down her forehead.

"Aye, they were there. They saw everything and chose to keep our friendship anyway. They even thanked him for saving them." Eleanor paused for a moment to think through the memory, and how surprised she'd been when they'd demonstrated their exceptional acceptance. "I think sometimes there is a kinship between people who saw too much during the war. We understand each other in a way that no one else can."

"I'm glad." Shruti whisked Eleanor up into a hug and then pulled away to reposition her dupatta by tucking it into her skirt and around her front, just as Babri had done the night before. "Edmund must have had some very unpleasant experiences with his secrets over the years. People are so quick to go raving mad with fear."

"You are very right about that," Eleanor agreed. She glanced at her improved appearance in the mirror. The emerald silk looked particularly striking with Mélusine's talisman and Shruti's costume jewelry. "Thank you for making my hopeless red mop presentable."

"Your gorgeous spritely locks," Shruti corrected her. "It was my pleasure, Eleanor. Now, shall we go introduce you to the maharani?"

Eleanor took a deep, calming breath. "I suppose if I've already met a goddess today, a maharani should be quite easy."

"You have absolutely nothing to worry about, Eleanor. Just be yourself. Now come. Father had two cases of Chateau Margaux delivered for you while you two were… er… experimenting. It is the best wine in India. He had to bribe the viceroy's importer with an astonishing sum to get it."

Eleanor pulled Shruti into a final hug.

"Thank you for everything, Shruti."

"Someday I hope to do something that really matters for you and Edmund. In the meantime, I'll have to settle for offering you minor conveniences. It is not enough."

Eleanor squeezed her hand, and with a few more deep, calming breaths, she set off for her next unexpected Indian encounter.

"Eleanor!" Mr. Valov exclaimed, breaking off a jovial Czech conversation with Edmund as she and Shruti reached the foyer. He glanced up and down assessing her appearance, and then stifled a subtle sigh of stress, replacing it with a wide, cheerful smile.

"Hello," Eleanor said questioningly as he pulled her into an awkward hug.

"I need to talk to you alone *now*," he whispered into her ear with his natural British accent.

"I'm glad to see you weren't swallowed up by the port! Now, tell me, Mr. Valov, where are our trunks? I have a few items I've been missing that perhaps you can help me dig up?" Eleanor despised the farce, but she played along anyway.

"Yes, yes, of course!" Mr. Valov agreed with the thick Czech accent he used as part of his cover. "The porters have just taken them to your room. Perhaps I can help you look."

"Just give us a few minutes," Eleanor said as she smiled reassuringly to Edmund and Shruti.

Mr. Valov bowed politely before heading straight down the hallway towards their room. Eleanor rushed to keep up with him, wondering in passing how he'd figured out which room was theirs in the first place.

As soon as they reached her room, he slammed the door closed.

"Tell me what happened last night, Eleanor. Tell me every detail!" Mr. Valov demanded, returning to his natural voice.

"What we do in our honeymoon bed is hardly your business."

"The murders!" Mr. Valov hissed. "Tell me about the bloody murders!"

He pulled a cigarette out of his front pocket case. As soon as he lit up, he began pacing back and forth.

"The murders?" Eleanor thought back to the prior evening. "Do you mean the blood in the fountain? Ravi's had investigators here all day, as far as I know they haven't found a thing."

"That is because my people found the corpses before they did." Mr. Valov dropped into a whisper as he glanced past her to the open veranda beyond. "Two British agents, both working for MI-5, were found dismembered in the garden of the Maharaja of Gondal's summer home next door."

"Good lord," Eleanor murmured. "Did you know them?"

"By reputation only." Mr. Valov took a long drag of his cigarette. As he noticed her attention, he offered her one.

"Those things will kill you, you know," she refused.

"They'll have to get in line. Now, this isn't about my feelings, Eleanor. This is about protecting Edmund, and the rest of the world."

Eleanor didn't like Mr. Valov's tone one bit. "The rest of the world?"

"Tell me honestly, Eleanor, were you with Edmund every second of the day yesterday? Did he have any opportunity to sneak away, perhaps while you were sleeping?"

"To sneak away? To murder two men in cold blood? What kind of question is that?!" Eleanor couldn't rein in her anger at his outrageous insinuation. "You've been living with him for years, *Mr. Cumberland*. He's better off than he's been since the bloody war! Surely you must trust him by now."

"Eleanor, please," Mr. Valov implored. "Lower your voice. We can't be overheard!"

"I want you to explain to me why you are accusing my husband of murder without one smidgeon of evidence."

"What makes you think I have no evidence?"

"Well, he didn't murder anyone, so whatever you have must be entirely circumstantial."

Mr. Valov reached into his pocket and pulled out a note. Eleanor read it several times. There was something unsettlingly familiar about it.

We are very bad men. We are foolish firang spies who steal what isn't ours and oppress for the sake of oppression. We cannot live with ourselves being such scum of the earth. May the next generation learn from our mistakes. Jai hind.

"This was found amongst the body parts," Mr. Valov whispered. "It was written in blood with an old-fashioned quill."

"What does *jai hind* mean?"

Mr. Valov lowered his voice even more. "It is a rallying cry for Indian nationalism. This is very, very bad, Eleanor. Even if Edmund didn't do it, it's bad for him and for the Bidkars. I'm up to my ears trying to protect all of them from the wrath that is itching to come down on someone, *anyone*. Heads will roll for this."

"And you're telling me that *Edmund* is the top suspect less than one week after he saved seven hundred British citizens from the foolishness of MI-5 on board that steamer?"

"He is *my* top suspect, Eleanor. The rest of them are perfectly happy to use this as an excuse to arrest Ravi Bidkar for murder and treason."

"WHAT?! NO!" Eleanor exclaimed.

"Please, Eleanor…" Mr. Valov coughed as he choked on the smoke of his cigarette. "Please keep your voice down!"

"You must do something! You know they didn't do it! You know deep down that *Edmund* didn't do it! Find a bloody solution worthy of your position, Mr. Cumberland!"

"There are too many elements now, Eleanor!" Mr. Valov exclaimed. "General Kettering has already covered up the steamer incident so well that the MI-5 agents in India don't even know about it! All they care about is snuffing out subversion in the army, and you and Edmund frolicking about in the home of an Indian nationalist of Mr. Bidkar's reputation, dressed as if you are natives does not help the situation one bloody bit! What the hell is that on your arms, anyway. Are those *tattoos*?"

"That is enough!" Eleanor shouted.

"Sshhh!"

Eleanor took a deep calming breath before continuing. "They are temporary. They are stains from the root of some plant. I rather like them and so does Edmund." Eleanor inspected her mehendi as she thought through her next words. "My husband is happier and more carefree than I have ever seen him. He is reveling so fully in his return to his homeland that he hasn't mentioned the war once since we arrived yesterday morning. I think you will agree that that is a record, Mr. Cumberland. Now, I will not stand in the way of his recovery, and neither will you."

"His homeland?!" Mr. Valov exclaimed indignantly. "He was born in Bath! He is the son of the bloody King of England!"

"He was *raised* in Hyderabad," Eleanor shot back. "And you know as well as I do that he is the son of the ancient king of Lanka. That is apparently Ceylon, for those of us not versed in the Indian epics."

"How do you know that his father was from Ceylon? Did his guardians tell you?" Mr. Valov asked, returning to a whisper. "We never had any record of where he was born. We assumed he was English!"

Eleanor sighed with annoyance at her unintentional revelation. "I know a great many things, Mr. *Cumberland*. More than you, more than my husband, more than almost anyone on Earth. What I will tell you with certainty is that despite its current political position, England is not the center of the world and it never has been. Even the illustrious Mr. Johnson is from Ceylon, and his impact on the world has been far greater than you can possibly imagine."

Mr. Valov thought carefully about her assertion and his next words. "*I* am not the one making judgments about your fraternization with the locals, Eleanor. But they are judgments that are being made by those with enough influence to make your lives extremely difficult. Frivolously dismissing them will only make things worse. If you aren't careful, Edmund will lose his position in the army."

"What a tragedy that would be! I'm sure that Earth's future messiah won't be able to find anything else to do with his time if he is forbidden from coddling the king's horses."

"What do you mean by that?" Mr. Valov asked with piqued interest.

"Never mind..." Eleanor was mad at herself for letting another important secret slip in her passion. "What about the Maharaja of Gondal? Why isn't he a suspect? The bodies were found in his garden."

"Don't you think I checked that first, Eleanor?" Mr. Valov returned to pacing back and forth as he lit a second cigarette, placing the remnants of his first in a purpose-built compartment of his cigarette holder.

"Does Edmund know how much you smoke?" Eleanor asked with sudden curiosity.

"I hide it from him as much as I can. He knows I only do it when I'm under stress. It tips him off to interrogate me every bloody time, always at the most inopportune moments. He's too bloody smart, that husband of yours. Too bloody smart…"

"Smart enough to stop himself from murdering on a whim."

"We aren't on opposite sides, Eleanor." Despite his fresh infusion of tobacco, Mr. Valov was not able to hide his growing desperation. "I'm trying to find another bloody suspect! *Any* suspect! The Maharaja of Gondal is in Switzerland with his wife getting surgery, and they took along their entire staff."

Eleanor paused to consider the intel. "Still, the note isn't in Edmund's handwriting. I'm still waiting to see your evidence. As far as I can tell, there is nothing linking Edmund to the crime. The last time I checked, being old enough to appreciate quill pens didn't qualify as evidence for murder."

"Don't you see, Eleanor? It is the same handwriting as the note in Paris! The note on the bodies of the thieves who shot him and beat you at Montmartre!"

"What?" Eleanor's mind raced as she recounted the unpleasant memories.

"The M.O. is exactly the same in both cases! And there was a third case! The captain of the steamer who was found dead with the French note. You and Edmund were there all three times!"

Eleanor took back the letter and inspected the handwriting again. He was right, it was the same as the note they'd found on the captain's body.

"I agree that the timing is suspicious, but that isn't Edmund's handwriting."

"What were the chances that a murderer with the same M.O. would be on the same route as your honeymoon? Each time he dismembered the bodies without any hint of a struggle or a weapon—just like Edmund did on the Orient Express—and then he left a note that tied the killing to some form of greater justice."

"I was with Edmund the entire time. He didn't kill anyone," Eleanor reiterated.

"You were not with him the entire time on the steamer. You left him alone for hours on end," Mr. Valov reminded her.

"Well, he and I were together the entire time in Paris and every moment since we arrived in India. Surely two out of three alibis should count for something, and you still haven't explained the handwriting."

"What if he isn't in his right mind when he's committing the crimes," Mr. Valov posited. "We have both seen him struggle to control himself. He is like a different person when his demon is aroused."

"You're suggesting that Edmund has some Jekyll/Hyde complex? A complex so severe that he has different handwriting in his altered state? You'd best get your head out of the penny dreadfuls, Mr. Cumberland," Eleanor scoffed. "I was a nurse for the criminally insane for fourteen years. Never once did I come across a real Jekyll/Hyde complex. Each and every time it turned out that the conniving bloke was concocting the whole charade in some crafty effort to expunge his full sentence."

"Edmund is not an average person," Mr. Valov whispered. "Think about who we are talking about, Eleanor. You have witnessed the scope of his dichotomy just as much as I have."

"I have witnessed him control his shell-shocked episodes with a level of discipline rarely found in this world," Eleanor countered. "Your theory is still rooted in wild speculation. Your strongest evidence is the timing of the murders. What about other people who were on the same route? Oz and Yvie were on our route, as were those poor Ridgeways. Surely there were others who made a stop in Paris and then boarded our steamer? What about the entire steerage deck on their way to Australia? Perhaps you should check into them. They have criminal backgrounds, don't they?"

Eleanor held a straight face as Mr. Valov struggled for a response.

"I hope you realize that my ridiculous assertion there was just as ridiculous as your accusations against Edmund. Besides, we heard the ruckus that resulted in last night's murders. There was a loud crash that felt like an earthquake right in the middle of the children's dance performance. Edmund was beside me the entire time. There is absolutely no way it was him, even with his speed."

"Dance performance? So there was an illicit performance last night?"

Eleanor rolled her eyes. "If by illicit you mean that there were little girls in adorable costumes flitting about a stage in front of their parents, celebrating their ancient traditions, then yes. And you'd best not stoke my anger at the pointless sassanack oppression of other cultures, Mr. Cumberland. My great-great-grandfather had his kilts burned by the British, and my family still has not forgotten."

"For god's sake, Eleanor, we don't have time to argue about trivialities!"

"Cultural oppression is only trivial to you because you are not oppressed," Eleanor rebuked.

Mr. Valov straightened his bowtie. "Those two officers were infiltrating the Bidkars' because someone called in a tip that there would be some sort of debauched sexual dancing involving children. Now tell me honestly, Eleanor, what exactly happened?"

Eleanor guffawed. "That is the most absurd, ignorant assertion I have ever heard in my life. You've been stewing about here long enough to talk to the Bidkars. Do they look to you like the type of people who would put on some sort of child pornography cabaret in their living room?"

"Mr. Bidkar married a prostitute. I would put nothing past him," Mr. Valov countered.

Eleanor worked hard to control her growing anger. "Reya was *not* a prostitute. Do you know how the Bidkars met Edmund? Two British officers were going to rape Reya and her seven-year-old daughter! They said that Reya was a madame pimping out her

166

daughter on the streets, and they would have gotten away with it if Edmund hadn't stopped them!"

"I do not understand the connection you feel to these people, Eleanor. You've just met them!" Mr. Valov exclaimed. "How do you even know that what they've told you is true? Does it sound right to you that two officers of the British Army would try to rape an innocent mother and child on the streets of Bombay?"

"I do not hold the sassanack army in the high regard that you do, Mr. Cumberland. And I shouldn't have to remind you that last week your beloved British military put the lives of seven hundred innocent citizens at risk just to catch my heroic husband using his talents." Mr. Valov humphed his concession. "Besides, I have exceptional judgment of character. Supernatural judgment, as it turns out."

"What do you mean by that?" Mr. Valov asked with raised eyebrows.

"Never mind. It doesn't matter. The more important point is that Edmund loves and trusts the Bidkars, and he has for over a decade."

"Edmund is too easily manipulated. Every native with a sob story from here to Timbuktu can weasel his way under his protection like a puppy in need of an owner."

Eleanor was taken aback by Mr. Valov's harsh words, and his racist undertone. "Like you did, Mr. Valov, our dear exiled Czech spy?"

"Pah," Mr. Valov scoffed. "In fact, yes. You are exactly right. Do you know why I have enslaved myself to this absurd Slavic accent for years and years? Because we didn't think an average British sob story would be sufficiently enticing to guarantee my position under his wing. So yes, Eleanor, you are entirely correct."

"If you don't respect Edmund's judgment, perhaps you should recuse yourself entirely and choose a replacement who will not hold the elevated status in our household that you do."

Mr. Valov looked as if she'd slapped him, and she suddenly regretted how far she'd taken her argument. "Are you suggesting that I resign?" She could feel a sudden emotion in his voice.

Eleanor took another deep, calming breath. "I'm suggesting that you wash your hands of whatever nationalistic nonsense has been hammered into your head since yesterday and remember why you have devoted your life to helping Edmund Marriner. If you are unable to do that, you should recuse yourself. To be quite honest, I'm shocked by your ignorance. I expected more from you, and I'm certain that Edmund did too."

Mr. Valov sat down on the edge of the bed and put his head in his hands. He lit up a third cigarette and smoked several drags in silence.

"You have no idea how perilous my position is, Eleanor. It's worse than it's ever been. I don't know if I'm going to be able to protect Edmund, and his treasonous friends? Pah. You have been surrounded by magic for too long. You've lost your sense of how difficult these things are in the real world."

"Magic... yes, magic! That's exactly what we need!" Eleanor exclaimed. "Kuveni?" she whispered. "Kuveni, can you join us? Please? Just for a minute?"

With a pleasant breeze, Kuveni materialized in the form of Kate, clad in her sparkling black beaded flapper dress.

Mr. Valov finished off his cigarette and stood up to greet her with an awkward handshake, which she accepted unenthusiastically before pulling Eleanor into a loving hug.

"I shouldn't be here," she whispered. "Lord Vibhishana will be livid if he learns that I've ignored his orders again... We don't want to push him too far, Eleanor... No, we really don't want that. He can get very, very testy..."

"As testy as Lord Shiva with the fire of Durga burning within him?" Eleanor asked innocently.

Kuveni froze in her position as she looked Eleanor up and down questioningly. "Yes... one might say that."

"Did Edmund murder two British agents while I was sleeping yesterday?" Eleanor changed the subject bluntly. "You've been watching us every moment, right?"

"Well, I wouldn't say *every* moment..." Kuveni hedged. "I couldn't get into that cave you were trapped in earlier today."

"What cave? You were trapped in a cave today?" Mr. Valov interrupted. "Why didn't you tell me? Did the Bidkars see any of Edmund's superhuman talents? Bloody hell, I don't have time for this..."

Eleanor ignored him and addressed Kuveni instead. "Uma must have wanted privacy." She watched carefully for Kuveni's reaction.

"Uma? You stumbled upon Uma? Yes... yes, that makes sense, actually. I wonder if it means what I think it means..." Kuveni trailed off and began muttering to herself in a very foreign tongue, until Mr. Valov's impatient sigh distracted her. "You'd best point your finger elsewhere, Mr. Cumberland. My beautiful boy hasn't murdered anyone."

"There, you see!" Eleanor exclaimed triumphantly.

"Shall we go down to the MI-5 headquarters at Victoria Terminus so that you can make a statement to that effect?" Mr. Valov asked cheekily. "Unobserved witnessing of a crime is admissible in British courts, as long as you don't admit that you were literally invisible."

"If you simply need a witness to keep the Bidkars out of trouble, I will go with you right now," Kuveni said seriously. "Although, first we must agree on who we are going to accuse in their stead."

"Who did it?" Eleanor asked. "Kuveni, you must know, right?"

"I do not. I'm not omniscient, my dear girl. I have my unique ways of keeping tabs on those I love most, but neither you nor Edmund were at the scene of the crime... any of the crimes... and so I am as lost as you are, I'm afraid. So, Mr. Cumberland, do you have a wanton murderer for me to accuse? Perhaps one you are sure is a serial killer but hasn't yet been convicted? That would be the most just course, I think, given the circumstances. Shall I make myself male for my accusation to be given adequate weight?"

Kuveni morphed herself into her jolly, rotund male form of Mr. Quince.

"Oh, for god's sake, I was only being sarcastic," Mr. Valov said as he sat back down on the bed and lit up his fourth cigarette.

"Those really will kill you," Kuveni warned him. "Horribly painful deaths they cause too, eating you from the inside out."

"I have bigger things to worry about," Mr. Valov countered.

Eleanor startled as a light knock at the door distracted her.

"It's Shruti," Kuveni whispered.

"What do we do?" Eleanor panicked.

Kuveni squeezed her hand reassuringly and waltzed right over to the door, swinging it open with a flourish.

"Shruti, my dear girl, what a pleasure it is to finally meet you in person!" Kuveni exclaimed as she pulled Shruti into the room and slammed the door behind her.

"Is everything alright? I thought I heard shouting." Shruti addressed her question to Eleanor. As Eleanor struggled for a response, Shruti eyed Kuveni's male form suspiciously. "How did you get past the guards?"

Kuveni looked down at herself, and then dissolved completely, reappearing in the form of Kate.

"Never you worry. Your guards are just as competent as always, my dear. I just popped in for a moment, and I will pop out soon enough. Now, we need to figure out how to keep the British dogs off of you and your father, my dear girl. What would you suggest?"

"I'm sorry?" Shruti asked with even more bewilderment as she blinked several times, observing the results of Kuveni's magical transformation. Mr. Valov looked intensely annoyed at the development, but he said nothing.

170

"Oh, I'm sorry. How silly of me. I'm Kuveni. I am one of Edmund's Yakshini guardians." Kuveni offered her hand with an affected aristocratic handshake.

"A Yakshini?" Shruti murmured. She poked at Kuveni's hand, but didn't shake it. "Yakshinis are real? Yes… yes, I suppose if Rakshasas are real, Yakshinis must be real too…"

"Many things that you can't see are real, my dear girl. I am no different. Now, Eleanor might have mentioned me, or perhaps Uma did. We were very good friends, Uma and I. I was sorry to see her embrace her fate as a recluse, but to each her own, I suppose. How is she doing, by the way? Eleanor tells me you had a lovely little chat earlier today?"

"She's dead," Eleanor whispered. "Uma killed herself at the end of our visit. She said she was relieving herself of her sacred throne, and the tiger went with her."

A look of sadness in Kuveni's expression quickly morphed into resignation. "She was waiting a long time for you to come. I'm glad she got what she wanted."

Mr. Valov cleared his throat and readied himself to speak, switching back into his Czech accent. "I will think carefully about what we've discussed and get back to you with a solution, Eleanor. I'd best make sure that the colonel has everything he needs for his dinner with the maharaja."

"They could use some help in the kitchen opening the wine," Shruti suggested. "None of the servants are very skilled at using that odd device for removing the corks."

Mr. Valov nodded his agreement, bowed, and left them alone.

"Edmund's butler knows all about him? About you?" Shruti asked as soon as the door was closed again.

"He knows enough," Kuveni replied. "Too much, perhaps, but we will just have to wait and see how strong his character turns out to be. I am still cautiously optimistic, despite his most recent foray into nonsense… But, Shruti, dearest, we have more important matters to discuss, now that it's just us girls."

171

Kuveni guided her to the messy bed, and gestured for Eleanor to join them as she sat down on the edge.

"Are you… are you an avatar too, Kuveni? Your name sounds familiar, but I can't remember the story," Shruti asked timidly.

Kuveni smiled. "I am not an avatar, my dear girl. But I know why you'd think so. I am just a simple Yakshini who has devoted my life to supporting the Avatars of Light. The rest of my story doesn't matter anymore. It was many thousands of years ago."

"Thousands of years ago…" Shruti murmured. She snapped her fingers, and her bangles jangled with the gesture. "Wasn't Kuveni the ancient Yakshini queen of Lanka? The queen who was betrayed and exiled by her human husband?"

"Yes, my girl. I can see you were well-educated in the classics," Kuveni replied with a resigned sigh.

"Kuveni, you were a queen? Why didn't you ever say anything?!" Eleanor exclaimed.

"What was there to say, Eleanor? I'd rather leave the past in the past. Now, do tell us, Shruti dearest, what did the Singhs find in their investigation today?"

"Nothing. My father hounded them for an hour, ensuring that they'd left no stone unturned, but they were just as surprised as he was at their lack of results. They said it had never happened before. No fingerprints, no footprints, no evidence for where the blood came from or where the rest of it went. It makes me quite frightened, to be honest. I have always felt very safe in our home."

"Oh, my dear, dear girl…" Kuveni pulled Shruti into a hug a bit more forcefully than Shruti expected. "You will have nothing to worry about. I will take care of everything. Now, if anything strange happens, anything at all, you just need to whisper my name, and I will help you, and I mean *anything*, Shruti. If British officers come sniffing around, summon me, and I will help you deal with them any way I can. I will even help you and your father escape to Shambhala if you need to."

"Shambhala?" Shruti's eyes widened at the reference. "You live in Shambhala?"

"That is what I call Lord Vibhishana's estate in Bath," Kuveni explained. "It's a bit of a joke, really."

"Is that where Edmund... Lord Kalki was born? Just like the scriptures said he would be?" Shruti pushed.

Kuveni did not give away any panic at the turn of the conversation, nor did she seem remotely surprised by the mention of Edmund's divine future title. "My, my, Uma did have an earful for you, didn't she? You must be very special for her to share so many secrets with you. Now, we won't be repeating the details of Master Edmund's destiny very loudly to anyone, will we, my girls? It is very important that it stays a secret, especially from him, until the time is right."

"Yes, Your Highness," Shruti agreed. "Although, I already told my father... and Yvie was there in the cave with us. I hope we haven't already said too much?"

"There is no need for honorifics with me, my dear girl. After five thousand years surrounded by gods, my deposed royal status means absolutely nothing to anyone, especially not to me. Now, be careful with whom you share your special knowledge, and everything will be perfectly fine. Uma would not have entrusted her secrets to you if you weren't worthy."

Kuveni closed her eyes and grimaced with a silent argument. "I'd best be going. Remember, Shruti, summon me if you need my help."

"Thank you, Kuveni," Eleanor whispered. "Oh, and thank you for the rain!"

"It is my pleasure as always, Mistress Eleanor." Kuveni pulled Eleanor into a parting motherly hug. "Although, I think you will need to thank someone else for the rain. I find it as surprising as you do."

"Huh..." Eleanor humphed.

Kuveni squeezed her one last time, and then dissolved.

"Your life is so strange, Eleanor. I always thought that my father was one of the most powerful men on Earth, but I have learned today that the world is so much bigger than I ever thought it was... It's really quite daunting..."

Eleanor squeezed her hand reassuringly. "Please don't be shy in seeking Kuveni's help, Shruti. You are right that she is very powerful, and she means everything that she says. You must protect yourself and your father, no matter what happens."

"Why are you so worried about it, Eleanor? Why were you shouting at your butler?"

"Two dead British officers were found in the garden next door last night. Their deaths were brutal, and the residents were all out of the country, which could throw suspicion on you. Mr. Valov was warning me of the danger, but our conversation got a little out of hand."

Shruti gasped. "How horrible."

"The murders are still a secret. They are being investigated by the British Army."

"That's not good..."

"The British authorities might try to pin the murders on you or your father. You must not let them, do you understand? After we've left, if you need our help, Kuveni will be able to find us in a heartbeat. Don't let yourselves be victimized, please? For Edmund's sake and for yours."

Shruti nodded her solemn agreement.

"Memsahib!" Babri's voice called from the hallway. "Memsahib! Dinner is served! Sahib is very unhappy that you're late!"

"We mustn't keep the maharaja waiting." Shruti stood up, but then she stopped. "You must do this all the time, mustn't you, Eleanor? You must pretend as if you know nothing, when the truth is threatening to burst right out of you."

"It is my life now," Eleanor sighed.

174

Shruti squeezed her hand in solidarity. "Come, we will be sisters in arms and in secrets from now on."

"That is exactly what I need."

And together, the sisters in arms rushed through the hallway, preparing themselves to dive right into another elaborate web of lies on behalf of Edmund's secret divine destiny.

CHAPTER 9 – THE FIRST MAHARAJA

Shruti led Eleanor into an even grander banquet hall than the lavish dining room they'd eaten their dinner in the night before, and Edmund broke off his conversation with Oz and Yvie to greet her. He triumphantly handed her a large glass of red wine he'd been waiting to offer her for some time, as his glass and Oz's were already empty.

"Thank you, darling. Chateau Margaux, Shruti tells me?"

Edmund nodded happily. "Surely the best wine I've ever had in India. It is a luxury I didn't dare to dream of during my decades in the British Indian Army."

"It is certainly our pleasure, Edmund," Shruti said with a polite curtsy.

"You look even more lovely in that lehenga underneath the chandelier lights than you did before, dearest," he whispered.

"Where are the other guests?" Eleanor asked, disregarding his praise as she eyed the empty place-settings suspiciously. Suspicious of what, exactly, she wasn't even certain. She hated the feeling.

"Ravi had some business to attend to, as always," Edmund explained casually.

"I will go check on them now." Shruti made her way across the room, but as she reached an arched doorway, the door flew open from the other side, and she shrieked with surprise as two servants dressed in matching uniforms guided Ravi, followed by a very fashionable couple adorned in traditional silk clothing even heavier with sparkling beads than Shruti's, straight through the door.

"Shruti, my dear, are you alright?" Ravi asked concernedly.

She laughed as she worked to slow her racing heart. "I'm perfectly fine, Father. You just startled me."

"Shruti, you are a woman now!" the maharani exclaimed with perfect British intonation. "I can't believe it's been so long since we saw you last!"

"It has been too long, Your Highness," Shruti replied as she offered her a polite *namaste*.

"Come, come, let me introduce you to our other guests of honor." Ravi led the couple straight to Edmund. "Edmund, my lord, may I present the Maharaja and the Maharani of Gwalior."

Edmund and Eleanor cringed simultaneously at Ravi's error, while the royal couple both offered polite *namaste* greetings as they eyed the four *firangs* clad in Indian clothing.

"I see Babri has been busy," the maharani laughed. "What a task for her, to dress four unsuspecting *firangs* in India's finest! Oh, and the mehendi! How lovely! You didn't have this done for your wedding in England, did you?"

Eleanor and Shruti both relaxed at her casual tone.

"Shruti did it last night." Eleanor held out her arms to observe the intricate designs again. "I've been meaning to thank her again for doing it. I like it more and more as the color darkens."

"Yes, it is really quite striking on your fair skin." The maharani reached forward and squinted to take a closer look. "What do the

178

other British women think? They must have been in an uproar when they saw you!"

"Well, I'm a Scot actually, but I haven't had the pleasure of finding out what the other *firang* women think of my choices in fashion," Eleanor admitted. "I've been lucky enough to avoid the confrontation so far."

"Well, never let those cats corner you," the maharani winked. "And if they manage it anyway, be a falcon, not a songbird."

"That might be the best advice I've ever heard for dealing with British women," Eleanor laughed.

"*Oui, je suis d'accord!* I agree!" Yvie interjected.

"Oh yes, please forgive me. May I present Mr. and Mrs. Helmsworth," Ravi said as an afterthought.

Oz offered them a polite *namaste*, and the maharaja chuckled. "I see Sri Bidkar has been training you!"

"He has offered us quite a bit of sage advice," Oz agreed.

"*C'est un plaisir de faire votre connaissance*," the maharani said as she shook Yvie's hand demurely.

"*Vous parlez français?*" Yvie asked excitedly.

"*Oui, j'ai étudié depuis quinze ans…*"

As Yvie and the maharani slipped into an amicable conversation in French, Eleanor refocused on the men.

"Now, tell me, Edmund Sahib, was it? What is this business about you being a lord? Which lord? Of what house? My son Georgie is a godson of King George and Queen Mary. Perhaps we have some common acquaintances beyond Sri Bidkar, although his glowing praise of your unquestionable virtue and warrior prowess do make me wonder if perhaps you are Lord Rama himself."

Eleanor shifted uncomfortably at the reference, and Shruti threw her a nervous look.

As Edmund moved to correct Ravi's mistake, Ravi rushed to interrupt him. "Please forgive me. It was simply a slip of the tongue. Might I present Colonel Edmund Marriner of the British Army and his wife, Eleanor."

"Colonel Edmund Marriner…" the maharaja repeated his name questioningly. He looked up at Edmund, noticing seemingly for the first time exactly how tall he was (especially in comparison to the maharaja's petit stature), and a wide grin spread across his face. "Colonel Marriner, we have met before! I must admit, you have aged far better than I have!"

"Have we?" Edmund asked, hiding his nerves in a casual tone. "When?"

"The last time we met, you were a young captain in the British Indian Army in need of an unbiased ear to whom you could complain about your workplace woes, and I was a jilted groom in need of some exceptionally sage advice after that wretched Delhi durbar convinced my fiancée that it was a fine idea to break off our engagement so that she could marry some handsome cad for *love*."

"Madho Rao?" Edmund asked as his nerves morphed into genuine excitement.

"You do remember me!" the maharaja exclaimed.

"You did not tell me that you were a maharaja," Edmund pointed out.

"You didn't ask!" the maharaja countered jovially. He leaned in and whispered confidingly. "I can see that I'm not the only one in need of a few moments of respite from my royal title from time to time… my lord." As Edmund moved to protest, the maharaja patted him on the back. "Ravi Bidkar's tongue never slips, my friend. But think nothing of it. You shall be Edmund, I shall be Madho Rao, and you may call my wife Rane."

She broke off her French conversation with Yvie to acknowledge him. "What luck, Madho Rao! What were the chances that you would already know Sri Bidkar's virtuous *firang* soldier?"

"Lord Vishnu works in mysterious ways," Ravi practically squealed with excitement. Shruti threw him a disapproving look, and he straightened his turban and pushed forward. "Now come, let's eat as the old friends that we are."

As Ravi guided them to the table, Edmund grabbed Eleanor's hand and squeezed it. She found his delight at the reunion contagious, and she was ever so glad that he hadn't noticed anything amiss.

Just as the thought crossed her mind, Mr. Valov rushed into the banquet hall, expertly balancing a precarious tray with six open bottles of wine and several extra crystal glasses. He silently set about refilling each person's glass, finishing off his rounds (as if he were simply an exceptional butler) by offering wine to the royal couple, who accepted gratefully.

Madho Rao took in a long, savoring sip. "I'm glad you heeded my advice, Ravi. The Chateau Margaux is unbeatable, don't you think, Edmund?"

"It's perfect," Edmund agreed as he downed half his serving in one controlled Rakshasa gulp.

"I will be forever grateful to you for your kind suggestion, Madho Rao," Ravi said as he eyed Edmund's reaction with complete satisfaction.

As they seated themselves, Madho Rao glanced at Eleanor and smiled oddly. "I'm glad to see that you have many more pleasant things to keep you occupied than Lord Curzon's whims these days, Edmund."

"I do," Edmund agreed as he squeezed Eleanor's hand.

"Lord Curzon's whims?" Eleanor asked curiously. "I don't think I've heard that story yet."

Edmund finished off his wine, and Mr. Valov immediately refilled his glass. "I was his glorified errand boy for quite some time. He found my linguistic talents especially useful. Despite the promotions he bestowed upon me, our close time together is what led to my less than glowing impression of his leadership. It wasn't until I met Lord Kitchener and he decided that the British Indian Army had a more important use of my skills that I was released from my duties as a consummate pansy."

Madho Rao laughed heartily, while Ravi seemed more pensive about Edmund's flippant description of his past plight.

"What a waste," Ravi muttered. "What a bloody, useless waste… Think of the better state India would be in now if you had been our leader, Edmund… I can't think of it. It depresses me too much."

"Father," Shruti hissed.

"I don't believe that Viceroy of India was on my list of career prospects, old chap. Even Lord Kitchener couldn't manage it for himself, and he had a far more impressive dossier than I ever have," Edmund said as he took another long swig of his wine.

"Yes, but, Edmund, it is your right!" Ravi argued. "You can still do it! You can lead us now! That is why you were born in the land of the conquerors! So that you could lead them and us together! You can lead the whole world!"

"Father!" Shruti kicked him under the table.

"You think far too highly of me, Ravi," Edmund countered with more calm than Eleanor knew he was feeling.

"Really, Ravi, the surprises never end with you, do they? Haven't you been talking my ear off for years about independence?" Madho Rao asked. "And now you are suggesting that a British military officer become our leader? No offense to you, Edmund, old friend, of course. Still, we must all keep each other honest, mustn't we?"

"Edmund is not a Brit. He is a man beyond any one nationality," Ravi humphed.

Shruti kicked him again.

"I did grow up in India," Edmund admitted.

"See!" Ravi exclaimed. "I knew it! Wait, really? Where?"

As Edmund squirmed, Shruti came to the rescue. "The maharaja was considering a holiday to Paris. You were there recently, weren't you? Perhaps you can give him some travel advice, or perhaps you could tell them your suggestions, Yvie?"

Yvie was startled by the attention. "I would be glad to," she said politely as she took another sip of her wine.

"Paris is the city of love, is it not?" Madho Rao asked, allowing Shruti's deflection to stand. "A perfect place for honeymoons?"

"It is," Edmund agreed.

Eleanor felt lightheaded for a moment as Edmund's burning love infused her. She was glad that Ravi's assertions had not unsettled him too much.

"Are you in search of a romantic locale?" Edmund asked, gratefully continuing along with the mundane turn of the conversation.

"I'm always on the lookout for a romantic locale," Madho Rao smiled.

"Oh, Madho Rao," Rane laughed.

"I'm glad that your premarital woes did not hinder your happiness. You mentioned you have a son?" Edmund asked.

"And a daughter," Madho Rao replied as Mr. Valov swooped in to refill their glasses again. "I've had all a man could possibly want in this life, thanks to Rane." He glanced back at Eleanor. "Wife is life, Edmund. Always remember that. Happy wife, happy life."

"Sage advice, indeed," Edmund winked. "Out of curiosity, do you know how the bold young lady has fared? The one who broke off your engagement by letter to marry her handsome lover?"

"Ha! You will not believe this, Edmund! Really, I hardly believed it myself! She married him in a London hotel room without a single witness from her family to support her. Truly scandalous, it was! We all thought she was done for! But by the grace of God (that I still do not understand one bit), she too is a maharani now! Within a year of their illicit marriage, the cad inherited his brother's title!"

"Well, she married the most drunken maharaja in all of India," Rane interjected. "And that is what she gets for disgracing her family to marry a sweet-tongued cad for *love*." She rolled her eyes. "He'll be dead by year's end, I've heard, and she'll be a widow with *five* children. In the end, karma will be satisfied, as always."

"Oh my, how sad," Yvie commented politely as she finished off her first glass of wine, and Mr. Valov poured her another.

"At least she wasn't forced to bear the children of a man she didn't want to be with. How horrible for a woman to give up her body against her will…" Eleanor realized as soon as she spoke that her statement might be offensive, and yet she couldn't bring herself to apologize for saying something she felt so strongly was true.

"My mother would have agreed with you," Shruti whispered under her breath.

"She should have trusted her family's judgment. Madho Rao is a far better husband than that cad she married has ever been," Rane countered.

"He is a far better husband to *you*," Eleanor argued. "But, honestly, Madho Rao, would you have been as good of a husband to a woman who detested you?"

"She had no rational reason to detest me," he replied. As Eleanor noticed his subtle discomfort, she realized that she was letting her tenacity push her too far.

"Do you not believe in marrying for love, Rane?" Eleanor softened her tone. She found their shared attitude of disdain for the concept particularly puzzling when paired with Madho Rao's effusive support of his wife.

"True love grows from stability and nobility," Rane replied. "When either of those are missing, trouble is never far behind. Families are far better at identifying those traits than silly children are, especially silly children infused with lust, and Indira's current plight only underscores my point. Madho Rao and I have built a life together. Our love has grown from our shared commitment to each other and to our families."

"I suppose I fell in love with a man who exudes stability and nobility. I was lucky to never have to choose between them." Eleanor was glad to be reminded of her great luck in meeting

184

Edmund, especially against the backdrop of the continuous surprises that had distracted her from the original, mundane reasons she'd found him so intriguing. He squeezed her hand lovingly, and she stroked his cool palm.

"You were hardly a lustful child making your choice. Maturity breeds wisdom," Rane pointed out.

The comment stung momentarily until Eleanor realized that Rane did not mean her statement disparagingly. In fact, based on her body language, she appeared to mean the statement as a compliment.

"Oh, Eleanor, you chose the most noble husband in the world," Ravi sighed, rescuing her from having to muster a response.

Edmund shifted uncomfortably at his overly effusive praise, and then steered the conversation away from himself. "It would seem that Indira did you a favor, in the end, didn't she, Madho Rao? Opening up your options so you could meet Rane?"

"Indeed, she did. As you probably remember, I didn't think so at the time… But it was really you, Edmund, who deserves the credit. Before you talked me out of it, I was planning on holding her to our arrangement out of spite. At least for a while, you know, to really make her squirm. In any case, I would not have had room in my heart for Rane. You freed me from myself."

Ravi looked like he might explode. "Lord Vishnu works in mysterious ways!"

Without a moment for Shruti or Eleanor to demonstrate their displeasure with his statement, he clapped his hands, and a troop of servants rushed into the banquet hall, each carrying a huge silver platter, followed by another troop of servants bearing silver serving spoons in an absurdly formal fashion, each carrying their spoon before them as if it were a sword readied for battle.

As Eleanor watched them approach the table, she noticed for the first time that each place was set with a full spread of somewhat gaudy new silverware, with so many forks and knives that she didn't even know what some of them were for.

"Put the Goan fish curry at the end, between Rane and Edmund," Ravi instructed them.

"*Fish* curry?!" Shruti exclaimed. "Father?! You have never allowed meat in our kitchen. Never ever!"

"If it's good enough for Edmund, it's good enough for us." Ravi straightened his posture as he reiterated his uncomfortable plan to himself. "Besides, I brought in a Konkani chef just for the occasion."

"Really, Ravi. You didn't need to go to the trouble," Rane said as the servant lifted the cover of the platter, and she took in a deep, satisfied whiff. "It does smell delicious, though. Just like home."

"Rane is from Goa in the west originally," Madho Rao explained on her behalf.

"Please, eat!" Ravi urged them.

Edmund waited politely as the servants served out equal portions to everyone, while Ravi inspected the chunks of white fish meat bathed in a rich red coconut curry sauce with subtle disgust. Shruti threw a desperate look to Eleanor.

"Ravi, really, it was so kind of you to accommodate your guests, but you really shouldn't eat anything that you don't want to eat. No one should." Eleanor reached under the table to squeeze Edmund's thigh, hoping that he would understand her request for backup.

"I agree entirely." Edmund caught her pass and ran with it. "Ravi, please do not eat anything that does not make your stomach growl with hunger. There is so much delicious food here to choose from."

As soon as the maharani began eating, Ravi watched Edmund collect a large chunk of fish with his bread and stuff it into his mouth, as gracefully as anyone on Earth could accomplish the task with such a large portion. Ravi, on the other hand, pushed his curry around on his plate unenthusiastically for a solid minute, until Eleanor got another idea.

"Shruti, wasn't Babri just talking about how hungry she was after her night of sewing? About how she could think of nothing better than a meat curry?"

"Why, yes!" Shruti exclaimed. "Yes, she was! Father, perhaps we should send both of our portions to Babri before she falls asleep for the night."

"How thoughtful!" Edmund added for good measure.

"Yes... yes, what a thoughtful idea, Shruti," Ravi finally agreed.

He whispered something to his footman in Marathi, and two servants swooped in to collect their plates, followed immediately by two more servants replacing them with fresh ones. When the deed was done, the servants served them both all of the vegetarian dishes, and Ravi sighed with subtle relief.

"So, you are headed to Agra, Colonel?" Madho Rao finally spoke after several minutes of silent, satisfied chomping.

"It is on our itinerary," Edmund agreed as his footman refilled his plate for the fifth time. "A tour of India wouldn't be the same without the obligatory homage to the Taj Mahal."

"Don't make it sound too romantic, darling," Eleanor teased.

"I never dreamed it could be as romantic as having you by my side to combat the masses, dearest."

"Then you must join us on our private train tomorrow," Madho Rao proposed. "I was already convinced to take on two strange *firangs* by Ravi's exceptional powers of persuasion, but it would be such a genuine pleasure to host you on our train, Edmund. It is the least we can do after all you've done for us."

"And you can meet the children!" Rane exclaimed. "Georgie and Anya! Oh, they will be so excited to meet you. They are reaching the age that they feel actively left out when we leave them at home with the governess for dinners like this one."

"You can ride with us all the way to Gwalior," Madho Rao added. "It will get you within a few hundred miles of Agra, and you can stay with us at our home for as long as you want before you head off to Agra. There is a direct train from Gwalior with an adequate first class carriage."

"What do you think, dearest?" Edmund whispered.

"I think it is a rare opportunity to ride on the private train of an old friend of yours, darling," Eleanor whispered back.

Edmund smiled. "That is very kind of you, thank you. We won't be too much trouble, will we? We also have my man, Mr. Valov, traveling with us."

"We have an entire carriage just for the servants," Madho Rao reassured them. "I'm sure Mr. Valov will find it comfortable enough."

"Alright, then, I suppose it's settled!" Edmund exclaimed.

"I suppose we'd better start packing... whatever packing is necessary..." Eleanor whispered to herself. The idea of moving on saddened her. She'd already come to feel at home with the Bidkars, and she stopped for a moment to contemplate how quickly the feeling had developed—she'd hardly spent two days with them.

"I have already had Babri drop off a few more outfits for both of you, for when the fancy strikes to wear something more interesting than those bland British suits and trouser-less shirts," Shruti winked.

"It's hard to believe that we'll be in Perth by the end of the week, isn't it, Yvie?" Oz said with an ambivalent sigh.

"*Oui*, Ozzie, it is. We will be so sad to say goodbye."

Eleanor worked to push back her emotions. "We will come and visit. I'm sure of it."

"Oh, please do!" Yvie exclaimed. "We get so lonely down on the edge of the world! Good friends are impossible to come by!"

"Really, mates, you should come and stay as long as you want," Oz reiterated.

"Well, we mustn't start saying our goodbyes yet," Edmund declared as the footman served him another portion.

"You got that right, mate. You're not even halfway through your dinner!" Oz teased him. "Why, that reminds me, did I ever tell you about the time I won the skippy pie eating contest down in Margaret River?"

"Do I want to know what skippy is?" Eleanor asked semi-seriously.

"Definitely you don't!" Yvie exclaimed.

"Well, it all started when we set out for the cattle fair, not knowing that fate had a very different plan in store for us…"

As Oz enticed the entire group into one of his most grandiose tall tales, Eleanor focused on her meal (the spiciest she'd tasted yet), adamantly avoiding an air of depression that threatened to dampen the former air of joviality.

Edmund must have sensed her struggle, and as he squeezed her thigh under the table, he leaned over to whisper in her ear. "We will visit them in Perth, Eleanor. Perhaps next year, or sooner if the fancy strikes. The world is our oyster now. There is nothing stopping us from doing what we want."

"I love you, Edmund," she whispered back, hoping that he wouldn't sense the ball in her throat.

He squeezed her hand, and together, they sat in silence, mourning the impending separation from their first friends as man and wife.

CHAPTER 10 – BITTERSWEET

Eleanor awoke in Edmund's cold arms to a flurry of action in the hallway beyond. She didn't want to get out of bed. She snuggled into the nook of his arm, but an extreme sense of unease wouldn't let her settle. She rolled away from him and covered her head with a pillow to block the bright morning light shining in from the open veranda. It was much warmer already than it had been since her heat stroke two days before, and she was not looking forward to combatting the heat and her fatigue at the same time.

She hadn't slept well at all, as the impending separation from their new allies ate away at her consciousness, opening the door for a flood of repressed anxiety to torment her.

First and foremost, there was the unsolved murder mystery which had already claimed *seven* victims since their unfortunate night in Paris, followed closely by the unjust axe threatening to come down upon the Bidkars. The two problems were inseparable, and both were unquestionably her fault—hers and Edmund's. While they had rolled around in bed pretending that they were just a normal honeymoon couple (how foolish!), some sort of serial killer had followed them across the globe, wreaking havoc on innocent people with gruesome deaths. Well, not entirely innocent people, she had to admit. Those thieves in Paris were certainly not innocent, and the French captain didn't seem like an upstanding citizen either. She had little sympathy for the MI-5 agents who had infiltrated a private home on an errand of ignorance, but dismemberment was, of course, an outrageously harsh fate for such a crime... She cringed as she pushed an image of their painful demise from her mind.

Her thoughts wandered back into the same cycle that they had used to torture her throughout her mostly sleepless night. To the unusual lack of evidence of the most recent crimes, to Mr. Valov's accusation against Edmund, to the irrefutable point that the deaths had followed them across the world and that each victim had some trouble in mind for them... She was even more certain than she had been the night before that Edmund was not the culprit, but what about his guardians?

She'd met five so far: Mélusine, Kuveni, Vibhishana, that strange priest in Bulgaria... what had Mélusine said was his name? Thomas... yes, Thomas... and then there was the stern Yaksha companion of Mélusine who had quietly managed security at their wedding in Basingstoke. The ones she knew well didn't seem like the type to dismember humans on a whim, but some of them she hardly knew, and then there were the ones she hadn't met yet at all.

She tried to force herself to focus on the positive. Kuveni had promised to protect the Bidkars, that was something... and Mr. Valov was extremely resourceful and well-connected. She was certain that if he put his mind to solving their immediate plight, he would be able to protect the Bidkars... but what would it take to convince him to do it? She was still taken aback by his harsh judgments of them, and of his distaste for the Indian culture that Edmund loved so much. Was he simply annoyed that his job had gotten harder since their arrival in Bombay, or was there more to it? She wondered if perhaps he was subtly unhappy that Edmund's shell-shocked weakness was quelled now that he was surrounded by old friends… if perhaps at the core of Mr. Valov's displeasure was the simple fact that he didn't feel as important now that Edmund was stronger and had more allies. She hoped he'd find his honor before it was too late, as Edmund would have put it…

Without a knock, the door to their room burst open, and Mr. Valov rushed inside. Edmund sat straight up as he took in his awakening Rakshasa breath. He took a moment to observe his surroundings, and Eleanor caught a flash of his black demonic eyes before he calmed himself.

"I'm sorry. I didn't mean to startle you." Mr. Valov had dark bags under his eyes, and his voice sounded unusually tired. "You are running dreadfully late. If you want to join the maharaja on his train, you will need to dress and depart immediately."

"Well, I suppose we'd better get moving." Edmund stood up and gathered a silk robe from the ground.

Mr. Valov rushed to the closet and collected the only two outfits hanging inside that he had presumably chosen for them while packing the night before—a rather frumpy brown wool British suit for Edmund and a similarly frumpy short sundress for Eleanor.

"I'm not wearing that, Mr. Valov," Eleanor said bluntly. "It was made abundantly clear to me that showing one's bare legs is not acceptable in India."

Edmund looked at his option with a similar lack of enthusiasm, and as Mr. Valov noticed Edmund's eye wandering to the pile of flamboyant silk kurtas Babri had stacked in the corner the night before (and that Mr. Valov had conveniently forgotten to pack while he was supposedly completing the task during dessert), Mr. Valov sighed his disapproval loudly.

"Colonel, please. I beg you. You are in a very precarious position. You mustn't draw attention to yourself."

"By wearing a blue silk shirt?" Edmund asked with puzzlement. "On the private train of a maharaja on the way to his home?"

"Do you have a specific reason why wearing Indian clothing will be detrimental to Edmund's position?" Eleanor pushed.

Mr. Valov shook his head. "I shouldn't have to explain to either of you why rocking the boat is a bad idea when multiple spy agencies are after you."

"What do you mean, they're after us?" Edmund asked with a burst of anxiety. "I thought we got all of that nonsense on the steamer sorted. Did you hear something to the contrary when you were back on the steamer collecting our luggage?"

Mr. Valov looked rather desperate. "It didn't feel entirely settled to me, Colonel. It seemed like some were still intrigued by your unique talents."

Eleanor threw him a disdainful look at his lie. Based on what he'd told her before, no one in the spy agencies in India had any idea Edmund was unique; they were simply concerned about a colonel in the British Army having too much sympathy for the "natives."

"Oh, really, Mr. Valov? And what gave you that impression?" Eleanor poked at his lie. "Did you see spies disembarking from the steamer to trail us?"

Edmund looked at him expectantly for his answer.

Mr. Valov looked towards his pocket with his cigarette holder, and then held off. "No. I didn't see any spies specifically. Still, it is not wise to rock the boat. Things are not as easy as they used to be. The Hindu-German Conspiracy during the war put many people on edge, and they haven't forgotten it."

"How do you know so much detailed information about the British Army's politics, Mr. Valov? Did your Czech contacts inform you?" Edmund asked with more curiosity, bordering on suspicion.

Eleanor was so frustrated with Mr. Valov that she didn't even care how close he was to blowing his cover.

"I don't understand how wearing Indian clothing on our holiday in India is rocking the boat. Edmund isn't here on official business. He didn't even bring his uniform!" Eleanor pushed. "Besides, modern fashions are changing all the time. Who's to say that those lovely silk shirts won't be on the runways in Paris next year? Didn't Lady Curzon herself wear Indian fabrics?"

She wanted him to say what he really meant. If there was a real danger, she wanted to know what it was. If there was not, if his distaste was simply a form of the same ignorance that had led to her great-great-grandfather's kilts burning in the town square, she wanted him to bloody realize it!

Mr. Valov shrugged his concession. "You are free to do what you want. I will help you dress, or you can dress each other. I await your orders, Colonel."

Edmund looked to Mr. Valov and then looked to Eleanor as he mulled over the question that should not have been nearly so difficult to answer.

"I will follow your lead, darling, whatever you want to do. If we wear normal clothing, I will need something suitable with trousers."

Edmund eyed the bland brown suit and the stack of colorful kurtas, and then he straightened his posture. "We are in India. There is no occasion better than the present to embrace it, and I will never have the chance to wear such beautiful fabrics in England."

He walked over to the stack of silk kurtas, collected one in a rich royal blue, and slipped it on, pairing it with a fresh pair of white linen pyjamas.

"Perhaps, dearest, you should wear a different color. It is a bit silly for us to wear matching fabrics in public, I think."

As Eleanor joined him to examine her choices, Mr. Valov lit up a cigarette and walked out onto the veranda.

"There is a bee in his bonnet," Edmund whispered. "And I don't believe it is rooted in his opinion of our fashion choices."

"I think… I think perhaps I've usurped him a bit," Eleanor admitted. "It used to be just you and him, and you, darling, have become quite a bit more assertive in these last few months. Perhaps he was used to you complying with his suggestions regularly, and now he doesn't know what his role is."

The assertion wasn't wrong; it simply didn't include the vast bottom of the iceberg.

"Perhaps I will have a talk with him." Edmund glanced over to observe Mr. Valov's fatigued, unenthusiastic posture as he paced back and forth, smoking deep drags of his cigarette. "Yes. I will have a talk with him as soon as we have a few minutes to ourselves."

Eleanor chose a green silk salwar kameez, similar in style to the one she'd worn the day before to Elephanta, with a high, straight neckline, almost like a blend between a dress and a long coat, over flowing baggy trousers made of a less embellished version of the same emerald silk, paired with a matching dupatta scarf in a more delicate, sheer silk. She collected some slightly gaudy emerald earrings from a stack of matching jewelry left behind by Babri, and put them on.

Edmund smiled his support. "That salwar kameez is beautiful with your coloring, dearest."

She shivered as he buttoned up the back and kissed her neck.

"Darling, I'm going to use the powder room to finish up getting ready. Perhaps you should talk to Mr. Valov now."

Edmund kissed her again gently on the lips, and then naughtily slapped her bum as she headed towards the bathroom, leaving the door open. While she focused on wrestling her wild hair into something presentable, she listened carefully (and slightly guiltily) to overhear their conversation.

"Those things will kill you, you know." Edmund began with a less than diplomatic point. "I've known too many men who died very unpleasant deaths from them."

"Everyone dies, it's just a question of when and how," Mr. Valov replied.

"Well, I for one, would like you to live as long as possible, Mr. Valov. You have been a dear and loyal friend to me over the years, during the most trying time of my century on Earth."

Mr. Valov finally stopped pacing. "I appreciate the compliment, Colonel, but I am not your friend. I am your butler. I think perhaps we've blurred the lines too much."

Edmund paused for a long, awkward silence. "Do you really feel as if we have no friendship, Mr. Valov? Would you really prefer a more formal service relationship? I have always appreciated our time together, not just because you make my life easier, but because I enjoy your company."

"You do not need my company anymore, Colonel." Mr. Valov gave away a quiver of emotion in his voice.

Eleanor wondered if the root of the problem really was more simple than she'd realized—if Mr. Valov's personal feelings about Edmund (and his sadness at the loss of their one-on-one relationship) really was the core of everything else they'd been arguing about.

"Oh, come now!" Edmund exclaimed. "Of course I need your company!"

"Flattery is pointless at this juncture, Colonel."

"It is not just flattery," Edmund countered sternly. "You are the most loyal man's man in the world, Mr. Valov, and I have found your company indispensable over the years. I have no reason to believe that will not continue to be true in the future."

"I am not loyal enough, Colonel. Not for you," Mr. Valov whispered.

Edmund suddenly shifted with anxiety and lowered his voice. "Have you revealed my secrets to someone, Mr. Valov?"

"No!" Mr. Valov exclaimed. "No, never, Edmund! I will *never* reveal your secrets! I have sworn it to the death!"

Edmund relaxed. "That level of loyalty is not necessary, Jarek. Your life is worth more than my secrets."

"I beg to differ. The life of a man with so many flaws is not worth so much, Colonel. I think that perhaps you would be better off without me."

"Hogwash!" Edmund exclaimed. "Oz told me several times that he tried to coerce you into leaving me, and you steadfastly refused. Surely my time enjoying the pleasures of marriage on my honeymoon isn't enough cause for you to change your mind; it certainly hasn't changed my opinion of you. If anything, I feel closer to you than I ever have. Until last week, do you know how many people had ever known my secret other than you? Two! Eleanor and Edward. You were the third, Jarek."

Mr. Valov paced back and forth silently for almost a minute before deciding on his response.

"Edmund, my name isn't really Jarek," Mr. Valov confessed in a barely audible whisper.

They both paused for another minute of awkward silence, and Eleanor's heart raced in anticipation of Mr. Valov's full revelation.

"I lied to you about my name," he whispered. "There was too much going on back then... I didn't realize what you would become, what I would become... I didn't realize how complicated it would be, or how much I would care..."

Eleanor could feel him tottering on the very edge of throwing his arms up and revealing everything. A large part of her hoped that he would, and then she would be done with one of her most infuriating farces.

"I lie to everyone about myself all the time, Mr. Valov. It would be intensely hypocritical of me to judge those who see fit to do the same," Edmund reassured him.

"You are too forgiving, Edmund." Eleanor could hear him battling with a ball in his throat.

"Would you like to tell me your real name now that you know my deepest darkest secrets?" Edmund asked with a particularly fatherly tone.

Mr. Valov paused to battle with himself, and then he lowered his voice even more. "My Christian name is Leopold. You'd best not use it too often, Colonel. Too many people know it. It could get both of us in trouble."

"It is nice to meet you properly, Leopold," Edmund whispered as he shook his hand.

"Colonel…" Mr. Valov paused.

"Do speak your mind, Mr. Valov," Edmund coaxed.

"Colonel, I have done things… horrible things… in the line of duty… things that should not be forgiven. Things I haven't told a soul. I am certain that you would not approve of my actions…"

"So have I, Mr. Valov," Edmund reassured him with a slap on the back. "It is the curse of our generation, I think. Or perhaps the curse of men in every generation. All we can do now is learn from our mistakes and set ourselves up for more peaceful lives in the future."

"I'm not sure that's possible for me," Mr. Valov admitted. "I don't think I will ever be able to escape. I buried myself too deep to ever scratch my way out."

"Well, you will have a refuge in my household all the same, Leopold." Edmund guided him back into the bedroom from the veranda.

"You do not want to know what it is I have done?" Mr. Valov asked nervously.

"There is nothing you could have done that would compete with the darkness that the war unlocked inside of me," Edmund replied. "Unless you'd like to tell me, to get it off your chest?"

Mr. Valov paused for a long moment considering the option. "Not yet, Colonel. It isn't time yet. But it makes me feel relieved to have the option. You are too kind to offer it."

"It is nothing compared to the kind and forgiving patience you've demonstrated with me over the years."

"So you really want me to stay?" Mr. Valov asked like a child seeking approval from his father.

"I cannot imagine my household without you, Mr. Valov," Edmund reiterated.

Mr. Valov gave in and hugged Edmund, and Eleanor caught a tear in his eye.

"Please forgive me, Colonel. Forgive me for everything. I'm really very tired," Mr. Valov admitted as he self-consciously wiped the tear away. "I haven't slept more than a few hours at a time since I met up with you in Paris."

"Perhaps you should stay here with the Bidkars for a few days and rest up," Edmund suggested. "I'm sure they would be more than happy to accommodate you."

"No!" Mr. Valov gave away too much of his underlying emotion. "No, thank you, Colonel. I wouldn't dream of imposing on them. I would feel most comfortable remaining with you and Eleanor from now on, so I can be of more direct assistance."

"Whatever you prefer. Eleanor and I will endeavor to be more self-sufficient from now on, so that you can get some rest."

"There is no need to change your behavior, Colonel. It is my pleasure to be useful, and a man needs to be useful, doesn't he?"

"Indeed he does," Edmund agreed.

"I'm sure a night or two of good sleep will be enough to get me back to my normal self," Mr. Valov said as he stood up. "Now, we'd better get on the road. It will be excessively rude to keep the maharaja waiting. The departure of his private train had to be worked into the station's schedule, so he must leave on time."

Eleanor quietly closed the door to the bathroom and then rushed to finish her mundane hygienic tasks while Mr. Valov dutifully packed their Indian clothing and the heavy pile of matching costume jewelry into the trunks.

When she finally emerged, he threw her a solemn nod of acknowledgment. "Eleanor, do you remember what we discussed last night, while I was helping you find those items in your trunk?"

"Yes?" she asked with a pang of anxiety.

He straightened his bowtie and pushed open the door for them. "I took care of it."

"Really? All of it?" She couldn't tell what aspect of their argument he meant. He'd found their serial killer? He'd cleared the Bidkars of suspicion? He'd told his fellow agents to stop being such sassanack wankers?

"All that mattered," he replied vaguely as he glanced at Edmund, who politely allowed them the privacy of their exchange without interrupting with prying questions. "Now, please. Mr. and Mrs. Helmsworth are waiting to say goodbye to you in the foyer, and Mr. Bidkar's car is waiting out front to take you to the station. I will manage the porters with your trunks and follow behind in a separate car."

Edmund took her hand, and they held each other especially tightly as they prepared for their goodbyes. When they reached the foyer, Ravi and Shruti were standing with Oz and Yvie, chatting politely. The conversation fell into silence as soon as they approached.

"You'd better get moving, Edmund. You don't have very long to get to the station. Traffic can be quite bad at this hour," Shruti suggested. "Same for you." She addressed Oz and Yvie.

Yvie rushed to Eleanor and pulled her into a tight hug. "What luck that we met such wonderful friends. We will impatiently await the news of your upcoming visit to Perth."

Eleanor couldn't fight back the ball in her throat. She realized in that moment that in her entire life, she had never had a friend that she liked as much as Yvie.

"We will come as soon as we can manage it," Eleanor agreed. "I hope you have a relaxing return to Perth in the meantime. Perhaps with a break from the drama of our company?"

"I have always loved drama, Ellie."

Eleanor squeezed her again. "I wish you the best, Yvie. I really do. I hope that whatever your heart desires comes to you straightaway."

Yvie kissed her on both cheeks, and wiped away her tears. "*Et a vous, aussi.*"

"It's been an honor, Colonel," Oz said as he shook Edmund's hand.

Edmund pulled him into a brotherly hug. "Don't be a stranger, mate."

Oz nodded, avoiding eye contact as he worked to keep his emotions under control.

Ravi, on the other hand, was a lost cause. As Edmund turned his attention towards him, Ravi's tears were already flowing freely. He took off his turban and bowed, but Edmund wouldn't let him get away with his pious gesture and pulled him into a hug instead.

"Thank you once again for your exceptional hospitality, Ravi. It feels more like home every time I come here, and this time is no different. We are brothers in arms now, I'd say? If that's alright with you?"

"It is an honor I never dared to dream of," Ravi whispered.

"We will see each other again soon, old chap," Edmund said as a fresh round of tears flooded down Ravi's face. "I'll make a point of stopping by on our way back to England. How's that?"

Ravi nodded his effusive agreement. "We will count the days."

"Sisters in arms and in secrets," Shruti whispered as she hugged Eleanor.

Eleanor hugged her back. "Don't hesitate to summon Kuveni. Protect yourself and your father, Shruti, from everything that might try to ensnare you. We will do anything we can to help you."

"Thank you, Eleanor," Shruti whispered. "Thank you for everything."

"Thank you, Shruti," Eleanor reiterated.

"You need to go, or you will miss the train," Mr. Valov interrupted.

Edmund nodded his agreement and escorted Eleanor to the first of three waiting cars. He opened the door for her, helped her inside, and then closed it behind her. The novelty that she cared so much about parting from these people she had only met a few days earlier was almost enough to overwhelm her sadness at the parting… almost.

As Edmund sat down beside her and closed the door, Harjeet nodded his acknowledgment to Ravi, and they waved back at their tearful friends as he took off down the driveway.

"I have never cared more about leaving somewhere than I cared just now," Edmund murmured as he took her hand tightly into his. "It is such a bittersweet feeling—wonderful and frightening at the same time. It is, I think, how I feel about my love for you, dearest."

"I know exactly what you mean, darling," Eleanor agreed. "*Exactly*."

And in contemplative silence, the two lovebirds sat together as they sped away from their new troop of loving allies, straight into the great unknown.

PART TWO
INTO THE HEART

Mr. Valov was in an absolute tizzy over the time as their car crawled through traffic to the entrance of Victoria Terminus. Eleanor wiped a flood of sweat from her forehead with her dupatta scarf, silently chastising herself for not preparing for the heat with a single handkerchief.

"Colonel! We must hurry! The train is scheduled to leave in five minutes!" Mr. Valov exclaimed as he rushed out of his trailing car and reached their open window. Behind him, eight porters from Ravi's staff stood in formation, holding their large trunks.

"I'm sorry, did you say that it is *scheduled* to leave in five minutes?" Edmund asked.

"Yes, Colonel! We must go!" Mr. Valov reiterated.

Edmund relaxed. He slapped Harjeet on the back and offered him a few parting words in Punjabi, to which their chauffeur laughed heartily, and then he nodded his agreement with a sly smile, and let Mr. Valov guide them out of the car.

"I reckon your haste will not be rewarded, Mr. Valov," Edmund said as he helped Eleanor up.

Eleanor glanced self-consciously at a huddle of fashionably dressed British women standing just inside the station who were watching their arrival with great interest and a chorus of shocked whispers. Eleanor looked down at her elaborate mehendi and beautiful Indian suit, and she straightened her posture and forced herself to remember the maharani's advice.

Falcon, falcon, falcon, she repeated in her head as a mantra.

Just as she was getting her nerves under control, she noticed another huddle of fashionably dressed Indian women, also waiting just inside the station on the other side of the archway from their British counterparts, pointing and whispering with similar interest.

As several begging children walked into each other, knocking over the youngest one as they stared with their eyes glued to her fiery red hair, Eleanor repositioned her dupatta to cover her hair, as she'd seen many Indian women do throughout her time looking out the window of Ravi's car.

Edmund reached into his pocket and handed each of the children a coin, offering them some advice in Marathi before he let them rush away to show their friends their new booty.

"Be careful, or you'll cause a riot, Colonel," Mr. Valov muttered.

As Edmund noticed the brewing crowd of beggars at the far corner of the building who were inspecting the children's intake, he quickly escorted Eleanor into the station, and Mr. Valov followed with similar haste.

When they entered the station, Eleanor avoided eye contact with all of the other women, and instead focused her attention on the vast windows and cathedral-like architecture of the neo-gothic space. The ceiling did not look like a train station at all, but the bustling chaos around them at ground-level did its work in reminding her. Edmund, on the other hand, was loving every moment of the hubbub as he looked around, taking in a deep, satisfied breath as he swam in the ambiance of British and Indian crowds intermingling with loud porters and vendors. He let off a similar series of nostalgic sighs to the ones he'd voiced when they'd arrived at the port two days earlier, while Mr. Valov's loud stressed sigh punctuated Edmund's, bringing them both back into the moment.

"We must find the maharaja's train," Mr. Valov reiterated.

Edmund stopped the closest local man in an official-looking uniform. "Excuse me, sahib. Might you direct us to the Maharaja of Gwalior's private train? We will be traveling with him at his earliest convenience."

The man's eyes widened as he looked Edmund up and down, observing his fine clothing, and then moving his attention to Eleanor, who smiled self-consciously, and then to Ravi's well-dressed porters dutifully holding their large trunks in perfect, militaristic formation. Eleanor caught the British women eyeing them as they listened in to overhear their conversation, and she couldn't help but smile to herself at their strangely posh position. *But, of course, we're riding with the maharaja! Who wouldn't ride with a maharaja these days?* She pictured Martha's reaction to the statement, and then she pictured her mother's…

While Eleanor's mind wandered to some guiltily satisfying fantasies of countering her mother's misconceptions about the "savages" of India with some photographs of their exceptionally luxurious travels, Edmund noticed the man's attention and engaged him in a jovial conversation in Hindi that the man seemed to find both confounding and invigorating.

Without any regard for whatever else he might have been doing, their new ally enthusiastically guided Edmund straight into the crowds. Edmund grabbed Eleanor's hand, and Mr. Valov followed with Ravi's porters, expending great effort (and some shouting at those who stood in their way) to keep up.

They walked straight to the other side of the large station to the farthest platform, where a completely modern five carriage train awaited, flanked by ten Sikh guards in full Indian military-styled uniforms of crimson and gold, with large turbans and long, curved swords.

Edmund paid their guide several coins, to which the man bowed and thanked him emphatically, and when the closest guard noticed them, all ten guards bowed in unison.

"Lord and Lady Marriner, we have been expecting you," the guard said in a deep baritone voice with lilting Indian intonation.

"You may call me Colonel Marriner," Edmund corrected him.

"As you wish, Colonel Marriner," the guard agreed. "I am Jaap Sahib. I am the head of security for His Highness The Maharaja."

Edmund offered him a polite *namaste*, and Jaap Sahib smiled and offered one back. Eleanor found the exchange delightfully civilized, until Jaap Sahib turned his head and shouted into the open door of the carriage in Hindi.

A young servant girl in a clean, bright yellow cotton sari and a young servant boy wearing a crisp yellow kurta and linen pants rushed to greet them with a deep bow.

"The maharaja and his family are readying to leave for the station now," Japp Sahib explained. "In the meantime, we will see to your needs. You, sahib, can have the porters load Lord and Lady Marriner's trunks onto the third carriage. It is the guest quarters." He addressed his suggestion to Mr. Valov and then returned his attention entirely to Edmund. "The first carriage is the royal master, the next is the children's suite, then your guest suite. This one here where you are standing is the family dining and lounging carriage, and then the back one there is the kitchen and the servants' carriage. Each sleeping car has a WC, and there is an extra bunk in the servants' carriage for your man."

Mr. Valov worked hard to hide his displeasure at the idea, but Edmund already had his back. "How many sleeping berths are there in the guest carriage?" he asked.

"Two," Jaap Sahib replied. "My lord and my lady are free to sleep in separate berths if you prefer."

Eleanor almost laughed at the idea, but managed to hold in her reaction.

"Thank you kindly for the suggestion, but I think we will have our man sleep in the second berth so he can see to our needs with as little delay as possible," Edmund suggested with calm authority.

It was clear that Jaap Sahib did not approve of the suggestion, but he dutifully held his tongue. "As you wish, my lord."

Mr. Valov threw Edmund a grateful look, and then guided the porters per Jaap Sahib's instructions to load the trunks into the guest carriage.

"Please come, my lord, my lady," Jaap Sahib suggested as he pulled open the door. "Please seat yourselves here. The servants will remove and store your shoes by your luggage, and then they will wash your feet before you enter the living area. The maharaja considers his train an extension of his home, so we must show it the same courtesy."

Edmund helped Eleanor up the stairs, and as they sat side by side in elaborately carved thrones that were fancier than any she'd seen in England (even while dining in aristocratic households), Jaap Sahib slammed the door behind them, closing them into the compartment, which was at least ten degrees cooler than the scorching air outside. Eleanor hoped that Kuveni wasn't playing another dangerous meddling game.

The two young servants rushed to remove their shoes, handing them to yet two more servants who whisked them away without a word. The servants then crouched at their feet with basins of warm soapy water and washcloths. The luxury of the setting was even more absurd than Eleanor could have imagined, but the pleasure of the clean water on her feet combined with the strikingly cool air were so nice that she couldn't find fault.

"Welcome to India, dearest," Edmund winked.

"Is this normal?" Eleanor whispered.

"It is for some. Not for me, of course, but the Indian aristocracy knows far more luxury than their British counterparts could ever imagine… and all the better for the world, I think. When Lord Curzon realized the sheer variety of luxury that was available to him in his position as viceroy, he became a bit Napoleonic, if you know what I mean."

When their foot bath was finished, another male servant, older than the others, waifishly thin, and dressed in a crimson kurta with ivory pyjama trousers, arrived from a neighboring carriage to greet them.

"Welcome, Lord and Lady Marriner!" he exclaimed. "I trust your journey from Sri Bidkar's estate was pleasant?"

Edmund moved to protest again at the incorrect title, and then gave up on the lost cause. "Yes, it was perfectly pleasant, sahib?"

"Your lordship may call me Dev Sahib," the man replied. "I am the head of His Highness The Maharaja's staff."

"It is a pleasure to meet you, Dev Sahib. You may call me Colonel Marriner, although, you are welcome to continue referring to my wife as Lady Marriner." He smiled mischievously at Eleanor as he made the suggestion.

"As you wish, Colonel Marriner," Dev Sahib agreed. "Please come inside."

He guided them to a mahogany dining table that was big enough to seat at least ten people. The décor of the entire train was just as opulent as everything in the Bidkars' house, down to the flowing silk curtains and the soft persian carpets underneath their bare feet.

"It will be at least an hour, probably two, before the maharaja and his family arrive," Dev Sahib informed them. "We have prepared a British tea to tide you over until the late lunch that we will serve upon our departure."

Mr. Valov approached from behind Dev Sahib, looking entirely bewildered. Eleanor noticed that his bare feet were damp and his trouser legs were haphazardly rolled up just past his ankles.

"You may wait there for Lord Marriner's orders," Dev Sahib suggested sharply to Mr. Valov as he pointed to a position in the

212

corner of the carriage. Eleanor threw Mr. Valov an apologetic glance at the rigidity of the plan. Dev Sahib bowed to Edmund, and then backed through the door, into the kitchen carriage.

Mr. Valov looked around the carriage, and then without any intervention from Edmund, he unenthusiastically sulked across the room to his standing position in the corner.

"So, darling, what shall we do for the next two hours?" Edmund asked casually.

Eleanor could tell he was up to something, so she played along.

"I suppose we will be having a long, relaxed tea service worthy of a lord and ladyship, darling."

Mr. Valov's stomach growled at the suggestion, and Edmund glanced over at him.

"Yes, I am looking forward to seeing how many tea sandwiches I can fit into my mouth at once. Do you think I can fit all of them, dearest?"

"You are a man of many talents, darling."

After a sufficient pause to let Mr. Valov settle into looking miserable, a sly smile spread across Edmund's face, and he laughed at his little joke and gestured for Mr. Valov to join them.

"Come, Mr. Valov. Please join us at the table for tea," Edmund suggested loudly so that any silently observing servants could hear him.

Mr. Valov sat down beside Edmund, but glanced guiltily towards Dev Sahib's position in the kitchen car.

Edmund followed his gaze. "You have never been to India before, I surmise, Mr. Valov?"

"No, Colonel, I have not," Mr. Valov admitted. "It is… er… more foreign than I anticipated."

Edmund chuckled. "It isn't Britain, is it?"

"No, it certainly isn't."

"I have three pieces of advice for you, Mr. Valov, if you are interested?" Edmund offered amicably.

"I have clearly proven that I need all the advice I can get." Mr. Valov sounded rather defeated, and Eleanor realized that her sympathy for him had finally returned after his heart-to-heart with Edmund at the Bidkars'.

"It is quite normal for Europeans to be overwhelmed when they first arrive, but you will come to love it, Mr. Valov, I'm sure of it." Edmund smiled reassuringly, but Mr. Valov looked less than convinced. "Firstly, you mustn't expect the rigidity of Britain when it comes to adhering to rules, including timetables. You will simply drive yourself mad. You must relax a bit, and let the pace of the world around you drive your actions, otherwise, you will spend a lot of your time waiting around. When you accept that you have less control here, you open yourself up to unexpected adventures that are far more interesting than anything you'd stumble upon back home."

"But how will the train leave the station at any semblance of a reasonable time? It's lost its position in the departures queue," Mr. Valov asked with genuine concern.

Edmund chuckled. "A wealthy maharaja's train will leave when he fancies it. The authorities will find a way to make it work, and he will make sure they reap the rewards of their support so that next time he will be given an even more plum position. That is, at least, how these things worked in the past when I lived here."

Mr. Valov humphed. "I still don't understand why the maharaja's staff would have told us to be here at eleven o'clock if they meant one o'clock. What is the point of stating a patently incorrect time for a meeting?"

"It is the way of things, my friend. If you try to fight it, you will just be throwing yourself against a mountain."

Mr. Valov shrugged. "What else should I know?"

Edmund glanced down at Mr. Valov's bare feet. "Always take your shoes off when you enter a private space. Let me guess... the porters dropped off our trunks just inside the carriage, and Dev

Sahib was very unhappy with you when you attempted to walk through our living area with your shoes on?"

"He called the guards on me," Mr. Valov admitted. "They escorted me back to the entrance, made me remove my shoes *and* my socks, which they subsequently confiscated, and then they made me wash my feet while four servants frantically cleaned the floor where I'd walked."

Edmund smiled knowingly. "Make sure your feet are thoroughly dry whenever you're done washing them. Otherwise, they will crack and bleed and become very difficult to manage."

"Does that happen to you?" Mr. Valov asked curiously.

Edmund smiled at the novelty of being able to offer a truthful response. "As you know, my friend, I do not have any trouble drying off, but I've certainly witnessed enough soldiers suffering the consequences of poor foot hygiene."

Suddenly, an unpleasant thought occurred to Eleanor. "Darling, did the servant boy who washed your feet notice that your skin was perfectly dry as soon as you took your feet out of the basin?"

"If he did, he did not say one word about it," Edmund said as he glanced at the boy who was returning into the carriage from disposing of the dirty water. When it was clear that the boy did not seem in the least bit concerned, all three of them relaxed.

"And your third tip?" Mr. Valov asked.

Edmund lowered his voice, and Eleanor and Mr. Valov both leaned in. "Social hierarchy here is even more rigid than it is in Britain. Servants are a dime a dozen, and they are expected to act like servants. What may seem obsequious to our modern egalitarian sensibilities is expected behavior here for a household staff."

"I've noticed," Mr. Valov sighed.

Eleanor wondered if Mr. Valov, as a highly skilled secret agent, had always been unhappy with his subservient cover story, or if it had only really started bothering him recently, when her presence had forced him to act more like a real butler.

"It is a great privilege to be in the service of a wealthy or royal house, even more so here than in Britain. They will expect our butler to act more subservient than you do in our liberal household, Mr. Valov, but I have a little trick up my sleeve that just might work…"

Just as Edmund spoke the words, Dev Sahib returned from the kitchen, followed by four servants. One carried a tall, tiered silver tea platter with sandwiches and adorable tiny pastries, followed by another carrying a large silver tray with a teapot and two cups, followed by two more servants, each carrying a silver place-setting, porcelain plate, and Belgian lace napkin.

When Dev Sahib noticed Mr. Valov seated at their table, he didn't hide his disapproval.

Edmund stood up and gestured for Dev Sahib to follow him to the corner, while the rest of the servants silently set up the meal.

"Dev Sahib, I must admit something to you that I did not share with the maharaja. It is not for discussion amongst polite company, but I trust that you will be discreet."

Dev Sahib nodded his dutiful agreement.

"Mr. Valov is not just my butler; he is my cousin. He is in the service of my household as a favor to my dear late aunt who left him penniless four years ago upon her tragic death (she married a Czech count, you see, whose title is thoroughly useless ever since the war). Jarek has endeavored to make himself useful to us in return for our kindness in taking him in, but he is really as royal as I am, which is why he holds such an unusually elevated status in our household."

"I see…" Dev Sahib looked thoughtful as he considered the intel. "But it is highly irregular in India for a servant to eat with his masters, my lord. What am I to tell the maharaja? Surely you do not expect your butler to take meals with you and the royal family?"

Mr. Valov stood up and slowly made his way over to them. "I know my place, Colonel. I will be more than happy to eat with the servants. Although, I would very much like to take advantage of your kind offer to let me sleep in the neighboring berth so that I can be of direct assistance to you."

"Is that acceptable to you, Dev Sahib?" Edmund asked.

"It is, my lord," Dev Sahib agreed.

As Mr. Valov's stomach growled, Edmund looked rather pleased that the embarrassing sound had come from someone other than him.

"I haven't eaten since I disembarked from the steamer," Mr. Valov admitted. "I don't take well to spices."

"Well, I have the solution for that problem, as well," Edmund said cheerfully. Eleanor found his diplomatic management of the situation to be strangely arousing. "The maharaja and his family are still hours away. I would like very much to use this time for baksheesh." He glanced out the window to the dirty fields just beyond the station filled with beggars and paupers going about their business in the baking mid-afternoon heat, clad in filthy rags.

"For baksheesh, my lord?" Dev Sahib asked confusedly.

Edmund switched into Hindi, and then into Marathi, and Dev Sahib didn't hide his surprise at Edmund's linguistic talents as he asked him a series of follow-up questions in Marathi. He looked increasingly bewildered as Edmund answered each one amicably. Eleanor could see Mr. Valov subtly squirming at his inability to understand what they were saying, until Edmund slapped Dev Sahib on the back, and he nodded his reluctant agreement.

"Mr. Valov, you should stay here with Eleanor and enjoy tea time on my behalf," Edmund suggested. "I will be outside giving alms to the poor. It is an old habit that I learned in my childhood in Hyderabad that I have not indulged in many years. Mr. Valov, if you will be kind enough to come and fetch me when the maharaja arrives, I will join you then, and you can return to your butling corner."

"Yes, Colonel," Mr. Valov agreed as he eyed the poor masses through the window.

"Dev Sahib, might you show me to our trunks? Sri Bidkar was kind enough to help me prepare a purse just for the occasion," Edmund asked politely.

Dev Sahib nodded his agreement and gestured for Edmund to follow him into the next carriage.

"Don't worry," Edmund reassured them. "You will both be able to keep an eye on me. I assume, dearest, that you don't wish to join me? It can be rather unpleasant out there."

Eleanor glanced again at the desperate paupers baking under the powerful noon sun. "I will be quite happy to stay here with Mr. Valov." She meant every word of it, although she was fascinated to watch Edmund go about his plan. The fact that he had explicitly prepared for the occasion made her even more curious.

As soon as Edmund and Dev Sahib disappeared into the guest suite, Mr. Valov sat down across from her in the place set for Edmund, and the servants who had served the tea service disappeared back into the kitchen, leaving them alone.

"I don't like his plan one bit." Mr. Valov slipped back into his natural British voice. "He is asking for trouble."

"You have to admit, he is far more comfortable here than you are," Eleanor pointed out.

"You're right. I'm already at my wit's end, and I've been off the boat for one day. I've never been anywhere that felt so foreign. For the first time since I was a junior officer, I have no bloody clue what I'm doing."

Eleanor poured Mr. Valov a cup of tea, and then she poured herself one.

"It is important for a man to recognize his own limitations. It is the only way to improve himself."

Mr. Valov drank down a long sip. As his stomach growled again, Eleanor smiled. "Please, eat whatever you'd like... Leopold? Is that really your name?"

"It is. My mother chose it. It is a Czech name as well as an English one. The lads back at school used to call me Leo, but it has been many decades since anyone has called me that... or Leopold, for that matter."

"Really?" Eleanor asked. "Not even your family?"

"Family is a luxury one gives up to join the Secret Service, Eleanor."

"You don't even keep in contact with your parents?"

Mr. Valov sighed with resignation. "My mother died when I was ten. My father lives in York, and we were never close. I am closer to you and Edmund than I ever was to my own family. If the agency knew that, I would be sacked and hanged."

Eleanor was somewhat taken aback by the idea. "How sad."

Mr. Valov gathered several tea sandwiches onto his plate with his hands and immediately ate two, following them up with another long sip of tea.

"I surmised that you were listening to my exchange with Edmund earlier. Really, Eleanor, you would've been an exceptional spy. It's a shame for Britain that women's talents are not taken nearly seriously enough."

"Yes, it is," Eleanor agreed, letting him change the subject as she collected several sandwiches for herself. "Although, I don't think I would have ever been willing to give up contact with my family, despite my mother's many faults. They are too much a part of who I am. It keeps me awake at night sometimes, thinking about how I'll deal with them when Edmund miraculously returns to youth."

"It keeps me awake at night too," Mr. Valov admitted.

"We will find a way to make it work. I hear Perth is beautiful, and we have an open invitation."

Mr. Valov finished his first cup of tea and poured himself another. "I meant what I said to Edmund this morning, Eleanor. Every word of it. I'm sorry for what I said yesterday, and I'm grateful that you reminded me of my priorities. I am not in my position because it is easy. I'm in my position because I am the best at what I do, and you were right that I wasn't acting worthy of my position, within the agency or within your household. I will attempt to rectify my errors from now on."

"I appreciate the sentiment, but really, Leo, was there a good reason for your intense distaste for our Indian wardrobe? I don't understand your aversion."

"Did you not see how those women were looking at you when you arrived at the station?" Mr. Valov asked as he ate another sandwich.

"I'm used to deflecting the evil eye. I've dealt with that since my infamous father shot himself in the streets of Edinburgh."

"Oh yes, the illustrious Robby MacLeod. I stumbled across that media circus as soon as Edmund brought you home to London. He was livid when I showed him the *Evening Herald* article about it. It was the closest I've ever come to getting myself sacked. It turned out you'd already told him your deepest, darkest secret. I knew then that things were about to change, although I didn't realize they would change so much. It is quite a task to keep up with you."

"Did you really think he'd have any reaction other than that?" Eleanor asked curiously. "Even if I hadn't told him, he isn't the type to care about the sins of the father... for good reason."

"He doesn't know that his father is a monster."

"Still, he thinks he's a bastard," Eleanor reminded him. "Bastards never have a particularly illustrious background, myself included. But you didn't answer my question, Leo. Were you skillfully misleading me away from it? Why were you so adamant that we wear the frumpiest British clothing you could find?"

Mr. Valov finished off his second cup of tea and refilled his third. "When there are unnecessary eyes on you, you are more likely to get caught doing things that you don't want people to know that you're doing, Eleanor. It is a fundamental lesson for spies, but it goes for Edmund too, for anyone with secrets that they don't want to have observed…"

He trailed off as they both watched Edmund tiptoe across the refuse, donning his absurd golden Rakshasa shoes (the same ones provided by the Bidkars' confused cobbler for their Elephanta trip, rather than the more tasteful ones that he had worn to the station from the Bidkars' final offering of clothing).

"Bloody hell." Mr. Valov shook his head with disapproval. "My case in point. He is going to have an ogling audience for his riot in no time, and then *I* will have to go clean up another mess in a country that I do not understand one bloody bit."

"Speaking of which, how exactly did you take care of our outstanding problem? Did you find the murderer?"

"I did what was necessary. The Bidkars will have nothing to worry about. Oh, and I also submitted the necessary paperwork for Edmund's lordship."

"I'm sorry, you did what?" Eleanor laughed, assuming he was being facetious.

"Ravi Bidkar referred to him last night at dinner as a lord. Why, though, is still a mystery to me, since Edmund himself was quick to deny it." Mr. Valov observed her reaction, and she settled into her tried and true stalemate poker face until he gave up. "Anyway, as I was saying, the Maharaja of Gwalior is one of the most well-connected maharajas in all of India. If anyone bothers to check, Edmund will be Lord Marriner, Earl of Easton from now on, and you will be Lady Marriner. Congratulations, my lady."

Before Eleanor could muster a response to the shocking development, she and Mr. Valov were equally distracted as a large crowd surrounded Edmund.

"Blimey," Eleanor whispered.

"Here we go," Mr. Valov muttered.

Edmund began handing out coins from a small pouch tied around his wrist to each person, closing his offerings into their hands, smiling, and chatting with them amicably with increasingly enthusiastic gestures on their part and on his.

As the crowd grew, he continued on with his alms, holding each and every person's hands as he gave them a coin, and as more and more people began arriving from every direction, Edmund's audience quickly fell into a disorganized approximation of a queue, rather than dissolving into a chaotic riot as Mr. Valov had predicted.

There was something about Edmund's peaceful demeanor that appeared to be contagious. It made him look especially saint-like, and as Eleanor glanced over to spy Mr. Valov's reaction, she could tell that he saw it too.

They sipped their tea in silence for quite some time, watching Edmund calmly manage the growing crowd.

"Eleanor, what was it that you meant yesterday, when you said that Edmund was Earth's future messiah?" Mr. Valov finally asked.

"I shouldn't have said anything."

"Did one of his guardians tell you something to that effect?" Mr. Valov pushed.

"Please do not interrogate me, Leo. You know that I am the most skilled civilian liar on the planet. If you are meant to know Edmund's secrets, they will be revealed to you in due course, just as they have been revealed to me."

Mr. Valov poured each of them another cup of tea, and they returned to watching Edmund in silence until the tea was long gone and Mr. Valov had finished up each and every morsel on the tiered silver tea tray.

Eventually, Dev Sahib returned to their carriage, but his eyes were also glued on Edmund through the window. Eleanor realized that he must have been watching the scene himself from the neighboring carriage.

"The maharaja and his family will be here shortly. Their motorcars have just arrived at the station," Dev Sahib said distractedly. "Jarek Sahib, please go fetch his lordship. Your shoes are waiting for you at the door of his carriage, and I will have the servants prepare an extra soapy cloth to wash him upon his return. Perhaps then you can help him change his clothes before he greets the royal family?"

Mr. Valov stood up and nodded his agreement. He bowed to Eleanor, but he and Eleanor both noticed Dev Sahib's change in tenor. He was now using a respectful address for Mr. Valov, and his reverence for Edmund was genuine, rather than polite as it had been before.

"Dev Sahib, my husband will probably be quite thirsty after so much time outside in the hot sun. Could you please have the servants prepare several carafes of water for him? Or perhaps several pots of tea?"

"Yes, yes, of course, my lady," Dev Sahib agreed, snapping himself out of his stupor. With a respectful bow, he backed into the kitchen.

Eleanor stood up and hopped out of the way, but kept her eyes focused on Edmund as a troop of servants rushed to collect the used dishes and clean up the table. Shortly, Mr. Valov appeared outside, attempting with great difficulty to push his way through the crowd.

Eleanor was startled as the door to the carriage flew open.

"I told you I'd beat you!" a young girl's voice squealed.

"No fair, you cheated!" a young boy countered.

As two plump, school-aged children, decked out in intensely beaded outfits that looked like miniature versions of the ones Ravi and Shruti had worn, rushed up the stairs into the carriage and threw themselves down in the thrones, flipping off their shoes and tossing them with their feet towards the kitchen carriage, Eleanor braced herself for the next storm.

Two servants rushed from the kitchen with washbasins and immediately began scrubbing their feet.

"Sherlock! Come here, boy!"

"Sherlock is mine, you can have Watson!"

"Sherlock isn't yours! Babu is yours! Sherlock is Papa's!"

Two fluffy tricolor cavalier king charles spaniels were dropped into the carriage by two servants, followed by a third servant who coaxed a macaque (clad in a regal outfit made up of a beaded crimson silk vest and matching poufy trousers, complete with a tiny turban) off of his shoulder and into the carriage. The servant slammed the door, blocking the children and the zoo inside alone with Eleanor and the two foot-washing servants.

The cavaliers barked excitedly as they rushed up to Eleanor and jumped up against her legs, while the macaque screeched and rushed across the floor to search for loose crumbs underneath the table.

"Hello, lads!" Eleanor cooed as she kneeled down to scratch the dogs' ears. At the attention, their barks became even more enthusiastic.

Both children startled and stood up from their foot baths to stare at her, spilling soapy water all over the floor to the great chagrin of the servants.

"Geez, Georgie, she really is paler than Queen Mary!" the girl exclaimed.

"Silence!" the maharaja boomed as he entered the compartment from the guest carriage.

The dogs sat. The children stood up straight. The foot-washing servants rushed back into the kitchen, and the macaque hopped into the corner under a chair.

It was only at that moment that it occurred to Eleanor for the first time that perhaps a public train would have been perfectly sufficient.

CHAPTER 12 – LORD AND LADY MARRINER'S DEBUT

"You must forgive my children, Lady Marriner. They must be reminded of their manners on occasion, just like the dogs." The maharaja glanced disapprovingly at his children as he spoke. "Their governess has taken ill and is remaining in Bombay indefinitely, and so it falls on me to remind them."

"Sorry, Papa," the girl said quietly with her eyes averted.

"Sorry, Papa," the boy added in exactly the same fashion.

"You must address your apologies to Lady Marriner for your callous remark," he said sternly.

"I'm sorry, my lady," the girl said with a curtsy. "Being paler than Queen Mary wasn't meant as an insult. You look like a porcelain doll!"

"Tsk!" The maharaja's face turned red. "Do we ever comment on how people look, Anya?"

"No, Papa. I'm sorry."

The macaque slowly came out from under the chair, and Anya coaxed it up her arm and onto her shoulder.

"Really, it's quite alright," Eleanor said as she straightened her posture to address the maharaja, hoping to end the disciplinary session. "You are not the first to notice my resemblance to a doll. My red hair is often a topic of conversation, not just in India, but back home in Scotland as well."

"Well, Lady Marriner, you are far too forgiving," the maharaja said as the dogs relaxed and began panting. "Now, may I introduce my children, Georgie and Anya."

They both offered her polite *namastes*.

"Georgie and Anya, meet Lady Eleanor Marriner, Countess of Easton." Eleanor's eyes bulged at his immediate use of the false title Mr. Valov had seemingly cooked up on a whim in the middle of the night.

"You can just call me Eleanor," she suggested.

"Yes, yes, what fun it was to use our first names at dinner last night. Perhaps we should continue it for the rest of our journey," the maharaja agreed amicably.

"This is King Babu," Anya added as she wiggled her finger in a subtle command and the monkey bowed regally from his perch on her shoulder.

Eleanor laughed. "King Babu? King of what?"

"He's the king of our zoo," Georgie said as he joined their conversation. "I crowned him myself!"

"Where is Edmund?" the maharaja asked as he suddenly noticed his conspicuous absence.

"He is… er… outside giving alms to the poor," Eleanor said as she glanced out the window. Mr. Valov still had not managed to make his way through the crowd.

"He's doing *what*?" The maharaja crouched down to look out the window for himself, and his children joined him. "Good lord…"

"Mr. Valov is trying to rally him, but it looks like he isn't assertive enough to make his way through the crowd… Clearly, he's never been at an Edinburgh pub for last call," Eleanor attempted to lighten the mood.

"Jaap Sahib!" the maharaja boomed.

His guard rushed in from the guest carriage.

"Go relieve Mr. Valov of his duty at once and inform Lord Marriner that we are ready to leave…" He paused as he watched Edmund coo at a baby and then give an extra coin to its mother. "At his earliest convenience."

"Yes, Your Highness," Jaap Sahib agreed. He rushed straight back to where he'd come from.

"What is all this noise?" the maharani asked as she passed Jaap Sahib in the hallway to greet them. "You are looking lovely again today, Eleanor. The British cats at the station must have been going positively mad when they saw you."

"But…" Anya moved to protest, surely at her mother's immediate thwarting of the rule to not comment on how people look, but the maharaja threw her such an intense look of disapproval that she stopped herself before another word came out of her mouth.

"They did look quite shocked," Eleanor admitted. "Although the Indian women seemed to be similarly interested in the novelty of my fashion choices."

"I'm sure they were!" The maharani dropped her amicable tone as her husband grabbed her hand and directed her attention out the window. "What is it, Madho Rao? Is something wrong? Good lord…"

Mr. Valov looked intensely relieved as Jaap Sahib took his place, gently but forcefully working his way through the crowd. When he finally reached Edmund, Edmund nodded his acknowledgment, glanced towards the train offering a subtle apology for his tardiness, and then he worked his way through the crowd, giving coins to everyone left in the orderly queue, and ignoring those who had crowded in behind him in an effort to skip to the front.

Eleanor rushed into the guest car to greet him, and the maharaja's family (and his zoo) followed.

Edmund hopped up the stairs and took his position next to Mr. Valov in one of the thrones, thanking the servants in Hindi as they took his shoes and scurried away. "I knew those absurd jester slippers would come in handy as soon as I saw them!"

Eleanor could feel his excitement in the air, and his power, normally a gentle, pulsating hum, was bursting off of him in waves that almost overwhelmed her.

"Oh Eleanor, did you see how happy they were? I had so many wonderful conversations. It was just like my childhood when Abdul Barr and I would give alms by the Mecca Masjid on Fridays. We will go there in a few weeks, when we reach Hyderabad."

"It looked like everyone was having the time of their lives, darling," Eleanor said as four servants arrived. Two carried basins of soapy water, while two more carried steaming towels. Edmund looked surprisingly natural as he let the servants do their duties. Mr. Valov, on the other hand, worked to hide his bewilderment while he kept a hawk's eye on the reactions of the servants who were dealing with Edmund's unusually absorbent skin.

Madho Rao and Rane approached, standing behind Eleanor to watch the scene with a bit too much interest for Eleanor's comfort.

"I'm sorry to keep you waiting. I hope I didn't inconvenience you?" Edmund asked as he noticed their attention.

"Please, do not think of it for one moment. Dev Sahib is informing the station master that we wish to depart. It will probably be at least ten minutes until they can accommodate us," Madho Rao reassured him. "Edmund, my lord, I would like you to meet my children, Georgie and Anya."

Rane coaxed the children in front of her, but as the monkey spied Edmund (and Edmund spied the monkey), it began screaming a high-pitched, blood-curdling screech, and he cringed.

"That is enough!" Madho Rao shouted.

The monkey did not heed his command. Instead, it screamed and screamed, scrambling across Anya's shoulders to get away from Edmund while Anya and Georgie began screaming, until the same servant who had dropped it off in the carriage several minutes earlier rushed to the rescue, grabbing the creature and whisking it away into the children's carriage.

"Please forgive us, Colonel," Madho Rao said testily as he eyed the direction of the monkey's keeper. "It is usually a well-behaved monkey, as monkeys go, at least."

"Monkeys and I do not tend to get along." Edmund threw Eleanor a knowing look. "It would be best, I think, to keep him away from me for everyone's sake, especially his."

"Yes, yes, of course. It will stay in the children's carriage for the remainder of the journey," Madho Rao agreed. "Jaap Sahib! Make sure that monkey stays in the children's carriage!"

"Yes, Your Highness," Jaap Sahib called from somewhere in a neighboring carriage.

As the servants finished up their washing ritual, Edmund stood up to officially greet the maharaja's children.

"Shall we try this again? Edmund, my lord, might I present my son, Georgie, and my daughter, Anya," the maharaja said as he nudged his children forward. They offered another round of *namastes*.

"I'm named after the king!" Georgie declared.

"Why I suppose I must be too, then. George is my middle name," Edmund replied amicably.

"Which King George would that be?" Madho Rao asked. "The mad one or his dandy son?"

"Madho Rao," Rane hissed.

"Yes, I suppose neither of those Georges were particularly worthy of being one's namesake. Perhaps then I was named after a different George. I suspect there were many millions to choose from."

Eleanor could see the wheels turning in his head as the idea that his middle name possibly reflected his father's name occurred to him for the first time, and she glanced at Mr. Valov who was doing an admirable job of concealing his concern.

As Madho Rao realized his faux pas in insulting two of Britain's former monarchs at once, he cleared his throat and returned to seriousness. "Georgie and Anya, this is Lord Edmund Marriner, Earl of Easton."

"Am I?" Edmund asked with a combination of confusion, skepticism, and curiosity. "Did Ravi tell you that?"

"Oh yes, I understand." Madho Rao placed his finger on his nose. "Mum's the word. We've already decided for the rest of the journey to use our given names like old friends, unless that is too presumptuous?"

"I would absolutely prefer it," Edmund agreed as he threw Eleanor a subtle questioning look.

As Dev Sahib approached from the dining carriage, the dogs rushed into the hallway, straight to Edmund.

"I see we haven't met the whole family yet!" he exclaimed as he squatted down to rub their ears. He laughed as they licked his face.

"This is Sherlock and Watson," Georgie introduced them on his father's behalf. "Sherlock is Papa's, but Watson is mine!"

"He is not!" Anya exclaimed. "He's Mummy's!"

"Sshhh," Rane hissed.

"They must be excellent at solving mysteries," Edmund said diplomatically, calming all of them at once with his subtle air of authority. He led the dogs through a series of standard commands, eliciting a perfectly parallel sit, lie down, stay and release from both of them at once.

"Good lord, they've never been so obedient," Rane whispered. "Perhaps you should keep them, Colonel."

"What?! No!" the children protested in unison.

"They just need a firm but supportive hand," Edmund said as he scratched their ears affectionately. "Just like army cadets."

"And children," Madho Rao agreed.

"Oh, Madho Rao," Rane whispered disapprovingly. "How many times have I told you not to compare our children to dogs?"

"Too many to keep track, lovey."

Eleanor was mesmerized by watching Edmund interact with the dogs, who looked as if they had fallen thoroughly in love with him as their tongues hung out of the sides of their mouths. They rolled onto their backs, presenting their tummies for rubbing, but as she felt another bout of lightheadedness from a burst of love emanating off of him, she leaned on Rane for support.

"Are you alright, Eleanor?" Rane asked. "Perhaps you should sit down. It has been quite hot today. Dev Sahib, please ask them to turn down the temperature of the mechanical cooling system."

"So that's why it's been so comfortable in here," Eleanor murmured as she regained her strength. "The wonders of technology can solve any problem these days…"

"Yes, Your Highness," Dev Sahib agreed with a bow. "We will be departing shortly. If you will be kind enough to seat yourselves in the dining car, lunch will commence as soon as the train is moving."

Edmund noticed Eleanor's weakness and rushed to her side. "Are you alright, Eleanor? Is it the heat again?"

The dogs followed him dutifully.

"I'm perfectly fine," she insisted. "But, Edmund, darling, I think you must be parched after all that time in the sun. Don't you want some water?"

Dev Sahib clapped his hands, and two servants, each carrying a carafe of water, rushed to his side.

"My lord, if you will be so kind as to take your first serving of water in here and then change your clothes before entering the family car, we will be most grateful." Dev Sahib glanced nervously at the maharaja as he made his suggestion.

"Change my clothes?" Edmund asked.

"So as to not bring the filth from outside… inside." Dev Sahib shifted uncomfortably as he explained euphemistically what he really meant.

"Right, okay then," Edmund agreed as it occurred to him that they found his close physical contact with the paupers outside to be unclean. "Mr. Valov, perhaps you can help me navigate our trunks for an acceptable alternative."

"Eleanor will have better judgment than I do on the fashions, Colonel, but I am happy to be of assistance," Mr. Valov demurred.

"I will help you, darling," Eleanor agreed.

"Please, take your time," the maharaja suggested. "We will have two and a half days together on this train. There is no need to hurry."

With nods of acknowledgement all around, the maharaja and his family left them alone, whispering with Dev Sahib as they went, leaving only the two young servant boys who dutifully stood in position presenting their carafes of water to Edmund and the two dogs who awaited his next command.

Edmund watched to make sure his audience had disappeared, and then he drank down the first carafe in one long Rakshasa gulp. The servant boy watched with wonder, but said nothing, and Edmund moved on to his second. When he was finished, he said something to the servants in Hindi, and they scampered off to follow the maharaja.

"Come, Colonel, I will show you your choices," Mr. Valov said with a hint of new humility as he led them to their trunks, which were now stacked neatly side by side inside of a large closet. He kneeled down and began pulling the colorful Indian kurtas out one by one, and Eleanor appreciated that he had finally given up on his mission to pressure them into British frumpiness.

"How about that one?" Eleanor suggested as Mr. Valov pulled out a brocade crimson vest, paired with a loose linen shirt and trousers. "It looks more comfortable than the ones you've been wearing, don't you think, darling?"

"I find all of them to be more comfortable than a British suit," he admitted. "But I do quite like that one. It is similar to what I wore as a boy in Hyderabad."

Mr. Valov handed Edmund the stack. "There is a dressing room just there, next to your berth. There is a door inside of it to the WC, which has a washbasin but no shower or bath, and from the WC, you can also go directly into your berth—it sits between the bedroom and the dressing room... a rather clever idea for your privacy, I have to say."

The dogs charged after Edmund as he headed towards the dressing room to change his clothes.

"Have I unwittingly mutinied the command of this zoo, my furry friends?" He laughed as he let them into the dressing room with him and closed the door.

"Eleanor, I have something for you," Mr. Valov whispered as soon as Edmund was out of earshot.

Eleanor pushed back a pang of embarrassment as Mr. Valov dug through stacks of her underwear in the other trunk, but then she gasped with a combination of surprise and excitement as he pulled out a small silver pistol.

"I took so long on the ship partly because I was procuring this for you," Mr. Valov whispered. "You've proven you know how to use it already, so I assume I don't have to show you."

Eleanor took it from him and held it up to examine it. "I hope this doesn't demonstrate your secret knowledge of another enemy?"

"You've fought off muggers, revolutionaries, pirates, and spies in just two weeks, Eleanor. I think it's safe to assume that there will be more enemies to come."

"I suppose you're right..." She aimed it at the edge of the closet. "Did you give this to me in secret so that Edmund wouldn't know I have it?"

"You can tell him what you want, Eleanor. I wanted to give you the choice. You are better at anticipating his reactions than I am."

Eleanor was flattered by the concession.

"But, Eleanor…" Mr. Valov trailed off, rethinking his next words.

"Yes? You aren't going to start up again about Edmund being our murderer, are you? I don't want to be tempted to use this gun on you." She winked to make sure he knew she wasn't serious, but when he shifted uncomfortably, her friendly jab morphed into actual disappointment. "Really, Leo, are we still on about this? He didn't bloody do it!"

Mr. Valov lowered his voice into a barely audible whisper. "I am not worried about Edmund anymore, but Edmund is not the only one of his kind… Eleanor, the way the bodies were torn apart… We've seen it before. It is how several of George IV's enemies at court were found dead in their homes… It happened to several advisors who were conspiring to have Edmund's mother quietly and permanently removed from the scene."

Eleanor's mind raced at the many unpleasant implications of the suggestion. She focused on the most mundane to start with. "Do you mean that the advisors were going to have her killed?"

"They believed that another child from another affair would destabilize the crown too much. But they were dismembered long before she actually became pregnant. Their concern was a general one based on his growing affection for her. They were not in the group who knew his true identity."

"And you think Edmund's father, the ancient Rakshasa King of Lanka who quietly steals the thrones of the most powerful nations on Earth is following us, offering brutal death to random hooligans who inconvenience us?"

"I think it is a possibility that we must consider. As far as we are aware, Edmund is his only living child, which would make him his heir. If somehow Edmund's guardians gave away his

234

whereabouts, it would not be out of character for Edmund's father to come to take what's his."

"Blimey," Eleanor whispered. "But a gun isn't enough to stop Edmund or his guardians. Surely it won't be enough to stop his evil father."

"It will slow him down long enough for you to call for backup. If it is him, you must call for Kuveni and Mélusine immediately. You will need all the help you can get."

"But how will I carry around a weapon like this? I have no pockets and no purse most of the time."

Mr. Valov lifted up his foot and rested it on the edge of the trunk. He pulled up the cuff of his right trouser leg to show Eleanor a small pistol strapped to his leg.

"I always carry a gun, and no one has ever discovered it. As long as you are wearing trousers, you should be able to do the same. If you'd like, I can procure some similar straps for you."

"Thank you, Leo. Yes… yes, please do." Eleanor was touched by his support.

"I will have to figure out where to find something of the sort in this godforsaken country, but I will do it as soon as I can."

As the door to the dressing room flung open and the dogs came charging out, Mr. Valov scrambled to pull down his trouser-leg. Edmund laughed as he watched the dogs rush straight to Eleanor, but as he noticed the pistol in her hand, his joviality dissolved. She breathed in a deep sigh of relief that he hadn't seemed to notice Mr. Valov's compromising position.

"Darling, Mr. Valov thought that perhaps I should keep this gun just in case we run into trouble like we did on the steamer. Isn't it adorable?" She hoped to deflect his anxiety with feigned cheer.

"It is dangerous," Edmund countered. "More people have been accidentally shot by their own guns than thugs have ever been warded off."

Eleanor was annoyed by his response. "Does that mean that you don't trust me to use it responsibly? Do you have less faith in me than you had in the thousands of teenaged boys you inducted into the army over the decades? Did you tell any of them that guns were too dangerous?"

As Edmund struggled for a response, she caught a look of subtle respect in Mr. Valov's eyes at her tactic, and she didn't like it one bit. She did not want a seasoned spy to be impressed by her ability to manipulate her husband.

"That's not what I meant," Edmund replied.

"Then what did you mean?" Eleanor felt her fiery temper working its way to the surface, as she was quite sure that, in fact, that was exactly what he'd meant.

"Eleanor, everyone knew how to act around guns in the army. *Everyone.* If someone stumbles across this weapon here, they might accidentally shoot themselves or someone else. What if the children found it?"

She hated to admit that he had a valid point.

"I will lock it into your trunk, Eleanor," Mr. Valov offered. "I will put it with your jewelry in the top compartment. Does that suit you, Colonel?"

Eleanor could see that Edmund was still struggling with the idea of her carrying a gun, but Mr. Valov had cornered him, and she was grateful.

"Yes, I suppose that will work for now. I hope you won't need to use it, Eleanor."

"Me too, darling. Now, let's not keep the maharaja waiting."

She handed the gun to Mr. Valov with a subtle nod of thanks, and then she took her husband's surprisingly warm hand into hers and led him into the family carriage, followed by their two fluffy new companions.

"But, Papa, we don't need a new governess! I'm almost eleven years old!"

"I will not hear any more protestations. Do you want me to send you to boarding school in England where even the dirtiest servants will think they're your superiors?"

"No, sir."

"Then we will begin the search for your next governess as soon as we reach home. In the meantime, you will behave yourself with the conduct expected of a royal position like yours. That goes for you too, Anya. No more shouting. No more running indoors. No more rude commentary."

"Yes, Papa. But... is Memsahib Jyoti going to be alright?"

"You needn't think about Memsahib Jyoti ever again," Rane interjected. "God will see that she faces the appropriate consequences for her irresponsible actions. God *always* punishes those who deserve it."

Anya whimpered, and Madho Rao threw his wife a disapproving look.

"But Mummy, Memsahib Jyoti was so nice!" Georgie protested. "Why would God punish her?"

"That is between her and God," Rane replied haughtily. "Now, no more questions."

Eleanor squeezed Edmund's hand, hoping that he would notice the suspicious tone of the conversation they were overhearing, but the dogs rushed around them, alerting their hosts to their presence, and her few moments of spying came to an abrupt end.

"Ah, I see your tour of our local fashions continues, Edmund!" Madho Rao exclaimed with just a bit too much enthusiasm as he jumped out of his seat and escorted them to the dining table, which had already been set with silver for six.

Edmund looked down at his vest with satisfaction. "It has been too long since I've had the privilege."

"Come, Lord and Lady Marriner, please sit. We are all quite famished. It has been an unusually trying day," Rane urged.

"Unusually trying? How unfortunate! Has something unpleasant happened?" Eleanor asked casually.

As Edmund and Eleanor joined the royal family, Mr. Valov took his official position in the corner (with a subtle sarcastic flourish that only Eleanor recognized), and Eleanor focused her attention on assessing the discomfort of their hosts at the prospect of answering her straightforward question.

After too long of a pause, Madho Rao finally gathered his wits for a response. "The children's governess has fallen ill. She has been with us since Georgie was born. It is very unfortunate that we will need to find a replacement, but sometimes these things are unavoidable. Now, let us not speak of such mundane problems. Sri Bidkar tells us that you command the Household Cavalry back in London, Edmund? Anya and Georgie are both quite interested in horses. Perhaps you can tell us all about your interesting work."

"Well, there isn't much to talk about, really," Edmund demurred. "But Eleanor grew up surrounded by the best horses in the world. Her father was a thoroughbred trainer back in Scotland."

Eleanor's heart jumped into her throat at his reference. She hoped that they wouldn't ask any follow-up questions that would reveal that she was one of the infamous Robby MacLeod's fiery bastards. Edmund felt her tense, and he squeezed her hand in apology.

"I want to be a thoroughbred trainer!" Anya exclaimed.

"You will be a maharani," Rane countered authoritatively.

Anya sat back in her chair, crossed her arms, and sulked.

"Scotland was a wonderful place to train horses," Eleanor said politely. She was beginning to dislike Rane, as she sensed a certain type of self-righteousness that reminded her far too much of her mother. She fought off the feeling. "I used to ride the finest thoroughbreds in the Empire as a lass…"

Eleanor skillfully avoided the topic of her father as she initiated their requested conversation about thoroughbreds, and

Edmund chimed in every so often with his supportive opinions until the servants rushed in from the kitchen car and served them each a dainty portion of daal in silver bowls.

Edmund's stomach growled especially loudly, and Eleanor realized he'd gone all day without a bite to eat (she was thoroughly impressed by his lack of complaining on the matter), but as he observed the bright yellow color of the lentils and brought the bowl to his nose for a somewhat uncouth sniff, he sneezed three times in a row, barely putting the bowl down without spilling it all over the table. As soon as he got himself under control, his posture deflated. "There is turmeric in that daal, isn't there?"

"Why, of course there is, my lord," Dev Sahib replied as he moved in from his observational corner to address him. "Turmeric is important for digestion. It is one of the healthiest spices in the world."

Edmund prepared himself to deliver the bad news. "Perhaps it is for everyone else, but I learned long ago that I have a wicked allergy to it. I promise you wholeheartedly that none of us want to experience what happens when I consume it." Eleanor snorted at the understatement. "I hope that my deficiency will not cause you too much trouble? Is there anything in the kitchen that does not have turmeric in it?"

Eleanor could not have been more grateful that Edmund had noticed the detail before a horrific revelation, and as she glanced over to Mr. Valov, she noticed his appreciation of Edmund's foresight as well.

"I'm sorry, old friend, turmeric is the backbone of Indian cooking," Madho Rao replied. "We have the staff use it for all of our meals. Sri Bidkar should have warned us."

"Please do not hold him at fault. It is my frustrating deficiency. I have missed out on many mouth-watering dishes over the years with this irritating constraint."

"Dev Sahib, is there anything the colonel will be able to eat in the kitchen?" Madho Rao asked.

"Certainly not," Dev Sahib replied.

"Perhaps we can stop at the next station, and the staff can collect some food from the market?" Anya interjected.

"What a thoughtful suggestion!" Eleanor exclaimed, genuinely impressed by the young girl's empathy for his plight.

"I suppose that is one solution," Rane said unenthusiastically. "It will set us back by hours."

Edmund looked utterly put out by the development. "Please, do not let me be a burden to you."

"Are there any more of those tea sandwiches that you served earlier?" Eleanor asked as the thought occurred to her.

"I suppose we could make some more," Dev Sahib agreed.

"Then do it!" Madho Rao boomed, startling Eleanor with his sharp tone. "Lord Marriner must have something to eat while we take our meal!"

"Yes, Your Highness." Dev Sahib bowed and rushed into the kitchen.

"Please, do not wait for me to begin." Edmund's face was a deeper red blush than Eleanor had ever seen it.

The royal family was not convinced by his plea, and so she tasted a spoonful of daal, offering them the signal they needed to begin their meals while Edmund watched miserably.

"So, you were telling us about how much painful, dirty work it is to train horses, Eleanor?" Rane asked the loaded question with a knowing glance towards her daughter.

"One might put it that way, yes. But I find that there is great value in hard work. It gives me a sense of accomplishment and meaning impossible to achieve by any other means."

Eleanor smiled to herself at her excellent retort, and the group continued on with their polite conversation as the staff served Edmund a heaping plate of cucumber sandwiches while switching the rest of the group to the second course. Edmund gazed longingly at the aromatic fish curry that filled the plates of his fellow diners as he gobbled down his first sandwich in one

Rakshasa bite, to the silent entertainment of Georgie and Anya, whose muffled giggles at the sight served as a pleasant contrast to Rane's subtle expression of disapproval.

After what felt like hours of work to keep the conversation going while Edmund slowed his pace to eat each sandwich in a perfect impression of a well-mannered human diner, Eleanor noticed Mr. Valov shifting uncomfortably in his position in the corner, and she decided that they'd all had enough.

"This has been a thoroughly enjoyable meal, but I am rather tired. I think I would like to take a wee cat nap," she declared.

"Yes, the children should rest as well," Rane agreed.

"But, Mummy!" they protested in unison.

Rane hissed her disapproval in Hindi, and they mumbled their agreement.

Eleanor stood up and took Edmund's hand. "Shall we, darling?"

"Please, relax and take your time. There is very little to do on the long journey," Madho Rao suggested. "We will schedule an extra stop to collect food for you in Thane, Edmund."

"Please, do not trouble yourself," Edmund suggested (rather disingenuously, as he would obviously need something to eat for the next two days).

"It is no trouble at all!" Madho Rao replied, again with a bit too much enthusiasm.

"Well, I thank you kindly for accommodating my deficiency."

"It is nothing," Madho Rao reiterated.

Eleanor nodded her thanks and then guided Edmund straight into the guest car. She yawned as soon as Mr. Valov followed them inside, accompanied by the two cavaliers. He shut the door behind them as the dogs took their position seated before Edmund, awaiting his next command with enthusiastic panting.

"That was the most interminable meal of my life," she sighed.

"I found it thoroughly unsatisfying," Edmund grumbled. "That damn turmeric got me again."

He rubbed the dogs' ears as a consolation.

"We're all lucky you were so proactive, darling. It would have really gotten you if you hadn't noticed it was there until it was too late."

Edmund commanded the dogs to lie down before him with a subtle gesture. "You're right. I will need to be even more careful from now on. I've been away from India for so long that I've gotten out of the habit of asking. The consequences will be worse than ever if I slip."

As Eleanor sensed his anxiety tick up at the thought, she stood on her tiptoes and kissed him gently on the lips. "Mr. Valov and I will both be here to help you remember, darling. You aren't alone anymore."

Edmund pulled her into a passionate embrace, and she almost collapsed with a bout of lightheadedness at his effusion of love.

"Are you alright, dearest?" he asked as she leaned on him for support.

"Perfectly fine, darling. I'm just too tired. I didn't sleep well at all last night with the excitement of everything that happened yesterday."

"Shall we explore our berth, then?" Edmund suggested as he guided her towards a mahogany door.

"Biordinar!" Eleanor exclaimed as he pulled it open. "This must be the most luxurious train on Earth! I might be ruined for life."

A king-sized bed with an enormous mound of silk pillows awaited them inside the largest moving bedroom she'd ever seen. An ostentatious crystal chandelier over the bed tinkled with the rumbling movement of the train, and there was even room in the corner for a rocking chair with an electric reading light that protruded directly from the wall. Thick silk curtains blocked all of the outside light, and the temperature was just as wonderfully cool as the rest of the train cars had been with the help of the magical mechanical cooling system (which you, Ellie, would certainly recognize as a prototype of a modern air-conditioner—a marvel only available to the top tier of privilege back in 1923).

"How extraordinary," Edmund said excitedly. "I won't have to curl up like a dog to fit in the bed!"

At his cue, their fluffy entourage proved their intelligence by racing each other straight onto the middle of the bed. Edmund and Eleanor both laughed at the sight, but Mr. Valov was less amused.

"You don't know where those mongrels have been. It's filthy outside, you know, and dogs roll around in god-knows-what…" he grumbled.

"Oh, come now, Mr. Valov, you are not a fan of dogs, I take it? Those dogs look cleaner than we are!" Edmund dove onto the bed and giggled as the dogs pounced right on top of him, and then he sighed nostalgically as they cuddled right up against his sides. If the sight hadn't been so adorable, Eleanor might have felt a pang of jealousy as they stretched out to fill her favorite spot in the nook of his arm. "I miss having dogs around. They were my sole companions for forty lonely years in Basingstoke."

As Eleanor assessed the space on the bed left for her, Edmund's expression turned to concern. "They haven't usurped you, dearest. I will make room." He nudged them both to the foot of the bed and gestured for her to join him in her favorite spot. "You do like dogs, don't you, Eleanor?"

Eleanor nestled into his nook. "I love them, darling. We had them until my father died, and then when we moved to the one-room cottage, my mother made us give them away. I haven't had any since."

Edmund kissed her on the forehead. "Perhaps when our honeymoon is over, we will procure some fine puppies to join us in Basingstoke."

"I would love that, darling," Eleanor said as she took in a deep, relaxing breath. Her aching joints from her night of tossing and turning immediately began to settle, and she glanced over to

Mr. Valov who was watching them with an expression that she couldn't quite identify. Some combination of sadness and joy.

"Knock on the door of the other berth if you need me, Colonel. I will try to catch up on my sleep now," Mr. Valov said with a bow.

"Sleep well, Leopold," Edmund declared.

"And you… Lord and Lady Marriner." Mr. Valov smiled at his little joke, and before Edmund could comment, he closed the door and left them alone.

"I will have to ask Ravi about how that misnomer came to be," Edmund said with a wide yawn.

"Does it really matter?" Eleanor asked as she closed her eyes, focusing all of her attention on the lulling rumble of the train.

"I suppose not…" Edmund trailed off.

And so, alongside their two fluffy companions, on the most luxurious train in the world, Lord and Lady Marriner slept.

CHAPTER 13 – ON THE PLATFORM

Eleanor awoke to the chirpy warning bark of one of the dogs at the foot of the bed. Edmund stirred, and the other dog sat up straight and growled his own warning. The train was completely still. Eleanor had no idea where they were or how long they'd slept, and she hated the disoriented feeling.

"Georgie, we're going to be in so much trouble," Anya hissed from the hallway just outside the closed door to their berth. Eleanor looked down in a panic, and relaxed slightly as she noticed that she and Edmund were still fully clothed.

"This is our only chance to explore, Anya! When have we ever been stopped at a station all night long?"

"You heard Dev Sahib. We ran out of coal, and we have to wait until morning for the delivery. Papa was already angry, but now he will be furious if he catches us!"

"Where's your sense of adventure, Anya? Tonight is our only chance in a lifetime to be explorers! Papa will replace Memsahib Jyoti, and then we'll have another governess watching our every move! And then you'll get married off to some fat old maharaja…"

"No, I won't! I'll run away just like Indira Devi did!" Anya countered. "I won't marry anyone I don't want to! I'll be a famous thoroughbred trainer and make my own way in the world! Even Queen Mary said that I was a horse whisperer."

"Queen Mary was just flattering you, Anya. She was flattering Papa by complimenting you when your riding was only mediocre at best. Ow! Hey!" A sisterly slap echoed through the corridor.

"Was that mediocre too?" Anya asked snarkily. "Ow! You can't hit a girl!"

"Watch me!"

As the sibling slapping in the hallway escalated, Eleanor reached up and pulled the thick silk curtain away from the window to spy their position. It was dark, and the train was parked on a platform of a small station. Flickering gas lanterns hung from an old-fashioned wooden awning, and an old man with a cane propped up between his legs sat sleeping on a bench. A large Victorian clock read a quarter to four. Eleanor couldn't believe they'd slept so long, although it had felt like weeks since she'd had a proper night's sleep.

As the friendly fight continued with louder banging and squeals, Edmund took in his awakening Rakshasa breath and sat up. "What is it, dearest? Is something wrong?"

"I don't think so." Eleanor coaxed him into lying back down. "The children are having a sibling spat in the hallway."

"Why aren't they in their own carriage?" He welcomed her back into the nook of his arm.

"I believe they are using our carriage as a shortcut to sneak off the train and explore the station by moonlight."

"Do you think we should we stop them?"

"It seems rather harmless to me. My sisters and I wandered about the fields of Elphinstone looking for fairies by moonlight quite often, and nothing ever happened to us. But what do you think, darling? You know India far better than I do."

"It depends where we are. Certainly there are neighborhoods where children shouldn't go wandering about at night. But I myself have spent many a night on a platform bench after missing the last train of the day."

"I have no idea where we are. Do you, darling?" Eleanor sat up and propped open the curtain to show him the station.

"It looks rather commonplace to me. There are hundreds of stations like this across India now. It doesn't look particularly dangerous."

They both watched as Anya and Georgie stumbled down the stairs from the guest carriage onto the platform, still clad in the formal beaded outfits they'd been wearing earlier in the day, although the buttons of Georgie's shirt were askew, indicating that he had redressed himself hastily in the dark. Anya wrapped her dupatta around herself and shivered, even though it did not look particularly cold outside.

The old man sleeping on the bench startled and opened his eyes, and then leaned on his cane as he stood up and hobbled away, muttering to himself. The children were oblivious to their observers as they tiptoed past Edmund and Eleanor's window to check that all of the guards were inside the train sleeping soundly.

Eleanor smiled at their childish choice, as Georgie pulled King Babu out of his vest and let the macaque climb up onto his shoulder.

"There you go, boy. You don't have to stay locked up either," Georgie whispered.

King Babu screeched and swung down Georgie's sleeve onto the ground. He squatted down and relieved himself right there on the platform.

Eleanor couldn't help but laugh at the sight. "What a disciplined monkey!"

"Disciplined? He looks rather mischievous to me," Edmund grumbled.

"He must not have gone at all while he was locked up in the children's carriage all day and night," Eleanor explained. "Besides, not all monkeys are your enemies, darling. We met a few just yesterday who came to realize you were their... er... friend." Eleanor narrowly avoided saying what she really meant... that those monkeys at Elephanta had realized that Edmund was their *lord*.

"Perhaps you can remind King Babu of that the next time you chat, preferably while I am elsewhere, not getting screeched at."

Eleanor snuck a kiss. "I will, darling. I'm sure he'll come around."

Anya looked down at the monkey's refuse and then looked guiltily back at the train. "Georgie, this is a bad idea! Now there's evidence that we were out here! If Jaap Sahib catches us, we'll be hanged!"

"Aw, come on. You're just scared. Just like a girl."

"I am not!"

"Prove it! Clean up King Babu's poop!"

"Ew! You're the one who brought him out here. You do it!"

"No you!"

"No you!"

More slapping ensued as the children made their way across the platform, farther and farther from the train... and King Babu's mess. King Babu followed them, deviating from their path to sniff around for dropped morsels, and then catching up and climbing back up Georgie's arm. Georgie left Anya alone by the closed window to the ticket office as he skipped to the edge of the small building and peered around the corner.

"Looks boring." He turned back towards his sister and glanced around the station. "I guess it's more interesting than this spot. I'm going to see what the front of the station looks like. This alleyway looks like it goes through."

"Georgie, don't! It could be dangerous!"

Georgie disappeared around the corner, and Anya sighed with discomfort and walked straight up to the door of the station. She pulled hard on the handle, but it was locked. She muttered curses in Hindi, and then followed him around the corner, into the darkness.

Edmund sighed with resignation and sat up, dangling his legs off the side of the bed.

"They should not go wandering about alone in the dark streets of an unknown city at night. I will go alert Jaap Sahib."

"Is that really necessary, darling?" Eleanor asked, feeling perhaps a bit too much empathy for their desire to escape their heavy destiny with a harmless nighttime adventure.

"Eleanor, if they were our children, and our guests caught them doing something foolish and dangerous, would you not want them to intervene?"

"I suppose…" It was the first time in her life that Eleanor was forced to truly empathize with the parents rather than the children. "But surely we don't need to involve Jaap Sahib. Perhaps we can go wrangle them ourselves."

"Eleanor, please, let me go alone. It could be dangerous for you." Edmund stood up and checked that his clothing was all in acceptable order.

Eleanor laughed as she felt the heat rush into her face alongside her fiery temper. "Darling, for the sake of our marriage, I will pretend that you didn't just say that."

She stood up and walked straight to the door. "Are you coming?"

Edmund shrugged his concession, and as the dogs tried to follow him out into the hallway, he gently nudged them back into the berth and closed the door.

"We will be back after the mystery is solved, my friends," he whispered apologetically as the dogs voiced their disapproval with high pitched whining.

As they made their way through the dimly lit hallway, Eleanor momentarily considered collecting the silver pistol from her trunk, but then she let the thought pass. Edmund had agreed that the station wasn't dangerous, and she didn't need to prove her husband right about their prior argument by pulling a gun out at the slightest provocation.

"It does seem odd that none of the guards are around, don't you think, darling? You don't think the children drugged them just for this little adventure, do you?"

"Certainly the children wouldn't even know how to do such a thing," Edmund replied, reassuring himself. Eleanor could see the growing concern on his face. "It is odd that all of the guards are asleep, though. Certainly at least some of them are supposed to be awake. Perhaps whatever happened with the governess kept them awake last night."

Eleanor stopped, rather taken aback at Edmund's astute observation. "I didn't realize you were paying such close attention, darling."

"I learned a long time ago that one must always pay extra close attention to the servants in an Indian household. They are often the bearers of important knowledge that their employers are too embarrassed to discuss. They are usually the most useful allies, in fact."

Eleanor was speechless. Once again, her husband had blindsided her with a moment of surprisingly shrewd social awareness. She fought back a pang of arousal.

"Come on, we'd best find the children and bring them back before Jaap Sahib awakens, or else I see quite a memorable punishment in their future." Edmund squeezed her hand as he guided her to the door.

"Should we try to find our shoes?" she asked as she glanced around for them.

"I'd rather find the children posthaste," Edmund said as he pushed open the door. Eleanor's pulse picked up as she sensed his growing sense of urgency. "They've been gone too long to have only taken a peek around the front of the building. I do not want them to get lost."

She shivered as her bare feet hit the cool stone of the platform, and she suddenly realized why Anya had done the same, even when the air was pleasantly warm.

"Perhaps we should split up," Eleanor suggested. "We can cover both alleyways at once."

Edmund looked pained at the suggestion, but before he could protest, a high-pitched squeal followed by the angry screeching of King Babu echoed from the alleyway where the children had disappeared.

Eleanor's heart almost exploded, and Edmund's eyes turned black.

"Darling, remember, you don't have to kill anyone. Do what Percy taught you and knock them out cold!" Another scream rang out, this time littered with pain as well as fear. "Go!"

With Rakshasa speed, Edmund disappeared down the alleyway, but as Eleanor debated running back onto the train to alert the guards and grab her pistol, Anya's screams echoed from the other side of the station. Without another thought, she rushed down the other alleyway to the rescue.

As Eleanor turned the corner, two men were pushing Anya up against the side of the building, while a third was giving them orders. Eleanor had seen the same wild look of violent desire that blanketed their faces too many times before, especially during the war when horny, half-mad soldiers were channeling their fearful energy into unfocused lust.

She took a deep, calming breath, readying herself to stop them, just as she had seven times before over the years.

Anya cried as one of the men ripped her gold bangles off her wrists, collecting them into a small pouch. She squealed with disgust as the one collecting the jewelry reached forward and licked her cheek.

"No, please! Please don't!" Anya whimpered.

Eleanor rushed towards them, hoping the surprise of her appearance might simply scare them away, but as they noticed her delicate female disposition and her wild red hair, they were suddenly rather interested in learning more about her. The leader licked his lips.

As fearful men's shouting and stomping footsteps mingled with King Babu's screeches, echoing from closer than they had been before, perhaps even from the platform, Eleanor wasted no time. She ran straight up to the lip-licking leader and kneed him in the groin. His companions were so shocked by the development that they watched, dumbstruck, as the man collapsed onto the ground, cradling his crotch and whining.

"Who's next?!" Eleanor exclaimed, gazing threateningly at the thug who was still holding Anya up against the wall. He let go of her, took one final look at his boss and at Eleanor, and then took off running towards the front of the station.

The final thug who had already assaulted the young girl with his tongue was still holding the bag of Anya's jewelry. He looked torn as he glanced between Eleanor, his boss, and the young girl he was still coveting, but as more of Georgie's screams echoed from the platform, Eleanor decided not to give him another moment to think about how surprising it was that *she* had disabled his pathetic little gang, and she punched him in the nose. As a burst of pain exploded in Eleanor's freshly bleeding hand, the man dropped the bag of Anya's jewelry and ran after his companion towards the front of the station, leaving his boss in a fetal position on the ground.

Anya was shaking as Eleanor coaxed her arms away from the wall where the man had been holding them.

"He... he... they... they..." Anya stuttered.

"You're safe." Eleanor guided Anya into a gentle hug. She wiped Anya's cheek with her silk dupatta where the man had licked her. "We will get you cleaned up in no time, and tomorrow I will teach you how to do what I just did. From now on, you will be able to stop any man who tries to do the same."

"Georgie," Anya whispered as she squeezed Eleanor with all her might and buried her head in her chest. "There were so many men who wanted Georgie! They said they were going to ransom him! They knew who we were! They knew Papa was a maharaja!"

Eleanor rubbed her back soothingly as she let the girl cry in her arms. "Your brother has nothing to worry about, Anya. Edmund is a decorated war hero, and he is rescuing him now. He will be safe just like you are."

Eleanor hoped desperately that Georgie's screams had not been directed at a bloodbath initiated by her overly stimulated, out-of-control Rakshasa husband.

Suddenly, the same two thugs whom Eleanor had already thwarted turned the corner from the front of the station, rushing back into the alleyway and shouting frantically in Marathi.

"Come on. We won't give them another chance." Eleanor grabbed Anya's hand and dragged her, squealing with fear, back towards the platform.

As they turned the corner, Georgie lay on the ground, cradling his arm and wailing, surrounded by five thugs who were all unconscious on the ground with bruised shoulders and various bleeding surface wounds.

There was one thug, however, at Georgie's feet whose neck was broken, bent back in a grotesque unnatural pose.

Edmund was leaning up against the wall, whispering his self-control mantras desperately, and King Babu was lying limp by Georgie's side. In his moment of weakness when he'd killed the thug, Eleanor hoped that Edmund's adrenaline hadn't also enticed him into killing the family pet in front of the little boy. She felt almost no guilt that she cared more about the monkey's fate than the man's.

"Georgie?" Anya whimpered. She ran to his side and kneeled down. "I told you this was a terrible idea!" Her eyes landed on the dead body, and she squealed.

"Anya, they broke my arm!" Georgie whined. "They really broke it! And then... then... Edmund... Lord Marriner... He ran faster than anyone ever runs. He killed the one who was holding me hostage with his bare hands!"

"Eleanor saved me just like that too!" Anya exclaimed. "I mean, she didn't kill anyone, but still. She knocked him straight to the ground!" She looked back towards Eleanor who was debating whether to tend to her struggling husband or Georgie's broken arm. "She said she'd teach me how to do it!"

Georgie leaned towards his sister, glancing at Edmund and lowering his voice. "Edmund isn't normal, Anya. You should have seen how fast he moved..." He lowered his voice even more. "And his eyes, Anya. I don't think he's even human!"

"Aw, come on, Georgie. You're such a liar!" Anya countered.

"I'm not lying! It's true! Edmund's some sort of... I dunno... something! Like a creature from Jules Verne... or Sherlock Holmes!"

Anya suddenly looked pensive, and Eleanor didn't like it one bit.

"My god..." Jaap Sahib murmured as he climbed down from the train. As soon as he observed the mayhem, he dissolved into a panic at his obvious failure. He shouted something into the train, and then rushed to inspect the unconscious thugs. He glanced towards Edmund as he examined the dead man, and then he shook his head with personal castigation. "You have done my job, Lord Marriner. I must beg your forgiveness for leaving the dirty work to you."

Edmund did not respond.

"Please forgive him, Jaap Sahib. My husband has been terribly upset by violence since the war, especially his own," Eleanor replied on his behalf.

"It should not have come to this," Jaap Sahib said angrily as he turned his attention onto Georgie. "You should have known better. You could have gotten yourself and your sister killed! What were you thinking locking me in your carriage? I am here for your protection. For the protection of your entire family."

"But you were asleep! I didn't think it would do any harm," Georgie protested half-heartedly.

"What would have happened if Lord Marriner hadn't been here? Answer me, boy!" Jaap Sahib demanded with fatherly authority.

"Something terrible," Georgie admitted. "They said they were going to ransom me! They knew Papa was a maharaja!"

Jaap Sahib shook his head. "Of course they knew, boy. Do you think anyone other than a maharaja would arrive in a private train? We have been parked here for ten hours. The whole town knows who we are by now." Jaap Sahib cringed as he observed the fall-out again. "I should have been more aggressive in guarding the train… I thought locking the riff raff out would be sufficient…" He glanced down at Georgie. "It would have been if you little fools hadn't run amuck. Now a man is dead, and I will have to clean up this mess on behalf of Lord Marriner, whom you should be thanking."

Georgie glanced over at Edmund. "Thank you, Lord Marriner," he whispered fearfully. Edmund still did not respond, and Georgie whimpered with pain as he tried to reposition himself to see what Edmund was up to.

Eleanor looked back and forth between her struggling husband, the unconscious men, the stiffening corpse, Jaap Sahib, and the children, but as the two remaining thugs who'd attacked Anya turned the corner onto the platform, Edmund looked up with his black eyes, saw their proximity to her, and in a blur observed clearly by both children and Jaap Sahib, he approached the thugs, slammed his hand onto the spot that Mélusine had shown him on the nape of their necks, and knocked them out.

They collapsed onto the ground, flanking Eleanor's position. A subtle clank caught her attention as she watched a knife fall out of the closest assailant's hand. Edmund noticed it too, and leaned over, looking as if he might be sick, closing his eyes and whispering his mantras.

"Bloody hell," Mr. Valov murmured as he stood in his pajamas at the door of the guest carriage pointing his pistol at the former position of their adversaries. He glanced over to Jaap Sahib and the children, whose eyes were solidly glued on Edmund, and then he shook his head with resignation as the maharaja, clad in red silk pajamas, leaned his head out the door of the train from his master suite.

"What in god's name is going on?" Madho Rao demanded to Jaap Sahib.

Just as Eleanor entertained a moment of hope that the maharaja had not noticed Edmund's demonstration of superhuman speed, Madho Rao's gaze moved from Jaap Sahib to Edmund.

"Sri Bidkar wasn't mad after all," he murmured.

"What in the world is going on here?!" Rane demanded as she stepped into the doorway behind her husband.

"We… we… we were attacked." Anya's voice quivered. Her gaze moved from Edmund to the unconscious assailants and the corpse. "They… they… they said they were going to ransom Georgie! They… they… were going to hurt me too…"

As Anya burst into tears, Rane pushed past her husband and rushed barefoot with a dupatta wrapped around her sleeping gown to crouch between her two children.

"Georgie? My god, Madho Rao, he's injured! He's covered in blood! Dev Sahib! Dev Sahib, come here this instant! How did this happen?!" Her tone morphed into the angry roar of a lioness. "Jaap Sahib! How could you let this happen?!"

He finally broke his gaze from Edmund to address the maharani. "Your Highness, I render my resignation to you now for my abhorrent failure. I do not deserve my position, and I will relieve myself of it now."

"That is hardly necessary, Jaap Sahib," Madho Rao intervened. "We must calm ourselves and consider the situation rationally."

"I will say what is necessary!" Rane boomed as she gathered Anya into one arm and squeezed Georgie's uninjured hand with the other.

Eleanor could feel Edmund's struggle increase with the energy of their confrontation, and she began rubbing his back and whispering in his ear. "Darling, take deep, calming breaths. You are almost back under control."

"He could have killed you, Eleanor." They both glanced over at the knife again, and then he noticed her injured, bleeding hand. He took in a deep, pained whiff. "I want so desperately to kill him. So bloody desperately, Eleanor. I don't know how much longer I can hold it together."

Eleanor positioned herself to block the others' view of him, and then she whispered into his ear. "He didn't kill me, darling. I saved Anya. You saved Georgie. And now everything is perfectly alright, and only one man is dead. I am so proud of you, darling, really. There is no need to ruin this triumph with vengeance. Now, you must get yourself back under control so I can check on Georgie's injury."

"Just go, Eleanor," Edmund whispered. "Your bleeding hand is arousing me."

Eleanor self-consciously wrapped her hand in her dupatta. "Is that any better, darling? I can't just leave you here while you're like this. We must get you back under control."

"Please, dearest. Go help the boy," Edmund implored. "You should have heard his screams when they broke his arm. It was like my men's screams the first time they were injured in the trenches. It was the sound of children realizing what real pain feels like." Violet tears began flowing.

"We must get you under control first, darling." She glanced at Mr. Valov who awkwardly put the pistol in his pocket and climbed down from the train in his pajamas to join them.

"Go, Eleanor," Mr. Valov whispered as he relieved her of her duties and took his position by Edmund's side. "I will stay with him until he's back under control."

Eleanor kissed Edmund gently on the cheek, and then left them to tend to Georgie. She kneeled down beside him, but Rane gave her a wild look. The look of a desperate, overprotective mother.

"I have been a nurse for twenty years. Let me take a look at his injury," Eleanor said calmly.

"Ow!" Georgie screamed as Eleanor barely touched a blackened bruise on his arm.

"Don't hurt him!" Rane cried.

"Hand me your scarf," Eleanor replied, refusing to let Rane distract her. When Rane hesitated, Anya pulled off her own scarf and handed it to Eleanor. Eleanor carefully tied it into a makeshift sling, ignoring Georgie as he and his mother cried and whimpered while she secured it.

"Well, it's certainly broken," Eleanor sighed. "And a nasty break it is. You mustn't move your arm, and you will need to keep it elevated to avoid swelling. It would be ideal if you had some remedy for the pain in the meantime. Do you have anything on board the train for that?"

"Dev Sahib!!!" Rane shouted. "Dev Sahib, come here this instant or you will be sacked just like Jaap Sahib!"

"Yes, we do have some herbs for pain on the train," Madho Rao addressed Eleanor, countering his wife's panic with calm. "I'm sure Dev Sahib will prepare them as soon as he can."

"We locked him in the servants' car," Anya whispered. "We locked all of them inside so they wouldn't stop us from exploring."

"You did what?!" Madho Rao exclaimed. "Do you know how dangerous that was?! Of all the irresponsible, careless, wicked things to do!"

"I'm sorry, Papa," Anya dissolved into more tears.

"Please go let them out, Jaap Sahib," Madho Rao said as he took a deep breath and returned to his feigned calm.

Jaap Sahib nodded his agreement and rushed back onto the train.

"Lady Marriner, how is my fool of a son?" Madho Rao asked as he gazed at Georgie with such intense disappointment that his expression almost made Eleanor cower.

"He will need more medical attention when the world wakes up in the morning. Does this city have reliable doctors? It would be best to take him somewhere with competent medical personnel and good facilities where they can properly set the wound before it gets infected. We must be very careful to keep it clean."

"We will leave first thing in the morning, as soon as we have our coal," Madho Rao sighed. "I will have Dev Sahib call ahead to make the arrangements in the next civilized city."

Jaap Sahib emerged from the train and took his position beside Madho Rao. "Dev Sahib and the other men are free. They are dressing themselves now."

"Mummy, it was all my fault," Georgie whispered. "And now God is punishing me for my foolish actions, just like he's punishing Memsahib Jyoti."

"Nonsense," Rane countered. "Just lie quietly, and Mummy will take care of everything."

"But, Mummy, it was all my idea. I convinced Anya to break the rules and sneak off the train. We locked Jaap Sahib in our carriage while he was sleeping so he couldn't follow us, and then we locked everyone else in too," Georgie whimpered. "God knew what we did, just like Memsahib Jyoti, and he taught us a lesson!"

"Memsahib Jyoti was a foolish woman who couldn't keep her legs together," Rane snapped. "Her loose morals are what God is punishing, and I will not hear another word about it. You are nothing like her!"

"You will not speak of Jyoti in that way," Jaap Sahib declared.

"I beg your pardon?" Rane was taken aback.

Jaap Sahib straightened his posture. "As I am no longer in your employ, I will be leaving on the first train in the morning back to Bombay, where I will marry Jyoti. I am the father of her child, and I would have married her years ago if Dev Sahib had allowed it."

The drama was finally sufficient to distract Edmund from his plight, and he and Mr. Valov both looked over to observe each person's reaction to the revelation. Suddenly, the mysterious illness of the governess and the unexplained tardiness in the morning made sense.

"You were copulating right under our noses?! Near the children!" Rane exclaimed. "Of all the indignities!"

Anya and Georgie threw each other a shocked look as their mother shouted the word 'copulate' for all to hear.

"I knew it!" Anya exclaimed. "I knew they were meant to be together! God made it happen with a baby!"

Eleanor was glad that the girl was not too traumatized by the attack to enthusiastically participate in the conversation.

"Silence!" Rane boomed. "You, Jaap Sahib, will never work again. Have no doubt I will see to that."

"Rane, let's discuss this privately," Madho Rao implored as he glanced over self-consciously to Edmund, who was leaning on Mr. Valov, watching them with his eyes finally returned to their human hazel. "We must get everyone back on board the train. Georgie must be made comfortable until we can find a doctor, and most importantly, we mustn't make a scene."

Jaap Sahib leaned down to help Georgie, but Rane slapped him away. "You will not touch my son."

He stepped back. "You are welcome to move him yourself, Your Highness. I will watch with great interest as you try."

260

Eleanor liked Jaap Sahib more and more with every unhindered reaction. He was suddenly so much more human to her than he had been when she'd met him in the morning.

Dev Sahib finally emerged from the train, but his eyes were glued on Edmund. Eleanor wondered if he'd been watching the scene unfold for too long through the window of the train.

"I'm sorry, Your Highness. We were locked inside." He threw a ferocious look at Georgie. "Tell me how I can serve you."

"Help me pick up Georgie and get him inside," Madho Rao suggested.

Dev Sahib looked to Jaap Sahib with confusion.

"I have rendered my resignation. I will be returning to Bombay to marry Jyoti tomorrow," Jaap Sahib informed him.

Dev Sahib's expression of shock turned to concern and then embarrassment as he glanced at Edmund for his reaction, and then at the maharaja.

"Dev Sahib, we must avoid a scene, if you will be so kind as to help me carry Georgie inside," Madho Rao reiterated.

Dev Sahib nodded his obedience, but Eleanor could see the skepticism in his expression as he contemplated how the two of them would lift the boy, who was markedly better fed than other children of his age.

Edmund ignored his discomfort at addressing the group after they had witnessed his unusual talents, and approached them.

"Perhaps I can save you the trouble," he suggested.

Jaap Sahib, Dev Sahib, and Madho Rao stood back with a combination of deference, curiosity, and fear, while Anya and Georgie watched with wide eyes as Edmund kneeled down to lift the boy into his arms, carefully avoiding placing any pressure on his broken arm.

Georgie shivered as Edmund lifted him up, but said nothing. He only gulped fearfully and held his tongue, a development that made Eleanor far more nervous than if the boy had said anything at all.

"Shall I take him to the children's carriage?" Edmund asked Rane directly, avoiding the attention of the rest of the group.

"Yes, Colonel. Please do," Rane agreed. Eleanor realized at that moment that Rane was the only one who hadn't observed Edmund's show and tell, and she was exceedingly grateful for the minor boon.

"No! We have to bring King Babu!" Georgie squealed.

Eleanor looked over at the limp monkey. She reached forward and felt for whether or not the animal was still alive. As she pinched its tiny wrist, it awoke with a start and scrambled to get away from her. It squawked as it observed its surroundings, landing on Edmund holding Georgie, but instead of screeching as it had before, it gulped silently and took a look around at the unconscious villains.

"Dev Sahib, please bring the monkey," Rane ordered as she followed Edmund and Georgie onto the train.

Dev Sahib collected King Babu and followed them up onto the train, and Eleanor finally returned her attention to Anya. "You're still in shock," she said as she felt Anya's pulse and her clammy hands. "You should follow them inside and try to rest. You have been through a frightening ordeal."

"I should have stopped him," Anya said angrily. "I knew it was wrong, and I let him convince me to do it anyway."

"Well, now you know better," Eleanor reminded her. "You will not let anything like this happen ever again, I reckon."

Anya nodded her emphatic agreement, and Eleanor helped her up.

"Now go on inside, wrap yourself up nice and warm, and I will ask Dev Sahib to bring you and Georgie some warm milk." Eleanor felt strikingly motherly as she said it. "I will join you in a few minutes to make sure you're settling in."

"Eleanor..." Anya looked around at the seven assailants littering the ground, landing her gaze on the dead body. "Is Edmund really an avatar like Sri Bidkar said?"

Eleanor straightened her posture, and Mr. Valov moved in beside her. "I thought Sri Bidkar would be more discreet."

"He didn't tell *me*, per se... I was listening in on his telephone call with Papa." She avoided eye contact with her father as she made her confession. "I wanted to know who would be on the train with us. Mummy and Papa were so excited about your visit, I thought you might be Queen Mary and King George."

"I thought Sri Bidkar had gone stark raving mad," Madho Rao admitted. "But he wasn't mad, was he?"

"You mustn't say anything to anyone," Eleanor warned them.

"So he really is Lord Kalki?!" Anya exclaimed.

"Anya," Madho Rao hissed. Despite his embarrassment, he looked straight at Eleanor, hoping for an answer.

Eleanor considered her options as she glanced down at the corpse and then back at her attentive audience. A virtuous avatar was certainly an easier explanation than having to prove that Edmund wasn't a demon. It was, she supposed, in some ways, a Hindu equivalent of an 'angel in disguise'—the excuse that had been so effective recently at defusing their witnesses' fear of Edmund's frightening Rakshasa traits. Still, he actually *was* Lord Kalki... admitting it was a dangerous move.

Just as Mr. Valov straightened his posture, readying himself to step in, Eleanor gently grabbed his arm, and dove right in. "You mustn't say anything to anyone. Not even to Edmund. Lord Kalki gets very unhappy when people know who he is. He can only help the world in secret right now, and keeping his secret is a sacred duty."

She found the term odd—*sacred duty*—she'd heard it used before, but she couldn't for her life place exactly where. If felt strikingly familiar, and yet she hadn't meant to say it at all. The words had just tumbled out of her.

"Lord Kalki..." Madho Rao and Anya repeated in unison with fear and awe.

"Can I trust you to keep all of this between us?" Eleanor reiterated. "You mustn't tell anyone. Even Rane. She did not see Lord Kalki use his divine talents."

...*Divine talents*... Again, the words felt foreign and yet familiar. What had she meant to say? She couldn't even remember now...

"Yes... yes, of course..." Madho Rao murmured.

"But... but... we must tell Georgie! He must know to keep the secret!" Anya exclaimed. "He's going to go around telling everyone that Edmund is a monster from Sherlock Holmes!"

"He would do nothing so foolish..." Madho Rao did not seem entirely convinced by his own assertion.

"I think we mustn't assume so," Eleanor countered as she glanced around at the fall-out of the children's failed adventure again.

"Yes... yes, you are right, Lady Marriner," Madho Rao conceded. "I have been forced to accept new depths of foolishness in my son tonight. Perhaps you can speak with him. We will speak with him together to help him understand the importance of his compliance."

Eleanor reached down and helped Anya up.

"Eleanor... Does that mean that you're an avatar too?" Anya asked shyly.

"Yes," Eleanor replied.

She hadn't meant to say *yes*! Every fiber of her being had tried to say *no*. A burst of anxiety rushed up from her gut. Where had the declaration come from?

"I am the vessel of Uma, Avatar of Shakti. I will connect her with her next incarnation," Eleanor continued, against her will. She knew as soon as the words forced their way out that they were true. She felt Uma's morbid power tucked away, pulsating somewhere deep inside of her. "And I suppose that is all I have to say about that," she said, finally pushing the words out.

264

"Uma…" Anya whispered. "But isn't Lord Kalki the Avatar of Lord Vishnu? Isn't he supposed to marry the Avatar of Lakshmi? Uma is a form of Parvati, Lord Shiva's wife, isn't she, Papa?"

"She is," Madho Rao replied pensively.

"Well, Edmund married me, and here we are," Eleanor said curtly, hoping desperately to escape from the conversation.

"No wonder you look so pretty in those Indian clothes," Anya said as she took Eleanor's hand.

"Thank you, darling." Eleanor glanced down at the blood-stained dupatta that she had used to wrap her injured hand, and then to the sparkling silk salwar kameez that she'd been wearing for too long. She was grateful for the girl's simplicity. It distracted her from the raging conflict that was brewing inside of her. "I am glad to see you've stopped shivering. You are recovering nicely. Now, let's go check in on your brother, shall we?"

Madho Rao rushed to follow her suggestion, stepping out of her way as she led the girl to the stairs of the children's carriage. "Jaap Sahib, please secure all doors to the train and then call the authorities to collect these worthless thugs. We will tell them that you and your men fought them off."

"But, Your Highness, would you not rather have one of my men do it? Rajiv Sahib is a fine candidate for my replacement," Jaap Sahib replied.

"Please, Jaap Sahib, it is no time to train your replacement now. You must help us tonight, and tomorrow we can discuss your future," Madho Rao implored.

"I must return to Bombay to be by Jyoti's side," Jaap Sahib reiterated, glancing self-consciously towards Eleanor. "I was too cowardly to admit my folly, but it is done now. I will do whatever I have to do to be with her." He kneeled down to address Eleanor from a position of prostration. "I hope that you, Lady Eleanor, will forgive me for all of my sins?"

"Me?" Eleanor asked confusedly. "Memsahib Jyoti is the one whose forgiveness must be sought."

"But, my lady, if I go to Bombay with the blessing of the Goddess, surely Jyoti will be healthy throughout her confinement?" he asked timidly. "You see, we do not have the money to pay for a great deal of medicine, and without employment for either of us, we will have even less money, even in the best of circumstances."

"Good lord," Eleanor muttered as she realized that he was treating her with pious reverence, just as Ravi had treated Edmund. She took a deep breath and considered her response carefully. "I am happy for you, Jaap Sahib. I am greatly impressed by your commitment to Jyoti, but I have no control over the natural order of things. In fact, I have no bloody clue what being the vessel of Uma or Parvati even means." She glanced down at her bleeding, bruised hand. "As you can see, I still suffer from human limitations, regardless of whatever else is lurking inside of me."

"I see..." Jaap Sahib whispered. Eleanor did not like the fearful look on his face. "I'm sorry for asking, my lady. I do not deserve your blessing after all of the things that I've done."

Eleanor sighed with stress. She suddenly understood more about Edmund's precarious position (and his aversion to religion) than she ever had before. She was doing a terrible job of convincing this poor man that her inability to answer his prayers was not some sort of divine curse, and he wasn't even Hindu, she was quite sure. He was Sikh! She made a mental note to learn more about the mysterious distinctions between the religions she had never thought much about before diving into Edmund's complicated world...

Suddenly an idea occurred to her. "Jaap Sahib, go to the Bidkars' estate in Bombay. Tell them that Edmund and I sent you. Tell Shruti that we would like very much for Jyoti to convalesce in the safety and comfort of their home."

"Do you mean it, my lady? I could not dare to impose," Jaap Sahib replied with a hint of hope in his voice.

Eleanor liked the mundanity of her plan more and more. "I suspect right about now they are seeking an experienced guard to add to their staff. You would be of great help to them, and Sri Bidkar would enjoy having a baby around to keep his mind occupied."

"Thank you, my lady." Jaap Sahib took her hand into his and kissed it. Eleanor pulled it away awkwardly.

"Please, Jaap Sahib, you must stand," she implored.

He obeyed, but averted his eyes as he towered over her.

"Mr. Valov, I trust that you can give Jaap Sahib the Bidkars' address?" Eleanor suggested.

"Yes, my lady," Mr. Valov replied. Eleanor didn't like his tone either. "Perhaps you should write a note on his behalf so the Bidkars' will believe him."

"Yes, yes, of course. I will do it before morning," Eleanor agreed. "Jaap Sahib, perhaps in the meantime, you can make sure that our position is secure, and that there aren't any more foolish thugs to worry about?"

"Yes, my lady."

As Jaap Sahib set about checking and locking the doors to the train cars, Eleanor urged Anya up the steps into the children's carriage. "I will join you shortly," she said as she encouraged Madho Rao to follow. He reluctantly refused. "Please, Your Highness, I need to have a word with my butler."

"Please, my lady, there is no need for honorifics with us, especially now," Madho Rao replied.

Eleanor's patience was at its end. "Fine, Madho Rao, please leave us alone for a few minutes. I need to sort some things out."

He nodded his agreement and followed Anya up into the carriage. Eleanor watched him go, waiting anxiously for them and Jaap Sahib to be out of earshot. As Jaap Sahib disappeared around the other side of the train, she began pacing.

"Are you alright?" Mr. Valov asked with his natural voice as he pulled out a cigarette and lit up.

"No, I'm not alright!" Eleanor exploded. *"Yes, I'm the Avatar of Parvati? Lord Shiva's wife?* I didn't have any control over my words, Leo. None! It was like someone else was talking through me."

"Your eyes glowed green as you said it. I've never seen anything like it," Mr. Valov informed her. "It was quite different than what happens to Edmund when he loses control."

Eleanor stopped in her tracks. "You have a wretched sense of humor, my spying friend. Just wretched." She watched his reaction, and her anxiety only ticked up another notch. She knew he wasn't lying.

"I rarely joke, Eleanor. And never about such things," Mr. Valov replied calmly. "Has this ever happened before?"

"No. Never. I have always just been fiery, irreverent Eleanor MacLeod, the uninteresting, untamable human nurse."

"Well, something is different," Mr. Valov countered. "Do you think some aspect of your... er... relationship with Edmund has affected you... er... physically?"

"Yes." Mr. Valov was almost as surprised as she was by her admission. "But not in the way that you're thinking." Her heart raced as she thought about the idea. "I met the Avatar of Uma when we were in the temples of Elephanta just a couple days ago. We had a lovely little chat, and then she zapped me with green lightning from her magical trident and killed herself."

Mr. Valov raised his eyebrows at the absurdity of the story.

"Yeah, I know it sounds utterly mad. It was even madder at the time. Her pet tiger disappeared along with her body after the deed was done. It's all bloody bonkers."

"But how was Edmund responsible for this incident?" Eleanor could tell that he was trying his hardest to keep the conversation sounding sane.

"She said that I had a great destiny and whatnot, that there were prophecies, and that I, as Edmund's wife, was the key to *everything…*" Eleanor rolled her eyes as she said it. "But I'm just boring old Eleanor MacLeod! None of this, *none of it*, would have happened if I hadn't fallen in love with that bloody Rakshasa god in there. None of it! I should still be collecting bedpans and coaxing madmen into their clothes. If *I'm* that important, the world is doomed."

"I believe that your husband has a similar attitude about his place in the grand scheme," Mr. Valov pointed out. "Do you think he's right?"

Eleanor humphed. "Of course he isn't. He's going to be the world's bloody messiah at some point, alongside his wonderfully powerful, gorgeous Indian wife, who will not be me."

"Are you sure?"

She suddenly felt like she was enduring a counseling session with one of the army doctors. "Yes, I'm bloody sure. He will marry some girl named Padma who will be the Avatar of Lakshmi, the avatar he was *supposed* to marry. According to the Bidkars, the Hindu scriptures say so, and I've caught several references from Kuveni and Mélusine. They are not always the best at hiding important details." She glanced around, in case Kuveni was listening.

"So the name Lord Kalki comes from Hindu scriptures, and Edmund's guardians admit that he is this godly character?"

Eleanor didn't have the energy to evade him. "It is the name he will take when he fully ascends. According to our magical friends, it won't happen for another century or so, so it won't be much use to you and the Secret Service."

"Do you think I'm reporting all of this back to the Secret Service?" Mr. Valov sounded hurt.

"Aren't you?"

"I have been reporting back half-truths for years, Eleanor. You have no idea how difficult it is for me to maintain the web of lies I've woven."

"I have an excellent idea of it," Eleanor countered simply.

"Yes, I suppose you do," Mr. Valov conceded. "You are the only one in the world who knows exactly how heavy my burden is."

They both stood in silence, contemplating the idea until Mr. Valov spoke.

"Those scriptures weren't particularly right about Edmund. Were they? It's hard to believe that the Hindu scriptures foretold of the coming of a British savior."

Eleanor laughed. "I agree, it's rather absurd. If someone told me that the Scots were waiting for a British savior, I'd tell them it was some sort of sassanack propaganda. Apparently, they thought he would be Mongolian. It was the land of the conquerors at the time the scripture was written. And he is, I must point out, only half British. His father is Indian (or Lankan, I'm still not quite sure which), and who knows about his mother. Do you know?"

"She was French," Mr. Valov replied. "She pretended she was British due to the political situation in France, and she got away with it because she spoke perfect English. She was a refugee from a very powerful family. She was one of only two of her line who survived the revolution, thanks to the help of a scullery maid in her household who helped her escape in disguise."

"Huh... so Edmund really isn't British at all... Perhaps you should tell him what you know about his mother sometime. It eats away at him not knowing."

"He is legally British. He was born in Bath," Mr. Valov countered. "And how, exactly, do you propose I tell Edmund all the secrets I know about him without giving away my real identity?"

"I see your point. My poor husband could drown in the secrets that are floating all around him."

Mr. Valov took another drag of his cigarette, and then returned to his original point. "It is beyond contention that Edmund is not Mongolian. Perhaps the scriptures were wrong about you too, Eleanor. Perhaps you are the woman who stands by his side."

"You are very kind to me, Leo." Eleanor's posture relaxed. "But there is quite a bit of evidence that there will be another wife in his future. What I am in the meantime, though, I have no bloody clue. Apparently, I'm the vessel of Uma… or Parvati… or both, whatever that means. There is a goddess named Durga involved as well, but I'm not entirely sure how."

As Mr. Valov dropped his cigarette butt on the stone platform and pulled out another cigarette from his case, she rushed towards him, and he flinched. She took a moment to calm down, and then took one for herself.

He shook his head with resignation and lit it up for her. "These things will kill you, you know."

She took in a deep drag anyway.

"You've done this before," Mr. Valov observed.

"They were my greatest solace for almost fifteen years," Eleanor admitted. "I quit ten years ago when one of my patients died from a particularly ghoulish battle with lung cancer. If you'd seen his disgusting state, you would have quit too."

"Your husband would rip my head clean off if he saw me help you start up the habit again."

"He'll have to get through me, which apparently isn't as uneven a fight as it used to be." She held up her injured hand. "Although, who knows? It still hurts like hell, and this was just from offering up a punch in the nose. I didn't inherit godly healing powers from Uma, it would appear."

She walked past the unconscious men and the stiff corpse and sat herself down on the lone bench where earlier in the night the old man with the cane had been sleeping. She thought about the fortuitous timing of his exit, and then she let the thought pass. She had far more unpleasant worries on her mind.

"I don't know anything about the world anymore," she sighed. "Everything I thought I knew... *everything*... is wrong. I don't even know who I am anymore."

"I know the feeling," Mr. Valov commiserated.

"Have you ever had another person speak through you?"

"No, I can't say that I have. But I sure as hell didn't see myself here, as I am now. I was a cold-hearted bastard, Eleanor, and I liked it. I was the best spy the Empire had ever known. Now I find myself wishing that I really were just Edmund's devoted butler. It is utterly shameful, at least to my ambitious former self. But I've come to realize that Edmund changes everyone he encounters. Absolutely everyone."

Eleanor sighed. "I swore I'd never change for a man. Now I don't even know what species I am. Did I mention that Uma was a Vanara—an enormous monkey?"

Mr. Valov leaned over to inspect Eleanor's chin playfully. "You still look human to me."

She finally cracked a smile. "Well, that's something, at least."

Mr. Valov returned to seriousness. "I don't think anyone chooses to change around Edmund. It simply happens. His wake is more powerful than he realizes... as is yours, Eleanor. It has been that way since I met you for the first time, so I can only assume you were like that long before you met him. Perhaps you have not changed as much as you think you have."

Eleanor took another long drag as she thought about his assertion. "Maybe. But what do I do now? You saw how Jaap Sahib reacted. What a bloody mess! At this rate, all of India will know that the avatars have arrived by the time we reach the Taj Mahal."

"I'd suggest you try to stay out of trouble, but I know it's a futile suggestion. Trouble is certainly finding you."

"You've got that right." Eleanor laughed and then coughed. She threw her half-finished cigarette onto the ground, but stopped short of stamping it out when she noticed her dirty bare feet.

"Smoking isn't nearly as satisfying as it used to be. In fact, it is rather grotesque, isn't it? I can feel it burning my lungs. I won't be able to hide it from Edmund—my mouth already tastes like tobacco."

"I love it. I haven't been able to quit, no matter how hard I've tried. I used to smoke three packs a day. Getting it down to one has been the triumph of a lifetime."

Jaap Sahib returned from his security survey of the train, and approached them tentatively. He noticed the cigarette butt by her feet, but said nothing about it. "My lady, if it pleases you, might I ask that you board the train? We will call the authorities to take care of these men, and it would be best for you to be locked safely inside with everyone else. In these small towns, even the death of a thug can be very dangerous. If his family finds out before we have left the area, there is no telling what might happen."

"Yes, yes, of course," Eleanor agreed as she stood up. "Thank you for your counsel, Mr. Valov. Perhaps you can help Jaap Sahib with cleaning up this mess."

"Yes, my lady," Mr. Valov replied. This time he did not say the honorific jokingly, and she sighed subtly with resignation.

As she approached the train, she was startled by the sound of footsteps accompanied by the squeaking of an unoiled wheel. From around the front of the station, down the same alleyway where Georgie had met his attackers, a small Indian man dressed in a simple traditional loincloth pushed a wheelbarrow full of coal onto the platform.

"Someone called for some coal?" he asked with a thick accent in English.

"You are hours earlier than we expected!" Jaap Sahib exclaimed.

"You are the first of my deliveries." As the man caught Eleanor's eye, he winked, and she suddenly recognized him, despite his excellent disguise.

"Kuveni," she whispered.

He smiled, and pushed his wheelbarrow straight to the door of the locomotive, completely ignoring the carnage as he passed by. "Come, we have no time. The village is waking up, and you'd best be out of here by the time anyone reaches the station. The dead man has five brothers who are going to want revenge."

Jaap Sahib rushed to open the door of the locomotive, and he barked orders inside. Several servants rushed down to help Kuveni make her delivery.

As soon as they were finished, Jaap Sahib reached into his pocket and pulled out a pouch of money.

"For your trouble," he whispered. He handed her an extra handful of coins from his other pocket. "And your silence."

"As you wish, sahib," Kuveni replied. "Now, I'd better be off!"

She skipped away with the empty wheelbarrow back into the dark alleyway.

Mr. Valov threw his last cigarette butt onto the platform and joined Eleanor by the open door to the guest carriage. "Was that one of... yes, of course it was. I don't know why I even bothered asking."

Eleanor threw him a glance of agreement, and then guided Mr. Valov into the carriage.

"Please sit, the servants will wash your feet." Jaap Sahib dropped his pious tone in favor of a pragmatic one as he rushed to close the door behind them. "Hold on tight; we will be departing as soon as we possibly can. We are incredibly lucky that he came when he did."

"Indeed, we are," Eleanor replied.

Jaap Sahib stopped to contemplate her statement with too much thought for Eleanor's comfort.

"Thank you, my lady." He averted his eyes, and Eleanor sighed with annoyance at her backward progress. "You have saved us from an even worse catastrophe."

Without waiting for a response, Jaap Sahib closed them into the carriage. As the loud roar of the engine began, Eleanor sat back in one of the thrones, beside Mr. Valov, and sighed again, this time with stress.

"I'm glad you didn't resign, Leo. It is priceless having an ally I can talk to, especially with these things that Edmund mustn't know. I'd be going mad if I had to keep everything to myself."

"I'm glad to be of service, Eleanor. Really. A man needs to be useful, and finally I am again."

Eleanor squeezed his hand supportively, but pulled away guiltily as two servants rushed into the carriage carrying basins of soapy water.

She sat back, closed her eyes, and felt the rumble of the train picking up momentum. It mixed strangely with the subtle hum of power emanating from her core. She tried to relax and focus on the sensation of the warm soapy water on her feet, but she couldn't shake the unsettling feeling that she was no longer alone in her body.

Uma, what have you done? She thought.

Do not fear, my child. Someday all will become clear. The familiar voice resonated from deep inside of her.

Someday does not sound like today, Eleanor sighed.

No, my child, it is a long way off. Now is the time for you to revel in Lord Kalki's arms. There is nothing more for you to do.

If you're going to ride around inside of me, can you please leave my voice and my actions under my control from now on?

I will try, my child.

CHAPTER 14 – JUST A MAN ON A HORSE

When the servants were finished with their footbath and the train was rumbling along at a steady pace, Dev Sahib approached Eleanor and Mr. Valov with his head bowed in humility.

"Your husband wishes for you to join him by Georgie's side in the children's carriage, my lady," Dev Sahib whispered.

"Yes, I suppose he does," Eleanor said with feigned cheer. "I've left him alone a bit too long, I reckon. Mr. Valov, please help Dev Sahib and Jaap Sahib with whatever they need to deal with Edmund's... er... mess. Oh, and see to the dogs! We left them in our berth! Blimey, they're sure to have left us a few reminders of their displeasure at being locked inside, poor things."

"We will see to it at once!" Dev Sahib declared.

"Perhaps let Dev Sahib lead the way," she whispered into Mr. Valov's ear. "And don't think too poorly of the dogs. It was our fault for leaving them inside for so long. We should have let them out onto the platform hours ago."

Mr. Valov nodded his agreement and helped Eleanor up.

Madho Rao approached from the children's carriage. "Please, my lady, follow me. We must talk to Georgie, but I fear the situation is not as you expected."

"What do you mean?" Eleanor asked with a burst of anxiety.

"You will see," Madho Rao replied.

Eleanor could sense his heart racing, but he did an admirable job of hiding his nerves as he guided her into the children's carriage, where Rane was pacing back and forth in the hallway.

"Why does my son not want to see me?!" she exclaimed. "Madho Rao, you must fix this!"

"Don't worry, lovey. Everything will be perfectly fine." He kissed her on the cheek. "We've all been through an ordeal tonight, and everything will be resolved straightaway. The coal came hours earlier than expected, and Dev Sahib has already called ahead to the hospital in Nashik. They will have a private room set up for us, and Dev Sahib's cousin's cousin's uncle will meet us at the station with a car."

Eleanor was relieved to see their display of affection (and to hear their mundane plans, none of which involved prayer to her or Edmund), and she smiled at Rane but said nothing as Madho Rao knocked on the door of one of the berths and then pushed it open before receiving a reply.

Inside, Edmund sat beside Georgie's bed, while Georgie lay above the covers nursing his arm, which remained in Eleanor's makeshift silk sling. Under the covers, a shivering lump cuddled up by Georgie's side. The conversation looked thoroughly amicable as Edmund smiled to greet them.

"Dearest, are you alright? I expected you sooner. Georgie and I have been having quite an interesting conversation, haven't we?"

Georgie smiled, but Eleanor could still see a hint of fear and guilt in his expression.

"I'm perfectly fine, darling." She sat down in a chair on the opposite side of Georgie's bed. "Mr. Valov and I were just working on logistics for cleaning up the little problem at the station."

"You mean the body," Georgie said miserably.

"Yes, I mean the body," she agreed.

"It was all my fault," Georgie muttered angrily to himself.

"It was a painful mistake that you must learn from. You must be wiser next time to prevent more tragedies," Edmund reminded him. "You are lucky that your greatest mistake only caused pain to some worthless thugs. It could have been much worse if something had happened to someone you love."

"Yes, sir." Georgie reached forward to pet the quivering lump through the blanket, and it squawked and nestled deeper into his side. "Lady Eleanor, will you tell Anya I'm sorry?"

"As soon as she is rested, you can tell her yourself," Eleanor suggested.

Madho Rao closed the door, locking his wife out of the room, and then he took a seat in a chair by Georgie's feet.

"Georgie, we must discuss something very important." He leaned in and dropped his voice to a whisper, glancing at the door suspiciously. "You mustn't tell anyone that Edmund is Lord Kalki. Do you understand? Not even your mother."

Eleanor shot the maharaja a fierce look of disapproval, but Edmund reached over the boy and took her hand.

"I was just telling Georgie how all I really am is a man on a horse who sometimes helps people in need," he explained. "Just like Lord Kalki. He was Ravi's metaphor that I finally agreed with, wasn't he? Did I get the name right?"

Eleanor worked harder than she ever had to hide her bewilderment. "Yes, darling, that was his name."

"Well, good. We have that sorted then." Edmund squeezed her hand. "You won't tell anyone anything about me, I reckon, Georgie?"

"No, my lord," Georgie agreed.

"You needn't use honorifics with me. I far preferred our game of informality." Edmund addressed the boy and then landed his attention on Madho Rao. "If it still suits you, old friend."

"Whatever you desire, my lord…" Madho Rao replied, "I mean Edmund, if it really is what you prefer."

"It is," Edmund agreed. "Now, I'm rather famished, if Dev Sahib might be able to dig up some of those adorable tea sandwiches for me."

As he moved his hand away from Eleanor's, the quivering lump under the covers squawked with fear.

"Is that King Babu?" Eleanor asked.

"He's still scared of Edmund," Georgie explained. "I told him not to be, but he won't listen."

Take the child's hand, Eleanor, Uma's voice resonated in Eleanor's head.

Eleanor looked away from Edmund as she awkwardly reached for Georgie's hand.

No, not that one! King Babu's. What an absurd name for a monkey, I must say…

Eleanor stealthily changed her plan and lifted up the covers to address the fearful monkey, blocking everyone's view of her glowing eyes as she addressed him. When King Babu saw Eleanor, he froze in position, and she gently took his little hand into hers.

Uma communicated the message without one spoken word. *Do not fear, my child. Lord Kalki is not to be feared by any virtuous creature. Did he kill you when he had the chance?*

King Babu squawked as he nodded his head in the negative.

That's right. He saved you and Georgie. His Rakshasa nature is irrelevant. You must obey him and learn to love him. It is a great privilege to be in his presence.

Eleanor let go, and King Babu dropped into a bow before her. She coaxed him out from his hiding place onto a pillow next to Georgie.

"Extraordinary," Madho Rao murmured as he watched the phenomenon.

"You have a way with monkeys, dearest. Perhaps you should have stayed with the men in Elephanta," Edmund said half-jokingly.

"You're right, darling, I certainly should have," Eleanor replied. *Then I wouldn't be in this mess, channeling the Queen of the Monkeys…* her inner monologue added.

Now, now, Eleanor. Someday you will appreciate my presence.

Eleanor closed her eyes.

Please don't speak to me now! Not in front of Edmund! He will see the green glow of my eyes.

Excellent point, Eleanor. You are a worthy partner.

"Dearest, is everything alright?" Edmund asked.

Eleanor opened her eyes and smiled. "Yes, darling. I'm perfectly fine. King Babu seems to be recovering from his episode, don't you think, my little friend?"

King Babu turned towards Edmund and dropped into another bow.

"There we go!" Eleanor cheered.

"He has always been a very trainable monkey, as monkeys go," Madho Rao murmured.

"Georgie, how are you feeling?" Eleanor asked, returning to her mundane medical persona as King Babu crawled into the nook of Georgie's unbroken arm, forcing himself to look at Edmund. Eleanor examined the boy's black bruises and the ugly break. Luckily, the bone had not cut through the skin, but it was still clearly visible from the outside.

"It hurts, but the medicine helped," Georgie replied. "I don't deserve it, though. I deserve to feel more pain. Don't you think, Edmund?"

"I think you have already learned your lesson, Georgie," Edmund replied simply.

Georgie sighed with relief.

"Now, shall we invite your mother to tend to you?" Madho Rao suggested.

Georgie humphed. "Only if she doesn't tell me how wonderful I am again. What I did was so much worse than what Memsahib Jyoti did. All she did was love Jaap Sahib! I almost got my sister killed!"

Madho Rao squeezed Georgie's leg approvingly. "I will tell her to keep her unwarranted praise to herself."

King Babu shifted fearfully as Edmund stood up, but then he and Georgie both watched as Edmund put his arm around Eleanor and guided her out of the room.

"Georgie!" Rane exclaimed as she rushed into the room. "How are you feeling?! Why didn't you want Mummy's help?!"

Eleanor tiptoed across the hallway and peeked her head into Anya's berth. The girl was already sleeping soundly, wrapped tightly in many layers of blankets, cuddling a small stuffed tiger. Eleanor closed the door without making a sound.

Dev Sahib approached them with a deep bow.

"His lordship has requested some tea sandwiches," Madho Rao informed him. "Please bring as many as the staff can make and leave them in the guest carriage along with some masala chai."

"Yes, Your Highness!" Dev Sahib backed away and then turned around to run back to the kitchen.

"Thank you, Madho Rao," Edmund said amicably. "I am quite famished after our ordeal."

"I cannot thank you enough for saving my children. Both of you." Madho Rao glanced between them. "I don't know what we've done to warrant the privilege of your presence, but we will endeavor to be worthy of it, my lord... Edmund, and my lady Eleanor."

"We were glad to be of assistance," Edmund spoke distractedly as he looked towards the door to their carriage, and Eleanor suddenly couldn't hold back a yawn. She realized that her salwar kameez had become thoroughly painful after its eighteen hours of continuous use.

"Darling, I'd like to take some time to unwind... privately."

"Please, take all the time you need!" Madho Rao interrupted on Edmund's behalf. "We are dreadfully behind schedule anyway, and we will continue to be behind with Georgie's appointment at the hospital in Nashik. Please, take all the time to yourselves that you desire, and do not hesitate to ask for anything that will make you more comfortable."

"Thank you," Edmund and Eleanor replied in unison. Edmund took her hand, and she shivered at his Rakshasa frigidity.

"Let's go have some chai, darling," she whispered.

When they arrived in the guest carriage, the door to their berth was open, and a folding table was already set up inside with a steaming silver pot of tea and a heaping plate of tea sandwiches. Eleanor looked around, wondering if Kuveni had beaten the staff to their task.

"I hope it is to your liking, my lord!" Dev Sahib exclaimed as he rushed in from the dining car, carrying a large plate of pastries, similar to the ones they'd served during tea the day before. "We had these prepared for your dinner last night. You don't mind that they've sat for a while?"

"This is perfectly sufficient, thank you," Edmund replied.

"Dev Sahib, if you don't mind, could you please leave us alone now? Can you tell the staff to avoid transiting through our carriage unless it is absolutely necessary?"

"Yes, my lady!"

Dev Sahib rushed to place the tray of pastries on the table, and then backed away from them, maintaining a deep bow as he went. Eleanor tried to take in a deep breath as Edmund closed and locked the door to their berth, but she once again felt the painful constraint of the clothing she'd been wearing for too long.

"Please, darling, can you help me out of this top? I'm finding it dreadfully uncomfortable."

Edmund kissed her neck as he unbuttoned the back, and Eleanor felt her skin tingling as it breathed in the cool air. She finally took a deep, calming breath.

"I suppose I've gotten used to being naked with you, darling. It is so much more comfortable than being clothed."

As she stepped out of the dress-like kameez, a burst of arousal overwhelmed her. Her skin was still tingling, and she suddenly couldn't think of anything other than ripping Edmund's clothes off and riding him to the rumbling beat of the moving train.

"Darling, I want you so badly it hurts," she whispered as she ripped off his shirt and frantically pulled out the drawstring of his pants.

"Dearest, you're so vigorous!" he exclaimed as he ripped off her pants and pounced onto the bed beside her.

She climbed on top of him and held his arms above his head with all her strength as she moaned and sighed with the pleasure of feeling him inside of her. It was more electric than it had ever been, as if their energy, their life-forces were combining into one more powerful being.

"It is my turn to ravage you, darling. Do you like it?"

As Edmund moaned his approval, the first of many bursts of pleasure exploded inside of Eleanor's tingling loins, and together, for the first time of many, the two lovers experienced the utterly unique pleasures of two avatars becoming one.

CHAPTER 15 – IN THE LOOKING GLASS

When Eleanor awoke in Edmund's cold arms, the sun was peeking in through the thick silk curtains, and the train was moving at a steady pace. She sat up to observe her surroundings, smiling as she noticed the empty trays of tea sandwiches and pastries that her husband must have snuck after she'd fallen asleep.

The strange tingling sensation that she'd found so arousing the night before continued, and she reached down to feel her breasts, which pulsated with a combination of pain and pleasure.

"What on earth…" she murmured as she looked down.

Her breasts were markedly larger than they had ever been before. Her whole life she'd embraced the simplicity of being thin and flat, a shape perfectly conducive to modern tomboy fashions, but now… now! They were enormous! Two copious handfuls!

Edmund sighed and turned over as she jumped out of the bed in a panic. She glanced around for a mirror, but there was none, and then, before a whiff of her fear aroused her husband, she rushed into the WC and locked herself inside.

She turned on the electric lights and looked down. They were even bigger than they had looked in the muted light of the bedroom.

"Kuveni!" she hissed in a panic. "Kuveni, please come!" She fought back tears.

With a warm, pleasant breeze, Kuveni materialized before her in the form of Kate.

"What is it, dear girl? What has you so upset?" Kuveni moved to pull her into a hug, and then fully noticed her naked state.

"Look at me, Kuveni! Look at my body!"

Kuveni furrowed her brow as she observed Eleanor's large breasts. "It looks like marriage has been quite healthy for you, my dear girl. You were just skin and bones before!"

Eleanor's fear morphed into frustration. "Kuveni, human women do not just grow a set of enormous breasts overnight. They went from apricots to grapefruits! Never! It *never* happens like this, especially not at my age!"

"It is strange," Kuveni admitted as she glanced down. Eleanor blushed self-consciously until she noticed what had caught Kuveni's eye. Her hips were also markedly wider. It wasn't the worst development, as she'd always felt like she was too petite, but the jarring nature of the change could not be ignored.

"Do you think…" She gulped with acute fear as she spoke. "Do you think I'm pregnant?"

Kuveni grabbed Eleanor's hand. "We will find out at once."

With a pleasant breeze and a moment of lightheadedness, they rematerialized inside of Mélusine's crystal cave, the same cave with sparkling black walls and the eerie glowing well where they'd taken Edmund after his unfortunate overdose of turmeric in Turkey.

"What is it? What's wrong?" Mélusine said as she materialized right beside them. She took in a deep whiff, gathered Eleanor's injured hand into hers, snapped her fingers, and wrapped a fresh bandage with her Roman remedy around it. Eleanor had completely forgotten about the injury, but she was grateful that it still hurt. It was one small piece of evidence of her humanity.

"That's not why we came." Eleanor finally lost her battle with tears. "Mélusine, am I pregnant?!"

Mélusine took a moment to observe Eleanor's naked body, and then she placed her hand gently on her abdomen and closed her eyes. As a sense of warm well-being rushed through Eleanor, Mélusine pulled her hand away.

"No. You're not pregnant."

"Are you sure?" Eleanor asked as she wiped the tears from her eyes. "Look at me! In one night, my breasts are almost as big as yours!"

Mélusine smiled reassuringly and pulled Eleanor into a gentle hug. "I am certain, ma chérie. I *always* know. It is one of my special talents."

"Then how could this happen?" Eleanor gave into another round of tears. "I don't know anything about myself anymore."

Kuveni rushed to her side and pulled her into a motherly hug.

"Now, now, my dear girl. We will get to the bottom of this." Kuveni snapped her fingers, and a tall standing mirror appeared before them. "Let's take a look at you together, shall we?"

She guided Eleanor in front of the mirror and stood behind her as Eleanor observed herself. Her skin and her breasts continued to tingle as she looked at her new body. It was even worse than she'd imagined. Her thin waist, which was wider than it had been before but still looked slim in comparison to her new curves, accentuated the figure of her breasts which were almost the size of small melons. She leaned forward to observe her face and her hair, which mercifully looked how she remembered them. Then, she reached up and held her breasts in her hands, gently pushing them together to create copious cleavage that rivaled Mélusine's. A pang of arousal annoyed her as she observed herself in her new state. Some part of her liked it.

"Something is different," Mélusine said as she stood behind Kuveni.

"Obviously!" Eleanor exclaimed.

"I don't just mean your physicality, ma chérie," Mélusine replied calmly. "There is something else that is different about you."

"Perhaps that would be the goddess who has taken up residence in my body," Eleanor said snarkily. As soon as the words came out of her mouth, Eleanor realized the connection. "Uma! Uma, did you do this to me?!"

"Uma?" Mélusine asked with intrigue. "You met Uma?"

"She zapped me with her trident, killed herself, took up residence in my body, and here I am." Eleanor looked down at her new cleavage. "All of it against my will, I might add."

"*Mon dieu.* So that was what the prophecy meant…" Mélusine murmured.

"Uma! Was this your doing?!" Eleanor looked at herself in the mirror until her eyes flashed momentarily with the same bright green of Uma's trident.

I'm sorry, my child. I did not realize that my presence would affect your physicality. But Shakti does what Shakti wants.

"Great. Uma says that Shakti has decided that this is how I'm going to look," Eleanor said angrily. "How about I get a say in how I look?!"

"Oh dear," Kuveni murmured. "Shakti does tend to like certain proportions for her avatars…"

"These proportions?!" Eleanor exclaimed. "These absurd, Victorian pin-up proportions?!"

My child, does any human really get to decide how she looks? Is it not determined from birth by factors beyond her control?

"Is it normal for a goddess's vessel to hear someone else's opinionated voice in her head? Because I'm already tired of this. I value my freedom, and the silence of my own mind," Eleanor griped.

288

"Ma chérie, it is not unusual for an avatar to hear her elders in her head. It is perfectly natural, and many before you have learned to live with it. You are partners now, and Uma is a wise and fair queen. She is a much better partner than some are left with… But you are still in control, Eleanor. Isn't that right, Uma?" Mélusine leaned in and looked Eleanor straight in the eye. "You will let Eleanor remain in control of her own faculties?"

Of course, mon amie.

"She said, 'of course, *mon amie*,'" Eleanor translated with an eye roll.

"See, *c'est vrai*. Exactly as I said."

"Mélusine, do you hear someone else's voice in your head?" Eleanor asked as she focused her attention on the subtle power emanating from Mélusine's being. It was quite different from Uma's, even more so now that she had Uma lurking inside of her for a direct comparison. Mélusine's power was softer, warmer, lacking a certain edge.

Mélusine laughed. "Ma chérie, I must seem very powerful to you, but I am not an avatar. I am simply the Sacred Rakshini of the Roman Era, and the guardian of the Yaksha people."

Careful, Eleanor. She doesn't know her destiny yet.

"I'll take that as a no," Eleanor humphed.

"This must be very frightening for you, ma chérie. It is very unusual for a human to become an avatar so suddenly. In fact, you are the only one I've ever encountered. Avatars are usually born that way. They discover their destinies at an early age."

"Edmund wasn't. He has no bloody clue he's an avatar," Eleanor pointed out.

"You're right, ma chérie…" Mélusine trailed off for a moment of thought. "Think of how fortuitous it is that you are experiencing this pain now. You will be able to prepare him for his destiny like no one else can."

"But I never asked for any of this!" Eleanor's emotions at her powerlessness overcame her, and she burst into tears. "I was willing to marry my gentle demon prince, to protect his secrets and help him become the man he was before the war broke him, but I *never* agreed to anything that would change *me*! Not like this!"

Kuveni snapped her fingers. While a red silk robe materialized in her hand, a velvet Roman chaise materialized beside them. She wrapped Eleanor up and sat her down on the chaise, letting her cry into her chest.

"I can't even tell Edmund what happened!" Eleanor sobbed. "What in the hell am I supposed to tell him?! I'm possessed by a goddess, just like he is possessed by a god that he doesn't even recognize yet?!"

"No, my dear girl, you most certainly cannot tell him that," Kuveni whispered as she kissed Eleanor's forehead.

"I know! I can't tell him anything anymore! Our bloody spying butler knows more about me than my own husband does! I want to confide in Edmund! I want to cry in *his* arms!"

Kuveni looked searchingly to Mélusine, who was also at a loss. She sat down on the other side of Eleanor, encompassing both of them into a warm Yakshini hug.

"Cry all you want, ma chérie. Time is stopped in this cave, so you needn't rush. Sometimes there are things we simply can't control—tragic, horrible things that destiny puts in our path to thwart us and to kill our spirit. But you are stronger than that, ma chérie. You are stronger than all of us."

"I used to control my own destiny. I was a skilled spinster nurse who didn't have to do anything she didn't want to do. I was as free as a woman could be. But that Eleanor MacLeod is dead now, isn't she?"

"Change is inevitable, ma chérie, and control of destiny is only an illusion. It is a tragic truth for us, as well. The world we knew when we were young is unrecognizable now, and even with our power, there was very little we could do to alter the course of history. Every time we tried, destiny proved far more powerful. That is just the way of things."

Eleanor cried into Kuveni's chest until she felt like she had no tears left, and then she closed her eyes and lay in their arms for a while, contemplating her misery as a few more rogue tears worked their way to the surface.

Finally, she took in a deep, snorting breath and sat up, wiping her eyes. "What do I do now? What do I tell Edmund? I don't even have any clothes that fit."

"My dear girl, just tell him how jarring the change was and that you don't know what caused it. You've helped him through many similar situations, and now it's his turn to help you. He will be very grateful for the opportunity; I'm certain of it." Kuveni snapped her fingers, and Eleanor's trunk appeared at their feet. "Now, don't you worry for one second about not having any clothes that fit. I will make you a whole new wardrobe with your new measurements, starting with your favorites from your trunk."

Eleanor leaned forward and began digging through her clothes. "They aren't going to look the same. The styles won't even work. They'll look absurd on me now. I'll probably look like a common prostitute... or a frumpy old maid."

"We will update the styles, my dear girl. We have all the time in the world to make you things that you will love. Perhaps for now you should choose the fabrics you like, and I will use them as inspiration."

Eleanor reached over and hugged Kuveni as she fought back another round of tears.

"Now, now, Mistress Eleanor. You are not alone in any of this. You will never be alone again... unless you really want some time to yourself."

Eleanor nodded her agreement as Kuveni wiped away her most recent round of tears, and then Kuveni reached forward and began sorting the clothing in Eleanor's trunk into piles on the floor.

Eleanor gathered her wits and joined her, creating piles of clothing she liked and that she didn't, relegating most of the remaining items from Edmund's thoughtful (if a bit frumpy) Paris collection into a sentimental pile for safekeeping. As soon as she had a collection of fabrics she loved, mostly flowing silks, structured linen, and intricately beaded patterns, Kuveni began her work.

Mélusine watched from the sidelines as Kuveni whipped up garments in each of Eleanor's favorite fabrics – dresses, skirts, and stylish pant-suits, varying the collars and waistlines to give Eleanor more options to try than if she'd walked into the largest department store in London.

As soon as Kuveni had one collection ready, Mélusine hopped up to help Eleanor dress herself, although her presence was more moral support than actual help, as Mélusine was rather lost with the nuances of putting on human clothing.

Eleanor took a deep breath as she looked up from her first option, a beautiful midnight blue silk dress with sheer sleeves, a flowing skirt, a dangerously low princess-cut neckline, and a tight cut around her waist that accentuated her new curves. Eleanor could hardly believe that she was looking at herself in the mirror as she leaned in to observe the tasteful cleavage that defined the look, a look she had never once dared to attempt in her life.

"What do you think, my dear girl?" Kuveni asked. "I won't be offended by whatever you say. You are the boss!"

"I love it, Kuveni. I never thought I could wear anything like this. It's so elegant… Do you think Edmund would like it?"

"I'm certain he would, my dear girl. You are simply stunning!"

Kuveni happily helped Eleanor out of the dress, and then muttered to herself as she snapped her fingers, producing several more evening gowns of similar cuts with various flourishes in fabrics far finer than anything Eleanor had ever worn.

Eleanor more enthusiastically began trying them on, now that she knew it was possible to like how she looked, and with each new dress, she felt her anxiety disperse. For the first time in her life, she was having fun trying on clothes, perhaps because the experience was so full of surprises. It felt almost as if she were dressing a doll, a body that wasn't hers at all, and yet it was. She could feel the new weight on her chest as she hopped around trying to get into the dresses, and the tingling of her skin still distracted her.

Kuveni continued on tirelessly, producing matching pant-suits that looked as if they were straight off of the Paris runways, casual dresses that were far more flattering than the wide-waisted boyish ones Eleanor had been wearing for years, and even a set of salwar kameez and lehengas to replace the ones that Babri had made.

After hours and hours of diligent work by Kuveni and minor suggestions from Mélusine (each of which resulted in a distinctly Roman look that Eleanor adored), Eleanor stood before the mirror, modeling the final lehanga, and turning around to observe her bustier profile in the perfectly fitted blouse as her large, supple breasts gave way to her porcelain waist.

"How am I going to explain this to the maharaja's family? The change is so obvious!"

Mélusine stood behind her, nodding her approval. She morphed her own white medieval dress into a similar lehenga, and stood beside Eleanor, comparing her handiwork to Kuveni's.

"It suits you," Eleanor smiled. "Perhaps you should wear Indian clothing more often."

Kuveni snapped her fingers, producing her own lehenga of the same violet beaded material she'd used for her favorite flapper dress. "Do not worry about the maharaja's family. You can wear the less fitted outfits until you arrive in Gwalior, and then you will never have to explain yourself again. No one will know how you looked before. The game of managing our changing forms in front of observant humans is something we have quite a bit of experience with."

Eleanor pulled them both into a tight hug.

"Thank you," she whispered. "Thank you for everything."

"It is our pleasure, Mistress Eleanor," Kuveni replied with a kiss on her forehead.

As Eleanor's stomach growled, Mélusine smiled and snapped her fingers, producing a baguette sandwich.

Eleanor gratefully devoured it, and when she was finished, a fanciful thought occurred to her. "If Shakti wants me to have these measurements, do you think that means that I can eat anything I want? Any quantity, just as Edmund does, and I will remain the same size?"

I told you that you would not always detest my presence, my child, Uma replied. *You should revel in the pleasures of your humanity now, more than you ever have.*

"Ha! Uma says yes!" Eleanor exclaimed triumphantly.

Mélusine smiled and produced another sandwich, but as Eleanor finished it up, a burst of anxiety dissolved her remaining appetite.

"I will have to discuss this with Edmund immediately. I will not be able to hide it from him."

"Perhaps that is a blessing, ma chérie. It is one fewer lie you will have to tell."

"Yes… yes, I suppose. But I hate change! I always have! I refused to cut my hair because I was so afraid of change! And *this*," Eleanor looked at her cleavage again. "Oh, it will be so painful to discuss!"

"You will get through it, my dear girl, just as you always have," Kuveni said with a final hug.

She snapped her fingers and all of the new clothes whooshed through the air, straight into the trunk, neatly folded. Mélusine held up the new red silk robe for Eleanor as she took off her lehenga, and then she took one final look at herself in Mélusine's full-sized mirror, observing her new shape through the thin silk of the robe. Another pang of arousal shot through her.

"You look lovely, Eleanor. Just as you always have," Kuveni reiterated. "Now, shall we get you back to your husband's sleeping arms?"

Eleanor nodded her agreement, and Mélusine kissed her on both cheeks. "Everything will be alright, ma chérie."

Kuveni snapped her fingers and the trunk disappeared, and then she gathered Eleanor into her arms, and with a pleasant breeze, they were back in the WC of the rumbling train.

"Go to your husband. Confide in him," Kuveni whispered. She hugged Eleanor one last time, and then disappeared.

Eleanor looked down at her body, sighed, rolled her shoulders, and pushed her way back into the bedroom. She pulled off the robe and slipped back into the bed, into the nook of Edmund's arm. Her breasts still tingled.

She leaned over and nibbled his ear. "Darling? Edmund, darling, wake up."

He took in his awakening Rakshasa breath and pulled her tighter into his arms.

"Good morning, dearest. The rumble of the train is so relaxing, isn't it?"

"Yes, darling, it is…" Eleanor prepared herself. "But, darling, something happened in the night. Something very odd…"

Edmund sat up, now fully awake. "I didn't do something strange, did I? My… er… elements didn't ooze out of me?"

Eleanor smiled. "No, darling. This time the mystery is all mine."

Eleanor sat up beside him and looked down at her breasts. "My body just… changed." Edmund sat up and followed her gaze down to her chest.

"Blimey," he whispered. "They are much bigger than they were before, aren't they?" A smile crept across his face. "You don't think, dearest… you don't think that perhaps you're pregnant, do you?" The hope in his voice ripped a hole in her heart.

"No, darling. Women have a way of knowing these things. I'm not pregnant."

He quickly hid an expression of disappointment, and then he gently cupped her breasts in his large hands. They filled them entirely, and Eleanor felt him perk up with excitement. She climbed on top of him so he could have a better view.

"I have no rational explanation, darling. I hope it doesn't upset you?" she asked with a rare bout of timidity.

Edmund reached up and gently massaged them. "You are the most beautiful woman I've ever seen, Eleanor. It was true yesterday and it is true now. They don't hurt, do they?"

"No, darling. Your cool touch feels perfect."

He squeezed her gently and pushed her breasts together. Then he sat up and licked the crevice between them. A burst of arousal rushed through Eleanor. She had never had enough cleavage to feel the sensation of someone's tongue between her breasts before.

She leaned down and moaned with pleasure as he set about exploring the new sensations.

"I am rather glad that something like this happened to you, dearest," Edmund admitted as she lay down beside him and he took his position to straddle her. "It makes me feel more normal to know that humans also experience these kinds of changes."

"Darling, I understand you better now than I ever have," she said truthfully.

She sighed with relief as he entered her and she felt the same electric connection that had aroused her so much the night before. He leaned down and licked her breasts, and the tingling sensation erupted into a burst of pleasure unlike anything she had ever felt before.

And so together, the two lovers set about exploring each and every new sensation afforded by Eleanor's unexpected transformation.

CHAPTER 16 – THE ACCIDENTAL TRAIL

Eleanor awoke to a gentle tapping on the door. She looked up, behind the silk curtains to spy the sky burning with a bright orange sunset… or sunrise. She assumed that if someone was awake to tap on the door, it was probably sunset.

After she'd returned from her time with Kuveni and Mélusine, she and Edmund had ravished each other for hours, until they finally grew tired and fell back asleep… She couldn't have slept another fifteen hours, surely…

The tapping repeated, this time with slightly more force.

She tiptoed out of bed, gathered up the red silk robe, looking down at her strange new body, half-expecting that the whole incident had been a dream. Her new large, tingling breasts were still there. She rapped herself up, and as the tapping began again, she cracked open the door.

"Dinner will be served in half an hour, if you and Edmund are interested," Mr. Valov whispered. "The maharaja did not want to disturb you, but I thought you might be hungry after so many hours of… er… vigorous exercise."

Eleanor snorted a laugh. "Were we that loud?"

"You were not the loudest I've ever heard, but you were rather conspicuous... I'm glad you were enjoying yourselves."

"I hope we didn't offend them. We know what Rane thinks about *copulating* near the children." Eleanor laughed as she impersonated the maharani's tone. Somehow, a weight had been lifted, and she found herself in a better mood than she had felt in days.

"I think that you can get away with almost anything at the moment, Eleanor, with everyone who is aware of your divine status, which, as far as I can tell, is *everyone* on the train but Rane."

"Were the servants watching Edmund's rescue through the window?"

"Yes, and Anya was not the only one listening in on Ravi's indiscreet telephone call with the maharaja. Dev Sahib was also on the line. I suspect his cold greeting was due to his annoyance at the assertion, but Edmund's saintly time with the poor and his rescue of the boy seem to have convinced him. Now the entire staff is in a tizzy to please you."

"Blimey."

"I don't think there's anything you can do now to undo the damage."

"And you're not going to try to manipulate their silence with another lie, like you did with our witnesses in Europe?"

"It is not a security risk for uncivilized natives to worship British authority figures."

"Uncivilized natives?! Worship British authority figures?! We're not on some cannibalistic island, Leo!" As Mr. Valov glanced nervously around, Eleanor noticed her outburst and lowered her voice. "We're on a subcontinent that has had its own vibrant cultures for *thousands* of years! These people are just as civilized as anyone in Britain. In fact, the maharaja is more reasonable than any British aristocrat I've ever encountered!"

"That is exactly how my superior phrased his opinion of the matter. His misunderstanding is our gain, Eleanor. It means that the trail of worshippers you're unwittingly gathering is of no concern to the British authorities. It is one less thing for us to worry about."

"I suppose I'll take what I can get," she sighed.

"I agree completely. Now, shall I tell the royal family that you'll join them? The entire staff has been slaving away on a turmeric-free Indian dinner all day."

"Yes. Yes, of course. We have been rather antisocial, I think. I'll rouse Edmund. Can you bring us some clothing from our trunks?"

"I am at your service, Eleanor."

Mr. Valov left her alone to begin his task, and she closed the door and sighed with stress, anticipating the moment when he too would notice her new curves. She pushed the thought away and crawled into bed beside her husband.

"Edmund, darling. It's time to wake up." She kissed him gently on the lips, and he took in his awakening Rakshasa breath and pulled her straight into a deeper kiss.

"Good morning, dearest."

"Good evening, darling. Dinner will be served in half an hour. Would you like to eat? They've been working on an Indian masterpiece without any turmeric."

Edmund sat up, and his stomach growled. "I cannot think of anything I would rather eat… well, almost anything…" He dove down to lick her playfully, and she squealed with happy approval at his spontaneity. He worked his way up, landing on her breasts, lingering long enough for her to enjoy another burst of arousal until Mr. Valov's tapping at the door interrupted their fun.

Edmund ran his finger through her cleavage one last time before standing up. "I half expected that our morning games were just a delicious dream."

"You aren't disappointed that it's real, are you?" Eleanor asked self-consciously.

Edmund kissed each of her breasts and then her lips. "I love you, Eleanor. There is no possible way I could ever be disappointed, and now is no exception."

He gathered up his linen pants from the floor, and Eleanor scampered under the covers as he opened the door.

"Thank you, Leo!" Edmund said cheerfully. "I reckon we might have slept through another meal without your help."

"I'm glad to be of service, Colonel. I will wait out here to assist you however you need me."

Edmund gathered the stack of neatly folded clothing and brought it to the bed to lay out, while Mr. Valov closed them back into their room.

"This is lovely!" he exclaimed as he held up one of Kuveni's new lehengas in a striking violet that was not dissimilar to the color of Edmund's Rakshasa plasma. "Look at the bead work!"

Eleanor's gratitude almost overwhelmed her anxiety. She'd forgotten to specify that Mr. Valov should find one of her loosest fitting outfits, but she loved the gesture that he had chosen one of the most flamboyant Indian outfits in the collection for her to wear.

Edmund held up a rich cerulean sherwani for himself. "I think Leo finally understands our taste!"

He pulled on his new silk pants and the heavily beaded jacket in time to kiss Eleanor's neck as she pulled on the new blouse. It all felt real now that he was helping her dress, rather than the dreamlike experience in Mélusine's magical lair. Eleanor looked down as soon as he was finished, and spied a hint of cleavage that she hadn't noticed the first time she'd tried it on. Edmund noticed it too and kissed her as he snuck a tickling feel with his cold finger.

"You look beautiful, dearest," he whispered into her ear.

"They're going to notice," Eleanor sighed. "I look so different than how I looked yesterday, and this outfit accentuates it."

300

Edmund helped her pull up the flowing, beaded silk skirt, and she shivered as he reached around her to tie the drawstring, copping a pleasant feel of her bum before he finished his task.

"Are you sure they'll notice?" he asked. "Perhaps we just notice it more because we are so well acquainted with your lovely naked body."

Eleanor sighed as she pulled the dupatta up and held it behind her back, thinking through how she'd seen Babri and Shruti tuck it. "It's possible that you're right, but it seems unlikely."

As Mr. Valov tapped on the door again, Eleanor sighed with resignation and readied herself for a test that she desperately wanted to avoid. "Open it, darling. We will see what Mr. Valov thinks of this development."

Edmund nodded his agreement and pulled open the door.

"The maharaja asked me to tell you…" He trailed off as he took in Eleanor's new look. He blinked several times, took in a deep breath, and then struggled to continue his thought. "He asked me to tell you that there will be cocktails before dinner, if you'd like to come now."

"Thank you, Mr. Valov. We'd love to," Edmund said as he followed Mr. Valov's gaze back to Eleanor.

"Eleanor… you look… er… especially stunning tonight," Mr. Valov said as he looked around desperately for an out. "I'd better go tell the maharaja that you plan to join him…"

"You're going the wrong direction, Mr. Valov," Eleanor pointed out.

"I need to visit the WC first," he squeaked as he ran away from them.

"I think it was obvious," Eleanor humphed. She sat down on the bed and looked down at her cleavage. "He could hardly contain himself. That's never, ever happened to me in my life."

"Eleanor, I can hardly contain myself most of the time that I'm around you. You drive me mad with desire."

"You don't count, darling. You know what treasures lie beneath." She finally cracked a smile. "And they are at your beck and call."

He sat down beside her and coaxed her into a gentle kiss. "Shall I collect a different outfit for you from your trunk? I'm rather impressed that this one fits, to be honest. Babri's genius must know no bounds."

"I suppose," she conceded. "I think there is a looser salwar kameez in there with a scarf I can drape over the front."

Edmund snapped his fingers with an idea. "First, let's try this…" He gathered her dupatta and draped it over her with a slightly different but similarly effective technique to what Babri had used, tucking it into her skirt and wrapping it around her with great skill. When he was finished, despite not using a single pin, her front was covered with graceful pleats folded into the scarf, and only the sleeves of her blouse showed clearly. Her sides were still bare, but the bulk of her revealing front had been successfully covered.

"Dare I ask how you know how to do that?" Eleanor asked.

"I learned a thing or two in my decades in India, dearest," he answered vaguely. "Does it work for you?"

Eleanor stood up and walked to the door of their WC to use the small mirror. "It should suffice, I suppose. Thank you, darling. This was very clever."

She noticed her wild hair as she caught a glimpse of herself in the mirror.

"Perhaps I should take a moment for some human hygiene, darling."

"Yes, yes. Of course," he agreed, leaving her alone without another word.

She frantically worked her fingers through her wild hair, with more success than she had anticipated.

Let me help you, Uma suggested. Eleanor ran her fingers through her hair more slowly, and the wild wisps calmed themselves into the gentle ringlets that only Kuveni had ever been able to produce.

When she was finished working her hair into a loose, old-fashioned up-do, Eleanor noticed her cosmetic bag on the counter by the washbasin and made a note to thank Mr. Valov for his thoughtful unpacking... as soon as he was not overwhelmed with lust for her. She sighed. She had always been grateful that her shape wasn't conspicuous enough to attract such attention. She was not ready in the slightest to deal with yet another inconvenience; although, she was intensely grateful that Edmund had not seemed to be jealous at Mr. Valov's reaction.

She finished up her mundane business, put on some perfunctory makeup, moved the mirror around to make sure the dupatta was properly covering her cleavage, and pushed her way back into their bedroom.

Edmund was chatting amicably with Mr. Valov, who looked intensely relieved by the modest update to her outfit.

"The maharaja is waiting," he informed her.

Edmund offered her his arm with the archaic Victorian gesture that always made her laugh, and as Mr. Valov offered her a questioning look, communicating, no doubt, that he hoped for more of an explanation in a private setting, she took her husband's arm and readied herself to face the world.

As they entered the dining room, the dogs and the children rushed to greet them.

"I got a splint!" Georgie exclaimed as he waved his broken arm towards them. "Just like a soldier!"

"You look... very beautiful in that lehenga, Eleanor," Anya said shyly. She looked over to her mother, who didn't offer her the standard chastisement for commenting on Eleanor's looks.

Instead, Rane stood up to greet them.

"You are glowing, Eleanor. No doubt from hours upon hours of honeymoon bliss... a blessing afforded only to those responsible individuals who have been joined together in holy matrimony in the eyes of God," she added, addressing her children directly.

Eleanor and Edmund both blushed.

"Here, here!" Madho Rao interrupted as he directed a servant carrying a silver tray with four cocktails garnished with delicate floating lemon peels to present the offering to Edmund and Eleanor. "My lord, my lady, it is our greatest privilege to toast to your marriage."

Edmund and Eleanor each took a cocktail, and the maharaja collected the other two, keeping one for himself and handing the other to his wife. Another servant followed, offering delicate crystal champagne glasses filled with a thick, orange juice to the children.

"Mmm! Mango!" Anya exclaimed.

"Anya," Madho Rao hissed as she took her first sip before the rest of the group.

Eleanor clinked Edmund's glass, and their relaxed reaction calmed the maharaja, who followed their lead.

"I'm glad to see the children are recovering nicely." Eleanor took a second sip of the surprisingly flavorful mix.

"Sri Bidkar mentioned that you like cognac. We called ahead to the British Imperial Hotel where Ravi has arranged for you to stay in Agra and asked them for their recipe suggestions. This is what they offered. It is called a sidecar, and apparently, it is all the rage in Paris right now."

"It's delicious, thank you," Edmund replied with another toast. He drank down half the cocktail in one controlled Rakshasa gulp.

It was strangely delicious, a bit too sweet with whatever had been added to the cognac, but the lemon added just the right amount of tang. It was a dangerously drinkable drink.

Eleanor was proud of Edmund for having anything left in his glass at all, and as she contemplated Uma's suggestion to fully embrace the pleasures of her humanity, she decided at that moment to begin a little test. She matched Edmund's pace.

Madho Rao, looking rather pleased at their reaction, nodded towards Dev Sahib, who rushed into the kitchen with the server, whispering his orders to prepare another round.

Rane looked less impressed by their enthusiastic consumption. "Temperance is a virtue that should rarely be ignored, but one's honeymoon is a very special time. It is a reward for making a lifelong sacred commitment," she explained to her children. "Someday, if you are good, you too will be able to enjoy many grown-up pleasures on your honeymoon."

"I'm never getting married. I'm going to be a thoroughbred trainer!" Anya declared.

Rane threw her a piercing look. "You will last one hour shoveling manure before you decide that being a maharani is a far better fate. Perhaps when we are home, we can arrange for an apprenticeship in the stables for you."

"That's not a bad idea, actually," Eleanor interjected. Rane was not pleased by her support of the idea that had been offered as a threat. "It's good to understand the work that goes into training horses, Anya. If you don't like it, you can find other work that fulfills you."

"You will be a maharani," Rane reiterated. "Shoveling manure is for those who were not born to a position like yours."

Madho Rao cringed as his wife offended Eleanor, but as Eleanor looked around, spotting the servants whispering fearfully as they waited for her reaction, she smiled and let the maharani have her moment.

"The Queen of England spends quite a bit of time with her horses. Perhaps you can be a maharani and still enjoy your riding, Anya. It isn't the worst thing in the world to let someone else shovel the manure."

Anya chugged down the rest of her mango juice and then humphed down with her arms crossed in the corner in a singularly adolescent move.

"Lady Eleanor shoveled manure, and she's even more important than you are, Mummy," she declared as a final blow against her mother.

Rane was genuinely confused by the assertion as she threw a questioning look towards her husband and then towards Eleanor, but with perfect timing to defuse the conversation, Dev Sahib returned with another tray of cocktails, and Eleanor used the excuse to chug down the remnants of her first so that he could replace it with a new one.

"I'm simply famished," Madho Rao declared, changing the subject. "Dev Sahib, it is time to serve dinner!"

"Yes, Your Highness!" Dev Sahib agreed, stealing a reverential glance at Edmund before rushing back into the kitchen.

Eleanor checked that her dupatta was still covering her front as she took a seat beside Edmund at the richly decorated table. The idea of checking that her clothing was sufficiently modest was not something that she was used to, and she hated it.

Anya took a seat beside her, to Rane's obvious displeasure, but Madho Rao whispered something into his wife's ear, and she humphed her begrudging agreement.

"Do you think I should be a thoroughbred trainer, Eleanor?" Anya whispered as Georgie took a seat beside her.

"I think that you should focus on school and building your character for now, and when the time comes, you will be able to make an educated decision about your future." Eleanor was rather pleased by the diplomacy of her answer.

"I wish I could go to school," Anya sighed.

Eleanor almost spilled her drink at the development. "You don't go to school?"

"Mummy doesn't think it's proper," Anya explained. "And she doesn't think that a maharani needs to know too much. She says too much education makes girls ornery."

"That is enough," Madho Rao hissed. "The children have the best tutors in India," he explained to Eleanor. "They study a wide range of subjects far beyond the capacity of the best schools in the province."

"I see..." Eleanor found the maharaja's concern with her opinion of their household to be disconcerting. She was used to having an opinion and working hard not to bring the conversation to a grinding halt by sharing her radical feminist views.

"Please do not think poorly of us, my lady. We have always done what we thought was best for the children," he added, rather desperately. "The only better education they might get would be in England, but we did not want to send them away."

"I understand completely your desire to keep your children with you, Madho Rao. You have a very wholesome family compared to most I've encountered." Eleanor hoped that the compliment would dispel his fear before Edmund could smell it.

Madho Rao's face lit up. "Thank you, my lady!"

"I thought we weren't using honorifics this evening, Madho Rao?" Rane asked sharply.

"Yes, you're right, lovey. I will work harder to remember." He threw a humble, apologetic glance towards Eleanor.

"What are your subjects, Anya?" Eleanor asked.

Anya straightened her posture and smiled at her inclusion. "Painting, literature, Sanskrit, English, Hindi, Marathi, music, dance, history, political science, and geography."

"That sounds like quite a healthy range of subjects," Eleanor praised. "Maths and Science seem conspicuously absent, but still..."

"What good would Maths and Science be to a maharani? Is she going to discuss the latest scientific journals with her peers? Or perhaps discover a new planet through her hobby telescope?

Certainly the humanities are more valuable to a young woman of Anya's stature. She will keep India's culture alive while being able to discuss the most interesting topics at any dinner party."

Eleanor worked hard not to guffaw. Planning an education around dinner party conversations seemed utterly absurd.

The maharani is not wrong. Eleanor closed her eyes as Uma chimed in. *The girl doesn't have the freedom that you had, Eleanor. They are training her to fulfill her destiny just as I and so many others were trained as young girls. She will be a great leader, and her education must prepare her for all of her duties, including dinner parties.*

Eleanor felt rather ornery at Uma's assertion, perhaps as a result of her over-education.

You are ornery, my child. Wonderfully ornery. It's one reason why I chose you to be my vessel. But you must realize the impact of your words on these people. They live in a world that you do not fully understand yet. Be careful what you criticize. They will take your words as gospel.

Eleanor opened her eyes and smiled, tempering her fiery reaction as she thought about her point more carefully. "Perhaps Anya has the best scientific mind in India. If she never gets any education on the topic at all, who knows what knowledge will be lost to humanity? What a loss for the world if that were the case."

"Perhaps one of the millions of farmers tilling their fields has one of the best scientific minds. What a tragedy for India that they are not educated enough to know. Shall we go collect all the farmers from the fields in an attempt to teach them equations?" Rane countered. "Perhaps they can count the nation's shrinking supply of rice as a homework assignment."

Madho Rao looked visibly distressed by her assertive discourse with Eleanor, but Eleanor rather liked it. She liked that *someone* was not afraid to argue with her, and Rane's cheek reminded her of why she had liked the woman the night they'd met.

"I have always believed in free education for the masses. We should be educating brilliant scientists out of the fields and into universities. Perhaps they will even invent a technique that will increase the food supply with exponential results. The ones who don't succeed will be left to till the fields, just as they always have been, and you will still have your rice."

"Ha!" Rane laughed. "It will never happen in India. Never."

"That is what my mother said about Scotland twenty years ago, and here we are with a fully literate populace," Eleanor countered. She found the escalation strangely invigorating.

"Please, Rane. Let it be," Madho Rao whispered.

"Why? You agree with me!" she exclaimed. "Why should I not voice our opinions on *our* train to our guests with whom we are on a first name basis?"

"Perhaps… perhaps I was mistaken…" Madho Rao looked nervously at Eleanor, and Rane followed his gaze.

Rane lowered her voice, working unsuccessfully to hide her annoyance at her husband. "Madho Rao, you said just last month during our dinner with the viceroy that India needs its peasants to be peasants. It is the only way the social order will work. Where is this change of heart coming from?"

Madho Rao's face turned red as he struggled for an answer. "I… I… I have learned things in the last few days that have led me to reconsider my position on many issues. We were… perhaps too rigid in some ways, lovey."

"Rigid?!" Rane exclaimed.

"God helped Memsahib Jyoti and Jaap Sahib," Anya interjected. "God didn't punish them after all."

"What does our pregnant governess have to do with peasants tilling fields?!" Rane was quickly losing any semblance of calm, and Edmund finally looked up from his conversation with Georgie to observe the wide eyes of the many servants who were watching their escalating argument from their positions around the room. He took in a whiff of their fear with puzzlement.

"Is everything alright, dearest?" he asked.

"Yes, darling. We stumbled into a heated debate about politics."

"Please forgive us, my lord," Madho Rao whispered.

Rane looked her husband up and down skeptically. "Perhaps, Edmund, you can explain why my husband is so humbled in your presence. It is a state I have never observed in him before."

As Edmund struggled for an explanation, Madho Rao finally stepped in. "He saved the children, lovey. Lord and Lady Marriner saved our children. Jaap Sahib was locked inside the children's carriage when they were being attacked, and Edmund is the one who disabled all of those men."

Eleanor was exceedingly grateful for his skilled half-truth.

"Then Jaap Sahib did nothing?" Rane asked with disbelief. "One man disabled seven?"

"Eleanor helped!" Anya exclaimed.

"We owe Lord and Lady Marriner our children's lives, Rane," Madho Rao whispered.

"Why didn't anyone tell me?" she asked with a combination of anger and disappointment. "You have all conspired to keep me in the dark? Why?! Is this all about Jaap Sahib's position?"

"I asked them not to discuss our involvement in the rescue," Eleanor jumped in. "I thought it would make things easier."

"How does lying to me in my own household make things easier?" Rane pressed.

Without her permission, Uma reached Eleanor's hand forward and grabbed the maharani's hand. *Because there are truths that you are not ready to know, my child, and now is not the time to discuss them. It is Shakti's will.*

"I'm sorry, Rane," Eleanor said simply for the rest of the group to hear. "You are right to be angry at being excluded from a secret in your own household. I would feel exactly the same way if I were in your position."

Rane was speechless as she nodded her forgiveness.

Eleanor pulled her hand away and looked back at Edmund, who was observing their exchange with heightened interest. She hoped that from the angle of his seat next to her, he hadn't caught a glimpse of the green glow of Uma in her eyes.

"Please forgive my outburst, my lady," Rane whispered.

Eleanor sighed with resignation as the last bastion of normal conversation dissolved into a subtle tone of reverence.

It had to be done, my child, before Lord Kalki was exposed.

"I rather enjoy debates," Eleanor reassured Rane and Madho Rao, trying desperately to bring back the casual tone. "I find that discourse is often a useful avenue for expanding one's own views on a topic."

"How enlightened," Rane murmured.

"Well, Georgie was just telling me all about his interest in mechanical engineering. It's a topic a bit beyond my schooling, I must admit," Edmund said cheerfully. Eleanor appreciated his intervention, although she wondered how much he'd understood about their odd exchange.

"I was telling Edmund how steam engines work!" Georgie exclaimed.

"Please, do tell the rest of us. I have always wondered myself how they work," Eleanor encouraged him.

As Georgie embarked upon a detailed description of engine construction techniques, Dev Sahib and a troop of servants silently carried in enormous silver platters, far too big for the six people seated at the table to finish.

Edmund's stomach growled with anticipation as the servers lifted up the silver covers to reveal plates of crispy fried vegetables.

"Pakoras!" Georgie interrupted his own point to exclaim. Madho Rao slapped his hand as he reached forward with his fingers to grab one.

"Edmund will go first!" Madho Rao declared. "Sri Bidkar thought you would like these. Nothing on our menu tonight has the tiniest hint of turmeric," he said directly to Edmund with a softer tone.

"They look wonderful," Edmund reassured him. "Thank you so much for accommodating me."

"It is nothing," Madho Rao said sincerely.

Edmund waited politely as the servants served him and everyone else a small plate, and Eleanor continued her silent attempt to pace her husband, eating just as many pakoras as he did and drinking just as many refills of the cocktail while Georgie chattered away, and the maharaja and his wife watched Eleanor and Edmund with silent curiosity.

The pakoras eventually gave way to a bright red chicken curry, and despite the rich flavor, Eleanor soon realized that pacing her husband was an unpleasant endeavor on many fronts. In her second helping of curry, she realized that her stomach simply couldn't fit anything else, and she sat back and contemplated her discomfort while Edmund took over the conversation from Georgie, engaging the entire family in a jovial discussion of classical English literature that she didn't care about in the slightest. Anya, however, had quite a bit to contribute to the conversation, impressing Edmund and her father equally, while Rane only offered Eleanor a subtle knowing glance that she apologetically relegated when she noticed Eleanor's attention.

When the meal was finally over, Madho Rao rubbed his stomach happily.

"I must admit, I didn't think it would be as good without turmeric, but I didn't taste the difference at all."

"Everything was scrumptious," Edmund directed his praise towards Dev Sahib, who looked like he might explode with excitement at the compliment.

"Thank you, my lord!"

Madho Rao leaned in as he returned to business. "We will arrive in Gwalior tomorrow afternoon. Ravi has already arranged for your transport to Agra. We are a day behind schedule, so you'd best hurry along, or else poor Sri Bidkar will be terribly upset. He's put quite a bit of effort into planning your next adventure."

"Well, we needn't ruin Sri Bidkar's plans," Edmund agreed.

Eleanor was eager to get away from her attentive audience, back to a place where no one knew her, and where she and Edmund were simply a pair of delightfully well-dressed foreign tourists.

As Eleanor stood up, she realized that while her stomach was disgustingly full, she didn't feel the effect of the copious cocktails at all. The feeling was both pleasant and disappointing. She rather enjoyed her tipsy evenings, when she could escape from the harsh realities of her complicated life, even if she paid for the escape with a painful hangover in the morning.

"It was a lovely dinner. Thank you so much," Eleanor declared as she made a bee-line for the door. Edmund followed her hurried exit, offering the maharaja a final nod of thanks.

"Are you alright, dearest?" he asked as they tumbled into the hallway of the guest carriage.

"I ate too much…" she admitted. "I thought I would see if I could pace you."

"Good lord, why?!" Edmund exclaimed.

Eleanor laughed and then groaned with pain. "It was a foolish idea, I agree. I'm paying for it now."

"Eleanor?" Anya followed them into their carriage without knocking. "Eleanor, will you teach me that move before you leave? The one you did yesterday to knock out the bad man?"

"Yes, yes, of course! I'm sorry. I completely forgot!" Eleanor agreed.

"Hurry, before Mummy realizes I didn't go to my room. She doesn't want me to learn how to fight."

Edmund was intrigued.

Eleanor ignored the cramps in her stomach to begin her demonstration, using Edmund as a volunteer, but as Anya took her place next to Eleanor to mime her, Rane pushed her way into the carriage. Anya stiffened up, and Eleanor readied herself for another confrontation.

"Anya has asked me to show her how I disabled her attacker yesterday. It is a useful skill for all women to know." Eleanor spoke with her most authoritative voice.

Rane moved to argue, and then she thought better of it. "Perhaps you can show me as well, my lady."

"Right then, perhaps you can take a position beside Anya. Both of you can copy my moves." Eleanor was not expecting such an easy concession, but as the maharani dutifully took her place, Eleanor continued her demonstration matter-of-factly. "First, you must take him by surprise…"

Madho Rao and Georgie tumbled into the hallway, and stopped as they noticed the odd position.

"Lady Eleanor is teaching us how to stop evil men!" Anya exclaimed.

Eleanor laughed. "I am showing them a technique for fighting off a male attacker. You are welcome to join."

Madho Rao looked timidly at Edmund, who smiled his agreement. "It is not only women who must know how to protect themselves."

"Right then," Eleanor suddenly found their attentive audience amusing, and Edmund's good cheer helped her relax. "Everyone follow me."

Madho Rao and Georgie took their positions behind Rane and Anya.

"So, as I was saying, the element of surprise is key. The longer he has to prepare, the more strength you will have to combat in your opponent. So, as you rush him, aim for the groin. It is any man's weakest spot. Position your knee so that it will engage the most sensitive part of the man's… er… manhood…"

As Eleanor demonstrated her suggestion by miming her attack on Edmund's crotch in slow motion, the children giggled and the

314

maharani blushed. Edmund winked and stood dutifully in position for Eleanor to finish off her demonstration.

"Then push all your weight into your thigh and your knee as you attack him."

The entire family copied her movements, miming them in the air.

"Yes, yes, that's good. Now push all your weight in… yes… very good!"

"You must keep an eye out for him to grab you by the neck, it will be his most effective move," Edmund chimed in as he reached forward and gently put his large hands around Eleanor's neck.

"Which is why you should keep your elbow ready to smack him at the pressure point that will disable his grip," Eleanor continued as she demonstrated what she meant.

As the entire family mimed her movements, Mr. Valov emerged from the dining car, carrying a tea sandwich. He stopped to watch them.

"Perhaps you can practice it on each other. Switching positions will give you a better sense of what you're combatting," Eleanor said as she fell out of position.

"Thank you, my lady," Madho Rao whispered.

"Thank you, Lady Eleanor!" Anya exclaimed as she pulled Eleanor into a tight hug.

"Now to bed!" Rane exclaimed as she rallied the children into their carriage. She stopped as they disappeared into their berths. "Thank you, my lady. Thank you both for saving my children."

Eleanor nodded and smiled shyly, and Madho Rao followed his wife into the children's carriage, closing the door behind them.

"I'm glad to see you got something to eat, Leo," Edmund said as Mr. Valov approached them.

"Dev Sahib was very accommodating," Mr. Valov replied. Edmund's cheer was not rubbing off on him. "Eleanor, if you have a moment, I'd like to discuss something."

Eleanor's heart began racing.

"Really, Mr. Valov, I'm sure you noticed something odd earlier, but now is not the time to talk about it."

"It's not that, Eleanor. I promise. I just have a few loose ends to discuss… er… privately." Eleanor nodded to Edmund, and he dutifully left them alone, closing himself into their berth.

"Really, Leo, I'm not in the mood to discuss my changing physicality," Eleanor whispered.

"All of the thugs were torn apart!" Mr. Valov blurted.

"What?"

"My back-up arrived thirty minutes after the train escaped, which was a close enough call as it was… we barely escaped a bloody riot! But by the time the Secret Service arrived, all of the bodies were dismembered, strewn about in the town square for all to see!"

"What? How?"

"He's becoming more aggressive, Eleanor! And there is no question now that he's on your trail!"

"Who?"

"Ravana! Edmund's father!"

"Do you have any more evidence that Edmund's father is the culprit?" Eleanor asked as she worked hard to keep calm.

"He doesn't leave evidence, Eleanor! He's too good for that! He leaves only what he wants us to see, what he wants the world to see. That is *always* how he has operated."

Mr. Valov reached for his cigarette case, and then with a moment of fortitude, he aborted his plan and took a big bite of his sandwich.

"Do you think the maharaja and his family are in danger?" Eleanor asked, focusing on the most immediate concern.

"So far the victims are still people who have threatened you," Mr. Valov replied. "But there's no telling what he'll do next. He's a brutal monster, Eleanor."

"Well, what do we do? Run? Run where? How do we possibly run without Edmund figuring out what's going on? We aren't even certain it's his father behind this."

"I don't have any bloody idea what to do. This is utterly beyond me, Eleanor."

Eleanor thought about the predicament for several minutes while Mr. Valov paced slowly, finishing off his sandwich.

"We must continue moving forward," she sighed. "Short of hiding under a rock, or in Mélusine's cave, I don't see any other options. We have to let this play out, and be more careful than ever that our presence is not endangering the people around us..." Suddenly another unpleasant idea crossed her mind. "The maharaja isn't in trouble with the authorities, is he? They don't think that Jaap Sahib and the other guards did this, do they?"

"I have been using all of my influence to keep your allies safe, Eleanor. I've done things... things that you and Edmund would not approve of..."

"Like what?"

"You do not want to know, Eleanor. I promise. But even with my tactics, I don't know how much longer I can keep it going. This crime was horrific enough that it is sure to be in every newspaper in India by tomorrow morning, and we do not need that attention! I'm using all of my influence to keep you and Edmund and the maharaja and his men out of it!"

"Jaap Sahib!" Eleanor exclaimed. "Where's Jaap Sahib?! I forgot to write his letter to the Bidkars! He's not in trouble is he? He's not taking the fall?"

"You can take that worry off your mind, Eleanor. I've kept him out of it. He's already in Bombay, and I called the Bidkars on your behalf while he was in transit."

"You really are an excellent butler."

Mr. Valov smiled, and Eleanor felt him relax in a way that she had never seen him relax before. It was a familiarity that only came from a 'body-carrying' friend (or a comfortable lover), and she let

317

herself accept the positivity of the development without dwelling on his newfound lust that complicated the situation more than she was willing or able to deal with.

"That's not all," he continued without acknowledging her wandering mind. "Shruti already collected Jyoti from the women's ward of some horrific mission convalescent home. You have done that girl a great service, I reckon."

"Well... that's at least something..."

"So..." Mr. Valov shifted uncomfortably. "Are you going to tell me what happened to you? To your... er... figure?"

Eleanor shrugged. "Apparently, the goddess who's inhabiting my body has decided that this is how I'm going to look from now on. Kuveni had to make a whole new wardrobe to accommodate her whim."

"Blimey, Eleanor. So you just woke up... changed?"

"That is exactly what happened. It was bloody awful."

"Well, it doesn't look awful."

Eleanor raised her eyebrows. "Yes, Edmund and I were both well aware of your appreciation."

Mr. Valov straightened his posture and cleared his throat. "I'm sorry, I won't say one more word about it. Your husband is waiting for you. I will pack your trunks and wake you in the late morning if you are not awake before that. We will disembark at the station in Gwalior and board the first-class carriage of the train to Agra. It will be a British train, Eleanor. Shall I keep out English or Indian clothing for you?"

"I think it is time to embrace our heritage again," she sighed.

"Thank god," Mr. Valov murmured.

"You're welcome." Eleanor winked.

"Good night, Eleanor."

"Good night, Leo."

As Eleanor entered the bedroom, the smoke of Mr. Valov's freshly lit cigarette wafted in behind her, and Edmund was topless, pretending to snore, cuddled up with the two dogs sprawled out

318

on both sides of him on the bed. He waited patiently for her reaction to his little joke.

"I suppose I'll just have to sleep in the hallway," she sighed. Then, without warning, she pounced onto the bed beside him, nudging the dogs out of her way so that she could reclaim her position in the nook of his arm.

"The element of surprise?" Edmund asked as he enticed her into a kiss.

"One cannot underestimate its importance," Eleanor agreed as she ran her finger along his bare chest.

"Can I ask you something, Eleanor?"

Eleanor did not like his sudden return to seriousness.

"Of course, darling." She tried to keep her anxiety under control.

"Were you smoking with Mr. Valov on the platform last night? Is that why you took so long to board the train?"

That was not the question she thought he was going to ask.

"I was, darling. I smoked half a cigarette. It was the first in ten years, and I couldn't even finish it, I found it so grotesque. Please don't be mad at him. I insisted."

"Please do not do things that will kill you, Eleanor," Edmund implored.

"Ditto, darling," she replied with a gentle kiss. "Now get me out of this blouse!"

Edmund helped her undress, and she helped him, and then they both cuddled up naked under the covers with the fluffy dogs curled up happily at the foot of the bed.

As Edmund copped a pleasant feel of her breasts, she nestled into his arms.

Uma, can you lock up my raging fear until morning?

As you wish, my child. Sleep well.

And in her husband's loving arms, with the help of her new divine partner, Eleanor slept.

PART THREE
BRITISH INDIA

CHAPTER 17 – CULTURE SHOCK

Eleanor awoke once again to a gentle tapping on the door, and the dogs both sat up straight with their ears perked. Edmund stirred and then rolled over with a snore, and she tiptoed across the room, slipping on her robe as she went. She cracked open the door, taking extra care that it wasn't open enough for Mr. Valov to catch an arousing glimpse of her figure under the thin silk, but the dogs did not heed her plan as they pushed their way past her, trampled past Mr. Valov, and raced into the children's carriage. Eleanor sighed with annoyance as she covered her cleavage with one hand and returned the opening back to a crack with the other.

Mr. Valov's discomfort was only given away by the sweat on his forehead. "The maharaja and his family are finishing up a late breakfast now, and they have saved a large platter of Indian pancakes for you. We will be arriving in Gwalior in less than two hours. Here are your clothes."

He held up a stack of neatly folded linen and silk, and Eleanor blushed as she opened the door wide enough to take them.

"Thank you, Leo," she whispered hastily as she slammed the door shut, just in time to keep her robe from slipping open in front of him. She sighed with resignation as she looked down at her large breasts.

She put the clothes on the bed and began inspecting Mr. Valov's selections. For Edmund, there was a suit made of starched white linen that he was sure to love, although she found it a bit too... American in style. For her, Mr. Valov had selected one of her favorite new pant-suits from Kuveni's collection. High-waisted flowing white linen pants paired with a two-piece midnight blue silk top—a solid silk structured camisole that gave away quite a generous view of her new cleavage underneath a sheer silk blouse with baggy flowing sleeves that tapered into tight buttoning cuffs. When she'd tried it on with Kuveni, she'd found the peek-a-boo effect of the cleavage and the tight fit of the camisole underneath the baggier sheer silk rather arousing, but now she wasn't sure she was ready to show it to the world... or Mr. Valov.

A wide-brimmed hat of perfectly matching midnight blue felt with white beaded accents made the outfit look like something meant for the races, but she loved it anyway.

As she contemplated whether or not she had the courage to wear her new outfit outside, Edmund stirred and turned over, and she decided not to wake him. It had been too long since she'd had leisurely time to herself to laze about at a bathroom vanity getting herself ready. She grabbed the hat and took it with her into the WC, leaving the rest of the outfit laid out on the bed.

She sat on the stool in front of the small mirror at the washbasin and carefully brushed her teeth, washed her face, and began putting on a slightly thicker layer of makeup than she'd been wearing, including her old favorite red lipstick, but as she powdered her nose and leaned in to look at her eyebrows more carefully, she noticed that her green eyes were much greener than they had been before.

"Uma..." she muttered. "This better be the last change."

Her eyes began to glow.

My child, I know as much as you do about the physical effects of my presence. I did not expect you to be conscious of my presence at all.

Really? You planned to just ride around silently inside of me? How wretched!

That is how it has always been for avatars. This arrangement between you and me is unique, my child. I have never heard of anything quite like it.

Then couldn't you just return me to my former state? Do I really need such green eyes and such large breasts?

It is not my will, it is Shakti's.

But aren't you Shakti? Or Parvati? Or Durga? I don't really understand the difference. As far as I can tell, there are three goddesses involved, not including you, and I have no bloody clue which one is which.

Shakti is the great goddess. She is the underlying energy of the universe, and she manifests in many forms. One of her divine forms is Parvati, the benevolent aspect of the Transformer of the Universe, and the wife of Lord Shiva. Durga is one of her warrior forms. She is a fierce aspect of the Transformer who uses her great power to fight evil. I am Shakti's avatar of transformation, and so are you.

I am nothing but a human with a goddess lurking inside of me.

You are wrong, Eleanor. You are much more than an average human. I have waited for you for centuries.

I don't believe you. I am as ordinary as ordinary can be. I'm the daughter of a bloody bigamist, for god's sake!

There is always meaning in our circumstances, my child, especially the difficult ones. What better way to learn earthly forgiveness? Those who are perfect do not feel the same empathy for the fallen as those who have clawed their way out of an abyss.

I'm too human, Uma. I have too many vices. Are you sure you weren't supposed to pick Shruti? She is much more virtuous than I am, and she has learned many useful things from her upbringing with Ravi and Reya.

I am never wrong, Eleanor.

But I don't even understand Hinduism. Even now, I don't understand the distinction between these different goddesses. Surely you were meant to pick someone who understands everything!

No one understands everything, my child. Those who think that they do understand the least. And it is an unbiased mind that can best see the forest for the trees. The most profound truth is that we are all connected, and you and I are both vessels of Shakti's transformational aspect. It is why you must be more careful from now on to avoid catalyzing unintentional changes in those you encounter.

Great...

It is as much a gift as it is a burden, my child. But it is up to you to make it so.

My stomach felt like it was going to explode last night.

So eating massive quantities of human food is not part of this gift. Now you know.

Neither is healing. Eleanor looked down at her bandaged hand. It still hurt as she moved it.

You are still human, Eleanor. You must always remember that. You are not immortal, and neither was I. You must take precautions accordingly.

As Edmund began stirring in the bedroom, Eleanor finished up her grooming by gathering her fiery ringlets into a loose, low bun and pinning the hat stylishly askew.

You look lovely, my child.

Don't you mean that we look lovely?

I will endeavor to leave your body and your mind to you, my child, unless my intervention is absolutely necessary. Lady Mélusine is very wise.

Yes, she is.

Eleanor stood up and pushed her way back into the bedroom. Edmund was already dressed in his new suit.

"Good morning, dearest!" he greeted her cheerfully as he finished tying his tie. He perked up as he noticed her open robe. "Back to British India today, I suppose. I will have to save the rest of Babri's offerings for another time."

He gathered her into a naked embrace and squeezed her bum playfully as he stole a kiss.

"Good morning, darling." She wiped her red lipstick off of his lips.

"Just look at the artistry of your hat!" Edmund exclaimed as he inspected it. "The subtly of the beadwork is thoroughly impressive!"

She stood on her tiptoes and kissed him again, letting her robe fall to the floor with a gentle tug of her sash. She felt his appreciation through his new trousers, and she fought back another pang of arousal.

She tore herself away from him and more thoroughly wiped her lipstick off of his lips. "We will be arriving soon, and there is a platter of idlis awaiting us in the dining car."

Edmund's stomach growled, and he helped her step into her new trousers. Then he watched with continued excitement as she put on her new blouse.

"Dearest, I don't know if I'm going to be able to contain myself with you wearing that." He ran his finger along her cleavage.

"You and every other man I encounter," Eleanor sighed with frustration. "Should I wear something else? I've never had to plan around this before."

Edmund pulled her into his arms and kissed her again. "Eleanor, you're lovely. You should wear whatever you want. Besides, I have it on great authority now that you know how to defend yourself."

She gently brought her knee to his groin like she had during her self-defense demonstration for the maharaja's family, and they both laughed.

"I love you, Edmund." She was more emotional about the statement than she'd intended to be.

"I love you, Eleanor." He kissed her again. She wondered if she had any lipstick left...

She gathered up her jewelry from the bedside table, including Edmund's mother's ring, Mélusine's green sapphire talisman necklace, and the paste emerald earrings from Babri's collection she'd been wearing upon their arrival.

"You look very smart, dearest."

"Thank you, darling."

Edmund playfully snapped at her fingers with his teeth as Eleanor wiped the final round of red lipstick off of his lips. Then she took a deep breath, preparing herself to face the outside world as he pushed open the door for her.

Mr. Valov was pacing in the hallway, surrounded by the dogs, who rushed up to greet Edmund with cheerful barks and sloppy licks.

"'Tis almost time to part ways, my fluffy friends." Edmund squatted down to let them show their affection, scratching their ears and rubbing the spot just above their wagging tails.

As Mr. Valov saw that they were fully dressed and ready to leave, he smiled with relief, and then he noticed Eleanor's blouse and looked away.

"Breakfast is waiting for you in the dining car. I will pack your remaining items into your trunks."

Without another word, he rushed past them and disappeared into their room.

Familial chaos emanated from the children's carriage, but Edmund's stomach led the way, and the dogs followed them as they took their seats in the dining car. Dev Sahib rushed in from the kitchen carrying an enormous silver platter, followed by two more servants who carried smaller bowls of bright red sambar and white coconut chutney.

"Sri Bidkar said that my lord enjoys idlis. I hope that they are to your liking," he declared as he lifted the platter's lid.

"Mmm…" Edmund sighed happily. "They look wonderful."

"Thank you, my lord!" Dev Sahib bowed and rushed back into the kitchen.

"Are you ready to return to British India, darling? I don't even really know what that means yet. We've spent all of our time with your Indian friends."

"To be honest, I'm a bit worried about what it means now myself," Edmund admitted. "When I was a soldier in uniform there was a certain order to things. I could influence precarious situations without a mess of trouble following me, but I'm not so sure that will happen now… for many reasons."

"Trouble does seem to be stalking us…"

"Well, we will find out soon enough what British India has in store for us." Edmund forced himself back to cheer and piled his plate high with idlis. Eleanor took a human portion.

She gazed out the window as the sunburnt countryside passed by in a blur, enjoying the simple silence as Edmund finished off plate after plate, until all of the idlis were gone.

"Well, that was thoroughly enjoyable." Edmund rubbed his full stomach and stretched. In light of her recent attempt to pace him, Eleanor wondered more than ever where he had room to physically store all of the food he consumed.

"It was thirty-three this time. I think that's an all-time record. I'll have to tell Edward about it the next time I see him."

Edmund sighed nostalgically. "Edward Rutherford… yes, what a wonderful chap. He was a wonderful ally in India. Together we kept many skirmishes at bay. I miss him even more now that I'm back. He and I were together here for the last decade of my time in the Colonial Army."

"I'm sure he wishes he were here." Eleanor was quite sure that her statement was true as she thought about Edward's shrew of a wife.

"Perhaps… but those little girls are enough to keep any man settled no matter where he is. I've never seen Edward happier than he has been with his children."

Mr. Valov mercifully interrupted before the topic of children escalated. "We will arrive shortly, and we'll need to hurry. Our arrival is several hours later than we expected, and the train to Agra is waiting for us. As it is a British train, I assume the timetable means something?"

"Perhaps," Edmund winked. "Don't worry, Leo. We won't dilly-dally."

"It may be easier said than done, Colonel," Mr. Valov said as he glanced towards Dev Sahib's position. Dev Sahib was standing with a troop of timid servants, each holding elaborate jasmine and marigold garlands. "When we arrive, I will direct the porters with your trunks. You will need to work your way through the crowds to the other train."

"The crowds?" Eleanor asked.

"The maharaja expects that his people will be gathered to celebrate their return... and the maharaja and his staff... er... would like to celebrate your presence here with an offering."

As Mr. Valov spoke, the maharaja and his family gathered behind him, each holding their own enormous jasmine garlands. Edmund and Eleanor stood up, and Edmund smiled knowingly as he guided her to address the maharaja.

"Thank you, Madho Rao. It was wonderful catching up with you." Edmund offered him a polite *namaste*.

"It was an unmatched pleasure to host you, my lord. Words cannot express our gratitude," Madho Rao said as Edmund leaned forward and let him place the first garland around his neck.

"What luck for us to reconnect, old friend." Edmund shook Madho Rao's hand jovially. "Thank you kindly for your hospitality."

"It is nothing, my lord. Nothing!" Madho Rao exclaimed.

Rane nodded to Eleanor that it was her turn, and Eleanor followed Edmund's lead, leaning forward so that Rane could place the garland around her neck.

"I hope that I did not offend you, my lady. You have witnessed our circumstances during a particularly trying time... first with Jyoti, and then the incident on the platform..." Rane whispered nervously. "I didn't realize… I didn't realize how special you were until it was too late."

Eleanor took both of her hands and squeezed them.

Don't worry, my child. Sharing one's own mind is not a sin. Go forward with Shakti's blessings, and do not forget the value of keeping an open mind.

"I look forward to another heated discourse in the future, Your Highness. Perhaps we can take on a religious topic instead of a political one next time."

"It would be my greatest honor," Rane whispered.

"Thank you, Eleanor!" Anya exclaimed as she rushed to hug Eleanor. She squeezed her so long that Rane leaned forward and whispered a gentle admonishment, and then Anya nodded dutifully and put the second garland around Eleanor's neck. "Come visit us some time? We have a swimming pool that's so big it has a boat in it!"

"It sounds like quite the novelty." Eleanor smiled and squeezed Anya's hands goodbye. "Don't forget what I taught you, agreed?"

"I'll never forget! Never, ever! I promise, Eleanor!"

Georgie stepped forward with King Babu on his shoulder. Edmund readied himself for the monkey's reaction, but as Georgie placed the garland around Edmund's neck, King Babu held onto his shoulder and bowed dutifully.

"Remember everything that we talked about," Edmund whispered. "You have a great capacity for good deeds ahead of you. Use your clever mind to improve the circumstances of your people. It will be much more rewarding, and much safer, than using it for mischief."

"I will, my lord. I promise."

When they were finished saying their goodbyes, Madho Rao nodded to the servants, who approached behind Dev Sahib's lead.

Dev Sahib whispered hushed mantras as he placed the third garland around Edmund's neck, and each of the male servants lined up and politely waited their turns to offer Edmund a garland until his neck was entirely hidden by layers and layers of fragrant white jasmine, pink bougainvillea, and yellow marigolds.

The female servants lined up for Eleanor, and with each and every offering, Uma reached forward and took their hands to deliver an unspoken message. *Take with you Shakti's blessings, my child.*

As the last girl finished, the train slowed its pace, and Eleanor held onto Edmund for balance.

"You must go first, my lord," Dev Sahib addressed Edmund.

Edmund laughed. "Even I know enough as a *firang* to know that the royal family should disembark first."

"You are quite right," Madho Rao interjected. "That is normally the protocol. But honored guests are an exception, and you, my lord and my lady, are the most honored guests in the world. Please do us the honor of going first."

Edmund looked to Rane, who nodded her agreement.

"If you insist," he agreed.

As the train screeched to its final stop and each person balanced themselves against the furniture, Mr. Valov rushed into action.

"Go, Colonel. I will follow the royal family and meet you with your trunks at the other train. You will be in carriage number one, premium first class."

Eleanor took a deep breath. She wasn't sure she was ready to face the real world yet. As they reached the door, all of the elaborate shoes of the royal family were laid out, as were a pair of tasteful leather loafers for Edmund and a beautiful pair of sparkling heeled sandals with midnight blue accents that matched her outfit perfectly. She slipped them on, and with some orders barked by Dev Sahib out the front door of the kitchen carriage, a different guard in the same elaborate uniform that Jaap Sahib had worn pulled open the door for them.

A blast of heat assaulted her as she held on tightly to Edmund's hand, and he guided her down the stairs and off the train, into a crowd of cheering well-wishers who waved flags and threw flowers in the air. The crowd's excitement morphed into intrigue as they realized that their maharaja had not stepped out first. Eleanor glanced around at them, hoping that their attention was not solidly focused on her chest, but they seemed to be equally intrigued by Edmund's unusual height and her fiery red hair. She held onto her stylish hat, pulling down the brim slightly to block their full view of her face, and followed her husband into the crowd.

The masses parted, staring intently at them as they passed. Edmund guided Eleanor swiftly across the platform to the only other waiting train, which was markedly smaller and older than the maharaja's. Eleanor felt slightly awkward as she thought about what her sisters would say about her reaction to its dirty, dumpy façade. *Eleanor Mary MacLeod, you've become a sassanack snob!* Martha's imaginary voice echoed in her head.

As they scampered up into the first-class carriage, an Indian conductor in another elaborate uniform that looked vaguely like a Paris bell-hop with various Indian flourishes, including a matching turban that looked a bit like a costume piece, welcomed them aboard.

"Lord and Lady Marriner, it is an honor!" he declared. "I am Mr. Garg, the first-class conductor. I will see to your every need."

Edmund sighed with resignation. "Are those the names Sri Bidkar put on our tickets?"

"Yes, my lord! Lord and Lady Marriner, Earl and Countess of Easton! Honored guests of the Maharaja of Gwalior himself! Please, follow me!"

Edmund reached into his pocket and pulled out several coins, placing them in the conductor's hand. "I trust you will wait for our man to board with our luggage?"

Eleanor found the ease with which her husband paid the tip to be mildly arousing.

"Yes, yes, of course, Lord Marriner! Please excuse me. I must go ensure that the stationmaster knows that we must wait!"

Eleanor smiled as she watched the man scamper along to fulfill his new duties. "You really are at ease here, aren't you, darling? It is your native home."

"I suppose it is. Now, shall we go find our seats amongst the sassanack conquerors?"

Now Eleanor was entirely aroused. She snuck a kiss, wiping off her rogue lipstick from his lips, and then she squeezed his hand as they entered the first-class seating area.

A haphazard group of white foreigners dressed entirely in western clothing and exuding an air of annoyance looked up at them silently as they entered. Several women wore short dresses similar to the ones Eleanor had stopped wearing after her first embarrassing entrance at the port, and most of the men wore dark wool suits with high collars that looked utterly unbearable in the heat. The temperature of the train was markedly warmer than the maharaja's train had been with his novel mechanical cooling system, and many of the women fanned themselves with paper fans, while the men simply sweated silently, looking miserable.

Even in the first-class car, the train felt more like a commuter train than a proper long-distance train, with the seating arranged with couples facing each other in groups of four with a small table attached to the window between them, just like the train she used to take from Elphinstone into Edinburgh as a lass.

"So you were the stragglers that held us up for a bloody hour," an old man with white hair and a Yorkshire accent muttered.

Edmund moved to respond, and then he stopped himself, refusing to let the impolite comment engage them in what was certain to be an unpleasant conversation.

Instead, he guided Eleanor to the only two seats left, across from a young couple dressed in conspicuously inappropriate eveningwear, the man with greasy black hair and leathery skin wearing a white tuxedo that was several years out of date, and the woman with fake, platinum blonde hair and bright red lipstick that looked particularly odd with her otherwise plain features, wearing a garish rainbow flapper dress that was so short that only inches of her bare thighs remained a mystery to the world. Eleanor hoped that she herself didn't look so unstylish wearing her red lipstick with her plain features. She took a mental note to gaze at herself in the mirror with more scrutiny the next time she made herself up.

Do not worry, my child. You are beautiful with and without your lipstick. You look nothing like that little trollop.

Eleanor almost snorted at Uma's miserly insult. It sounded for a moment like her mother was in her head.

As the man offered her a toothy smile, Eleanor looked down self-consciously at her chest, realizing with great relief that the stack of garlands was providing her with an unusually thick layer of modesty. Then she crossed her legs, offered him a polite glance, and re-took Edmund's hand, hoping that no one would comment on her henna, which was quite visible through the sheer silk of her sleeves.

"Can you believe there's a bonafide maharaja here? It's like a storybook!" the man exclaimed loudly with a thick Texas accent. Eleanor had heard the distinct dialect several times during the war, and she was quite sure that she had never come across a form of English that she liked less than the loud Southern twang.

"Oh, Bo. Isn't it just magical?" the girl swooned. "Maharajas and tigers and elephants and the Taaaj Maa-hal! I mean, we haven't really seen any of those things yet, but we're close. I can feel it!"

"It's all for you, darlin'. I called God right up and said, 'Lord, Betty needs a fairy tale vacation,' and he said, 'Bo, that sounds like a fine idea!'" He smacked her bare thigh so harshly that Eleanor wondered if the girl would bruise from it.

"Oh, Bo," Betty giggled. "You're such a tease."

"I ain't teasin', Betty! Clear as day, the Lord gave us this little trip!" He leaned forward confidingly to Eleanor. "I won us here two round-trip tickets to the Taaaaj Maaa-hal from a newspaper contest in Dallas. Can you believe it?"

She was quite sure that he was asking a rhetorical question, but as he stared her down waiting for an answer, she responded awkwardly. "You do seem to be in India, so, yes? I do believe it?"

"Ha!" Bo exploded into booming laughter, catching the attention of many of their unhappy fellow passengers. "You're a funny little lady, ain't ya?"

"Yes, I'm hilarious."

Something about him was rubbing her entirely the wrong way. She wondered if she had simply become a sassanack snob, or if there was more to it. She'd often found the simplicity of corn-fed American soldiers to be endearing during the war, but this man wasn't like them at all. She'd forgiven plenty of them for calling her things like 'little lady,' so perhaps it was his references to *the Lord* meddling in newspaper contests that she wasn't liking, as if any god had time to care about such trivialities...

Bo was undeterred by her lack of interest in joining his conversation. "I mean, we almost didn't come, mind you, because I wasn't sure that the Lord really wanted us to spend time with godless savages, you know, in case it rubbed off or somethin', but Betty here said that we oughta go, and Betty gets what Betty wants, even if her Bo don't give a lick about it..."

"Oh, Bo. You wanted to come. You said you'd show those injuns a thing or two, just like President Andrew Jackson did! He put 'em in their place back at home, you see. Those injuns were goin' around killin' all sorts of God-fearin' folk."

"You do realize that American Indians are not related in any way to India?" Eleanor did not want to get dragged into their asinine conversation, but she couldn't help herself. She could tell from their surprised expressions that they did not, in fact, know that the two were unrelated.

"Well, a savage is a savage in the Lord's eyes," Bo argued matter-of-factly. "Why, did you know that these here natives are bonafide cannibals? I read it in the newspaper! A nice ol' Christian reporter went lookin' for a story about a tiger, and they cooked

336

him right up like a hog on a spit! The Devil was dancin' that day, I say! If I'da been there, I'da shown those savages a thing or two about the Lord's way." He was speaking so loudly that several of the other passengers threw him dirty looks and unfolded their newspapers to provide a barrier.

"Perhaps you should check your sources," Eleanor suggested at the very edge of her prickly Scottish temper.

Bo blinked several times trying to process her statement, and then he changed the subject. "So, what brings you two lookers to this corner of the world? Looks like you've had a mighty fine time already. Are those tattoos on your arms? By golly, they look mighty strange. Where'd you get all those flowers from, anyway? I oughta get some for Betty, here!"

"We're on our honeymoon," Eleanor replied with a volume she thought was more appropriate.

"Your honeymoon!" Betty squealed. "Say, are you Irish? I always wanted to go to Ireland. My grandma came from there! She stowed away on a big ol' boat to New York! Lucky for her, she found a job as a seamstress, or she woulda been a hooker for sure!"

"I'm Scottish," Eleanor replied curtly. She had rarely in her life felt more cultured than any of her companions (except perhaps for her late evenings at the Edinburgh pub surrounded by the local bricklayers' bureau), but she found both of these people to be excessively irritating.

"And how about you?" Bo addressed Edmund.

"I am also on my honeymoon. Eleanor and I are on our honeymoon together," he replied.

Eleanor was grateful that he too was finding them annoying.

"No, silly! Where are you from? Are you Scottish too?"

"It is a long story," Edmund replied. "For the sake of simplicity, I am British."

"That's what I thought. You talk different than the Mrs.," Betty declared as if her observation were a revelation.

As Mr. Garg approached, one of the grumpy, white-haired men grabbed his arm. "Is this train ever going to leave? I don't care what kind of bloody maharaja is in town, you people have to keep your trains running on time, like civilized folk."

"We will be leaving momentarily, sir," Mr. Garg replied far more politely than Eleanor felt he should have. He approached her and Edmund and bowed. "My lord, your butler is on board, and the maharaja wishes you a pleasant onward journey. On behalf of the people of Gwalior, he thanks you once again for your service."

"Lord?" Betty whispered.

"Butler!" Bo countered.

"Maharaja!" Betty practically screamed her excitement.

"Your man is guarding your luggage in the storage car. He said that he will stay there until we arrive at our destination. It is a two-hour ride to Agra." Mr. Garg leaned in to whisper. "He asked if we might bring him a sandwich. Is that acceptable, my lord?"

Edmund laughed. "By god, man, bring the man a sandwich! Bring him all the sandwiches! Mr. Valov is to have anything he wants from your menu. Absolutely anything, you understand? Fine cognacs included. In fact, send him a taste of your finest with my compliments."

"Yes, my lord!" Mr. Garg agreed. Without offering another glance to the many other passengers, he rushed to fulfill Edmund's request.

"So, you're a lord?" Bo asked casually. "That sounds mighty important. I'm Bo Ralston, but my friends call me Bo... and this is Betty here. People call her Betty."

He reached his hand forward far enough that Edmund could not politely ignore it.

"Colonel Marriner," Edmund said curtly as he shook Bo's hand.

"A colonel and a lord?! You must be mighty, mighty important. Lord almighty, we must be gettin' somethin' mighty nice comin' to us with such important company sittin' right across

338

from us. To think, you just sat right down in our laps, like the Lord brought ya!"

Bo shook his hand until Edmund had to awkwardly pry his away. Eleanor could tell that the man's unctuous tone was getting under Edmund's skin.

"I know exactly what a colonel does... you know, army things and stuff, but what exactly does a lord do?" Betty added with her own attempt at nonchalance. "Other than a-leapin'!" She exploded into laughter.

Eleanor had absolutely no idea what she was talking about.

"You know, the Christmas carol!" Betty began singing in a strikingly off-key, high-pitched impersonation of an opera singer. *"Ten lords a-leapin', nine ladies dancin', eight maids a-milkin'...* Aw, rats. I never remember what comes next... is it seven, Bo, or six?"

"It's seven, Betty. *Seven.*" He patted her hand like he was forgiving a small child, and then he leaned in confidingly to Edmund. "If the Lord wanted the girl to count, he woulda filled her head with numbers instead of air, don't ya think?" He laughed heartily, but even Betty didn't join him. He straightened his bowtie. "So, Lord Colonel Sir, what does a lord do other than leap?"

Edmund looked pained, but then Eleanor noticed a subtle mischievous twinkle in his eye. "Well, I gather up unreasonable taxes from the peasants who break their backs tilling my fields, and then I use the money to buy myself ostentatious toys and outrageously oversized palaces so that all of the other lords will see how powerful I am, and my people will prosper from better trade deals with other villages. It is really a wonderful system in which everyone benefits equally... Although, I do wish that I could be a peasant. Their lives are so wonderfully simple. But the Lord had other plans for me."

Edmund delivered his cheeky answer with such dead-pan earnestness that Eleanor almost laughed out loud. Instead, she worked her hardest to keep a serious face, while secretly falling more in love with her husband.

"Well, I'll be," Bo replied, acting as if he were thinking seriously about Edmund's answer. "Sounds mighty interestin'! What kinda toys?!"

Edmund looked as if he was already regretting his little game. "It is not, in fact, an equitable system, and I do not, in fact, do anything as a lord. I am a colonel in the British Army. I command the king's Household Cavalry." They stared at him blankly. "The king's horses."

"Golly," Betty murmured. "Just like Humpty Dumpty…"

"I'm sorry," Edmund couldn't help but ask. "In what way am I like Humpty Dumpty?"

"Well, I didn't mean you're an egghead!" Betty exploded into high-pitched laughter. "All the king's horses and all the king's men, couldn't put Humpty together again!" Betty looked exceptionally proud at remembering the nursery rhyme.

Edmund finally offered her a bemused smile. "Yes, I suppose I am one of the king's men."

The train finally started moving.

"It's about time," their grumpy, white-haired peer muttered.

Eleanor relished Edmund's cool hand and subtle pulsating power as the train picked up speed, and she reveled in the silence as Bo and Betty were finally distracted, looking out the window as the few glimpses of Gwalior dissolved into the rocky, sunburnt countryside.

Mr. Garg returned to the carriage with a silver tray bearing a dusty bottle of cognac and two crystal glasses.

"Sri Bidkar sent this ahead for you to enjoy on your journey," he said as he placed the tray on the small table.

Bo licked his lips covetously at the offering, while several of the older passengers whispered their disapproval of the afternoon tipple.

"Oh, and Mr. Valov thanks you for the sandwiches, but he says that he cannot finish all of them. What am I to do, my lord?"

"All of them?" Edmund asked.

"Yes, my lord. We followed your orders and gave your man all of the sandwiches. He was only able to eat three."

Eleanor stymied a giggle at the man's literal interpretation of Edmund's joke.

Edmund smiled. "Perhaps other people on the train would also like a sandwich, like that gentleman there." He pointed at one of their white-haired detractors, conspicuously avoiding eye contact with Bo and Betty. "I'm sure if you ask around you can find some takers."

"Oh, but sir, the first-class dining car has much better food than that. It has mutton stew and mushy peas—a taste of home for the Britishers. The meal is already included in the ticket price."

"A taste of home, darling, did you hear that? With mushy peas!" Eleanor swooned sarcastically. She'd already become so accustomed to the flavorful local food, the idea of going back to the bland palate that she had known her whole life felt surprisingly unappealing.

"Are there spices in the stew?" Edmund asked with minor interest.

"Oh no, sir! Not at all! Of course not!" Mr. Garg declared.

Edmund glanced around at the other passengers and sighed with subtle disappointment. "I suppose that's ideal for your audience."

"What about the second-class passengers?" Eleanor asked, returning to the matter at hand. "What do they have to eat?"

"Nothing, my lady. We only had sandwiches for them. Now we don't have any left."

"Because you gave all of them to our man?" Eleanor pushed. She found the circular logic of the conversation to be somewhat amusing.

"Yes, my lady."

"Then I have the solution for you!" Eleanor declared. "Please gather up all of the sandwiches that Mr. Valov did not eat and offer them to the second-class passengers, compliments of Lady Marriner, Countess of Easton."

"Yes, my lady!" Mr. Garg disappeared to follow her orders without even glancing at the rest of the first-class passengers.

"Well, I never!" one elderly woman exclaimed. "There are other first-class passengers! I've never had such shoddy service in my life!"

Mr. Garg rushed back into the car with an afterthought. "Lunch is ready in the dining car!" he called.

"I shouldn't have been so flippant with him," Edmund whispered guiltily as he watched Mr. Garg disappear again to tend to Eleanor's request. "It would have been very bad for him if I'd been serious and he'd interpreted my orders as a joke."

"Really, darling, how could you not have been joking? Buying all the sandwiches from the entire train so that everyone in second class had nothing to eat? He shouldn't have even let you do that!"

"I'm sure he gets absurd requests all the time, from Britishers and locals alike. It isn't fair to make him distinguish the difference, and I must remind myself of the rigidity with which others of an elevated position expect things to work. It was his duty to tend to a lord's request, especially one who had just gotten off of the private train of a maharaja. I'm just not used to having such an elevated status here, and Ravi's game isn't helping. I must be more careful, and, dearest, I hate to say it... so should you."

Eleanor leaned over for a gentle kiss on his cheek. "You're a very thoughtful man, darling. I will follow your lead."

As he kissed her on the lips, the shifting of their annoying companions pulled them right out of their moment.

"That bottle sure does look mighty old." Bo eyed their cognac covetously again. "Are you supposed to drink it so old? Seems like it might be spoiled to me, but I'd be happy to test it for ya."

"It is perfectly fine to drink old cognac," Edmund replied.

Several passengers stood up to make their way to the dining car, and one old couple pointed and stared as they took in a closer look at Edmund and Eleanor. They stopped right by their seats, blocking the line of people behind them. The woman whispered into her husband's ear, and he leaned down to address Eleanor.

"My wife finds the scent of your garlands disturbing. You know flowers are grown in filthy conditions here. Just filthy."

"You mean... they're grown in dirt?" Eleanor asked, only half-jokingly. "And how are English flowers grown?"

The woman gasped her excessive offense at Eleanor's comment, and her husband escorted her into the dining car in a huff. The rest of the passengers followed them, gazing down at Edmund and Eleanor with varying degrees of disapproval and curiosity.

Eleanor glanced at Bo's continued attention and switched into Gaelic to whisper in Edmund's ear. "What did he want us to do, throw the garlands out the window?"

"He just wanted us to know that they disapproved of our support of anything native," Edmund whispered back. "It is not an uncommon problem. You'll notice that none of them have taken even the slightest effort to conform to local norms. It is like they are threatened here by the world being so utterly foreign, and so they hold even more rigidly onto their own cultural ideals. It has been that way since I moved here in 1895, although there is a certain edge to it now, a certain sense of self-righteous entitlement that wasn't so prominent earlier on. I suppose there weren't so many tourists earlier on. Perhaps that was the difference. This might be the most touristy train in India, and these people want their holiday to feel like a weekend trip to Brighton."

"Well, I suppose we'd better eat, Betty. Mutton stew sure sounds yummy to me." Bo stood up and made an exaggerated stretch, displaying his hairy pot-belly that had been hidden by his cummerbund. "Ya fancy lord and lady comin', or do you have better things to do than eat free food?" He directed his aggressively phrased question at Edmund.

343

"We are still quite full from our late breakfast," Edmund declined politely.

"Your loss," Bo shrugged.

He escorted Betty to the dining car, leaving Edmund and Eleanor alone with only a few sleeping passengers seated several rows away from them.

"Good lord," Eleanor murmured. "It's like we're aliens here."

Edmund opened the bottle of cognac and poured them each a full glass, squinting to read the remnants of the old writing.

"Hine, 1848. This should be delicious," he said as he clinked her glass.

She took in a deep whiff, relishing the rich vanilla scent mixing with caramel and old leather undertones that denoted the cognac's age. She paced Edmund as he drank down half his glass in one Rakshasa gulp, and then she topped them off.

"I must admit, dearest, I was a bit worried that when we arrived in India, you'd turn out to be like these people. You already seemed too good to be true, and people change here. It is quite common that they become rather tiresome."

"Really?" Eleanor laughed. "You really thought there was a chance that I'd end up like that? *Your fresh jasmine is disturbing my nose.*" She imitated the old man's whining tone.

Edmund snuck a kiss. "I suppose it was a foolish fear. Once again, you have proven to be more perfect than I could have ever imagined a wife to be, Eleanor."

"Thank you, darling," she sighed. "I'm glad to be setting the standard." *For comparison with your Indian avatar bride...* her obnoxious inner monologue added.

They sat for a long while, enjoying the silence. Eleanor wondered if Edmund could feel Uma's power pulsating from the core of her being, but as he dozed off, she decided that if he could sense such a drastic change, he certainly would have mentioned it. After all, he wasn't a consummate liar like she was.

She gazed out the window, fighting back the many fears that threatened to overtake her—a Rakshasa monster stalking them, hunting for Edmund and killing anyone who took a wrong turn in their path... The danger they'd put their loving allies in, Ravi, Shruti, Madho Rao, Anya, Jaap Sahib! What if Mr. Valov couldn't keep the British authorities away from them? Had the world woken up to a sensational headline about dismembered bodies in some rural township, somewhere in the vicinity of the maharaja's private train?

Then there were all the unsanctioned changes to her body, care of Uma's uninvited presence... Her mind wandered to a nightmarish fantasy about facing her sisters with her new busty figure... '*Ellie, what on earth happened to you!*' Mary's voice echoed, "*You look like a common prostitute!*" her mother's voice added... The thought moved along to pregnancy, *Rakshasa* pregnancy— whatever that really meant (she didn't want to find out), and explaining to Edmund the dangers of his innocent desire for children... Mortality... The word snuck up on her wandering mind. Even Uma was mortal. There was no escaping the day when she would leave her gentle divine demon alone in overwhelming misery, it was just a question of when...

"Why, I reckon you missed a mighty fine meal, Your Majesty," Bo interrupted her painful reverie. She wasn't sure what she'd rather deal with, his annoying presence or her tormenting thoughts...

Eleanor poured herself another tall glass of cognac.

"I see, a liquid lunch." He held up a bottle of whisky. "Well, you won't be drinkin' alone now! What're vacation afternoons for, anyway, if they ain't for drinkin'?"

Eleanor took a long sip of the cognac, wishing terribly that Uma's presence had not eliminated her ability to use tipsiness to dull the effects of such unpleasant company.

You will thank me later, my child. I promise.

"Golly, look at that whopper!" Betty exclaimed as she noticed Eleanor's wedding ring. Eleanor looked down self-consciously to see what she was looking at, hoping that her shirt hadn't somehow come undone.

"It is my wedding ring," Eleanor replied.

"Your hubby must be pretty rich to buy a ring like that!" Betty said as she squatted down to the level of Eleanor's hand to inspect the ring without Eleanor's permission.

"It is a family heirloom that belonged to his mother." Eleanor shifted uncomfortably and took her hand back as Betty noticed the henna. "The tattoos are not permanent. They are an Indian wedding tradition, and they will fade in a few weeks."

"You had an injun weddin'?!" Betty exclaimed. "That must of been somethin'!"

"We did not have an Indian wedding. We had a British wedding, in England. An Indian friend did the design for a celebratory evening a few days back."

"Whew," Betty said as she plopped down next to Bo and took a long swig right from their whisky bottle. "For a minute there, I was worried you mighta had a pagan weddin'! God don't like those, you know. They make him mighty angry. The Bible says so."

She handed the bottle to Bo who chugged down several servings in one go, and Eleanor poured the rest of the cognac into her glass and took a long, savoring sip.

"Really? In which scripture does God comment on his opinion of Indian weddings?" Eleanor asked innocently.

Let it be, my child. There is no point in arguing.

"All of 'em, silly!" Betty said matter-of-factly. "The Bible says that God hates all the sinners who don't do as He says. They're all gonna burn in Hell."

"Oh yes, those passages. They are my mother's favorites as well," Eleanor said as she took Uma's advice.

"What's your favorite?" Betty asked. Eleanor didn't like her tone, as if the question were a test.

"Matthew 7:12," she replied. "I hear it's the Lord's favorite as well. Perhaps you should read it sometime."

"Which one is that Bo?" Betty asked.

He furrowed his brow as he thought about it. "Why, I'm mighty sure it's the one where the Lord kills all the sinners with the flood, makin' way for God-fearin' folk like us to inherit the earth."

"Do unto others," Eleanor corrected him. "As you would have them do unto you. From the Sermon on the Mount... It is one of the most canonical lines of scripture for those who take the time to actually read the teachings of Jesus."

"I don't need to read," Betty explained as she took another long swig. "The preacher does all the readin' any of us needs."

Eleanor couldn't help but sit up straight and engage. "Are you saying that you can't read?"

"It ain't good for girls to read. It gives us all sorts of sinful ideas," Betty replied. "Besides, I have Bo, and he graduated the seventh grade, so why would I need to read?"

A wild look crossed Bo's face, and he grabbed her hand and squeezed it until she squealed with pain. "It was the eighth grade, Betty. How many times do I have to tell you?"

"Sorry, Bo," Betty sulked as he let go of her hand, and she wiggled her fingers. "You know I ain't no good at countin'."

As Eleanor struggled for a proper response, Mr. Valov approached and squatted down to address her. He looked Bo and Betty up and down, pausing for an extra-long moment on the half-empty whisky bottle in Bo's hand, and then he glanced at Edmund's soundly sleeping state. Bo and Betty leaned in uncouthly to listen.

"We..." Mr. Valov threw them a dirty look, and they backed up, still listening intently. "We will be arriving soon, my lady."

Betty squealed with excitement at his use of the honorific.

Uma reached Eleanor's hand forward to touch Mr. Valov's, and she tipped her hat so their attentive audience could not see her eyes.

Speak Czech, my child. I will translate for Eleanor.

Mr. Valov worked his hardest to act nonchalant at the development as he dropped into a whisper and continued in Czech. "Your... er... transportation will be waiting for you at the station, and I will follow in a hotel car with your luggage. I'd like you to know, Eleanor, that all of this was planned by Sri Bidkar. All of it. I had no hand it in, whatsoever."

Even though Eleanor could hear the foreign sounds of the Slavic language rolling off of Mr. Valov's tongue, she knew exactly what he was saying. Mr. Valov waited with a combination of skepticism and intrigue to see whether Eleanor had understood him.

"You are either incredibly modest, or something bizarre is about to happen," Eleanor replied. The words coming out of her mouth were still in English.

"This is a useful development for you, Eleanor. Now you will know what Edmund and I are chatting about. We'll have to be more careful about our topics of conversation."

"You are skillfully evading my point. Does that mean that we do have something bizarre in store for us?" Eleanor asked.

Bo and Betty looked like they might explode at the intrigue.

"I won't ruin the surprise. You'd best prepare yourself for a busy day." Mr. Valov glanced at the empty cognac bottle. "Are you going to be alright? It's scorching outside. Perhaps I should get you some water."

"Edmund and I could both use some water, but you needn't worry about me, Mr. Valov. I seem to have developed an exceptional stamina for cognac, along with those other recent changes."

"I will get you some water now. That Mr. Garg chap is surprisingly accommodating. Oh, and when he wakes up, thank Edmund for the sandwiches, and the cognac. The poor staff didn't know what to do when I refused to eat the whole lot. I'm glad you sorted them out… Oh, and the second-class cabin thanks you for your generosity."

"We aren't in Britain anymore, are we?" Eleanor winked.

"I am reminded of that fact every moment, Eleanor."

As Edmund took in his awakening Rakshasa breath, he paused for a moment, taking in their surroundings.

"Ah, Mr. Valov!" he said cheerfully as he sat up and straightened his posture. "Fancy meeting you here."

"We will be arriving soon, Colonel. I was just going to fetch you and Eleanor some water."

"Why, thank you!" As Edmund noticed Bo and Betty's attention, his cheer dissolved.

Mr. Valov nodded and disappeared to find Mr. Garg.

After a few minutes of silence, the train screeched to a halt. A large crowd of colorfully dressed locals was gathered in the Agra station, and Eleanor had a sneaking suspicion that Ravi Bidkar had something to do with it.

"Please, Lord and Lady Marriner. Please come quickly! You must disembark first!" Mr. Garg exclaimed as he rushed to help them out of their seats. Several of the elderly passengers grumbled their disapproval.

Edmund took Eleanor's hand, and she only offered their companions a minor nod of acknowledgment as she gratefully escaped from their presence.

"Have a mighty fine time, Your Majesties!" Bo called.

"God is smilin' on you!" Betty added.

As they stepped off the train into a blast of furnace-like heat, a large staff of colorfully uniformed guards held back the curious crowd, while two enormous elephants decorated with colorful paint, bearing enormous shaded compartments on their backs, screeched an enthusiastic welcome.

"Lord and Lady Marriner, your transportation awaits!" Mr. Garg declared.

CHAPTER 18 – PADMA?

"Good lord!" Edmund exclaimed. "Sri Bidkar has been busy! You'd think Lord Curzon himself had just arrived for the durbar!"

The elephants trumpeted their welcome again, and the crowd began throwing balls of fresh jasmine at them.

"I hope that miserly couple is ready to catch some filthy flowers," Eleanor laughed.

Several men stood waiting beside brightly painted portable stairs that were already positioned to help Edmund and Eleanor scale the massive beasts.

"Have you ever ridden an elephant before, dearest?" Edmund asked giddily.

Eleanor found his excitement contagious.

"Only three or four times," she winked. "When the train to Edinburgh was full."

"Well, we mustn't keep Sri Bidkar's elephants waiting," Edmund said as he guided her towards the smaller of the two elephants, twirling her around with a romantic flourish.

He held her hand as she climbed up the stairs, into the massive sedan. More strands of fresh jasmine hung around the four corners of the sedan's roof, and Eleanor wiggled herself awkwardly until she reached a reasonably comfortable position. She laughed and clapped as she watched Edmund ascend onto his elephant so gracefully that he looked as if he'd done it thousands of times before.

"Onward!" he declared with a silly salute. "Hold on, dearest, it's going to be a bumpy ride!"

The crowds cheered and threw more jasmine at them, as a large entourage of elephant handlers and guards guided them out of the station.

Eleanor caught Mr. Valov's eye and waved to him cheerfully as he directed eight porters (donning the exact uniforms of Ravi's staff in Bombay), carrying their trunks to the boot of a very large black car. He smiled and waved back, unable to ignore the novelty of the spectacle.

In that moment, all of her worries melted away, and Eleanor felt completely at ease for the first time in months, since before she'd met her beautiful divine demon. She felt as if she were herself again, as if she had regained some semblance of control, and as if all the pomp and circumstance around her was simply a manifestation of the same chaos of the nursing wards that she had spent years learning to love. If only her twelve-year-old self could see her now…

As the elephants exited the shade of the station, Eleanor braced herself for a blast of scorching heat, but she found that the sensation of the hot air on her skin was strangely pleasant. She did not feel any of the weakness that had plagued her on her first day in Bombay, and as she reached up to feel her forehead and her neck, she realized that she was barely sweating.

You're welcome, my child.

"Now that is a development I can live with," Eleanor whispered.

"Look, dearest! Do you see the minarets?" Edmund pointed into the distance where four white minarets jutted out from beyond the low-set, sandy-colored buildings of the town. Right in the middle was a tiny peek of the main dome.

The crowd from the train station followed them, while more curious onlookers joined, until the elephants were swimming in people.

"Are our followers in any danger, darling?" Eleanor called. "They aren't at risk of being trampled, are they?"

"These elephants are very intelligent and well-trained. As long as no one does anything foolish, everyone should be perfectly safe," he called. "How do you like it, dearest? Do you feel like a maharani yet?"

"I know why Lord Curzon went Napoleonic," Eleanor laughed. "I feel so powerful up here!"

They rode along through the crowded streets while Eleanor reveled in the wonderful heat, until the elephants reached a grand white marble colonial building made up of three stories of archways stacked on top of each other. The building was surrounded by lush lawns dotted with topiary, and several dusty black cars were parked in front, although Mr. Valov's hadn't arrived yet.

A troop of monkeys stopped a game of chase on one of the lawns to watch their approach, but as soon as they spotted Edmund, they squawked and ran away.

As another elaborately-clad staff rushed out of the hotel to greet them, Uma reached Eleanor's hands forward, placing them on the skin of the elephant.

Thank you, my child. Take with you Shakti's blessings.

The elephant screeched her approval, and Edmund looked over to see what had caused the ruckus.

"I think she's offering us her regards," Eleanor laughed.

Edmund reached forward and followed her lead, patting his elephant gently and praising her. With another trumpet call,

Edmund laughed, and the staff rushed to pull up another set of stairs.

"Welcome, Lord and Lady Marriner!"

A tall, grey-haired British man with a thick Manchester accent, donning a traditional butler's tuxedo rushed to greet them.

"I will have to have a talk with Ravi at some point about throwing around false titles. This is getting a bit absurd," Edmund muttered. "You may call me Colonel Marriner," Edmund corrected him.

"Yes, Colonel. Of course, Colonel. Please come!" the butler exclaimed. "Can I offer you some refreshments, my lord? Or my lady?"

Eleanor appreciated that he took the extra effort to look her in the eye as he addressed her, even if he had already failed at fulfilling Edmund's request.

"What did you have in mind?" Edmund asked with mild interest.

The man's posture deflated. "To be honest, sir, you don't have much time. You must leave for your sunset dinner at the Taj Mahal in an hour or you will miss it, and Sri Bidkar will be very unhappy."

"Sunset dinner," Edmund said happily. "Now that is something that Sri Bidkar is sure to do well. Perhaps he took my comment about the obligatory homage to the Taj Mahal more seriously than I intended."

"Please follow me. I am Mr. Dixon, but you may call me Dixon if you'd like, everybody does. I will be your butler during your stay."

"Ha! Don't let Mr. Valov hear you say that!" Edmund laughed. "We already have a butler, Mr. Dixon. He will be arriving any moment with our luggage."

"Yes, my lord. Of course, my lord. I shall serve as your concierge then. Please follow me. I will show you to your accommodations."

Dixon clapped his hands, and the entire staff stopped what they were doing and stood up straight as they passed.

"I must apologize, Lord Marriner. Sri Bidkar arranged for your privacy, but we already had several bookings that we could not cancel, and so we have accommodated you in this half of the building only. It is the half with the private gardens and the swimming pool, which will be guarded at all hours to ensure your sole access to it."

"Half of your hotel is booked out for us?" Edmund asked.

"Yes, I'm sorry we could not book it out entirely for you. If we'd had more notice, we may have been able to. Sri Bidkar was very upset, but we are the only colonial hotel in Agra, you see. We simply could not leave the other guests to find other accommodations. Many come here from across the world just to see the Taj Mahal."

"I'm sure that half of this grand hotel will be sufficient for our needs," Eleanor chimed in.

Dixon relaxed as she voiced her support. She held Edmund's hand as they followed Dixon through a hallway full of elaborate marble stonework, until they reached a set of french doors opening into a grand suite with a huge canopied bed covered in a delicate mosquito net. In the corner of the room there was a small vanity with a washbasin beside a door to a WC, and beside it, a large, old-fashioned Victorian bathtub was already filled with steaming water and floating jasmine. Three sets of french doors were open onto a vast green lawn which gave way to a large modern swimming pool that was surrounded by another set of whimsical topiaries. The white sheer curtains on each side of the french doors batted gently in the breeze, and a peacock walked right past the open window.

"He is the only creature you will see with these doors open, my lord," Dixon promised. "We have posted guards around the perimeter to make sure no uninvited guests disturb you, just as Sri Bidkar ordered, and we have employed the local monkey charmer to make sure you are not bothered by the little rascals."

"It would seem that Sri Bidkar knows our taste well," Edmund said happily.

"Oh yes, my lord, that reminds me. Sri Bidkar also sent a collection of the finest cognac in the Empire," he leaned in confidingly, "certainly the finest I have ever seen in India... and a generous supply of Chateaux Margaux. Per his instructions, we have left all of the offerings on the bar in the corner for you to drink at your leisure." Eleanor appreciated that Dixon did not bat an eye at the excessive quantity of alcohol.

Edmund slipped a bill into Dixon's hand. "Thank you, Mr. Dixon. You have been most helpful. If you will please leave us now and send Mr. Valov in when he arrives, we will be most grateful."

"Yes, my lord." Dixon offered a rigid nod of agreement. "But, sir..." He lowered his voice and shifted awkwardly as he avoided eye contact with Eleanor. "Sri Bidkar did suggest that I remind you that because we are on a strict timeline for this evening's sojourn, you should... er... hold off on diving into your honeymoon activities until later... after you return."

"Sri Bidkar does know us well," Eleanor laughed.

Dixon awkwardly straightened his bowtie. "You will be dining in the gardens of the Taj Mahal. Sri Bidkar suggested that you wear something appropriate for the setting."

"Thank you for passing along his suggestions. I can see you are a loyal enough man's man to pass along even the most uncomfortable of advice." Edmund guided Dixon to the door. "We will call you if we need you."

"Yes, sir!" Dixon agreed as he bowed one final time and then scurried away.

Edmund closed and locked the doors to the hallway, and then whisked Eleanor into a passionate embrace.

"Darling, we're going to be late!" She protested half-jokingly as she pulled the stack of garlands off of Edmund's neck and threw them onto the bed. He ripped hers off and threw them into the same pile.

A mischievous look spread across Edmund's face, and Eleanor braced herself for him to rip her new blouse off in one powerful move. Instead, he pulled her into his arms, and in a blur with a very loud splash, they were standing in the pool, fully clothed, and Edmund was laughing.

Eleanor glanced around, making sure no one had spied their Rakshasa entrance.

"He said not to dive into our honeymoon, but he didn't say not to jump!" Edmund declared triumphantly.

Eleanor was speechless as the thin silk clung to her body, and her hair collapsed into a wet mop.

"Forgive me, dearest?" Edmund said more seriously as he guided her legs into a gentle straddle around his waist. "I thought you might want to cool down. That ride was insufferably hot. My skin was flaking."

He held out his hand to show her, and he was indeed correct. A fine layer of his skin was flaking off like fish scales or a snake's outer layer. She found the sight slightly grotesque, but then she was grateful that his physical response to the heat was as grotesque as hers had been when she was sweating buckets and smearing her makeup all over her face.

When he noticed her reaction, he let go of her to submerge himself completely in the water. "A few minutes in here should be all I need to... er... hydrate. Then it will stop."

Eleanor sensed a sudden self-consciousness in him, and she gathered his hand up out of the water and kissed it. "I'm grateful that I am not the only one who feels dreadfully unattractive in the heat, darling. That's all I was thinking about just now. You are still the sexiest man I know."

He worked his hands around her back, unbuttoning her linen trousers and then lifting her silk blouse off over her head.

"That linen suit looks insufferable in the water. Perhaps your skin will hydrate faster without it in the way." Eleanor dove under the water and playfully helped him remove the fabric that was sticking stiffly to his arms and legs.

She wrapped her legs around him as they stood in the water with him in his thin boxer shorts, and her in her skin-tight silk camisole that clung to her large breasts creating a look that aroused both of them with equal measure.

"Mr. Valov isn't here yet. There's nothing else for us to be doing while we wait," Edmund said as he kissed her neck.

"Well, if we *must* keep ourselves occupied..." Eleanor sighed as he worked his way down to her breasts.

"I like this bathing suit of yours." He gently worked the strapless camisole down until her breasts were free of it.

"Anything goes at the beach these days..." Eleanor reached her hand into his shorts and copped a pleasant feel.

They played around, teasing each other with arousing wet licks and kisses, until a familiar voice interrupted their fun.

"Colonel?" Mr. Valov called from their room. "Eleanor?"

They both giggled guiltily, and Eleanor pulled up her camisole, which was certainly too sheer to qualify as a bathing suit, although she had seen some rather scandalous little outfits the last time she'd been at the beach in Brighton with her VAD friends.

"We're out here!" Edmund called. "In the swimming pool!"

After a minute of shuffling around inside their room, Mr. Valov approached with a towel for Eleanor, glancing around to make sure that no one was watching them.

"Mr. Bidkar is going to be very upset if you miss the sunset. He's called Dixon four times in the last twenty minutes just to make sure you're on time." He caught a glance of Eleanor in her wet, clingy underwear and then looked away as he dropped her towel by the poolside. "Shall I gather up some clothing for you? You need to be ready in fifteen minutes. I can gather your wet clothing from the pool after you've left for the evening."

"Yes, Leo. Thank you!" Edmund giggled guiltily again as he helped Eleanor out of the pool, slapping her wet bum as he

358

gathered up the towel and wrapped her up. Mr. Valov returned to their room without turning around to watch them.

"Something Indian, Leo!" Eleanor called. "Sri Bidkar said we must be appropriate, and what is more appropriate than wearing Indian attire?"

Edmund pulled her into a final, tongue-filled kiss and pulled her up against his aroused body. "God, how I love you, Eleanor."

When they scampered back inside, Mr. Valov had already laid out several choices on the bed for each of them, dutifully focusing on the most extravagant of the Indian outfits in their trunks. Eleanor smelled his cigarette smoke as he paced back and forth in the hallway outside their room.

"Look at that one." Edmund felt the delicate mint green and ivory silk of one of Kuveni's lehengas. "The craftsmanship of that silk is simply superb. It has no flaws at all... I don't remember seeing this in Babri's offerings. Do you, dearest? It is quite unique. The styling is almost... I don't know... almost Roman."

"The maharani offered me some of hers," Eleanor lied. "I couldn't resist, since I don't think most of Babri's will fit me now."

"That was very kind of her," Edmund said as he collected a silver and blue beaded sherwani for himself.

"Well, we did save her children. A few lehengas are only a small token of gratitude."

While Edmund dressed himself, Eleanor glanced over to make sure Mr. Valov was out of sight, and then she pulled off her remaining clothing, distracting her husband from his task. After letting him cup her naked breasts and kiss her neck one last time, she made her way to the vanity in the corner to deal with her messy mop of hair.

I will help you, but let us not give away too much to your unsuspecting husband, my child.

Eleanor ran her fingers through her hair, and the tangles calmed themselves into neat, damp ringlets. She gathered her hair into a lose ponytail and secured it with the same ribbon she had been using before, leaving several ringlets to fall down gently along the side of her face. As soon as she was finished, she noticed her cosmetics bag already laid out for her use, and she set about putting on the minimum amount of makeup she could get away with by her own personal standards of beauty.

"Colonel, you must get going!" Mr. Valov called from the hallway.

Eleanor rushed back to the bed, and Edmund helped her button up the low-cut blouse (much more low-cut than she remembered, showing copious cleavage), but she had no time to worry about it, and she pulled up the skirt, buttoned its delicate hidden buttons (an innovation unique to Kuveni, as far as Eleanor was concerned), and gathered the dupatta loosely across her back.

"Your elephant awaits, my lady," Edmund said happily as he offered her his arm.

Mr. Valov worked hard to keep his eyes off of her as he escorted them swiftly into the lobby where Bo and Betty, along with several of their other fellow passengers, were standing around looking bored.

"Look at those tattoos! She's like a bloody native!" the elderly woman who'd disapproved of their jasmine hissed to her husband.

Eleanor avoided eye contact with everyone, imagining their eyes following her henna up to her cleavage as she dashed passed them in the revealing outfit. She focused only on following Mr. Valov out to the front drive.

"Aw, where'd our elephant friends go?" Edmund whined melodramatically. "I was rather fond of them!"

"Sri Bidkar had a different idea," Mr. Valov said as he directed their attention to a guard who was escorting a noble white mare, donning an elaborate golden double-saddle, up the drive.

"Do you think Ravi had that saddle made just for us?" Eleanor asked amusedly.

"They are commonly used in Indian weddings. Perhaps he simply procured the most expensive one in the area," Edmund replied.

Mr. Valov braced himself for another awkward moment. "Sri Bidkar also asked me to give you this, Colonel. He had it shipped from Bombay by courier." From his inner coat pocket, he pulled out an exotic curved sword in a golden sheath attached to a matching belt that looked straight out of the *Arabian Nights*. "In case you run into trouble."

Edmund removed the sword from its sheath and tapped the sharp blade with his finger, and then he glanced back towards their growing audience in the lobby. Eleanor was quite certain that every guest at the hotel was now watching them. She half expected the staff to start handing out popcorn for the show.

"Well, better safe than sorry, I suppose," Edmund said as he put the sword back and slipped on the belt.

Save a jeweled turban, there was no detail left to make Edmund look more like a fairy tale prince. He seemed perfectly natural in his get-up, even more so with the sword.

"Er… Colonel…" Dixon emerged from the lobby, awkwardly carrying a silver and white turban with an enormous white plume extending from a cluster of glistening jewels. Eleanor did not want to know how much the thing was worth. Probably enough to feed half the country.

Eleanor shook her head with bemusement. "Oh, Ravi… you are a tenacious bloke, aren't you?"

Dixon presented the turban, glancing over at the other English servants and then the Indian ones. "Sri Bidkar had this couriered over for you to wear tonight. He seemed rather insistent. Do you want to… er… wear it?"

Edmund laughed jovially at the prospect. "I suppose, dearest, I won't have to procure my own now." He glanced inside at their attentive audience, landing his attention on the disapproving elderly couple who had complained about their jasmine garlands.

They were whispering cattily to each other. He took the turban and placed it securely on his head. "In for a penny, in for a pound, dearest?"

Somehow it suited him. He looked rather pleased with himself as he looked down at his full outfit, and Eleanor realized in that moment that *this* was possibly his most natural human state. Despite his fair skin from his French mother, he was, as it turned out, more native to where they were standing than he was to Britain. He was, she had to remind herself, the son of the King of Ceylon. The thought seemed so fanciful that she had trouble holding onto it, especially as her attention wandered back to their clucking audience.

Despite the combination of disapproval and amusement being vigorously emoted from their onlookers inside the lobby, Edmund didn't seem to care at all about their reactions, and Eleanor loved him even more for it.

"Hello, my friend. What a beautiful animal you are," Edmund said happily as he greeted the mare.

She offered him a friendly neigh.

"I can see that she's very well cared for." He addressed the servant who was staring at him silently has he handed over the reins. Eleanor realized that Edmund's statement was in Hindi.

"Yes, sir," the servant replied.

"Her name is Padma, and she is the pride and joy of our hotel manager," Dixon chimed in as he gestured for the enamored boy to leave them.

Eleanor almost guffawed at the name, and for a split second, for the first time since she'd heard Ravi speak of Lord Kalki's destined beloved, she felt a hint of hope that maybe, just maybe, the prophecies had gotten it wrong. Perhaps together as two joined avatars, they would ride Padma into the sunset…

"She is not normally a horse for hire, but Sri Bidkar was very convincing. You really are the commander of King George's Household Cavalry, are you not, Colonel?"

"Indeed, I am. Sri Bidkar was telling you the truth about that," Edmund agreed. "She will be in excellent hands."

"And you know how to get to the Taj Mahal? Sri Bidkar's staff will be there to welcome you. He has had the entire monument closed to the public so that you can enjoy the experience in privacy."

"Good lord, how did he manage that?" Edmund exclaimed.

Dixon cleared his throat awkwardly. "I believe, sir, by paying a great deal of money to a great many people."

Edmund laughed. "That is one of his talents."

"Do you need me to show you the way, sir?" Dixon asked.

"No, thank you, old chap. I know Agra well. I was a commander in the British Indian Army for two decades before the war."

"Very good, sir."

Dixon relaxed, and with the formalities out of the way, Edmund lifted Eleanor up onto the horse so that she could ride side-saddle behind him. The delicate layers of the lehenga's thin silk rustled beautifully with the minor breeze, although Eleanor fought back a vision of it flying open like a parachute when they actually started moving.

"Have you ever ridden in a gown like this, dearest?"

"Never," Eleanor admitted. She looked down at her bare waist and her bulging blouse, and then gave up on any semblance of modesty as she tightened her dupatta around her back so it wouldn't fly away in the wind. She felt a hot blush rush into her cheeks as she noticed the eyes of every guest in the lobby glued on her.

Edmund hopped up nimbly and took his position in front of her with the perfect posture of a seasoned rider, gathering up the reins and leaning forward to whisper a soothing hello into Padma's ear.

Uma reached out her hand to gently stroke Padma's soft hair.

The gods thank you for your service tonight, my child. Go now with our blessings and heed Lord Kalki's commands.

"You'd better get going, Colonel. The sunset is coming soon. I will stay in your room while you're out, guarding your belongings," Mr. Valov said with a friendly wave.

Eleanor grabbed onto Edmund as Padma bucked gracefully, and then, as she heeded Lord Kalki's commands, she trotted into the sunset.

CHAPTER 19 – MONUMENTAL

As the warm wind whipped through her hair and batted her flowing skirt, Eleanor laughed with exhilaration. The sky was already a bright magenta, filtering the light on them in a most surreal fashion. The scene was so absurd, so clichéd, yet she managed to subjugate her pessimism as she held on tighter to her gentle, divine, demon prince.

"Isn't it wonderful, dearest!" Edmund exclaimed.

"It is perfect," Eleanor whispered into his ear. "Simply perfect, darling."

The townsfolk all stopped to gawk at them as they navigated the small, winding streets, and Eleanor found herself wishing half-seriously that Edmund had brought his pouch of coins so that they could complete the effect by showering the villagers in alms as they went.

By the time they reached an imposing domed structure made up of red stone and white marble, a large group, all dressed in the uniforms of Ravi's staff, rushed to greet them. Eleanor hoped sincerely that they weren't going to bow and offer prayers to them, as Ravi had already proven himself to be less than the model of discretion.

As soon as they reached the gate, a bright flash startled her as one member of the staff took their picture. Edmund must have thrown the man a dirty look at the unexpected intrusion, because the poor bloke took off his turban and bowed.

"Please forgive me, my lord. Sri Bidkar thought that you would like to have pictures from this evening as a momento of your honeymoon. If my lord wishes to have no photographs taken, I will desist at once!"

Eleanor could hear that the man was speaking in Hindi, but she understood every word.

"Ravi employed him to document our evening," Edmund translated for her.

"I suppose it should be quite picturesque," she replied.

"You may continue, as long as you are not too intrusive," Edmund told the man.

"Yes, my lord!" The man stood up and readied himself to take another picture, holding the camera up and waiting for their next move.

Eleanor giggled at his immediate demonstration that he didn't share their definition of *intrusive,* but Edmund found his posture less than amusing.

"They will be lovely pictures, darling, that I'm sure we'll enjoy looking at later," Eleanor whispered into Edmund's ear.

Edmund hopped off the mare and helped Eleanor into his arms, and the entire staff (other than their devoted photographer) bowed in unison. Eleanor could see that their reverence was genuine, and some men in the back were even trembling.

"Very discreet, Ravi..." Eleanor muttered.

"Right then," Edmund said awkwardly as he too noticed their awestruck state. "I hear that Sri Bidkar planned a sunset dinner for us? We'd better get moving. The sky is already ablaze."

"Yes, my lord!" a man in the front exclaimed. "Follow me!"

Edmund guided the mare by the reins with one hand and held Eleanor's hand in the other as they emerged into an enormous garden filled with groomed trees and lawns, flanking glistening pools that reflected the rich magenta and blazing purple of the sunset. Just beyond the central pool, loomed the massive white marble icon. Even it had a tint of pink to it, reflecting the fiery sky.

Eleanor stopped to take in the astounding sight.

"Good lord," she murmured. "I've never seen anything so beautiful in my life."

"I agree." She looked over to catch Edmund gazing at her.

"Very romantic, darling," she giggled. "Jane Austen would approve."

Edmund brushed a rogue ringlet out of her eyes. "I am very serious, Eleanor. I have been here so many times, and I never cared very much about it. There are so many other monuments in India that are more interesting to me. But being here with you now... It is like a dream I never even knew existed has come true."

He put his cool hand around her bare back and pulled her into a gentle kiss.

She gave into a swoon, and for the moment, for one magical moment, she let him be her fairy tale prince, and more extraordinarily, she let herself be a fairy tale princess.

They stood together, watching the bright colors fade into darkness, until symmetrical pairs of servants lit up a series of flickering fire torches all along the edge of the glistening pool, creating a magical reflective effect worthy of a Yaksha palace.

"My lord, my lady. Your dinner is ready for you."

The servant gestured for them to follow him to a canopy that had been set up stealthily many meters behind them while they'd been distracted watching the sunset. Around it, more fire torches flickered, and underneath, two chairs were placed next to each other facing the Taj Mahal at a disproportionately large table, set with fine silver place-settings, enormous candelabras, and heaps of fresh jasmine atop a white linen tablecloth.

As soon as they were seated, eight servants approached, carrying massive platters and steaming bowls.

"Good lord, there's enough food to feed an army regiment," Edmund murmured as they removed the silver covers, revealing heaping piles of spiced biryani, burbling red and yellow curries, steaming fried vegetables, several different kinds of aromatic flatbreads, and glistening fresh salads. Another round of servants followed, bearing six bottles of Chateau Margaux. They said nothing about the outrageous quantity for two people, and dutifully poured them each a generous serving.

"Is it to my lord's liking?" their leader asked hopefully. "There is no turmeric in any of it. None at all!"

"It looks absolutely scrumptious." Edmund smiled as he took his first spoonful of biriyani onto his plate. "Perhaps, if you would be so kind... can you please leave us to it for a bit? We enjoy eating privately."

"Are you sure, my lord? It is our greatest honor to serve you!"

"We appreciate your earnest effort, my friend, but I would rather serve my wife myself on this romantic evening."

"Yes, my lord!"

The man barked some orders to the other servants, and they followed him back to a position about ten meters away from them where the entire staff stood in a rigid row, awaiting their next command.

"Ravi sure knows how to throw a party," Eleanor laughed.

The whole scene was, of course, utterly absurd, but it had crossed some threshold at which the absurdity had become amusing. Eleanor decided to embrace the feeling.

She gathered what she wanted onto her plate and ate slowly while Edmund plowed through his first seven servings.

As a yellow full moon rose high into the sky, the warm breeze blew her dry ringlets into her eyes and tickled her face. She took in a deep, calming breath, followed by a long sip of her wine.

"It finally feels like our honeymoon," she sighed. "This is so much more magical than I ever believed anything could be."

"I will have to thank Ravi again. He has really given us something extraordinary tonight. The Taj Mahal is usually a nightmare to visit, full of hawkers and loud tourists."

"He really is a thoughtful man." Eleanor reached up and rustled the white feather in his turban. "Perhaps a bit too thoughtful sometimes, but it is a forgivable offense."

Edmund chuckled. "He has always been very accommodating, ever since our first dinner when I surprised him with my manners. But this... this is different." He took off the turban to inspect it more closely. "This must be worth a fortune. These are certainly real sapphires, and this enormous one here is a diamond. If the king knew about these stones, he'd probably confiscate them to be added to the crowned jewels..." He trailed off as he was distracted by the aesthetics. "The craftsmanship of the settings is superb. I think they may even be a Moghul setting; if so, they are in exceptional condition for their age..." Edmund furrowed his brow. "I hope Ravi isn't bankrupting himself with all this."

"He does seem like he knows how to manage his money, darling."

"Yes... I suppose you're right." Edmund put the turban back on. "But he's different now. He has gone a bit mad, I think, after what he saw. I found it rather frustrating, to be honest, that there was simply nothing I could say that would temper his reverence. I considered momentarily listing out for him the horrific injuries I've imparted on other men... but then I didn't want him to fear me."

Eleanor took his hand into hers. "Sometimes we must let people see us how they want to see us, darling. Even if it isn't how we see ourselves." Eleanor wasn't sure if the wisdom had come from herself or Uma.

"It isn't healthy for him to think that I'm some sort of godly figure, Eleanor. The last thing I want is for him to change himself to impress me. Did you see his face when he was contemplating eating that fish? How foolish that was! And next time, I won't be there to coax him into following his own instincts. He'll simply embark upon a fool's errand because it's what he thinks I would do. It is a very dangerous proposition for him."

"Darling, Ravi is an intelligent man. He was given quite a shock when he saw your unique talents. It is not unusual for him to take some time to comprehend what it all means. He was already quite religious, and now he must work what he saw into his view of the world. Give him some time. And if he takes too long, we can always sell back the turban to bail him out of the poor house." She winked, hoping to bring back some relaxation to their evening. Edmund did not seem moved. "Darling, you must have faith in him. Perhaps I can telephone Shruti when we get back to the hotel to check in on how Ravi's doing."

"Would you really do that, dearest?"

"She and I are sisters in arms now, and she will give me an honest appraisal of her father's state. Oh, and we can check in on Jaap Sahib and Jyoti! I wonder if they're married yet!"

"Jaap Sahib?" Edmund asked.

Eleanor realized that with all of the hubbub, she hadn't included Edmund in her plan at all.

"Yes, he wanted to marry Jyoti but Dev Sahib had disallowed it."

"It is very uncommon for servants to be married in a distinguished household here," Edmund explained.

"Yes, well, whatever the reasons, when Rane fired Jaap Sahib, he used the excuse to do the honorable thing. He was worried about what losing his position meant for them financially, so I sent him to Ravi and Shruti. I thought that after the incident in the garden, they'd appreciate another skilled guard, and Ravi was rather preoccupied with wanting a baby around the house. I thought perhaps the whole thing would be mutually beneficial."

Edmund paused for a long moment considering her statement, and Eleanor began to worry that he disapproved of her plan. Instead, he squeezed her hand and leaned over to entice her into a gentle kiss.

"You are so clever, Eleanor. So wonderfully thoughtful. I'm sure they will all benefit from that situation. It is, in fact, better than any situation they could have had if Jaap Sahib had stayed in Madho Rao's employ. You have given them a life they could not have had any other way. You transformed their misfortune into a blessing."

"Well, Ravi and Shruti certainly must take most of the credit. They're the ones who are going to do all the work."

"Still, dearest, you used your influence to make it happen. Very few people could have done such a thing, and even fewer would have."

"It seemed far too easy to warrant such praise," Eleanor argued. "But I'm glad you approve of my plan. I should have told you sooner, I suppose, but there has just been too much going on."

"I love you, Eleanor."

Eleanor took a deep breath and allowed herself to return to the fairy tale romance of the evening, to the version of their special night when worrying about the yoke of their divine destinies was someone else's problem entirely. She kissed him gently on the cheek, and then poured them both another glass of wine.

"It is hard for me to picture this place overrun with tourists. It's so peaceful now."

Edmund took a long, savoring sip. "I believe this must be much closer to what Shah Jahan intended when he built it."

"Why did he build it? Is it a castle?" Eleanor asked.

Edmund smiled wistfully. "It is a tomb."

"Blimey, that takes the romance right out of it." Eleanor felt like she'd had the wind knocked right out of her.

Edmund took her hand and kissed it. "He built it for his favorite wife after she died in childbirth. He spent the next twenty years building this mausoleum for her... He, of course, did not actually build it with his own hands. Some historians believe that it took twenty thousand artisans."

Eleanor took another long swig of her wine. She wished more than anything that it could help her ignore the sorrow that was burrowing to the surface.

"Why did Ravi think it would be romantic for us to come here?"

"It is rather famous for being romantic. I agree, though, there is too much morbidity in the story for my taste. I have always found the idea that lost love is romantic to be paradoxical. Surely, losing someone who completes you is the greatest agony anyone can ever feel. There is no other reason Shah Jahan would have built this. It was the only way he could survive with his despair."

Eleanor grimaced as she envisioned her dead body lying on a slab inside the massive monument. "Do you think Tennyson was right? Do you think it is better to have loved and lost than to never have loved at all?"

"I didn't know you read much poetry." Edmund squeezed her hand. "I suppose there is still a lot about you that I don't know yet. It feels like we've been together for a lifetime already."

"I haven't really read much poetry," Eleanor admitted. "But there were several books of English poems floating around the VAD boarding house during the war. But, really, Edmund, do you think he's right?"

"I bloody hope so," Edmund admitted. "I'm sorry, Eleanor. I didn't mean to ruin the moment. It's just... I have always outlived the people I love, but I have never loved anyone like I love you. I cannot imagine losing you. The thought terrifies me."

"I know the feeling, darling. The thought terrifies me too."

She leaned over and put her head on his shoulder, and they gazed pensively into the distance, holding each other's warm, pulsating hands tighter than they ever had, watching the moon rise over the most iconic monument to an unsettlingly familiar ancient tragedy.

CHAPTER 20 – THE LOYAL MOUNT

After many hours of sitting side by side watching the moonrise and enjoying the ephemeral pleasures of each other's company, Edmund borrowed a torch from an obliging servant and led Eleanor to the mausoleum, walking her through all of his favorite details and pointing out the sapphires, jade, and lapis lazuli that had been painstakingly imported from the far reaches of the globe.

When they had examined all that Edmund could think of to share, they returned to their loyal row of Ravi's yawning servants and offered their profuse thanks. Edmund encouraged them to finish off the feast, and they refused steadfastly, opting instead to kiss his hand—a development that he didn't like at all.

He escaped them with the fewest words he could get away with and helped Eleanor back onto the patient mare, taking a more direct route on a wider, well-lit street back to the hotel.

When they arrived, Dixon was asleep in a chair by the front door of the lobby, and a sleepy valet let them inside and escorted Padma back to the stables.

"Are you tired, dearest?" Edmund asked as they reached the door to their suite.

"I don't know. Not really. We've slept a lot in the last few days," Eleanor replied.

Edmund smiled. "I was feeling the same way. Now that everyone's asleep, what do you think of taking a midnight dip in the pool?"

"A skinny dip?" Eleanor asked with a mischievous smile.

Edmund practically ripped open the doors. Romantic candles flickered from various surfaces around the room, and the french doors out to the garden were still open, letting in a lovely warm breeze. Eleanor paused for a moment of panic as she heard a suspiciously human noise, but as she looked around for the culprit, there on the bed, still fully clothed, lay Mr. Valov sleeping soundly.

She closed and locked the doors to the hallway behind them, and then tiptoed over to the bedside.

"We shouldn't wake him, don't you think?" she whispered.

Edmund unbuttoned her blouse and then hastily removed his belt, his turban, and his sherwani, leaving them in a messy pile on the floor.

"I wouldn't dream of it," he whispered.

Eleanor wiggled off her skirt while Edmund ripped off his silk pants, and then they scampered naked across the lawn and into the pool, jumping in together with a big splash.

Edmund fully submerged himself and then popped up to splash her playfully. She splashed him back, and they quickly devolved into a battle marked by booming laughter and loud squeals by both of them.

Finally, Edmund pulled her into his arms and held her up around his waist as she straddled him.

"Happy honeymoon, dearest." He sunk down so that only their heads were out of the water as he welcomed her onto him with a hushed sigh.

They set about secretly making love under the moonlight, relishing the game of keeping themselves quiet as they elicited gyrations of pleasure from each other.

When they were finished with a particularly successful round, Eleanor sighed. "I could use something to drink. Do you want something, darling?"

"I have never reached my maximum capacity for liquid," Edmund agreed. "Shall I get it?"

"I can get it, darling. Do you want the cognac or the wine?"

"I will drink whatever you'd like."

Eleanor braced herself, and then scampered out of the pool, across the lawn, and straight back into their room. When she eyed Mr. Valov, she slipped on her red silk robe from its position hanging on a hook by the bed, and then she tiptoed to the small bar to inspect their options.

She blew off a thick layer of dust from two of the cognacs, barely holding in a sneeze, but as she squinted to read the old writing, an unnatural rustling followed by several creaks and a clomp brought her straight to attention. She glanced back at Mr. Valov, who hadn't moved at all, and then she carefully put the bottles down and looked around the dark room again with more scrutiny.

Eleanor glanced towards the door where they'd entered, and then she focused in her attention on an old-fashioned wardrobe on the opposite side of the room. The distinct sound of something being dropped, something metal and slightly heavy, permeated through the door of the wardrobe.

"Blimey, what are you up to…" Eleanor glanced around for her trunk, hoping that Mr. Valov had left the silver pistol alongside her jewelry in the top compartment.

She tiptoed to her trunk and opened it up, but the pistol and the piles of costume jewelry that matched Babri's final offerings were all missing.

"Blimey," Eleanor whispered again as the full implications rushed through her mind.

She tiptoed to the bed and tried to awaken Mr. Valov, but as she nudged him harder and harder, she realized that he was sleeping too soundly. She leaned forward and listened for his breath—it was too shallow. She lifted up his eyelids, still with no reaction.

"Good lord, Leo, you've been drugged," she murmured.

She patted him down, hoping to borrow the revolver that he kept strapped to his calf, but as she felt nothing, and lifted up his trouser cuff, all that was left was the empty strap.

As another clomp resonated from the wardrobe, Eleanor thought momentarily about alerting her husband (a sensible choice, she had to admit), but then she thought about the gruesome deaths that had come to everyone who had recently offended him, and she thought the better of it.

She grabbed the crescent sword that Ravi had given him as part of his princely costume from underneath the pile of his clothing on the floor, but she paused as she looked down at it. The turban was missing. She readied herself to deal with the thief.

Following her own advice by maintaining the element of surprise, she rushed towards the wardrobe and ripped open the door, positioning the sword right at the throat of their intruder.

"Aw, hell and damnation," a familiar voice with a grating Texas accent swore. Betty looked up guiltily at Eleanor, wearing an enormous stack of the wilted jasmine garlands, and holding the silver pistol with a shaking hand.

"Drop the gun," Eleanor said as she tightened her grip on the sword and its position poised on Betty's jugular.

Betty obeyed, and Eleanor swooped down and picked it up, pointing it at Betty with her free hand.

376

"Now stand up," Eleanor ordered as she stood back and made room for the girl to exit the empty wardrobe.

As she moved, all of Shruti's costume jewelry fell out of Betty's shallow pockets, clanking as it bounced off the marble floor.

Eleanor glanced down at it. "You bloody little fool. Do you have any idea how much danger you're in? All for a handful of costume jewelry?"

Betty stuttered. "Well… uh… you ain't gonna hurt me, are you, Your Majesty? Not little ol' me? I didn't mean any harm by it, really!"

"You didn't mean any harm by drugging our butler with so much sedative that he is barely breathing? Or by stealing my pistol so that you could do no harm with a gun in your hand?" Eleanor asked sharply. "How many other people did you drug tonight? Dixon? The guards? How many?!"

"I dunno. Bo said it was just a little sleepin' sauce!"

Betty did not seem repentant at all, nor appropriately scared.

"So you drugged the hotel staff and our butler, and then snuck into our room to steal our personal belongings? To steal my jewelry?"

"You didn't need it!" Betty exclaimed. "You gotta have lots of jewelry! I mean, you're a like a queen or somethin'! Bo works mighty hard to give me the things I want, mighty hard, Your Majesty. And then the Lord gave Bo these tickets to the Taaaj Maaa-hal, and then He brought us to you! He plopped you right down in front of us on the train, and then you know what He did? He told Bo that He wanted us to have your jewelry! For bein' good Christian folk! It was our reward, and God almighty, we deserve a reward! We work mighty hard to be good Christian folk, mighty, mighty hard."

"*God* told you to steal my jewelry as a reward for being a good Christian?" Eleanor rolled her eyes with annoyed disbelief at that idiocy of the assertion.

"Don't ya have anythin' ya can spare for the normal workin' folks?" Betty's voice became shrill with anger. "You're selfish, I reckon, and God don't like selfish people! Bo said so!"

"You know *nothing* about me." Eleanor could feel her fiery temper bubbling up to the surface, but it was far more fiery than it had ever been before. She felt Uma's power bubbling up with it. "I've been a nurse for twenty bloody years. I've spent my entire life helping people. Normal people. People who worked harder than you can even comprehend and had families and dreams and didn't deserve the agony they were suffering. I've saved *thousands* of lives. Do you know what that number even means? It means that I've saved more people than you've ever met in your life." Betty gulped. "Don't you dare tell *me* what God likes, you ignorant little fool!"

"Why're your eyes all green, Your Majesty?" Betty whispered, with her first hint of appropriate fear.

"You are using God's will as an excuse for your own selfish crimes!" Eleanor couldn't contain herself. "Let me tell you a thing or two about God's will…"

Eleanor trailed off as the barrel of another gun touched the back of her head.

"I reckon, this here is God's will," Bo said as he released the safety with an ominous click. "Now drop these here weapons and let Betty go."

Eleanor's mind raced with her limited options.

Obey him for now, my child. We have other means at our disposal.

Eleanor dropped the sword and the pistol, and Betty reached down and collected the jewelry back into her pockets.

"Her Majesty claims these here jewels are fake!" she humphed.

"A mighty tricky lie," Bo said as he nudged Eleanor away from Betty towards the bed. As Eleanor slowly turned around to face Bo, he was wearing Edmund's turban and several of the wilted jasmine garlands. The door to the WC was now swinging open in the breeze, and Eleanor chastised herself for not noticing the obvious hiding place sooner.

"You have no idea how dangerous this is," Eleanor warned them. "If you value your lives, you will leave now. It might already be too late."

"What're you gonna do? Tell your injun prince to chase after us? We'll be long gone!" Bo exclaimed. "The Lord will lead the way! He even brought us that beaut of a horse out there for our getaway!"

As Bo backed her onto the bed beside Mr. Valov, Betty suddenly began pouting.

"Not now, Bo. We ain't got time for games! The lord colonel sir is around here somewhere. He'd be mighty unhappy if he caught you!"

"How's he gonna stop me, Bets? Huh? He ain't got two guns and a sword now, does he? The Lord gave 'em to us! He gave us everythin' we'd need to take what's ours!"

"But, Bo... It ain't right! You said you weren't gonna do it again! The preacher said you shouldn't!"

"Shut up, woman! Obey your husband, like the Bible says! If the Lord didn't want me to take my prize, He wouldn't of given it to me! And a mighty fine prize you are, ain't ya, Your Majesty? Just like a fairy tale princess."

He looked down at Eleanor in her thin silk robe and licked his lips covetously.

"Now come on over here Betty, and keep that beaut of a pistol pointed right up at her head. We don't need no screamin' now, do we?"

Betty reluctantly obeyed, with her hands still shaking as she held Eleanor's pistol aimed at her head so that Bo could have both hands free for 'taking what the Lord had given him.'

He tossed the revolver just out of Eleanor's reach across Mr. Valov's unconscious body, onto the far edge of the bed. As Bo unbuttoned his pants, Eleanor looked around desperately for any option that would not result in Edmund ripping Bo's head right off.

Do not fear my child. She is our loyal mount, and she heeds our commands.

She?

The growl of a tigress echoed from the hallway.

"Blimey," Eleanor whispered.

Bo and Betty both froze in position as an enormous Bengal tigress scratched at the french doors.

"Why, whaddya think that is, Bo?" Betty squeaked.

The beast paced back and forth several times in front of the closed door, humphing and growling with displeasure, and then, without a moment of warning, it burst through the glass and pounced right on top of Bo, grabbing him by the nape of his neck and dragging him across the room in one graceful move. Edmund's turban fell off and rolled away as Bo whimpered with fear and pain, unable to push out a coherent word while the tigress circled him, calculating her next move.

"Shoot it, Bets," he rasped. "Shoot the goddamned devil."

It was too late.

Betty choked on her own screams as the tigress slashed deep wounds into Bo's arms with her enormous claws. As Bo's body went limp, the tigress finished off his punishment by clawing a final set of wounds into his legs.

When she was convinced that Bo was immobilized, she looked up at Betty, staring her down with her glowing green eyes.

"The Lord has spoken," Eleanor hissed.

With one final squeal, Betty dropped the gun and ran in her bare feet across the broken glass of the french doors, into the dark hallway, and away.

"Someone help! There's a tiger! A tiger ate my Bo!" her voice echoed from the lobby.

The tigress leapt across the room, right into Eleanor's arms and knocked her over is it licked her face lovingly, paying great care not to injure her delicate human body.

I've missed you too, Sheranee, Uma communicated as she held the tigress's head in her arms and touched its forehead to hers. Eleanor found the sensation of utter fearlessness as she cuddled with the tigress to be strangely invigorating.

This is the longest Sheranee and I have been apart in five hundred years, Uma explained. *She thought I was dead until I summoned her.*

I don't think Edmund will let us keep a pet tiger, Eleanor pointed out.

Speaking of whom…

"Blimey," Eleanor whispered.

"Eleanor, dearest? Is something wrong?" Edmund called.

Keep your distance, Sheranee, Lord Kalki must not be alarmed.

Sheranee hopped up and walked over to the broken doors to the hallway, keeping her distance from Eleanor as they both listened to Edmund's footsteps approaching.

"Dearest, I was getting worried. Did I hear someone squealing?" Edmund's minor anxiety morphed into demonic rage as he reached the room and smelled the fresh blood from Betty's feet and Bo's wounds.

His eyes turned black, and Eleanor felt him lose control as he whooshed to her side. He spotted the two guns and the sword, and then he spotted Bo.

"Eleanor, what happened?!"

Like an unfocused beast whose pride had been compromised, Edmund glanced around the room in search of a target. Sheranee growled a low warning growl as his attention fell directly on her, but before Edmund could engage Eleanor's divine mount in ill-conceived combat, she threw herself in front of her.

"Stop! She's fine! She helped!" she exclaimed. "Bo and Betty were robbing us! Bo had me cornered with a gun in his hand and a snake in his pants, and she arrived just in time!"

Edmund gazed covetously at the bleeding wounds on Bo's arms. "That man was going to rape you, Eleanor? Why didn't you call for me?!"

In a blur, Edmund was leaning over Bo, who opened his eyes weakly and whimpered as he took in the terrifying expression on the face of his vengeful demonic foe. He began shivering with shock, and then closed his eyes again, whispering prayers.

Eleanor held Edmund back as she leaned down to whisper into Bo's ear. "Which God are you praying to now? The patron saint of rapists? The protector of thieves? What does the Bible say about God's punishment of violent, thieving bastards, eh? Why don't you ask Him what he thinks of your actions now? Are you ready to be judged?"

Bo's shivers increased in intensity until he was gyrating uncontrollably, and Eleanor stood up, calmed herself, and began rubbing Edmund's back.

"You are answering your own question, darling. I didn't call for you because I didn't want you to kill him. He's not dead yet, even after a tiger attack. We must let him be. Mr. Valov is drugged, and we don't need a riot with pitchforks coming after us."

As Eleanor heard the echoes of movement in the lobby, she grabbed Edmund's hand and dragged him to the washbasin, as far away from Bo as possible. She wrapped him up in a robe that was hanging on a hook on the wall and returned to rubbing his back. "Get yourself under control, darling. You must get yourself under control *now*."

He glanced back over at the tiger that was now pacing back and forth guarding the door to the hallway. With no sign of immediate danger, he gave into her command and whispered his mantras until his eyes returned to their human hazel.

"Very good, darling," Eleanor whispered. "Now let us think clearly about what we will do next. Betty has gone to rally anyone who's still awake. I have no idea how much of the staff they drugged, but someone will be here soon, and there will be a dying man for them to tend to… if the tiger will let them pass."

Edmund maneuvered himself in front of her as he watched Sheranee calmly fulfill her sacred duties.

"I've never seen a beast as controlled as this one," he whispered. "Certainly with the scent of fresh blood, a tigress should drag a wounded man away for a nice supper. And she made no attempt to attack you, Eleanor? None?"

"None, darling. I think she is our ally."

As men's shouting resonated from the lobby, Edmund's eyes turned momentarily black, and he whispered a final mantra, forcing himself back under control. He took a step towards Sheranee, who stopped her pacing to wait for his next move. He tiptoed towards her, keeping eye contact, and Eleanor followed closely behind.

"She has attacked a human," Edmund said as he slowly reached his hands forward to let her sniff him. "She must escape now, or they will surely shoot her. She must go far outside of the city limits. There will be a hunt until they find her."

Sheranee kneeled down into a languid stretch that looked remarkably like a pious bow.

"Go," Eleanor commanded her.

She and Uma both wanted to reach forward and pet the creature with a thankful blessing, but as Edmund maintained his guarding position between Eleanor and the beast, they gave into their responsibility to keep Lord Kalki in the dark, and kept their distance.

"Is there a tiger here? That loud American girl is up in arms! She's awakened the whole bloody lot of us!" One of their grumpy white-haired fellow passengers from the train stepped through the broken french doors, wearing slippers and flannel pajamas. "Good lord!" he exclaimed as he stood face to face with Sheranee.

Sheranee took in a deep breath and roared at him. He backed away, up against the wall, and Eleanor looked down at his freshly soiled trousers.

Go! Eleanor urged as Sheranee took one last look at the man. She obeyed, and took off running out the french doors, through the garden, and into the dark.

Will she be safe?

Do not fear, my child. She has already returned to her divine perch. She is awaiting our next command.

"That... that... that... that *was* a bloody tiger!" the man stuttered. His hands were shaking.

Eleanor took his arm and guided him into their room, seating him on a chaise that she had hardly noticed until that moment.

"The tiger got him!" the man exclaimed as he noticed Bo's wounded presence. "She was a man-eater!"

"Mr. Ralston and his wife were robbing us. They drugged most of the staff and tried to attack me. The tigress intervened," Eleanor explained. "If the tigress had not come, I don't know what would have happened. Something worse, I think."

The man paused to consider the intel, and then he leaned forward confidingly. "I've never liked Americans. They're a bunch of scoundrels, I tell you! The lot of 'em!"

Eleanor relaxed at his seemingly supportive reaction, if albeit a bit... generalized in his distaste for their common enemy.

"Well, Mr...?" Eleanor asked.

"Mr. Waverly," he replied. "And you're some duchess or something, I take it?"

"Lady Eleanor Marriner, Countess of Easton," Eleanor replied, avoiding eye contact with Edmund as she said it.

"I figured. Trains are always late when there's a lord and lady to wait for."

Three more men, all hotel guests clad in English pajamas, approached in the dark hallway.

"Is everything alright in here?" a round, red-faced, balding man asked. "Did we... did we hear a roar?"

"There *was* a bloody tiger!" Mr. Waverly exclaimed as they stepped through the broken doors. "In the count and countess's room! I saw it with my own eyes!"

The three men eyed Eleanor's immodest state in the red silk robe, shifting uncomfortably in an unsuccessful effort to hide their involuntary reactions to it, and then they glanced over to Edmund guiltily, and finally landed their attention on Bo.

"Bloody hell!" one exclaimed. "The tiger attacked him?!"

All three men ran to examine the wreckage, and Eleanor joined them as they approached Bo's body. She held her robe closed as she kneeled down, while Edmund kept his distance, maintaining his position by the broken door.

"I was a nurse during the war," she explained. "I've seen a lot of trauma. His injuries might be fatal, unless we can get him to a hospital. None of you are doctors, are you?"

They nodded their heads disappointedly in the negative, not, Eleanor was sure, out of sadness for Bo, but out of their inability to impress her.

"Are there any hospitals here?" one of the men asked. "You know, like real hospitals. *British* hospitals?"

"I have no idea, we just got here today," Eleanor replied. "Do any of you know?"

They all nodded in the negative, and she glanced back towards Edmund.

"There wasn't a British hospital in Agra twenty years ago when I was here last. I have no idea whether there is one now."

"Is anyone on the staff awake?" Eleanor asked.

"No!" the red-faced man exclaimed. "The lazy louts were all sound asleep! During a bloody tiger attack! I'll have to call the board of governors about this in the morning. It is utterly unacceptable."

He looked to Eleanor, hoping for some sort of praise. She did not oblige him.

"You needn't go to the trouble, Mr...?"

"Mr. Brown, my lady!" he exclaimed. "It is an honor to make your acquaintance!"

"Right, Mr. Brown." Eleanor was unmoved by his enthusiastic greeting. "You needn't go to the trouble. Even our butler was knocked out cold. Mr. Ralston and his wife drugged the staff so they could rob us. You will find handfuls of my jewelry in Mrs. Ralston's pockets."

Two of the men stood up with refreshed vigor. "Shall we go retrieve it for you, my lady?"

Eleanor moved to refuse, and then she reconsidered the prospect. "If you'd like."

They raced each other to the door.

"We'll go collect her at once!" the younger of the men announced as he disappeared down the dark hallway. His companion followed, and within moments, their voices echoed from the lobby.

"There *was* a bloody tiger! And Betty here is a thief! Her beau was attacked in the lord and lady's room!"

"I don't know what to do about him." Eleanor sighed, glancing between Edmund, Mr. Waverly, and Mr. Brown. "We don't have any way of getting him to a hospital with the entire staff asleep, and his wounds are so dire that bandaging him up seems futile."

"Do you think the tiger will come back?" Mr. Waverly asked nervously.

"I think if she wanted a snack, she would have taken it with her," Eleanor replied.

"Lemme go!" Betty whined as the two men dragged her kicking and screaming back into the room.

"My lady, what shall we do with her?" the younger one asked.

Betty whimpered as Eleanor approached her. As the men held Betty's arms behind her back, Eleanor gathered her jewelry from her pockets and dropped it on the floor with a series of loud clanks.

"Was it worth it for some paste?" Eleanor asked her. "Is this what God wanted? For your husband to die over some costume jewelry?"

"Bo! My Bo!" Betty burst into tears, but the men held her, unmoved.

Eleanor glanced around at the mayhem again, and finally formulated a plan. "I say we lock Betty and her beloved Bo in their room for the rest of the night. If you gentlemen will be so kind as to carry our injured thief, we can ask the staff to call the authorities and the doctor if he's still alive in the morning."

"Yes, my lady!"

"I will take the girl, if you two youngsters will take our thief," Mr. Brown offered as he observed Bo's girth.

The men obliged him, and Edmund looked away, whispering his mantras as they carried Bo away, while Mr. Brown dragged Betty along behind them.

"Edmund, darling, why don't we leave Mr. Valov to sleep off his ailment, and we can take the room next door. The entire wing is ours anyway. I trust, Mr. Waverly, that you can find your way back to your room?"

"You don't think the tiger will come back?" he asked again.

"Are you on the ground floor?" Eleanor asked.

"No, my lady. I'm on the second floor."

"Well, I didn't see the tiger fly, so I think you will be safe either way." She winked, hoping that her humor would calm his nerves.

Mr. Waverly finally relaxed. "Yes, my lady, you're right."

He stood up and self-consciously waddled in his soiled pajamas past Edmund and into the dark hallway.

Eleanor gestured for Edmund to join her as she sat down beside Mr. Valov on the bed. She felt his pulse, listened to his breathing, and nudged him a few times to examine his reaction to the stimulus. As he sighed and rolled over, she relaxed.

"He should be fine. He needs to metabolize the drugs. He isn't in a state to drink water, so we will just have to wait it out."

"Every time I relax for one bloody moment something dreadful happens," Edmund grumbled.

Eleanor stroked his cheek and pulled him into a gentle kiss. "And yet, here we are, safe and sound again, darling. Now, shall we get some rest? I'd like to be out of here in the morning. Do we have somewhere nice to go? I suppose we must be ruining Sri Bidkar's plans."

"The Taj Mahal is the main attraction in Agra." Edmund allowed her to pull him into a mundane conversation. "I hadn't decided where to go next. Originally I'd thought of heading to Dharamsala in the Himalayas, or perhaps Shimla. We could head down to the Golden Temple of Amritsar from there, but that is the opposite direction from Hyderabad, and I do feel rather inclined to return to Hyderabad with you in my arms as soon as possible. I also received an invitation from Mr. Rana to visit him in Baroda, but that is probably not the most interesting place we could go."

"Mr. Rana? From Basingstoke?" Eleanor asked curiously.

"One and the same. He has already returned to India to set up the Baron's charity. He chose Baroda because the maharaja there was very supportive of the idea. He even gave Mr. Rana a house."

"Is Baroda grand or ordinary?" Eleanor asked.

"I've only been there once. I think if we aren't staying in the maharaja's palace, it's rather ordinary. Perhaps we should go to the Golden Temple instead…"

Eleanor kissed him again. "Ordinary sounds perfectly wonderful, darling. I don't think I've seen ordinary India yet. It's been pomp and circumstance since we arrived."

"I love you, Eleanor." Edmund pulled her tighter into his arms, but as a gentle warm breeze fluttered the curtains, his eyes turned black and he pulled away.

"I need to get away from all this blood," he whispered. "Some part of me still wants to hunt that man down and kill him."

Eleanor took his hand, and as she guided him towards the french doors to the garden, she reached down and collected his turban. Without a word, she guided him onto the lawn and then straight into the empty neighboring room. While he watched her, she closed and locked the doors, and then she placed the turban on the bedside table, lay down on the bed, and opened her robe.

"Problem solved," she said as she ran her finger across her bare stomach and then her breasts.

Edmund dropped his robe onto the floor and climbed onto the bed to straddle her. She wrapped her legs around him and pulled him inside of her. She was determined to replace every horrific memory of Bo leaning over her with the reality of her husband.

"This is better than killing a man, isn't it, darling?" she asked innocently.

"You were so wonderfully brave, Eleanor. Braver than I've ever seen anyone be. There was a bloody *tiger* in our room!"

"And now, darling, there is a tiger in your bed!"

She growled and pulled him deeper into her.

"A tigress!" he declared.

She nibbled his ear, and then growled again as he thrust his pent-up energy right into her loins.

And so together, the two honeymooners set about replacing their many unpleasant feelings with the pleasure of each other's company.

CHAPTER 21 – THE DEVIL HIMSELF

The warm sunlight tickled Eleanor's face as she awakened in the strange bed. She leaned over and kissed her gentle sleeping demon, and then she took a deep breath and sat up. There was no time to dawdle. A mess had been made, and Mr. Valov was not awake to clean it up. She knew better than anyone that they needed to be out of there before anyone started asking too many questions.

She yawned. She walked over to the washbasin that was identical to the one in the room they'd been given. She splashed water on her face and then slipped into the WC. She sat staring at the carved mahogany walls, wondering whether Bo had died in the night. She hoped he had. She hoped Betty had watched. She hoped both of them had known in those moments how wrong they'd been. God didn't care one lick about them. In fact, God was glad they were suffering. Was He, really, though? Or was She? Surely Eleanor's vengeful human emotions had nothing at all to do with what any god really felt. She listened a bit for Uma, who remained silent on the topic.

A pang of sympathy for Betty resonated from somewhere deep inside of her. The poor girl was so stupid, so poorly educated, so entrenched in a culture that Eleanor knew only too well, a culture that lauded the submissive, uneducated wife, that she could hardly blame the girl for following the idiotic leadership of her villainous husband.

But that man… that man *deserved* to suffer. That man was going to rape her, and Betty was going to help him do it. Her sympathy for the girl immediately dissolved. Betty wasn't even surprised; she'd helped him do the same thing before. Eleanor hoped that the wanton bastard had prayed fearfully all night as he felt his life-force dissolving. As he'd awaited his reckoning…

She heard Edmund stir and finished up her mundane business.

"Darling, we should check on Mr. Valov." She washed her hands in the basin and gathered up his robe from the floor. "I hope he can get us tickets on the first train to Baroda… and that he's feeling better, of course."

She wrapped herself up in the red silk robe and didn't even wait for Edmund to acknowledge her. She unlocked one of the french doors and walked straight back to the mayhem of their room.

Mr. Valov was lying in the bed with his eyes half-open, blinking confusedly. She sat down beside him and smiled. His pupils were wildly dilated.

"Are you alright, Leo?"

"My limbs are too heavy," he whispered. "What happened?"

"Those lovely Texans drugged you. They tried to steal my jewelry and Edmund's turban, but we managed to stop them."

"Is anyone dead?" he asked as he struggled to sit up.

Eleanor guided him back into a resting position. "Lie still. You aren't fully recovered yet. I'll get you some water. It should help you get the drugs out of your system."

She collected a carafe of water from the bar and brought it to him, realizing only when she reached him that he would not be able to drink an entire carafe of water. She smiled as she realized that she'd already become accustomed to her husband's unusual habits.

She helped him sit up and take a small sip, but he choked before he managed to swallow.

"You didn't answer my question, Eleanor."

"I don't know yet. Edmund didn't kill anyone, but my divine tiger might have imparted a fatal wound. I will have to ask around to find out if our rapist thief died in the night."

Mr. Valov looked pained. "He didn't rape you, did he?"

"Do you think I would let any man get away with that?"

He sighed with relief and then changed the subject. "Divine tiger?"

"Yes. Don't tell Edmund that she's mine. The men who came to help us think she was a wild man-eater who just happened to intervene in our spat."

Edmund came in from the lawn, clad only in his robe, and took a seat beside them.

"You look like hell, Leo," he said as he took Mr. Valov's hand. "It appears that being in our service was dreadfully dangerous... again. I'm sorry, old chap."

"I'm sorry that I failed you, Colonel."

"What I don't understand is how they managed to drug everyone but the other guests," Eleanor said as she fed him another sip of water.

"Mr. Dixon brought me dinner from the staff's kitchen," Mr. Valov whispered. "Perhaps they poisoned only the food for the staff. Was Dixon knocked out too?"

"He was," Eleanor replied.

"I thought the shepherd's pie tasted rather awful, but I assumed that they didn't know how to prepare it."

"Well, Mr. Ralston certainly faced his punishment," Eleanor reassured him. "Now we need you to recover. We're planning on going to Baroda next, to visit a friend from Basingstoke."

"Now that's something I might finally understand," Mr. Valov said as he regained a hint of strength.

"He's Indian," Eleanor explained. "He was the butler of the Baron of Heathfield."

"I see. Then I will continue to navigate blindly," Mr. Valov sighed.

The crunching of glass underfoot brought Eleanor's attention to the broken french doors.

"My lord, my lady..." Dixon looked almost as bad as Mr. Valov, but he leaned on the door to hold his balance. As he noticed their scantily clad state, he averted his eyes. "My deepest apologies. I don't know what went wrong. Something went dreadfully, dreadfully wrong. And the other guests tell me that there was a tiger in here? Are you certain? There haven't been tigers in Agra in decades."

"Please don't apologize." Eleanor took his arm and escorted him limping to the chaise. She gestured to Edmund to join her with the carafe, and then she helped Dixon take a long sip. "Mr. Dixon, you've been drugged."

"Drugged?" he asked with a combination of relief and concern. "Why would somebody drug a concierge?"

"The staff was drugged by those swindling Texans..." Eleanor looked for a spark of acknowledgement from him, but saw none. She found his complete lack of knowledge about the midnight commotion to be especially unsettling. She wondered if he'd come straight to their room after awakening in his chair by the front door. "Speaking of which, have you heard anything about the Ralstons? Did anyone ask you to call a doctor?"

Dixon looked like he might collapse at the effort of answering her. "I thought that perhaps a rumor had taken hold of the other guests. Are you telling me, Lady Marriner, that there was, in fact, a tiger in your room last night?"

Eleanor reluctantly responded. She did not want a bunch of burly men gunning down every tiger in the province on her behalf. "There was, but she was not a threat to me. She intervened when Mr. Ralston attempted to attack me."

Dixon looked especially pained as he tried to stand up. Edmund reached forward to help him.

"Lady Marriner, I must ask you to come with me. Colonel, you'd better come too. Mrs. Ralston is in a ghastly state, and no one has been able to console her."

"Did someone let her out of her room?" Eleanor asked.

"She will not come. She has insisted that she must speak to you," Dixon explained. "She has been... er... inconsolable."

"Did her husband die in the night?" Eleanor asked. "We would have called a doctor or taken him to a hospital, but they'd drugged the entire staff. No one knew who to call."

"You know far more about the situation than I do, Lady Marriner. I must entreat you to help us."

"So Bo isn't dead?" Eleanor pushed. "If he's still alive, we must call the doctor at once. The tiger's wounds were quite dire."

"Please, my lady, if you could be so kind, you must speak to Mrs. Ralston on our behalf. We have not been able to make heads or tails of her mad rantings."

Eleanor did not like the twist at all. Where in the bloody hell was Bo in all this? She racked her brain for whether Betty had seen Edmund do anything unusual. Eleanor was quite sure that she hadn't. Surely her green godly eyes wouldn't have sent the girl into a fanatical state—the girl had hardly even noticed them during their confrontation.

Mr. Valov struggled to swing his legs over the side of the bed. "Please go, Eleanor. Find out what's going on. I will join you both as soon as I can."

"Well, we certainly can't go out like this." Eleanor looked down at her thin silk robe, and Dixon looked away.

"You're right, my lady. I will wait outside for you both to be ready."

Dixon limped into the hallway, and Eleanor heard him lean heavily up against the wall.

"I'd help, but I can still hardly move," Mr. Valov said as he lay back down. "My head is swimming."

"I will change in the WC," Eleanor said as she walked straight over to their trunks and began digging through hers. She gathered up another pant-suit that she had particularly liked during her session with Kuveni (including one of several modern bras Kuveni had made for her—an undergarment she'd never had to wear before) and scampered into the WC without even glancing at Mr. Valov.

She pulled on the high-waisted, flowing black linen pants and then the modern bra, sighing with resignation as her breasts came together into a hefty curve of cleavage that she still couldn't believe was hers. She pulled on a loose periwinkle silk blouse with black paisley embroidery on its elbow-length bell-shaped sleeves that still, despite its seemingly modest cut, gave away her sumptuous figure, and finished off her outfit with some modest black heels.

She ran her fingers through her hair, calming her wild frizz as Uma had helped her do the night before, and then she pulled it into a loose ponytail, tying it into place with a strand of her own hair—a technique she'd learned in the spartan boarding house of the VAD during the war.

When she emerged, Edmund was already dressed in a distinctly British khaki suit.

"Shall we face the firing squad, dearest?" he asked as he offered her his arm.

"You should drink more water, Leo" Eleanor said sharply to Mr. Valov, who was lying back on the bed, holding his head in his hands. "We're going to need you in tip top shape."

"If my eyes don't pop out of my head first," he whined. The fact that he had enough energy to whine made her hopeful about his imminent recovery.

She let Edmund escort her through the broken door, into the dark hallway where Dixon was waiting for them, and then into the lobby, where a number of guests, including all of their helpers from the night before, were waiting.

"It *was* a flying tiger!" Mr. Waverly exclaimed.

"Let us know when it's time to leave for the hunt, Colonel!" Mr. Brown called with too much enthusiasm.

"Colonel, Lady Marriner, please come with me," Dixon said as he attempted to act normal.

They followed Dixon into another dark hallway and up a dark staircase to the second floor, past several young servants who were cleaning out the rooms. Eleanor paused for a moment as a young girl scrubbing the floor caught her eye. The girl looked strikingly familiar, but she could not for her life place from where. The girl continued on with her duties without looking up, and Eleanor refocused on the more immediate problem.

When they reached the open door of a darker, dumpier room, two guards were standing on each side of the door. Inside, Betty's familiar voice was chattering to herself interspersed with explosions of sobs, as if she were having a full-blown row entirely in her head.

As soon as she saw Eleanor, she ran towards her and rung her by the shoulders.

"Your Majesty!!!" she screamed. "Please, Your Majesty, tell me what I have to do to bring him back! I will do anything, *anything* you ask. Please!!!"

Betty's eyes were red and swollen from many hours of crying, and she had bleeding scratches all over her arms. There were no other signs of struggle in the room, except that the sheets were stained with dried blood from Bo's injuries.

"Darling, why don't you wait outside," Eleanor suggested firmly as she felt Edmund cringe.

Without protest, Edmund left her alone and began pacing in the hallway, whispering his mantras.

"Tell me what happened, Betty. Where's Bo?" Eleanor asked calmly.

"The Devil took him!" Betty wailed. "The Devil himself! He came in the night and took Bo right out the window!"

Dixon threw Eleanor a knowing glance.

Eleanor guided Betty to a dusty rocking chair and sat her down. Eleanor kneeled before her, taking her hand.

"Do you mean that Bo died, Betty? He died in the night?"

"No! The Devil took him! He said that you would tell me what I had to do to repent! Please, Your Majesty, tell me what to do to get my Bo back!!!"

"You're saying that the Devil came into your room last night, literally?"

"He had horns and everythin'!" Betty exclaimed. "His skin was red, his eyes were a-glowin' yellow, and he had giant horns! Just like the preacher said he would!"

"Good lord," Eleanor muttered.

She had no idea what to make of the claim. Was the girl certifiably mad? But then, where had Bo's body gone? Surely Betty would have gone with him if he'd tried to escape...

Eleanor's mind raced through the possibilities... Was it possible that Edmund's father looked like Satan himself? Or perhaps a shapeshifter, *any* shapeshifter, any Yaksha or Rakshasa with a morbid sense of humor, was playing a wickedly mean game with the girl.

"Please, Betty, describe to me everything that happened last night," Eleanor said as she stroked her hand.

She now felt a great deal of pity for the girl, and she realized that no matter what her vengeful fancies were, she hadn't really wished true suffering on her… Bo, on the other hand, could burn in Hell… She hated that their suffering was linked. The poor girl's fate was tied inextricably to her brutish mate.

"Well, those mean men locked us in our room until mornin', and Bo was in a terrible state. He was a-whinin' and a-snivelin'— not like a real man at all! But then, the Devil just appeared in the room. Right there by the bed, clear as day, just like Mr. Dixon is standin' there. And he said that Bo had been a very bad boy, and that really God should punish us both, but because he was feelin' generous, he was only gonna take Bo! I begged him not to, I begged him, Your Majesty! Then he laughed and said that because he was so nice, he was gonna let Bo have one last chance, if I'd make a deal with the Devil! He said that you would tell me what I oughta do to make up for all of Bo's sins, and then he picked him up and took him out the window!"

Uma squeezed Betty's hand, and reached Eleanor's other hand forward to cup her cheek, just like a doting mother.

My child, you have been led astray. You have sinned too many times, and there is nothing left to undo what your foolish actions have wrought. Your Bo is dead. You must mourn him and go home. You must do whatever you can to make meaning of your life through helping others. Find a virtuous man who will not lead you into darkness like Bo did. Find a preacher who truly knows the Lord's will—who preaches about loving thy neighbor, not burning in Hell. And for God's sake, girl, learn how to read for yourself.

Eleanor couldn't tell whether the last sentence was hers or Uma's, but she generally approved of the message, except for the bit about finding a man to lead her…

This poor lemming cannot stand alone, Eleanor. You must learn to see what each person needs. It is not always what you need.

"Bo is dead," Eleanor reiterated. "You've gone mad, Betty. You must get help, and then you must go home. Mr. Dixon will help you make your immediate arrangements."

Betty only stared at her with wild eyes.

Eleanor stood up and sighed. She guided Dixon out into the hallway. "She must leave here immediately. Is there a nice place where she might convalesce for a while? Perhaps a mission where the nuns can care for her until she's ready to return home?"

Despite her general distaste for the pedantry of the church, she figured that nuns would be quite adept at calming people who believed they'd actually seen the Devil...

"There is an old Portuguese palace in the west by the sea where some British people have gone in times of... er... trouble," Dixon whispered. "It is managed by Konkani and Irish nuns. But, my lady, it is dreadfully expensive."

Eleanor glanced at Edmund who nodded his agreement, joining their conversation with his demonic urges under control. "We will pay for her. Just send us the bill. Mr. Valov will settle everything for us, if you can help him make the arrangements."

"Yes, Colonel... but, what happened to Mr. Ralston?"

"Tigers often return for their wounded pray. Perhaps the girl saw her husband taken, and the memory has made her go mad."

Eleanor couldn't tell if he'd just come up with a perfect lie, or if he actually believed the story to be plausible.

"Good lord," Dixon murmured. "From the second floor?"

"It is a very clever tiger," Edmund replied. "And its senses are surely impeccable. Tigers can smell fresh blood from miles away. I encountered quite a few feisty ones during my days as a commander in the British Indian Army."

"Should we organize a hunt, Colonel? There hasn't been a tiger here in decades. Do you think there's a chance Mr. Ralston is still alive?"

"No," Edmund said with complete certainty. "He died in this room, perhaps five or six hours ago." Betty squealed as she eavesdropped. "There are more important things for you to do than a hunt, Dixon. Securing the perimeter of the hotel with more guards will be a better use of men than hunting down a creature this clever. If she returns, perhaps you can reconsider, but I don't expect her to."

"If that's what you think is best, Colonel," Dixon agreed.

"I do. Now, Dixon, if you can work with Mr. Valov to make arrangements for Mrs. Ralston, we would also be grateful if you could arrange passage for us and Mr. Valov on the afternoon train to Baroda. I assume we will need to change trains in Jaipur."

"Yes, Colonel, I will see to it."

Eleanor glanced into the room one last time, and Betty looked up at her desperately.

"Bo is really dead?" she asked meekly.

"He is, Betty. And we will get you some help," Eleanor replied.

"Then I don't have to make a deal with the Devil?"

Eleanor's pity for her only grew. "No, my child, you do not."

Betty rushed towards Eleanor and flung her arms around her.

"Thank you, Your Majesty! I'll be good from now on. I promise! I'll do just what you said. I'll find a good man and a good preacher and I'll learn how to read!"

Eleanor hugged the girl awkwardly, hoping that neither of the men noticed that her advice had not been vocalized out loud.

Go find peace, my child.

"That sounds like a fine idea, Betty." Eleanor tore herself out of Betty's arms and steadied her. "Darling, let's go check on Mr. Valov."

She took Edmund's hand and led him down the stairs, leaving Dixon behind to deal with Betty.

"The room smelled like death, didn't it?" Eleanor whispered.

"Ghoulishly," Edmund whispered. "A violent, fearful death… but I don't think it was that tigress. She was far too civilized for such a beastly maneuver."

"You seem quite taken with her," Eleanor couldn't help but point out. "She responded well to you, in fact."

"I have often found that animals and I get along quite well, except for monkeys, of course. I have often wondered if the wild beasts and I share some unusual commonalities due to my unique condition. Sometimes I have felt as if I'm more connected to them than I am to humans... that is, until I met you, dearest. And Edward Rutherford. And Leo."

"You did have a way with the dogs... and the horses... and the tiger..." Eleanor thought through her memories in light of his astute observation. One of the things she'd fallen in love with first, ages ago at the Baron of Heathfield's estate, was Edmund's unusual synergy with the horses. Suddenly, Eleanor could not hold back a fanciful question. "Darling, what do you think about having a pet tiger?"

Edmund chuckled. "It is a great folly to try to tame a wild beast, Eleanor. It is not its nature to be a pet, and when you try to change a creature's nature, it is bound to be dangerous. And tigers, dearest, are really quite dangerous. She did attack Mr. Ralston, even if she did not come back for her meal."

"What do you think it was, darling?" Eleanor asked with genuine curiosity. "What do you think killed Bo?"

He paused as he thought carefully about his answer. "I think that girl encountered a foe she thought was the Devil himself... I don't know how to explain it... but there is something familiar about the whole thing... something I don't like one bit... Dearest, I was in your arms all night, wasn't I?"

"Yes, darling. You should not think twice about it. You would never do anything like this. Not in a million years."

"I really wanted to kill that man last night."

"You did not kill him, darling. Not sleepwalking or wandering in madness, or anything of the sort. I promise." Eleanor pulled him into a gentle kiss, and then looked him straight in the eye. "I promise, Edmund. You didn't do this."

"Then we should get out of here," he whispered. "Before the Devil comes for us."

"Amen."

PART FOUR
FATEFUL

CHAPTER 22 – BARODA

"Guess what, darling? Mr. Valov is on his way on the evening train!" Edmund skipped out into their quaint, verdant garden with two pitchers of lemonade on a wooden tray, and placed it on a small table next to Eleanor's lounge chair.

"That's wonderful, darling! I'm so glad he's finally recovered."

Eleanor didn't want to think about how bad the fall-out had been from Sheranee's rescue that it had taken Mr. Valov nine days to sort it out and catch up with them.

After settling their plans for Betty with Mr. Valov, they'd packed two smaller suitcases provided for them by Mr. Dixon, and then at Mr. Valov's insistence, they'd taken the first train from Agra towards Baroda without him.

They stopped in Jaipur to change trains, but the opulent desert outpost, with its ornate pink buildings and glassy lakes set against rugged brushy hillside, was so foreign and fascinating to Eleanor's Scottish sensibilities that despite all of their nagging troubles,

Eleanor suggested that they stay the night, which turned into three, as they toured the winding streets of the ancient city and explored some of Edmund's favorite examples of architectural artistry in India.

In a moment of self-sufficiency that made Eleanor more proud than she thought it should have, they'd managed to procure their own accommodations at an old palace hotel where Edmund had stayed during a prior visit several decades earlier. With Edmund's linguistic savvy, and without the influence of Ravi Bidkar, or their enormous trunks, or their butler, they had managed to fit in as colonial visitors, those unusual *firangs* who'd spent so many decades in India that they spoke the local tongues, ate the local food, and knew how things were supposed to work.

Eleanor's fading henna served as a useful demonstration of their integration with the locals, although rather than wearing the royal Indian clothing provided by Babri and Kuveni, they decided to stick to some of the more practical western clothes that they'd packed, as the locals in Jaipur wore such distinct clothing that the Indian styles they had were almost as foreign as the European ones.

Their time in Jaipur was perfect. It was all that Eleanor had hoped India would be, and she had to admit it was more like the honeymoon she'd envisioned, instead of the aristocratic farce they'd endured under the influence of Ravi's desire for the world to treat Edmund like a god.

With every day of normalcy, Edmund seemed to become more and more like the man he had been before the war, and the trouble that had been stalking them seemed to finally be at bay. With it, Uma's interjections had dissipated, Sheranee had remained in the clouds dutifully awaiting her next command (that is at least how Eleanor imagined her 'divine perch' without any more color from Uma on the actual meaning of the statement), and Eleanor could finally feel like she was alone with her husband on their honeymoon, being together as a normal married couple. It was wonderful. She wanted it. Always.

408

They'd then made their way to Baroda, which was a wonderfully ordinary place. Centered around the landmarks of the maharaja's palace and a small man-made lake flanked by a towering statue of Shiva, the rest of the city was mostly cute little pastel-colored houses with hanging gardens and trickling fountains, interspersed with miniature bazaars featuring just enough exotic goods for sale and sari-clad bartering housewives to remind her that she was on the other side of the world.

Despite being rather surprised that Edmund had accepted his invitation to visit, upon hearing their desire for a break from the adventure of their honeymoon, Mr. Rana had asked around and procured them a short-term rental of one of the cute little houses, containing the most spartan furniture Eleanor had seen since arriving in India, a small kitchen with only a wood stove and a two-person dining table, a WC with only a squat toilet, and a bathroom with only an old-fashioned pump in the sink with a sponge for bathing.

The house had its own little hanging garden with a trickling fountain right in the middle and tropical vines climbing down an imposing white-washed wall that provided excellent privacy from the neighbors. Half of the garden was shaded at all hours by the branches of a huge banyan tree growing in the neighbor's garden; and, built into the wall, barely visible through the rich foliage, was an altar to Shiva with a rusting metal Nataraja icon. Eleanor found its transitional state, slowly dissolving in the elements, to be perfectly fitting for a tribute to transformation. Every so often, while Edmund was occupied in the house, she'd pay it a visit and let Uma contemplate wistful thoughts that she didn't choose to share.

Outside the freshly painted red front door, a pair of white horses were tied up at a small trough, waiting patiently to fulfill their duties as ordinary transport. Everything about it, every imperfection and slight inconvenience was perfect. Eleanor finally felt like she was human again.

And so, as Eleanor's relaxed, cheerful husband joined her with two pitchers of lemonade, the news of Mr. Valov's imminent return made her feel rather ambivalent. Sure, she'd grown fond of her unexpected ally, but she was not ready to give up her guilt-free bliss. She hadn't had to lie openly to her husband in over a week.

Edmund poured her a glass of lemonade and sat down on a lounge chair several feet away from her in the shade of the banyan tree.

"Are you sure you don't want to join me in the shade, dearest? I don't want you to get burned. It's positively sizzling out here."

Eleanor took in a deep breath of the hot air. Uma's taste had certainly overwritten hers on the matter of comfortable temperatures. She couldn't get enough of the heat now.

"I'm finding it perfectly enjoyable, darling. I don't seem to be burning, do I? I think I look just as pale as always." She held out her arms and pulled down her sunglasses to inspect them. Then she looked down at her breasts, which she was only covering with a black silk scarf tied into a scandalous makeshift top, followed by her bare stomach and her legs, which were soaking in the sun thanks to a pair of outrageously short linen shorts that Kuveni must have secretly added to her collection.

Edmund drank down his entire glass of lemonade and refilled it with a second round.

"You surprise me every day, Eleanor. It's hard to believe that you had such a strong reaction in Bombay, and now you have more stamina for the heat than I do!"

"I suppose we all adapt and change, don't we, darling?" Eleanor hoped that he wouldn't keep pushing on the subject.

"Speaking of which, I have a proposition for you."

Eleanor sat up. His tricky tone had her interest piqued. "And what proposition would that be, darling?" She hoped it wouldn't involve the word *children*.

"What do you say we try to cook Mr. Valov a welcome dinner?"

Eleanor fully relaxed. "I warned you that I'm not a very good cook, darling. Are you a good cook?"

"Wretched. Every attempt I have ever made has been an utter failure. That's why the proposition is so adventurous. So, shall we try it? Perhaps with several buckets of water to keep us from burning the house down?"

Eleanor laughed. "Have you ever burned a house down cooking?"

"Never to the ground…"

Eleanor laughed again. "Darling, you've convinced me. Dinner for Mr. Valov it is. I suppose we should go to the bazaar then? What shall we fry up? I wonder what kind of oil they use for the pakoras, that might be acceptable for a fried pie and some chips. Do they have potatoes here?"

"Dearest, on an old-fashioned stove like this, we probably shouldn't bathe anything in oil. It's bound to catch the house on fire. Believe me, I've almost done it."

"But, darling, I only know how to fry things. I told you I was a bad cook, and I wasn't lying."

"Perhaps we can figure it out together. We could ask some of the ladies at the market what they recommend."

"Ha! Darling, I don't think that I can begin to master Indian cuisine."

"Then a chicken, maybe? I'm sure we could get one in the bazaar by the mosque. We could get a pot and some vegetables and perhaps some powdered spices, then just boil them all together. That doesn't seem like it should be too hard, don't you think?"

"Mr. Valov will not be very happy with the spices," Eleanor pointed out.

"Then salt and pepper, I suppose. Do you think boiled chicken is good?"

"I don't know, darling. I've only ever fried it."

"Curried chicken is boiled, isn't it?" Edmund thought out loud. "It must be… sitting in those wet sauces for hours and hours, but I suppose those sauces aren't water. Do you think boiling it in water will be bad? Or perhaps we should boil it in cream? But surely that would take too much cream… I can't fathom how they make the sauces so rich…"

"Well, Mr. Valov will have something presented to him for dinner. Whether or not it's edible is yet to be seen. Perhaps we should serve it on a silver platter, so he will think that whatever we did was entirely intentional." Eleanor loved the mundanity of the entire proposition.

Edmund looked up at the sun that was blazing down on them from high in the sky. "I reckon we should go to the market soon. We want to have some choice about the quality of the items we're buying. The later in the afternoon we go, the worse the options will be."

Eleanor stood up and enticed him into a kiss, and he pulled her into his arms and squeezed her bum naughtily up under her shorts.

"Give me two minutes, darling!"

She rushed inside and gathered up a pair of white linen trousers and a flowing pink silk blouse from the floor, sniffed them to make sure they weren't embarrassingly sweaty, and then finished off her quick change with a wide-brimmed straw sunhat that she'd bought in the hotel's shop in Jaipur.

When she was finished, she popped outside, and Edmund had already untied the horses. He lifted her up effortlessly onto the mare, and then swung his leg over and hopped right onto the stallion. She brought her mare to a quick trot, hoping secretly to engage Edmund in a little race, but he did not take her bait, and she sighed with minor disappointment as she slowed down to pace him.

"The best meat is usually in the Muslim part of town. Shall we explore there?" Edmund suggested.

Eleanor looked down self-consciously at her thin blouse clinging to her curves. "Do you think I'm dressed alright? If I'd thought about it, I would have at least brought a dupatta."

"I'm sure you'll be fine, dearest. You look perfectly modest to me, and I'll be with you the whole time."

"If you think it will be fine, I'm happy to explore another neighborhood, darling."

They rode through the leafy residential streets of Baroda, past the imposing gates of the maharaja's palace, until they reached an area with even smaller winding streets, and a profusion of women in dark niqabs with only their eyes showing. Eleanor felt slightly alarmed, thinking back on the attack at their wedding by Edmund's evil aunt who had used the disguise to hide her disfigured face, but with women all around them wearing the same outfit, she forced herself to ignore the feeling.

"Ah, it reminds me of Hyderabad," Edmund sighed nostalgically.

He hopped off his horse as they reached the entrance to a particularly narrow street, and then he helped Eleanor off of hers. He tied them up at a trough, handed a few coins to a teenaged boy who was tasked with managing the communal resource, and then joked with him amicably in Gujarati, to the boy's great amusement.

"I reckon the meat market is just down this road. The scent of death is on the breeze."

"Huh… going to the butcher must be quite unpleasant for you, darling, mustn't it?"

"It didn't used to bother me. I developed the sensitivity during the war." Edmund took her hand and led her into the narrow alleyway. "But I'm feeling much better now, Eleanor. I haven't felt so normal since the war began."

"I'm very glad to hear it, darling," Eleanor said as she squeezed his hand.

They rushed past each spice stall displaying massive drums of powdered turmeric, then Edmund ducked as they passed several shops with low-hanging items for sale. They stopped a few times to peruse various metal pots, until agreeing that they'd better know the size of chicken they were procuring before they settled on the rest of their plan. All the while, the curious locals watched them, and Edmund engaged various shopkeepers in jovial Gujarati conversation.

When they finally reached the block of the meat market, Eleanor and Edmund both cringed at the smell. Blood and rotting meat juices filled the air, bombarding their senses, although she was quite certain that Edmund was having a harder time of it than she was.

Skinned fresh mutton hung from one stall, while live chickens clucked from cages in several different corners.

"Ba-kaaah!"

The sound of a cleaver swiftly ended a chicken's final words, and Eleanor looked over to see who had just collected their dinner. She was shocked to spot a very fair-skinned blonde woman with grey eyes and rosy cheeks, dressed in a simple green cotton salwar kameez with her head covered loosely by a matching dupatta.

The woman thanked the proprietor in Gujarati as he handed her a sack with the fresh chicken in it, but as she turned around to make her way out, she stopped in her tracks as she noticed Edmund and Eleanor.

"Why, hello," she said with a perfect British accent. "I've never stumbled upon another *firang* in this neighborhood. Are you lost? Perhaps I can see you back to the mosque. Did you come to Baroda to see it? It does have some redeeming qualities, although the one in Ahmedabad is much more impressive. Oh, I'm terribly sorry…" She reached out her free hand, keeping the dead chicken in the other. "I'm Miss Mabel Smith. I'm the principal of the Maharani Girls' School over on the other side of town, but this is the best place in Baroda to get fresh meat, so, *voila*, here I am!"

Eleanor realized that she desperately wanted to be friends with this intriguing woman. She couldn't have been more than twenty-five, and yet her comfort at going about her business alone in this foreign place, even speaking the local language, made Eleanor suddenly feel like she had a lot to aspire to.

"Eleanor MacLeod Marriner." Eleanor reached out her hand and enthusiastically shook Miss Smith's. "Oh, and this is my husband, Colonel Edmund Marriner."

"Colonel?" Miss Smith exclaimed. "We don't tend to get a lot of elites in these parts, although, that's changing a bit as the maharaja continues his investments. He's starting to attract more of a British crowd with his unique programs for education and welfare for the poor."

"Perhaps we should connect him with Madho Rao... er... the Maharaja of Gwalior. I hear that he too is now looking to invest more in his people's welfare," Edmund said casually.

"Ha! That'll be the day," Miss Smith laughed.

Neither Edmund nor Eleanor understood what was so funny about the statement, and Miss Smith realized her faux pas. "I'm sorry, I forget how obscure the gossip of our little town is. You see, the Maharaja of Baroda's daughter was engaged to the Maharaja of Gwalior, and she broke off their engagement via a letter so that she could marry the Maharaja of Cooch Behar. It was quite the scandal... and so, I do not believe the Maharaja of Baroda is particularly keen on ever seeing the Maharaja of Gwalior again, perhaps more out of familial embarrassment than anything else."

"I have heard the story, actually," Edmund replied. "Although, it was from the Maharaja of Gwalior's point of view. He was quite happy with the end result, so I suspect the Maharaja of Baroda should not be so shy."

"Well, if it weren't so taboo to bring up the topic, I might suggest giving him the hint. He is a good-humored man, the Maharaja of Baroda. He is quite unique, in fact. I have never met a more kind-hearted aristocrat in my life... I'm sorry. I didn't mean to rattle on and on. It is rare that I have the chance to speak to other Brits these days. Are you here for good, or are you just passing through? I hope there aren't plans for expanded military presence in the province. It isn't remotely necessary."

Edmund smiled. "We're just passing through. We came to visit a friend, Mr. Rana, who has taken up residence here to create a charity that supports native Indians in British courts. It is sponsored by the estate of the Baron of Heathfield from Basingstoke, which is where we have our home in England."

"Mr. Rana is from England?" Miss Smith asked curiously. "I would have guessed the man was Indian based on his name."

"Indeed, he is," Edmund agreed. "You have been paying attention, Miss Smith. Mr. Rana was the butler to the Baron of Heathfield during his decades as a judge in India. He then accompanied the Baron when he retired back to England."

"Well, I hope to meet him soon," Miss Smith said cheerfully. "I'm sure we'll cross paths. Baroda is really a small town, especially amongst those with connections to the British Raj."

Edmund suddenly looked around, completely distracted from their conversation. He landed his attention down one of the bazaar's alleys, on a rather homely young Indian woman with beady dark eyes, an excessively large, angular nose, and quite a bit of excess weight all around, especially under her chin. Despite her physical features, she was dressed nicely in what Kuveni had described as an abaya-style anarkali suit—a floor-length gown with long sleeves and trousers, more Islamic in style than the other salwar kameez suits in Eleanor's collection—with a scarf wrapped loosely around her hair. The suit had some minor embellishments, but the rich green of her anarkali made her stand out quite conspicuously compared to the other local women in the neighborhood who were all wearing black niqabs.

She reached into a simple sack and handed a loaf of bread to an impoverished old man who was sitting on the ground, leaning himself awkwardly against a wall.

"Who is that?" Edmund asked with his eyes glued on her. "She's familiar to me somehow."

"That is Miss Radha Patel. Her family is the most influential in Baroda," Miss Smith explained. "They have quite a close relationship with the maharaja and his family. Miss Patel organizes various charitable activities, and she always gives alms on Friday afternoons."

Miss Patel knocked on a small door, and when an old woman answered, she smiled and went inside.

"But she's not Muslim with a name like Patel?" Edmund asked, continuing to watch the door.

"No, the Patels are certainly Hindu. Their estate lights up the entire city during Diwali, and Miss Patel coordinates a soup kitchen at the Shiva temple on the other side of town on Mondays. She does not limit her charity to Hindus, though, and she is rather beloved around town because of it."

"Yes, I can see why," Edmund murmured.

Eleanor found his distraction unsettling, and so she attempted to bring them back to their original plan. "Miss Smith…"

"Please call me Mae," Miss Smith insisted.

"Mae," Eleanor smiled, "can you offer us your advice on how to choose a chicken? And for that matter, how to prepare one?"

Mae laughed heartily. "The recipes here are rather complicated."

"I meant… any style. Other than frying. We've decided to cook dinner for our… er…" Eleanor decided in that moment not to use the word *butler*, "for our friend who is coming to visit, and with only a wood-burning stove, we were afraid of burning the house down with a vat of oil, which is the only way I know how to cook it."

"Well, I have always preferred roasted chicken, which isn't very easy to do here, because ovens aren't so common in houses. I procured a tagine in Morocco a few years back, and that is always what I use. It's quite a heavy ceramic pot that roasts the food slowly over coals or a wooden stove. Perfect for a whole chicken with some vegetables in a sauce of wine and spices… I suggest more of a chai-style masala to go with the wine—cinnamon, cardamom, cloves, and ginger—it will taste more Moroccan than Indian, but it will taste delicious all the same, especially if you include dates alongside your vegetables."

"Dates... Hrm. I don't think I even know what a date tastes like... this is going to be quite an experiment."

"Be sure to remove the pits," Mae warned. "In fact, check for pits in all of the exotic fruits and vegetables you find here. It's taken me years to figure them all out... unless you already know, Colonel?"

Edmund finally focused all of his attention back on their conversation. "Alas, I've always been a dreadful cook. I've never gone to the effort of figuring out how all of the fruits and vegetables work, in England or here. They just magically appear fully prepared on my plate. I think it will build some character for me to finally figure it out."

"Well, stay away from the bitter melons. They'll ruin anything," Mae warned.

"Bitter melon? That does sound rather unappetizing," Edmund replied.

"Is that er... tagine... available locally?" Eleanor asked hopefully.

"It isn't. Apparently, the brilliance of the Moroccan traders never made its way this far on the spice route. But you know, I think it's quite similar to a heavy casserole dish. They have almost the same function. If you look around the bazaar, I suspect you will find something similar. All you should need is a big, heavy pot with a solid lid. Do you need me to help you? Most people here don't speak English."

"And you speak Gujarati?" Eleanor asked.

"Hardly. I butcher the language with every ill-conjugated verb," Mae laughed. "But they are so pleased that I try that I can usually get what I want. So, shall I help you?"

"No, that is not necessary," Edmund replied... in Gujarati.

"Ha! I suppose not then. Colonel, you must know India quite well."

"I do," Edmund agreed.

"Actually, I'd better be going," Mae said apologetically. "In this heat, a dead bird in a bag isn't going to last very long."

Eleanor shook her hand again. "It was wonderful meeting you, Mae. I hope we see each other again!" Eleanor was surprised by how much she meant the statement.

"Cheerio!" Mae said cheerfully as she headed off into one of the alleyways and left them alone.

"Well, darling, I would say that so far our adventure is destined for success, don't you think?"

Eleanor did not like that Edmund was still eying the door where Miss Patel had gone inside.

"Darling, what was it about that girl that intrigued you so much?"

He finally snapped himself out of it. "I don't know. It's hard to explain. It just felt… as if I knew her somehow. But that isn't possible. She would have been a child when I left India, and I've only ever been to Baroda once. It's somewhat of an unsettling feeling, actually. Did she seem strange to you?"

"She was rather far away, darling. I could hardly make out her features. I don't think I could describe to you now what she even looked like."

"Yes… yes, I suppose you're right. It was silly of me to let myself be distracted while we chatted with that lovely woman. Miss Smith is a very rare gem, I'd say. I've always wished more Brits were like her."

"Well, perhaps we'll run into her again. Now, darling, I believe it's time for us to choose a victim." Eleanor glanced over to the many caged chickens, and several competing vendors noticed her attention and started shouting about their very good prices.

Edmund guided her to the stall where Miss Smith had bought hers. "It is always best to follow the locals. I'm sure she's tried each one of these, and this is her favorite," he whispered.

And so, with a few words in Gujarati and a few passed coins, Edmund and Eleanor procured the first step in their wonderfully mundane culinary adventure.

CHAPTER 23 – MR. VALOV'S RETURN

After many hours of heated bargaining and wandering around the bazaar looking for every item from Mae's suggested shopping list, Edmund and Eleanor headed home on their noble steeds, carrying a dead bird in a bag, another full bag of vegetables and spices (many of which they hardly recognized), and a cast iron pot so heavy that Eleanor couldn't even lift it.

When they arrived back at their little house, Edmund headed out into the garden with a plan to pluck the chicken, which lasted until he realized that he had absolutely no clue how to do it. Eleanor found his ignorance rather cute, and she showed him the technique she'd learned from her father back during the innocent days of her childhood when she thought that the world was fair.

When they were finished and there was a large pile of feathers in the corner of the garden, Edmund lit the stove, and they squabbled quite a bit as they dropped the chicken in the pot and covered it in chopped potatoes, onions, carrots, garlic, tomatoes, and several mysterious green vegetables, one of which had been rather unappetizingly referred to as a 'lady finger.'

Their squabble escalated as they contemplated what to do with the whole spices. Edmund argued that they must be ground quite finely, as no curry he'd ever eaten had been filled with chunks of whole spices. Eleanor didn't disagree with that particular point, but she argued that the spices must be cooked in their entirety in the pot, and then removed at the end, just like mulled wine.

Since it seemed like, indeed, they were making a version of mulled wine in which to cook the chicken, Edmund gave in, and they dropped all of their spices right into the pot along with some salt, and then poured an entire bottle of Chateau Margaux right on top (a travesty, they both agreed, but a necessary sacrifice for the cause of dinner).

Edmund closed the pot with a proud flourish. "I'd say we're ready for the Cordon Bleu, dearest! Perhaps we should open a restaurant."

"It does seem like an outrageous amount of food for three people," Eleanor said as she watched the pot begin to steam. "And we don't have an ice box."

"What do you say we…" Eleanor cringed as Edmund began his suggestion, hoping against hope that he wouldn't suggest that they invite the mysterious Miss Patel for dinner, and then she cringed again at her own foolish jealousy. She had always prided herself on not being the jealous type, on being so self-confident that the idea of her man being led astray was positively ludicrous, and by such a homely young woman! Eleanor chastised herself for thinking twice about it… "invite Mr. Rana over? I'd suggest we invite Miss Smith, but she already has her own chicken cooking."

"I think that sounds like a wonderful idea, darling. Do you want to telephone him? You should invite him to bring a guest… or two, or three. We're going to have plenty of food."

Eleanor grabbed one of their few remaining bottles of cognac that they'd packed from their hotel room in Agra and headed out into the garden while Edmund made his call. She couldn't resist saying hello to Shiva at his altar, and Uma subtly enticed her into spending an extra-long moment there in deep thought.

"Good news, dearest!" Edmund exclaimed as he came out into the garden to join her. He paused as he noticed her attention. "Mr. Rana is coming over for dinner. Now it will be four of us, and I do think that he and Mr. Valov will get on well, don't you?"

"Yes, darling. I think they will," Eleanor agreed as she ripped herself away.

"I have always found it rather funny that people here find every conceivable place to stash a religious icon," Edmund said as he looked at it. "They built this imposing wall, and planned from the get-go to have a little altar. It is so different from England... so wonderfully different."

"There are angels and such in English gardens," Eleanor pointed out.

"Yes... yes, I suppose you're right, dearest. Shall we sip some cognac while we wait for Mr. Rana? He said he could be here in an hour. He is just finishing up some business at the maharaja's palace. He's signing the lease for his new office! It's rather remarkable how quickly he's managed to get things together for this charity."

"It's nice that the Baron saw his potential. He'll have a second life of his own now that the Baron is dead." Eleanor glanced over at the icon of Shiva, and then refocused her attention on the cognac as she plopped down in one of the lounge chairs.

Edmund dragged his lounge chair over beside hers, as the entire garden was now shaded by the banyan tree, and a gentle warm breeze felt wonderful as they soaked in the late afternoon heat.

"How long do you think we should cook the chicken, dearest? Did Miss Smith tell you her advice?"

"Hrm... she didn't," Eleanor admitted. "You don't cook it very long when you're frying it, but I assume this must take a long time… don't you think? My mother would slave away in the kitchen for hours when she was making a whole bird. Although, I suppose she must have been roasting it in the oven. I don't even remember what she did, because I was always outside playing. She stopped cooking when my father died…" Eleanor trailed off as a moment of melancholy overtook her. "I remember vaguely moments when she was happy… moments before everything blew up. She was a completely different person. I suppose that must be true for everyone who is betrayed in the way that she was."

Eleanor hoped that her web of lies would never explode like her father's had, and suddenly the idea that she could lose Edmund in more than one way—not just through her mortality, but through more mundane methods—took its place in the subtle ball of anxiety that had become a permanent fixture of her life.

Edmund squeezed her hand. "I wish I could have met her before it all happened."

"So do I. I hardly remember her how she was," Eleanor murmured wistfully. "I suppose that means that in many ways, the woman she was died the same day as my father. She was replaced by the angry zealot that I grew up with. That is, at least, after I stopped her from killing herself…" Eleanor hadn't voiced the memory explicitly in her life.

"You never told me that," Edmund said as he moved his chair closer to hers.

"After the police came to our house with the news of my father's demise, I ran away to the barn to be with the horses. I found my mother tying up a noose."

"Good lord."

"It was bad enough for me to see it, but my sisters had followed me, and I had to protect them. Someone had to be the parent, and it wasn't my mother. I was so mad at her that I ripped that bloody rope from her hands, and then I slapped her. I chastised her so ferociously for taking the easy way out that she collapsed into the corner of the barn, up against the hay, and wailed for hours. We joined her, and it was really the last time that I spent time in my mother's arms. She was colder, more distant after that. It was like she'd flipped a switch in her brain to detach from her pain, and she detached from us then too. I was basically the mother to my sisters after that… although, Mary, mercifully, had learned how to cook before the tragedy. She taught Martha, and they made all the meals while I found work… that is, until I realized that I could make more money as a nurse than all four of us could make in any reputable work for uneducated women. That was when I ran away, and my Aunt Flora in Perth (the original Perth, in Scotland, of course) took me in. When she realized what a state we were in, she began sending money to my mother, and when I explained to her my logic—that I could support all of them with an educated career—she paid for my schooling until I became a nurse. Then I paid for all of them until my sisters married themselves off as young as they possibly could."

"You haven't spoken much about your aunt," Edmund pointed out as he handed her a glass of cognac. "Is she still alive?"

"No, she died just before the war. She wasn't a very loving woman… not in person, anyway. Her actions were quite kind, obviously, although she was my father's sister—I always thought that she helped us more out of guilt than out of love. She generally kept her distance, although she did ask about my progress and offer me various suggestions. She was a widow who had been a teacher before she got married, so she may have felt some connection to me in my desire for a career, I suppose just as I felt quite invested in encouraging Anya."

"It is interesting how much these interactions can mean to people. I've found that many of the young soldiers I encouraged were thinking about my advice years later. They've told me so often when I've stumbled across them at various points. I'm glad that Flora's legacy is in you now, dearest. I'm sure that Anya will think very seriously about everything you told her."

"She will be a maharani," Eleanor sighed. "Which is, I suppose, a far better fate than the choices I had ahead of me. I hope she can marry a man she loves, or at least whom she respects. I believe that her reticence is primarily based on a fear of being married off to an old man she finds repulsive. I hope that if she is faced with that possibility, she will come to me for help. Perhaps I'll be able to talk some sense into Rane, since it seems like maharajas are a dime a dozen here... there should be plenty of choices for Anya to choose from."

Edmund laughed. "I've always found the number of royal families in India to be surprising. Some are more influential than others. It is quite a coincidence that we seem to have paid a visit to the two principalities with the most famous feud in India."

"Tell me about the durbar, Edmund. Tell me about how you met Madho Rao. Was Lord Curzon really as horrible as he sounds?"

Edmund laughed. "Well, that is a long story."

"We have a chicken simmering all afternoon."

"Well, it all started when Lord Curzon decided that he and his wife must demonstrate the superiority of the British Raj with more pomp and circumstance than anything any of the maharajas had ever seen. If only the peacocks of India had anticipated his plan, they might have escaped with their feathers intact. As it was, there were so many peacock feathers adorning every blasted inch of Lord Curzon's entourage, that I don't think there was a peacock left in India who wasn't squawking about naked..."

Edmund set off on a lively story filled with amusing details, minor intrigue, and quite a bit of jabbing at Lord Curzon, and Eleanor sat back and relished just listening to his voice as the sky became hazy and then burst into the deep oranges of a summer sunset. She appreciated that she could sip the cognac in the heat without the typical consequences of an afternoon of tippling, although she did still wish that she could pick and choose when

426

the alcohol would affect her—she was still finding her new state of being to be a bit too consistently sober.

When the sun had just set, Mr. Rana knocked on their garden gate, and Edmund finished up his last anecdote and hopped up to greet him.

"Welcome to our humble abode, Mr. Rana!" he said cheerfully. "Come in!"

Mr. Rana presented him with a box of sweets that Eleanor had seen for sale at various market stalls. It was the first time Eleanor had seen him out of his butler's uniform, as earlier in the week Edmund had gone alone to pay him a 'hello' visit while she lounged about back at home. He still wore his long Sikh hair tied up in a poufy crimson turban, but along with it, he was now wearing a much more relaxed traditional kurta and pyjamas with a flowing crimson scarf draped loosely around his neck.

"Thank you for inviting me, Colonel. I have not met anyone in Baroda yet whom I know well enough to visit; although, I do believe that I am the one who invited you. I should be hosting you in my home."

He nodded his hello to Eleanor as he followed Edmund into the garden.

"Well, we've got all the time in the world," Edmund replied. "Would you like some cognac? I think we have a few sips left."

Edmund held up the bottle. There was only the tiniest dribble left at the bottom.

"Hrm." Edmund blushed slightly with embarrassment. "Well, we have another unopened one inside. Would you like some?"

"No, thank you, Colonel. I don't drink alcohol."

"Right… of course. Well, perhaps we should check on dinner. Our butler, Mr. Valov, is arriving on the evening train, so we were hoping to serve up dinner when he arrives."

"Very good, sir," Mr. Rana said politely.

He eyed the two-person table in the kitchen, and Eleanor suddenly realized that they had not at all planned for seating four people… or serving them… she wasn't even sure if they had enough plates. Then she realized that they had no appetizers to serve Mr. Rana, and no idea what time Mr. Valov would actually arrive… their first attempt at a dinner party was off to a brilliant start.

"Please sit, Mr. Rana!" Edmund escorted him to his vacant lounge chair in the garden, and Mr. Rana awkwardly sat down. "I will bring you some lemonade."

"Thank you, sir."

Eleanor followed Edmund into the kitchen. "How are we going to serve dinner to four people on this tiny little table!" she hissed.

"Do you… er… do you smell that, dearest? It's like burnt caramel."

Eleanor took in a deep whiff. She did smell it. She glanced around, landing her eyes on the pot over the roaring fire that was no longer steaming. Instead, little bits of smoke were escaping.

"The chicken!" she exclaimed.

Edmund ripped the lid right off the pot, dropping it on the floor with a deafening clank.

"Is everything alright in there?" Mr. Rana called through the open window from the garden.

"Yes, perfectly!" Eleanor lied.

Edmund turned his body so that Mr. Rana couldn't catch a glimpse as his Rakshasa plasma rushed to the surface to heal the sizzling burn that the lid had just imparted.

"We need a potholder!" Eleanor hissed.

"Not anymore, we don't," Edmund said dismally.

She looked into the pot, where a black, glistening blob was fused to the bottom.

"What happened?!" Eleanor exclaimed.

"Blimey, I have no bloody clue," Edmund said as his hand finished up healing.

428

"It must have cooked too long. But I thought Miss Smith said to cook it a long time…" She looked down at the vigorous flames. "Maybe the fire was too hot. I think it must have dried out and burned. All that Chateaux Margaux is wasted!"

"But a lot of things are slow cooked here. Practically everything!" Edmund argued. "How is everything not burned all the time?"

He reached into the pot and pulled out an unrecognizable blackened chunk. He sniffed it. "I believe this used to be ginger."

He held it up for Eleanor to sniff, and then, after a moment of intense disappointment, she burst into laughter.

Edmund was startled by her reaction, and then, with another moment of processing, he joined her.

"Cordon Bleu, indeed," she laughed as her eyes began watering. "Darling, I think our incompetence has compounded each other's. We've become an even worse chef than we were on our own."

"Speak for yourself, dearest. This house is still standing. I consider this a marked improvement for me."

Mr. Rana walked up to the window and spotted their guilty posture, but said nothing as he eyed the burned chunk of ginger in Edmund's hand. "A Miss Smith is at the gate, shall I let her in, Colonel?"

"How on earth did she find us?" Eleanor whispered. She could not have been more grateful. "Yes, let her in!"

She rushed outside as Mr. Rana opened the gate. Miss Smith paid her buggy driver, and Mr. Rana helped her maneuver a large basket containing a beautifully painted dish with an exotic conical top.

"Mae? How did you know?!" Eleanor exclaimed.

"Could you be so kind as to put that in the kitchen, sahib?" Mae asked Mr. Rana.

Mr. Rana took the basket inside, and Eleanor reached out her hand to shake Mae's. She held on for an extra-long moment to feel for any hint of Yakshini warmth, but there was none.

"Oh, I asked my housekeeper about this Mr. Rana bloke who's new in town, and about his *firang* visitors, and she asked her cousin who asked her cousin, and she knew the chap who rented you this house. I'm glad they were right. It's always about fifty-fifty odds."

"No, I meant… how did you know we'd already made an epic disaster out of our chicken?!" Eleanor exclaimed.

Mae laughed. "I had a nagging suspicion as I thought about the tone of your questions that I had created a bit of a monster. I'd given you enough rope to hang yourselves."

Eleanor let the imagery of the idiom wash over her. "Well, you were certainly right about that. Would you like to come in and see what we've done?"

"Shall I give you a post-mortem?"

"Yes! Yes, please!" Eleanor exclaimed.

She took Mae's hand and led her inside. Edmund had given up completely on their chicken, and was awkwardly squeezing some lemons into a pitcher for Mr. Rana's lemonade, while Mr. Rana watched him politely. Edmund hadn't actually cut the lemons, and so he was using his Rakshasa strength to smash them in the palms of his hands, in a gesture that looked mildly like something an abominable snowman might do.

"Oh dear… you cooked it on much too high of a temperature…" Mae inspected their glistening black blob. "And you didn't have enough liquid in the pot… You see, normally the steam doubles back in a tagine to continuously hydrate the contents, but you can see this pot here has two large steam releases. Your wine evaporated away when the steam was released, leaving it dry to burn. Is that ginger?"

"It was," Eleanor laughed.

"Why did you put it in whole like that?"

"Ah ha!" Edmund exclaimed triumphantly. "I knew we weren't supposed to put it in whole! We should have ground all the spices, I reckon?"

"Well, it really depends on the spice. For a dish like this, I don't typically grind the cinnamon because it can be scooped out later."

"Ah ha!" Eleanor countered.

"And as long as you take the cardamom seeds out of the pods, they will mix in nicely with the rest of the sauce."

Eleanor stuck her tongue out at Edmund playfully. "It would seem that neither of us considered that each spice should be treated differently."

Mae smiled. "A full root of ginger like that would have made it very spicy. I normally would have cut it into thin slices and used about a tenth of the amount that you used."

"I suppose then, dearest, we'll have to postpone our application to the Cordon Bleu until next year. Miss Smith, on the other hand, should seek a reference from us if she wishes to apply."

He lifted the cover of her tagine and took in a satisfied whiff. A beautiful golden chicken was surrounded by richly spiced, sweet-scented root vegetables in a stew of onions and caramelized fruit chunks. His stomach growled, and he quickly put the top back on.

"It smells absolutely scrumptious, but we had hoped to wait for our butler to arrive. Shall we keep it on the stove?"

"No!" Mae exclaimed, then she laughed. "Colonel, you'd have a second pot of ashes if you kept this tagine on a roaring stove like that. The heat should be very minimal. In Morocco they cook these on hot coals all day—no active flames at all. It is a very useful vessel that will keep its heat for quite some time. Perhaps we should leave it on the table for now. Where were you planning to eat?"

"We... er... hadn't planned that far in advance," Edmund admitted. "There isn't a table big enough for four... or five."

Mae laughed heartily again. "Well, all we need is a bit of *jugaad*... creative improvisation, for lack of a better translation...

Now let's see here…" She looked around the kitchen and then peeked into the small living room. "I propose that we eat Arabian style. We can all sit on the floor of the living room… I know it seems a bit strange, but millions of people do it every day."

"What a wonderful idea!" Edmund exclaimed. "Now, shall we open a bottle of wine while we wait?"

"I'd love some!" Mae exclaimed. "It's hard to get good wine around here. You didn't bring it from Europe, did you? Oh, what I wouldn't give for some drinkable French wine…"

Edmund grinned and disappeared into their bedroom to dig out one of the few remaining bottles of Chateaux Margaux. Mr. Rana added some water and sugar to Edmund's unfinished pitcher of lemon juice, and poured himself a glass.

"I'm sorry, Mr. Rana… as you can see, we're not used to hosting dinner parties… in fact, this is the first one we've ever hosted together," Eleanor said sheepishly.

"It is a rite of passage for a new married couple." He smiled forgivingly.

"Newly married?" Mae asked.

"We're actually on our honeymoon," Eleanor explained. "We've been married almost a month now, although it feels as if it's been a lifetime… in a good way, of course." She couldn't believe as she said it that their honeymoon had only been going for a few weeks. It really did feel like a lifetime.

"Your honeymoon! And you came to Baroda? I suppose at some point you will make your obligatory homage to the Taj Mahal."

"Already done," Eleanor replied. "It was one of the first things we did after we arrived in Bombay. It was adventurous enough that we decided to visit Mr. Rana in this lovely ordinary town instead of hopping straight over to another famous site."

"Oh yes, of course. Mr. Rana—the new stranger in town!"

"I am Rohan Rana," Mr. Rana said as he introduced himself to Miss Smith. Eleanor blushed with embarrassment that she hadn't even remembered to introduce them.

"Miss Mabel Smith," Mae replied with a polite *namaste*. "I am the principal of the Maharani Girls' School. It's the first English Medium school in the province."

"How impressive for one so young," Mr. Rana replied.

"I suppose. I'm already a spinster by local standards, so I'm not used to anyone thinking that I'm young."

"Still, you have accomplished a lot."

Eleanor thought that she noticed a hint of extra interest in Mr. Rana's expression as he spoke.

"Tell that to my mother!" Mae laughed. "She would rather I'd stayed back in Cambridge to marry the boy next door," she confided to Eleanor. "Anyway, I'm sure we'll run into each other, Mr. Rana. I'm in the maharaja's employ, and so I'm at his palace often discussing his designs for educational policy. I assume with his sponsorship of your charity, he will expect you to report to him directly from time to time as well."

"I look forward to it," Mr. Rana replied.

Edmund emerged triumphantly with their last four bottles of Chateaux Margaux in hand.

"Chateaux Margaux 1899... should be good," he said as he used a knife to stab the cork just enough that he could loosen it with his fingers and pull it out with his Rakshasa strength (a technique he'd spent many hours working on upon their arrival when they'd realized that they didn't have a corkscrew).

"Are you serious?" Mae asked. "I haven't had a wine so good since I moved here!"

Edmund poured them each a taste in the three remaining clean glasses from the cupboard, and as Eleanor nodded her approval, he filled their glasses right up to the brim.

"I consider this a worthy trade, Colonel. What a treat!" Mae exclaimed.

As Edmund's stomach growled again, he glanced covetously at the tagine. "Miss Smith, how accurate are the timetables for the arrival of trains here?"

"Oh, not particularly. We have mostly regional trains coming into town. There are only a few long-distance routes, and they're often delayed."

"Would it be… er… terribly rude if we ate now? We could set aside a healthy portion for Mr. Valov to eat when he arrives…" Edmund proposed awkwardly. "You see, we haven't actually eaten anything today, I realize now…"

"I'm sure he won't mind, darling. I'm sure he doesn't expect us to have any food for him at all…" Eleanor glanced over at their pot of failure on the stove… "and rightfully so!"

She opened the cupboard and collected four plates, noticing with annoyance that there weren't any more, and when she opened the drawers, she realized that the only cutlery in the entire house were cooking knives and serving spoons. She sighed with resignation. They would have to improvise.

"I suppose we will be eating Arabian style as well," she informed them. "What a fitting end to our culinary adventure."

Edmund gathered up the tagine, and they followed him into the living room, where he sat right down and crossed his legs in his favorite position from his childhood.

"Colonel, you've done this before!" Mae exclaimed.

"I actually grew up in Hyderabad," he admitted.

"Really, how did that come about? Was your father in the military, or was he a civil servant?"

"It's a long story."

"I'm sorry, I didn't mean to pry," Miss Smith said with another long sip of her wine.

Eleanor offered her a reassuring smile as she handed out the plates. "Tell us, Mae, how did you come to Baroda?"

"Well, it all started with a silly misunderstanding, actually. I was planning on going to Ceylon. I'd applied to both positions, you see, and I accidentally switched which position I sent my acceptance letter to. I was terribly upset about it at first, but my father reminded me that a commitment is a commitment, and so I came here to make the most of it. It turned out to be a very pleasant surprise. It is a lovely place to live, very peaceful and welcoming. You should think about settling here!"

As soon as Mae suggested it, the idea settled in Eleanor's mind. She had been happier during their week in Baroda than she had ever been in her life. She had finally given into the pleasures of simple domestic life, and she had managed to forget many times already about the plethora of non-human problems that plagued them. Was it possible that they could maintain this bliss?

"What do they think about employing married nurses here?" Eleanor asked.

Edmund looked rather excited about her interest in the proposition, which only fed her own excitement.

"You're a nurse, Eleanor?! Oh, they would be thrilled to have you!" Mae exclaimed. "The maharaja is already in the process of building a hospital, in fact. It will be the best hospital in India! What a gift you would be to the whole project!"

"It is a very intriguing proposition," Eleanor admitted.

The pessimistic voice deep inside of her was scrambling to crawl its way up to explain to her in great detail why such a perfect idea could never work, but she pushed it back. "Now, Edmund, darling, perhaps you can give me a lesson in how to eat this tagine Arabian style without any rice or bread."

He gracefully hopped up and returned from the kitchen with four cloth napkins. "We'll need these. Now, first you must put some on your plate, and then put your fingers like this…"

They all followed Edmund's lead, and sat back for hours of a relaxed, friendly dinner as Mae told them everything she thought they should know about Baroda, until a light outside coincided with a tired knock at the door.

Edmund hopped up to answer it.

"Leo!" he exclaimed. "Welcome home!"

Mr. Valov looked haggard as he peered in around Edmund, spying their position on the floor of the living room.

Edmund paid the driver of the donkey cart that had managed to haul Mr. Valov and their two trunks from the station, and then he nimbly lifted up the trunks and brought them into the foyer, to the driver's surprise.

"It took four porters to get those trunks on the cart," Mr. Valov muttered.

"Come, Leo, we have dinner waiting for you!" Edmund said cheerfully. "Now, it was no small feat, let me tell you…"

Mr. Valov glanced suspiciously at Mr. Rana and Miss Smith, and Edmund rushed to remedy the situation. "Mr. Valov, this is Mr. Rana and Miss Smith. Mr. Rana is our friend from Basingstoke, and Miss Smith is the principal of the girls' school here. She rescued us from a kitchen disaster. Come!"

Edmund guided Mr. Valov into the living room, and then he rushed into the kitchen, washed out one of their cognac glasses, and brought it to Mr. Valov along with the last of their wine.

"How was your journey?" Edmund asked as he collected the tagine and placed it right in front of Mr. Valov. "Please, Leo, eat. We saved this for you. We don't have any other plates or spoons, so you'll have to eat it right out of the pot like a caveman."

Mr. Valov inspected it, and when he smelled it, he finally gave in and used the serving spoon to eat it right out of the tagine.

"You made this?" he asked with surprise after his first bite. He began eating the rest more enthusiastically.

Edmund chuckled. "This was our intent, but our blackened disaster of a chicken has been abandoned in the kitchen. Miss Smith made this delicious dish and graciously brought it over to spare us from our own cooking."

Mr. Valov looked thoroughly overwhelmed by the entire situation. Eleanor wasn't sure if he had simply had a long day of travel, or if the degree to which they'd settled into the new home

436

in his absence was troubling him. She hoped that his state was not a reflection of the many unpleasant things he'd done to clean up their most recent mess.

Edmund must have sensed Mr. Valov's reticence, and so he engaged Mae in another amicable conversation about her most adventurous travels, and they let Mr. Valov sit quietly with his food until everyone's wine was finished, and Mr. Rana was yawning.

"Well, I'd say this was an unexpected success of a dinner party, with no thanks to us whatsoever," Edmund declared as he stood up and collected the plates. "Miss Smith you were a godsend."

"It was thoroughly enjoyable, Colonel. And, Eleanor, I do hope you consider staying in Baroda. Do you mind if I tell the maharaja about you? He may want to have a chance to convince you to stay himself. I have a meeting with him tomorrow."

Eleanor looked to Edmund. "Yes, why not. It doesn't hurt to learn about the possibilities, does it?"

Mae squeezed her hands excitedly and then pulled her into a hug. "What kismet that we met!"

"Mr. Rana, we owe you our great thanks for enticing us to come to Baroda in the first place," Edmund said as he shook his hand.

"Next time, dinner will be served in my home. I'd better invite Miss Smith here, to make sure we have some food."

They all burst into jovial laughter, and Mr. Valov watched them with tired, glassy eyes.

"Blimey." Edmund looked around the room.

"What is it, darling?" Eleanor's heart skipped a beat.

"We have absolutely nowhere for Mr. Valov to sleep..." Edmund looked guiltily towards him. "I'm sorry, Leo. We didn't think about it."

"Perhaps, Mr. Valov would be willing to stay in my home tonight. I have a guest bedroom," Mr. Rana suggested. "I don't live very far from here."

Mr. Valov moved to protest, and then he glanced at the marble floors and the thatched mat they'd been sitting on to eat, and he shrugged his resignation.

"I am really very tired," he admitted. "I would rather sleep in a bed. Thank you for your offer, Mr. Rana."

"We will escort you home, Miss Smith," Mr. Rana offered. "Do you live far?"

"I live in a cottage at the school," she said apologetically. "It's about a mile from here."

"Why don't you take the horses," Edmund suggested.

"You may ride with me, if it suits you, Miss Smith," Mr. Rana suggested. "You know how to ride?" he asked Mr. Valov.

"Of course I know how to ride," Mr. Valov grumbled.

Mr. Rana shook Edmund's hand one last time. "Thank you kindly, Colonel. We can board the horses in my garden for the night, and Mr. Valov can bring them back in the morning."

Edmund and Eleanor walked their guests to the door. Eleanor felt tremendously guilty for overlooking Mr. Valov's needs, and she hoped that he didn't take it as a lack of respect for all the help he'd been to them.

"Good night!" they called as their guests climbed onto the horses and disappeared into the night.

Edmund closed the door, and then sighed as he looked around the living room. "That felt... lovely. More lovely than I could have imagined. It was as if..."

"As if we were entirely human?" Eleanor asked.

"Yes, that is as good a way of putting it as anything," Edmund admitted. "I'm ashamed about Leo. We put so much thought into making him dinner, and we didn't think for one moment about where he would sleep. I suppose I'm not very good at planning."

"We both failed on that account, darling."

"And on account of the chicken." Edmund smiled.

"We'll get better at these things with more practice, I think. I've just never had to host a group of people."

438

Eleanor sat back down on the mat and unbuttoned her blouse. She suddenly realized that she'd been wearing one of Kuveni's modern bras for hours, and at the reminder, she couldn't wait to get it off.

"Darling, can you unclasp me?"

Edmund leaned over her and snuck a kiss of her neck as he unclasped the back. "This looks more comfortable than any corset."

"Did you remove many corsets, darling?"

"A few," he admitted. "Never with pleasure like this."

He ran his finger across her naked breast, and they both perked up with arousal. She began unbuttoning his shirt, and then they hastily ripped off the rest of each other's clothing, until they were lying next to each other on the floor.

"Shall we christen our new dining room, darling?" Eleanor asked naughtily.

"A perfect end to a perfect evening?"

"I couldn't have said it better myself."

And so, the two ordinary lovebirds set about reveling in the happy ending of their first married dinner party.

CHAPTER 24 – ACROSS A BUSY ROAD

Eleanor awoke beside Edmund in their bed, grateful that they'd had the sense to move upstairs after they'd enjoyed themselves for quite some time in the living room. The sun was already high in the sky, and the sheer curtains were billowing in the warm breeze. She took a moment to appreciate Uma's influence on her stamina for heat, as she was quite sure that if she had been left with her Scottish temperament, she would have spent most of the prior week complaining in bed with a wet washcloth on her forehead. Now, she might even consider living in India… in fact, the idea seemed better than it ever had…

Edmund took in his awakening Rakshasa breath and sat up. It was the first time she hadn't had to wake him in several days. "Good morning, dearest. It's another lovely day, isn't it? Perhaps we should clean up a bit before Mr. Valov arrives."

"Why? When he sees the pigsty we've made of our flat, I'm sure he'll feel more valuable," Eleanor winked. "More seriously, we must decide what we're going to do. We can't have him stay here in this flat, and it is unreasonable to expect Mr. Rana to host him."

"I was thinking…" Edmund trailed off.

"What, darling?" Eleanor coaxed.

"I was thinking last night that I'd gotten so caught up in our little approximation of domestic life here, that I'd almost forgotten to take you to Hyderabad. It really is something I've dreamed of doing for decades, dearest—to bring the woman I love to the place I grew up, where I spent so many good times with Abdul Barr. But I don't want to give this up. It's been so relaxing."

"We could do the same thing in Hyderabad," Eleanor suggested. "Perhaps we can rent a flat there for a bit, and relax as we spend time in the city."

"What a wonderful idea!" Edmund exclaimed. He kissed her and hopped right out of bed, dancing around as he pulled on his trousers. "Perhaps we can catch the sleeper train to Aurangabad and change there for Hyderabad."

"Darling, I think Mr. Valov might collapse from exhaustion if we leave so soon." Eleanor stood up less enthusiastically and began gathering up her stray clothes from the floor. "And I may have a meeting with the maharaja."

"Yes… yes, of course…"

"Perhaps we can leave tomorrow?" Eleanor said as she enticed him into a kiss. She didn't want to damper his spirits.

"Dearest, are you really serious about staying here? It sounds like something you might like to do?"

"What do you think, darling?" Eleanor realized as she asked the question that she was desperately hoping that he would agree with her. She *wanted* to stay. A whole new life had blossomed as a fantasy in her head, and it was more of a fantasy than any she'd let herself have in her life, even when she agreed to marry him. It seemed like maybe, just *maybe*, it could be real.

"Eleanor, I have missed India so dearly. I never imagined that I'd marry a woman who would love it enough to live here."

"But what would you do in Baroda, darling? Mae was right. An active colonel taking up residence would increase the military presence here. They'd probably send along a troop of cadets for you to command."

"I've thought... I've thought perhaps I might retire, actually..." Edmund glanced down at her nervously, waiting for her reaction. "Perhaps return to painting for a bit. I'd been holding so tightly to my work as a distraction from my shell shock, but now I have such wonderful distractions, Eleanor. I think I might be ready to walk away for good."

The idea blindsided her, but not in a bad way. She had always envisioned him tethered to the military, but as soon as he voiced the idea, her fantasies exploded. Without worrying about Edmund's employment, they could live anywhere!

"If that is really something you want, darling, I couldn't be happier about it. It would give us so much freedom. We could live however we want!"

Edmund pulled her into a romantic twirl and dipped her into a deep kiss.

"God, I love you, Eleanor."

Edmund startled as the front door creaked open downstairs. His eyes turned black, and then Mr. Valov's familiar voice called up to them. "It's just me, Colonel. I'm back with the horses."

"We'll come down shortly, Leo!" Edmund called back.

Eleanor hunted more aggressively for a single outfit that wasn't dirty, and then she sighed with resignation as she landed on one that only had a few stains. "If we live here, we'll have to have a laundry girl."

"We can have so many servants, Eleanor! A servant for every task. It will be a nice job for them to be employed by a kind and fair household, and it will make Leo's life easier too."

"Not if he has to be their boss."

"Hrm. I hadn't thought about that..."

"And where will we house all of these servants, darling? Will we buy a palace?"

Edmund stopped to think about it more seriously than Eleanor intended. "We could, but our domestic bliss has come from a humbler abode. I'm sure we can find something big enough to house a staff that doesn't have a swimming pool big enough for a boat."

"I suppose Gwalior is off the list then," Eleanor winked. "But do you think, darling, that having a lot of servants is a good idea? With so many things that we need to hide?" She wished she hadn't spoiled the mood as soon as she said the words.

"I don't know... I had many servants over the years in Basingstoke, and none of them ever suspected anything... but I suppose I have much more to hide than I did back then..."

"I'm sure that when the time comes, we'll figure it out," Eleanor said cheerfully.

She finished up dressing herself in her linen pants with a black silk blouse, and she waited for Edmund to finish tying his tie before swinging open the door and heading downstairs to sheepishly face their unaccommodated butler.

"Mr. Rana has invited you for a late lunch at his home," Mr. Valov said as he stacked their dishes in the sink, and then eyed the old-fashioned water pump questioningly.

"Please, Mr. Valov, don't worry about it. We'll be leaving tomorrow, and we'll pay for a staff to clean up."

"Tomorrow?" Mr. Valov asked, rather overwhelmed by the prospect.

"Yes, we're going to Hyderabad, to visit my home town." Mr. Valov raised his eyebrows skeptically at the assertion. "But we will plan to stay there for at least a week, maybe even two or three, in a flat, so that we can relax a bit. We'll be sure to get at least two bedrooms..." Mr. Valov did not look pleased by the development. "Does that suit you?"

"I'm sure it will be fine," he agreed disingenuously. "Shall I call Mr. Rana to confirm that you will be coming for lunch?"

"Why, yes. That's very kind of him to invite us!" Edmund was clearly trying to cheer Mr. Valov up with his enthusiasm, but it wasn't working.

"You'd best get on the road then, Colonel. It's already one o' clock. I got lost on my way back, and it took me much longer than I intended."

"Do you not wish to come?" Edmund asked.

"I ate breakfast with Mr. Rana, and I will stay here and pack your trunks, Colonel. I've had enough heat for the day."

"Ah, yes. It has been rather infernal. Suit yourself."

Eleanor wanted to stay back and ask Mr. Valov what horrific things had come to pass in their wake, but she couldn't think of a reasonable excuse to cut Edmund out of their immediate conversation, and so she squeezed Mr. Valov's arm supportively, and then climbed onto her mare.

"We'll be back in the afternoon, Leo. Is there anything you need us to bring back for you?"

"Nothing, Eleanor. Thank you," he said. "Enjoy yourselves."

He closed himself into their house, and without anything else to say, Edmund hopped onto his stallion, and they rode towards the center of town.

As soon as they crossed a busy road, filled with horse and camel-drawn carts, rickshaws, meandering cows, and a few motorcars, they were at the edge of Baroda's most sprawling bazaar that was teeming with locals clad in every color imaginable as they buzzed about their early afternoon shopping. Eleanor loved the frenetic energy of it.

"We should bring a gift to Mr. Rana," Edmund said as they passed the first stall. "I suppose it would be silly to bring him the ghee sweets that he brought us..."

"What else can we give him?" Eleanor eyed a flower stall. "I don't know what one should give a sober bachelor as a gift."

"I'm not sure either..."

"Perhaps we can give him different sweets? From a different vendor?" Eleanor pointed at several competing stalls selling pure ghee sweets.

"I suppose it will have to do." Edmund hopped off his horse. "Would you like to join me, or shall I just grab one while you watch the horses, dearest?"

"Are we in a hurry?"

"I'm not sure. It's hard to tell what Mr. Valov understood from Mr. Rana's invitation."

"I will wait then, darling."

Edmund walked right up to the closest vendor and began chatting amicably in Gujarati, asking him about the different sweets and which were the best to give as an afternoon gift, and Eleanor remained on her horse, holding the reins to Edmund's, watching the chaotic traffic correct itself and then gridlock in a predictable pattern that didn't seem to be connected to anything in particular.

Eleanor's interest was piqued as a sleek, black car pulled up––by far the best-looking car she'd seen since they'd left Bombay––and as Eleanor watched to see who got out of it, her heart skipped a beat as Miss Radha Patel stepped into the street. She was clad in a beautiful violet silk sari that looked quite good on her, despite her physical shortcomings, and she crouched down and gave the driver her orders, and then the car meandered back into traffic. But as Miss Patel paused for a moment to get her bearings, she spied Edmund, who was just finishing up his purchase, and just as he had when he'd seen her the day before, she stopped, mesmerized, to stare at him.

She stood in the road, oblivious to the gridlock that was forming around her, and as one camel-driven cart barreled towards her, Eleanor snapped out of her voyeuring, and called out a warning.

"Watch out!"

446

Her call had no effect.

Eleanor let go of the reins of Edmund's steed and raced across the crowded plaza to intercept Miss Patel before the camel had a chance to plow over her.

She made it to only a few feet away from Miss Patel before the girl broke out of her stupor and looked up at her confusedly, and then at the camel.

"Get on!" Eleanor reached down her hand, and Miss Patel hopped right onto the back of her horse without Eleanor even needing to stop.

There was now a crowd watching as Eleanor used her expert riding skills to double-back out of the road, narrowly missing the camel cart. She slowed her horse back to a trot, and returned to Edmund's steed, who was dutifully waiting just where she'd left him. The crowd clapped and cheered, and Eleanor blushed at their attention.

"Dearest?! That was glorious!" Edmund exclaimed. She was very pleased that he'd watched the whole thing, and that he wasn't complaining about her putting herself in danger.

Eleanor hopped off the horse, and then she helped Miss Patel off, but as Edmund made eye contact with the girl, they were both once again sucked into their odd connection.

"I'm Mrs. Eleanor MacLeod Marriner." Eleanor reached forward her hand to shake Miss Patel's, plopping herself right in front of Edmund to break their spell. "And this is my husband, Colonel Edmund Marriner."

Miss Patel finally blinked, and as she reached her hand forward to politely shake Eleanor's, Eleanor felt a very familiar shiver travel up her spine, followed by an even more familiar rhythm of subtle pulsating power. She held the girl's hand for slightly too long as she contemplated the odd feeling.

"I'm sorry, I'm quite cold. It runs in the family," Miss Patel said self-consciously as she took her hand back. "I'm Miss Radha Patel. Thank you, Mrs. Marriner, for rescuing me. I don't know what came over me." Miss Patel spoke with perfect British English, but her voice danced with a subtle Indian lilt that Eleanor found especially lyrical.

Miss Patel glanced at Edmund again, and then actively focused her attention on Eleanor, avoiding Edmund's gaze.

"Are you alright now?" Eleanor asked. Her mind was screaming all sorts of incoherent things. She worked her hardest to ignore it.

"Yes... yes, I'm sure I will be perfectly fine. Really it was very foolish of me to stand in the road like that."

"Well, I'm glad I could be of service..." Eleanor looked up at her dumbstruck husband, and suddenly she couldn't get away from the scene fast enough. "If you'll excuse us, we're late for a luncheon."

"Mrs. Eleanor Marriner..." Miss Patel repeated her name as she paid closer attention to Eleanor's physicality. Eleanor stood up straight, pushing back a bout of self-consciousness as she felt the girl's eyes travel past her chest to her fiery hair that was still especially messy after her hasty morning ritual and breezy horseback journey. "Are you the visiting nurse that Miss Smith was discussing with the maharaja this morning?"

"Yes, I suppose that is me," Eleanor agreed. "My, Miss Smith works fast."

"Yes, yes, of course!" Miss Patel exclaimed. "You are Mr. Rana's *firang* visitors!" Miss Patel settled into a friendly, casual tone. "Oh, you must both come to the ball I'm co-hosting with the maharaja at his palace tonight! It's a charity benefit for the new hospital. Have you ever taught, Eleanor? Do you think you could teach other women how to be nurses?"

"I taught all of the new VAD recruits for three years during the war," Eleanor agreed.

Miss Patel looked like she might explode with excitement, and she clapped her hands together happily. "Oh Eleanor, please promise me you'll come tonight! Come to the maharaja's palace!

There will be dinner and dancing, and it's sure to be great fun. You must give us the chance to convince you to stay in Baroda! You would be such a godsend!"

Miss Patel completely avoided looking at Edmund as she stared down Eleanor waiting for an answer.

"Yes, I suppose we could attend," Eleanor gave in. "We were planning on leaving for Hyderabad tomorrow, though. We're still on our honeymoon."

"Well, we must get our proposition into your head so it will stay with you on your travels," Miss Patel said matter-of-factly. Eleanor liked the girl's tenacity, and her passion. She did not like at all that she liked her. "Sunset cocktails will be served at six o'clock in the garden, dinner will be served at seven, with dancing to follow. Tell them your names, and I will have you on the list."

"Should we wear... er... Indian formal or western formal clothing?"

"You have Indian formal clothing?" Miss Patel glanced down at Eleanor's fading henna. "How wonderful that you have been here long enough to appreciate our fashions! Please do wear it! Even Miss Smith will wear a sari!"

Eleanor found her youthful enthusiasm to be rather cute, and there was a certain earnestness to her that made her seem younger than she looked.

"Then it's settled! We will see each other tonight!" Miss Patel squeezed Eleanor's hands in affectionate goodbye, and then skipped down one of the bazaar's avenues without a word or a glance at Edmund.

"I am certain that I know that girl," he finally said as her distance released him from the spell.

"Radha Patel?" Eleanor asked. She was singing inside that the girl's name wasn't Padma, but there were too many things about her that felt familiar. "Did you know any Patels?"

"Plenty. It is a very common name." He glanced one final time down the street where she'd disappeared, and then he looked down at the box of sweets in his hand. "We'd better get going. We shouldn't keep Mr. Rana waiting." Eleanor did not like that he was still so unsettled. "You were wonderful, by the way. A knight in shining armor if I've ever seen one."

"Thank you, darling. Perhaps I can have some armor made to my measurements." She looked down at her chest, and they both laughed. She was intensely grateful for their return to good humor.

She hopped right up onto her mare and Edmund followed her lead, and together on their noble steeds, they rode right into the blazing midday sun.

CHAPTER 25 – A SURPRISE IN THE CONSERVATORY

"Are you sure this looks alright? It's not too... er... busty?" Eleanor asked as she attempted to assess how her lehenga looked from the tiny circular shaving mirror in the bathroom. She was wearing a particularly flamboyant design that Kuveni had said was ancient Lankan in fashion, of magenta and mossy green netted silks embroidered with golden lotuses all around the skirt, with matching accents on the shoulder of the blouse and the dupatta. Like the blouse she'd worn to the Taj Mahal, the cut was much lower than Eleanor remembered it from her dress-up session in Mélusine's cave, and she made a note to corner Kuveni at some point and force her to confess to a bit of meddling.

"It looks lovely, dearest. Very exotic. I don't think I've ever seen anything quite like it. It looks quite southern, but it is not a standard southern silk..." He felt the netted skirt with his hand and inspected the embroidery. "The craftsmanship is superb. The maharani has excellent taste."

"Thank you, darling." Eleanor relaxed.

He was back in his blue and silver sherwani, the same one he'd worn to the Taj Mahal, minus the turban, which Mr. Valov had sensibly couriered back to Ravi Bidkar from Agra for safekeeping. Eleanor liked this outfit on him more than any other, and she wasn't sure if it was because she'd allowed herself to revel in the vision of him as a prince in it, or if it was because the color-scheme brought out the rosiness in his cheeks, a feature that reminded her of his vigorous younger self that she had enjoyed making love to immensely.

"Colonel, you need to leave. It's already a quarter past six!" Mr. Valov called.

"Tick tock!" Eleanor laughed. "It's nice to have an alarm clock sometimes. Are you sure that we should show up fashionably late? We won't be rude?"

"I am certain that if we had arrived on time, we would have been the only ones there for quite some time," Edmund reassured her. "It is the way of things here."

Eleanor used the excuse to rush back into the bathroom to check her hair—which Uma had helped her smooth into beautiful ringlets, tied back into a loose Roman style similar to the ones Kuveni had done for her—and her makeup, which she had been extra careful to do correctly as her mind beat down the tiny jealous voice that continued to buzz in her head at the thought of Edmund's reaction to Miss Radha Patel.

She was rather pleased with how the rich colors of her outfit brought out the unusually bright green of her eyes, and how they complemented Mélusine's green sapphire talisman and the paste emerald earrings that she was still frequently wearing from Shruti's collection.

"Ready!" she declared. She hadn't felt so good about her appearance since Uma's presence had changed her.

"You look positively royal, dearest. Perfect for a meeting with the maharaja."

452

He offered her his arm, and she giggled as she took it.

"I suppose we shouldn't bring up Madho Rao or Gwalior..." Eleanor strategized. "Although, it seems like he would get along with this maharaja from everything that Mae said... perhaps we could meddle just a bit, although meddling usually ends badly, in my experience..." She glanced around, throwing her jab invisibly at Kuveni.

"I think that we mustn't put too many constraints on ourselves about the topic of conversation. As long as we keep our secrets intact, we should say what feels natural, don't you think, dearest?"

"I think that is a very sensible plan, darling."

"Are you sure you don't want me to call you a car?" Mr. Valov asked as they reached the front door.

"I think arriving on horseback will be perfectly apt," Edmund refused. "Thank you, Mr. Valov. Will we see you later, or will you be at Mr. Rana's house?"

"I will wait for your return, Colonel, scrubbing out the mess from last night's dinner experiment."

"Oh, our poor little Cinderella!" Eleanor teased him. "Leo, we've already hired someone to do that. Mr. Rana helped us make the arrangements after our luncheon, and they will scrub up the whole place after we leave for Hyderabad tomorrow. Really, you should lounge about lazily. There is a final bottle of cognac in our room with your name on it."

"If you insist." Mr. Valov winked, and Eleanor realized that she'd been led right into a trap laid by the Empire's best spy.

"Leo, I'm glad you use your mischievous powers of manipulation for good causes." She meant the comment jokingly, but he straightened his posture, returning to seriousness. Perhaps the comment had hit too close to home.

"Please be careful, and do not hesitate to call if you need my help," he said as he opened the door for them.

Edmund helped Eleanor onto her horse so that she could ride side-saddle in the flowing skirt, and then he nimbly hopped onto his, and with a friendly wave, they headed down the street in the hazy orange twilight.

Eleanor's heart picked up its pace as they neared the maharaja's palace, a location they had seen many times from afar throughout their relaxed week going about town, but that she had had very little interest in seeing until Miss Patel's invitation. She felt the same anxiety as she'd felt before her various job interviews in the past, except that this time, it was mixing annoyingly with her jealousy and puzzlement about the mysterious Radha Patel.

The crowds at the night market parted as she and Edmund passed, and she no longer felt so self-conscious at their attention. She realized that some part of her liked it, as the little girls pointed and whispered to their mothers about the foreign princess who was riding past. She tried to hold onto her newfound confidence as they reached the imposing gate-house of the maharaja's palace.

"Colonel Edmund Marriner and Mrs. Eleanor Marriner. We are here for the benefit," he said to the guard.

"Yes, sir! Of course, sir! Miss Patel told us to expect you!"

The guard saluted as he let them pass.

"That was easy," she whispered. "I half expected that they'd turn us away."

"Miss Patel appears to be very organized."

They trotted along a meandering drive past acres and acres of manicured lawns and gardens dotted by massive banyan trees that loomed in the shadows of the last remnants of a rather uninspiring yellow sunset.

When they finally reached the intensely extravagant palace that Eleanor honestly felt looked more grand than the Taj Mahal (at least more decorated, with so many bulbous spires and archways that she couldn't even count them, although the stone of the building made it look somewhat akin to what she was used to in Edinburgh), a large staff in uniforms similarly styled to those of Ravi Bidkar's staff welcomed them.

Edmund hopped off his horse, and then he helped her off of hers, and the staff immediately took the reins and led the horses to the stables.

"Colonel and Mrs. Marriner," he told a Sikh guard at the door who was dressed in an even more elaborate uniform, complete with a decorative spear in his right hand.

"Very good, sir. I will announce you."

Eleanor threw Edmund an excited look at the idea. She had to admit, being announced at a ball felt very royal. They followed the man inside, through a massive hallway decorated with murals and inlaid marblework, until they reached a ballroom illuminated by the biggest crystal chandeliers Eleanor had ever seen. The palace made Ravi Bidkar's house seem like a humble little holiday home.

The sentry used his spear to knock on the floor three times to get the attention of the crowd. A quartet of musicians playing exotic instruments stopped in the middle of their song.

"Fashionably late, darling?" Eleanor whispered as she blushed with embarrassment. Clearly, Edmund's plan to be on time by showing up late had been wrong.

Hundreds of people dressed in a sea of glistening sparkles looked up at them.

"Colonel and Mrs. Marriner," the sentry announced.

The crowd watched with mild interest for a few seconds as they made their entrance, and then the musicians started up again, and the crowd went back to their hum of conversation.

A servant rushed to offer them some champagne, and Eleanor made quite the effort to sip it slowly, wishing once again that she could dull her anxiety at the foreign situation with just a little bit of tipsiness.

"Eleanor!"

Mae, looking beautiful in a sparkling sky blue sari that brought out the blue in her grey eyes, rushed to greet them. "I'm so glad you came! You must have received the invitation just a few hours ago!"

"Actually, we ran into Miss Radha Patel earlier today. She invited us," Eleanor explained.

"It must be destiny!" Mae said excitedly. She looked Eleanor and Edmund up and down again. "You just had these clothes sitting around? They're perfectly tailored!"

"We've already had quite an eventful honeymoon," Eleanor explained.

"How wonderful! I was so busy rattling on last night about my own travels, I only realized when I got home that we hadn't heard any tall tales from your trips." Mae's amicable demeanor began to calm her nerves. "I do hope we'll have more opportunities to chat. Last night was so much fun."

"I must admit, the idea of staying in Baroda was more appealing than I anticipated..." Eleanor trailed off as she followed Mae's gaze to Miss Radha Patel and several other impeccably dressed people who were parting the crowd, making a bee-line for their position.

"Looks like the Patels are coming right over to convince you," Mae giggled. "It is a great privilege to know them, Eleanor. They keep their distance from most of the people in town. I've only been able to work with Radha because of her interest in educational policy. Oh, Eleanor, I do hope that you stay!"

"Eleanor, I'm so glad you came!" Miss Patel declared as she greeted them with a polite *namaste*, and then shook both of Eleanor's hands. Now Radha's hands were pulsating with warmth, just as Edmund's did when he'd consumed enough hot liquid, and they were pulsating with something else, something too familiar. Eleanor knew exactly why Edmund was so perplexed by her. It almost felt as if she were shaking Edmund's hands. "Please, let me introduce you to my Auntie Maya, Uncle Rohit, and my uncle's business partner, Mr. Vishravan. My little cousin Rahul is also hopping about somewhere, probably up to a bit of mischief."

456

All three members of Radha's entourage offered them a polite *namaste*, but as Mr. Vishravan looked back and forth between them, Eleanor caught something in his expression, first confusion as he glanced at her again, and then a moment of panic that he immediately smoothed out into a friendly smile.

"Radha tells us that you are considering staying in Baroda to help us with our hospital project?" Maya asked.

"It is a rather new idea," Eleanor hedged. "But Miss Smith and Miss Patel have made compelling arguments."

"We would be so happy to have you." Maya reached forward and squeezed both of Eleanor's hands. Her hands pulsated with the same warmth. She looked over to Edmund. "And you, of course, Colonel. Although, I don't think we would have much work for you to do here. Baroda is a very peaceful place."

"I have many endeavors beyond the military with which I can keep myself occupied," Edmund replied politely.

"Yes, yes, of course!" Rohit chimed in. "Colonel, if you're interested, we could use a skilled liaison for our business. We have been looking to expand into the western markets, but it's a dastardly difficult prospect without a *firang* to rally the other foreigners. Don't you think, Vibhi?"

Mr. Vishravan gave away another split second of panic, and then he smiled. "Rohit is always looking for ways to expand the business. If you are indeed interested in staying, I'm sure we can find a place for you. So, Mrs. Marriner, you are a nurse?"

"Yes," Eleanor said questioningly.

Mr. Vishravan leaned in confidingly, and suddenly Eleanor felt faint. A familiar pulsating wave of power wafted off of him, and she took a step back, taking in the features of the tall, thin but muscular Indian man before her with large, soulful brown eyes, a kind smile, and a twisting mustache, clad in an especially elaborate glistening violet sherwani. She had never seen him before in her life, but she was certain that she knew him, just as Edmund was certain that he knew Miss Radha Patel.

"Mrs. Marriner, I've been suffering from a dreadful health problem. Would you mind terribly if we discuss it in private for a moment? I would be grateful for your advice."

"Yes… if you'd like," Eleanor agreed.

The Patels looked to each other with an expression of shared intrigue, but as Mae gathered them all politely into a conversation about the architecture of the maharaja's palace, Eleanor followed Mr. Vishravan through several empty hallways, noting with increased interest that none of the guards made any attempt to stop him, until they reached a glass-ceiling conservatory filled with blooming tropical foliage.

He closed the door behind them, and Eleanor's anxiety ticked up a notch as she realized how isolated they were.

"Don't worry, Eleanor, you are not in any danger."

He looked around, ensuring their privacy one last time, and then with a subtle wiggle and a flash of the violet metallic plasma that Eleanor knew only too well, Mr. Johnson was standing before her, clad in a stylish western suit. Eleanor only realized then, without the guise of a frumpy vicar's uniform, how attractive Edmund's virtuous Rakshasa uncle really was. She also recognized the subtle pulsating power that was emanating off of him. It was stirring something deep inside of her, a desperate longing that she didn't like one bit.

Uma, that must be you.

I'm sorry, my child. I cannot control it. He is my other half.

"Blimey," Eleanor whispered.

"I'm sorry for the surprise. It is often strange for humans to watch us transform for the first time. But you've seen it before, haven't you? Mélusine showed you once?"

"Yes." Eleanor suddenly realized how difficult their conversation would be without her getting Mélusine and Kuveni in trouble for their excessive meddling. She swiftly moved the topic along. "Will Edmund be able to do that someday?"

After a moment of consideration, he decided to give her a real answer. "I don't know. He's only half Rakshasa. Some hybrids can do almost everything, while other hybrids can hardly do anything at all. It is very unpredictable. I thought that Edmund was more of the latter, but with the emergence of his speed and his... er... struggles, I'm not so sure what to expect from him anymore. Has he developed any other talents since our cricket match?"

"No, not really," Eleanor replied. "He has become much better at controlling the speed, though."

"Yes, that isn't surprising. Once Edmund sets off on a path, he usually travels it to completion." There was a hint of fatherly pride in his voice. "But something is different..." He glanced at her, eyeing her figure for several seconds too long, with growing concern. "Are you feeling alright, Eleanor? You haven't felt too cold? Or any severe pain in your stomach?"

Eleanor was puzzled by the questions until she realized what he was asking. "Are those symptoms of Rakshasa pregnancy?"

He looked embarrassed. "Your measurements have changed, Eleanor. As has something else about you. I can't quite put my finger on it."

Uma forced her eyes closed.

Do not tell him the truth. It is not time yet.

Surely he'll figure it out.

He does not have the honed senses that you have, Eleanor. Your ability to sense the avatars is very unique. Only a few others have ever had it, and Lord Vibhishana isn't one of them.

"I'm not pregnant. I was worried about it too, but Mélusine confirmed it. I have no rational explanation for the change in my measurements. It has been dastardly unpleasant for me, actually. I was quite happy with how I was before."

He stared at her chest, until she looked down and noticed that his attention was not on her cleavage, but on Mélusine's talisman.

"Mélusine gave it to me for emergencies, in case I needed to summon her."

He broke himself out of his thoughts. "It is a sensible precaution as long as it's a last resort… So, she was certain that you aren't pregnant?"

"She was."

Eleanor didn't like the look of relief on his face, but he quickly changed the subject.

"Eleanor, please, you must be entirely honest with me. Did Kuveni somehow lead you here? To Baroda?"

"No!" Eleanor exclaimed. "Of course not!"

"It is a very obscure place for you to find yourselves," he countered suspiciously.

"Really, she didn't. I haven't seen her in… quite some time." Eleanor wasn't sure how convincing her half-truth was. "We came because a friend from Basingstoke invited us to visit him, and we were looking for an escape from… er… the action of the last few weeks."

He began pacing slowly. "This is very strange, then. It is too much of a coincidence. Destiny is in motion…"

"I've heard that one before."

"Did Mélusine say so? What prompted her statement?"

She found his interest in Mélusine's opinion even more intriguing.

"I don't even remember now. She's said it several times…" Eleanor knew she was in dangerous territory of getting her loving allies in trouble with their boss. "But if Baroda isn't important at all, why are you here? What is special about the Patels? There is something very strange about Radha."

He stopped his pacing, glanced at the door, and lowered his voice. "They're Rakshasas, Eleanor."

"Blimey," she whispered, "Of course."

As soon as she said it, she felt like an idiot for not fully recognizing it the moment she'd felt Radha's frigid hands.

"They are as virtuous as Rakshasas come, and they always have been. Maya is a full Rakshasa like I am, and Rohit is human…" he trailed off. "You're certain that Kuveni didn't lead you here?"

"Unless she was posing as Mr. Rana?" Eleanor meant the suggestion jokingly, but then she stopped to think carefully about it. "But she wasn't. I can sense the Yakshas. I've shaken Mr. Rana's hand several times, and he is entirely human."

"You can sense the Yakshas?"

"Yes. It turns out I can sense quite a lot of things… my lord."

Uma cringed as she said the words, but he didn't take her statement as she meant it.

"So you recognized me, even in my other form? It is very unusual for humans to be able to make such leaps. It is a standard limitation of a corporeal mind."

"Not entirely. In retrospect, it was obvious, but I wasn't expecting to run into you. In fact, I didn't really think that you'd be hopping about at a fancy dinner party."

He finally cracked a smile. "I am much more ordinary than people imagine, even with my many talents."

With another subtle wiggle, he was back in his gentle Indian form, although Eleanor found his flamboyant mustache to be rather amusing, and not particularly attractive. She was glad.

"This is my most natural human form," he explained.

"I suppose it makes sense that you're really Indian. I was wondering how you'd come to look so similar to Edmund, and whether or not the resemblance was intentional."

"This form is Lankan, actually," he corrected her. "But it is a pedantic difference in the modern world. The people of both nations have migrated back and forth as so many dynasties have risen and fallen that it's hard to tell the difference between them now."

"Huh… I hadn't thought about how all of the human populations around you must have changed physically over the millennia. Were there people five thousand years ago who looked nothing like any race on Earth today?"

He smiled wistfully. "There were thousands of races that don't exist today. And languages. And religions. And cultures. Millions of plants and animals that you can't even imagine, and that do not exist at all in the fossil record. They are lost to human knowledge completely. I have never been able to properly describe exactly how different it was. Perhaps the best example is that my Rakshasa family made no effort at all to hide our foreign nature. We lived completely out in the open as Rakshasas, and we were not the only ones."

"How sad that you've gone into hiding!" Eleanor exclaimed. "Edmund longs so dearly to not have to lie to the world."

"Someday the Age of Truth will be here, and his farces will come to a merciful end. He will not have to wait as long as I have, and I am grateful for him. One always wants their children and their wards to have an easier time than they did."

"Then why did you let him grow up in an orphanage?" Eleanor hoped that her aggressive question wouldn't stymie their honest conversation. "To be honest, I haven't been able to figure out why you went to the effort of making yourself look like his father. He still believes you're his father, by the way, despite your clear denial at our wedding."

He sighed with melancholy. "He needs a father. A good father. A man he can look up to. I simply cannot bring myself to lie to him about that. It is better for him to believe that I am his father for now, without me having to support the assertion with a farce. He has used what little he knows about me to create a role model in his head that serves as a good manifestation of his own conscience. He will need his conscience to be particularly well-developed when he learns the ugly truth about his real father."

"So you made that form as part of a plan looking forward centuries from the day he was born? Are you really that deliberate? I suppose I thought that the prophecies were more riddles than they were instruction manuals..." Eleanor didn't like the implications of the prophecies being so clear.

"How do you know about the prophecies, Eleanor? Did Kuveni tell you? Mélusine would have had the sense to keep our most dangerous secrets to herself."

Now she'd really let the cat out of the bag…

Tell him you met me, not that you are me. Tell him the Oracle revealed itself.

"I met Uma in Elephanta. The Oracle revealed itself."

Eleanor watched curiously for his reaction.

He began pacing as he considered the implications. "Could it have meant that? No, surely not… but destiny is in motion…" He finally looked up at her. "You're right that the prophecies are riddles. Riddles that I have misinterpreted plenty of times over the years. One must always approach them with healthy skepticism, or they can become very dangerous."

Eleanor brought him back to her original point. "Then how did you have the foresight to make a form that looked like it could be Edmund's father?"

"I have used the form Edmund knows when I have needed to look European over the centuries. It is purely coincidence that it resembles him at all. Edmund knows it because I was using it when he was a child, when my brother was meddling in the British royal family, and I have been forced to keep using it in his presence, so that he doesn't realize that we can change our forms. Over the years, as I have contemplated being more honest with him, I have come to the conclusion that it is better for him to keep his misconceptions about me close to his heart. Sometimes it's better for people to believe in comforting lies. It is a harsh truth that I have had to concede to over the millennia."

"So that's why you've kept him in the dark about all the things he can do? Are the Patels in the dark about the many things they can do? Do they know that they can fly?"

"How do you know that we can fly?" He raised his eyebrow with intrigue in an entirely human gesture.

Eleanor thought fast to keep Mélusine out of trouble. "Edmund dreams about it constantly... and the priest who checked up on us in Bulgaria asked him several questions about why angels have wings. It wasn't difficult to put two and two together."

"If I didn't know any better, I'd think you had a Rakshasa memory, Eleanor." Eleanor didn't let him evade her question. "The Patels' situation is entirely different from Edmund's. I have many good reasons for keeping him in the dark, and you must trust me and help me keep him that way. It is not time for him to know everything yet. Great misery will descend on all of us if we try to force these truths into the light before the time is right."

"You're right that he isn't ready," she agreed. "He is still quite fragile from the war."

He relaxed. "You are a worthy partner for him, Eleanor. I have waited a hundred years for him to meet a woman who was worthy of standing by his side. If you're interested, I will arrange for you to talk to Rohit tonight. You and he have a lot in common, as the human spouses of virtuous Rakshasas. He is a wonderful man who may be able to offer you some insight about marriage that no one else can."

"Does he have to lie to his wife constantly about what species she is?" Eleanor couldn't help but throw in some cheek.

He looked pained. "No, he doesn't. But together they must lie to their son. Young Rahul has not demonstrated a single Rakshasa trait, while his sister has advanced very quickly. Until he shows some Rakshasa aptitude, they have committed to simplifying his life by raising him as a human, at the expense of honesty in their household."

"I suppose we will have something to talk about then. I suppose you will be distracting Edmund with an expert farce in the meantime? It's utterly tragic that he won't know that he's in your company. He misses you so dearly."

"I promise you that it is as painful for me as it is for him, but my influence is too strong. He must develop on his own."

"The influence of Lord Shiva, the Transformer?" Eleanor asked. His avoidance of Edmund suddenly made sense to her, as she contemplated Uma's warnings about accidentally changing those she encountered.

Careful, Uma warned.

He was startled. "What do you mean by that, Eleanor?" She could see he was working hard to hide his reaction, but she could feel his fear, not in the way that Edmund could smell it, but as if it were a part of her. His fear was compounding her own.

I won't give away your position, Eleanor reassured Uma. *But I must move our hand forward...*

It is a dangerous move.

"I have always been an excellent judge of character, but it isn't just that..." Eleanor readied herself for her revelation. "I can feel the Yakshas' warmth, the Rakshasas' frigidity, and I have recently learned that I can sense the avatars with unusual accuracy... all of them, Lord Shiva."

As she said his name, he looked down at himself, and they both watched as his appearance began to transform. His sherwani dissolved and his silk pyjamas morphed into a tiger skin loin cloth, while his skin became an ashen gray. His mustache dissolved into a clean-shaven face, and his facial features remained otherwise the same, except for a third eye that emerged right in the middle of his forehead. His hair grew out, collecting itself into matted knots in a large bun on the top of his head, and around his neck a necklace of skulls was accented by a live white and yellow snake slithering across his shoulders and down his arms. In his right hand, he held a very familiar bronze trident. It was not exactly the same as Uma's had been, it was slightly larger and more angular, but despite the extreme foreignness of his look, he was completely familiar to her.

In a blur, he whooshed away from her to the corner of the room behind several large-leafed plants, as far away from the windows as possible.

"I'm sorry! I didn't mean to… er… unmask you like that," she called. "Are you alright?"

This is a catastrophe, Uma murmured.

She tiptoed around the conservatory until she found him. *Good lord, Eleanor. Look at what you've done now… You have him cowering in the corner.* She chastised herself for instigating the foolish turn of events, as Uma was entirely consumed with conflict and desire.

He looked up at her, and then at his ashen arms. He dropped the trident on the floor beside him, and the snake continued slithering, offering her a subtle look of recognition.

"How did you do this, Eleanor? It is very dangerous. No one can know this truth, do you understand? Absolutely *no one*. The fate of the world depends on it."

"I just… I just felt the nuances of your power, and as I learned more about the complexity of the Hindu pantheon, I was able to give it a name," Eleanor explained.

"That is not what I meant. How did you force this transformation?"

"You didn't do it willingly?" Eleanor asked.

"I did not." He looked down at his strange body with annoyance.

"Blimey," she whispered. "I have no bloody idea how it happened."

He looked even more alarmed. "That means that neither of us knows how to undo it."

She took a seat next to him, leaning up against the wall, as she had done with Edmund the first night of their acquaintance when he'd hidden himself away in the Baron of Heathfield's barn, battling with his shell-shocked episode.

"It is rather odd…" She waved her hand in front of his third eye, and she shivered as it followed her.

466

"This is my divine form. It is what Lord Shiva looks like as a corporeal being. My Rakshasa abilities allow it to manifest more literally than other avatars are able to show their divinity."

"Has this ever happened before?"

"A handful of times in five thousand years. Each time in a dastardly inconvenient moment, just like this one. Perhaps it is a game destiny is playing with me... But no one has ever called it forth, Eleanor. You are the first."

"I tend to have unusual effects on people. It isn't usually intentional."

The snake slithered from his shoulders onto hers, and she took in a deep, satisfied breath. It pulsated with life.

"He does not usually take to humans," he said as he watched the snake perplexedly.

"Is he your mount?" Eleanor asked curiously. "I would think that a snake isn't a particularly effective mount. Straddling him seems like it wouldn't make for a very divine entrance."

He finally smiled at the whimsical idea. "I don't need a mount, because I can fly with my Rakshasa wings. He is the snake of life. He embodies the cosmic energy of the universe... But it is very strange that he is choosing to stay with you like that, Eleanor. I have never seen him willing to be so far away from me."

"Animals often like me," she replied as he wrapped himself around her arm.

"He is not an animal. He is a manifestation."

"Gods tend to like me too," she winked.

He became too pensive about her comment.

"I was just joking."

"No, Eleanor. I don't think that you were." He stared her down with all three of his eyes.

"My wondrous abilities are not limited to sensing your inner light, my lord."

"You should call me Vibhi. Anyone who knows my most hidden secret should not be using honorifics."

"I thought that your most hidden secret was your sojourn in Jerusalem."

"That is perhaps my most dangerous secret, but many of my long-lived allies were there. It is not a secret amongst the Celestial Court. But *this*, Eleanor. There is no one alive today who knows this truth. My sister has had her suspicions over the millennia, but I have never once confirmed the truth for her. No one must know about this. Do you understand? Not Mélusine, not Kuveni, and absolutely not Edmund."

Eleanor held her tongue on the issue of Kuveni's knowledge, as she was quite sure from her earlier reaction, that Kuveni had already managed to stumble upon this secret.

"I won't tell anyone," Eleanor reassured him. "I am already a seasoned veteran at lying to my husband about himself, so I see no reason why it should be any harder to lie to him about you."

"You have sensed something special about him, as you sensed it in me?"

"He is Lord Kalki, is he not? Future messiah of the world?"

"You've been doing your homework, Eleanor."

"A few weeks in India are enough to change a girl." Eleanor almost laughed at the understatement.

"Edmund has not ascended yet. It will be a good century before he's ready. Until then, he is not Lord Kalki."

"Do you think he will be religious by then?" Eleanor asked curiously. "I find it hard to imagine him falling in line with any particular doctrine, but the Hindus seem to think that Lord Kalki will lead them in all capacities, including that one."

"He will lead them, but not in the way that they think. He must lead the world. All societies. All species. All religions. He must be liberal in certain ways, in the ways that he already is, for that to work. His understanding of virtue must transcend all dogma. It is why we focused his education so heavily on humanist philosophy and comparative literature. He was always required to identify the common themes across cultural contexts."

"I'm quite sure that that is not the curriculum that anyone would expect you to choose… I think they would expect it to be more… liturgical in nature."

"Yes, well, most of my simple messages of peace and acceptance were corrupted over the millennia by my brother's twisting of my words. I'm just grateful now that a few of them remained intact. If I'd known what he would do to humans on my behalf, I never, ever would have done what I did in the Holy Land. It was one of my greatest follies, for which the world is still paying dearly."

"Some people find comfort in religion." It was the first time she had ever made a remotely positive argument on behalf of religion. She found the fact that she was making it to him to be especially unbelievable. She thought about Betty, and then about the preacher who, despite his fire and brimstone message, had apparently told Bo not to go around raping women on God's behalf. "Some lemmings need someone to tell them what's right and wrong. A religious voice is a powerful one to guide them."

"You're right, of course. But it has as much power to corrupt as it does to provide salvation. It is my karmic punishment for my hubris to fight against its corruption indefinitely. Although," He looked down at his divine form again, "it is one of Lord Shiva's sacred duties to stomp down the dwarf of ignorance that corrupts human morality. This is all, perhaps, a natural and inescapable part of the universe's cycle. It doesn't make the battle any less tiring, or my guilt at my failures any less severe."

Eleanor took his hand into hers, and she felt a quickening as Uma's energy connected with his. He startled, as he noticed the feeling too.

"The world is lucky to have you here, fighting the invisible fight, Lord Shiva."

She pulled away. Vibhi gazed at her searchingly again.

That was all you, Uma. If he figures it out, you will take full responsibility.

469

I'm sorry, my child. I simply couldn't resist.

Vibhi finally dropped his silent inquiry and looked nervously towards the door.

"Someone is in the hallway. We cannot be discovered. *I* cannot be discovered like this."

Eleanor coaxed the snake off her shoulders and back onto his. "When Edmund is out of control, he whispers his mantras, connecting himself with his humanity until his eyes are no longer black. Can you use a similar technique?"

"I'm not battling with my inner demon, Eleanor. This is who I am. It is a more accurate manifestation than any other form I take."

"Then, I suppose you'd better go out there and announce yourself, Lord Shiva. They already have a giant statue of you in the center of town; I'm sure they'll be happy to learn that the real deal has been wandering about in their bazaars." She waited for him to react to her sarcastic suggestion, and he finally gave into her more sensible one and closed his eyes, whispering his own mantras.

Uma reached her hand forward and stroked the snake's head.

Go, my love. Free him of his burden for now. It is not time for us to be together yet.

In a split second, all of Vibhi's divine features melted back into his gentle Lankan form, and he was once again wearing his elaborate violet sherwani.

"Welcome back, Lord Vibhishana," Eleanor said as he opened his eyes and looked down at his form with intense relief.

As the door to the conservatory opened, he hopped up in a blur, and pulled Eleanor up to join him.

"This is going to look very suspicious," she muttered. "I hope Edmund isn't the jealous type."

"Mr. Vishravan?" a young boy called. "Mr. Vishravan? Papa is looking for you!"

"Yes, Rahul!" Vibhi called. "Tell him I will join him in a moment. Now be a good boy, and leave me to my business for now."

"Okay!"

Rahul slammed the door and rushed to follow Vibhi's suggestion.

"Eleanor... I... I honestly don't know what to say. It is an extremely rare occurrence that I am left without any words..."

Eleanor smiled, and fought back an urge to kiss him.

For god's sake, Uma. Will you stop that?! I don't need any more complications in my life!

"I am a model of discretion, Vibhi. With yours, and everyone else's secrets."

He nodded, and she suddenly realized that he too was fighting back his emotions.

"Words cannot express my gratitude, Eleanor. You are an utterly unique human. Unlike anyone I have ever met."

"It means a lot that someone so holy thinks so highly of me," she replied. "Now, Edmund must be wondering what we're up to. I will tell him that you had a particularly disgusting tumorous lump on your lower back. You'd best add a little pucker to your shirt to support our story. Now, I'm famished, and I'm certain Edmund is too. Perhaps I will see you later this evening."

"Yes... yes, of course..." he said distractedly.

"I will stop in the powder room on my way back to the ballroom."

"Goodbye, Eleanor," he murmured.

And without letting Uma take one more covetous glance, Eleanor left Vibhishana alone in the conservatory to contemplate the many confusing revelations that destiny had just placed before him.

CHAPTER 26 – MEETING MR. PATEL

When Eleanor returned to the ballroom, the cocktail hour had cleared out, and an obliging servant pointed her towards the dining room. She cringed as she anticipated her second late entrance of the evening, to be followed up by several bold-faced lies to her husband, followed by an especially elaborate Rakshasa farce all night.

The only redeeming factor about the whole situation was her burning curiosity about watching Vibhishana and the Patels as they went about their human interactions. Would she notice any Rakshasa habits, or would they be so good at human farces that they'd hide every tiny clue? She wondered if they'd all consume an army's worth of food like Edmund would.

When she entered the massive gilded dining room, a servant escorted her to her seat beside Edmund at the center of the largest single dining table she'd ever seen in her life. She had trouble imagining that Queen Victoria's table could possibly have been any bigger.

As she probably should have guessed, they were seated directly across from the four Patels, and she was seated next to Mae. There was still an empty seat beside Edmund, a seat, no doubt, reserved for Lord Shiva.

"I hope everything's alright," Edmund whispered. "You were gone longer than I expected."

"Perfectly fine." She jumped right into her newest web. "Mr. Vishravan had a tumorous growth on his back that he wanted me to look at."

"Good lord," Edmund murmured. "At a dinner party?"

Eleanor smiled. It was, now that he pointed it out, an absurd thing for their Mr. Vishravan to ask her to do.

"I'm a nurse, darling. I'm used to similarly uncouth inquiries. Many people are too afraid to go to the doctor, but when they meet a nurse at a social event, they somehow feel like I'm not going to give them bad news."

"Well, was it?"

"Was it what?"

"Was it bad?"

"Darling, it is not good form to discuss anyone's health conditions at the dinner table." She glanced over to the Patels, who were watching them with great interest.

"No… no, I suppose not…" He noticed the Patel's attention, and blushed slightly at his social faux pas. "Well, little Rahul here was just telling me about his interest in trains. He knows quite a bit for a boy his age!"

"I'm six!" Rahul exclaimed as he held up his fingers to show her how many.

Eleanor laughed. "Are you in school then, Little Rahul?"

"Oh yes, I've been in school for two years already," he said proudly. "I can write in Gujarati and English and Hindi now."

474

"Perhaps you should write to our little friend Georgie," Eleanor suggested. "He's about ten, though. He shares your interest in trains."

"Is he in England?" Maya asked. "It would be great fun for Rahul to have a pen pal in England."

"Actually, he is in Gwalior…" Eleanor suddenly realized the awkward nature of her suggestion. "He is the maharaja's son."

"Oh my, the Maharaja of Gawlior!" Rohit laughed. "I'm not sure he accepts any letters sent from Baroda anymore."

"Oh Rohit," Maya said as she smacked him good-naturedly on the arm. "Not here. The maharaja is just at the end of the table."

While Rohit continued to chuckle at his own joke, Edmund continued more seriously. "The Maharaja of Gwalior does not hold any resentment towards the Maharaja of Baroda. He has told me so from his own lips."

"He is a good chap, isn't he? That Madho Rao? I've met him several times at various business functions," Rohit replied. "To be honest, it is that sharp-tongued wife of his that our maharaja finds so frightening. I've told him that he should just call up Madho Rao and invite him over for a cup of tea, but he hasn't mustered the courage yet."

"Rane is more reasonable these days," Eleanor chimed in.

"Rane? Are you on a first name basis with them?" Maya asked.

"We are. We know them quite well," Eleanor replied.

"I have known Madho Rao for decades now, and I think that our feuding maharajas would get along quite well these days," Edmund added. "Perhaps I'll suggest that they try to mend their fences if it seems appropriate in the conversation later tonight."

"Better you than me!" Rohit said jovially.

"What luck that you have come to us, Colonel, and you, Eleanor. May I call you Eleanor?" Maya addressed her.

"Please!" Eleanor exclaimed.

"We do not get such useful visitors here very often," Maya confided.

"Useful!" Rohit laughed. "What an adjective to use, my love! They aren't horses!"

Maya blushed. Eleanor found the gesture absolutely fascinating, as she had always assumed that Edmund's blushing was a human trait he'd inherited from his mother.

"I'm sorry, I didn't mean it offensively." Maya looked to her husband for some sort of confirmation, and then she continued her explanation. "It is just... a nurse who can teach other nurses is a blessing we have needed for months as we've worked on the hospital project. And now you can also solve a silly spat that has troubled our maharaja for decades... it just seems too good to be true."

"Perhaps Lord Vishnu sent them to us," Rohit suggested, "just as he sent you to me."

"Yes, dear, perhaps," Maya conceded. She glanced at Vibhishana's empty chair, and then relegated a look of worry with a soft smile.

As an army of servants brought in the first course and served it with perfectly synchronous moves, Eleanor suddenly noticed that she recognized the footman who was serving Maya. He didn't even glance at Eleanor as he returned to his position behind Maya's seat against the wall, but Eleanor stared at him for a long while until she realized who he was. He was Mélusine's stern Yaksha ally who had helped at their wedding! He continued to keep his focus entirely on Maya.

As a delicate bell dinged, everyone at the table picked up their spoons and politely began eating their soup. Edmund watched carefully to pick up on the pace, and then perfectly emulated the rest of the group. The Patels did exactly the same thing.

Radha was unusually silent as she ate her soup, but Rahul filled the void by re-engaging Edmund in a conversation about trains, and Miss Smith did her part by engaging Maya and Rohit in a conversation about the many pleasant day trips that could be made from Baroda for the weekend.

They continued in polite conversation through three more courses, and Eleanor began to wonder what had happened to Vibhishana. She hoped that he hadn't thrown in the towel and escaped to avoid another farce with Edmund, but as the servants brought in the main course, he slipped in without the help of a servant and took his seat beside Edmund, offering them each a polite nod of acknowledgement.

"Is everything alright?" Maya asked with a hint of nerves.

"Perfectly," he replied with a smooth smile. "Mrs. Marriner was kind enough to discuss some rather awkward personal topics with me, and now I have more clarity than I had before. I hope that my absence was not noticed by the maharaja?"

"He hasn't been around yet," Rohit reassured him.

"Well then, I'm interested in hearing all about the Marriners' honeymoon adventures. Colonel, Eleanor was telling me that you took the Orient Express across Europe, and then a steamer to Bombay? It sounds like quite a story!"

Edmund replied amicably, describing the mundane details with the skill of a fictional writer, while expertly avoiding the many secret climaxes of the stories, and Eleanor watched curiously as Vibhishana picked at his meal, taking in only the tiniest sips of the curried sauce. She glanced over at the Patels, and noticed that Maya and Radha were doing the same thing, while Rohit and Rahul were enthusiastically finishing up every last bite of their own.

When they were all finished, the maharaja made a speech thanking everyone for their support of the hospital, and then with a toast and a round of applause, a full western orchestra began playing in the ballroom, and the guests stood up to move into the next stage of the party.

Vibhishana made his way over to Rohit and whispered something into his ear, glancing towards Edmund and Eleanor. Rohit's eyes widened with recognition, and with a subtle pious nod to Vibhishana, he translated the message to Maya, who also glanced at them with new interest. With only a few words exchanged between them, the Patels were ready to initiate their next farce. Eleanor was fascinated to watch how they would go about it.

"Colonel, perhaps we can talk about your interests? I am in charge of staffing," Vibhishana proposed. "We can see if there is a position for you at Patel & Vishravan Pvt Ltd."

Edmund looked to Eleanor for approval.

"Mrs. Marriner, perhaps I can tell you more about the plans for the hospital," Maya suggested. "Would you like to see the models? They are in the maharaja's library."

"Yes, of course, that seems like a sensible place to start," Eleanor agreed.

"Come, Colonel. Let's talk over cognac in a quieter place," Vibhishana suggested.

Edmund squeezed Eleanor's hand and then followed Vibhishana out of the dining room.

"Radha, dear, will you please watch little Rahul for a bit?" Maya asked.

"Yes, of course," she agreed. "Come on, Rahul, let's go watch the musicians."

"I'm going to play the sitar!" he exclaimed.

"Let's choose a western instrument too. How about the violin?" She took his hand and led him away.

As soon as they were gone, Maya guided Eleanor in the opposite direction, down several hallways until they reached an enormous library with imposing murals depicting a very familiar story, surrounded by walls and walls of books. Rohit followed them, offering authoritative nods to the servants as they passed.

As soon as Maya closed and locked the door to the library, she took Eleanor's hands into hers.

"I knew there was something special about you the moment I saw you. What a treat! It is very rare indeed that we stumble upon another good Rakshasa. We must have so much in common! Now, tell me, where did you come from, Eleanor? Were you born from a womb, or did you fall from the sky? Have you been free for long?"

"I'm... er... not the Rakshasa," Eleanor said awkwardly. *Fall from the sky?* Her inner monologue added. *How alien!*

Maya looked into her eyes questioningly, and then looked her up and down again, assessing her clothing, her figure, her hair, and then returning to her exceptionally green eyes. She reached forward and felt the fabric of Eleanor's lehenga.

"My love, that is a very rude gesture." Rohit stepped in, taking Maya's hand into his.

"Your clothing is so perfectly tailored, I assumed that it was an extension of your Rakshasa form. You mean this is your natural form? The form Lord Vishnu gave you?"

"Shakti gave it to me." Eleanor smiled at the literal truth of the statement.

"Oh, yes, well, we Patels are Vaishnavist Hindus, but Shakti animates God for us too, so I suppose we mustn't squabble about the details," Maya replied. "You are very well-endowed, Eleanor. It is very unusual for a human to have such divine proportions... such distinct features. This hair is natural? I have never seen any like it."

"My love, those are rude questions too," Rohit whispered. "Humans do not like to discuss their physicality in such open terms."

"Then who is the Rakshasa?" Maya asked.

"Edmund is half Rakshasa," Eleanor replied.

"But he ate so much human food!" Maya exclaimed. "Where did it all go?!"

Eleanor laughed. "I wonder that myself quite often."

"I suppose little Rahul eats healthy human portions... then is Edmund a very human hybrid? Can he do anything Rakshasa?"

"He can move very fast..." Eleanor assessed her audience. "And he is an exceptional soldier. He can kill an enemy before they even realize he's there."

Maya shifted uncomfortably. "Yes, well, I suppose for a soldier that is a useful talent. It is a talent I have worked quite hard to avoid."

"So does he," Eleanor replied. "Oh, and he can speak every language."

"That is one of my favorites," Rohit said amicably. "It is so much easier to travel when Maya is with me." He guided Maya to the door. "But now, my love, Lord Vibhishana suggested that perhaps Eleanor and I should have a little chat to discuss the unique pleasures of being married to such wonderfully foreign creatures."

"Am I really still so foreign?" Maya asked with a combination of disappointment and resignation. "Even after adapting enough to human life to produce two children? I carried Rahul for nine whole months!"

"You have your moments, my love. Moments that I cherish."

He kissed her gently on the lips. "Now, perhaps you should go take a rest in the washroom for a bit, so that Edmund does not become suspicious of our time alone in here... Oh, and Maya, he doesn't know very much about Rakshasas. Lord Vibhishana has used a similar plan to how we are raising Rahul. It is important that we do not give away his own nature to him."

Maya nodded her agreement. "I will wait outside for you, dear. Eleanor, I hope that I didn't offend you with my comments? They were meant as a compliment. It is very rare for a human to be so naturally beautiful."

"I was not offended," Eleanor reassured her. "I hope that we can spend more time together, Maya."

"As do I." She closed them into the library.

Rohit gestured for Eleanor to take a seat on one of several plush velvet couches in the center of the room, and he took a seat across from her.

"It is a great wonder of the world that a creature can be so powerful and so innocent at the same time. It's like they are aliens in this world, discovering every human nuance for the first time. Don't you agree?"

"Yes, I suppose I do." Eleanor wrapped her dupatta around her front to give herself more modesty, and then she sat back and let her muscles relax in the comfortable position.

"I never realized how hard we are to understand until I tried explaining human tendencies to Maya. Every time she thinks she has mastered her humanity, she finds a new detail that is utterly perplexing."

"I would never have known she wasn't human based on what I witnessed tonight. She has done a wonderful job of adapting. Perhaps a slightly better job than Edmund has. Will she eat when she gets home?"

"She will drink gallons and gallons of hot honeyed milk," he laughed. "Does Edmund like it? We bought a dairy outside of town just to keep our supplies consistent."

"Doesn't your Yaksha butler just snap his fingers and make it for her?"

Rohit raised his eyebrows with surprise. "You know Mr. Montero?"

"He helped Mélusine at our wedding in England. We have never met formally."

"He will not be happy that you recognized him. He likes to go about his job unencumbered by human relationships… except for mine, of course… Maya doesn't like the flavor of Mr. Montero's approximations. She prefers real milk, and as it is one of the only human foods she consumes, there really was no other reasonable option. She is so happy with the fresh milk, and she needs it now that she is sleeping in a human bed every night. Otherwise she gets dreadfully dehydrated."

"Does her skin flake off like a snake's skin?" Eleanor asked. She was beginning to recognize Vibhishana's wisdom in connecting them. Suddenly, she was able to ask all sorts of bizarre questions she'd never thought she'd be able to ask anyone.

"She doesn't have real skin at all. Pieces of her just flake off if it is too hot and dry. We have a very large, humid conservatory for the summer months, although sometimes, if it's too hot, Maya must stay in her Rakshasa bed all afternoon."

"Ah, the Rakshasa bed." Eleanor smiled knowingly. "Do you sleep in it with her sometimes? I find that it's too strange to have Edmund's liquid swimming all around me. It distracts me too much for me to sleep."

Rohit smiled. "You have a very honest relationship to know so much about him already. Maya hid her liquid form from me for years, even after we were married. I only discovered it when she was so tired that she couldn't hold her human form anymore, and she splattered into the fountain in the living room."

"Oh my. What made that happen? Did she accidentally eat turmeric?" Eleanor hadn't even considered the possibility that Edmund's liquid might just drip right out of him in the living room.

"Thank goodness, no. I have only ever seen her turmeric reaction once, after a dinner party in Bombay. She became stiff as a board for hours! I thought my wife had been turned into a statue!"

"Oh no!"

Rohit laughed. "Mr. Montero got us home alright without any witnesses, and after a few hours in her Rakshasa bed she was fine. No, she collapsed because she'd been hiding her liquid form from me for so long, refusing to rest, that her plasma just went on strike."

"Her plasma?"

"It is what we call their metallic liquid. I'm not quite sure where the term comes from, but Lord Vibhishana uses it as well."

"Hrm… I suppose it makes sense that there is a unique word for it. It isn't exactly blood, is it?"

"It isn't blood at all. It is… for all intents and purposes, *them*."

"What happened with your staff when she splattered? Did you have servants around that you had to worry about? Or was it just

Mr. Montero? Edmund and I have been discussing whether or not it's wise to have uninitiated human servants in our household."

"We were lucky that time. There was no one around to watch her melt. We do have a human staff that Mr. Montero manages. For the most part it works, because we have a strong ally in him. He is very good at getting them out of the way when there's an emergency. Do you have an ally you can rely on?"

"Yes, actually. We do. I think he would be very helpful in a similar way now that you mention it, although I'm not sure that even he would be ready to see Edmund splatter into a fountain."

"I must admit, seeing Maya as a puddle in the fountain was more foreign than I'd imagined, even though I grew up to stories about the other virtuous Rakshasas in our family line."

"You have always known about Rakshasas?"

"The Patels of Baroda have married virtuous Rakshasas for centuries. Lord Vibhishana has always kept a close relationship with our family, and so we have always known that Rakshasas are real. But before Maya, it had been a very long time since a virtuous Rakshasa woman had escaped from Ravana's court. The last one was during the Moghul era, so I don't have any recognizable Rakshasa traits myself. The red sapphires didn't even have an effect on my grandfather."

"Red sapphires?"

Rohit reached into his pocket and pulled out a large gemstone that sparkled strangely in the electric lights. He handed it to her for her inspection. "They are the most powerful weapon against any Rakshasa."

"And you carry it with you? All the time?"

"I must carry it, because Maya cannot."

"But why do you have it at all?" Eleanor didn't like the idea of keeping a weapon with her to use against Edmund, even with his shell-shocked episodes. "Does Maya lose her temper and kill her enemies?"

Rohit laughed and took the red sapphire back. "No, Maya is the best tempered Rakshasa in the world. Even Lord Vibhishana can give into his demonic rage from time to time, but I have never once seen Maya give in. I find it hard to believe that she has any demonic side to her at all... No, the red sapphire is to ward off the evil ones. The bloodthirsty minions who are tasked with bringing her back to Ravana for punishment."

"Minions?" Eleanor's interest was piqued. "There are evil Rakshasas hopping about, doing Ravana's bidding?"

Suddenly she had a new primary candidate for the serial killer that was following them, killing their enemies.

"Oh yes. Although, there are fewer now than there were a while back. Ravana disposed of too many of them in his most recent war."

"I wonder why Vibhi didn't tell me that. It seems like a pertinent detail... Why are the minions after Maya?"

Rohit became more serious. "She escaped from slavery. And Ravana does not let his slaves escape. He won't rest until she's punished in front of the others, to make an example out of her."

"I would never have guessed that Maya had been a slave... how impressive that she has been able to build her life with so much trauma in her past."

"She never talks about it. I have never wanted to push her, but I do sometimes wonder what it was like for her. I wish that I knew more so that I could understand her better. When she sleeps in the human bed, she often awakens with wild shaking from her nightmares."

"Edmund has nightmares quite often too. From the war. His shell shock was quite bad. He is improving now that he has marriage to focus on. I hope that it stays a useful enough distraction when our honeymoon is over."

"Yes, I think Maya improved markedly when we were married. She has not regressed."

Eleanor smiled. "That is a truly comforting thing to hear." Eleanor paused as a thought occurred to her. "Rohit, did you know? Did you know what you were really getting into when you married Maya?"

He laughed. "No one really knows, do they?"

Eleanor joined him in his good cheer over his fair point. "I suppose there are always surprises."

"I knew that I would be taking on a great burden that came with a great reward. Both were true. How they made me feel was not something I could have predicted. Being the feeble mortal of the family is not something that I have ever enjoyed... In fact, I dislike it even more than I thought I would... but having a family and a beautiful life with Maya is better than anything else I could have imagined. There is a magic to it that the rest of humanity doesn't even know exists."

"I couldn't have said it better myself," Eleanor sighed.

"So, do you really think you might consider staying in Baroda? It would be quite nice to have another virtuous Rakshasa family in town."

"We were thinking more seriously about it than I anticipated," Eleanor admitted. "But Vibhi lives here? I don't think that Vibhi will want us to move here. He wants Edmund to be far enough away that he doesn't unduly influence him."

"Really? Why? Lord Vibhishana is the sacred guardian of all of the virtuous Rakshasas. He keeps a permanent room in our household."

"His treatment of Edmund is different for a number of reasons..." Eleanor hedged. She was quite certain that Vibhi had not confided Edmund's divine status, nor his lineage during the few words he'd exchanged with the Patels in the dining room. "I think that if he wants to discuss his reasons with you, he will probably find a time to do it himself."

Rohit smiled. "You know our world well already, Eleanor. Leaving Vibhi's secrets to him is always the wisest path."

A subtle knock at the door was followed by Maya peeking her head inside.

"The maharaja is looking for Eleanor, dear. He's going to make his pitch for her to stay."

"Well, we mustn't keep the maharaja waiting." Rohit stood up and offered Eleanor his hand.

She maneuvered out of her comfy position with his help, and then followed him out of the library.

"Your husband is deep in conversation with Lord Vibhishana in one of the parlors," Maya informed her. "I'm not sure where the maharaja has disappeared to. He was in the ballroom a few minutes ago. Perhaps he's still there."

"Were you not waiting in the washroom?" Eleanor asked curiously, as she'd found Rohit's initial suggestion to his wife to be somewhat odd to begin with.

"Oh, I was. But Mr. Montero was keeping an eye on things for me," Maya replied.

They returned to the ballroom, where the guests were dancing and the servants were scurrying around the edges, offering refreshments to the many people who were sitting around watching.

"I'm sure he's here somewhere," Maya said as she looked around again. "We do so hope that you will stay in Baroda, Eleanor!"

"My love, I'm sure he will find Eleanor when he wants her. Shall we dance before we lose the opportunity?" Rohit offered Maya his hand, and she giggled like a schoolgirl as she took it. Eleanor loved watching their exchange.

She took a seat and accepted a glass of champagne from a passing waiter, but after watching the mesmerizing movements of the crowd for several minutes, Radha startled her as she took a seat beside her.

"Eleanor, can I talk to you for a minute?" She had a reticence that hadn't been there before.

486

"Yes, of course."

"Perhaps… somewhere quieter?"

Eleanor nodded her agreement, and Radha took her hand and led her through several archways, across a sprawling lawn, and out into one of several manicured gardens, surrounded by tall secluding hedges.

Radha closed her eyes and listened intently, and when she was satisfied that they were alone, she sat down on a stone bench in the middle of the garden and gestured for Eleanor to join her.

"I have a confession to make, Eleanor."

"Yes?" Eleanor's heart began racing, although she had absolutely no idea what the girl might be ready to confess.

"I was listening in on your conversation in the library. I overheard Lord Vibhishana's advice to my father, and then I followed you and hid behind the stacks."

"I see…" Eleanor wasn't sure what to make of the confession. If the girl was a Patel, then surely what they'd spoken about couldn't have been so alarming.

"You are married to a Rakshasa?" she asked.

"Yes…"

"And you know Lord Vibhishana?"

"Yes."

"May I show you something, Eleanor? Something I've never shown anyone?"

"If you'd like…"

With a subtle wiggle, Radha's homely, overweight form morphed into a beautiful young woman. Her wide, brown eyes and long eyelashes complemented the other delicate features of her face, and her long, silken hair twirled itself into an elaborate crown of thick waves, held back from her face by jeweled combs. Her sari morphed into a much more elaborate lehenga, with an iridescent look to the color that shifted between silver and blue as the girl moved. Finally, intricate mehendi began at her fingers, and Eleanor watched as a new design traveled up from Radha's fingertips all the way to the edge of her blouse's short sleeves.

"This is who I really am," she confessed. "And my real name is Padma Patel."

"Why are you scared, Eleanor?" Padma asked nervously. "You've seen a Rakshasa transform before, haven't you?"

"I have..." Eleanor's inner monologue was screaming incoherent rants.

Padma got up, and looked around the garden, making sure that no one had witnessed her transformation.

"Why are you showing me this?" Eleanor could barely bring herself to look at the beautiful girl, but as she glanced over at her, she noticed that Padma had exactly the same proportions that she had come to recognize in herself. *Shakti's favorites...*

"I thought... I thought... I just really wanted to tell someone!" Padma exclaimed. "This Rakshasa farce is insufferable! I can't even say that my parents are my parents! And my little brother? Don't even get me started on the lies that I have to tell him! Oh, Eleanor, it's so awful!"

Padma plopped herself down right next to Eleanor on the bench in a decidedly adolescent move and sighed.

489

"Radha Patel is just a character. She is a character I have to play until Padma Patel is as old in human years as she looks. It is the only way I will be able to be myself later in public, because Rakshasas age too fast. All of Baroda thinks that Padma Patel is off with some cousin in Madras, while Radha has come to take her place for a while. It's all such a pain to keep straight."

"And how old are you?" The girl looked like she was about seventeen.

"Nine," Padma humphed. "I'm only three years older than Rahul. But he got the human genes, and I got the Rakshasa traits, and now I have to pretend I'm someone else for *six* more years!"

"Blimey."

Everything about the situation was so utterly unexpected that she had no idea how to move forward.

"Being a Rakshasa is insufferable," Padma sighed. "I hate everything about it. It's like God is playing a very mean trick on me."

"I know the feeling."

Padma took Eleanor's hands into hers, and Eleanor shivered.

"Isn't Edmund cold like I am?"

"He is sometimes, yes." Eleanor hadn't shivered because of Padma's frigidity. She'd shivered because of something else... that familiarity again... Eleanor closed her eyes and felt for it. Subtly, ever so subtly, there was that familiar pulsating power, and it felt too familiar... it felt... *exactly* like Edmund's.

Eleanor closed her eyes to engage Uma.

For god's sake! Now I have to hand-hold my husband's future wife?!!! Uma, this is outrageous!!! Wait... is she your next incarnation? Are you going to hop right into her and leave me alone?

She is the Avatar of Lakshmi, my child. I am the Avatar of Parvati. They are different aspects of Shakti, and they cannot be combined in such a way. We will have to wait until the next Avatar of Parvati is born.

And so, in the meantime, I am to prepare this child to marry my husband?

490

I'm sorry, my child. Destiny can play very cruel games. But you and Padma are more alike than you think. You are complementary aspects of Shakti. You are, in many ways, like sisters.

So my sister is going to marry my husband after I die?!

In some ways, she is already married to him, my child. Lakshmi is Lord Vishnu's wife. It is only in the earthly plane that they are not yet joined. It is the same for Lord Shiva and I. It is why we feel such magnetism around Vibhishana. Padma and Lord Kalki surely feel a similar magnetism that they do not yet understand.

This just keeps getting better and better, doesn't it? Thank you, destiny, for being such a bloody wanker.

Padma pulled her hands away. "I'm sorry, Eleanor. Should I not have done this? I thought that because you had married a Rakshasa, you might be willing to listen to me. I'm so desperate to talk to someone honestly. I feel like I haven't been honest in years… in my whole life!"

Eleanor sucked up her wild Celtic temper and subverted it with all of her might.

"Please, Padma, tell me whatever you want. I am a model of discretion," Eleanor said as she took Padma's hands back into hers.

Padma smiled gratefully, and she was even more beautiful than she had been when her features had been distorted by her anxiety.

"I was born in the wrong body, Eleanor. I'm sure of it."

"Many people feel like that, darling."

"Not like this," Padma argued.

Padma let go of Eleanor's hands and held her palms up. She grew out some craggy, black claw-like fingernails. As her eyes turned black, she closed them, took a deep breath, and retracted her claws back into her delicate decorated human fingers.

"Edmund is frightened by his dark tendencies too, but he has learned to live with them, and so will you. Certainly, your mother can help you?"

"She doesn't know. I'm not even sure that she knows how to do that herself. I have a darkness inside of me, Eleanor. A darkness that terrifies me."

"But surely your mother would understand your struggles, darling. Children often think that their parents won't understand, but the truth is, parents have had many life experiences that they don't want their children to know about. Life experiences that make them excellent people to confide in."

"I'm not a child," Padma humphed.

"A young woman?" Eleanor suggested diplomatically.

She sighed a long, melodramatic sigh. "I don't know what I am. I'm ancient and young at the same time. My body is grown up, but I have the urges of an adolescent. And then I have these wicked Rakshasa traits. I hate it. All of it. I have never found life so challenging to restart."

"I'm not sure I know what you mean."

Padma looked around the garden again, and then lowered her voice. "I am... different, Eleanor. Different from everyone, even my mother. It isn't just that I'm a Rakshasa... I'm something else too. Something that makes me feel things that I shouldn't... and remember things that I shouldn't... It's as if I'm two people at once, Padma Patel and... someone else. Someone ancient and tragic."

Eleanor squeezed Padma's hands. "Darling, you are not the only one with this problem."

"I'm quite sure that I am."

No, my child, you are not. I am Uma, Avatar of Parvati, Incarnation of Shakti.

Padma's eyes widened as Uma made herself known. Uma reached forward and kissed Padma's forehead, and they both startled as a spark ignited.

You are not alone, my child. You are not Shakti's only avatar, and you are not the only one who finds the dichotomy painful. Eleanor finds it similarly insufferable.

"She's right, I do," Eleanor admitted. "Although, Uma has helped me appreciate India's heat. Having another being riding around inside of you isn't entirely bad."

Eleanor closed her eyes and prepared a little surprise to help her case. She hoped it would work, although where her sudden empathy for the girl was rooted, she wasn't entirely certain. It didn't feel as if it was simply Uma overriding her own opinion of the matter. It was more like the sisterhood Uma had mentioned was taking hold of her.

As she heard the heavy breathing and the shuffling footsteps of her mount approaching from just beyond the hedges, she smiled.

"Sheranee, come say hello!" she called.

The tigress bounded straight for them, licking Eleanor's face happily, while Padma watched with wonder. When she was done greeting her mistress, Sheranee turned to Padma and licked her hand.

"You're an avatar, Eleanor? You're the Avatar of Parvati, and you chose to marry a Rakshasa?"

"Yes. Both of those things are true. But why do they surprise you?"

"No incarnation of Shakti should be married to a creature of darkness," Padma muttered.

"A creature of darkness?" Eleanor laughed. "Is Vibhishana a creature of darkness? Or your mother?"

"They are not normal Rakshasas, Eleanor. It is normal for Rakshasas to be evil. It takes exceptional character and self-discipline for Rakshasas to change their nature."

"I will admit that it seems to take some work for Rakshasas to subvert their violent tendencies, but that is true for everyone, darling. I have all sorts of horrible thoughts that I don't share, and that I don't act on. Surely my actions count more than my fancies?"

"Shakti should be an Avatar of Light. She should be a creature that does not have to fight its own nature to champion the cause of peace."

"And yet, she chose to manifest in you and in me, a virtuous creature of darkness, and a prickly Scottish thistle." Padma did not find her casual description amusing. "One thing I will say for her, is that she knows what she's doing, darling. I will admit that I don't always see her scheme, but I do believe now that she has one."

"I don't agree," Padma argued. "Shakti has made too many mistakes. Terrible mistakes that have ended in misery. Everything I do now is to escape from the pain of my own ancient mistakes."

Sheranee put her head in Padma's lap, and Padma began petting her and scratching her ears. Sheranee's purring was so loud, Eleanor had a passing worry that it might be audible all the way back at the party.

"Do you remember someone else's life?" Eleanor asked. "I have Uma's consciousness in me, but I don't have her memories."

Padma massaged Sheranee in silence for a long time before answering. "I remember everything. Five thousand years of painful lives and tragic deaths. And now, I am *this* creature. This monster. I'm finally powerful enough to defend myself, and instead, I must battle an inner demon far darker than the wicked witch who has hunted me for thousands of years."

"A witch has hunted you? Are witches real then? I always assumed they were imaginary... although, I suppose a lot is real that I thought was imaginary."

"I didn't mean it literally," Padma replied with a subtle adolescent eye roll. "Surpanakha has hunted me for five thousand years. She always finds me, and she always kills me. I have never once been able to escape."

"I'm sorry," Eleanor said as she put her arm around Padma's shoulders. Sheranee returned to licking Padma's hands. "I've run into Surpanakha. She made a surprise visit to our wedding, in fact,

494

with an aim to kill us. She was a terrifying creature… madder than a hatter."

"She didn't used to be so mad. She used to hunt me entirely out of malice, but at some point, the madness began to reign. It made her more clever in how she went about tormenting me…" She trailed off, and Eleanor let her put her head on her shoulder as she grimaced at the memory. "You faced Surpanakha just recently, and you survived? Did you use Shakti's power to defend yourself? I have never been able to get her divine power to work."

"I believe that Surpanakha chose to let us go. I don't know what will happen when we face her again. Sheranee might be able to help."

"Be careful. She's ruthless. She could kill Sheranee, and she wouldn't think twice about it. She would probably revel in the pain."

"Can she kill Sheranee? I assumed that she was immortal."

She is very strong and very clever, my child, but she is not immortal. Surpanakha could kill her.

"Bugger. Uma says that Sheranee isn't immortal. So, I don't know what we'll do if we face Surpanakha again. Hopefully Mélusine and Kuveni will be able to help."

"You should not summon Kuveni," Padma warned. "Surpanakha would love to enslave her. You must keep Kuveni as far away from Surpanakha and Ravana as possible."

"Blimey, I wish she'd mentioned that sooner."

"The Yakshas do not like to discuss their weaknesses."

"It is a sensible plan."

Eleanor suddenly realized that it didn't feel like she was talking to a young girl anymore.

"You really are trapped between two beings, aren't you? You are this young Rakshasa girl, and you are…?"

"I am Sita." Padma pet Sheranee even more vigorously. "I have never told anyone that truth before, not even my mother."

"Sita?" Eleanor knew that she knew the name.

"The ancient queen of Ayodhya. The wife of Lord Rama. The Seventh Avatar of Lakshmi. The heroine of *The Ramayana*. And the most tragic woman in history."

"Blimey, that's a load of baggage, isn't it?"

Padma finally smiled. "Yes, it is."

Eleanor could not believe that she was about to give Padma a pep talk, but she hunkered down and banished every selfish voice in her head. "You have your own life, Padma. You are a young, powerful, charitable, loving girl. I watched you giving alms in the streets a few days ago, and Miss Smith told me how beloved you are in Baroda because of all your good work. You convinced a *firang* couple with very busy lives to consider moving to Baroda in less than a five-minute conversation! You have the ability to do all sorts of wonderful things that normal humans can't even imagine. You can make yourself into whomever you want to be."

"It is not so simple, Eleanor."

"Why not?"

"So many reasons…"

"Would you like to tell them to me?"

Padma sighed sadly. "I'm still married, Eleanor. I'm married to Rama, and Rama is alive. He is hopping about somewhere on Earth right now, hoping desperately to find me so he can woo me again. My fate has been the same for five thousand years. Rama finds me. Rama marries me. Surpanakha kills me. I'm trapped in a never-ending cycle of agony."

"Why don't you just refuse to marry him this time?" Eleanor couldn't believe she was suggesting that the girl keep herself open for a future with Edmund, but she cared more about solving the girl's woes than she cared about being selfish.

"I can't, Eleanor. We're already married."

"I'm not sure I understand," Eleanor admitted. "If you're already married, why do you marry him again in each lifetime?"

"I have never remembered who I was before. That pain is unique to this lifetime. In every other lifetime, I've gone about in blissful ignorance until my prince found me and married me, and then the monster killed me. Every time, every bloody time, it was a surprise. But now... now I know too much. I know that I am Sita, I can hardly tell the difference between her mind and mine, and Sita is still married to Rama." Her eyes turned black. "But Padma hates Rama. It is his fault that I'm trapped in this cycle. He ruined every chance that I have to ever be happy. He put his pride above everything else, and I am still paying for his mistakes five thousand years later. God, I hate him. But Sita is too weak to hate him. She's only lost, unable to stop loving him."

"That does sound confusing." Eleanor genuinely sympathized with the girl's complicated plight, more so now than ever with her own recent conflict between Uma's feelings and her own on the topic of Vibhishana. "When Uma and I disagree, it is very difficult to control myself. I must fight her with a kind of tenacious energy that is very draining."

"Does Uma hate Edmund?"

"No. I'm grateful that she doesn't."

"Then you cannot possibly understand the conflict that is tearing me apart. I am married to a man I hate, whom I haven't even met yet in this life."

"Could you... er... divorce him?"

Padma laughed. "Divorce doesn't exist in Hinduism, Eleanor. I would have thought Uma had taught you that already."

"But certainly death parts you? Were you not dead before you came back to Earth in this lifetime?"

"It is different for avatars. It is different for me, and for Rama. We cannot escape each other. Our fates are completely intertwined. Even if I wanted to be with another man, Lord Vishnu wouldn't allow it."

Unless he were Lord Vishnu... Eleanor barely held the thought in.

"Well, if I were you, I would banish Sita's voice and live my life, Padma. You have hundreds of years ahead of you to explore the world, to help people and find activities that fulfill you, and to avoid repeating history. Perhaps it's part of Shakti's plan for you to keep the memories that will free you from your past."

"They don't free me. They enslave me."

"Perhaps they will free you in the future, darling, after you've gained more life experience. You're only nine years old, after all. When I was nine, I had no idea what the real world was. I discovered that the next year when my father killed himself and my family was thrown into destitution."

"Shiva's wrath, Eleanor. Really?"

"Shakti chose the daughter of a polygamist as her avatar, Padma. Just like she chose a Rakshasa. Perhaps it is our shameful struggles that give us the strength to be braver and more powerful than we've ever been."

Padma pulled Eleanor into a hug. "Thank you, Eleanor." A violet tear worked its way into the corner of her eye. "So you really think that a Rakshasa can transcend her darkness? I'm so afraid of what I might do with the power of Lakshmi and my Rakshasa darkness combining."

"Darling, Edmund is one of the most virtuous men in the world. If Ravana's son can be the world's next messiah, then really, you have nothing to worry about."

As soon as the words came out of her mouth, Eleanor and Uma cringed in unison. Sheranee looked up, and Padma froze. She had just flippantly given away two of her most guarded secrets at once. If she could have buried herself in the earth at that moment, she would have.

"What do you mean by that, Eleanor? Are you saying... are you saying that *Edmund* is Ravana's son?"

"I... I... I..." Eleanor found herself at a rare loss for words. "I didn't mean it in that way..."

"He is, isn't he? I wondered where another virtuous half Rakshasa came from! Shiva's wrath, this can't be happening! It can't be true! Shakti can't be married to Ravana's bloody Rakshasa heir! Do you have any idea what that monster has done?! He should have no progeny, ever! His line should end when Rama slays him!"

Padma blurred to the edge of the garden, and Eleanor rushed in a panic to stop her.

"You can't tell Edmund anything, Padma. Do you understand? It is Lord Vibhishana's golden rule."

"*That* is not his golden rule," Padma shot back, channeling a moment of adolescence again.

"Fine, it is one of his rules," Eleanor countered. "You mustn't tell Edmund anything. He doesn't even know exactly what Rakshasas are yet. He thinks that Vibhi is his father."

"Shakti has a plan?!" Padma shouted. "Shakti knows nothing! It's just the same folly as always, except now the bloody monsters are running the show!"

She burst forth an enormous pair of golden falcon wings from her back, and in a blur, she disappeared into the night sky.

"Blimey," Eleanor whispered. "I've made a real mess of it this time, haven't I, Sheranee?"

You have seeded a great change, my child. We will have to wait for the eventual outcome, but Padma must not confront Edmund. It is pivotal that they stay apart for now.

Eleanor hugged Sheranee one final time, and then released her back to her divine perch. She stalked off into the darkness and disappeared.

Eleanor took a deep, calming breath, and readied herself to make her next move… what exactly that was yet, she had no idea.

She scampered across the lawn, back into the palace, and as she reached the ballroom, she noticed Maya's Yaksha butler standing in the corner, looking bored. She glanced around to make sure that Edmund wasn't around, and then she made her plan.

"Monty?" she whispered as she stood beside him casually.

He glanced down at her, barely giving away his surprise.

"Mr. Montero, I've made a mess. A terrible mess. I said something that I shouldn't have to Padma…" Now she really had his attention… "and she flew off in a huff! Do you know where Vibhi is? I need to ask him what to do!"

Mr. Montero gestured for her to follow him into an empty sitting room. He glanced around, scrutinizing all of the corners until he was sure that they were alone.

"Madame, who are you? How are you acquainted with Mr. Vishravan?"

"Blimey, Monty, I'm Eleanor! Eleanor MacLeod Marriner? Edmund's wife?! You were at my bloody wedding! You know, in Basingstoke, a few weeks ago?"

As a look of recognition dawned in his expression, he relaxed slightly. "Madame, I was only there for a few minutes, when Lady Mélusine summoned me."

"Well, now you know who I am, and I need your help!" Eleanor was losing her patience, and Uma reached forward and grabbed Mr. Montero's hand. It pulsated with Yaksha warmth.

Oberon, you must find Lady Padma. You must console her and be her ally. She will be too alone with her secrets and her sorrow without you. Go. Find her. Help her. It is Shakti's will.

Eleanor let go of his hand, and he looked at her again with a combination of fear and puzzlement.

"Don't tell anyone that I am the Avatar of Shakti," Eleanor whispered. "Not even Vibhishana."

Monty looked into her glowing green eyes one last time. "I am at your command, my lady."

He looked around, ensuring their privacy, and with a subtle pious bow, he dissolved to fulfill his sacred duties.

"Well, that was one option…" Eleanor muttered.

She looked around again, now at a total loss about what to do next. She took a deep breath, and then made her way back to the ballroom. She took another glass of champagne from a silver tray and guzzled it down, collecting a second one for the road, without the energy to care whether anyone was watching her impolite consumption.

"Dearest?! I've been looking everywhere for you!" Edmund grabbed his own champagne from the tray as he skipped up to her cheerfully. "The ball is almost over, and we've been so consumed with business that we haven't even had a dance!"

"Yes, I suppose we should dance…"

Mr. Montero will see to Padma. Be with Lord Kalki now, Eleanor. There is nothing more you can do.

He downed his champagne in one Rakshasa gulp and then whisked her into his arms. She gave into his lead, and this time, unlike at their wedding, as he twirled her around the dancefloor, she began to feel the pulsing of the beat and the rhythm of the other dancers, and she felt perfectly natural flitting about in Edmund's arms. She even improvised a few movements of her own, to Edmund's great enjoyment.

As they twirled and they twirled, she pushed all of her raging fears out of her mind alongside her guilt from her many failures and her pessimism about her future, and she let her gentle husband pretend for one more magical hour that they did not live in a painful, complicated world where creatures of darkness and avatars of light were one and the same.

She had a sneaking suspicion that she wasn't going to escape from the ugly realities of the real world for long. When the clock stuck midnight, she would be back in the arms of a tormented divine demon, and she would still be a conniving, dishonest wife, putting lofty visions of the greater good above her husband's right to know the truth.

She sighed wistfully. *If only the clock could stop.* But, alas, by morning, the real world would return, more complicated than ever.

PART FIVE
THE KNIGHT AND THE DRAGON

CHAPTER 28 – GRUMP DAY

Eleanor yawned as she threw her legs off of the side of the bed and looked around the room. Edmund was still sleeping soundly. Heavy silk curtains blocked most of the morning light, and she had very little sense of what time it was. She slipped on some silk slippers, and just as she was going to scamper across the cool marble floor to the WC, she heard the subtle swoosh of an envelope being pushed underneath the bedroom door.

"Mr. Valov, what are you up to?" she whispered as she gathered it up.

They'd been in Hyderabad for over a week already, and Mr. Valov had been even more secretive than usual. He had skillfully deflected all attempts that she'd made to learn what he'd been up to after they'd left Agra, and her reconnaissance had been made especially difficult by his annoying tendency to disappear for long swaths of the afternoon on supposed minor errands—laundry, groceries, and collecting the English newspaper—that Edmund insisted he shouldn't be doing himself at all with the profusion of eager local boys on the stoop downstairs begging for work.

With Mr. Valov's begrudging help, they'd procured a temporary rental from one of the Nizam's low-level administrators, and had taken out a month-long lease that Edmund had giddily signed without much forethought about the ensuing logistics.

On the plus side, it was a surprisingly luxurious three-bedroom flat in a well-kept building on a hill by the Nizam's seasonal monsoon palace with a grand, sweeping view of the old city. It had the modern conveniences of running water and electricity paired with nice balconies, tasteful Arabian-styled furniture, and so many designs inlaid in the marble of the floors, the walls, and the intricately carved mahogany ceilings that Edmund found himself distracted by appreciating the craftsmanship several times a day as he was just going about his business.

"Look here, dearest! The geometric pattern changes ever so subtly in this corner! It changes how the dimensions of the room look! Genius… pure genius…"

She was glad he had something to occupy his mind, as the downsides of their choice had become obvious rather quickly. Most importantly, the fresh air and beautiful views that had bewitched them came with the inconvenient concession that they were rather far from everything. Far from all but the most basic of restaurants. Far from the old city (and up a hill that felt torturously mountainous to climb in the heat, even for her). Far from cabs and horses and carts for hire. And very, very far (to Mr. Valov's obvious dismay) from the British garrisons housed in Secunderabad, a relatively new cantonment that had been built on the other side of the Hussain Sagar lake several decades earlier to house thousands of British troops who were enjoying the hospitality of India's richest and most well-connected princely ruler.

On top of the inconvenience of the location, they'd quickly come to realize that despite their cute balconies, they had very little outdoor space in which to lounge about, and most importantly, they had absolutely no privacy. Every time they took a seat on the terrace with a glass of wine, Memsahib Fatima next door found her way onto the neighboring balcony to stare at them disapprovingly until they gave up and went inside. But even inside, they had no refuge from the overly communal living situation. They could hear their barefoot neighbors shuffling about in the hallway at all hours, incessantly sweeping with an old-fashioned broom made of sticks, that she was quite sure only puffed the dust right up into the air for it to land right down again where it had begun. But the greatest challenge to their marital bliss had reared its ugly head on their first night, when they had become aware as the upstairs and downstairs neighbors respectively banged broom handles at them from the ceiling and the floor, that the neighbors could hear every peep emanating from their apartment… and from them.

The blow to their mood from their mundane tribulations had been more palpable than either of them had expected, although Eleanor had a sneaking suspicion as to why.

When she'd told her giddy husband the morning after the ball that she'd decided that Baroda wasn't the best place for them to live after all—that they should explore their options before jumping into a hasty commitment—he'd been noticeably disappointed. But, she'd convinced both of them that his home town was the best place they could have gone in the world to remind him that there were many good choices for their future abode, and so Eleanor had set out to do everything she could to emulate the relaxed domestic life that they had tantalizingly tasted in Baroda. It was a much harder task than she'd expected.

She'd been forced to increase her efforts when, after several days of searching, they discovered that the flat Edmund had grown up in with Abdul Barr had been burned in a fire several decades earlier and replaced with a non-descript building which now housed a very ordinary retailer of rickshaw accessories on the first floor.

After that dismal discovery, they'd spent several days wandering aimlessly around the Charminar bazaar, as neither of them were particularly interested in growing their collection of tchotchkes, and Eleanor was quite sure that she already had all the bangles she could ever need from Shruti's collection.

As the days wore on, she had been forced to admit to herself that Hyderabad wasn't the easiest city for her to live in. The very high percent of Muslim women in the old city made her stand out even more than she had anywhere else in India, and despite the freedom from passing gawkers that a niqab offered (she'd worn one around several times already), she didn't like hiding herself away. She had far preferred the liberal, multi-cultural city of the maharaja's 'golden age' in Baroda (as the locals had deemed it, a term Eleanor now wholeheartedly agreed with more than ever with her new comparison), where she could pick and choose how she wanted to present herself based on her mood.

She'd voiced a similar point to Edmund the prior day, to his great disappointment (although, he admitted that his childhood had been generally devoid of women, and so he had never paid much attention to how their experience was different from his in the city that he loved so much), and so he'd proposed that they take a day trip across the city to explore the ruins of Golconda Fort, a massive monument that had once been the fortress of a great Hindu empire, and, even more interestingly, that had been ruled by one of India's most famous queens—Rudrama Devi—a queen that many legends asserted was an incarnation of Shakti herself. Uma could not confirm nor deny the claim.

She refocused her attention on the mysterious envelope that had been slipped under the door of their bedroom. It was made of a delicate parchment, unlike anything she'd ever seen. She carefully broke through a red wax seal and removed a matching piece of parchment. In elaborate, old-fashioned cursive it read:

Happy Birthday, our dearest boy.
May you celebrate this day with joy in the arms of your beloved.

508

With all our love,
Kate Marriner & Sir Percy Blakeney

Eleanor looked back at the seal and smiled at the joke. As she ran her finger over the petals of a scarlet pimpernel, the seal miraculously returned itself to an untouched state.

"Blimey, Kuveni. I hope you know what you're doing. Vibhi will be livid if he finds out," she whispered.

"But you are a model of discretion, Eleanor dearest, and so we have nothing to worry about," Kuveni's disembodied voice replied.

Eleanor sighed with resignation and brought the letter to Edmund's bedside. She sat down beside him, and kissed his forehead. "Wake up, darling. I have a surprise for you."

He opened his eyes and took in his awakening Rakshasa breath, smiling as he observed her naked state.

"Good morning, dearest." He sat up. "Did you say that you had a surprise for me?"

He ran his cold finger across her bare breast, and she shivered.

"Waking up to my naked body is hardly a surprise, darling. It is a given."

"Marriage really is all it's cracked up to be then, isn't it?" He tickled her sides until she exploded into giggles.

"I have a better surprise for you."

She handed him the letter.

"What strange parchment. Where did it come from?"

"You should open it!"

He inspected the seal with puzzlement. "I haven't seen a seal like this in decades... not since I was living in Bath."

"Open it!"

Eleanor was finding the game rather exciting now, and she was glad that Kuveni had taken the risk for her entertainment.

He carefully broke the seal and read the note several times, furrowing his brow, and then looking around the room, scrutinizing the curtains and the door to the wardrobe, as if his guardians might be hiding inside, waiting to hop out and yell 'surprise.'

"What is it, darling?" Eleanor asked innocently.

"Apparently, it's my birthday."

"Apparently?"

"I have never known what day my birthday was. Apparently, they've known the whole time, and they decided not to tell me until now."

Eleanor was entirely certain that Kuveni had not anticipated this reaction.

"Perhaps they think you're ready to know more, darling." Eleanor repositioned herself to rub his shoulders.

"Still, it's taken them over a hundred years to tell me something so important about myself. It feels as if I have been wronged in some way."

Great misery will descend upon those who thwart destiny, Uma murmured. *Kuveni was not supposed to share this information yet. Now you can see, Eleanor, what happens when we give into our selfish desires. It only hurts the ones we love.*

"Darling, I'm sure that they sent you this letter out of love. They were probably thinking of you after our encounter on the steamer and decided to send you a little hello on a day that they cherish."

"I suppose."

He put the letter down on the bedside table and gave into her massaging strokes for a few minutes, until he sighed unenthusiastically, as if the wind had been taken right out of his sails.

"I suppose we ought to get dressed. It will probably take at least two hours to get to Golconda Fort. Possibly three or four if the roads are too busy. Today is the main market day. Hordes of people will be coming into town from the countryside, and they never know how to drive."

510

"We could always postpone our excursion, darling. We've rented this flat for an entire month."

"What else am I to do? Sit around moping?"

He was far more upset about the entire thing than Eleanor had predicted.

"We could do something nice to celebrate your birthday. We could explore the market, and ask Memsahib Basimah to make you a special birthday biriyani!"

At Eleanor's mention of the elderly woman downstairs who had been feeding them wonderful homemade meals for the last several days, ever since Eleanor had run into her in the hallway and engaged her, with Uma's help, in a jovial Hindi conversation, Edmund's posture deflated even more.

"And what am I to tell her, dearest? That we are celebrating my hundred and… something birthday? I don't even know how old I really am! And I am so much older than you are. Let's not forget to think about that. I'm practically a cradle-robber."

"Darling, I've been a spinster for decades," Eleanor argued.

"And I've been an old man for almost a century."

Eleanor stopped her massage and took her position next to him to look into his eyes. She put her hand gently on his cheek.

"What is it, Edmund? What's really bothering you? Surely a loving birthday card isn't the only thing on your mind?"

"I hate birthdays," Edmund griped. "Celebrating other people's birthdays has always reminded me how different I am. Now that I have one, it doesn't make me feel any better! I'm still the awkward stranger, being gawked at by everyone who passes by, and somehow, being here, I've remembered how lost I felt the last few years I was with Abdul Barr. I was longing so dearly for Mr. Johnson to come and collect me—for my father to come and take me home. And then he came and took me to Bath, but he didn't stay! It was a fine place, and Mrs. Hopper was perfectly kind, but it was not my home, and I did not have a family."

"But, darling, you have a family now. Shouldn't we celebrate the fact that you are in your hometown, on your birthday, with your wife?"

Eleanor enticed him into a kiss. He gave in only slightly, and then pulled away.

"I'd forgotten that I did not always love Hyderabad so much, and now I've brought you here, and you don't love it either. I thought it would be romantic, but it feels too empty. I suppose I was foolish to build up so many fantasies in my mind about how it would be, but really, dearest, the whole thing is making me quite a grump."

"Aw," Eleanor said as she kissed him again. "You're allowed to be a grump sometimes, darling. Especially on your birthday. I don't like my birthday either. It reminds me that I'm only getting older…" She cringed. She should have known better than to remind him of her mortality. "Well, shall we burn your birthday letter then? And say no to birthdays altogether?"

He smiled half-heartedly. "I suppose they only meant it nicely. I think we'd better just go about our business, pretending that it isn't Grump Day."

"So, to the fort?"

"To the fort."

She gathered up one of the simpler floor-length Islamic abaya-style salwar kameez suits that Kuveni had made for her and wrapped the dupatta loosely around her hair. Edmund, on the other hand, dressed himself up in his British khaki suit. Eleanor could tell then exactly how grumpy he was to pass up the opportunity to revel in the fashions of his youth.

"I'm curious to see what the Hindu part of town looks like," she said. "I assume it must be quite different than the Islamic center."

"It's not really the Hindu part of town either. The old Muslim rulers of Hyderabad built their tombs over there, and they added to the medieval fort with their own Moghul designs."

512

"Right then. At least we will have a little adventure."

Edmund walked to the door without even glancing back at her. "I'll go see if there's any roti left from dinner last night. The food in that part of town isn't usually very inspiring."

Eleanor hopped into the WC and then joined Edmund in the kitchen as he opened every cupboard and drawer, with increasing disappointment. His stomach grumbled.

"I hate birthdays," he muttered.

"Colonel?" Mr. Valov called. He was already dressed and looked like he'd been up for hours as he joined them in the kitchen.

"Tell me, Leo, is there anything in this house that a man can eat, or do I need to start grinding down the marble to make some bread?"

Mr. Valov threw Eleanor a questioning look.

"I can send the boy downstairs out to get some snacks. Remind me what to tell him to buy?"

"Chaat!" Edmund exclaimed. "It's called bloody chaat! You've only heard the word a hundred times in the last month. Are two languages the maximum that a human brain can handle?"

Now Mr. Valov was really alarmed.

"It is Edmund's birthday," Eleanor explained quietly. "But we are going to call it Grump Day from now on."

"Make that Hungry Grump Day," Edmund griped.

Mr. Valov cleared his throat and straightened his posture. "Colonel, the Nizam needs an answer to his invitation."

Edmund's eyes turned momentarily black, and Eleanor threw Mr. Valov an even more concerned look.

"Darling, what is Leo talking about?"

"The answer is still no!" Edmund shouted. "How many languages do I need to say it in, Leo? No, *Ne, Neit, Nein, Non, Nahin!*"

Mr. Valov glanced at the cigarette holder in his pocket, and then took a deep breath and abstained. "But, Colonel, it is a dangerous snub to keep refusing his invitations. You are risking a diplomatic situation, and the army is not going to be happy. It is your duty as an active colonel in His Majesty's army to represent Britain in its full diplomatic glory when the circumstances require it."

Edmund laughed with disbelief. "And, prey, Leo, how exactly will I be helping the glory of Britain by moseying down to the Nizam's outrageously ostentatious palace to perpetuate this wretched aristocratic farce with a smile on my face? How many times do I need to tell the bloody world that I am not the goddamned Earl of Easton?! You'd think Ravi Bidkar had bestowed the real bloody title on me!"

"Colonel, I have reiterated many times in my discussions with the Nizam's administrators that you do not acknowledge the title, and they don't care. The Nizam is becoming very unhappy at your continuous snubbing of his invitations to dinner, and his support is important to the British Raj. He recently discovered that you are on a first-name basis with the Maharaja of Gwalior, and that you attended a ball at the Maharaja of Baroda's palace, and now he is even more obsessed about wooing you into attendance for one of his lavish dinners. He has even offered to host you at Falaknuma palace up the hill for *your* convenience. Do you know when the last time was that the Nizam did anything for someone else's convenience?"

"Bloody never, and this is no different. He just wants to add me to his collection of pansy lord acquaintances, like he collects his cars and his diamonds and his concubines. I won't be an object for the richest man on Earth to covet for the sake of petty greed, Leo. You can tell them all to go to Hell."

Leo let out a long sigh of stress and walked out onto the terrace to light up a cigarette.

Edmund watched him, and then began pacing.

"Darling?" Eleanor began with the tone that she used when she was coaxing her patients into telling her the truth. "Please talk to me. You have been refusing invitations from the Nizam? Why didn't you tell me?"

"It didn't matter. The answer was no."

Eleanor worked hard to keep her Celtic temper at bay at his blatant exclusion of her from his decision.

"Darling, it is clearly bothering you. I thought we shared everything?" She stomped down a burst of guilt at her lie. "Why are you so reluctant to accept the invitation? We have had two quite pleasant interactions with princely leaders in India in these last few weeks. Did the Nizam do something to make you dislike him?"

Edmund finally stopped his pacing and plopped himself down on a divan, leaning forward with his elbows on his knees and his head in his hands as he thought through his response. Eleanor took a seat beside him mirroring his position and waited patiently for his explanation.

"I don't deserve to have dinner with the Nizam, Eleanor. I have done nothing to deserve it. I earned our invitation onto the Maharaja of Gwalior's train, and you earned our invitation to the Maharaja of Baroda's ball, but the Nizam's interest in us is purely out of misguided self-interest, believing that another visit from an English lord will make him feel more important."

"But, darling, we don't have to earn every tiny thing in life, do we? Sometimes things just happen. Invitations are given, opportunities are placed in front of us on a silver platter. I agree that I value earning my keep, but surely we shouldn't turn down opportunities simply because they were handed to us? Perhaps we can earn our position at his table another way. Perhaps there is something that he needs to hear that only we will be able to tell him."

"That sounds a bit more religious than I expected from you, dearest. Do you really believe that there is some grand order around us? Some order that cares whether or not we attend an aristocratic dinner party?"

Eleanor smiled. "Well, when you put it like that, it sounds a bit foolish, but I will admit, darling, that the great fortune of our meeting has me optimistic that there is, perhaps, some meaning in all of it that I didn't believe was possible before I met you."

He stopped to think about the idea for a long while.

"When I was a child in Hyderabad, the Nizam was like a god. He was on an untouchable plane above all of us. When Abdul Barr took me to the palace to paint his portrait, I couldn't believe my eyes. It was as if I'd been transported into a completely different world, and despite the beauty of the artistry all around, I felt sick when I saw it. It was as if the gods were lounging about in the lap of luxury while the people were starving outside. There had just been a famine, and Abdul Barr and I had spent weeks giving alms. I'd thought the whole time that the plight belonged to all of humanity, but when we entered the palace through the servants' door to the kitchen and I saw the colossal volume of food ready to be served, I couldn't contain myself. It took Abdul Barr hours to console me as I cried in the corner."

Eleanor took his hand gently into hers. "That must have been very jarring for you as a young boy."

"It was the first time I realized exactly how unequal the world was. Throughout all my time at the orphanage, and in Abdul Barr's spartan care, I had no concept of what excess was afforded to a select few as a birthright. Abdul Barr told me that Allah had designed it that way, and then I asked him why he worshipped a god who would design a world where some men would gorge while others would starve. He told me that I should look into myself for such answers, and so I did."

"And?"

He sighed. "I came back with nothing. I still don't understand it one bit. I understand it even less after watching so many virtuous boys die horrific deaths in the trenches. The only conclusion I can make is that there is no order, because if there were, such inequality would be intentional, and I choose not to believe in a god who would be so cruel."

Eleanor kissed him gently on the cheek. God, how she loved her husband. Every time she dug deeper into his complicated, noble psyche, she loved him even more.

"You've managed to accept some aspect of luxury in your life," she pointed out. "Do you feel the same disgust when you are at Ravi Bidkars'? Or when we were on Madho Rao's train?"

"I have learned to live with the world around me," he shrugged. "But Ravi and Madho Rao are both virtuous men. They use their privilege to help the less fortunate. If I were them, I'd like to think that I'd do more, but I suppose I too have a weakness for hedonism. If I didn't, I'd have spent my entire fortune helping the needy decades ago…" He trailed off with a grimace of guilt.

"One man can't change the world single-handedly, darling. You have done quite a bit to help worthy causes. We had four tables at our wedding made up entirely of the leaders of charities you'd patronized."

He sighed with resignation. "It is never enough. If I think too much about it, it depresses me, and I don't need anything else to depress me on Grump Day."

"I am always glad to meet a man who knows his own limitations." Eleanor kissed him again. "Now, given your extra century of experience, are you sure that you don't want to give the Nizam's invitation a shot? Perhaps you can subtly comment on his excess in a way that will make him think twice about it."

Edmund shook his head. "If I go have dinner under the Nizam's crystal chandeliers, served by his obsessively deferential servants, sitting amongst the beautiful village girls he has acquired for his harem, it will be wrong. I don't belong there."

"He has a harem? In 1923?"

"He doesn't call it that anymore, but it is what it is. The set-up is allowed by Islamic law, and he sees no fault in it."

"I suppose he's given excess a whole new meaning."

Edmund guffawed. "You have no idea, dearest."

Eleanor kissed him again and then stood up and pulled him into her arms. "I love you, Edmund. I love you more and more every time I learn something new. You are such a beautiful person."

He twirled her into a romantic dip, but as she giggled, another round of broom banging from the apartment brought their moment of cheer to an abrupt end.

"We will be going out for the day, Leo," she called. "If you could please procure us some dinner for when we return home, preferably from Memsahib Basimah, or from anyone else who does not need to grind marble into bread like an ogre, we would be most grateful. And perhaps you should raid our stash of wine. I suspect we will be leaving Hyderabad sooner than we'd originally planned."

"Thank god," Mr. Valov muttered.

"So you don't like it either?" Edmund practically shouted the question.

Mr. Valov dropped his cigarette butt onto the balcony and squished it out with his shoe. Edmund watched the gesture with displeasure, and then admonished him more sternly than Eleanor expected. "I've told you many times now, Leo, you should take your shoes off when you're inside."

"I'll try harder to remember, Colonel."

"You didn't answer my question," Edmund reiterated without softening his tone.

"To be honest, Colonel, I don't like it here. We are miles and miles from the British garrisons, and I find these Mohammedans dastardly difficult to read. Every time I think I know what's going on, they do something bizarre."

"Perhaps, Mr. Valov, you are not communicating properly. You are in their city. Did it ever occur to you that you should be accommodating them?"

Leo couldn't hide his frustration with Edmund's assertion. "This is British India now, Colonel. I shouldn't have to remind you."

Eleanor took Edmund's hand as she felt his heart tick up at the confrontation. "Darling, we have had a nice time here. Why don't we plan to continue along our honeymoon adventure? What was that place you were talking about a few days ago? Munnar? Tea plantations in a cloudy jungle sound lovely, and you and Mr. Valov will both benefit from a break from the heat."

"Anything to get out of this bloody nightmare." He let her distraction stand, although his foul mood had returned with even greater force.

Eleanor led him to the door.

"Thank you for your help, Leo!" she called.

Without waiting for his response, she guided Edmund down the two staircases and to the road. It was deserted. So far, every day there had been a cart or two that they'd been able to procure from the begrudging owners for an exorbitant foreign premium, but now the street was completely empty.

"Birthdays…" Edmund muttered.

"I'm sure we will be able to get one on a bigger street."

Eleanor led him down the road, to the next road, and then the next, until they finally reached a haphazard traffic circle that was trapped in complete gridlock. They had found the carts.

An entire troop of water buffalo joined the crowd meandering in between the rickshaws, the donkey carts, and the horse-drawn carriages. Every single rickshaw was packed to the brim, some with four people squeezed into a space designed for one, while the poor drivers looked like they might collapse from the weight. The scorching sun made their precarious situation look dreadfully unbearable.

"I always hated market Mondays."

"Ah… I see… this is the traffic you were referring to. Then, darling, why don't we just go home? We can go to Golconda Fort tomorrow."

"What are we going to do at home? We can't make a peep without the whole bloody building getting up in arms!"

"Alright…" Eleanor was both annoyed that he was being such a whiner, and grateful that her divine demon had the capacity for such mundane complaining. He seemed entirely human in that moment, and she realized how much she loved that he was not, for the most part… human. "There's one! Just there!"

She ran to hail a rickshaw as a family of three, a couple with an infant, gave up on the traffic and decided to walk the rest of the way.

"Wait!" She ran after it. "Can you take us to Golconda Fort? We will pay double your going rate!"

The driver looked skeptically at Edmund as he caught up with her. "Dearest, don't run into traffic like that! You could have been run over!"

"It was hardly moving!" Eleanor argued. "Now, do you want to go to Golconda Fort or not?"

He eyed the small platform and the meagre driver.

"Dearest, this man cannot pull us all the way to Golconda Fort. It is too far away for a man to walk there carrying our weight. We must find a donkey cart or a horse."

Eleanor's posture deflated. She reached into her pocket and offered the man a coin for his trouble, and he inched away, towards another packed alleyway.

"Well, what do you want to do? We can either wander around until we find a cart for hire, we can give up and walk to the market instead, or we can go home and mope. It's your Grump Day. You have to decide."

"Let's go home."

"Alright, a decision has been made," she declared.

They walked slowly back up the hill towards their flat, and as Eleanor felt a drip of sweat on her forehead, she looked over and noticed that Edmund's skin was flaking. She decided she was not going to say anything.

"Out of the way!"

As they turned the corner onto the steepest part of the street, a young boy, who couldn't have been older than twelve, barreled past them, whipping his donkey and yelling at them. Edmund grabbed Eleanor, harsher than he'd probably intended, and whisked her out of the road and onto a stoop.

"Watch where you're going!" he yelled angrily in Hindi.

"Does sahib need a ride?" the boy asked.

"Not in a death machine like that," Edmund replied.

"Does sahib want to hire my cart? I will give you a very fair price. It is an auspicious day. My cart will have a driver that is better than I am!" He burst into hyena-like laughter.

"Do you want to do it, Edmund? Now is our chance." She hoped that Edmund wouldn't notice that she had understood their entire exchange in Hindi.

Edmund glanced up the street towards their flat, and then at the grinning boy who was slowly backing his cart up the road to greet them.

"Fine."

"A Grump Day decision has been made!" Eleanor declared.

"That will be two pounds," the boy said as Edmund approached the cart.

"Never mind. We will go home."

He started back up the hill, and Eleanor joined him, until the boy turned the cart around and chased after them.

"Wait! Wait, sahib! I will give you a very fair price! How much do you want to pay? Name it!"

Edmund walked up to the boy, staring him down with a piercing look. He reached into his pocket and held out some coins.

"Take it, or leave it. Either way, make up your mind, and we will be on our way."

The boy grabbed the coins and hopped off the cart, leaving the donkeys without anyone at the reins.

"You can collect your cart tomorrow at our flat. It is just up there at the corner. You can be sure the animals will be in a better state than they're in now."

"As you wish, sahib!"

The boy skipped down the street without another glance. Eleanor wondered in passing whether or not he'd actually been Kuveni, but he seemed too harsh for that. There was something about him that was still rubbing her the wrong way.

Edmund hopped up onto the cart, and Eleanor followed him, noting to herself that he was so distracted with his foul mood that he hadn't even remembered to offer her his hand. He took the reins and dropped the whip into the back of the cart, and without a word, only a hunched over posture and a scowl, they headed towards Golconda Fort.

After an interminable several-hour ride in market traffic, they arrived at the gatehouse. The heat was even more intense, and a thin layer of Edmund's skin was visibly peeling off of his hands and his neck.

"Darling, you need to drink some water. You are becoming terribly dehydrated."

She was so concerned with his deteriorating state that she hardly paid any attention to the imposing stone fort built up on a massive hill, flanked by the biggest boulders she'd ever seen.

"Maybe they have a little café. Is this a tourist attraction?"

Edmund helped her off the cart, noticing his own grotesque state as a sheet of his discarded skin fell to the ground and floated away in the hot wind.

"For god's sake, I bloody hate birthdays."

He put his hands in his pockets, and she followed him as he approached the gate.

"Is there a café inside?" he asked a man who sat on a stool fanning himself with a paper fan inside the gatehouse.

"It's closed!" the man shouted unreasonably loudly.

"The café is closed? Then where can I get some water?"

"No, the fort is closed!"

Edmund looked like he might explode.

"What do you mean the fort is closed? The fort is never closed! Not even on Fridays!"

"It is closed today," the man shrugged. "The Nizam declared it."

"Bloody hell," Edmund muttered.

Eleanor couldn't even take his hand to calm him down, as he had both hands solidly stuffed into his pockets.

"Where can we get some water? Or perhaps some lunch? Is there a restaurant near here?" Eleanor asked cheerfully.

The man was surprised by her question, as was Edmund.

"Just over there, there are two restaurants. The one on the left makes better dosa, but the one on the right makes better chaat."

"Well, darling, what will it be, dosa or chaat?"

"Dosa…" Edmund murmured.

"Perfect. Thank you very much, sahib!"

Eleanor guided Edmund across the empty road to the restaurant with the better dosa.

"Two for lunch, please."

A waiter eyed them curiously, and then guided them to a table by the open window. He pointed to a chalkboard. "Choose your dosa."

"How about one of each?" Eleanor asked. The man looked annoyed. "I'm not joking. One of each, please." Eleanor took out a handful of coins and dropped them onto the table. "And all of the cold drinking water you can spare."

The man collected the money into a pocket in his apron and left them alone.

"Eleanor, when did you learn how to speak Hindi?" Edmund asked with a combination of surprise and suspicion.

"Was I speaking Hindi?"

"You were."

"I don't know, darling. I suppose I just picked it up. I speak Gaelic quite well, even after only learning it for a few years as a child. Maybe I'm good at languages. I was always wretched at French, though…"

The man returned with two small glasses of water. Edmund picked his up and drank it down in one gulp, and then Eleanor pushed hers towards him, and he finished hers up with a gurgle.

"More water, please," Eleanor asked sweetly. "I was not joking when I said to bring us all of your cold drinking water. I assume we paid you enough for it?"

Without another word, the man disappeared into the back.

"But, Eleanor, you're speaking in very complex sentences. Where did you even hear this vocabulary?"

"Darling, people have been speaking Hindi all around us for weeks."

"Not in Baroda. They were speaking Gujarati. And not on the maharaja's train. They were speaking English. And not in Ravi Bidkar's house…"

"Darling, what do you want me to say? Do I scrutinize you when you do strange things? I don't know why I'm so good at Hindi. Perhaps I was Indian in a former life."

Edmund became too pensive about her flippant remark.

"Darling, please relax. You're more insufferable than I've ever known you to be. Tomorrow your Grump Day will be over, we will leave Hyderabad, and we will continue along our romantic honeymoon. It will all be alright. I promise."

"It will not be alright when you're dead, Eleanor. I will have no reason to live."

The statement knocked the wind right out of her.

"Is that what this is all really about? My mortality?"

524

Edmund looked down at his flaking hands and refused to answer.

"Darling, it disturbs me just as much as it disturbs you. Do you think that I want to be the weak mortal of this relationship? The wife whose death will torment the king until he builds an outrageous monument to her memory? It's all bloody unfair! But, darling, life is unfair. Now, we can give into our melancholy and ruin our beautiful day with our fantasies about our future misery, or we can enjoy our time together. It's your choice. Do we let the pain of the future ruin the joy of the present, or not?"

The waiter returned with a pitcher of water and left it on their table without a word.

"You're right," Edmund conceded. "We'd better get out of grump-erabad as soon as we can. I am a version of myself I've never met before, and I don't like him one bit."

Eleanor reached forward and squeezed his hand. "Darling, it is a very good sign for your recovery that you're feeling grumpy. It is a very normal feeling that we often cannot feel if we are struggling too much for survival at a base level. It means that your shell shock is beginning to subside."

He refilled her glass with the water pitcher, and then held it up for a toast. "To Grump Day."

"To Grump Day," Eleanor declared.

He drank down the entire pitcher, and then they waited for several minutes while the restaurant filled up with the rich aroma of freshly fried-up dosa. Edmund's stomach growled even louder.

Finally, the waiter and two young boys emerged from the kitchen carrying nine plates with the largest pancakes Eleanor had ever seen, rolled up around a variety of colorful steaming fillings.

The waiter waited for their shocked reaction, but Edmund only cracked his knuckles and dove into the dosa closest to him.

"Mmm... aloo masala..."

The staff watched as Eleanor tasted a bite or two of each one, while Edmund set about using his Hyderabadi table manners to demolish every dosa on the table, until there was not a crumb left on any plate.

"Perhaps two more of that sweet potato one?" he called.

The waiter looked to the two boys, and they all shrugged and headed back into the kitchen.

"And two more of the egg dosa!" he called.

"I'm glad you found it acceptable, darling," Eleanor winked.

"I have missed Hyderabadi dosa," he said as he sat back and observed his success with the empty plates. "I'm glad we had some before we left the city. Shall we go to Munnar tomorrow? We can take the train to Mysore, and then hop over the mountains to the west from there. The jungles there are wonderful. Full of wild tigers and elephants and the most enormous squirrels!"

"It sounds fascinating," Eleanor agreed. "Do they speak more English there? Mr. Valov will be pleased to be somewhere he can navigate more easily."

"Oh yes, Munnar is a hill town. It will feel like we're in an English suburb."

"Really?"

"No. Not really." Edmund finally cracked a smile. "That is what many of the English tourists think. It is India, of course. Wonderfully so. But there are a lot of Brits who go there to escape from the heat of lower elevations, so we should have no problem finding acceptable wine and bland food for Mr. Valov to eat."

"It sounds like a perfect destination."

Eleanor sat back and finally relaxed as Edmund finished off his last four dosas and another three pitchers of water. When his skin looked like it was fully rehydrated, she nodded her thanks to the waiter and the boys who were watching them, and then guided Edmund back out towards the fort.

"It looks very impressive from here," she said. "I think I've seen enough of it."

"I don't even remember what is particularly interesting about the inside of it," Edmund admitted.

"Then I'd say we had a fine Grump Day feast, and now we can return home, pack our trunks, and feel accomplished. Don't you think?"

Edmund was suddenly distracted. Eleanor followed his gaze back and forth between the gatehouse, the restaurant, and the place where they'd left the cart... and then she noticed it too: The cart was gone! There was absolutely no sign of it.

"I hate birthdays," he muttered.

"We can buy the boy a new cart." Eleanor looked around for any alternative transportation, and just as she was about to sigh with resignation, she noticed the exceptionally odd sight of an absurdly decorated palanquin held up on the backs of eight skinny, muscular young men wearing dark suits and red fezes. She and Edmund squinted simultaneously to spy who was inside, but as they both realized that it was empty, a middle-aged man with a twisting moustache, clad in a more formal grey western suit accompanied by a tall red fez marked by a golden seal glittering in the afternoon sun rushed towards them from the gatehouse of the fort.

"Lord Marriner?" he called as he ran towards them.

Edmund's face turned red, and he looked like he might explode with anger, although mercifully his eyes did not turn black.

The man bowed as he reached them and struggled to catch his breath. "Lord Marriner? Please forgive me. I am Amir Sahib, and I am the senior administrator for His Highness, the Nizam. I have been looking all over for you."

"You had quite the fortune then to run into us in this massive city," Edmund grumbled.

"We... er... followed you here from your flat," Amir Sahib explained awkwardly. "Dinner will be served at six o'clock at the Falaknuma palace, and you must freshen up and change into appropriate attire before then. If you do not have time to stop at your flat, we have prepared a room for you at the palace."

"Did my man fail to communicate our refusal?" Edmund asked, barely holding in a shout.

Amir Sahib shifted uncomfortably. "The Nizam did not accept your refusal this time, my lord. He is determined to make your acquaintance, and it is best for everyone if you comply. He is all-powerful in Hyderabad, you see. He closed the fort just to demonstrate a point, and now he has sent one of his palanquins to collect you. It is a very rare treat that you should not take lightly."

"I will not ride on the backs of other men as if they are chattel," Edmund countered sharply.

"But our chauffeurs said that you refused the Nizam's motorcars that had come to collect you at your flat!"

"I refused the invitations completely!" Edmund exclaimed. "What more must I do to convince you people!"

Amir Sahib lowered his voice. "You must not refuse. The Nizam will take it as a personal affront. He demands to know what he has done to offend you, and he will have his answer."

Edmund leaned in to hiss his response, and a shiver ran down Eleanor's spine as a wave of divine power, stronger than any she had ever felt from him, wafted off of him. Amir Sahib shivered too.

"You tell the Nizam that when there is not one starving person left in Hyderabad; when every man, woman and child has had a proper modern education; when there is not one man left in this principality beating his wife; and when every single person has free and unquestionable access to modern medical care, *then* and only then will I take a seat at his table, and not a moment sooner. And you can tell him that if he sends another bloody mango to an unlucky pauper, I will come for him in the night and personally help him understand that there is a higher law than the archaic Moghul traditions he uses to exploit the innocent feudal peasants that he is supposed to be protecting. He has inherited the means to make Hyderabad the model of human society, and instead he is hoarding jewels and collecting cars like a spoiled rotten teenaged boy, and I will have none of it. Got it?"

The man was so shocked by Edmund's blatant insults that he stuttered and then gave up on any defensive response. "I cannot tell him that, my lord. He will have my head."

Edmund sighed a long sigh of disapproval. "I suppose he will, my friend. Then you tell him that you missed us completely. Your spies trailed the wrong two *firangs*. We were simply two unimportant commoners, not worth the breath in his lungs for a conversation."

The man moved to argue, and then he gave up. "But, my lord, how will you get back to your flat? My men watched your cart being stolen an hour ago."

"We will walk," Edmund declared.

"My lord, your flat is too far from here for you to walk."

Edmund glanced over to the men who continued to dutifully hold up the empty palanquin. "We will a have a much easier time of it than those poor blokes would carrying the weight of two lazy louts on their backs."

"You are not like any English lord I've ever met," Amir Sahib murmured.

"That's because I'm not," Edmund replied simply. He took Eleanor's hand. "Good luck with your task. I don't envy your role as the messenger, my friend, but I cannot give you better news to bear."

Without another word, he led her down an alleyway, and then another, until they were clearly out of earshot. Then he leaned up against a wall and sighed.

"I don't know why I'm so emotional about this, Eleanor," he admitted without looking at her. "I was so angry just now, I wanted to rip that palanquin into shreds."

Eleanor rubbed his back. "You had many vivid experiences as a lad here, Edmund. It is obviously bringing up old unpleasant memories, old feelings, that you haven't thought about in decades.

It is perfectly natural for you to feel this way." He took in a deep calming breath as she felt him relax. "Are you going to tell me what your comment about the mangoes meant?"

Edmund finally turned towards her. "The Nizam's grandfather built his wealth on the backs of his people. It was a Moghul tradition to send mangoes to his subjects, and in return they were required to pay him a hefty duty of gold coins. It bankrupted many, including a man in Abdul Barr's building who killed himself after he couldn't pay for his wives."

"His wives?!" Eleanor exclaimed.

Edmund shrugged. "That was the culture, and I never questioned it. It is still very common for men to have many wives, and it is legal as long as they can pay for them and their children. That man was a good man, Eleanor. His wives made dinner for Abdul Barr and me quite often, even when they were struggling to make ends meat for themselves."

"I'm sorry, darling. I didn't mean to distract you."

"The Nizam had enough precious jewels to pay for all of India to live on for centuries, but he saw it as his birthright to just keep demanding more and more from his hard-working populace. As far as I could tell, he did it purely for sport. It was as if people weren't even human to him, just like those coolies weren't human to him today. It's like a century has passed and nothing has changed."

"Darling, I'm proud of you for standing your ground." Eleanor kissed his forehead, but as a pair of women in niqabs turned the corner into the alleyway and tsked disapprovingly, she straightened her posture and stepped away from him.

"My little rebellion has left us without a means to get home," Edmund said with frustration.

"It wasn't so far. I'm sure we can walk." She sighed with resignation as she wiggled her toes in her uncomfortable shoes and sucked up her discomfort.

She took his hand and guided him down the street, retracing the steps of the donkey as her feet became more and more sore in her sparkling black sandals.

The sun dropped low in the sky and then it set as they slowly made their way back to the center of town. Edmund had been right that it was very far for those poor men to carry them. She was feeling bad enough walking it herself, and she let herself give into a moment of gratitude that he had pointed out the men's plight. She'd watched so many rickshaws pulling the weight of too many men already that she'd stopped noticing it completely.

As they treaded farther and farther, her feet developed blisters, but instead of fighting the pain like she usually did, she embraced it. She realized, in those moments, that the feeling was a small but important connection to the vast swathes of humanity who didn't have the choices that she had.

You are very wise, my child, Uma praised. *Shakti chose well.*

It had been dark for at least an hour by the time they got home. Edmund had hardly spoken a few words.

"Darling, we survived, and your Grump Day is almost over. Shall we see what delicious dinner Mr. Valov has procured for us? I'm sure we will have excellent wine to go with it. The best wine in Hyderabad, I reckon, and we can glug it down with reckless abandon if we're heading out of here tomorrow."

As they climbed the stairs, the rich scent of a fresh biriyani wafted into the hallway, and Edmund's stomach growled again.

"See! Memsahib Basimah made you a Grump Day biriyani! It's not all bad! We will have a nice, relaxing end to the day, and tomorrow we will leave here for good."

Eleanor pushed open the door to their flat and tossed her sandals across the room with her feet, wiggling her toes on the persian carpet and sighing with relief.

"That wasn't so bad, was it darling? You made a point, you feasted on dosas, and we got plenty of exercise."

"Leo, we're back!" Edmund called.

When Mr. Valov didn't answer, Edmund turned on the hallway lights and walked through the sitting room to the kitchen. Eleanor followed him.

"Leo?"

Edmund startled as he pushed open the door. Memsahib Basimah in her full niqab was standing at the stove in front of a huge covered pot of biriyani.

Edmund relaxed. "Thank you, memsahib. A birthday biriyani is just what I needed."

She burst into loud, cackling, mad laughter.

"Happy birthday, Young Edmund!" she cooed. "Your birthday surprise has just begun!"

She lifted up the lid of the pot, and a thick puff of sparkling black smoke filled the room.

Edmund coughed and gagged.

Eleanor's throat closed up.

As the woman's laughter echoed with greater and greater ferocity, Eleanor fell onto the floor. Edmund fell beside her.

Darkness ensnared her.

CHAPTER 29 – THE GAME

When Eleanor awoke, her head was pounding, and she didn't know where she was.

Golconda Fort. Refusing the Nizam. Long walk home. Dinner. Memsahib Basimah?

Her limbs were so heavy she could barely move them, and a thirst unlike any she'd ever felt burned her throat.

She struggled to open her eyes. The world was blurry. She was in a dark room, but there was a light coming from somewhere, perhaps outside a window. A warm, gentle breeze wafted in, tickling her face as it flitted through her hair.

"Edmund?" she rasped.

As she forced her eyes all the way open, she looked down to observe that she was not wearing the abaya-style salwar kameez she'd been wearing earlier. She was wearing the elaborate lehenga that she'd worn to the ball in Baroda. She had no memory of changing into it.

She sat up and felt her back. The blouse was not properly buttoned, and her skin was sore from open scratches. There was still a minor amount of fresh blood when she ran her fingers across the wounds.

She stumbled across the room to the source of the light.

A full moon illuminated the bulbous towers and spired minarets of the city. It looked rather romantic. It was a different angle compared to the one they had from their flat; it made the city look more fantastical, as if it were right out of a storybook. She looked down. The building she was in was massive and ornate, perhaps one of the Nizam's palaces, and her position was very high up—at least several hundred feet, with a steep fall down into a gorge below.

She looked around the room. It was similar in style to their flat, with intricate geometric patterns inlaid into every surface, except that the materials were more on par with the grandeur of the Taj Mahal, with sparkling gemstones decorating the marblework. There was no furniture, and the walls were curved. She was inside one of the city's many bulbous towers.

She glanced over towards the door. It was heavy and wooden, and it only had a small barred window. She was locked up. She went straight to the door anyway to try to push it open. It didn't budge. She threw all of her weight against it. Her arm ached.

"For god's sake, that bloody Nizam doesn't know what he's messing with," she murmured.

She chastised herself for not realizing sooner that the richest man on Earth, whom her husband had blatantly insulted, might go a bit Napoleonic on them. But to kidnap her and lock her away in a tower seemed too draconian, too melodramatic for the modern world, even in a city where men still had many wives.

She glanced around again, making sure that she hadn't missed any wardrobes or WC doors, but there was nothing. She was alone, and she was trapped.

She paced back and forth for a while contemplating her circumstances, wiggling her feet to try to awaken her heavy limbs.

Uma, do you know what happened?

534

I do not, my child, but we must be very careful as we combat this clever enemy. We are in grave danger, and so is Lord Kalki.

She heard the echo of footsteps in the hallway beyond, and her mind began racing as she strategized what she was going to say… "How dare you capture us like this! We are British citizens! My husband is a colonel in the British Army! The king himself will have your head for this!" Her blurry mind wandered. "Do you know who we are?! We're the bloody gods, you wanker! You've kidnapped the bloody gods themselves! You think you're so bloody powerful? I'll show you power…"

As she envisioned Sheranee tearing him apart, the footsteps passed, dissolving into silence, and Eleanor's heart raced even faster. She felt sick, and leaned up against the wall, crouching down against it and holding her aching hands against the cool marble as a bout of hot nausea rolled over her.

She sat for many minutes, trying futilely to regain her strength as she swallowed painfully with her scratchy, parched throat.

Just as her heavy eyelids were giving into another round of drowsiness, a raven landed on the windowsill.

"Rapunzel!" it cawed. "Rapunzel!"

Eleanor looked down at her hair. It was loose and wild, but not particularly reminiscent of Rapunzel. She blinked several times, trying desperately to wake herself up, but as she felt the cool marble on her hands and then pinched her own arm, she became quite convinced that she was already awake.

The raven cackled. "Wishing you were asleep, Rapunzel? But why? Living out your dreams in the waking world is so much more permanent!"

As the raven hopped off the windowsill and landed on the floor, Eleanor was at a total loss. The entire situation was utterly absurd.

"I take it you don't work for the Nizam?" Eleanor asked somewhat facetiously.

The raven almost choked on its laughter. "I work for no man, especially not a worthless human wanker like him. I have annexed a turret of his palace for the time being. It was necessary for my thoughtful little gift."

It suddenly began to grow, morphing into a black dragon with shimmering scales that was several feet shorter than she was, more like the size of a dwarf.

"Shall I breathe some fire on you?" it asked. "What do I have to do to get you to be a princess, Darling Eleanor? Your fairy tale has just begun."

Eleanor glanced down, looking for her talisman to summon Mélusine, and then she noticed it hanging around the dragon's neck. *Blimey.*

"I am not a princess." She struggled to stand up, leaning heavily against the wall as she went, and the dragon just watched her curiously. She straightened her posture, working her hardest to hide the weakness she was feeling, and then she walked around it slowly, taking in its perfectly formed black scales, razor-sharp claws, and spiked ridges. "I am an ordinary nurse."

"Ha!" It laughed. "Lie number one! You only get three lies, Eleanor. That is how our game will work. Now, will you be more of a princess if I refer to you by your official title, Your Majesty?"

The words were too familiar. Betty. Bo. But they had been entirely human, she was certain.

"I am not a queen," Eleanor insisted.

"Wrong! Lie number two. Eleanor, you must be very careful. The punishment for three lies will be severe. I thought you'd have more sense. More of a whimpering, fearful obsession with self-preservation, just as you've always had."

"I have never whimpered," Eleanor replied. "I don't know what you're talking about."

"Lie number three!"

In a blur, the dragon whipped up its tail, wrapped it around Eleanor's forearm, and snapped her bone.

She screamed with agony, and then looked back at the dragon with freshly enraged eyes. She took in a deep breath, grabbed her broken bone, and pushed it back into place. Her fiery Celtic temper began mixing dangerously with Uma's power. She was not going to let this creature torment her.

She glanced around the floor, spotting her dupatta in the corner where she'd first awoken. She walked nonchalantly over to it, picked it up, and folded it into a sling.

"I have never whimpered," she repeated.

Careful, Uma warned. *You are still mortal, Eleanor. We must learn more about this enemy before we can combat it.*

The dragon exploded into cackling laughter. Eleanor recognized it. She had heard it twice before. *Surpanakha.*

Shiva's wrath.

You know her?

Too well. Be careful, Eleanor. She will lull you into a false sense of security. She does not even know herself, and she cannot control the demon that burns her from within.

"Good show!" the dragon exclaimed when it had calmed itself. "Eleanor, you are just full of surprises! That's why I brought you here. Oh, this will be so much fun! Everyone will win. Young Edmund will be the prince, you will be the princess, and I will be the evil dragon! Isn't it the best birthday present in the world? He will win back his manhood!"

"I can assure you, he never lost it."

The dragon threw itself on the floor, rolling around with booming cackles for several minutes, while Eleanor assessed her exit options with more urgency.

"Oh, Eleanor! I like you so much. SO MUCH! It's no wonder you seduced our prince. If only you weren't my ultimate nemesis, I really think we could be friends."

"I didn't realize I had a nemesis. What did I do to offend you?" Eleanor was genuinely interested in the answer to the question.

"Oh, my poor, sweet, innocent little Sita. You never know, do you? Every time you are so surprised. You take pity on me, or you invite me in for tea, as if I haven't murdered you a thousand times before. And no matter how many times I do it, I still get so much pleasure out of killing you."

Padma's descriptions of her dark fate over the millennia as Surpanakha had ruthlessly hunted her rushed into Eleanor's mind. *She thinks I'm Padma! I will not die in her bloody place just so she can marry my husband!*

Eleanor's entire being erupted with burning defiance.

"I am *not* Sita."

"You always say that, and you are always wrong," the dragon replied.

Suddenly, Eleanor made another realization. *She is the one. She's the one who can sense the avatars, and it has driven her mad.*

She cannot sense the difference between us, Eleanor. We must keep that secret until we can use it to our advantage.

It began circling her. "But now… now destiny is really playing games with me! With us! She is really the cruelest beast I know. She is so much crueler than I am. What am I to do with you, my sniveling Sita? Do I off with you, like always, or do I play a longer game? You see, Young Edmund's place in this game changes everything."

"Really? How?"

The dragon's tail whipped around, knocking Eleanor into the marble wall. Her broken arm exploded with another round of burning agony, but she would not let this creature see her pain. She held in every sound that was itching to burst out of her, pushed her broken bone back into place, stood up, and faced her.

"Do not get clever with me, girl. I have been doing this for five *thousand* years."

As Eleanor caught a hint of madness in its eyes, she decided on a new plan. She was going to treat it exactly how she treated her madmen. Her murderers. The criminally insane wankers she'd tended to for two decades to support her ungrateful mother.

"Then do tell me, my dragon lord, if I may call you that, what exactly would you like to do now? Do we wait for my prince to rescue me?"

The dragon cackled and then clapped its hands with approval. "Yes, this is much, much better! Young Edmund will be the knight in shining armor that you never let him be! Oh, how mean you are, Eleanor! Always saving yourself! What is a knight to do? He must feel so useless!"

Eleanor walked right over to the window. "Edmund?!" she called into the warm, whipping breeze. "Edmund, darling?! Edmund, my love, come and save me! I'm in the tower, and there is an evil dragon! Can't you please slay it for me?! Its skin would make such a lovely rug!"

Surpanakha rolled around on the floor with laughter, clapping her hands.

"Oh, Eleanor, why can't we be friends?!"

"Perhaps we can," Eleanor said as she moved out of the immediate vicinity of the window, in case her mad captor decided to push her out on a whim.

"We cannot, Eleanor. Destiny will not allow it. Now, tell me, my princess, what do you make of your circumstances?"

Eleanor looked around her prison again. "I have been kidnapped, on my prince's birthday, which is very unfortunate for him, since he already hated his birthday, and now he must rescue me from a dragon who has held me up in Rapunzel's tower. It is a rather muddled fairy tale, I'd say, full of mixed metaphors, but perhaps that is what will make it interesting."

"That is a very astute observation. For that you have earned one white lie."

"I will hold it close to my heart."

"You'd better... now tell me, Your Majesty, what should I do with you? Should I kill you? Or should I let you live?"

"I suppose it depends on what you want to get out of this whole thing. It's important to keep your final objective in mind when making these types of decisions."

The dragon stared her down, but she refused to look away. "You are a very curious Sita, indeed... very curious."

"Why?"

"You are really not going to plead for your life?"

"Why? To make it more fun when you kill me?"

The dragon exploded into another round of cackles.

"If I didn't know any better, I'd say you knew me already!"

"Perhaps I do."

"You don't!"

The dragon moved to attack her again with its tail, but when Eleanor didn't even flinch, it reconsidered its plan.

"Tell me more about my strategic options," it suggested instead.

"Well..." *Be careful, my child. This is a dangerous game.* "You could kill me, which would torment Edmund unlike anything else. His inability to save me would haunt him for eternity, and I suspect he would dislike dragons mightily. In fact, I suspect that he would loathe all Rakshasas, as he would eventually realize that you are the same kind of creature that he is. It would create quite a bit of unhappiness for him, so if that is your aim, it would be very effective at ruining his life."

"That is NOT the objective!" the dragon declared. "The objective is to HELP Young Edmund. To make him feel like the prince that he is! The royal position that my worthless little brother has stolen from him, and that you have trampled all over with your silver pistol and filthy nursing and *modern* womanhood!"

"Ah. I see. Then you don't believe in women's rights? You think we should all be married off to produce a troop of bouncing babies instead of doing what we want with our lives?"

"*Edmund* deserves a wife who lives only for him. The rest of the women in the world can do what they want."

"If only they could," Eleanor sighed.

"Most of them want to be a princess."

"That is because they don't know any better."

"You don't want to be a princess?"

"I would rather be a nurse."

"So you say. Shall we bring in some humans who are rotting at death's door so you can wipe off their excrement and change their filthy sheets?"

"I did that for twenty years, and I would certainly rather be doing that now. Will you let me go if I go back to nursing? You can watch me go about my business as long as you don't hurt anyone. I've made a vow to do no harm."

"That is NOT ACCEPTABLE! You are a princess. You will act like one!"

A wild look darkened the expression of the dragon, and Eleanor realized that she was in exceptional danger. Surpanakha was battling a blooming wave of madness.

"Edmund, darling?" she called out the window again, this time with even more affection. "Won't you rescue me? The dragon is getting very cross!"

"That's better. Now, you have not finished your analysis. Will I kill you, or will I let you live? My game will be ruined if Edmund arrives and you are already dead. It won't be any fun at all."

"Let us talk of a different strategy then. Let's say you keep me alive. Edmund will find me, rescue me, I will swoon, and he will slay you. I assume he won't be using a red sapphire sword, and so you won't die. He will feel like a prince, I will be his princess, and you will get to watch."

The dragon began pacing. "Yes... yes, I like this plan better... but I cannot let you live... no... no, you must suffer your karmic punishment... It is my sacred duty to inflict it... but... but, yes... yes! If he knew, oh, if he knew... Oh, yes! He will know! We will show him, and that will be worse than if you were already dead! Yes! Oh, this will be wonderful!"

Eleanor held her tongue, hoping that Surpanakha would give away more details of her incoherent plan.

"Rama will just die when he finds out! Oh, but how will we orchestrate it? How will we make it sufficiently poetic? Let me think… My little birthday present is the perfect start. Young Edmund will show you his true nature, and then you, my dear, will see what kind of prince you've really married, and then together we will all show Rama your happy Rakshasa family! Oh, yes… oooohhhh, yes. We will invite him over for tea so that he can see with his own eyes the Rakshasa prince whom you have already married in his absence… we will have to work out the details later… and then we will bring him over to see you again when the time is right. We will force him! We will capture him and force him to see what his Sita has done when you're dying in your bloody bed, screaming in agony to bring another Rakshasa child into this world. Another Rakshasa heir! Yes! He will see you die bringing forth Ravana's progeny! Oh, my dear, you have done all of my work for me! Now all we must do is wait for your prince!"

"Edmund will not like this outcome," Eleanor pointed out.

"Edmund will have no choice. He is a Rakshasa. You are a human. It is nature."

Eleanor hated that she was right. She didn't care one lick about Rama, but the rest of the story was right. If Eleanor ever gave into her urge for children, she would end up dying in her bed, bringing forth the grandchild of one evil wanker.

"Have I saddened you, my sniveling Sita?" the dragon asked with some combination of real and fake concern.

"I love Edmund. I don't want him to suffer." Eleanor hoped that the truth of the statement would cut through some of her madness.

"Love ruins us all," she replied. "Love is a horrible, useless weakness that only ends in pain."

"It feels pretty bloody good when you're in the midst of it. My jury is still out about whether it's worth the pain, though. Edmund will learn soon enough, and I'm glad that I won't be around to witness it."

"You are a most curious woman, Eleanor. You are nothing at all like the other Sitas. They were all princesses."

"They should have changed more bedpans," Eleanor quipped. "So, what have you done to Edmund? How long do I have to wait for him to rescue me? I hope that he will have enough energy for a happy ending to his birthday."

The dragon laughed and clapped again with approval. "It depends how long it takes him to give into his true nature. Any self-respecting Rakshasa could finish the task in a few minutes, but my brother has wasted our nephew's talents for a century. I am cultivating his talent! But will he thank me? Never! No one ever appreciates my hard work."

"Perhaps he should be allowed to take his own time to cultivate his talents."

"That would be no fun at all! Young Edmund must figure it out before morning, or there will be more dead humans in his wake, and that butler of yours will not be able to cover them up again."

"Mr. Valov is very resourceful." Eleanor's heart suddenly skipped a beat. "You didn't hurt him, did you?"

"You care about this butler?" Surpanakha asked with piqued interest. "About a lowly human servant?"

"He is a member of our household. *Edmund* cares deeply about him. They have been together for five years."

"Young Edmund made quite a good move, recruiting a human minion to cover his tracks. They are easier to control than Rakshasas, and much easier to track. I plan to take up the technique myself, although Edmund seems to have convinced him to do it out of his own free will... I will never understand the unique talents of that boy. Humans are always so deliciously afraid when I ask for their help that I can't help but tear them apart. They bring it upon themselves."

"It was you, then? You're the one whose been following us and killing our enemies?"

The dragon bowed a deep, melodramatic bow. "And what thanks do I get? None! That's gratitude in this modern world. I even went to the effort to let you play along when I left that ignorant little trollop alive, and did you thank me? Did you give me anything entertaining to watch? Nothing!"

"Do you mean Betty? The poor girl who thought the Devil wanted her to make a deal for the life of her rapist thieving husband?"

The dragon exploded into more cackling laughter. "She offered me his soul for hers. I told her that both of them were at the front of the line. I almost hid the man's body as a favor to your butler, but I simply couldn't resist. I left it crucified in the swimming pool, which made all of those stories about a tiger impossible to explain!"

"I'm sure he found a way."

"He will not find a way next time. Not unless Edmund claims his birthday present. That boy must find his bloody strength, or everyone will pay!"

"What have you done to him?"

Surpanakha cackled. "I've shown him who he really is."

"Great misery descends upon those who thwart destiny."

"Where did you hear that?!"

Surpanakha flung out her tail and wrapped it around Eleanor's waist.

Hold steady, Eleanor. We will fight her only when we know what she has done to Lord Kalki. We must find him, before it's too late.

"Mélusine!" Eleanor squeaked.

The dragon looked down at the talisman she had stolen.

"Ah yes, Melysium. You have her wrapped around your little human finger, don't you? I have never seen her so enthralled with a human before. It's disgusting. After everything they've done to her... *you've* done to her."

"I've done nothing to her."

"You have weakened her with human emotions."

"She seems strong enough to me."

"You know nothing about her!"

As Surpanakha reached her dragon wings up into the air, Eleanor flinched, and a look of primal excitement crossed her face.

"Yes! Yes! There is the fear I've been waiting for! The fear I've been craving! You are too bloody brave, Eleanor, but your fear is so tantalizingly delicious! I must have more of it!"

Surpanakha grew out one of her claws into a blade, but before she could execute her horrific plan, she froze and looked towards the window.

"Yes! Yes, yes, yes!!!" She left Eleanor alone to stand by the window and watch. "Come, Young Edmund! Come rescue your damsel in distress! She *needs* you!"

Across the night sky, a dark figure approached.

With a pleasant draft, Edmund flew right into the window, but instead of the golden falcon wings Mélusine had shown Eleanor, he flew with enormous black bat wings that looked rather sinister. He dissolved them immediately as he landed in the middle of the room. He wore the same blue and silver sherwani that he had worn to the ball, and his eyes were already black with rage.

"How could you do this?! How could you do this to your own flesh and blood?!" he boomed.

"But, Edmund? Edmund, darling, I love you! It is a gift! From your Auntie Surpanakha! You were so unhappy earlier today when I gave you my cart. Now you can fly! You can save your princess! You can use your most powerful and natural form! You will not need me to kill your enemies for you anymore!"

"You have been killing my enemies?" He looked her up and down assessingly. "That was you leaving the trail of bodies?"

"They were all evil men!" Her tone became shrill with madness. "They deserved to die!"

He glanced past Surpanakha to Eleanor. Eleanor took a moment to get over the image of Edmund with his sinister wings, and then, as she considered her options, she rushed past Surpanakha with a loud swoon.

"Edmund, my prince, you saved me!"

She threw her uninjured arm around his neck and pulled him down into a kiss, but as their lips touched, a spark ignited. The spark of two halves of one whole uniting.

Eleanor felt herself give in as the rich taste of milk and honey filled her mouth. Suddenly, she had to have more. All of the voices inside of her sang *more, you want more!*

She ignored the clapping and cackling as Surpanakha watched their reunion with glee, but as she let Uma hold on too long in her long-awaited embrace, Surpanakha suddenly went silent.

"No!" Surpanakha hissed. "NO!"

Eleanor broke away. Instead of the dragon, there stood the tall, slender woman who had attacked them in the forest after their wedding. Surpanakha grew out her silky black hair into an elaborate up-do not dissimilar to the one Padma had produced during her revelation to Eleanor, and she wore a black lehenga that matched the style of Eleanor's, paired with the same unnatural iridescence of the dragon scales. If it weren't for her grotesquely disfigured face and ghoulish claws, she would have been beautiful, and Eleanor suddenly found the dichotomy sad.

"The sherwani was a human sherwani! I ripped it, and the beads spilled all over the ground! THIS IS ALL A LIE!!! Do you think I was born yesterday?!!!" Surpanakha screeched.

In a blur, Surpanakha ripped Eleanor out of Edmund's arms and threw her across the room. He pulled a crescent sword in a leather sheath out from a hidden pocket in his sherwani. As he removed the sheath, the red sapphire blade glistened eerily in the moonlight.

"You wouldn't dare!" she hissed.

She threw herself at him in a blur, and in the blink of an eye, they were rolling around on the floor, then throwing each other up against one wall and then the other, cracking the marble and shaking the building with the power of their impact. Eleanor could hardly see their moves, until suddenly, Surpanakha slammed Edmund up against the door with the red sapphire blade at his throat.

"Let's see if you can survive this," she spat. "A weapon forged by Lord Shiva himself."

No.

In one split second, Uma's rage bubbled up to the surface, mixing violently with Eleanor's. A burst of heat engulfed the room, and as Surpanakha and Edmund looked around for the source, Uma's green glowing trident was fully formed in Eleanor's uninjured hand.

"I told you I wasn't Sita!" she exclaimed as she pointed the trident at Surpanakha.

"Durga?! How can *you* be the Avatar of Durga?!" Surpanakha hissed.

The trident burst into green flames as Eleanor rushed forward and slammed it against Surpanakha's back.

"Drop the sword!" she commanded.

Surpanakha dropped the sword on the ground, but as it bounced off the marble, the red sapphire blade grazed her foot, and it melted into red metallic liquid. The reaction traveled up her leg, and she looked pained as she struggled to keep her form.

"Get on your knees!" Eleanor commanded.

"No! No, I didn't mean it! You must forgive me, my lady! I beg you! I am your servant! I am your most devoted follower!"

Her voice and Uma's became one as they declared their orders. "You will leave us! You will never kill anyone on our behalf again. You will never seek us out again. You will do as Mélusine commands you from now on, and you will repent for your sins! It is Durga's will!"

"Yes, my lady!"

Eleanor used the trident to escort Surpanakha to the window, and then she gathered Mélusine's talisman into her hand and yanked it right off of Surpanakha's neck.

"You will not touch anything of mine ever again. That includes my husband and my Yakshini allies."

"Yes, my lady."

"Now go!"

She pushed Surpanakha out the window, but instead of falling, Surpanakha burst forth enormous black bat wings and blurred into the sky.

Edmund glanced at the red sapphire sword on the floor in front of him and then at the flaming green trident in her hand.

"Shiva's wrath," he whispered.

"Eleanor? How can this be?" he asked with a combination of fear and wonder. "*You* are the Avatar of Durga?"

"It is as surprising to me as it is to you, believe me."

She held the trident up and observed it with minor curiosity. Its power vibrated, making her hand tingle pleasantly. She closed her eyes and let it dissolve back to its divine perch.

She let Uma take his hand into hers, reveling in the magnetism, and then she let Uma have one final kiss.

He pulled away. "Eleanor, I am not..." He couldn't help himself as he gave into the magnetism again. "I am not... I am not Edmund."

She forced Uma to let go, and when she opened her eyes, Vibhishana was standing before her in his gentle Lankan form looking exceptionally guilty.

"Eleanor... I... I... I don't know what to say. I thought... I hoped... I hoped you'd be able to use your special talent to know that I wasn't Edmund."

"I knew you weren't Edmund. That moment of godly fireworks was for you and Uma, who has taken up residence deep inside of me, and you will not get another one. If Edmund ever knew what a mess we were in, I think he'd forgive us just this once."

"Uma..." he murmured. "So that's what the prophecy meant... That is not at all what I thought... Shiva's wrath, this changes everything..."

She intertwined her fingers with his.

My love, Eleanor is my vessel now. It is still not time for us to be together. We have been patient for centuries, and we can be patient for a little bit longer.

"That's how you called forth my divine form," he murmured. "And it's why I've been feeling so strange."

"There are strange feelings all around, I can assure you."

Eleanor picked up the red sapphire sword and gathered up the leather sheath from the ground. Once the blade was safely guarded, she handed it back to him, and he stowed it safely away in the hidden pocket in his sherwani.

"That seems dangerous, keeping a red sapphire sword so close to you."

"It is inside of me, actually," he corrected her.

Eleanor chuckled. "I suppose it is less dangerous than Uma, and she is inside of me."

"She's inside of you, but she's separate? You're conscious of her?"

"We talk often. She agrees, it's a very unusual arrangement."

"So this happened recently? After you and Edmund were married?"

"Three weeks ago." Eleanor couldn't believe it had only been three weeks. It felt like a lifetime. "It is her presence that changed my measurements. Apparently, Shakti prefers a curvier figure than I was originally endowed with." He looked away from her awkwardly, and Eleanor sighed with resignation. "Why she didn't curse me with it to begin with, I'll never know, but I suppose I

550

should be grateful that I lived the first thirty-seven years of my life with more simplicity and less leering than I'm living with now."

"I'm sorry, Eleanor. I didn't mean to... er... notice. Rakshasas often have a very keen eye for detail. It helps us make our impressions of human bodies necessarily precise."

"Please don't apologize. You'd have to be blind not to notice, even Edmund did. I'm sure I'm supposed to learn some lesson from the transformation, but it doesn't matter right now... Where is Edmund? Is he recovering? Did he realize it was you who rescued him? He must be worried sick about me. We shouldn't keep him guessing."

"We must move fast." Vibhishana forced himself back into action. "You must rescue Edmund. It is the only way."

"Wait, what? You found him, and you just left him? To rescue me?!"

"Eleanor, you are the weaker of the pair... or at least I thought you were. But I did not just leave him. I couldn't get him out. You will see why when we get there. We must go quickly. It might already be too late. But first, I have to show you something."

He took a step back, took in a deep breath, closed his eyes, and burst forth a hideous demonic form. Black spikes protruded from his skin, which was now patches of bright blue, green, and yellow. Familiar black eyes and fangs sprouted from his monstrous face, and his fingernails grew out into craggy claws, similar to the ones Padma had revealed in the garden in Baroda.

"Good lord," she murmured.

"This is our demonic form. It is what is manifesting in Edmund's eyes when he loses control. You must take a good look, and get over your shock."

"You really are ugly like that, aren't you?" She reached out her hand and touched one of his black spikes. "Have you considered being a dragon instead? I found Surpanakha's dragon to be rather cute."

"Eleanor, you must take this seriously. You must not feel any fear when we rescue Edmund, or it will compound his condition."

"He is like this? Right now? And you just left him lying in a ditch somewhere?" Eleanor could feel her anger mixing dangerously with her fear, not *of* Edmund, but for him.

"He is in a dungeon," he corrected her.

"Even better!" Eleanor exclaimed.

"Eleanor, I *couldn't* rescue him. Even Mélusine couldn't. We need you to do it."

"Well, where is he? Let's go!"

"Eleanor, he will not be dangerous to you, not even in this form. He has too much self-control for that. Are you sure that you have mastered your fear?"

"Of course, I'm sure!" she exclaimed. "I've never feared him, or you. Not before and not now. Let's go! Let's rescue my poor, suffering husband! He is sure to hate birthdays for good now!"

"You are an utterly remarkable woman," he murmured.

He morphed back into his gentle Lankan form and burst forth his wings, but this time they were not the sinister bat wings that matched Surpanakha's, they were the sparkling golden falcon wings that Mélusine had shown her, and that looked conspicuously similar to the ones depicted on the walls of the cathedral in Bulgaria.

"Hold on tight," he whispered as he gathered her into his arms, carefully avoiding her sling.

He stepped up onto the windowsill, and with one graceful flap, they were soaring over the twinkling city.

As the golden light of an impending dawn inched its way into the horizon, she let Uma swoon for the duration of their flight.

They flew across the old city, then over several lakes illuminated by the golden light, and then over dark patches with only the light of haphazard campfires flickering from the ground, until they reached the imposing fortress of Golconda Fort.

He brought them down beside a set of massive stone columns, and Eleanor startled as she looked down and spotted a detached finger at their feet.

"Good lord!" she exclaimed.

"It was part of my sister's game. She left a blood-scented trail to your tower all the way across the city. It is how I was able to find you so quickly."

"I hope that finger belongs to an evil wanker. Perhaps a murderer? Or a rapist?"

"It's hard to tell. She gets sadistic pleasure from different forms of torment. The fear of the innocent ones always tastes the best."

"Blimey," Eleanor murmured. "No wonder Rakshasas have such a bad reputation…"

"Legends are usually based on a kernel of truth. The ones about us are no different. Now, prepare yourself, and watch your step. The ruins of the staircase down into the dungeon are uneven."

She followed him down a dark staircase, until the fledgling daylight was completely obscured by the stone structure. When she could no longer see anything useful, Uma closed her eyes, and when she reopened them, everything around her glowed green. She could see everything.

That's a useful trick!

You're welcome, my child.

The smell of a rotting corpse assaulted her senses. She knew only too well what hours-old violent death smelled like after so many years of the war. She pushed forward. She could see that Vibhishana's eyes were now black, but he was holding back the other evidence of his demonic struggles.

As they reached a small stone cell, Eleanor gasped. She peeked through the bars. Edmund was unconscious and blindfolded, crouched in a fetal position on the ground with his wrists and his ankles bound in metal cuffs and chained to the wall. His sherwani was ripped into pieces with blood-soaked beads strewn all around. His skin was covered in bright patches of blue, green, and yellow, and black spikes jutted from every inch of his body. His fingers were clawed, and his mouth was filled with sharp fangs. He was rather ugly, although he was still clearly recognizable—much more so than Vibhishana had been in his especially ghoulish demonic form.

Beside him, several parts of a human corpse lay dismembered. Rotting blood made the ground all around him a grotesque color of reddish brown.

"Did he do that?" she whispered.

"He did not. My wicked sister did it to arouse his demon."

The bars on the door of the cell glistened an eerie red, even without any natural light.

"The red sapphire will melt us, Eleanor. We could not get the bars off or the door open. I don't know exactly what my sister did to make it so difficult, but there is a Yaksha trap there…" He pointed to an old unlit lantern in the corner. "If Kuveni had tried to intervene, she would have been enslaved."

"Blimey," Eleanor whispered.

"There is a reason I give the orders that I do. I'm grateful that just this once she had the sense to summon Mélusine."

"Is Mélusine immune to Yaksha traps?"

Vibhishana nodded. "Her Rakshasa lineage protects her from most of the Yakshini weaknesses. But we have both failed here. It is extremely rare that Mélusine and I together cannot solve a problem."

"Perhaps Durga will have better luck."

"I did not realize that we would be lucky enough to have such divine intervention." There was no hint of sarcasm in his tone. "It is a twist that has utterly blindsided me, Eleanor."

"I know exactly how you feel."

"When this is over, I will stay away from you both. You will not have to worry about Uma's desires again."

"I will cherish your absence and the beautiful simplicity it will bring back to my life, Lord Shiva. Now, let's rescue the man we love, shall we?"

Eleanor wrapped her hands around the smooth, strangely warm bars. They vibrated with power—a different power than her trident, but not totally dissimilar. It felt more dissonant and unnatural, almost alien.

Uma, shall we summon the power of Durga?

As you wish, my child.

She squeezed the first bar. It glowed green, and then crumbled into ashes.

"Shiva's wrath," Vibhishana murmured. "That is a useful talent, Eleanor. I've never seen anything like it."

Could you do this before, Uma?

I never had a need, my child. Red sapphire is usually used to kill Rakshasas, and in my experience, they have usually deserved to die.

Perhaps things are changing. Destiny is in motion.

Yes, my child. It most certainly is.

Eleanor quickly set about completing the task for the other bars, and then she squeezed through the opening. She crouched beside Edmund and gathered his head into her lap, carefully avoiding his many sharp spikes.

"Oh, darling. My poor, gentle, tormented husband. What are you going to think when you wake up?" She looked up at Vibhishana. "What can we do? How do we get him out of this state?"

"We must take him to a safe place, a place where there is nothing to stimulate his demon. He must have the time and the space to return to himself, and then he and I are going to have to have an honest discussion."

"He has been longing for honesty from you. Perhaps it isn't entirely bad."

"The time isn't right, Eleanor. Great misery will come from this meddling. I'm certain of it. Now, where can we take him? I cannot have him in his demonic form in my Lankan palace. My people are not prepared to accept this aspect of our lives."

"Mélusine's crystal cave?"

"You have been to the Sacred Well?"

"It was an emergency. Edmund was horribly poisoned by turmeric in Turkey."

"Yes... she told me about that... She did not tell me that she brought you to the Sacred Well."

"Perhaps you should trust Mélusine's judgment more, and she wouldn't have to lie to you so often. She is very wise, you know, and she is an avatar, although I haven't figured out which one yet."

"It is not time for her to know her destiny yet."

"Yes, Uma said so as well... but she does have a very convenient cave where she can stop time for emergencies like this one."

"We should not take him there yet. If he wakes up, we will not be able to explain ourselves. We must minimize the impact of Surpanakha's meddling."

"What about the Patels?" Eleanor suggested.

"We cannot take him to the Patels. Rahul cannot see him like this, and neither can Padma. She had quite a scare just recently. I still haven't been able to figure out exactly what she witnessed." Eleanor held her tongue.

"The Bidkars!" she exclaimed. "We can take him to the Bidkars' in Bombay! Shruti will help! She knows everything. She knows he's Lord Kalki, and she even knows that he is Ravana's son."

Vibhishana was not pleased by the development. "Eleanor, how many people know Edmund's most guarded secrets now?"

"A few..."

"This is bad... very, very bad."

She took off the blindfold and ran her fingers gently across Edmund's forehead, avoiding his spikes.

"Vibhi, darling, we don't have time to worry about it now— the city is already stirring. Let's get him out of here. If we don't, we will have a demon to explain."

Vibhishana joined her in the cell. After taking one last conflicted look at Edmund, considering their imperfect options, he gathered up Edmund's body into one arm, and Eleanor into the other.

In a blur, they were out in the open by the columns of the fort where they'd landed. The sun was now a glistening golden disk, rising swiftly over the massive boulders of the fort's hill.

"I assume you mean the Bidkars on Malabar Hill?" Vibhishana asked. "Ravi Bidkar is not the type of person who will accept us, Eleanor."

"You know him?"

"I have made it a point to know Edmund's closest friends. Ravi Bidkar is too religious to accept truths that do not align with his interpretation of scripture. It is common for people who have suffered like he has to grasp especially tightly onto literal dogma, and he is no exception."

"He loves Lord Kalki and Lord Vibhishana. Maybe he will surprise us… or maybe it will be a disaster. But Shruti is reasonable, and she will help us."

Vibhishana sighed with resignation. Eleanor could feel his fear, but she didn't care. She cared about one thing: helping Edmund.

Vibhishana pulled her and Edmund more tightly into his arms, and with a blast of incredible Rakshasa speed, far faster than an airplane, he spirited them away, into the warm morning sky.

It was raining when they landed with a thud in one of the open tropical gardens of the Bidkars' home.

Vibhishana let Eleanor out of his arms, gathered Edmund into both of his, and then dissolved his golden falcon wings.

She scampered out of the garden, bringing with her a trail of mud from her dirty feet and the hem of her lehenga.

She glanced around in a panic. It hadn't occurred to her until that moment that Shruti might not even be home. She hoped that they were all still sleeping, and that she could awaken Shruti and get her help before Ravi Bidkar even noticed.

"We should go to Shruti's room." Eleanor did not wait for Vibhishana's agreement.

As she ran through the hallway, Babri, clad in an especially flamboyant pink lehenga with enormous poufy sleeves, was meandering slowly, muttering to herself as she returned from the kitchen with a plate of biscuits and some chai.

Babri startled as she noticed Eleanor.

"Babri, where's Shruti?" Eleanor asked. "Is she asleep in her room?"

Babri looked her up and down. "Skinny doll? Skinny doll what has happened to you? You are a breasted doll now! None of your suits will fit! Memsahib will be very upset, very, very upset …"

"Babri, we don't have time for this!" Eleanor hissed. "Take me to Shruti, right now!"

Babri glanced past Eleanor, took one look at Edmund's demonic state, and then exploded into shrill screams. She threw the plate of biscuits and the cup of chai in the air and ran down the hall towards Shruti's room.

"And, we're off to a swimming start…" Eleanor muttered.

At the commotion, two guards rushed into the hallway. Eleanor panicked, and then she recognized one of them. *Thank god!*

"What is going on here, Babri?" he boomed. "The masters of the house are still sleeping!"

"Jaap Sahib! You are a sight for sore eyes! Please tell me that Shruti's home!" Eleanor exclaimed.

He took one look at Eleanor's dismal state. "Viraj Sahib, go fetch Shruti now!" he ordered.

The other guard rushed to obey him.

"What has happened, my lady?" Jaap Sahib asked as he eyed Vibhishana. His eyes widened as he glimpsed Edmund's demonic features.

"Something terrible has happened, Jaap Sahib. A great evil has played a horrible game with Edmund. We need a place where he can rest and recover *without* too many people seeing him like this."

"Yes, yes, of course!"

Eleanor sighed with relief as Shruti, clad only in a silk robe, ran down the hallway to greet her.

"Eleanor?! Eleanor, what's wrong?! You look horrible! How did you get here? Did Jaap Sahib let you in?"

"Go guard the door to Shruti's room, Viraj Sahib!" Jaap Sahib shouted down the hallway, before his fellow guard got close enough to see what exactly was going on.

Eleanor guided Shruti straight over to Vibhishana.

"Shruti, *this* is Lord Vibhishana," Eleanor said with her best impression of calm.

"My god," Shruti gasped as she saw Edmund. "What happened?!"

Eleanor debated momentarily how much she should share. "We rescued Edmund from Surpanakha. She forced him into this horrific state, and now we must help him escape from it."

"Surpanakha..." Shruti murmured. "Lord Vibhishana?!" She dropped into a deep bow.

"Shruti, there's no time for that. We need your help," he reiterated. "Lord Kalki needs your help. We must get him somewhere private *now*."

She stood up and gathered her wits. "We must get you away from the staff, and my father! He can't see Edmund like this! He won't understand!"

She took Eleanor's hand and led her down the hallway towards the guest room where they'd spent their first nights together in India. As soon as they were inside, Eleanor rushed into the bathroom and immediately began drawing the bath.

"Jaap Sahib, guard the door! Don't let anyone in!" Shruti ordered.

"Yes, memsahib," he agreed. He took his position in the hallway in front of the bedroom door.

"Shruti, dear? What's going on? Why are the guards up in arms?" Ravi called.

Shruti threw Eleanor a panicked look.

"It's nothing, Papa!" she called.

Eleanor shook her head with resignation. Shruti had just given away their position.

He barreled right past Jaap Sahib, through the cavernous bedroom, and into the bathroom.

"What is going on?" He trailed off as he spotted Eleanor, Vibhishana, and then Edmund. "My god..."

Vibhishana gently put Edmund down under the running water in the bath and took in a deep, calming breath.

"Mr. Bidkar, I am Lord Vibhishana."

"No," Ravi whispered. He backed away with his eyes glued on Edmund.

"Father, we must help Lord Kalki," Shruti whispered. "He is in a terrible state! It is our sacred duty! We can finally make up for everything he's done for us!"

"NO!" He finally tore his eyes away from Edmund, landing his burning gaze on Vibhishana. "Lies! Lord Vibhishana would never dirty himself by touching that... that... that *thing*!"

Eleanor could feel Vibhishana's temper rising. "I am one of those *things*, Mr. Bidkar. You know the epics well enough to know that."

Ravi's expression became more desperate as he looked Eleanor up and down, landing his attention on her chest. "Shruti, get away from them! They're Rakshasas! They're trying to trick us! They are dirtying Lord Kalki's name with insidious lies!"

"Father," Shruti hissed. "This is Edmund! He is *our* Edmund, and he needs our help!"

"Guards!" Ravi called. He took off running out of the bathroom.

"Stop him, Jaap Sahib!" Eleanor shouted.

Jaap Sahib threw himself in front of Ravi before he made it out of the bedroom.

"You will let me pass!" Ravi boomed. "You will let me pass now, or you will be out on the street!"

Come, Sheranee, come help us.

With a roar of excitement, Sheranee raced through the hallway, straight into her guarding position in front of the door.

562

"My god!" Ravi cowered.

"Let him pass, Jaap Sahib," Eleanor called. "Sheranee will keep Ravi Bidkar exactly where he needs to be."

Sheranee let out another resonant roar.

"What... what... what is happening?" Ravi whispered. He sunk back into the room, while Jaap Sahib backed slowly away from the tigress. She let out a long, low warning growl.

"Eleanor," Shruti whispered. "Is that... Uma's tiger?"

Uma took Shruti's hand. *It is, my child. Eleanor is my vessel now. Together, we are the Avatar of Shakti, and Sheranee heeds our commands.*

"Tell me what to do, my lady," Shruti whispered as she averted her eyes.

You must help us fix this, my child. Help us bring your father back into the light.

"I will stay with Edmund. Shruti, please talk to your father," Eleanor suggested.

Vibhishana stepped forward and leaned in to whisper into Eleanor's ear. "Eleanor, you mustn't stay with Edmund right now. Your broken arm and the bleeding scratches on your back will slow his recovery. They will keep his demon aroused."

Eleanor looked down at her blackened, bruised broken arm in the makeshift sling and sighed her resignation.

"I will stay with him," Vibhishana whispered. "Perhaps my energy will help him transform back."

He glanced over at Ravi, who was watching them with glassy eyes, and then, in one subtle movement, he transformed into the attractive British form Edmund knew. Ravi and Shruti gasped in unison, while Jaap Sahib watched with dutiful silence.

"I will be the father he recognizes when he wakes up, so that we can discuss unpleasant truths as a family."

"Please let me join you as soon as he can bear it," Eleanor whispered.

Vibhishana nodded his agreement, and Eleanor guided Shruti out of the bathroom, closing the two divine demons in together.

"My lady, shall I re-button your blouse?" Shruti whispered. "You only have one button holding it together, and it is in the wrong hole."

Eleanor blushed. She'd been so distracted that she hadn't even noticed that Surpanakha had apparently failed at dressing her up in her princess costume. She was grateful the scratches on her back weren't more severe as she thought back on Surpanakha's particularly sharp clawed fingernails.

"Yes, Shruti. Thank you."

"Don't touch it!" Ravi rushed forward to stop Shruti, and Sheranee's growl increased in volume and displeasure.

"Father!" Shruti hissed.

"It is evil, Shruti! It's a demon!"

Eleanor reached forward and grabbed Ravi's wrist.

That is enough, my child. Calm yourself. Shakti commands it.

He stepped back and tried to pry his wrist away from her, but she held it steadfastly.

Do not awaken the wrath of Durga, Sri Bidkar. You know as well as anyone how fiery her temper can be.

"How are you doing that?" Ravi whispered. "How does a Rakshasa have such power?"

"I am *not* a Rakshasa."

Ravi changed his tactic. "Please, let Shruti go. I will stay. You can have whatever you want. You can have all of my money. It really is so much money, if only you let her go."

"Ravi, Shruti has no desire to go," Eleanor said matter-of-factly. "She knows that she is safe and that it is her sacred duty to help Lord Kalki."

"Shruti, please go. Please run! These demons are playing a wicked game with us! This woman isn't Eleanor! She isn't even the right shape!"

Eleanor rolled her eyes with annoyance. "I didn't realize you were paying such close attention before, Sri Bidkar."

"I was," he said with a burst of anger. "And you will not get away with your lies! Lord Vishnu will make you pay!"

Eleanor had reached the end of her patience. She closed her eyes and silently called forth her trident, coaxing it to come slowly enough that Ravi Bidkar could watch. She stood before him and held her unbroken arm out.

Shruti whispered quiet prayers while Ravi watched with total astonishment until the green, flaming trident was fully formed in Eleanor's hand.

"Come, Sheranee," she called. "Come to your mistress."

Sheranee obeyed, gracefully slinking across the room and bowing at Eleanor's feet. Ravi froze with fear as the tiger took its position beside him.

Eleanor let Uma's consciousness mingle with hers until they could speak with one voice. It resonated eerily, and Eleanor felt waves of her own power wafting off of her as she spoke. "I am the vessel of Uma, Avatar of Shakti. I wield the transformative energy of Parvati and Durga. And you, Ravi Bidkar, will heed my commands."

"The Avatar of Shakti…" Ravi Bidkar thought through the idea for an extended moment as he eyed Eleanor and her trident again, and then he threw himself onto the floor in prostration. "Please forgive me, my lady! You… you… you… do not look how you should! How I thought you would look! Nothing is as it's supposed to be!"

Eleanor was rather pleased at his appropriate level of trembling, but after almost a minute, when his trembling began to worry her medical sensibilities, she relaxed and released her trident back to its divine perch. She kneeled down and coaxed him into looking at her.

"Looks can be deceiving, Sri Bidkar, as can your fantasies."

"I do not understand any of it," he murmured. "That monster was Edmund? The *real* Edmund?"

"I expected you, of all people, to understand that his physical appearance is not a representation of his character. I thought that you would be able to see past his wounded outer shell, just as Reya saw past yours. You have greatly disappointed me, Sri Bidkar."

He stared down at the ground for many minutes of increasingly frenzied mantras peppered with mutterings of personal castigation, until he finally got himself back under control and looked up at her.

"My lady… it does not seem to me… if you will forgive me… if you will forgive my ignorance… I do not see how the two are comparable." He glanced up at her, and then he returned his eyes to the floor. "I was wounded in an accident. My shell is grotesque, but it is not a manifestation of evil… But that creature I saw… that creature was a *demon*. Are demons not dangerous? The great goddess Durga herself slayed the demon Mahishasura. Didn't she?"

"Are tigers not dangerous?" Eleanor asked as she gestured for Sheranee to come to her. She rubbed her ears and under her chin, and then kissed the top of her head. Sheranee rolled onto her back to present her tummy for rubbing. Eleanor obliged her, and as she rubbed the soft fur, Sheranee began purring contentedly.

"But, my lady, your mount is not an ordinary tiger. It is a divine tiger… an animal worthy of serving the great goddess."

"I see. So there is a difference between tigers, Sri Bidkar? Between a wild beast stalking a deer in the jungle and Sheranee here?"

"Yes, my lady. Of course, there is!"

"Then why, my child, do you not see a difference between demons?"

Ravi's posture deflated. "So he is a demon?"

"So is Lord Vibhishana, Lord Rama's ally and friend. If Lord Rama could accept a Rakshasa, the *brother* of his greatest enemy, into his innermost circle, why can't you?"

566

Ravi sat back and stared at the floor for several minutes of contemplation.

Finally, as the heavy footsteps of several guards approached, and Sheranee hopped out of her relaxed position to return to her post at the door beside Jaap Sahib (who was remarkably relaxed about the whole thing), Ravi broke himself out of his stupor.

"Leave us!" he called to them. "Guard all of the doors. No one is to come into this wing until I say so!"

Shruti walked over to her father, helped him up off the floor, and guided him to sit next to her on the bed. She took his hand and held it. They sat in excruciating silence for a long time. Ten minutes, twenty minutes, an hour? Eleanor couldn't tell. She paced back and forth across the room, waiting for news, throwing Jaap Sahib a grateful glance every so often that he returned with a pious nod.

"But... but... Lord Kalki is not a Rakshasa," Ravi finally murmured. "How will he defeat the demon Kali if he is himself a demon? There can be no victor if a demon wins."

"Father, perhaps it will take a good demon to defeat a bad one. He will understand Kali better. He will know what his weaknesses are."

"But how will he lead humans back to righteousness? Lord Vishnu cannot possibly expect that humans will follow a demon!"

"Lord Vishnu works in mysterious ways, Father."

Vibhishana emerged from the bathroom and closed the door behind him. Eleanor rushed across the room to greet him. "How is he?"

"He has returned to himself, but he is still sleeping. We will have to wait and see how much he remembers. I will plan our discussion accordingly."

As Ravi observed Vibhishana in his British form with fresh eyes, he suddenly gulped with fear. "Shruti... Shruti, I have made a terrible mistake!"

"Yes, Father. I think we all know that." Shruti glanced at Eleanor, who offered her a supportive smile. "But now Shakti has helped you see the error of your ways. It is a great privilege to know the Avatar of Shakti, don't you think?"

"Yes... yes, it all makes sense now!"

Ravi stood up and hobbled over to Vibhishana and Eleanor. He awkwardly kneeled down and bowed piously.

"Please forgive me, Lord Vibhishana. I have wronged you and your son. I did not understand... I was callous and ignorant... but now I understand! Lord Vishnu chose your son as his vessel! The son of the Chirangivi of Righteousness!"

Vibhishana looked torn for a moment as he considered the situation, and then he smiled and guided Ravi up out of his prostration. Ravi shivered as Vibhishana touched him with his frigid hands, but he said nothing.

"Lord Vishnu works in mysterious ways," Vibhishana reiterated.

"Yes, my lord! But... but..."

"Speak your mind, Sri Bidkar. You have already done so too much today."

"But, my lord, I didn't think that you were really a demon. None of the images ever show you as a demon. Did you not... escape from your demonic nature when Lord Rama anointed you?"

Vibhishana held out his hand, palm up, and Ravi watched nervously as Vibhishana brought forth his blue skin, black spikes, and craggy claws. With a subtle wiggle, he dissolved them back into his smooth, fair human skin.

"We do not escape from who we were, Ravi. It is always a part of us. But I have chosen not to use my demonic form except for the rarest of occasions in which it serves the cause of peace. Instead, I prefer to take forms that make humans comfortable, and that allow them to accept me without fear and loathing."

"And Edmund does the same?" He sounded like a child seeking confirmation from his father.

"Edmund is half human. The form you know is his natural physicality."

"It is the form Lord Vishnu chose?"

"It is. But tonight, Surpanakha forced him into his demonic form. A form he didn't even know existed, because I kept it from him."

"Surpanakha! But she's supposed to be dead!"

"And yet, she is not." Vibhishana glanced at the bathroom door. "He's stirring. Eleanor, please wait here. I will call you in when he's ready. Ravi, Edmund does not need any more trouble. You will say nothing about any of this. If you cannot be around him without fear, you will excuse yourself now."

He slipped into the bathroom and closed himself inside.

Ravi finally turned his attention back onto Eleanor. "Durga married Lord Vishnu? There is no scripture about that..."

"It is a long story that isn't over yet," Eleanor replied. "I am quite sure that when I am gone, he will eventually marry his Padma, but it is not time yet. It is not time for him to know who I am, either, Ravi. You cannot tell him that I'm an avatar. Do you understand? It is Shakti's will that you keep your silence."

"Yes, my lady."

"I mean it," she said sternly. "Keeping your silence does not mean telling those whom you think should know."

Shruti stood up and joined them. "Father, what is she talking about?"

Ravi suddenly looked very sheepish as he struggled for an answer.

"Madho Rao and Rane and their children now know all about us, as does their staff," Eleanor glanced over to Jaap Sahib, "and the entire staff who served us at the Taj Mahal."

"But… but… they needed to know! They needed to treat Edmund like Lord Kalki should be treated! They might have treated him like an ordinary *firang*!"

"That is not for you to decide!" Eleanor felt Uma's voice joining her own for her admonishment. "From now on, we will decide who knows our secrets. Do you understand?"

"Yes, my lady," he whispered. "Please forgive me, my lady."

Sheranee growled a low warning, and Eleanor glanced over to see what had aroused her. Standing at the door, holding a stack of freshly stitched clothing was Babri.

"Let her pass," Eleanor commanded.

Shruti threw her an apologetic glance, while Ravi grimaced in anticipation. None of them had any idea what to expect from their simple genius. She'd already seen Edmund's demonic state, and had apparently decided to make him a suit.

"Busty doll's skirt is ripped. The buttons are all wrong. Spiked giant had no shirt at all," Babri explained as she handed Eleanor the stack.

"Thank you, Babri. That was very kind of you." Eleanor held up a sparkling black silk lehenga with a tasteful, modestly cut blouse. She smiled. "It's perfect."

She handed it to Shruti so she could hold up the kurta made of the same black material for Edmund. She worked her hardest to hold in her laughter. Every inch of the lehenga was dotted with tiny holes cut into it for his spikes.

"Thank you, Babri. This is more thoughtful than I ever imagined someone could be." Eleanor felt strangely emotional about the simple gesture.

"It is my own invention!" Babri exclaimed. "He doesn't have one, does he? Spiked giant doesn't have a kurta like this one?"

Eleanor chuckled. "No, Babri. This is his first."

Babri grinned and clapped with self-satisfaction. "Shall I go make another?"

"No, my darling girl. Edmund will not have spikes when you see him next."

Babri's posture deflated.

"But he will still have the most unique kurta in the world," Eleanor reassured her.

Babri smiled.

"Thank you, Babri. Can you go tell the kitchen staff to prepare a breakfast feast without turmeric?" Shruti suggested.

"Yes, memsahib." She skipped past Sheranee, and then stopped, turned around, and patted her on the head, and then she skipped down the hallway towards the kitchen, as if nothing strange had happened at all.

"Babri was wiser than I was," Ravi Bidkar admitted dismally. "Babri did not offend Lord Kalki and Lord Vibhishana and Shakti in one go."

"Perhaps, Father, that should be a lesson for you," Shruti pointed out.

"It will take me the rest of my life to fully understand tonight's lessons," he admitted.

"Eleanor?!" Edmund's voice called out desperately.

She handed Shruti the kurta, slipped into the bathroom, and closed the door behind her.

"Edmund, darling? I'm right here." She kneeled down beside him and took his hand.

"Eleanor?!" Tears streamed down his face as he kissed her hand. "Eleanor dearest, I thought you were dead!"

"I'm not dead, darling. I'm perfectly fine. I'm right here, and we are both safe and sound." She kissed his forehead.

He noticed her broken arm in the sling.

"But it was real?" He looked back and forth between Vibhishana and Eleanor. "It wasn't all just a nightmare?"

"It was real," Vibhishana replied as he took Edmund's other hand. "But this is real now too. You are safe, my dear boy, and we are here by your side."

"But… but what happened? It was a nightmare! All of it! A horrible, wicked nightmare!"

"Darling… Do you remember that creature from our wedding? The one who tried to lead us astray in the woods? It kidnapped us as a cruel game. But we escaped, and it is gone now."

"You killed it?" he asked Vibhishana. "You killed it and saved Eleanor?"

"My boy, Eleanor saved herself and then she saved me. The madwoman will not be bothering you anymore."

"But how do you know?! She was too powerful! She did things! Horrific things! She killed an innocent man. She ripped him apart and tried to force me to… to… to eat him!"

"I know, my boy, I know. She is a monster. She lost her mind a very long time ago, but she will not be bothering you again. I promise."

Edmund looked down at his bare chest. "I felt… I felt like I was going to crawl out of my skin. She blindfolded me, and put the warm corpse right there… right there beside me… and then she chained me up and told me that I had to break free… that the blood would free me… but the scent of the blood… it was just like the godforsaken trenches in the bloody, wicked war…" He trailed off into tears.

Vibhishana stroked his forehead like a doting father. "It is all over, my boy. You are safe, and Eleanor is safe, and the monster will never be back again."

As Edmund's tears morphed into sobs, Eleanor crawled into the bath fully clothed and maneuvered Edmund's head against her chest. She stroked his hair while he cried, and Vibhishana waited patiently, holding Edmund's hand tightly in his.

Eventually, Edmund's emotions calmed down, and he looked up at Eleanor and smiled sadly. "The whole time, Eleanor, all I could think about was you. I sacrificed you, dearest!" He gave into a fresh round of tears.

"Darling, you did nothing of the sort."

"All I had to do was eat him… if I ate him, she said she would let you go," Edmund whispered.

Vibhishana's eyes turned black with rage at the thought before he got himself back under control.

"I couldn't bring myself to do it, Eleanor. Even for you."

"Darling, I could not eat a man to save you. It doesn't mean that I love you any less."

He cried more.

"Darling, perhaps there is a small blessing in this." Edmund did not look convinced. "You have been tormented by the beastly urges from your shell shock. You have been terrified that you might act on the hunger that the war ignited in you. And now, even to save me, the woman you love most in the world, you couldn't bring yourself to eat him. Surely, you will now have confidence that no matter what your stomach tells you, you will not give into those urges. Don't you think?"

Edmund kissed her hand.

"I love you so much, Eleanor."

"And I love you, Edmund. Now more than ever. We will get through this, and next year, your Grump Day will be a million times better. I promise."

He finally smiled. "I hate birthdays."

A gentle knock at the door distracted them. Vibhishana got up and cracked it open.

"Might I… might I offer my help, Father Johnson?" Mr. Valov's familiar voice asked.

Vibhishana let him in.

"Leo, you look like hell," Edmund sniffled.

Eleanor was intensely grateful that Edmund had the wherewithal to joke, although Mr. Valov really did look bad. He had large bags under his eyes, his color was off, and his right hand was blackened with his fingers broken. He glanced at Eleanor's sling.

"Perhaps Eleanor can help bandage me up after she fixes up her own war wounds."

"How did you get here?" Edmund asked. He looked around the room with more scrutiny. "Are we in Bombay? At Ravi Bidkar's house?"

"It has been a long night, darling," Eleanor said, hoping he wouldn't push on how exactly they'd managed to get from Hyderabad to Bombay in a few hours.

"I… er… flew… in Lord Blakeney's plane," Mr. Valov replied.

"Is that how we got here? In a plane?" Edmund asked.

"More or less," Eleanor replied. "I'm glad to see that you're alive, Leo. You had me worried."

"It looks like the gods decided to let me live another day," he shrugged.

"Is he here?" Edmund asked hopefully. "Percy?"

"Why do you ask, darling?"

"It is a rather silly idea, actually…" He became shy as he glanced up at Vibhishana. "I thought… I thought that perhaps my birthday could be redeemed… in some small way. I have always wished that I could have a birthday, and I suppose when I envisioned what it would look like, it would have my family around me. Percy is related to me in some way, I'm quite sure… and you are here, *Father* Johnson, and my beautiful wife… and the Bidkars are here?"

"Yes, darling, everyone's here," Eleanor agreed.

Vibhishana reached down his hand and helped Edmund up. Edmund leaned woozily against him as he regained his balance, and then he pulled Vibhishana into a tight hug.

"Happy birthday, my dearest boy," Vibhishana whispered into his ear. "You make me prouder and prouder every time I see you. You have a strength of character that is unmatched in this world… except, perhaps, by your wife. You are a perfect pair."

Edmund would not let go of their embrace, instead he only squeezed Vibhishana tighter.

Mr. Valov rushed forward and helped Eleanor stand up awkwardly in her soaked lehenga. "Leo, if you would be so kind… Shruti has some clothes for us," Eleanor whispered.

Mr. Valov nodded and slipped out the door to get them.

"Will you stay, then? Just this once?" Edmund asked hopefully.

"It will make me happier than anything else in this world," Vibhishana agreed.

Mr. Valov slipped back into the bathroom, holding up the bizarre black kurta for Edmund. "Is this right?"

Edmund took it into his hand to examine it more closely. "Each of these holes has been pricked into it. What painstaking work! But it looks very odd, doesn't it?"

Eleanor smiled. "It was Babri's invention, darling. She made it just for you."

Edmund laughed. "You know, now that I think about it, it probably is quite cool! She's made a summer kurta that will keep me from peeling!"

He slipped it on, and then Mr. Valov handed him some matching, similarly airy black silk pants.

He held out his arms and watched good-naturedly as the light filtered through onto his skin. "Well, I suppose it would be rude to refuse such a thoughtful gift, but perhaps I will wear it just in the company of family."

Eleanor could see a giddiness in his expression as he said the words to Vibhishana.

"I'm sure Babri will be thrilled that you like it, darling."

She took the black lehenga from Mr. Valov. "If you will excuse me, gentlemen, I would prefer it if my husband helped me."

Mr. Valov took her cue and Vibhishana dutifully followed him out of the bathroom, closing the door behind him.

Eleanor stood onto her tiptoes and wrapped her one good arm around Edmund's neck, enticing him into a kiss. He gave in for a wonderful moment of simplicity, but then he pulled away.

"I thought you were dead, Eleanor. I thought that you were dead, and that it was my fault. I wanted so badly then to die myself, and I realized that I don't even know if I can. There was absolutely no option to escape from my torment."

"Darling, you mustn't give up so easily. I'm glad that you didn't have the means to act on your sorrow. You are so much stronger than you realize. Look at what you survived tonight! It was more horrific than anything we've ever faced. It was, in some ways, even more horrific than the war. And yet here you are, kissing your wife and readying yourself for a birthday party with your family. Do not let my mortality be the demon that defeats you. Not now, and not ever."

"You are so wonderfully strong, Eleanor. Stronger than I ever imagined anyone could be." He pulled her into a kiss, carefully avoiding her injuries. "You really defeated her? You defeated the monster who had *me*, with all of my power, tied up in a dungeon? How did you do it?"

"I didn't give up, darling. I didn't let the first or the second or even the third blow stop me. And neither will you."

"I suppose then, we will have to call the silversmith," Edmund said resignedly.

"Why?"

"So that he can start fitting you for your armor, dearest. I don't think they will have any knight's armor on hand that will fit you."

He finally cracked a smile at his silly joke, and Eleanor tickled him until he burst into roaring laughter. "I know how to vanquish you, darling! With pleasure and love and uncontrollable laughter!"

"It is the best way to be vanquished," he agreed as he escaped her attack with a speedy Rakshasa move and whisked her into a romantic twirl. When they were finished with a particularly

576

delicious kiss, Eleanor felt the pull of the many people waiting just outside the door for them.

"Darling, can you unbutton me? I have a matching lehenga to put on with my husband's help." She turned around and pulled her wild curly tendrils away from the back of her blouse.

Edmund kissed her neck as he unbuttoned her blouse, but as he reached the tender scratches, he sighed with resignation.

"I am certain that this is my fault. If it weren't for me, this creature would never have touched you."

"If it weren't for you, darling, I'd be changing the bedpans of madmen right about now. Our life is stranger now, but it isn't worse. In fact, it is markedly better. Don't you think? The pursuit of ultimate perfection is a fool's errand. It distracts us from appreciating the beauty of imperfection all around us, and we, darling, are beautifully imperfect together."

"I suppose."

"I do think, though, that perhaps it is time for our honeymoon to come to an end. I think that we have both had enough adventure for now. What do you say we hop down to Munnar and see if they need a medical clinic and a painter to take up residence in one of their most pastoral houses? It is cool but humid there? With plenty of tea and wine? That should be quite nice for both of us, and for Mr. Valov."

"Do you really want to stay in India, dearest? Even now, after everything that's happened?"

"I cannot think of anywhere I'd rather be, darling. Can you?"

He pulled her into his arms and crushed her into a tongue-filled kiss. "Nowhere."

As they heard the shuffle of the others in the bedroom, he finished buttoning up her new blouse.

Sheranee, please go. Lord Kalki cannot know you yet.

She pulled him into a final kiss.

"Darling, I have decided that Tennyson was right. It is better to have loved, no matter what happens next. Now, shall we go celebrate your Grump Day once and for all? Here on out, we're going to have to call it your birthday."

"As you wish, Eleanor. I will never have a reason to be grumpy again."

She took his hand tightly into hers and pushed open the bathroom door.

There, Mélusine in the form of Percy stood holding an enormous tiered birthday cake, surrounded by the rest of their friends and allies.

"Happy birthday!" Vibhishana, Mélusine, Mr. Valov, Shruti and Ravi all cheered.

"Welcome home, Edmund," Ravi said as he timidly offered him his hand to shake.

Edmund pulled him into a hug. "Brothers in arms, and in spirit?"

"It would be a privilege, old chap." Ravi hugged him back.

Eleanor threw Shruti and knowing smile, and Kuveni clapped her approval.

And so together, surrounded by their truest friends and family in their home away from home, Edmund and Eleanor said goodbye to their honeymoon and hello to their new married life.

EPILOGUE

Ellie let her triumph and relief wash over her as she waited in the hallway just outside of the auditorium for her father to break away from the uproarious crowd and join her. She'd done it. Two hours in front of hundreds of snarky adolescents, answering all sorts of prying questions without giving away how incredibly painful the experience was. She'd beaten down the urge to run away so many times, and she'd made it through with only a few supportive thumbs-ups from her father and Charlie.

You were wonderful, Ellie-bean.

Her mother's voice echoed in her head. She wondered if it was real, or just imagined. She had imagined her mother's voice in her head so many times growing up, but now she wasn't so sure what to believe.

I'm real, my darling. You must read Supriya's manuscript, then you will understand.

Mum?

Oh, how I love you, Ellie-bean.

How is this possible? Why is it possible? Why now? I've wanted so badly to know you my whole life!

My darling, it is the Age of Truth now. So much has changed—the world, your father, and you. It is finally time for us to know each other, and for you to help me complete my unfinished business.

Have you always been here?

I have, Ellie-bean. Through every triumph and every folly. It was my curse to share your pain in silence, but what a blessing it was to know your joy.

Why? Why didn't you stop me? Why didn't you tell me what an idiot I was being when I married that abusive wanker?

Darling, you must walk your own path. You needed to make your own choices and your own mistakes. I know myself only too well how difficult it is to keep a foreign voice inside of you under control. I did not want you to have to fight me.

I wouldn't have fought you.

My darling, that is an even more dire proposition. You needed to develop your own judgment and your own sense of self, and now you've finally done it. Ninety years have finally given you the experience you needed—they've given you the independence to know me, and to help me.

What do you need me to do?

It is not quite time yet, Ellie-bean. You will know. For now, I will leave you to yourself. Lord Kalki is on his way.

No, Mum. Don't go!

"Ellie-bean!" Edmund pushed through the door into the hallway with Charlie by his side and pulled her into a hug.

"Ellie, you were great!" Charlie exclaimed.

"Are you alright?" Edmund asked as he sensed her reticence.

"Yes… yes, I'm fine," Ellie lied.

"Dad said that Sabrina is making carpenter's pie for dinner!" Charlie exclaimed. "I hope it's as good as Kuveni's!"

"I'm sure it will be," Ellie said distractedly.

She grimaced as Grace pushed her way through the door, followed by Dr. Higgins.

"Ms. Downey, please wait…" Dr. Higgins implored.

"Wait for what? To see my son?" Grace snapped.

Edmund, Charlie, and Ellie all tensed as her attention landed on them, and Dr. Higgins threw Edmund an apologetic glance.

Grace ignored him as she straightened her posture, squeezed the rosary in her right hand, and focused her attention on Ellie.

"That was a lovely speech, Ellie. I had no idea that you had such interesting experiences as a girl. I'm sorry that I didn't have the chance to talk to you about them years ago… back when we were… er… a family."

Ellie threw her father a surprised look. She had no idea how to respond. Grace had been a heartless, judgmental shrew the entire time she'd known her. She still couldn't believe, after everything, that her father had made such an egregious lapse in judgement to ever let the woman into their lives.

"Well, er… thank you, Grace. I'm glad you enjoyed it," Ellie replied.

"Since you are here unexpectedly, from undoubtedly far away, I thought… er… I was thinking… I was just wondering if you… if both of you…" she looked at Edmund, "would like to join us for dinner back at home?"

"Well… er… thank you kindly for the offer, Grace…" Edmund's mind was racing for an appropriate response as he realized that his offer to Charlie had been made a bit prematurely without considering Grace's plans at all. "Actually, we've been invited to the Rutherford home for a family dinner, and we thought that Charlie would like to join us… but perhaps you would like to come as well?"

Ellie threw him an annoyed glance.

Ellie-bean, she's trying. It's good for Charlie if we can get along as civilized people. Ellie shivered as her father's voice echoed in her head through the green sapphire necklace that she wore always now as her secret Rakshasa connection to him. She still didn't like the alien effect, but after months of needling by Neha to get her to use it, she had finally given into the convenience of the option.

"Oh, I see…" Grace did not look pleased, but as she observed Charlie's hopeful expression, she took a deep breath and collected herself. "I suppose Charlie would like to spend more time with you…" Charlie nodded emphatically. "I suppose… I suppose, if it's not an imposition…"

"Join us, Grace," Edmund reiterated. Charlie looked just as shocked as Dr. Higgins did at the development, as the media had already spent many thousands of hours dissecting every detail of the annulment of their excruciating marriage. "Ellie was just telling me how much she misses our time together in Cambridge. Weren't you, Ellie?"

She hated to admit that he was right… that perhaps what she really needed was a slap in the face to remind herself how unpleasant her old life was in Grace's company. She wondered how intentional her wise father's actions were on that front…

"It does seem like it has been too long since we've all spent time together with Charlie," Ellie begrudgingly agreed.

As several unruly children tried to push their way through the door into the closed-off hallway, Dr. Higgins shouted his disapproval and left them alone to manage the crowds.

"We'd better go before the paparazzi find us. It's a wonder they haven't been hounding us for hours already," Ellie suggested.

"I can drive," Grace offered. "Unless… unless you have another suggestion?" Ellie couldn't tell if there was hope or fear in Grace's question… perhaps a bit of both.

Edmund looked between the three of them, contemplating his limited options. He was not going to carry all three of them in his arms, and he hated to bother Kuveni with mundane requests for Yakshini public transportation.

"That is a fine idea," he agreed. "It has been quite some time since I've been in a car. Almost a year now, actually. It's funny how time flies."

"Time is not the only thing that flies these days," Ellie winked.

"Indeed, it isn't," Edmund smiled. "Shall we?"

582

"I'm parked out back, in the faculty carpark. Dr. Higgins was very accommodating," Grace said as she led the way.

Charlie took Edmund's hand and skipped happily alongside him as they followed Grace through the empty hallway.

When they reached the parking lot, Ellie noticed her father tense as a horde of paparazzi aimed their cameras into the locked gate, snapping away as they approached Grace's modest old mini, a car that had sparked more than one raging row over the years, as it was possibly the least practical car on Earth for a man of Edmund's height to stuff himself into.

"Blimey," Ellie muttered.

With a warm, pleasant breeze, Kuveni was standing beside her in the form of Kate, dressed in a stylish modern wool pant-suit.

She glanced disapprovingly at the paparazzi. "Selfish swine they are, the lot of them. Making a living from others' misfortune. If I could curse them all with disgusting human diseases, I would do it… and that is, perhaps, why I am not an avatar. I've never had the discipline, I must admit…"

"Thank god you're here, Kuveni," Ellie whispered as she welcomed Kuveni with a hug. "Everything is so bloody hard these days, isn't it? Just getting in a blasted car to drive home is an event on the six o'clock news."

"It is my pleasure to help you, Ellie dearest," Kuveni said as she squeezed her affectionately. "We will get you all sorted."

"Kuveni!" Charlie exclaimed as he noticed her and rushed straight into her arms. She swung him around and then gathered him into a grandmotherly hug.

Edmund could not have been gladder to see her. "Grace, perhaps you can collect your car later, when the mobs have dispersed. Are they like this often? I thought we'd made it clear that we disapproved of their uninvited presence."

Grace glanced over to the wall of paparazzi, and sighed with resignation. "They are more aggressive than usual, certainly because you are here, but there are usually a few camped out in the bushes every morning."

"*Every* morning?!" Edmund exclaimed. "Grace, why didn't you say anything?! We have ways of making them comply with our orders!"

Grace suddenly looked panicked. "Please don't smite them… it really isn't so bad… I'm sure that they just need a bit of religious counsel. Perhaps Father Flannigan can talk to them…"

Edmund rolled his eyes with frustration. "I didn't mean that we'd throw lightning bolts at them, Grace."

"Yes… yes, of course. I'm sorry, Edmund… I didn't mean to offend you…" Her spicy fear bothered him even more.

"Grace, what I meant was that we can ask Kuveni to put a Yaksha shield around the house. They won't be able to hide in the bushes. No one who is uninvited will be able to cross the threshold."

"Oh…" Grace glanced over to Kuveni who was now chatting amicably with Ellie and Charlie, watching for a cue from Edmund to intervene. "Yes, I suppose that would make things easier… if Kuveni can manage it…"

"Of course I can manage it!" she exclaimed as she rushed over to pull Edmund into a motherly hug. "Anything for my beautiful boy, and his beautiful boy!" She winked at Charlie. "But first we must deal with these ruffians. Now, Ellie dearest, are you able to fly yet, or do you need a Yakshini escort?"

"Me?!" Ellie exclaimed.

"My dear girl, if Supriya can fly, certainly you can too. You are more Rakshasa than she is! Have you not been trying at all? Not even a little bit?"

Ellie had banished the idea from her mind many times throughout the past year as she'd fought against her foreign nature more than she had in decades. She'd been grateful that her magical relatives had all been so preoccupied with their own endeavors that they hadn't noticed her excessive level of avoidance.

"Do you not want to fly, my dear girl? It's really very freeing, you know." Kuveni pulled Ellie into another hug.

"I just… I…" Ellie glanced back over at the wall of paparazzi who were voraciously consuming every word. Ellie took Kuveni's hand. *I didn't want to try and fail,* she admitted. *I've never been a very skilled Rakshasa… Supriya has always been able to do more than I can. I assumed it was because her mother was so powerful.*

Oh, my dear girl, that is utter nonsense. Your mother was just as powerful.

She was? How?

Hrm. I see you haven't taken her memories yet.

I've been avoiding them…

Well, it doesn't matter right now. Your father went more than a century with no Rakshasa traits at all, and now look at him. You have it in you, Ellie. I'm sure of it, but we needn't make a scene.

Kuveni followed Ellie's attention to the paparazzi. "Now, shall I call Mélusine or Sabrina to join me? Together we can take all four of you. You needn't do anything that you don't want to do, darling girl, especially in front of an audience."

Ellie glanced over at Grace, and then at Charlie who was squirming excitedly as he waited for her response. Edmund left Grace to approach her. "Are you alright, Ellie-bean? Why don't we just have the Yakshinis transport us for now, and we can work on honing your talents together somewhere more private?"

Do it, Ellie-bean. Just banish your fear and do it!

Ellie took in a deep breath, closed her eyes, and focused on her mother's voice.

Come on, come on, come on…

She shivered and squealed as the bizarre sensation of a cold, wriggling fish swimming up her back exploded into a burst of weight throwing her off balance. As she struggled to stay standing, the cameras clicked and clattered. The paparazzi shouted with excitement and then began fighting with each other to get a better view.

Grace screamed. "Ellie?! What... what... why?! How?! They're... they're... they're evil!"

"Silence!" Edmund boomed. Everyone but Kuveni shivered as a burst of divine power wafted off of him. "You will not say one more word, *Grace*!"

"Yes, Your Holiness," Grace whispered as she backed slowly away, squeezing her rosary.

Ellie looked over her shoulder and almost collapsed with a bombardment of confusion, fear, and frustration as she observed a pair of ghoulish black bat wings that matched her evil grandfather's.

"Bloody hell!" she exclaimed.

Edmund blurred to her side and whispered into her ear. "Ellie-bean, this is perfectly natural. Mine did exactly the same thing when I first produced them, remember?"

"If I'd realized this could happen, I never would have tried it in front of the whole blasted world." She glanced over at the paparazzi, who responded with another round of clicks. "Bloody, bloody, bloody, wicked bloody hell."

Edmund gathered her into a gentle hug. "It will all be fine. I promise. Now, shall we get out of here, or do you want to try to change them into a form you like first?"

"Do you think I can?"

They stretched out and flapped several times. The sensation of the extra appendages was stranger than anything she had ever imagined. She had some control, but they also seemed to have a mind of their own...

"I know you can, Ellie-bean. Producing them at all is the hardest part. Forming them to your will is a natural talent for Rakshasas. They will be how *you* want them to be. You mustn't give them a choice. Now, picture the wings that you want to have in your mind. Focus on the image, relax, and make your plasma do your bidding. It will know what to do if you let it."

He took her hands into his. *Tell them who's boss, Ellie-bean.*

586

"She's got bloody demon wings!" one of the paparazzi shouted.

"Like a bloody vampire, she is!" another added.

"Shut up!" Charlie shouted.

The crowd exploded into more camera shutters clicking away, punctuated by loud, aggressive jeering.

Edmund's eyes turned black. "You will leave here now! The lot of you!"

Ellie shivered as another wave of power wafted off of him, and then she felt something stirring deep inside of her. Something that had scared her since her earliest childhood, since a girl at school had knocked her over in the schoolyard, sneering about her crippled, ancient, scrooge-like father. It was a fiery Celtic temper just like her mother's, mixing dangerously with something powerful, something dark and morbid.

"No need to make a scene, my loves," Kuveni said nervously. She whispered a quiet mantra, and Mélusine materialized beside her.

"*Qu'est-ce que c'est?*" Mélusine asked with minor annoyance until she noticed their predicament. "*C'est un disastre incroyable!*"

"Go!" Edmund shouted again at the paparazzi, but as his tone exploded into the roar of an angry father protecting his young, a real roar echoed from the road beyond.

The back row of the paparazzi horde began shouting and running. Within a few seconds, the entire group was frantically dispersing with fearful shrieks.

"Good lord..." Ellie murmured as an enormous tigress approached the gate.

"*Mon dieu,*" Mélusine whispered. "That is what the prophecy meant..."

Kuveni snapped her fingers and the gate dissolved momentarily, letting Sheranee right through, and then re-solidifying to block out their unwelcome audience.

"God almighty." Grace backed away, against the wall of the school's gymnasium. "Don't let it in, for God's sake!"

"You aren't a Rakshasa, are you?" Charlie ran straight up to greet Sheranee, and Grace screamed, but Sheranee only licked his hands.

"Dad? What's going on?" Ellie asked with equal parts curiosity and nerves.

Edmund approached the tigress and stroked her head and then her ears. Suddenly, a look of deep melancholy blanketed his expression.

"Sheranee?" he asked the tigress. She purred her agreement. "If only I had known you better."

She licked his hands, and then she leaned forward, bowing languidly before Ellie.

A few of the bravest (and most foolish) paparazzi returned to the gate and began snapping away again.

"Ellie, this is Sheranee. She was... she was your mother's mount," Edmund said as he stroked the soft fur on Sheranee's back.

"Her mount?" Ellie asked as she cautiously reached her hand out. Sheranee licked her, and Ellie shivered with a jolt of electricity as their energy connected.

"You will know who she is when you read Supriya's most recent manuscript. Your mother was a powerful avatar, as it turned out. She was so powerful that she was able to keep that truth from me long past her dying day. But now... now, I don't understand." He glanced back at Mélusine. "How is she here now?"

Ellie watched her hand reach forward to take Edmund's, but she was not the one controlling it.

It is almost time, darling. It is almost time for my sacred duty to be fulfilled. Only then will Uma and I be released from our sacred throne.

Edmund pulled away and looked searchingly into Ellie's eyes. "Eleanor?"

"Blimey, this is weird," Ellie murmured.

588

"I'm sorry, Ellie-bean," Edmund whispered as he glanced around, observing their audience. "I don't know how to feel about it either. It is like... it is like your mother's ghost is haunting me still, but I hardly even know who she was anymore. Everything I thought I knew about her was wrong. She was... she was much more powerful than I ever realized... much more in control... and much more courageous. I wish that I'd known her better. I think that I would have loved her even more."

Eleanor reached Ellie's hand up to take his wrist again. *I love you, darling. Thank you for forgiving my atrocious web of lies. Now, let us leave this momentous occasion to our daughter. It is not every day that a girl meets her mount.*

"She's mine now?" Ellie asked with wonder as Sheranee nuzzled her hand and began another round of affectionate licking.

"Yes... I suppose she is," Edmund murmured as he struggled to comprehend the implications.

Sheranee pounced forward and licked Ellie's face. She giggled and gave into the utterly odd sensation of connecting with the monstrous beast without any fear at all, but then, as her ugly wings flapped reflexively, she glanced back at Grace, and then at the enamored paparazzi, took in a deep breath, and reveled in rebellion against their unfair judgment of her intensely private struggle.

To Hell, the lot of you. I will have my angelic falcon wings!

She shivered as she felt another wave of wriggling, cold plasma exploding from her back.

"*C'est magnifique!*" Mélusine exclaimed.

Charlie and Kuveni cheered, and Sheranee roared victoriously as Ellie looked over her shoulder to observe her iridescent, glistening green falcon wings, just like the most beautiful hues of a peacock.

"I always did like green." She laughed giddily at her triumph.

"Ellie-bean, I'm so proud of you!" Edmund exclaimed as he twirled her around. "How lovely they are! And utterly unique! Mélusine, does anyone else have green wings?"

"She is most certainly the first," Mélusine laughed.

Kuveni gathered up Charlie and Mélusine to join their group hug. Ellie reveled in her triumph, and then she glanced back at the paparazzi.

"We're not bloody vampires," she called. "And you should all know that by now, or do we have to save your planet from a second bloody apocalypse?"

Sheranee roared her agreement, and Ellie laughed.

"Shall we skedaddle over to the Rutherford house?" Kuveni suggested. "Sabrina is ready for us, and Lady Neha has gathered up Lady Supriya from the Mexican desert to pop in for a bite and a tipple."

Ellie flapped her wings with a flourish. "I think I'll fly. Dad? Are you coming?"

Edmund grinned and burst forth his sparkling golden falcon wings, and the paparazzi exploded into an even more frenzied wave of clicks.

"We will take the others and meet you there," Kuveni declared. "Even Sheranee will come with us. There is nothing more fitting than for you two to take your inaugural flight together."

"Relax and let your wings do the work, Ellie-bean. They will know what to do," Edmund advised as he squeezed her hand and smiled.

And so, to a chorus of awe from the ogling photographers and cheers and roars from her loving allies, Ellie Ariadne MacLeod Marriner took off beside her effusively proud father straight into the cool afternoon sky, readier than she had ever been in her long life to conquer whatever surprises destiny had in store.

~TO BE CONTINUED~

GLOSSARY OF HINDU REFERENCES

Hinduism, the world's oldest continuously practiced religion, is an exceptionally diverse collection of philosophies and rituals practiced by over one billion people globally. There is no single institution and no single written text that defines the 'rules' of Hinduism, and thus it varies widely in practice and belief across the world.

While there is a pantheon featuring a plethora of gods and goddesses with various regional names and stories, there are also numerous sects who worship Vishnu (Vaishnavism), Shiva (Shaivism), Shakti (Shaktism), and combinations/permutations of these major gods and goddesses, and their manifestations (including avatars), as representations of the one supreme being.

The vast and fascinating complexity of Hinduism cannot be captured in a short glossary, and it is not the author's intent to do so. This glossary is meant to give the uninitiated reader some basic context for references throughout the Ashley Mayers universe. Further research is recommended for those interested in digging deeper.

Agni (uh-**gnee**) – 'Fire' in Sanskrit, Agni is also the god of fire and the conveyor of sacrifices to the gods. It is Agni's role in the Hindu pantheon that is invariably linked with the many rituals, both daily and for special occasions, that require a *yajna*, or sacred fire.

Artha (**ahr**-tah) – One of the four aims of human life in Hindu philosophy, sometimes 'meaning, sense, or purpose,' *artha* generally focuses on the 'means to live the life you want,' including but not limited to wealth, career, and financial security. It can perhaps be thought of as 'why you do work.'

Asura/Asuri (ah-soo-ruh/ah-soo-ree) – Originally a term used to describe divine, powerful beings, good or bad, the term later came to represent primarily darker powered beings in Hinduism and is sometimes (but not always) synonymous with demons. Rakshasas are sometimes described as one type of *Asura*. *Asuri* is the feminine form of *Asura*.

Avatar (**ah**-vuh-tuhr) – In Hinduism, an avatar is a deliberate descent of a deity to Earth. The term is most commonly used to describe incarnations or manifestations of Vishnu, but has been used with other deities, including Shiva, Ganesh, and Shakti. The lists of avatars and consensus around them is dubious. Some sects believe that Shiva, as a formless entity, will never have an avatar, while others believe that Hanuman is an avatar of Shiva. The lists of Vishnu avatars range from ten to twenty-five avatars, and some characters in epics are referred to as 'partial' avatars, such as Rama's brother, Lakshmana, sometimes being considered 'one-quarter Vishnu.' One major thematic element throughout the Ashley Mayers universe explores what exactly it means (and doesn't mean) to be an avatar.

Ayodhya (ah-**yoh**-dyuh) – An ancient city located in Uttar Pradesh in Northern India that remains inhabited today, Ayodhya is considered to be the birthplace and ancient kingdom of Rama. In modern times, tragedy and controversy, fuelled by Hindu/Muslim animosity, have plagued the city after a violent uprising in 1992 that led to the destruction of the 16th c. Babri Mosque, which many people believed was built upon the site of Rama's original temple.

Bhoomi (**boo**-mee) – The embodiment/personification of 'Mother Earth.' Bhoomi is referred to as the mother of Sita, and at the end of *the Ramayana*, when Sita's suffering becomes unbearable, she returns to her 'mother,' being swallowed by the earth.

Ceylon (say-lon) – The historical, British colonial name of modern-day Sri Lanka, Ceylon is a key setting in *the Ramayana*, as the home of the Rakshasa king, Ravana, who kidnaps Sita and takes her back to Lanka to woo her (while she is imprisoned).

Chiranjivi (chee-ruhn-**jee**-vee) – Seven immortals in Hinduism who remain on Earth to lead humans in various paths of righteousness. In this series, we have two: Vibhishana, Hanuman.

Dasara (**Duh**-suh-ruh) – Otherwise known as *Dussera*, *Dushera*, or *Vijayadashami*, depending on the region and language, Dasara is a holiday at the end/culmination of Navaratri, the nine-night autumn festival devoted to the Goddess. Dasara traditions vary across India, ranging from sacred dances of Garba and Dandiya in the north, to a candlelight vigil and elephant parade in Mysore in the south, a city that considers itself the namesake of the Goddess in her defeat of the demon Mahishasura (sometimes referred to as *Mahishasura-Mardini* from the Sanskrit holy mantras). It coincides with the culmination of Durga Puja in Bengal, and always involves great cheer, festivities, and often fireworks and light shows.

Devi/Deva (deh-**vee**/deh-**vah**) – 'Heavenly' or 'divine' beings in Hinduism, *Devi* can be synonymous with 'god' or 'deity' but primarily refers to powerful beings who are 'good,' and can sometimes be contrasted with the 'evil' *Asura*. However, the designations of 'good' versus 'evil' are far less clearly defined in Hinduism compared to Judeo-Christian religions, and so, for example, Kartikeya, the god of war, is still considered a *Deva*. In Hinduism, an *Asura* can ascend and become a *Deva*, with Vibhishana being a prime example, demonstrating that birthright is less important than actions on Earth to define one's character and virtue.

Devi Mahatmya (deh-**vee** muh-**hat**-myuh) – The *Devi Mahatmya* is a religious text (from the *Markandeya Purana*, one of eighteen primary religious texts in Hinduism) devoted to the Great Goddess (Shakti). It recounts her manifestation on Earth in the warrior form of Durga to protect the innocent by defeating the shapeshifting buffalo demon Mahishasura, and her subsequent return of balance and virtue to the world. A text revered by Hindus across many sects, the *Devi Mahatmya* serves as a primary text for Shaktist Hindus, who believe that the Goddess is the Supreme Being. It serves as the inspiration for the festivals of Navaratri, Durga Puja, and Dasara/Vijayadashmi.

Dharma (**dahr**-muh) – One of the four aims of human life in Hindu philosophy, with many meanings, *dharma* is roughly translated as virtue, morality, righteousness, obligations, and correct conduct. The Hindu epics, *the Ramayana* and *the Mahabharata,* both demonstrate that there is often no single clear path to *dharma*, as various 'right' paths often conflict and need to be prioritized, with each difficult choice producing complicated consequences and satisfying drama.

Diwali (Dih-**vah**-lee) – Also known as Deepavali in many South Indian languages, Diwali is one of the most important festivals across Hindu tradition, and celebrates the triumph of light over darkness, knowledge over ignorance, and hope over despair. Based on the Hindu calendar, the festival of lights typically falls between mid-October and mid-November each year, and its observance dates back to ancient times. The rituals vary across the many cultures who celebrate the holiday, but it is generally consistent that people light candles and offer prayers to Lakshmi.

Durga (door-**gah**) – A principle form of the Goddess (Shakti), who manifests physically in many different forms depending on the task at hand, Durga is also called Maa Durga or the Holy Mother (not to be confused with the Christian/Catholic Holy Mother Mary). The primary hero of her own epic, the *Devi Mahatmya*, Durga is most famous as a warrior for justice who wields the power of the entire pantheon, coming to Earth with many arms and weapons to defeat the shapeshifting buffalo demon, Mahishasura. Her triumph in defeating an insidious, ever-changing manifestation of evil can be viewed as a model of perseverance that can be applied in everyday life. Every year her triumph is celebrated during the festivals of Navaratri ("Nine Nights," each celebrating a manifestation of the Goddess), Durga Puja (five nights celebrating her defeat of Mahishasura, primarily celebrated in Bengal), Dasara (the culmination of Navaratri celebrated across India), and Diwali (the Festival of Lights, celebrated across the Hindu world and by other related religions). As the Great Goddess, she is sometimes referred to interchangeably with Parvati, wife of Shiva, and she is sometimes said to manifest as Lakshmi and Saraswati in their roles as the primordial energy that animates the universe. Across most sects, Durga is worshipped as the underlying creative, preservative, and destructive energy of the universe (Shakti), who exists as a formless entity always, and sometimes takes form within the gods or goddesses, to fulfill tasks on behalf of the universe.

Durga Puja (door-**gah poo**-ja) – A five-night festival primarily celebrated in Bengal, Durga Puja coincides with the festival of Navaratri in other parts of India, all in celebration of the Great Goddess (Shakti), manifested as Durga for her defeat of the shapeshifting demon Mahishasura. Known for its *pandals* (elaborate temporary altars to the Goddess), Durga Puja is celebrated with costume, dance, food, special rituals, and bright firecrackers, making the streets of Calcutta one of the liveliest (and most crowded) places in the world to experience the frenetic energy of the Devi in one of her most beloved forms.

Garuda (**guh**-roo-duh) – The 'mount' of Lord Vishnu, Garuda is a large bird, sometimes a humanoid bird, who flies Lord Vishnu around. Sometimes represented as a large phoenix, eagle, or kite, Garuda also exists in Buddhist mythology.

Hanuman (**hahn**-oo-mahn) – Rama's right-hand man and a beloved star of *the Ramayana*, Hanuman is a Vanara, a monkey-like humanoid race who fought by Rama's side in his attack against Ravana in Lanka. In *the Ramayana*, Hanuman uses his flying ability to track and eventually make contact with Sita while she is incarcerated by Ravana, but she refuses to go with him back to Rama. Various interpretations of this interaction range from it exemplifying Sita's purity through her refusal to be in another man's arms, even to be rescued, to a valid observation that had Sita agreed to go back to Rama with Hanuman, the entire war between Rama and Ravana might have been avoided. Hanuman is consistently referred to as one of the *Chiranjivi*, representing loyalty, courage and devotion.

Harihara (**hah**-ree-**hah**-ruh) – A combined form of Shiva and Vishnu (Transformation and Preservation), Harihara is sometimes used to explain/describe the complementary nature of the two gods as aspects of one supreme being. The symbolism evokes the necessary balance (and tug-of-war) between the two primary aspects of existence, each keeping the other in check.

Hiranyakashipu – (**hee**-ran-**yaak**-shih-poo) – A demon evil enough to warrant the Preserver of the Universe coming to Earth (as Narasimha, the fourth avatar of Vishnu), Hiranyakashipu gained a boon from Lord Brahma so that he couldn't be defeated by man or beast, thus requiring Lord Vishnu to take a more clever form, in his case, as a half-man, half-lion, to defeat him.

Lakshmi (**luhk**-shmee) – The female aspect of the Preserver of the Universe, often referred to as the goddess of prosperity (material and spiritual), and the wife of Lord Vishnu, Lakshmi (or Laxmi), is one of the principal goddesses of the *Tridevi*, or 'Trinity of Goddesses.' She is said to be the life-force of Lord Vishnu and is worshipped during the major festival of Diwali every autumn. As the wife of Rama, seventh avatar of Vishnu, Sita is an avatar of Lakshmi.

Kali (kuh-lee) – Hinduism's primary apocalyptic demon—not to be confused with Kali, a fierce incarnation of Shakti (spelled the same in English but not in Sanskrit)—this demon is often depicted with a dog's head. He is said to fan the flames of human greed, violence, and iniquity during *Kali Yuga* ('The Age of Vice'), an era that many Hindus believe describes the modern world. It is sometimes said that Ravana is an incarnation and/or devotee of the demon, Kali, and that Lord Vishnu will incarnate in his ultimate avatar form, Lord Kalki, to defeat Kali and bring the worlds into *Satya Yuga* ("The Age of Truth").

Kali/Kaali (Kah-lee) – A fierce incarnation of the female life-force of the Transformer of the Universe, Kaali (often spelled Kali in English, but too easily confused with the demon Kali), is one of the most misunderstood incarnations of the Goddess. Often referred to as the goddess of time, and represented with blue or black skin, her tongue out, standing on the dead body of her husband, Shiva, wearing a skull necklace and holding a severed, bloody head, she is often thought of as a ghoulish character by those who don't know any better. However, the symbolism of the imagery of her standing on Shiva's body is meant to represent that she is his life-force, and without her, he is lifeless. The life-force of change is fierce, and the ravages of time often frightening, which are two reasons why she is depicted in such a monstrous style. She is, however, a natural manifestation of the destruction required for our ever-changing universe to exist.

Kalki (**kuhl**-kee) – Lord Kalki, 'Destroyer of Filth,' the tenth and final avatar of Vishnu (the Preserver of the Universe), is believed to be the only avatar who has not already been on Earth. Legends tell of him being born in Shambhala, a mythical place of great spiritual power north of Tibet, a place of great interest to the sages when the stories were written, due to its association and proximity to the homeland of the invading Khans. While references to Lord Kalki can be conflicting, it is consistent in texts that Lord Kalki will come to Earth to defeat the demon, Kali, and restore balance and order, bringing humans back to the path of virtue, and ushering in the Age of Truth.

Mahagauri (**Maa**-huh-**gau**-ree) – A manifestation of Maa Durga (considered her eighth of nine manifestations by some sects), Mahagauri is worshipped on the eighth night of the festival of Navaratri in some parts of India. She is said to be "the fair one," with a fair complexion, who offers forgiveness and protection to all of her followers.

Mantra (**mahn**-truh) – Words or sounds, often repetitive, that are used in prayer.

Moksha (**mohk**-shuh) – One of the four aims of human life in Hindu philosophy, meaning 'release' or 'liberation,' *moksha* primarily refers to release from the reincarnation cycle of birth and death on Earth.

Naraka (nah-**rah**-kuh) – In Hinduism, Naraka, or the underworld (somewhat similar to Christian purgatory), is a temporary place for expiation of sins to be endured between a soul's mortal death and its return to Earth. There are many different forms of Naraka, each featuring colorful punishments that are related to a person's sins, such as murderers being eaten alive by Rakshasas. As positive and negative actions do not 'cancel each other out' in Hinduism, a soul can repent through their punishment in Naraka and enjoy the peace of *Svarga* (a heavenly place), both before their return to Earth.

Narasimha (**Nur**-sim-haa) – Regarded as the fourth avatar of Vishnu, Narasimha is a manifestation of the Preserver of the Universe who comes to Earth as a half-man, half-lion to defeat the demon Hiranyakashipu, who has immortality against "all men and beasts." He is considered a protector of the innocent and warrior for justice, as well as an example of one of Lord Vishnu's many clever responses to the inconvenient ancient boons held by his enemies.

Navaratri (Nuv-**rah**-tree) – Otherwise known as "Nine Nights," Navaratri is the primary festival of the Goddess and takes place at the beginning of autumn, typically three weeks before the festival of Diwali. Traditions and details of each night's symbolism differ across regions and sects, with fasting and the wearing of special colors to honor various manifestations of the Goddess being common across regions. In Gujarat, sacred dances known as Garba and Dandiya, enact Durga's battle and defeat of the demon Mahishasura.

Parvati (**pahr**-vuh-tee) – The wife of Shiva and one of the three chief goddesses of the *Tridevi* or 'Trinity of Goddesses,' Parvati is the benevolent female aspect of the Transformer of the Universe, and is often referred to as the goddess of power, love, fertility, and devotion. She is also sometimes referred to as an aspect or alternative name of Durga (the root form of creation, preservation, and annihilation), Shakti (the cosmic energy that underlies all life in the universe), and 'one thousand' other names/personas. In the Shaivism sects, Parvati is considered an inextricable force, without which, Shiva (and therefore God) would cease to exist, for it is her life-force that gives them both power and energy. Parvati is the benevolent form of Shiva's wife (a complementary aspect to the fierce form of Kali), and the mother of their two sons, Ganesh and Kartikeya.

Puja (**poo**-ja) – A prayer or offering, puja describes the manifestation of worship and reverence in Hinduism. Often involving offerings of light (candles or diyas), flowers, water, or food, along with prayers (often in the form of mantras), puja rituals are an important aspect of religious life for most practicing Hindus, and are particularly common and elaborate on holy days, during festivals, and to celebrate major life events such as weddings, funerals, and baby-namings.

Rakshasa (**raahk**-shuh-suh) – Shapeshifting demons in Hindu mythology, Rakshasas have been referred to with various characteristics throughout Hindu and Buddhist literature. Ravana, Vibhishana, Surpanakha, and Kumbhakarna are Rakshasas in *the Ramayana*. Due to the varying (and often conflicting) representations of Rakshasas throughout the literature, this series has expanded on the mythological depictions with far greater detail than has been generally used in the past. While there has been a parallel drawn between some vampire representations and Rakshasas, they are not considered to be the same, in the mythology or in this series. The origin of Rakshasas on Venus was entirely invented by the author, upon the suggestion of Neha, as she was writing her own story.

Rama (**raah**-muh) – The main protagonist of *the Ramayana*, Rama is generally considered to be the seventh avatar of Vishnu. Often referred to as 'the ideal king' and 'the ideal husband,' despite the miserable ending of his wife, Rama is still a beloved figure in modern Hinduism. While there is significant debate about whether Rama should be considered infallible, this series explores the dichotomy between the divine and human aspects of his character, in line with major historical representations across the Hindu world, including the iconic version by the ancient Sanskrit poet Valmiki, that demonstrate his crooked path to virtue in great detail. The festival of Diwali, one of the most popular Hindu festivals celebrated by hundreds of millions of people every autumn, celebrates the triumph of light over darkness, as embodied by Durga's triumph over Mahishasura, and Rama's triumph over Ravana.

Ramayana, the (**raah**-mah-yuh-nuh) – One of the most well-known and beloved of the ancient Hindu Sanskrit epics, *the Ramayana* follows the many triumphs and tribulations of Rama, the seventh avatar of Vishnu, and Sita, his wife and the avatar of Lakshmi. While the epic covers a range of stories and characters, the primary conflict centers around Rama's battle with Ravana, the Rakshasa King of Lanka, after his capture and incarceration of Sita. While there are many versions of *the Ramayana* referenced across Southeast Asia including in India, Nepal, Thailand, Cambodia, and more, the most famous version is credited to the storyteller Valmiki. *The Ramayana* of Valmiki contains seven *kandas* or 'books.' The seven-book structure of *The Sita Chronicles* is meant to be a nod to the original epic.

Ravana (**raah**-vuh-nuh) – The main antagonist of *the Ramayana*, Ravana is the Rakshasa King of Lanka. He is said to be a devotee of Shiva, and to have received the 'nectar of immortality' as a boon from Lord Brahma that allows him to withstand any injury from any creature, other than a human. Lord Vishnu comes to Earth as the human, Rama, to take advantage of this epic loophole.

Sanskrit (**sahn**-skrit) – The primary sacred language of Hinduism, it has many forms and served as the foundation for many modern languages in Southeast Asia. Its role in spreading Indic culture throughout the region can generally be compared to Latin's role in disseminating and communicating literature, religion, and secular education throughout Europe for the two millennia spanning the Roman Empire to the end of the 18th century AD.

Saraswati (sah-ruh-svuh-**tee**) – The female aspect of the Creator of the Universe, Saraswati is also considered the goddess of knowledge, music, arts, learning, and wisdom. Saraswati is the wife of Brahma, and one of the principal goddesses of the *Tridevi*, or 'Trinity of Goddesses.'

Satya Yuga (**saht**-yuh **yoo**-guh) – 'The Age of Truth,' *Satya Yuga* is said to be the peaceful era that will return to Earth after the Preserver of the Universe vanquishes Kali, ending Kali Yuga (the 'Age of Vice').

Shakti (**shuhk**-tee) – The Great Goddess, the primordial cosmic energy of the universe, and the personification of the 'divine mother,' Shakti has many manifestations, including the *Tridevi*, Durga, Lakshmi, Saraswati, and Parvati. She is said to manifest on Earth as the embodiment of creative power and fertility, and of life itself. Some sects believe that Shakti is responsible for all creation and is the agent of all change, as it is her energy that animates everything in the universe, including the gods. In Shaktism and Shaivism, Shakti is worshipped as the animating energy of the Supreme Being.

Shiva (**shih**-vuh) – One of the primary deities of Hinduism, and one of the *Trimurti*, or 'Trinity of Gods,' Lord Shiva is considered to be 'the Destroyer,' 'the Transformer,' and 'the Regenerator.' He is represented by hundreds, possibly thousands, of different epithets. He is often represented as conflicting personas: He can be 'fierce' or 'benevolent,' and he is portrayed as a 'householder' with his wife, Parvati, and their sons, Ganesh and Kartikeya, but he is also portrayed as an ascetic yogi (chaste and focused on solitary prayer)—two lifestyles that are mutually exclusive in traditional Hindu society. Shiva's wife, Parvati (also referred to as Durga, Shakti, Kali, and many other names), is considered to be his life-force. In Valmiki's *Ramayana*, Ravana is a follower of Shiva, and Shiva is said to have given him a divine sword with the stipulation that if he uses his sword for unjust purposes, it will be returned to 'the three-eyed one' (Shiva himself). Shiva is often considered to be 'formless,' and it is common to worship him through the formless idol of a 'lingam' (internet image search recommended).

Sita (**see**-tuh) – The main female protagonist of *the Ramayana*, Sita is Rama's wife and an avatar of Lakshmi. Often referred to as 'the ideal wife' for her desire and ability to make the deepest personal sacrifices on behalf of her husband, Sita's tragic suicidal ending is controversial in modern academic discussions of the ancient epics.

Sugriva (soo-**gree**-vuh) – The king of the Vanaras (non-human intelligent primates who can fly), Sugriva's support is crucial to Rama's defeat of Ravana in *the Ramayana*. It is with Sugriva's army that Rama attacks Lanka. Many discussions around historical validity of *the Ramayana* have centered around the assertion that Rama led Sugriva's army over a formerly existing land bridge from mainland India to the island of Sri Lanka, as NASA images show that a series of lightly submerged sandbar islands do appear to have, at some point in the past, connected the two land masses.

Surpanakha (**soor**-puh-nuh-khuh) – The sister of Ravana, Vibhishana, and Kumbhakarna, Surpanakha is a primary female antagonist in *the Ramayana*. She is often considered the catalyst of the main events of *the Ramayana* (often taking the blame for Ravana's despicable actions). Surpanakha's story is also complex, as one of her primary scenes in the epic is when she falls in love with Rama. When she is rejected and humiliated by Rama, Rama's brother, Lakshmana, permanently maims her by cutting off her nose with a divine weapon. Surpanakha's hatred of Sita and her anger at Rama's rejection is a driving force of her character's antagonistic actions later in the story and in this series.

Tridevi (tree-**deh**-vee) – The 'Trinity of Goddesses': Saraswati ('the Creator'), Lakshmi ('the Preserver'), and Parvati, ('the Transformer'), serve as the female aspects and underlying energy of their male, godly counterpart husbands. Together they create balance between the three main aspects of existence. Each one individually, and the group as a whole, manifest Shakti's energy as is necessary to participate in worldly endeavors on behalf of the gods and goddesses, usually to support the cause of righteousness and restore balance.

Trimurti (tree-**moor**-tee) – The 'trinity' of Hindu gods: Brahma ('the Creator'), Vishnu ('the Preserver'), and Shiva ('the Destroyer' and 'the Transformer'). Together, the trinity complements each other, representing a descriptive model of various aspects of life on Earth.

Valmiki (**vahl**-mih-kee) – The most widely attributed author of *the Ramayana*, he is credited with inventing the poetic structure of epic Sanskrit literature, somewhat akin to Homer's role in codifying ancient Greek verse. In Valmiki's *Ramayana*, he participates as a character in his own work, being said to have taken Sita in after her trial by fire when Rama banished her to the jungle to raise their twin sons alone. Valmiki's own voiced admonishment of Rama's behaviour in the final chapters serves as a valuable, if controversial, reminder of the story's main point of demonstrating the complex and imperfect paths to *dharma* (virtue), along with its tragic consequences.

Vanara (**vaah**-nuh-ruh) – An ancient race of nonhuman, intelligent primates, the Vanaras are supporters of Rama and serve as his primary troops in his battle against Ravana. Sometimes referred to just as 'monkeys,' other times referred to as 'half-man, half-monkeys,' the literature is not consistent in its depiction of Vanaras. Hanuman and Sugriva are the most famous Vanaras, from their important roles in *the Ramayana*.

Varuna (vuh-**roo**-nuh) – The god of water and the celestial ocean, Varuna was the original chief god of the Vedic pantheon and later appeared throughout Sanskrit literature, primarily as the ruler of the sea. He plays a secondary role in *the Ramayana*, and is often referred to as a symbol of *rta*, an ancient vedic concept believed to encompass cosmic order and divine balance or justice.

Vibhishana (vee-**bhee**-shuh-nuh) – The youngest brother of the villain demon king, Ravana, Vibhishana is an important ally of Rama in *the Ramayana*. In *the Ramayana*, Vibhishana attempts to convince Ravana to return Sita to Rama, but his efforts are not successful. He then joins Rama and provides important intel that leads to Ravana's eventual defeat. Rama crowns Vibhishana the King of Lanka after Ravana is dead. Vibhishana's role in *the Ramayana* is a complex one, as he betrays his family and his race in order to follow a path he considers to be more dharmic. Still, there is no perfect path towards *dharma* (righteousness), and so, he is also considered a traitor. Vibhishana is one of the *Chiranjivi*, one of the seven immortals of Hinduism, who are said to remain on Earth to this day to guide humans on the path of righteousness.

Vishnu (**vih**sh-noo) – One of the primary deities of Hinduism, Lord Vishnu is considered to be 'the Preserver of the Universe.' Lord Vishnu is one of the *Trimurti*, or 'trinity' of Hindu gods, along with Brahma and Shiva. Together with his wife, Lakshmi (or Laxmi), who is considered his life-force, Lord Vishnu is mentioned throughout numerous Sanskrit texts and is worshipped as the supreme being by the Vaishnavist sects of Hindus. Rama is generally considered the seventh avatar of Vishnu among the *Dashavatara* ('ten avatars of Vishnu'). Some Hindu texts/sects refer to more avatars of Vishnu, including Mohini, a female avatar.

Vishrava (**vih**sh-**rah**-vuh) – The father of Ravana, Vibhishana, Kumbhakarna, and Surpanakha, he is described as a powerful rishi or 'seer.' He is said to have left his wife, Kaikesi, the mother of his four Rakshasa children, to return to his first wife after he became unhappy with Ravana's conduct.

Ya Devi Sarva Bhuteshu (yah deh-**vee** sar-vuh bhoo-teh-**shoo**) – The beginning of the *Devi Suktam*, one of the primary prayers/mantras to the Goddess (often sung in worship), these Sanskrit words celebrate the Goddess's embodiment of power, peace, knowledge, and many other necessary and beautiful aspects of existence in the universe, allowing the worshippers to feel the Shakti, or energy, of the Goddess within themselves, while bowing (figuratively or literally) to the greatness of all that is.

Yajna (**yahg**-nyuh) – 'Sacrifice, devotion, worship, or offering,' it refers to any ritual done in front of a sacred fire, often with mantras.

Yaksha/Yakshini (**yahk**-shuh / yahk-**shee**-nee) – A powerful nature spirit with shapeshifting abilities, generally considered to be the caretakers of Earth. The feminine form of a Yaksha is a Yakshini.

Yama (**yah**-muh) – The god of death, lord of justice, and the gatekeeper of the underworld, Yama is one of several deities who participates in the management of the afterlife. The gatekeeper of Naraka (roughly Hindu 'purgatory'), Yama is said to be one of the judges of human life/morality and 'the first mortal to have died.'

Pronunciation Key:
Rather than using the international phonetic alphabet that is not commonly used by the average reader, these pronunciation notes use references to common sounds in American English, more similar to a foreign language guide for casual travelers. Note that an "h" does not represent an aspiration in this transliteration; it is used to demonstrate various vowel sounds in English. Also note that the consonants have been simplified for an English speaker and do not fully represent the nuanced differences in the Sanskrit alphabet, such as aspirated v. non-aspirated consonants, that a native Hindi speaker would recognize.

Ah – as in "car" and "hard"
Aah – hold "ah" as in "car" and "hard" longer
Uh – as in "under" and "bus"
Ih – as in "in" and "interest"
Eh – as in "extra" and "excellent"
Oh – as in "over" and "ornate"
Ee – as in "cheese" and "beast," note that this does not indicate an elongation
Oo – as in "choose" and "I do," note that this does not indicate an elongation

This series is dedicated to the Goddess who resides in all of us.
May she give us the energy, inspiration, and perseverance to triumph over
all that holds us back, no matter what forms our enemies take.
"We are told too often what we can't do."
May we do it anyway.
Jai Mata Di.
~Ashley Mayers